Alizedriel

AND THE DREAMER'S INTUITION

J. J. PAULINO

MPOWERING LEGACY PUBLISHING

Published in the United States by MPowering Legacy Publishing, a sub-company of MPowering Legacy, LLC, Mississippi.

www.mpoweringlegacy.com

J. J. Paulino

Alizedriel and The Dreamer's Intuition

Version 1- October 2025

Ebook ISBN: 979-8-9938642-3-5

Print ISBN: 979-8-9938642-4-2

Manufactured in the United States of America.

Printed in the United States of America

Dedication

To the readers who believed in my writing before I had the courage to use my real name as an author.
To my family who always let me be my weird self, and to my love, who sat through all the rough drafts.
I hope this story sparks your own imaginations so that a greater narrative can unfold with your own direction.

Contents

1.0 A Warrior is Not Always a Hero

"*In my youth, I asked a good friend a single question. I am sorry to be this way, inconsiderately vague, but it was so long ago that I have forgotten the exact wording, or any of the language that was used. I do remember that he replied to me with a question of his own...*" a soft rattle, like the sharp intake of a baby's breath oozed through the fabric of reality.

"*What do you call someone who throws their life away in a desperate gambit to save their loved ones?*"

"*I'll admit, it's something that stuck with me like a catchy jingle due to the circumstances that we found ourselves in, and I have found myself repeating the question whenever I am dreaming of a nicer future. Ha, my point is. Many years later, more than I can actually count, I still don't know if that person's question was asked out of an omniscient understanding of what keeps happening or if he just made a stupid decision at a difficult time. I guess that I am just trying to rationalize after coming to terms with never getting to talk with anyone else after this again."* The single breath rose and fell in the same rhythmic beat as a heart.

"Maybe I'm crazy for doing this. But fuck it, right? Why would I want to know the answer when things like this keep happening even after that moron's sacrifice? I know it's my lot in life being what I am, but I cannot keep dreaming about the past. Ahem. So, HERE IT IS. The gift of the present, and a dream of a better future. Live, love, laugh, and live. Flourish children," an improbable wave resonated with an impossible timbre, a self-deprecating chuckle, and a wholesome disdain that threatened to become vitriolic. This inconceivably pissed narrator pulled its voice and emotion from an inky void of absolute nothing and manifested as an undercurrent throughout all of what was, is, and is probable. The distinction there is heavy, worming its way into minds that have yet to form personalities or into the restful who were in the throes of a deep slumber or state of soullessness. If one were to blink, or think, or zone out to allow their thoughts and daydreams to flow unbidden, anyone would see this omnipresent imprint. This figure, vaguely present at the corner of one's perception, was the specter of an ever present observer and co-author in life.

In this moment of deep and altering consciousness, and on a scale so minute all things became full and meaningless and whole and distinct, purposeful intelligence and mindfulness forced physicality in a lapse or perhaps, a calculated effort to change. Letters, numbers, symbols, and thoughts given physical representation and form, warped and folded into chains of muted blacks and grays and instantly scrawled itself into, around, and across this amorphous shade at the corner of one's vision, fixing to the oculus that one called consciousness. This tangle of intuitive angst entrenched itself in reality, layer by layer, and unwittingly burned holes across all of creation, spurred on new life, and crushed ancient beasts and entities once thought to be immortal and immeasurable by comparison only.

In a breath, the figure completed its manifestation and sharpened alongside a pulse of blinding light that brought inspiration into the thoughts of those willing, fortunate enough, or fated to listen. Similar to a rushed heartbeat or ragged intake of breath, color buzzed and scattered across an endless nothing. Then, there was a reflection. Like an angler fish seeing the sun for the first time, the figure, bloated, held together only by the chains that ripped through the vacuum of space-time to contain it.

"Pay attention. This is as much as I can do to help. Hm, actually, this is just the limit to what all of you can receive without my interference being found out." The blinding being of condensed language, imaginary shapes, and uncanny features, pleaded at first.

"That said, ahem, please fix this if you can. We deserve a happy life, as much struggle as it is to create, maintain, and better it." Gradually, the being's tone trailed off toward an adopted helplessness.

"Don't you all think?"

The question burned in an endless expanse, a blank canvas save for the halting and haunting radiance of a singular dot that received the ripples and waves of mental input. The entity, the being, the unfathomable creature hung onto the words and waited, waited for a response. The chains of language ceased their shifting and, in a moment of hesitation, the abstract entity allowed itself to unravel and slip through the chains. Within the desolation, the void, the emptiness that defied and refiled the notion of spacetime, light, and the cosmic dance between different states of matter, something beyond comprehension and description moved and encircled thought given form. Before a single ripple could be emanated from the singular drop, the figure cowered.

"I'm sorry," it cried. An entity, something far older, vaster, and infinitely more unfathomable in power, splintered into a storm of massless and unavoidable force. In the blink of one's eye and without any struggle, the amorphous cloud that distilled its own chains, swirled into a slender hand reminiscent of a dead night sky. One only distinguished from an abyss by a blanket of mountainous landscapes, fog, and the movement of clouds as the cosmos peeked from behind the skyward curtain.

"I'm sorry." The word imprinted and coiled around the delicate hand, dispersed, then reconstituted not even a second later.

"I thought that I could help. I tried to help, to do better for me and you." The words instantly resonated and trailed into a sloppy text, similar to one looking away from their parents' eyes after getting caught doing something punishable.

Almost instantly, the slender hand was joined by another. The words *"Would you believe me if I said that I have no clue how I got here?"*

The emptiness, the depth of nothingness that clasped all around the text bubble, suddenly exploded with light and life as though an infinite number of galaxies were born in the blink of an eye. And in this moment, a face, one so horrifying, so beautiful, so perfectly flawed, and incomprehensible, narrowed its eyes and mouthed, " ". The word was defined and spoken in the absence of what was said around the face, as if existence itself was frightened to illuminate or bring genuine shape to the massless thing that was. As soon as that being's lips met once again, the vibrant and watercolor splash of creation instantly dimmed and returned to a dreary and surreal emptiness. With it, the chains of vocabulary and thought no longer contained the notion of perception. The phantom of thought and the nothing that caught it vanished in a blur and, following their exit, in the blank canvas of nothing, the singular dot rippled, sending out a wave into the expanse around it.

"Where have you gone, *my love? And what just hit me?"*

A new, lighter in voice, regal in tone, and undeniably different from the heart-rattling resonance, graced the stage with a sense of panic and sorrow. Lingering in the air as though it were cotton candy being spun, an electric light that sparkled with all observable color, and all shades thereof, poured into and wrapped around the speaker's body. His withered and outstretched hand clasped around a railing that was embedded in a solid pillar of petrified wood and stone. Before he was given a chance to think, a different and just as sudden lightning bolt pierced through the wall and, in what felt like slow motion, speared directly toward his heart. The wall, slower than the lightning that pierced it, rippled, and tore open with a deafening crackle as tongues of brutal energy lashed out in every direction. On a macrocosmic scale, a lightning storm that swallowed everyone's vision cascaded across the entirety of reality as some lament or cry of the Heavens.

Some found themselves completely obliterated, de-atomized, or disintegrated; others were not explicitly targeted by the downpour and instead suffered from burns, severe electrocution, or the loss of a limb as though a blade of pure plasma sliced clean through. Very few, similar to the new narrator, found an odd force of will blossoming from their own minds that took on a tangible protective barrier. That said, these changes were purely mental.

The main target of such a violent outburst, a creature beyond the lightning's ability to destroy, lurched forward unyieldingly. Walls of twisted flesh and screaming faces crushed entire mountains underneath their weight, oozing across the land with a deafening rumble. The silken-lightning weaved cocoons, constructed from a purely mystical and mental energy, solidified around and protected dozens if not hundreds of the individuals just like the old man. After a few moments, after the first wave of meat and death reached its trough, the dazed soldiers and warriors farthest from the combat were released from their bondage.

Unlike the defensive lines that instantly collapsed due to a physical storm of meat that they were under equipped to withstand and unlike the Vanguard that pushed too far and were rolled over before their protection fortified, these released individuals, almost simultaneously, moved forward in unison. In the blink of an eye, a sort of unspoken communion and understanding coordinated a symphony beyond just the individual as each person, regardless of their physical differences and creeds, acted in concert. Like the rays of sunlight peeking over and through a cloudy horizon, these people spearheaded a defiant resistance. The eldritch wall of flesh collapsed in on itself, creating a domino effect that halted the enemy line that rode atop the amalgam like unholy surfers of a vacuous horde.

Somehow, above and apart from this nightmare, the old man glared at the electric wisps that pricked his arms and face as one of the very same cocoons dissipated around him. Unlike the others, the new narrator gripped the back of his neck with a dissatisfied and ugly frown as many of the coils and streaks wormed into something that he had in or on himself.

"It's acting up again, which implies that something I didn't account for happened. As for this spell, it is certainly at or above the 7th Star in rank." The new narrator thought back on the words that shot up his spine and into his mind but found nothing of use in what the disembodied voice said. Decidedly, the narrator cast it aside and focused on regaining his footing amidst the rumbling world.

"It doesn't matter right now. Focus Ark." The man clutched a railing near him and peered through a broken hole and into dark clouds

streaked with falling stars. Amorphous beings writhed and shambled across the landscape beyond the slurrious gore. The titanic and lumbering beasts stumbled over withered, rotting, and parasitized flesh.

"I know you are out there. Knowing you, the challenge you are facing is likely one of such a scale that it could bring all of this to an end before we even have a chance to put up this struggle." The man steadied himself, putting aside the writhing imagery that decorated his exposed nape. Mistakenly, he swallowed a mouthful of fumes that suddenly wafted up the staircase. Rightfully, he doubled over and coughed out several mouthfuls of blackened spit and phlegm with a rotten expression on his face. In the blink of an eye, quite literally, the man stepped away from the ruptured wall with speed unbefitting his age. An eyeball the size of roughly two blue whales appeared by the recently blasted window and stared directly at him.

"Your Holiness," a light voice, one tinged with exhaustion and fear, echoed for a moment before the world once again turned into a blurred mess of nonsense under the bombardment of some type of thunderous munition. The man nodded and took a moment to restart his ascent, but the eyeball's blood vessels suddenly turned to crags along its watery surface.

"Get down." The massive pupil shattered into an uncountable number of yellow and green irises that pulsed along the crag-like capillaries. Similar to the splitting of a cell, all the yellow and green eyes except for one rerouted to other parts of the entity's body. A sweltering heat and optical phenomena similar to an eclipsed sun engulfed the older man, forcing him to lean against the parallel railing and shield his face with a gilded sleeve.

"Excuse my rudeness." The single pupil lowered itself subtly then blinked away just as it appeared. In that same moment, the lightning all over the wall dispersed and allowed the gash to repair itself. The exposed green of the wood leaked an amber and viscous sap that near instantly closed up the structural wound. The narrator, physically shaken but not rattled, regained his wits and ascended only a dozen steps before another explosion ripped open yet another window to the outside.

Rather than a cloud of dust and debris, a multicolored mist wafted in and clung to the air like a specter. Everything that touched the mist curled up and liquefied into a dark and sizzling goo. In less than a single second, the right side of his body deteriorated into a putrid slurry. In response, a braid of silver and red metal and clear jewels glittered resplendently atop the old man's bald head. In a single breath, the crown's light twisted into a stunning wireframe of the old man's face and repaired the damage across his entire body. The sparkle of life and intelligence in his eyes dimmed as several dozen extra explosions, their sounds, and chemical fumes, inconsiderately ruptured and liquefied his internal organs in a nonstop cycle. Blood and muscle vibrated loosely within the robes but did not leave the confines of his clothing as the luminous crown cracked against the strain of the restorative pressure. Just as the old man slumped to the floor and released his final breath, the crown shattered into two distinct powders. The silver surrounded his body in a shield while the red dust filled in the glowing wireframe, pushing and setting him into a physical state beyond his initial withered and decrepit self.

"This makes my forty-two thousand five hundred and forty-third death this year." The man whimpered out a single line and put his now bulging arms underneath him. His earrings, long and layered with gems and several malleable scales, dimmed and rusted at an unfathomable pace as the mist was directly ripped away from his face and skin. In the same instant, like a chain reaction, another item randomly shattered. The blackened goop that sloughed off of his body as decay

and rot bloomed with life and limb, allowing him to rise to his feet. Several other charms and accessories shattered in this moment of fated reversal. With every single less laborious breath, the unwoven threads of some articles of clothing rebound themselves to the man's now larger and robust figure.

"I shouldn't have too many more Arcanum left." Like a rubber band, the old man snapped to a standing position and grimaced. His attention quickly moved from his own circumstances to an undeniably infectious laugh that ricocheted from the top of the steps. Hearing such joyous laughter, however, the long-eared old man did not smile. Without even noticing, his pupils constricted to pinpoints. It was only after a deafening roar and another planetary rumble that he collected his emotions and pounced up the steps with a vigor unbecoming. The gilded and glittering embroidery all over his opulent clothing, stained black and brown with rot and an overwhelming stench of decay, drained of color and luminance with each step.

To offset the drain of the mystical energy used to facilitate this physics-defying transformation, the old man reached into his pockets, clenched, promptly crushed handfuls of multicolored buzzing rings and neon toothpicks. Like shattered glass, fractals and shards fell as it logically should as a solid, but before they could reach the floor, each speck and granular piece of matter evaporated into a cloud of flickering light that instantly funneled up toward the old man's blanching clothes.

BANG. The sound barrier popped several times over as he shattered handful after handful of glowing items in a tunnel of frozen light, skating up the winding steps in a defiance of gravity. The old man moved so fast that he didn't even notice any of the other deafening explosions that followed in his wake. A different kind of problem followed not too long after as something circular broke, pierced through the ceiling, and just barely nicked the bridge of his nose with light that had bent into straws around it. Much to his own surprise, the blowback of leaning away from the sudden attack instantly shattered some of the more delicate weaves and burned holes all over the regalia.

Dizzy from the whiplash and trapped in a field of mystical energy, light, swirling gems and broken ring fragments, the old man did not notice the extensive damage that he caused to his body with the sudden stop and miscalculated the speed of the crumbling ceiling and Bang! Heat, molten rock, and gravel of slag pelted him from above as several more blinding explosives engulfed his location seemingly purposely. Over the course of a few seconds, several charms on the collar of his brightly ruffled and singed cloak warped into dull studs as they released a glowing emerald mist that entered his nose. The old man regained consciousness with a snap of his eyes and immediately pressed the inside of one of his rings. A mystical halo of glowing and interlocked plates bubbled out of his burned skin and generated a tangible and thick exoskeleton, reducing his musculature by a few degrees. Another ring released an audible hum as mystical energy and heat gradually illuminated numerous hairline fractures that spread along the exoskeleton, all of which originated from the right side of his body. His towering height was reduced by not an insignificant margin as hell itself rained down and pelted his skeletal armor. The old man pushed aside most of the debris just a second before an implosive cascade of gases refilled the initial vacuum. He scampered out of the molten debris with the heart rate of a rabbit rattling within his ribcage, climbing and rising through the steps with a vigorous determination. He could not help looking down, however, toward the kiln that snapped and now crackled with a hellish black flame that cast green-tinted shadows. Its spread was only halted by a viscous amber liquid that dripped and oozed from the damaged walls above and beside him.

Soon after reaching a platform with more staircases that led in different directions, a thunderous grinding sound scraped against his ears. The entire structure around him, incapable of maintaining its integrity, collapsed almost all at once as the once and only momentarily halted flames burned through the mostly wooden structure. Breath caught, pupils dilated, and with a clawing flame reaching toward him, pulling him downward, the man clenched his fist around a third ring.

With a tap of his big toe on the air beneath him, swirls of chaotic winds turned into spring pads that launched him upward like a rocket. The soles of his shoes, right after, glimmered as paper-thin platforms miraculously appeared wherever he needed to maneuver. One leaped in an elegant jump from one falling fixture to another; the man avoided falling into a fiery pit. BANG! Another explosion ripped through the air just as the old man hopped to a stable location. BANG! His exoskeleton shattered as yet another explosive and sound-shattering round directly collided with his body from some inconceivable distance. Disoriented and covered in cuts and scrapes, the old man assessed his situation with a ragged breath and gulped upon seeing the mangled state of the left side of his body this time.

Without a single thought in his mind, the man gripped his blackened shoulder and activated another ring. With a breathless scream, he stepped forward and tore his own mangled arm to bound up the collapsing steps without any impediment. In the same motion, he reached into his breast pocket and took out a crystal vial filled with a deep sapphire liquid. The instant he used his teeth to remove the cork, the liquid turned red, but the detail practically escaped his notice as he forced his consciousness to remain and drink. In the blink of an eye, his missing arm and exposed ribcage completely regenerated, which was not the same for his now missing sleeve and all the jewelry that he left behind.

That said, the old man mused that beggars couldn't be choosers and right now, he was begging and praying to every known divinity, demigod, celestial, neumen, God or Goddess, and any other divine rated being within the known universe. Sadly, he was well aware that only adrenaline, mystical items, and some mysterious elixirs were his only companions in this moment as they pushed him forward with an unquantifiable superior strength than his own. Unfortunately, he heard the same melodious laughter break through the surrounding sounds of war.

"It's good to be back. Haa. This is quite the welcoming party, don't you think, my little empress?" The speaker chuckled at a set of angry roars. Yells and shouts that immediately turned into screams and the unmistakable tearing sound of flesh being sliced through with a cleaver.

"How? How did that man get through the defenses so quickly? I know the Immortal Hero Affix is supposed to be strong, *but how is this allowed by the* gods? *How is this fair? How? Oh my love, anyone. If you are listening. Please don't let that monster touch my daughter."* The old man shuddered, since he knew deep in his heart that all the mortals were alone in this conflict. For the most part, that is. His mind flashed briefly toward the mysterious meteor shower that preceded the electric webbing of tangible thought.

Not too far from the elderly man's climb, a scene ripped straight out of a madman's power-hungry, blood-splattered fantasy just about reached a climax. A human with pale skin and dark hair that swooped into an altogether flattering but messy side part stood in the middle of a slaughterhouse. His innocently beaming eyes and charming smile conveyed a sense of childishness that would have filled anyone who didn't know his character with the instinctive urge to protect him. His voice—well, it has been described as melodious and easy to fall asleep too, but because of the overall amalgamation of his altogether too perfect features, the man gave off an uncanny and uneasy presence. At least, all of this would be the opinion of the old man that serves as our new Narrator.

"Tree hugging idiots. You will all die before even giving me a scratch if you charge like that." The barbarous man laughed as he stabbed through the slitted visor of a bloodied soldier on the floor. As he did so, a thin figure clad in streamlined body armor darted at him with a speed that bordered untraceable by any modern observational device. The thin knight unleashed a torrent of piercing thrusts and flickering slashes while using an estoc forged from pure light and stardust, an artifact that left a blinding trail as it attempted to match its wielder's speed. The innocent intruder simply let out a stream of laughs and berating taunts with each deflected or sidestepped attack.

"Left flick, right, riposte, thrust, there you go. You can hit me. Keep trying. Go ahead. Haa. Time, hit, wow! You are so skilled. Quinte, Pfth, Haa. Moulinet. You got it." Another knight, majestic and tall, strode forth with an unyielding demeanor as cracks exploded out all over the floor with every step. A massive two-handed falchion tipped forward in an unstoppable charge that, unlike the kindred thin knight, produced a cascading and resonating sound wave of pure power and mystical energy rather than light, plasma, and radiation. Devastation swallowed the valiant knight's immediate surroundings.

"Whoa there, champ. A big guy like you shouldn't be moving so fast. How about you chill?" The haunting thing casually waved its hand and sent out a matching wave of mystical energy that canceled the surging tide of pure power before it could create anything more than a slightly powerful gust of wind. The valiant knight, despite the cancellation of his mystical effect, slashed out no less than a dozen times in concert with the thin knight that buzzed and stung toward the hero with no issues.

"Weak and stupid. How boring." The intruder sighed and twisted himself into a snake-like pose only achievable by the greatest of contortionists. Like a viper bites, twin black swords forged from soot and ash snapped across empty air and faded into wisps of smoke as they pierced the two knights almost unimpeded.

"It's like, ha, do you people genuinely not learn? Like, am I wrong for killing them? My little empress, I'm so sorry for this. Your parents must hate you if this is the quality of their guard. Don't worry, I will take care of and protect you from now on." The uncanny intruder combed through his admittedly luscious hair and produced a gentle smile on par with a Cheshire grin. To the man's left, his wicked smile and disgusted eyes burned into the retina of a decapitated head. Almost simultaneously, the two vertical halves of the valiant knight's body fell to the hero's right. Not so much as a drop of blood leaked from either of the bodies since each wound smoked with the sickly sweet aroma of cauterized flesh and sacrament-colored embers.

The Intruder locked eyes with a third knight, a stationary giant who wielded two spiked shields the size of an average human. In this knight's hands, however, they appeared as small bucklers or large gauntlets. The handsome intruder wiggled his eyebrows as a challenge, then bent at his waist to look up toward a pedestal with three high-backed thrones. A shivering girl glared at him from the middlemost seat.

"My empress, this is the third and last time that I will make this offer. Let me help you become your best self." The man's intention, at first glance, seemed pure, but the subtle manner in which he licked his lips and shifted his impressively ornate utility belt.

"You are a filthy, vile, and disgusting creature. You are a disgrace to all of humanity and a stain on my mother's grace. Die now, and you will be allowed a fair trial in the afterlife." Despite a shaking voice, the girl maintained her posture and kept her head tall as she looked down on the hero.

"Ah. You look so cute trying to look commanding. Sadly, that is not the response that I was going for." In less time than it took for a spark to fly off a piece of flint, the third knight lost sight of the intruder. In that minuscule moment, a sudden wall of metallic dust and soot kicked up and clung to the air, blurring and dulling the giant's senses. Out of nowhere, a small thread of condensed ashes slipped through the knight's chest and trailed along the air just behind her massive frame. The human floated just above this line for a moment before he dropped to the ground with a careless roll of his eyes. The ash and smoke throughout the room instantly clung to and forcefully stuffed the giant's body, creating a sort of soft immobilizing and internal combustion effect.

"Aww, don't look at me like that, my precious. I mean, just think about it for a moment. This is fate. You are fated to come with me. Ever since the day that you were born, I worked tirelessly to ensure that you would be safe and happy. I worked harder than your own parents." That man casually waved an arm to the indescribable sounds of horror and bloodthirsty chaos that he wrought.

"Look at the armies that I raised for your empire, practically free of charge. Do you see what happens when they listen to my commands?"

The guy laughed and ducked underneath a crystalline tablet that the girl threw at him.

"And don't forget what I've done for you. I put an end to the curses and sicknesses that made everyone's magic go out of control." He raised a finger and dropped a multi-sided, almost spherical container that swirled and glimmered with a deadly, almost caustic, light.

"I got rid of the Hexed Beasts causing issues for the people of Furja." He flared out his own clothing.

"Oh, I forgot about this one. I went over to that stupid desert and cleared how many of those graves for your idiot explorers?"

He pretended to count on his hand then threw them up in exasperation.

"Ha, then even after all of that, I cleaned up that idiot's prison for your mother and single-handedly restored this stupid place's physiks for your aunts and uncles. I asked for nothing then and did what I had to for the survival of this entire shitty empire." The guy lashed out and let go of the string that held the giantess in place. Hearing his mistake in the ear-splitting sound of her armor moving, he spun on his heel and pulled at it with both hands.

"Haa, I may have spoken out of order in my anger, Haa. But please understand, my lady. I put up with all of that for you." The man took a single step with each and every mention, then stopped and covered his face with a hand after tightening the smokey thread around his forearm.

"HaaHaa. You know, now that I think of it, I've dealt with so much crap for all of you ungrateful ass people. I survived so many crappy situations, and fixed so many of this world's stupid fucking problems. Haa. I finally finished everything. I got all the side quests done. I finally decided to finish up the main stuff and settled myself down after so many years. I was happy doing my thing, you know." The guy tugged on the wire and brought the giant to her knees.

"But then, your crappy parents went ahead and ruined everything. Fuck me, do you think it's fair, my little empress? After all the crap that I've put up with, after everything I've done for you, do you think it was right for them to lock me away in a Terrarium and Blip me away after taking everything that I built for myself? Haa. That's wrong, don't you think? Bad manners, right? A real bitch maneuver, yeah? Haa." The intruder slowly wrapped the thread of ash around his finger and pulled on it softly as he combed through his hair once again. The massive knight's muscles produced an audible series of pops as she roared to the heavens. With a bloody tearing sound and a bloodthirsty side glance, the knight swiped with a backhanded slap even as the ash ripped through her bloodstream and severed each muscle fiber slowly and in the most painful way possible. The gargantuan protector ensured that the spikes were the first to greet the overconfident whelp of a human. Sadly, the intruder was beyond being faster and simply tugged his finger a little bit harder.

In the blink of an eye, the giant fell apart like she was a ruptured bag of wet ground meat. Her massive frame was consumed by a ghoulish flame faster than the blink of an eye the moment that the crown of the giant's helmet began to descend. Only the massive knights' equipment clattered to the floor, and even then, the metal turned into a dull slag at the hero's feet before the spike hit her. Without missing a beat, the intruder wiggled his finger at no less than three dozen knights that barged through a wall of molten metal and black- green obsidian. Within a second, all of their bodies contributed to the mounds of disfigured meat and heated slag all over the floor. With another wave of his hand, the smoke, ash, and remains rushed to cover the open gates. A dark and slightly sagging substance once again turned into a strong mystical alloy.

Beside the outermost of the three thrones, two Valkyrian guards in gleaming armor narrowed their eyes and readied weapons as the man walked along a stained silver carpet. Unlike their allies, these two Valkyries waited and prepared to strike only after the monster before them breached the condition for them to leave their charge. The short sword and shield holder and the spiked mace wielder with massive studded greaves, respectively, undulated and hummed with a sort of divine radiance in their wait. Almost instantly, their masked faces appeared on either side of the intruder the moment he reached the first step up toward the girl that sat upon the resplendent, central throne.

The devilishly handsome man bent backward and then flipped using his hand as a springboard. He blocked nearly a dozen strikes with a series of light-absorbing bladed whips that coalesced from ash and soot. In the midst of his acrobatic backflips, he kicked the shield bearer and rebounded across the room in the blink of an eye. Against expectations, the man landed to a complete stop with only one hand in contact with the ground. He flicked his wrist with such strength that his entire body went from a dead stop to being propelled toward the mace wielding Valkyrie at a 45 degree flight path from the straight line he once had, cutting off the route that she attempted to route him with.

The Valkyrie managed to catch herself despite the unexpected appearance of the human and spun the mace in her hand to greet the man's piercing thrust. The clash gouged out the floor and made a rugged conical imprint for as far as the eye could see. Just a split second before the hero's blade met with the full resistance of being deflected and locked within an awkwardly shaped spike, he let go of his blades and spun like a top as he caught his sword in a reverse hand grip. The thrust twisted into a gliding slash that allowed him to once again spin on the floor and roll into the Valkyries' personal space. In the same fluid motion, his thrusting and now free hand lashed out in a crushing straight that ejected the guard back like a rag doll. Without looking, he used the reversed blade to parry a bright white sword that chopped toward his exposed back. Instead of contesting the shielded knight, the intruder allowed himself to be catapulted and thrown across the room, where he opened his palm and pulled on black threads that were connected to where he punched the mace wielder. Like a marionette, the hero pulled the mace wielder closer and interfered with her ability to reorient. Unexpectedly, his pursuit was met with another impediment as several throwing needles covered in a citrine glow pierced toward him without any delay.

The intruder, as if he could peer into the future, spun and released his connection to the mace wielder and twitched all the muscles on his free hand. Several thousand ashen threads exploded out and wrapped his body like a cocoon. Wherever the citrine light passed through, dozens of permanent splattered holes remained. Those same fuming and needlepoint-thin marks peppered the full body shield that the man used. It was as if the coating was so potent even space-time corroded and left behind a sinking void.

The heroic intruder, seemingly unbothered, instantly contorted his covered body and released an axe kick that pulled all the threads in the room. In the blink of an eye, the man disappeared, closed the distance, and shattered one of the mace knights' greaves after turning his momentum into a devastating spin kick. The shield bearer once again cut off the uncanny human's pursuit and unleashed a torrential assault that he simply couldn't get past.

"How about?" Before his gums could flap, instincts kicked in. He avoided a chop that cut away some locks of his hair and shaped the ashen sword into a massive hammer that he smashed into the shield user that cut at his backside without any warning. BANG! The resulting sound wave and rebounding shattered the hammer and created a blinding smoke cloud.

Halos buzzed into existence atop the two Valkyries' heads as the faint mystical presence around their bodies thickened into a physical crystalline coating. Their pupils also turned into an opalescent mixture of light, magic, and electro-magic feedback. Without any communication, the Valkyries regrouped at the bottom of the stairs and stood back to back within the ashen cloud. The shield bearer tried to disperse the cloud, but it clung to them like smog in a densely populated city.

Seconds passed, but nothing untoward happened — that is, until they heard an amused chuckle. Neither of them expected it as an endless stream of random cuts and crushing blows descended upon their glassy forms The mace wielder, being more agile than her ally, relied on evasion more than defense and tried to maintain her position but all it took was a single millimeter out of formation and BANG! The mace wielder suffered a devastating blow to the midsection that left her winded. Unable to react in time, the shield bearer could only watch as the entire cloud surrounding them collapsed onto her ally. BANG! The smaller Valkyrie shot out toward the end of the grand, football stadium-sized throne room. The hero was prepared to chase and finish the job, but the shield-wielding knight stood in his way before he could adjust his grip on some threads and balance on the tightropes that he created.

"Oh? Maybe the two of you aren't as weak as I expected. I completely expected to blow a hole in your friend's stomach there. Are you at the eighth rank or have you just entered the ninth? I can't tell even with my High Grade [Examine] Spell." The intruder raised an eyebrow and smirked as he retreated and hopped a few times to keep himself limber. His ashen sword spun like the tail blades of a helicopter in his hand before it came to an abrupt stop. Dozens of multicolored knives with the colors of gemstones and equipped with varying mystical effects clattered all over the hall along with the wispy dematerialization of several dozen black threads. The studs on the mace wielder's remaining gauntlet hissed and vibrated with some kind of intense energy as tiny motes of light gathered in the empty holes of the projectile firing mechanism.

Desperate and out of breath, the ejected Valkyrie twisted just enough with the added help from using her gauntlet so that her greaseless and outstretched hand could claw into the ground and leave a long enough chasm to stop her from leaving the building. A gush of blood poured out of her fearsome helmet. In a single movement, she dropped to a knee and held her stomach. The armor sloughed away as if it were made of mud. Her barely noticeable almond skin was nowhere to be seen as the exposed and heavily blistered muscle congealed to a soupy mess that writhed and pulsed with black- green flame. The Valkyrie immediately administered a combination of a mystical phenomenon that mixed a wavering distortion of space and time with a leafy green radiant light. A very noticeable frost spread from that pulse and covered the Valkyries' entire armor as she aimed to quell the near invisible ripples of heat and death that burrowed into her.

The shield bearer, in the meantime, followed the intruder with cat-like and glowing eyes that cut off any route he would have taken to finish off the mace Valkyrie.

"Speed is most definitely not your specialty. Being fucking annoying is." BAM, the intruder appeared in front of the shield bearer and attempted to instantly end the fight with a whiplash of spiked smoking threads to her blind spot. Unchallenged, the shield Valkyrie withstood dozens of strikes and parried dozens more, stopping each attack just a finger's length away from her ally. Suddenly seeing an opening in the hero's growing annoyance, the Valkyrie returned a calculative clawing slash that forced this "wicked stranger" away from both the throne and the mace-wielding Valkyrie despite being less agile. It was clear that she was a master of positioning and defense.

"You dishonor everyone of your predecessors and every true hero that has held an Alignment Series Affix." The shield's muffled voice hissed with disgust and reached the "hero" just as he regained footing with an amused scoff. His clothes and skin sported dozens, if not hundreds of bright red cuts that showed how outclassed he was. Worse for him, the injured mace recovered and looked to rejoin the skirmish despite the hole in her armor. In fact, the smaller of the two knights had already concluded her attack before the man could even register the change with his cocky smirk.

The "hero's" arm snapped in half and gushed with dark red and almost black blood before he was thrown across the room with a nasty spike lodging into and burrowing into his side as if it were a living carrion. Dozens of poisoned blades trailed and intercepted him from directions he simply couldn't defend himself from as they pierced his back like a porcupine's sprouted quills. That's not even mentioning that he couldn't even make a move with the shield cutting off his movement in general, ping ponging him back into the horrifying batting of the mace that spun and pierced through his skull in a gruesome manner. The inherent skill behind the Valkyries and their joint techniques only paused when the hero's blood began glowing. Sensing danger and a troubling shift in the dynamics, the Valkyries instinctively moved away. The intruder suddenly exploded with flame and ash, cleaning the board and melting everything around him.

The Valkyries did not even attempt to engage with such a move as a dark sphere that obliterated even light particles suddenly shaped around him as if he had turned into a black hole. In less than a second, they saw the "hero" standing upon a glassed surface as he observed his sudden litany of wounds. A cauterized hole closed up on his temple, and his blackened eye reduced in swelling at a visible rate as soot filled in the vacant hole. His body trembled and generated an almost audible quake across the entire throne room—no, across the entire structure.

"I don't think you idiots get it yet." Suddenly, like a pressure valve had just been released, an intense heat and weight bore down on the Valkyries as the structure that held the room wavered. The duo was forced to take a few steps back as the glassed and super-heated domain around the "hero" slowly expanded. His naturally cocky smile turned sour and explicitly annoyed as he randomly pointed his sword to the path of destruction left in his wake.

"Nothing you do hurts me. Not a single attack even scratched my clothes." The hero jeered as his wounds vanished as if it was all some kind of sick mirage.

"Actually. That's not entirely true. You morons have actually damaged my clothes." The hero spun on his heel and showed off the gleaming and metallic quality of his "restored" clothing. The Valkyries were given a clear view of how the metal slag and the bone fragments of their allies floated over and fortified the hero's equipment. Even the dents, chips, and warping of their own armor and weapons added to the hero's defenses as pieces floated over and packed into the man's body.

The wicked intruder waited for some kind of astonished or upset response, but he was destined to feel stunned. The knights finally threw their heated weapons to the ground. The shield bearer even took the preparation a step further and examined exactly what the hero did to her armor. In less than a second of deliberation, the Valkyrie stripped herself of the most affected and heavy gear. Her hardened jaw and scar-covered face were set on the monster in front of her. The mace tactfully observed the same thing not only in her armor but in her own rapidly deteriorating midsection and followed with an infuriated look of disgust directed at the hero. A stunning dark skin beauty with milk-white eyes and braids so tight, they seemed as though they were magnificent carvings on the woman's skin, came out of the second shell of armor. Both women lowered their stances and waited.

With a wide smile, the so-called hero put a single arm up and shifted his other arm behind his back mockingly. In a flash, both of the Valkyries were upon him. Each guardian knight unleashed an onslaught of jabs and kicks that combined into a stunning dance of destruction.

With a shatter and a rolling chime, the Valkyries released the crystalline energy that had been contained to just around their armor. Each created a different phenomenon, but together, they unleashed bursts of shrieking windstorms and shredding blizzards of ice and hail. With their rapid movements, they coalesced all of their power into a dome around the hero. Using that energy and the storms held inside, the Valkyries dispersed the hero's ash and smoke and charged with a flurry of weaponry made of nature. A sickle of wind, a spear of ice, a whip of water and other constructs flooded pelted the "hero" in a never-ending tide. Hard pressed even to evade, the man eventually felt his back press against a cold surface that turned into a wall of shackles and spikes. Using his rapidly falling internal body heat as the kindling, the monster collected and manipulated his own blood and generated a flicker on his finger. In less than a breath, the hero pressed the super-heated finger behind his back and into the icy surface of the wall. In that same moment, the green spark contained just underneath his nail turned into a flashbang of searing light that burned through the dome.

Both of the guardian knights gave more than 200% of their maximum effort to exert this much speed and power simultaneously, yet they were still completely caught off guard by the sudden and searing explosion.

"This is boring now." With a look of disappointment, the man clicked his tongue through the burning vapors and in less time than it took to blink, the abominable hero vanished from between a flurry of pincer attacks. Before the tall and scarred Valkyrie could even register the heat, the hero snapped her neck with a singularly swift motion, similar to how one might snap the neck of a small chicken with a single thumb.

The mace Valkyrie forgot the opponent for just a split second and in a blind rage, she used both arms to chop at the man's waist with an icy great sword twice her size. The sword's needlepoint edge simply cleaved everything in its destructive path with little to no resistance and effortlessly erased the form-fitting clothing underneath the man's costume and armor. The massive sword even nipped at the man's skin. The moment it did so, the blade lit up with intense heat and turned into a harmless steam that moistened his body. The second Valkyrie died not too long after that. There wasn't even a need to trick her as she exploded into a bonfire of green flame starting from her midsection. She was incinerated without a single bit of resistance, from the inside out.

"Stupid fucks. I mean, honestly, it's like no one hears what I'm saying. I am better than you." The man casually picked up a nearby piece of debris and covered it with smoke and ash. With a flick of his wrist, the stone sailed through a would-be escapee, who pretended to die during the influx of low-level grunts. Sadly, the "hero" did not measure his strength and tossed the stone with such speed that it burst out of the building entirely. The debris drew a fiery line out the side of a sky-piercing tree surrounded by mountains of bodies and fallen branches so large they were indistinguishable from mountain ranges.

Secondly, the tiny piece of ashen stone ignited with a flame so bright it illuminated a hellscape beyond the scope of a simple war. True mountain ranges with expansive lengths as vast as entire galaxies collapsed under the weight of fallen soldiers and monsters the size of moons or small planets. Of the few rivers with widths only slightly larger than the Milky Way that did not dry up in the flames of conflict, flowed with so much runoff blood that the waters glistened like rubies.

Any land that didn't sport an ongoing war was either barren and collapsing into dusty or icy canyons, was covered in ash and the wandering bones of undead, or swirled around unstably either in gravity wells, vats of magma, or toxic multicolored sludge. After a long and eye-catching arc, the ash-covered stone crashed into a mass of swarming bodies. Instant vaporization was granted to those lucky enough to be right where the glistening pebble landed. Those off on the fringe screamed in pain as armor and weapons fused to exposed skin. A ghoulish green and black flame expanded in the blink of an eye as pockets of air immolated with hellish intensity and rained like napalm. Sticky and inextinguishable until there was nothing left to burn. The so-called hero turned toward the intricate throne and smiled.

The young lady who sat upon it quaked. Her face.... Well, she tried to wear a rigid mask befitting royalty, but tears pooled at the sides of her shifting eyes. Her breath shortened and rattled unevenly as her bleeding fingers dug into the armrests at her sides. She glared at the disgusting creature in the guise of a man and let her thoughts race.

"That abominable—no, that horrid and despicable animal! No, even that's too gracious. That piece of..."

"My goodness. Your stare is so intense. Dare I say, disrespectful!"

"You vile creature. If you lay down your life before me right now, I will petition my holy mother to give you a quick end." The girl raised her head defiantly even as the Hero bore holes in her clothes with his gaze.

"Ah, you know what. I was going to be gentle when I brought you back home but, ah, fuck. But look at this mess you've made me create on your behalf, my troublemaking little empress." The animal cracked the steps up to the throne. A black flame with a ghoulish green tint snaked its way through the corpses littered throughout the room and surrounded his body. For a single moment, insatiable hunger and lust flashed across his eyes as he overlooked a subtle ripple in a corner of the throne room. He was too busy trying to unfasten his gaudy belt.

1.1 Wretched Heroics

"**G**ET AWAY FROM HER."

"Look at this. Another white kni...ght? Huh?"

The hero swiped with a blade of ash and fire in an attempt to parry a sudden attack, but a pure line of annihilation simply cut his body and soul in two.

"Sorry. I'm late. Xylos decided to make a fuss at the reunion. I put it back to sleep, the poor thing." The silently crackling disturbance pulled to a complete stop near the topmost step. In an implosive flash, a crouching figure stood and sheathed a glass blade just in front of the little girl that sat upon the throne. Once closed, the air, light, and trailing space snapped like a metal wire being pulled taunt and ripped the beast in two... or should have. The primal scream of an imminent and painful death quickly turned into a maniacal cackle as flame spewed from the animal's chest. The mysterious and tall figure in a wide brim hat narrowed their eyes and stepped back, hand on hilt.

"Who knew the old bitch lived? How have you been all these years? How'd you handle those useless fucks? An eternal recurrent temporal seal like the Graves you Gods are all so proud of? Dimensional expulsion like those idiotic prisons? Haa, wait. Let me guess again. Did you agree to give those old monsters a second chance with you?"

"Haaha. Oh my Haa, oh man. This is too precious. Did I hit the mark with the last one? Haa." The *hero* suddenly stopped laughing.

"Change that look on your face before I fuck it up. It's disgusting." The lady beneath the wide brim hat didn't glare; she wasn't even angry or annoyed or even disappointed. What she saw in front of her was not a human; it wasn't even a stain or smudge. Even nothing was better than this living trash by an incalculable amount. This thing was a lifeform with no brain capacity or a soul capable of understanding its own actions, so it saddened her to no end that such a senseless pestilence came this far in life.

That said, her hand tightened on the hilt of her blade. For a moment she closed her eyes and inhaled whilst the lecherous beast prattled. If one could see the imaginary image that this woman held in her mind, they would see a balding and wrinkled old man, fit for his age but obviously withered, covering a little girl's mouth as he dragged her away from the throne in silence. A small hidden door silently and subtly closed behind them. To anyone else, the young empress remained on the throne, cowering in fear and hope. Seeing the truth of the situation in her mind's eye, the woman exhaled and narrowed her slitted pupils on the monster in front of her.

"I am ready for this world to come to an end. You can take over now." The outline of a young man stepped out of the woman's shadow with an expressionless gaze. He adopted the woman's stance and, all in the same instant, their blades seamlessly overlapped. The hero, by this point in time, had recovered, albeit not enough to protect himself. In a flash, the lady vanished with a speed so unfathomable, she left all light, space, and time right behind her as a shadow. Her sword simply whipped across the hero as if the next slash had always been there. The hero could not overcome or even comprehend this level of power and simply remained wide-eyed and red-faced even as his body simply erased from existence without any struggle or fanfare.

Powers greater than his own activated for the sake of self-preservation. The ashen flame blade in his hand generated so much heat that its distortions created an inverted implosion of light against the women's movement. A sphere of aggravated reality pushed outward from the remains of the rapidly vanishing hero. In this sphere, the cataclysmically fatal strike moved in slow motion even if he appeared to have already been bisected. In response, a bladed tail of flame sprouted from his tailbone and matched the woman's slash. The initial erasure was replaced by a cosmic exchange of strikes, one contained to the small bubble around the two individuals.

The young man who superimposed himself on the woman, expecting some type of resistance, clashed several dozen times with the tail before even a nanosecond passed outside of the inverted and distorted space. Even now, the hero maintained his stupid expression, completely unaware of anything happening beyond his vision. Thankfully, the ashen flame writhed and moved the hero's body like a puppet. As a perfect example, burning hands ripped out his back like wings and behaved like a massive pair of shields covering the hero's blind spots. Stoney scales of crawling ash burst along his skin and moved whenever the flaming shields could not defend him. Sadly, with this next spurt of power and flame, the superimposed figure found themselves taking a step back. Minutes, hours, months and then years passed as a never-ending back and forth unfolded between the hero and this woman with a wide brim hat. Not even a second had yet to pass outside. The woman, due to external factors limiting her strength and the handoff of the combat, could not keep up with the hero and in a brief split second of inattention.

The tail effortlessly cut the woman's limbs at their joints in what felt like slow motion as the fractured space-time bent to the flames' will. In a breath, in a second, time rippled and returned to normal. The backed-up energy due to such a conflict exploded outward and pressed on the entire throne room, similar to an indestructible balloon expanding within a tube. Fire roared and tore through everything except for this small pocket where there was nothing left to immolate.

"You're too slow, fucking hag...." The hat fell off her head and scattered to ash as flames licked away her skin.

"Damn. Too bad there's not much left of you I can use." The animal sneered and lunged at the woman's breasts with his hands. Before he could squeeze, her body dried out and collapsed inward.

"That look in your eyes is filthy, you foolish child. Can you really not see what you have become? How many times must you go through this before you understand? How many more times will you do this before you realize your truth?"

The woman's dark hair unfurled and framed her long pointed ears and dark skin for only a moment before it frayed to cinders in the heat. Her cut limbs fell to embers around the young man, and her sword clattered to the ground harmlessly from the clenched fist that turned to ash. The person who was speaking, however, was not a woman as the spectral image of a young man swapped places with the ethereal beauty that once was in control.

"Ah. I would be mad.... IF. I. WASN'T. ALREADY. FUCKING. FURIOUS. YOU GODDAMN BITCH. I TOLD YOU. NOT. TO. LOOK. AT ME, LIKE THAT!"

The animal picked up her torso and tossed it onto the cracked throne with so much force, the chair and the entire throne room rumbled. Massive fissures expanded, which caused the ceiling to cave in noticeably. In the blink of an eye, he stomped on her chest repeatedly. The entire time, she didn't let out a whimper. The ghostly mirage of the man called Finch shook his head in disappointment, turned away, then vanished alongside a gentle sigh.

"Haaaa. God dammit. Stupid fucking immortal my ass. Ha. Right. Let's get back to it then." The abomination turned, looked left, then right, then back at the throne covered in the ashes of a supposed immortal. He looked behind it with another look of bewilderment.

"Where did my empress go? Did I squish her?" He wiped away the ash on the throne, expecting to find the crushed body of his girl, but there was no one. The entire throne room was empty, aside from the piles of ash that accumulated due to the ghoulish green flame that licked at his skin like a pet.

"Ah. I see. It was an illusion. My darling little empress probably escaped once her wretched mother got in the way of our love yet again." A twisted smile cracked across the animalistic hero's face as he sat down and spread flame everywhere. Ghoulish creatures with long and twisted forms scattered in all directions as they cracked and ripped out the floor, walls, and ceiling of the throne room.

"I can't...." the old bald man, our now standard narrator, collapsed to the floor as the very last golden thread on his clothing dulled to a blanched or washed out color.

"Can't run...." A handful of rings fell out of his now empty pockets, but they were so dull and chipped, it would be a miracle if he could use them to power even a single fiber of his mystical clothing.

"Anymore." The girl did her best to keep the old man from dropping to the ash-carpeted ground, but even her will to stand was nowhere to be seen as she fell to the ground with her father. A rain of soot and blood descended upon the two. Waterfalls ran down the poor girl's face as darkness stained her alabaster skin and gleaming clothing. The memory of an oceanic emerald forest, endless farmlands, and a towering citadel now burned and unraveled. Towering behemoths roamed and tore up millennia-old roots with every step while warriors and soldiers of all sizes and creeds lived and died together in a hopeless struggle.

"If only I had accepted the hero's offer and accepted whatever he would've done to me, *then my people, Everyone wouldn't be."* The girl trembled at the horrifying sight before her, mainly because the earth itself rumbled and collapsed under the titanic weight of various creatures in the distance. One such towering beast with a reptilian appearance but a humanoid shape, blindsided a roughly shaped ox that twisted with writhing flesh.

The carcass of a massive squished eyeball with thousands of burrowed holes in its body dropped to the ground from the horns of this massive ox. Hundreds of its tentacles flashed in the direction of the humanoid reptile and released blinding lights from a similar number of eyes at the end of each tentacle. The ox's back writhed a moment afterward, rerouting innumerable tendrils of flesh and spiked bone to reinforce itself. Initially, these eyes and tentacles moved independently to skewer the lifeforms below and around it.

The humanoid dragon effortlessly stepped to the side in a reactionary flash of movement and with a thunderous flap of its gargantuan wings, the dragon pounced atop the twisted ox and ripped into its wiggling spine and back with such savagery and desperation, one would assume it possessed the same origin as the cryptic beast. The difference lay in the dragon's eyes. They were bright, alert, and snapped in each direction to inform its movements and assess dangers to its wellbeing. They also shone with fury and sorrow and grief near unbearable as green blood stained each and every tear that fell from its purple eyes. As the monsters traded blows, a titanic creature with three more segments and twice as many appendages when compared to an anatomically correct spider, leaped from the shadow cast by the two larger combatants and skittered up the dragon's back. Though its size dwarfed in comparison, its spear-like appendages ripped flesh and distracted the dragon long enough for the ox to gain its four jointed and several dozen legs and roll. The dragon, pulled back and slightly paralyzed by the spider, could do nothing as the ox used its immense size and weight to break the dragon's wings and a leg. With another death roll, the ox reared its head and prepared a devastating blow. The dragon released a condensed beam of white-purple flame even as another spider nipped and paralyzed the other side of its body. In a grand display, a pillar of light parted the dust clouds just as the ox's split skull slammed down and pierced through the dragon's head.

The dragon's emerald blood and decaying flesh drowned and crushed friend and foe alike as the huge scaled beast was eaten by a swarm of spiders that rushed in from every direction to use the corpse as a breeding bed. Despite the insane distance, the princess could clearly see the execution atop one of the massive hills made from the branches of the planetary tree. Her people suffered loss after loss. Protectors, large and small, received deadly blows and were devoured by an endlessly increasing horde. The tips of the princesses' long ears drooped. The tidy braids that kept her hair up in a tight bun fell apart. Shades of rose mingled with small splotches of green and highlighted her person and vision. Blood-stained dust and fog filled the corrupt air and painted everything.

"It's over. No one is coming to help. They all left us stranded just because of that ... That, PIG!" The girl, the child, clenched the ash and cried, mostly out of frustration and the inability to help.

"Your highness, the empress. Your mother. She stayed behind so that you could get to a safe location. In any case, all is not yet lost. As long as you live, we can beat that tyrant even if...." The old man quickly controlled his breathing and knelt beside his daughter with a shudder and fearful glint. He examined everything around him in almost a panic as he attempted to get the girl to stand. A piercing laugh, more of a cackle, lit up the bloodied night.

"That's. Our home!" The girl's color drained just as her father's did.

"Dad?" she gripped the hand of the person who stood up to support her despite his own exhausted body.

"Daddy?"

He shook, almost as if he were caught in an earthquake. The old man's already ragged breath shortened to pleading gasps as he choked on the thickened air. An inferno, the likes of which could rival a sun's primordial ignition, consumed the world as a campfire would dry weeds. Tens of thousands turned to ash in the instant immolation; even more choked on the stifling air and immediately died as a flame burned their lungs and blood. A tree that had been around since the conception of vegetation as an idea, vanished without a single trace. The being that took shape within the flames twisted and writhed.

A nightmare beyond description, and such a monstrosity just turned its molten eyes toward his daughter. Faster than the time it took for lightning to strike, a snake of fire reached over hundreds of thousands of kilometers like an outstretched finger across the length of a page in a book. A person rose out of this liquid flame as if nothing could faze him. The abomination of a hero that took shape smiled at the new toy he was about to acquire.

"Dad, let's go!" The girl pulled her father away even with tracks of sparkling tears along her face. Energy she didn't recognize filled her body as everything screamed to survive and protect the frail old man beside her. He pulled himself together under the strong tug of this tiny future empress, but a thought suddenly printed itself in his mind.

"What would this monster do to my daughter if I hold her back? She's slowing down for me. She has been since I took her away from the throne room." The old man collected as much as he knew of the hero and realized it could be summarized as:

"This 'Hero' saved the world no less than a dozen times and retired not too long ago. He founded, funded, and became the principal *of a new institution for the young and gifted on the northern continent. There have been some complaints, rumors, and severe accusations against him in the few years his establishment has been running. Despite that, no evidence has been found. All in all, my wife and I decided against sending our baby. I expected and planned for his world renown temper after we turned down a direct* invitation, but *why? NO, it's what. What cruel fate will our baby have to endure because of my mess up? No, it's too unimaginable. He needs to die. Here. Now. Somehow."*

The man spat venom in his heart, hardened his resolve, and let go of his little girl's hand without any regard for his old bones. He dashed towards a living and unmerciful flame that embodied rage, frenzy, and sickening desire.

"RUN!"

Ultimate, unending, eternal power coursed through the old man's hand as the twin powers of justice and retribution coiled in his fist. This strike would end everything. BANG.

"Huh? Who? OH. Hey old guy, did you just hit me?" Instead of lashing out, the hero paused in his steps in genuine surprise and stared at the old man, who clenched his own bleeding wrist and exposed bone.

"Ha. You have no ranked stars. Haa. No way. Low grade. Haa-ha. LEVEL ONE. No fucking way. Haa. A normal squire mouse or etheroach is stronger than you, but you actually managed to hit me without me noticing." The affront to the living actually broke out in laughter and doubled over. Innocent, joyful laughter at the prospect of this old man's simple existence.

"I don't even want to know how you survived this long. I mean, look at your stats; a blade of grass has more magic than you. Wait, you! Ah, you must be the fabled Cursed Scholar, the Imperial prince consort. Haa. Your Highness." The false hero bowed.

"Haa, you know what? I have nothing but respect for you, old guy. You managed to fuck your way to the top of the world, so good on you. Honestly,...." Something miraculous occurred. A shred of humanity flashed behind the steaming excrement's eyes. No, humanity is too strong a word. Blinding arrogance created the illusion of humanity as he generously healed the old man's broken wrist by melding the wound closed.

"Imma let you live, seeing as you're the first person to genuinely hit me in years. Though, I don't know how long you'll survive out here all alone. I'm sure you only survived the effusion of those monsters because of my princess over there and your, well, your Arcanum are pretty much trash now aren't they." The jackal laughed some more, periodically looking back at the helpless old man to reignite his chuckle. The inherent cruelty of leaving a defenseless and useless person in a chaotic, magic-fueled war zone, in the ruins of THE Empire, wasn't lost on him. At a loss for words, the old man crumbled to his knees in fear while the heartless flea approached his daughter.

The girl barely stood up against the fright that coursed through her own bones now. Her legs carried her no farther than two steps before she fell, unable to fight against crippling fear without a parental figure by her side. No, if one could read her thoughts, they would have noticed that she realized something and stopped herself from taking that third step.

"Dad will get crushed by the radiation and effusion if I leave." She tried to run away, really, but seeing her father's soulless eyes as he mouthed for her to run, begged her to run. He even fell backward and crawled, millimeters at a time, to separate himself. A resounding snap overpowered her sniffles as a heavy object crushed her foot and ankle. Something else slapped her to the floor and rattled her thoughts.

The old man's eyes sharpened. The choking fear that gripped his throat and left him unable to even take a breath turned into a weight on his heart that filled him with volcanic rage. His body stopped trembling and rushed at the abomination's back. No thoughts, no plan, just pure instinct. He was slow, and old, and really only moved in more of a flustered shamble due to the sudden aching pain coursing throughout his entire body but it was the greatest speed he could muster without his tools, mystical equipment that allowed him to at least secure his meager existence.

"Absolutely not. NEVER. I will not allow my child to be harmed in such a way, not right in front of me!" The moment his mind caught up to his body, his gait steadied and speed increased. Sadly, he was just too slow overall and could not cover the two steps his daughter took. Two steps, in this case, being several dozen meters due to her extraordinary speed and strength. The hero, however, had no trouble covering the distance as he lifted his foot and stamped down to grind her ankle to dust. Before her scream could get loud enough, the hero reached out and gripped her jaw with wild abandon. The tiara atop the girl's tiny head fell to the side as the hair being held in place curled up and burned under the heat of his touch.

"Look at what we have here? Hmm Mn MN. You are fucking cute. I'm a bit disappointed, though. I thought you would be more like your mom. She had those slutty eyes despite the way she looked at me— a big rack too. She was a real woman. Though girls like you also have their own type of charm." The deranged shadow of a hero licked his lips with a disgusting look in his eyes. Not caring about shame, the age difference, or his own humanity and morality. Thankfully and also unfortunately, the girl's now naked body could not be seen as the man's out-of-control flames burst out with impatience and charred nearly 90% of her skin into an indescribable mess. The unfortunate part is here: the guy was sane enough to prevent the wounds from spreading so deep that he died. Instead, the wounds toed the line of being irreversible.

"AH. Fuck. Dammit. I got too excited. Tch. I did all of this for nothing now." The hero dropped her half-dead body to the ground with a disappointed sigh. Her cries now fell silent as the heat choked and melted her airways.

"Such a shame. You would have grown up a bit if you were with me. Too bad. You aren't in any state to come live with me right now." It frowned as it examined the girls' burned figure.

"I guess. Hm, if I fix you up a bit, maybe I could still use some parts of you. Oh, that's actually not a bad idea. I killed your mom too quickly, but if I could get a proper healer over, you could be saved." It narrowed its eyes. Despite the charred skin and despite being unable to properly breathe or move, the little empress glared through her half-sealed eyes and sneered at the disgusting animal that pretended to still have standards. The lust and undeniable greed in his eyes and the bulge in his pants showed that he was not planning to give up on "his" princess even if he had to travel to the underworld and back. This was all just some kind of sick and twisted, self-satisfying foreplay.

"You. Fucking. Bitch. Stop looking at me like that. Right Now. Or, Ha. Fuck! I will seriously kill you." The thing stomped on her legs and arms, absolutely infuriated, but the girl didn't even let out a breath.

A frail and old fist carried the wrath of a God and none of the power. The old man, who had been forgotten, lunged at the godforsaken hero's back. Though even that may not be entirely true. His wedding ring, the only piece of jewelry that did not have a gem or some glowing inscription, the only piece of jewelry that rebound itself to his person in a silent and unassuming manner, writhed with dark twisting runes. A shadow, as dark as night and as ever promising as the release of death, forcefully opened his clenched fist with a silent whisper. The ring transformed into a dagger.

"This time, I will die. I accepted your arrangement long ago, Lady Death, Shemishier. It would seem as though I belong to you now. Ha, I just hope my little baby can get past this, and become just as strong as her mother. Look after her for me, as a favor to an old friend." The old man plunged the tip of the dagger into the abomination's hunched over back, straight towards its heart. A ghastly black flame shot out in response to the blade.

"No, actually. You don't have to. I'm sure her mother will find a way to guide our baby on the right path. I can see it now. Surrounded by smiles, laughter, and love. She is already the greatest little Empress, the best our people could ever pray for. So, Lady Shemi, if she ever meets you in any of the accursed events that have guided my life thus far, please let her know that I love her..." The old man saw an immeasurably hot flame blast in his direction before he could even blink and in that moment, everything came to an abrupt halt.

1.2 Unexpected 2nd Chance

"*There are a lot more details in this nightmare compared to my other ones.*" A bright-eyed and bushy-haired boy briefly overlapped with the old man at this moment of cinematic pause.

Unimpeded, the face pushed forward and hovered away as a legless and mint-colored apparition. He even pushed through the accursed hero with an innocent glint in his eye and a look of confusion. Images of the old man running up the steps and of the hero's one-sided massacre flashed on the sliver within the boy's eye and informed him of the dreams' contents.

"*Why am I sleeping though? I was just camping out with Fell. I'm sure I was just pointing out the* sights, *so* it *couldn't be that I ....*" The ghostly apparition of a boy frowned as he floated through the chaotic war zone.

"*Did I fall out by accident or faint? Hm, it also took me longer than usual to enter a somewhat lucid state.*" The boy hovered in a brief circle and patted down his half-formed legs. After a few moments, he paused over the old man and the hero.

"Ah well. I still have to check my setting, regardless. I have to make sure that I am where I am and what I'm supposed to be. It would suck if this were all some elaborate illusion or a terrarium, or a sim. Can a Sim have this type of quality?"

The boy flew up toward the ash-filled clouds and clicked his tongue at the state of the sky. Well, sky was not the right word for what he was seeing. Blinding explosions and pillars the size of entire nebulae attempted to pierce and push against a dark red and almost black mass of pure emptiness and razor-sharp mouths, so not emptiness. The boy crossed his arms and pouted as the mass chewed through everything.

"That monster, I think Mom called it an Aberrant Verechen hump-back—a void whale. It is supposed to be extinct." The boy clicked his tongue for the second time.

"I suppose this type of dream is more of a nightmare than any of my other nightmares. It's not as scary as my training, though." The ghostly apparition shivered for a moment and then swam through the air and hovered around the head of the old man.

"As per usual, I was expecting to see some versions of Mom or Dad pulling some strings somewhere. Maybe a roided-out giant chasing me as this decrepit old man or some lightning demon shooting at me from halfway across the world." The boy suddenly remembered the lightning and odd narrator from the beginning of the dream and frowned.

"I don't suppose that counts?" The boy touched his neck with a look of incredulity and decided to let the story unfold. He dove back into the old man's chest and let the world return to a functional pace.

Almost instantly, the old man's perspective, emotions, and thoughts directed the narrative of the nightmare. As such, he roared not only in his own mind but also in the ears of the boy who viewed everything through his eyes.

"THIS ABSOLUTE WASTE OF LIFE! You will never lay your hands *on anyone ever again. You disgusting BASTARD OF A MON-GREL AND A REVLIAN. I would've tortured you for the rest of your conceivable human lifespan if only I* weren't *cursed. DIE!"*

The dagger that fused to his burned skin ripped even further into the animal's body. Shredding muscle and scraping bone. The blade's tip and edge met with a snow-white wall of flame that shielded the hero's almost exposed heart. Time stuttered awkwardly as everything around the old man's hand shimmered and warped. The illusion of a folding and shattered glass sphere shone with a blinding opalescence and dark haze. The edge of the old man's dagger sparked and chipped under the solidifying reflections. The dark haze of the blade shrouded his arm and dispersed the opalescent and mirror-like flame in a spiral behind the old man's shoulder.

"... DIE!" The old man roared out loud as the chipped dagger slipped through the glassy flame and pierced the hero's heart. All of existence expanded and then contracted around this singular moment. The boy raised an eyebrow as he floated within the old man's pupils. Without any warning at all, the boy felt a searing heat burn across his own spectral neck and spine as something tugged him out of the old man's body toward the opalescent implosion of flaming glass and divine haze. The weightlessness of being in some control of his nightmare flipped into a sickening dread the moment his body began to solidify.

"Am I waking up?"

The boy felt everything go dark, but that solid sensation turned to an ethereal chill deep in his core. In the blink of an eye, he was thrust towards a horizon where the glittering flame and the all-encompassing haze harmoniously intermingled. To the boy, it appeared as though two cosmic entities were locked in a gripping conversation. In one swift moment, the boy crashed onto the floor. From another point of view, however, he simply rose from the ground. Either way, he stumbled in an attempt to gather his footing.

"This is new. I've had dreams in dreams, nightmares in nightmares, and I've even had them suddenly intermingle as I lost and regained my consciousness inside of a sim. But this? This, however, is something very different and frightening. My soul, I think, has just been pulled out of my body." The boy examined his very physical and very solid state. Well, most of his solid body. Faintly, as if someone dusted his clothes with sparkling dust, he lit up with all manner of colorful sparks, and if he focused, he could see through his own body.

"Mom said if I ever found myself glowing in this manner in a dream or in illusion, then it's a sign that I am most likely in a magically induced coma, I have died, or am dying. Hm, Lady Death was mentioned earlier, meaning I subconsciously already know that I am either dead or dying since if I were in a coma, I would have already woken myself out of it." The boy crossed his arms and tapped the floor with his toe.

"Why can't I remember anything? What was I doing to end up this way?"

The boy touched his hands together only to find that they could slip through each other if he pressed hard enough, though with the same resistance of wading through jelly.

"This form, it's similar to when Dad taught me how to astral project, but it feels much weightier." The boy shuffled forward after gathering his body and thoughts.

"The environment is odd. Despite the solid nature of every structure, it's as soft as Karrellien Sheep. Softer?"

He touched the walls and floor around him and marveled at the firmness and springiness that seemed to change with the pressure and force that he applied. His hand, when being firm, created heavy lines that held distinct 3 dimensional impressions of color and depth but also allowed him to phase through the surface and melt into shadows they cast. All in all, he could both see and see through most, if not all, the things in his environment. Pillars held the corridor ajar, but they also stretched as far into the sky as they were infinitely reflected into the ground, similar to how his hand could both move through and touch the solid ground. Beyond that, he could still see the white, self-mirroring flame, and the dark divine haze. As he moved, the incorporeal mesh of structure twisted into the distinct overgrowth of wild plants, clipped hedges and bushes, and flowers of indescribable cultivation and beauty. Nature's wild and tamed aspects seemed to mingle here perfectly as the plants floated all around in patches of multicolored soil that did and did not actually have a material form.

And the simple yet complex architecture, just sublime. For instance, the endless walls were crafted with a snow-like marble that reflected runic veining of a dark black mineral and the purest gold. But when he looked through the physical material, the entire universe unfolded and overlapped into a clouded pool of seemingly random shapes and colorful splashes that somehow reflected the organized room inside. Like the concept of inside and outside, this and that, up and down, all of it was just a matter of perspective and what he intended to concentrate on at the moment.

By some miracle, the boy managed to pull himself away from the Ouroborus of trying to understand the chaos and shut down any attempts to figure out why he couldn't remember anything prior to this nightmare. He ruled out the possibility that he was dead since he didn't want to come to grips with it just yet, and he focused himself on what mattered.

"I have this feeling I shouldn't be here. Everything is beyond me." He paused, ready to be found and removed, but the burning sensation that planted itself on his neck did not diminish in the slightest. Despite the distance he felt to the environment, something compelled him onward.

"I probably shouldn't investigate based on this feeling, but being stuck in this spot will not do anything for me." He briefly touched his neck while biting his upper lip and decisively followed the only path available to him. Throughout the journey, the long-eared boy tapped his fingers over the casually strewn plants and flowers, delicately appreciating the beauty they had to offer while also respecting their arrangement so as not to damage the leaves, petals, or stems. Most of the walk, he marveled at the intricate designs of the architecture, mouth agape. Interestingly, as he ventured further into the unknown, the environment became less intangible and see-through. His focus only broke when he heard a horrifyingly familiar voice.

"Have patience? Ha. Let me think about it." The boy's steps slowed as he cleared his ears with an unsure expression.

"*Erm. My nightmare was just* that, *right? A nightmare. There's no way that a fictional hero I conjured up is a real person.*" The boy flinched.

".... No, you see. I've come to the conclusion that you tricked me, ya fucking asshole. You promised me that nothing in the world could kill me when I got reincarnated." The boy froze on the spot as his blood curled.

"The blade that pierced your heart and its wielder are inconsequential. Instead, think about why you died. I will be gracious and give you a hint, hubris." Whatever that thing was, snorted. Almost disdainfully, considering the tone.

"*Reincarnation,* huh? *Of* course, *a human got another shot at life. It's people like him* who *make it so hard for everyone else to study and revive the mysticism behind such a phenomenon. Tch, but that thing must be his divine patron. Damnit parents. I understand the training and your fear of my* events, *but neither of you informed me that things like this could happen. Damned curse.*" The boy thought to himself, slumped against the wall, and closed his eyes as he felt a searing pain rocketing through his body. He scratched the side of his neck with a look of annoyance and released a heavy sigh. A massive and colorful tattoo snaked up and around his neck to his spine.

An incomplete infinity symbol swirled behind his long ear for exactly five seconds before a jumble of nonsense symbols, letters, and numbers flashed with the words, "**CHANCE EVENT**" and all the details of said encounter. Though it can be determined from how dejected the boy was, he did not know what these runes or symbols meant. Against his better judgment, the long-eared boy opened his eyes and ears to pay attention. The skulls of men and monsters grazed his fingertips as moldings engraved in the wall.

"Bullshit. The fucken asshole had a God-killing weapon. Like, the old shit stabbed me with an item that's rated with nine stars. How did a shitty, old-ass elf have a weapon like that? The star-rating restrictions? The level requirement? Where the fuck was any of that, huh?"

The animal roared and stomped. His eyes nearly popped out of his skull.

"I'll give you another hint, boy. Willfully ignorant. You would have perished in that moment regardless of your foolish actions. Thus, the dagger and the LERIAN who used it are inconsequential."

"LIAR. Fucking Liar!"

The animal shook violently, like a kettle ready to blow, as he directed the tantrum toward a vast being that stretched across infinity. Its viewable flesh writhed in some parts and in others, it resembled a stone wall carved with monstrous hieroglyphs that danced with life. Above the vast "thing" was a halo that illuminated heavenly and shadowed cosmic bodies. The halo and bodies spun and surrounded a teardrop-shaped jewel that crowned the massive creature's head.

Despite it all, the oddest bit about the whole being was the shape of its face. It pinched into a comfortable and plush throne of cushions.

Sitting there, a humanoid person in a featureless mask. Golden discs pierced through where the eyes should have been. A lion's mane of thick forested, blood red hair, drooped over the person's shoulders like a scarf. Legs crossed, fingers raised into a faux smile on the mask. The boy, having gathered the courage to move and gaze upon this being, rounded his corner and skulked through the hall. He stood in the shadow of a massive pillar to observe the ongoings that he should not be privy to under normal circumstances.

"That being's visage is not depicted in any modern or ancient mythos. It's possible that it's a principal deity of an unrecorded era. Hm, or is it some kind of celestial from the voided era like the God of monstrosities Xylopherus? Maybe this is Xylo considering the physicality of the thing. That obviously is not right given the context clues. Its appearance is somewhat reminiscent of an old hymn about the Primogenitor of Absolution, the perceived end of creation and the creator of the Eternal lovers." The boy thought to and kept to himself upon noticing how one of the many eyes of the throne instantly latched onto his location before he even entered the hall.

"YOU DICK. I WAS BASICALLY A GOD! Did you see my stats?! My gear?! I even one-shot that stupid bitch! Fuck, what's his nam e... Whatever, the Incarnation of the Abyss. YOU KNOW WHAT,

NAH! You planned this shit. You killed me using that old fuck, right!?!"

The animal barked, foaming at the mouth in absolute madness. His eyes bulged as he tore at his own skin in absolute insanity. Going from hero to 0 really must have hurt.

"This man's mouth is worse than an Ashen Drem's after a mug of Swamp Ale. What is this entity thinking? Allowing such crass behavior in its presence. My mom would have popped me on the mouth for raising my voice out of turn and my dad would have stuffed me inside a century's worth of looping simulations for using such vulgar language," the boy shook his head and simply took in everything from the side.

"Young one. Hear us. The world we brought you too, holds more secrets than you could possibly know or even understand...."

"Brought to? Is this hero from another universe as well as a reincarnator? Is he from the Storm, the Graves, or outside of Eternity?"

The boy took in every word with a consistently deepening frown.

"I had power, freedom, and love! Everything I've never had. Then you take it all away? FUCK THAT! IT WAS MY RIGHT! IT WAS ALL MINE! I paid my dues and earned everything with hard work and good behavior, so it's not fair." The animal reached the point of insanity where the world returned to a semblance of normal once more.

"You planned for me to die there? You're just like those bastards who took advantage of me, trying to 'help' in their own way." By some miracle, a hint of recognition flashed through the animals' eyes as he remembered who this being actually was and lowered his voice to almost a whisper.

"Young one, we want you to have all the things you couldn't have before. To do that, you have to understand yourself more..."

"Then why did you kill me? I was doing my best with the powers you helped me unlock. I did my best to help everyone, like I was asked. I was just having a bit of fun at the end... I just... I didn't realize how bad..."

"Firstly. Do not cut us off again. We cannot harm you by right, but you are not untouchable. So, we advise you to steady yourself. Secondly, you do not understand what has been given to you or what you have gained. Perhaps you may have had an inclination when you were still in control of your soul, but now? You let yourself be consumed almost completely by your own corruption. Know that if you lose yourself and fall into your own self-induced insanity, the status that you do so enjoy turns to dust, and all of those that are waiting for such a thing to occur would no longer be stayed by my hand." The being pointed at the animal with a dismissive wag of its free hand. Its voice even and cold throughout.

"Thirdly, and as I have said before, your death is your own fault. Why did you let your guard down when you are personally aware of what a desperate person is capable of? Were not you also desperate to survive at one point during your first few years of traveling in this new world? Were you not also such a person in your previous life? Desperate to do your best, to do the right thing, to be a good person and ultimately to survive? Is that not why you strive and work for more?" The being closed its golden discs, showing a small glimpse of a vast abyss beneath the mask.

"Finally, and back onto the topic of yourself, have you ever stopped to look back on your actions after you've gained the freedom and limitless power you now hold in this new lifetime? Have you rooted out the core of your being?"

"I... I uh..." The animal blinked in fear. Memories flooded back up and reminded him of what he's done and seen since he was given this new lease on life.

"Have you ever stopped to appreciate and understand what the people around you had to go through to get you to this current position?..."

"No. NO!"

"Furthermore, when did you decide that it didn't matter if someone accepted you as an equal? Imposing yourself on whomever and whenever you fancied. Why did you change so much? Did you change at all?"

The image of a kindhearted and naïve nice young man overlapped with an insane monster in the animal's mind.

"That wasn't me! NO. It wasn't me. Stop."

"And your actions, each of them, slowly desensitized your humanity. Who or what corrupted your personal beliefs? Were you ever paused by the acts you were committing? When was it that you presumed to know the nature of this world's mysticism, rules, its people, or yourself?"

"It wasn't me. The Devil—no, Mortis—made me do it. No, the voices, the fire? Yeah, it was that damned burning spirit. I couldn't control it. I tried to fight back, but..." The animal backed away with each pointed statement. The image of a tiny living opalescent flame being caged, abused, and turned into an unintelligent, impure shell by the animal flashed through his mind.

"No? It wasn't you? What about the other times you did not choose him as your guide through life? Why is this outcome so recurrent?"

More images of the young man overlapped as several thousand recurring lifetimes suddenly filled his mind. More often than not, the monster would show its head, regardless of how his circumstances changed.

"Believe me. Please. It wasn't me. I'm not like that. I'm not. Give me one more chance, please. That's not me. Believe me. Please." The animal was forced to remember entire lifetimes that were reset by this entity. All of the second, hundreds, thousands, millions and even more chances constantly looped and reminded the insane hero how his actions never really changed.

The boy could see the fog of images that flashed around the animal. He clearly saw the choices of entire lifetimes burrow into the man's eyes and mind, reminding him of his own beliefs and failures even as he fought to make himself better. The animal curled up on the floor. A babbling mess of tears and throw-up. No, the hair all over the boy's body tingled as a chill swept through his body. The bastard hero was actually smiling and holding his wet crotch through the fear-stricken and tearful display.

The masked person clapped once and chuckled as they leaned onto their palm to relax their posture.

"...Sure. I'll believe you. Even if Reality and Death themselves wanted to mop you up, even if Fate decreed that you would forever be who you are, even if Life's infinite variables began to repeat and you made the same mistakes. I will plead on your behalf, for it is my job to help those even my parents and family do not deem fit enough to exist. So chin up. How about I give you another try? You'll start fresh. No memories of anything you've done previously, no record of your past sins, just you and an infinitely promising clean slate of a future. Let's see if you can figure it out this time. From the very beginning, one more time..."

"*NO!*—NO!"

The boy bit his lip but dared not scream out as the fallen hero did. Sadly, the bastard hero could not put up a single iota of resistance as the masked being snapped their fingers.

"Boy, please forgive that troubled youth for what he has done and what he may do in your future. As an aside, thank you for understanding yourself, Alizedriel. We are delighted with their ability to find their place in the world. Hmm. Also, take great care in not cheating on her when the time comes." The being spoke directly into the boy's soul and sent him away with a casual flick of a finger.

The boy crossed his arms and tilted his head with confusion written across his forehead as he was pulled back across the hallway that he had previously walked. He fell or rose through the floor and fluttered across an expanse of a clashing divine haze and a white, almost refractory, flame. Seconds later, the boy crashed through numerous glassy reflections and back out of the gray-scale implosion at the hero's back. Unwillingly, the boy called Alizedriel slammed back into the long-eared old man's chest and resumed the nightmare that he did not find scary.

The gray shades all around the hero and old man blurred into a view of nonsense images that manifested as sickening cracks that would have disoriented the kid if he wasn't about to wake up.

1.3 Minor Issues

A silent scream ripped out of Alizedriel's mouth as every fiber of his being screamed to run away from the fire that roasted his soul. Unaware of his own physical state and rather precarious placement, the kid accidentally rolled out of bed and crashed onto the ground. Before the child even had time to scream again, a litany of temporary splints and makeshift casts displaced and cracked with a soft and practically inaudible hiss as blood sprayed out of the wrappings. One of the splints, however, pressed onto his windpipe and forced his silence. The poor kid had no other choice but to collect his ragged thoughts and match the insane changes, that or choke to death. Seconds later, and infinitely calmer, his head tilted over and restored his ability to breathe.

"I'm alive! Why am I so happy about that?"

The nightmarish burns that he felt just one second ago vanished to the back of his mind as they were replaced by a whirling storm of uncomfortable, shocking jolts, and fathomless chills that threatened to remove or numb his sensations altogether.

"What is wrong with me?"

Alize stretched his neck to get a good look at his location and his body, carefully circumventing the cracked protrusion that pressed on his throat not even two seconds before. Thatched and wooden walls and several pieces of rudimentary furniture immediately stood out. There were three leathery drapes drawn over a window at each face of the boxy room, and a massive ornate carpet hung over the doorway. As for lifting his head and looking down at himself, he found that it was currently impossible.

"This all looks remarkably familiar, but why can't I place it? Did I lose any memories? It's certainly possible if I hit my head just right, which is quite possible considering my horrible headache." Alize closed his eyes and checked himself again. Through squinted eyes and choking breaths, he could just barely make out a minty green aura emanating from one of his arms and lower body area. With an even harder squint, he noticed how the compact light turned into a soft mist towards his midsection and chest as well as his joints. Being far-sighted sucked in this particular case, but he made do by extending his neck as far as his horrible condition would allow.

His strenuous endeavor bore some result as he could just make out the features of a braided rope harness. The item lit up with fractals of icy blue mist and a soft gray haze that spread to his entire body. With a steely resolve, the kid lifted his head against the broken neck brace, cutting his throat, and examined the device while a knife of plaster cut off his airflow. A blue circle of indecipherable runes floated in a small crystal casing on the chest piece of the harness, somewhat resembling a heartbeat as it pushed out one layer of ice mist after the other.

"In for a penny..." The kid felt the hard plaster attempt to pierce his larynx as he pressed the numbing sensation to its absolute limit. Just faintly, he could see his stomach squirm like an injured serpent.

Presumably, some rather aggressive medicine tore through his body like hell on wheels and caused such an odd movement in his bowels. The kid's head quickly slammed back into the ground as he gasped for breath.

"This all really is too familiar. I've seen all of this before, but it's all blurry. Maybe if I try to focus on what's missing, I can fill in the blanks with what I do remember."

Alizedriel slowly closed his eyes and let a ragged breath escape his lips.

"This is my bedroom. I'm home right now, but I should be outside celebrating my best friend's birthday weekend. Since I have returned home in such a state, I can only assume something went horribly wrong. I do remember I fell. I mean, yeah, I just fell out of bed, but hm, something is wrong." The kid opened his eyes and scanned the room for anything out of place now that his memories and muddled senses began to sharpen.

"My bed frame still has the same number of notches, my constellation charts are still on the desk and are in the same meticulously detailed order, every poster on the walls is arranged how I left it with not a single detail out of place. Yet, my current state still doesn't make any sense." Alize narrowed his eyes and looked over everything a third time, even his own body, but found nothing out of the ordinary.

"My instincts are screaming at me right now. Something is wrong." The kid felt his fingers get swarmed with pins and needles and twitched them with a look of surprise.

"Considering the variety and depth of illusion spells that are banned, hidden by the Empire and Guilds, lost to history, or any of the other options." Alize turned the twitch of his hand into a functional level of motor control with a few strenuous exercises.

"I have to slow down. EPA. Exhaust, Prepare, Act. Okay. What can I do to counter or assuage my instincts? What am I going to do now? The first conclusion that I can come to, since nothing looks off at first glance, is I have somehow fallen into a Grave Terrarium. The second possibility is an instantly cast Bifurcation Loop of Internal Physiology or in cast Blip, but that type of terrarium would alert my parents before it managed to consume me..."

The boy quickly looked over toward his bedside table. It held nothing but three books and a small floating and glowing orb that hovered over a magnetized base piece. One of the books was held open by a pen, pencil, eraser, and a variety of sticky note packages with different colors and shapes since it was a simple art book. "Odd Observations #09" and "Dream Journal #89" were written on the spines of the other two of the books in bold letters that were made of glued sticky note scraps.

"Mom and Dad have shown me that they are more than capable of pulling me out of that magical anomaly before it disappears when we were in the Sim-Terr. That fact leaves Ual Jisse Majori and Minori that I learned about. These phenomena are normally localized to a completely different continent, but despite the astronomical likelihood, it's possible that I fell into one of those at some point in my future and now I am in a storm that's replaying my childhood. If that's the case, my life up until now has been mostly fabricated." The boy scanned his room for anything out of place, missing, or even just discolored in a way it should not be for the fourth and fifth time as he slowly trained to raise and hold his arm.

"The next most likely possibility is an attack by some creature or the defensive mechanism of some plant that I managed not to detect or identify while camping with that snack gremlin. But again, it doesn't fit my situation since this particularly familiar space is not falling apart

at the seams, nor are the shadows or textures acting funny. There is also my missing memory of what exactly happened. A low-level or graded illusion would have filled in the gaps with what I do remember, causing anomalies the more I think about it. It's also not likely that any stronger individuals or creatures cast such an elaborate illusion since they would have been found and eliminated by Mom before getting to me. It's also not possible to keep me in such a state since any animals or plants who could cast such a high graded illusion are in a region of Jordaine that's on the other side of the country." Unsure of what had even happened to him, Alize took stock of his memories and compared the possibilities.

"Alright wait! I'm starting to remember. Let me take a step back. Starting with the more obvious approach, I did fall. I fell, not here obviously, but somewhere else, and it was a pretty bad one considering. It explains the bandages, casts, and splints. If I go with this logic, most likely, I was already in a near-death state before I fell. But that would imply a purposeful ambush or an attack of such magnitude that Mom could not protect me and I could not defend or evade. Which implies an enemy much, much stronger than anything that I have practiced against. An impossibility since Mom was nearby, hunting for dinner. Unless, did Wynifell attack me?" Alize frowned at the jolt that locked his stretching hand into a chicken claw of a clench.

"No. That girl is way too much of a crybaby and muscle-head. It is more likely that something tried to attack her, and I got in the way. Or was I just in the way of it doing something? Dad told me that back when the Ashen were called the Bludhauzshe, the ages 10, 50, 100, and 150 held some type of religious and mystical significance. Could I have gotten in the way of some mystical milestone? Ha, ancient history and religious studies aren't really in my curriculum right now, so I don't know the particulars, but could it be possible that my idiot friend has an ancient

mana or aura profile and something happened there? Tch. What a joke!" Alize slapped his forehead, losing all of his will to think of the matter.

"I sound like a nut. Ha. There's no point in exhausting myself if I cannot even move more than a single arm." Like a horse, his gums flapped with the pressurized release of a breath he didn't even know he held onto. Gasping for fresh air, the kid did nothing but think about himself. In fact, the first thing he analyzed was the tiny crystal dome fixed onto the harness covering his torso.

"It's a Quill Bank, a Quibe. A magical battery capable of storing a single spell. It has, let's see, it appears to be a C. Type spell. [Stasis] perhaps? Dad must have cast it on the bank and rigged it to the harness to spread the effect to the rest of my body. It explains the icy chill and gray mist around my joints." He moved on to the bandages and medical supplies that covered his entire body. The bandages and casts were actually woven, sprinkled, or somehow infused with tiny green fibers resembling glass. In the exact same way the golf ball size crystal held an indecipherable rune inside of it, the crystal green fibers held miniature scriptures that would make one's mind boggle since they were only visible on a cellular level. Evidently, multiple Quill Banks or magical batteries were woven into the bandages.

"There is definitely a D-type spell, perhaps a mixed variation of [First Aid] and a few others considering the coloration and illustrations." His head bobbed from side to side softly as all the initial anxiety whittled away under his mechanical approach to understanding his situation.

"Finer, more exact details like this are impossible in a standard-grade illusion, never mind a low-grade one. It's possible with a high grade, but again, there is the matter of my missing memory. It's possible to mix it up and use some mind-controlling spells, but those are strictly regulated and are basically nonexistent in the consumer market." The boy stared straight at nothing for a few seconds.

"To summarize a complicated scenario: I've been given another chance at life through some means that I, as of now, have yet to ascertain," Alize tried to raise his other arm but found that it did not obey his thoughts just like the rest of his body.

"I skimmed over it, but..." The boy rubbed his eyes with a bull-dog-like frown as he remembered the frightened expressions on his parents' faces as they explained the mystical and terrifying phenomenon that was an Affix.

"If this is all real and I'm not in an illusion or a terrarium, then my injuries are the result of a coincidence orchestrated by my curse. Supposedly, my Affix is considered rarer than the death of an Immortal, of which there have only been a few recorded instances. That said, this unicorn only has a single job in my life, which is to get me involved with random garbage problems at seemingly preordained times and places." The boy touched the side of his neck with his only working arm and pressed onto a tattoo that squirmed like a living, breathing entity. An infinity symbol tattoo with a gap in its endless line slowly twisted and warped into two broken circles that were set right next to each other. As he pressed onto the empty partition of the tattoo, words, numbers, and symbols constantly flashed and bubbled like a pot of water on a heated stove.

"If I follow that train of thought, then my current situation is pretty damn explainable. My weird fall can be counted as the primer for some future insane event, or it is the capstone for some previous event that I failed to resolve or succeeded in surviving through. That said, the odd encounter in the middle of my nightmare, where my soul left my body, must've been the setup for some other event. Most likely, it's something like a grand finale, prepared for my final moments in this life. If I can make it to living as an old man." Alize paused, inhaled deeply, then

grumbled as if he were an old war vet staring down the barrel of an enemy's loaded rifle.

The boy's frown deepened with each passing moment until something like a feather grazing one's skin touched his hand. The covered tattoo somehow leaped from his neck to his palm. He brought it to his face and squinted really hard. The chattering infinity symbol put all the symbols and weird characters on display and replayed the message three times before the infinite line stretched to resemble the loading circle that appeared on a frozen or lagging page. Exactly ten seconds later, the loading circle faded away and reappeared on the side of his neck.

"I'll have to write down what I saw this time and ask Mom and Dad to take a look. Ha, one of these days. I will learn how to understand the cooode, oh mother! FuaHaa, OW! This is starting to actually hurt!"

Thankfully, something new caught his attention. His torso regained some semblance of feeling beyond a dead cold. Sadly, it was not a good development as it felt like millions of centipedes crawling and cutting through his chest cavity and all along his bones. The pulsing gray heart pumped chaotically as a thick mist of icy fractals pierced his muscle and once again numbed the pain, but it was noticeably less effective than when he first woke up. As with all brief reprieves, miss fortune decided to help reality kick in. The chaotically pumping gray heart dimmed to the point of destabilization after just a few more seconds, cycling the pain once again.

"Dammit. I'm going to have to get back into my bed. Just to be on the safe side. I can already see Mom and Dad overreacting if they see me on the floor like this." So, true to his thoughts, Alize grabbed at the bedsheets and attempted to pull himself up. A fiery and electric jolt rocked through his entire body as even the parts he couldn't feel screamed in protest.

"Nope. I'll just let one of them rush in and pick me up. Dad, prefer- ably. He's calm and logical so unless he loses control of his emotions, I will be..." Alize casually thought to himself as the ice thinned but a massive clatter and the shattering of glass and ceramic reached his ears and cut off the rails that his train of thought used.

"Fine? Is that? No, he didn't! Did Dad just lose his temper? Nah, that must have been Mom working out her emotions or something." Alize froze in body and mind as he heard even more glass and ceramic shatter on the floor. His father's voice, soft and beguiling like that of a man willing to trade your good life and soul for his own benefit, suddenly rang out with a muted thunder that he had never experienced. That drum beating timbre and mind-numbing tone of voice left Alize in disarray.

"If Dad sees me like this while like that, I'm afraid he might do some- thing stupid. The last thing we need is to get caught by the authorities while I'm hurt." Despite being a kid, Alize hissed through the pain and tried to leverage his body weight against the bed frame by his side. Fire spread through his forearms as blood stained the entirety of the white and slightly green wrappings. More specifically, his fingertips left deep stains on the bedframe and sheets. A sigh escaped his lips upon falling back to the ground.

"Fuck. Okay. Wait. I really can't just leave it alone. I have to know if I am in danger or not." Alize looked over toward the distant noise for a second and breathed rapidly to calm his suddenly tense nerves. The casts on his legs and waist splintered and cracked even more due to his movement and revealed completely soaked through ruby bandages. Some kind of steel gray paste was smeared over the bandages and created this stunning red ice block that prevented the blood from escaping. Interestingly enough, as he laid still, the blood cleared up and recirculated through his system, similar to how water seeped through

sand. In less than a minute, the bandages beneath the casts returned to being snow white with hints of green. In that same cursory scan, the boy also realized that the icy mist on the top half of his body had completely vanished, leaving only the insects to stir within his chest.

"*I cannot keep moving. The magic keeping me alive is running thin. I believe the medicine in my system is also losing its effect.*" Almost as if the universe timed it to confirm his suspicions, the bubbling of his stomach slowed to the normal groans and aches of digestion. Once again, Alize steeled himself with a deep breath and attempted a third swift and efficient tug. He pulled at the blanket and mattress. Gradually, he lifted himself to a stable upright position with his back against the roughly carved and homemade nightstand. Its bark softly grazed against his soaked back.

"*Ha. It would be something if this is all just another one of their tests. I would really lose it if I were in a Sim.*" Alize shot a stale breath and bit his numb lips to keep the lead out of his batting eyes. The pain stole the air right out of his lungs and even tried for his life, but ultimately, he persevered. One deep breath led to another, and one chaotic thought led to a struggling stream of consciousness that fought against a symphony of voices that screamed at him to just lay down and sleep.

"*I have to heal myself or, at the very least, stop my body from giving up before I can gather. Ha. My. Helf. My. Wake. Stey. Up. I can't, Cant. Can. Ha...*" For a second, the kid's head slumped over to the side as blood gushed out from his waist, and for a moment, his bright eyes glazed over as all the voices came to a sudden and eerie halt.

"*So...*" The hot and cold flashes, the metaphorical centipedes that crawled through his body, and the weight of his problems and hard future, it all faded away.

"Warm." Alize exhaled and did not attempt to catch his breath as a warm hand attempted to wipe away his tears and the blood on his mouth. Thankfully, he had managed to pull himself from this exact feeling countless times in a simulated space. Instantly, his mind shot back into gear like the slowdown had only been a wind-up for something more.

"Healing, healing. My health. I cannot do anything physically. Then, fuck the worst-case scenario for my future. Parents, I am sorry. Right now, I have to live. My profile is a standard utilitarian mix, albeit slightly skewed towards the Ballast type. My capacity is also higher than average." Alize's chest inflated and dipped with a soft rhythm, almost like he flicked a manual switch and breathed with purpose, with determined focus.

"Easy. This is easy. I've practiced more times than I can count in the Sim. I just have to breathe properly, say the words, focus, imagine, understand the process behind my intent, and concentrate on the outcomes." Alize shut his eyes and pressed his entire thought process onto the words he printed in his thoughts.

"Accoty Mihca loge Fullbore. Taulge barea: Stacon," Alize chanted the spell in his mind and then focused on the rhythm that shook his entire body. In a second, the pulse turned into a tangible feeling, similar to waves of sand washing over the skin but from the inside moving out.

"STABILIZE!" Outloud and in a strained whisper that did not exceed the sound of his own breathing, Alize screamed the shorthand for the spell. Instead of words, blood erupted from his mouth like a geyser.

*Stabilize: Doesn't heal or mend the target; rather, it puts a halt to any external or internal processes that adversely or beneficially affect the target. Such as the aging of cells for a moment, or the effect of heat on a metal coil that's about to melt so it doesn't lose its shape. It breaches the authority of reality itself.

With a single thought, tiny green veins of light branched out along his entire body exactly where he specified in the spell. In terms of what the words actually meant, the language reformatted to "***Accord Type Minor Cast Heal: Stabilize Condition. Release Location (General): Full body. Target Area (General): Full body.***" A spell could be as specific or as general as one wanted as long as their imagination and knowledge behaved as sufficient enough supplements to bear the weight of imprecision. Right now, Alize was in no condition, nor was he practiced enough to actually chant the several pages long spell that specified the exact release of his magic or the precise flow of where and what he wanted to be affected. He used his imagination and intent as the driving force, forcing his magic to bend and work harder—a benefit of being young and willful.

Thus, after the initial blooming release, he basically let one of the many divine Lords or Ladies take the wheel and allowed the spell and magic to behave as it needed. That said, the tiny green veins slowly thinned and spread out until the entire surface area of his skin was covered. The mystical energy washed over him only a single time before it sank back into his flesh due to his fragile and weak state of mind. As a result, he was given exactly five seconds of reprieve as the mystical energy slowly faded away in a similar manner to a muscle being strained to the point of exhaustion.

"*Haa. It worked. First time. Damn right it worked. Let's do it again then. [Stabilize].*" Another wrapping of green threads tied his body together to prevent his wounds from getting worse. Again, the effect lasted one second and faded over the course of five.

"*[Stabilize].*" The mystical effect washed over him a third time, but the difference here was Alize exhaled with a shudder and then lifted himself to a proper upright position. The green veins faded over three seconds this time around.

"[Stabilize]!" With another mindful shout, the kid scrambled to catch his breath and focused on recovering from the emptiness that filled his chest. Once the buzz settled and the invisible weight in his thumping heart returned, he called out an altered version of the spell.

"Accoty Mihca, loge Lobore, ta lobarea: Stacone." The translation wasn't much different from the first, but this more specified general variant of the spell focused on the lower half of the body and required a slightly altered emphasis of words, a pronunciation difference, and most importantly, a more regimented cadence. For its active duration, the spell ensured his waist wouldn't suddenly snap in half or that he wouldn't fall in on his legs like an accordion. All in all, the kid swallowed his bile and forced himself to keep an upright position before he leaned over towards one side. Prepared and ready, for the spell's inevitable collapse only after two seconds this time, the kid cast the spell only on his arm, shoulder, pectorals, and all the other associated muscle groups that helped him grip the nightstand and bed to keep himself sitting upright.

"A dozen more of these and I'll be able to at least get back in bed. Ah, who am I kidding? This is amazing. I have managed to cast three successful variants of a Minor heal. Profiles be damned, I am incredible." Alize reared his head with a silent laugh as the rules and regulations for slinging spells passed through his mind. Though his chuckle looked more like a full-body spasm than a laugh.

1.4 (Magical) Options

"*Wait. I should calm down. [Stabilize]. I need to keep myself occupied. Occupied. Thoughts. Thinking. What should I think about? Right, my curse. If everything really is just a shitty co-incidence. Then, it managed to get me into this horrid state, it also created some noticeable interference in my nightmare. Noticeable? Ah, is it possible that I didn't notice such things before?*"

Alize tilted his head slightly to examine one of the many towering bookcases that made it impossible to see the walls of his room. Three rows of the shelf were filled to the brim with the spines of similarly designed journals, the only difference being the colorful words that were glued to the spines.

"*My dream journals...*" The kid's eyes suddenly fluttered as a horrible thought suddenly flashed across his mind.

"*My dreams are usable. That's why I had to keep track of them. Magic is now in the deck of cards as well.*" His eyes bulged in absolute terror as a slight burn filled in the gap on the loading circle symbol.

Almost immediately, the circle folded in on itself and turned into a single, vibrating dot.

"So that's why they only let me practice casting in the sim. Ha, why did I never second guess them on this obvious matter?"

Following the striking feeling, he used the same trick of putting his hand over his neck to see the changes.

"Alright then. What if, by chance, and in a worst case, I lose the ability to cast anything? The nightmare practically spelled it out for me. I am supposed to be a magic-less anomaly towards the end of my life, equipped with only the Arcane tools and finerys of a Ballastrate's trade, even if the specifics were exaggerated in my dreamscape. What can I do? What should I do to prepare for such an outcome?" Alize shook his head and immediately locked onto Dream Journal #8.

"Accord type's main draw, contracting, comes to mind. But who or what would be willing to accept someone with an Affix like mine? There are not many patrons who would willingly give their divinity to someone without any magic in return." In an imaginary landscape of clouds and mental fog, the boy stepped through a vast corridor of information. Metaphorical cobwebs and literary dust swirled as the winds of change washed over him. With a single step, a phantom book on the long corridor of mist buzzed with a blue light and projected several lines of information. In a single breath, the data reconstituted itself and simplified into a quick and easy-to-read excerpt that floated over his head like a signpost.

*Contracting: A magical binding that ties a caster to a powerful natural or divine source of physical or mystical energy. The contracting party can utilize the vast powers of their chosen Patron in exchange for a good or service. Usually, a portion of the contractor's magic is given to the patron of their choosing. Think: magic trust fund. The more magic a contractor puts into this "contract", the more mana or aura they can take out.

As for the terms aura and mana, he decided to let the basics fall into the explanation of contracting as other blue lights lit up in the fog of his mind.

*Aura: A household name for an unforgivingly named phenomenon by someone else who also did not think of a useful way to shorten the term. It essentially compiled everything related to the innate capacity for change and growth within a person or thing's body or form. In simpler terms, the term gauges how much someone can manipulate and push beyond the limitations of nature and fixed biology.

*Mana: Is the household name for a similar ancient phenomenon that was not named for the convenience of future generations. Basically, it is an ID that someone is born with that allows them to interact and alter specific natural phenomena around and outside of their own body through various mediums.

Aura and mana were essential components of a person's mystical identity. Similar to how one's mind, flesh, and the intangibility of the soul represented the requisite components of a complete physical life. That said, Alize's parents were very clear that his curse or any in general was a physical representation of a third kind of profile marker similar to how abstract and weird the soul was. An Affix was something that did not play by the rules or laws of physics or mystics. Thanks to his curse, he could lose his physical form, his sanity, gain an extra limb every time he blinked, or even lose his soul if he breathed funny, even his profile could be altered or lost within a second if the Affix generated an event that coincidentally possessed the conditions for such a change. In thinking that far, Alize decided to review what an Affix was in terms of mystical studies.

*Affix: A profile mismatcher. It's a type of mana, aura, or both or possibly even neither, that completely alters the way everything else works for the person attached to it. Generally, there is only one of each Affix despite uncanny similarities. They are split into three different subcategories. The first being the prefix variant, which are fixed to places, times, or throttled by limitations and widely ranging prerequisites. In other words, they are only active during certain cosmic times, in particular places, or until a condition has been met. Alternatively, there is the suffix variant that can only be active after certain physical or emotional states, or after a condition has been met. Then there is the universally accepted worst variant of the bunch and the poster child of what people usually talk about when they bring up a curse. The Affix. They are on at all times, passively working behind the scenes, creating stepping stones to some great or terrifying end.

"[*Stabilize*], *going back to contracting, there are 5 or 6 dozen divine-ranked beings that would be willing to grant their protection to someone who doesn't want to be effectively enslaved. There's also my Affix to consider as it could change the terms of a contract at any given point if it's related to an event it generates. There are even fewer forces capable of assuring me of the stability that I want.*" Alize pulled up a mental web of every single powerful mystical force from every folktale or piece of myth he's ever learned about. He didn't have many in-depth details or any choices past a certain date since the historical religions class he was forced to take was more of a broad-strokes setup, but he still managed to pull up several dozen pantheons and their principle members.

Therefore, he started with the oldest and least known, the creation myth deities, both of which he crossed out immediately. He unfolded small pamphlets and excerpts that confirmed and denounced the existence of the Lost Eras divinities, the Dark Age's Primogenitors, the Succession cycle's main Provinces, the Blessed eon's 108 numen, the near infinite Void Eras, and the countless Celestials that forged names in that trash fire of a time period, and the more recent but still Ancient pantheons of supreme beings and Outer demiurges that may or may not still exist out on the fringes of reality. Obviously, Alize did not forget to pursue the idea of the Principal Gods and Goddesses that currently served as the heads of the many churches in the world or the up and coming modern divinities called Archons. He remembered their personalities (if they had one), actions, and associations until he narrowed down the benefits and issues of each possibility.

Of course, like all things, not all the pantheons he knew of showed up in his filtering system. One particular group quickly showed up and was immediately thrown into the garbage. It was the Void Era's Terran Gods. There were names such as Space Cowboy, Gadget, The almighty yeti, The Godfather, Pollo de Fuego, The one-eyed One, The Real Godfather, Eledagid, or the Leather Daddy Gimp Demon, G.O.D or Goat over Death, Lucielle the Morningstar, Bambi, Pepe, and other names that simply made one either laugh or cry. There happened to be a lot of overlap in the void era pantheon lists, so Alize really didn't have much of an issue with his filtering or striking the Humans from his record almost entirely.

"[*Stabilize*]. *There's only Gnoll, huh? That is the name of the divine spirit supposedly responsible for all curses. I'll expand my possibilities to include sources that have historically restored their original contracts due to an Affix's interference. With that, five potential sources fit my requirements now. Ugh. Six if I keep Gnoll in mind.*" Alize felt a sudden and very unnatural gust of wind brush against his rapidly heating skin. He opened his eyes to observe the unnatural change and noticed that something near invisible pushed aside the curtain at one of the windows.

"A second option is offloading. The older me in the nightmare seems to have gone with such an option based on his gear and the use of disposable Quibe and Links. That said, I can start preparations early and store all of my excess magic for future use. Similar to the gem on the harness or the fabric woven into the casts and bandages, I could create or utilize bespoke Arcanum. A practice that could actually work if I can get through the initial paywall. [Stabilize]. The only downside, according to my parents, would be making myself a target to practically everyone, from low-life thieves to the gods themselves if I manage to make a name for myself. Hm, I would have the potential to craft and design some very dangerous things, especially with the information Dad has given me." Alize sighed before gathering his breath. Even though he was only thinking, the very act of holding himself in an upright posture became laborious.

"Then there's offloading without a proper permit, workshop, and unionization. The act would be the same as a singular person becoming a legal arms factory and dealer. But if this is my choice, I would be limited to one personal craft a year. Not to mention, I couldn't create or prepare anything more than what my permits and union would allow. And if I offloaded illegally, the Hounds of Ferrasi would immediately come knocking." Alize decided to lower his head under the cooling and sudden breeze and give standing up a go.

"[Stabilize]. Hmm, it should be possible to accomplish offloading if I keep the results hidden or maybe if I have Mom and Dad help me by selling my items to them? I'm sure there's some type of loophole in the system. I can, oh. Oh wait. This wind!" Alize lifted his head completely and stared at his open window even harder. Minutely, almost imperceptibly, the air itself solidified like cotton candy on a stick and took on a humanoid shape.

"[Stabilize]. That should be Mom's Fae. Hehe. That old man, he's always on about how he is not dead just yet. Pfth. Okay, Grandpa, you

are not dead. You are still an ancient Galean warrior. Haa." He took a moment of personal time to take in, understand, and re-contextualize the actual impact of his injuries on the family unit upon seeing the old wind's physical state.

"[Stabilize] It's weird seeing Jarold look so thinned out, [Stabilize]. He must have been doing a lot over the time that I have been asleep." Alize frowned in unison with the ghostly apparition. Seconds passed like hours, but it was the Sylph that broke eye contact and motioned with its semi-transparent head.

"My journals and notebooks? What is so important about them?"

Alize felt his arms buckle oh so subtly under the weight and rising pain, so he did his best to lock his arms in place and raise his head to where Jarold pointed. In complete silence, the curly-haired Sylph pulled down and carried one of the boy's dream journals and dragged his near-invisible finger over some partially underlined words. Alize read the page with sudden disgust, fear, and panic.

It was a drawing of a faceless and long-eared child, himself, who had died after falling out of bed. He, in that moment of drawing whilst in a semi tired fugue state, spared no lack of detail in how his own body popped and splat against the floor like a balloon covered in holes that only inflated due to the glue and tape holding it together. A few of the side notes and details were related to an indeterminate shadowy figure drawn in at the edge of the image. Swirls and scrawling lines highlighted the feverish pitch that Alize was in at the moment of scribing his own nightmares. The disproportionate limbs and sinking facial features of the shadow were hidden by a deep cowl that had familiar iconography but an un-placable demeanor that left the kid more confused than anything. It left his mouth full of cotton. Alize cleared his throat and scanned the towering bookshelf with dancing eyes. Jarrold, the old man who put the similarities on the map, looked at the image with a gulp and waved his finger. With magic, there is no such thing as a coincidence; there is no such thing as an unfortunate accident or weird overlap. Something was always at play, and the old man was the first to put the puzzle pieces together, or maybe... No. Alize shook his head and ignored the memory of the worried faces that his parents shared more often than not.

"An Affix capable of creating events under any and all circumstances would not be constrained by the limitations of when I am awake. It would be capable of generating events where my wildest dreams have the potential of coming true, the same would be for my nightmares." Calmly and expectantly, Alize let out a shuddering breath and remembered the rest of the book and some of his other journals.

"My conclusion on this recurring nightmare was that it was a silently developed fear of heights. The logical leap is pretty standard across my other journals since my nightmares always change the day that Mom alters my training regime. This one started after she taught me how to free climb." Alize maintained his form and stable breathing as he paced around in a fog of imagination. The nightmare where he fell out of bed and died played on a loop as he recalled every day that he woke up in a cold sweat due to it.

"Of course, I had to learn how to lucid dream. No wonder they forced me into it. I need to have a similar level of awareness even in my sleep. Everything they have trained me for relates to my Affix." Alize suddenly recalled some talks his parents organized. The boy's face went from an oiled tomato to white as a sheet of paper, to green and blue due to a sudden dizzying sense of sickness, and back to red from the physical strain and pooling blood.

On the other hand, we have the cool, calm, and frighteningly stoic Jarold flashing through several pages at once with an ever-deepening frown. The Fae retrieved a slightly glowing glassy sheet that floated above Alize's bed and opened up a calendar on the opaque face. The old man parsed through the first four weeks of a seven-week month and found a particular event written down in Alize's calendar. The usual three-day weekend was extended to four days due to some school holiday, but Jarold focused his finger on the words leading up to this mini-vacation. "Sleepover preparation" was written in red for the four days leading up to the extended weekend, while a calming green smiley face covered two days out of the four mini-vacation days. The calendar showed miniature boxes of all the other twelve months surrounding the maximized month of Ujen. Each one possessed a standard number of 56 days and 7 weeks and over a dozen months that were as follows: Boa, Ao, Den, Teres, Fjern, Main, Presen, Ujen, Juen, Oxsis, Nova, Autoten, Concluse.

"So today is still Fell's birthday weekend, huh? That's good then. I have only been unconscious for a few hours, by the looks of today's current date and time." With a gentle sigh, the boy examined the silent sylph's actions. The windbag condensed the room's dust particles into hair-thin lines that he layered atop the undetailed calendar that Alize illustrated within the dream journal.

"Ujen 54th, 4048 D.A. This is. Horrible. Absolutely terrible." Aghast, Alize tried to control his emotions, but the completed infinity symbol that burst out of the dot on his neck sent a jolt of electricity coursing through his body, almost as if the curse wanted to congratulate him on finally and fully understanding one of its most basic functions.

"Ha, how am I even supposed to notice and narrow down potential problems if they can actually be set up in this way? I mean, I wrote it down. I drew a picture. I knew about it somehow, but how?"

He briefly scanned over the spines of each and every journal that HE WROTE, with a ragged breath and began to tear up as he realized the absolute gravity of his situation. He had been told never to use his magic for anything until he learned how to read and gauge his curse, but now? It would be a miracle if he didn't die on the side of the road due to some malfunctioning spell halfway across the world.

Suddenly finding himself in a spiral of both rising physical pain and mental anxiety, the kid closed his eyes and held his breath. Jarold, in the midst of understanding his godson's revelation, kicked up a breeze and pulled all the stagnant and dirty air out of the room. He returned the calendar and book with a swish of silent wind that rapidly congealed around his jolly but rough features. Thanks to the dust, he entered a more detailed state. At the height of around 130 cm or 4 feet 3 inches, Jarold flexed his muscles with a deep and bearded frown. His cold and thoughtful expression was set on a wide and muscular frame, which calmed the boy in an odd manner.

"*[Stabilize]. Alright. Slow down. Don't jump to conclusions. Don't focus on negative potential results. EPA. Exhaust. Prepare. Act. Exhaust my options. Prepare countermeasures. Act based on the situation. Falling apart is not an option right now. I have options.*" Alize held the cold air in his lungs until his body screamed in protest. Upon repeating the process twice more, he fixed his slipping posture and prepared himself.

"*I just need to stabilize my condition and bring all of this up to my parents: my most recent nightmare, my failed memory, and now this coincidental overlap.*" Alize used his imagination to generate an imaginary space where he unpacked his thoughts in greater detail. He shouted, "*[Stabilize] in his mind one last time and engaged almost all the muscle he could get to listen to him.*" With a huff, the boy shot up in the air with a trail of rubies dropping from his fingertips and legs. Alize bounced onto the edge of the mattress and naturally rolled himself back into bed due to a slight but purposeful imbalance. The sheets were a mess, and his blood hovered in the air unnaturally, held there by dozens if not hundreds of green threads that connected to his bandages. Jarold paused in surprise and utter bafflement for a second before uncertainty and fear took place. He immediately floated to the window in a mad dash to return somewhere or to someone, but something kept him in the room as he stared at the boy who wore a hardened and defiant sneer.

"[*Stabilize*]. *Ha. That makes twelve. I have broken a few more bones and torn some already rough sections of muscle, but at least I am keeping myself awake. I have to keep busy. So, think more...me. What's next? What should I do now?*"

Alize gasped for breath and batted his eyes in an odd rhythm as exhaustion washed throughout his mostly un-feeling body. He was 100% sure that he would die if he fell asleep right now. The green fibers woven into his bandages began to turn an odd milky white before he even managed to throw himself into bed, nevermind right now as his blood fell and splattered before it could be re-injected back into himself. The bandages, which were pristine white and green, began to turn all shades of red, brown, and yellow from his leaking bodily fluids. In fact, he was entirely confident that if was not using a spell that specifically disallowed immediate death, his blood would have seeped through the bandages almost like water through a broken dam. Ah, but don't get confused, he was aware that one mistake with his spell and he would end up killing himself by stemming some necessary fluid leakage or if he was too slow in keeping with the monotonous casting, he would fall asleep and just pass away in an uncomfortably warm and numbing silence.

All the ice and frost from the harness and its [*Stasis*] spell also completely melted, ramping up the heat and sharpening the pain that his undamaged nerves could still receive. Jarold, seeing this and un-derstanding what the kid was probably going through, shook off his wonder and waved his fluffy and dust-colored gray hand. The wind in the room kicked up and cooled Alize as a replacement for the icy [Stasis] spell, but the breeze quickly died down as his semi-transparent and rough form thinned out at a noticeable rate. In fact, Jarold was barely strong enough to keep his own body stable as he quickly spun out and lost an entire arm. He muttered to himself in a deep, gruff tone that went unheard since his heavy voice couldn't reach anyone that he wasn't contracted to. As for Alize, the kid adjusted his spell again to match his rapidly declining mental faculties. Specifically, he restructured the spell to target his head and brain since he could feel himself nodding off.

"Accotype Mihca loge urbore tiske'r laivitspe fulbrenaa: Staconeht." This specified sentence was another universally standard variant of the stabilizer spell, which meant that in the relevant ancient language, the words meant, "Accord type minor heal cast, location general, upper body release, target inner skeletal region and full cranial cavity". A muted halo of green dots pulsed out of Alize's temples and the roots of his hair. After stabilizing his mental state, he was given half a dozen seconds to collect his thoughts.

"My Affix generates events that often lead to issues that have the goal to make me stronger, smarter, and faster, but the problems match or even outpace my capability to handle them. That is what I know; that is what I have been raised to deal with. Okay. According to my parents and the few experiences that they have curated, the curse uses my current limitations as the capstone for how beneficial or problematic something down the line will be. If I include Jarrold's discovery as part of the modus operandi of my Affix, then the dreams and nightmares that I have been keeping track of can be used as material to generate even crazier events. At a minimum, for example, using a nightmare scenario as the foundation, it can engineer factors beyond my immediate bubble of perception. Meaning, it means, what? The only thing this event

caused is my injuries. This isn't even the worst that I've ever been hurt, so what was the goal? How have I gotten better here? What's..." Alize slowly came back to the warnings that littered every single one of his mandatory lessons since birth.

"Magic." He rounded a mental circle and found himself staring at another train of thought that brought up the topic. Unintentionally, a sour note splashed across his pained grimace.

"It wanted me to start casting today by any means [Stabilize]." Branches of restorative energy shimmered through his matted hair and linked up with the Borealis of effusive fractals that faded around the rest of his body.

"The cat is out of the bag already, huh? [Stabilize]." While thinking, Alize continuously cast several different variants of the same spell, pinpointing, layering, and thickening his casting's regenerative effect across his entire body. In theory and in simulation, he was more than versed at accomplishing such a task; in reality and in practice, he was so slow that he could barely catch the previous spell before it faded. Thus, it appeared as though the kid would eventually die, at least Jarold thought so.

In the mists of his mind, Alize danced and matched his breathing to his incredibly slow heartbeat, where he then matched the casting rhythm of [*Stabilize*] to a song that he repeated in the back of his head. It allowed him to create a subconscious and automatic loop of casting while trying to recall how he was injured, contemplate the depths of his Affix, and ruminate on other factors that currently or were going to start affecting his life. On the other hand, Jarold's eyes shot wide while his jaw dropped. The extraordinary fluidity and control that the boy showed had left him bug-eyed since death was nowhere to be seen as he expected.

"*[Stabilize]. Mhhm, I'm getting better. I increased my casting speed by only one millionth of a millisecond, but it's better than nothing.*" Alize pierced the veil of his imagination, beyond the incandescent fog of his thoughts and paced through a seemingly empty hall.

"*Okay. What am I currently dealing with? Big picture stuff. One, I have to heal myself. It should take three and a half, maybe four months at my current pace if I rely on Minor Grade healing spells. A full recovery might take only a month if Dad can get more potion supplies. That's good enough. Second: Deal with and prepare for my Affix and its current access to magic, and before that, confirm if the damned thing has genuine manipulative capabilities. Third: Explain Jarold's finding and my new dream theory without sounding too insane. It shouldn't be too much of a stretch since they most likely have been keeping track of my journals and noticed the anomaly. No, if Jarold pointed it out so quickly, I'm 98% confident that they already know my curse is not limited to when I am awake. I'm sure they had some hints prior to this incident, maybe from when I was younger, like something I offhandedly said or did? Hm, that actually explains much of my childhood and the fact that we live in a Terrarium. It's possible that they learned that anything could be used as fuel for the shit fire that is my Affix.*" Alize touched his neck inside his imagination and found that the now completed infinity symbol on the back of his hand appeared like eyes. A shiver ran down his spine as the symbol faded.

"*How horrible is this situation? If I knew my writings and rambles were potential sources for events, I would have been more wary of something going wrong. No, it's possible that I would have even avoided taking Fell out this weekend. At least until the planned event passed by.*" Alize sat down in the fog of his imagination and watched as the spell for [Stabilize] came to mind. The words fell apart and turned into several dozen more ancient symbols that once again dissolved into pages of math formulas, diagrams, charts, and a legend that served as a little cheat sheet. Specifically, much of the information boiled down to snapshots of a musculature, organ placement, nervous system's pathings, and other things that focused on heat charts for thermodynamics, the displacement of kinetic energy, oxygenation, blood flow, and pretty much everything concerning the biology of a mixed Lerian (Pronounced Lie- Rune). Other diagrams were just imaginary drawings of some type of conceptual or theoretical process concerning the under-researched field of mystics rather than the reality of physics.

"Avoiding the event wouldn't have worked though, would it? As far as I know, all Affixes work like prophecies. The details are always vague, but the results are always exactly delivered, in some way, shape, or form." He was briefly reminded of a story that his parents hinted at sometimes. It concerned their past, but they narrowed it down by letting him know that at one point they were both cursed or blessed, depending on the perspective. That whole debacle involved an unnamed divine being that sent them on separate but intrinsically tied quests. Separately, their "blessings" were nothing that they could not handle, but as the story went on, circumstances led to them finding out that their prefix and suffix respectively could not be avoided, tampered with, or overpowered when they were together. The moral of the story—they had to deal with the cards that they were dealt and not get upset when their choices bit them right in the ass. They didn't tell him the whole story or any specifics, but the whole point of their epic was to inform him that he possessed an unstoppable gift. One that they were told was called the Infinite Event Generator as a reward for getting through their own ordeal.

The explanation they gave him was short and rather unhelpful since they only said that "the effect of the curse is that things will happen to you, a lot of things that are not necessarily good or bad in any overtly explicit way but these events will alway involve you, directly or indirectly." Despite being young and completely out of touch with the severity of that information, he simply did not show any worry at the time. When he was old enough to understand, his parents continued with, "we have never heard about such an Affix before but its similar in effect to some other documented cases so if you feel something from the depths of your heart or if there is ever a time that you feel it moving or being unusually still, be alert. You may be wrapped up in a consecutive, never-ending cascade of things just happening, so pay attention to everything." The interchanging and disembodied voices of his parents played like an audio file in the background of his mind. Alize could only nod since, exactly as his parents explained, he was always caught up in some insane situation when his Affix stopped buffering or when it began to conduct its elaborate symphonies. And that was with them acting as a buffer.

Without realizing it, the kid stopped focusing on using his magic and dozed off to the sound of his parents talking to him. The fog in his mind, almost as if coaxing him with candy, shifted and turned into a blurry representation of another rare moment of clarity.

"Why is my Affix part of the Infinite series when it alternates between working like a Suffix and Prefix?"

Through the fog, Alize could see most of his blurry mom as she helped him up from the floor. With a tear-stained frown, she silently and carefully wiped blood off his face and mutilated knuckles. After a few moments, she re-strapped a dented and bloody metal plate to a pole and crouched in front of him.

"You will understand when you are older. Right now, we need you to focus and prepare, okay? EPA. Danger will follow you for as long as you live, and oftentimes, you will not be able to understand how these things occurred or why they have unfolded in the way they have or are going to. Always remember that you don't need to know at that moment, okay?" The tall woman gave him a kiss on the forehead and turned away with a small sniffle that went largely unnoticed.

"*Okay, okay*?" Alize whispered his own lines like he was just a spectator at a movie he had seen hundreds of times before.

"Good. Now let's get back to training. After you learn how to defend yourself in a fight, we will train you to survive in the woods and beat the odds. You will be great. I promise. Even without us. Even..." The image slowly faded.

"*I might have been only two or three there. Ah, such horrible memories.*" He opened his drowsy, leaden eyes, and glanced at the numerous dream journals and the books titled Observations and Illustrations just above them. His attention immediately shifted to another tall shelving unit that sported odd contraptions, crafts, toys, and miniaturized tattered scrolls suspended in small clear cubes. In particular, he looked at a hand-sized pot sealed with a browning cloth that was capped with a once royal blue but now aged wax seal that was engraved with golden runes that retained their brilliance even under layers of dirt and grim. It looked exactly like a novelty item bought at a thrift store. In fact, the tiny paper tag on the exposed side of the item showed that Alize or his parents did exactly that; they bought the small but ancient pot-pourri from a yard sale at a town they visited on the way toward their new domicile.

"*If my nightmares are problems waiting to happen, then the Prefix of Folded Souls is being contained in that urn. As I understand it, that kind of 'curse' is practically a death sentence for people who are not scholars or in niche professions.*" Alize matched some of the other items that he had collected over the years, nine long years, to items that he wrote about in his journals and notebooks.

Jarold seemed to have the exact same thought process as his billowing eyes fluttered with tears made of clouds. The old man wiped away his emotions and hardened the lines on his face, as if he had just made a decision that would cost him his life. His only visible hand morphed into a sort of thin lance capable of becoming a projectile and pointed it at Alize. Instead of throwing it, the old man trembled, moving slightly to wind up his throw and then returning to a preparatory stance. Closing his eyes, the old sylph released his grip on the cloud's spear and looked out of the window with a look of sorrow and concern. He stared out toward a vibrant sun that crested over a distant black wall that pierced through the clouds.

"[*Stabilize*]." Alize and Jarold, miraculously, came to vastly different conclusions that revolved around the same information despite not sharing more than a single glance throughout their entire interaction.

As for the resident adult....

"He needs to eat something. Porridge, soup, a broth maybe! What else do we have? I, I don't know...." A middle-aged man with a medium set and somewhat plump build and a scraggly beard, swiped a bowl and dozens of ingredients off of a hand-chiseled stone kitchen island. The clatter resonated, sure, but it didn't have the impact of anger or the tone of absolute despair behind it that frightened Alize into attempting his grand feat of determination.

"Ark needs to eat something. Anything, but there's nothing left that he could digest in his state." Brows furrowed, the man exhaled and gripped his shaking legs. He leaned against an empty spice rack, tearful and ragged as his thoughts spiraled out of control.

"He wouldn't be in this much danger if I took care of his wounds on site. But no. I had to stay here and work. Fuck me, her speed nearly killed him. No, she nearly got all of us discovered. No, if I had just taken my head out of my own ass for one blasted moment, I would have gone with her when things turned south. No, if only I had paid more attention to the signs. It was right there; I knew. We both knew, even that old fart guessed the truth, but we still let him do what he wanted. Fuck Ark, oh. My son, I'm so sorry. I should have told you. We knew something would happen; it's just. We assumed. FUCKK!" The man slammed his fist into the wall beside him and created a massive fissure against a near-invisible crystalline shield. Thankfully, he pulled his punch at the last second, so the wall near the spice rack only shook and cracked a little bit despite the thunderous beat.

"Don't place blame. Just don't...." The man couldn't catch his breath. His entire body trembled.

"It's not her fault. It's not. It's mine. If I wasn't working, I could've gone with her. Stop. Just think. What can I do? I can hydrate him!"

The bearded man slapped himself and wiped the tears that fell without his permission. Without meaning to, he leaned his entire weight on the shelf as he reached for a semi-translucent container with some amber-colored liquid. The shelf broke in half. Porcelain and glass containers shattered on the floor one after the other, spreading grains or specks or whatever was left inside of them all over the floor. One rather small and markless container cracked and revealed a soft purple haze that tapered out around the mouth of the new opening. The man's breath lapsed as he lunged for the container with the amber liquid in hand. A gorgeous braid of wood sporting purple and teal veins sprouted from his fingertips as he gently popped it open. The man rushed to the fallen items and fished out a chipped bowl from the wreckage. He placed it on the table. A smoke-gray ring of mystic runes glistened on his free palm, which lassoed the moisture in the air, clumping it together. Without any ancient dialect or dubious prerequisites, the man skipped about a dozen steps to use a mana-oriented spell well within his means.

"[Create: Water]."

Altogether, the purified or perfectly distilled water that materialized on the spot drizzled into the chipped bowl. With a free hand, the older man sliced a glowing knifelike nail along the side of the gnarled root that contained more light blue veins than purple. He cut into the deceptively soft wood and released a thick, honey-like sap.

"We had one more Lochorn root. Hopefully, it's enough. She can make it back in time now, please make it back, love." The man dug his finger further along the smallest groove and cleanly split the root in two, exposing a lima bean-sized gel pouch within the thickest part of the veined casing. Filling the bowl, the man let out a sigh and used the cracked open braid to mix the glowing blue gel with the water, turning it into a crystal clear sparkling substance. On the other side of the wooden braid, the root's purple veins darkened and slowly leaked out a blood red extract. The potion, interestingly enough, took on a very dark red tint, nearly the same tar shade of the root's skin. The man searched the floor and periodically dumped some of the fallen herbs into the liquid, which cleaned the potion and heightened the red tint. Slowly, he added the amber liquid that he had gathered just moments before. Without a single step of hesitation, the man snapped his fingers to create a blinding flash that burned the tincture into something similar to liquid rubies. Amber sparks danced within the concoction as if life itself was distilled into this gorgeous medicine.

With that, the man ran out of the simple wooden shack that he was in and onto a pathway that cut slightly above a yard with a flourishing garden to one side. The other side showcased large amounts of logs and pulled stumps, all of which were piled next to freshly cut boards and beams. A rare few of the pieces were carved into partial sets of furniture and building materials, and next to it all were half a dozen boards full of blue grid papers and scrolls of odd colored parchment. Stone tablets full of runes and symbols so complex, a normal person's mind would be sent reeling, piled into waist-high columns and makeshift tables full of notebooks, rulers, and all manner of construction equipment. Not too far away, certainly within sight, a giant hole laid in wait for the foundations of a home.

With a frown, steady steps, and a nervous brow twitch, the gentlemanly-looking man ignored the landscape as he rounded the hill. The garden dipped into a chasmous, no man's land of pits and scorched earth full of broken statues and metallic contraptions that were warped into disfigured mounds of scrap. He followed the path toward the smaller of the two rough wooden huts placed atop and at the end of the gravel path. The man slowly moved the first curtain at the igloo-like entrance of the smaller building and felt a jolt of electricity shoot through his mind as something he couldn't quite notice before prickled his senses. Hundreds of times past his previous speed, as numerous crystalline barriers suppressed his full movement, the bearded man pushed away the second curtain. His thoughts became an uncontrollable mess of anger, anxiety, and helplessness.

"ARK!"

"Ah, this isn't good." Alize couldn't see his father since he was forced to close his eyes due to an intense measure of exhaustion, but his tomato red face, blood and sweat stained sheets and bandages, and grimace showed how much pain and danger he was in. Not only that, he was caught using magic by an impossibly inquisitive person. Alize's father, the nosy individual in question, rushed to his son's side and nearly spilled the concoction within the bowl.

"Can you hear me? Are you awake? What, uh, what is this? Are you doing this? We told you NOT TO. Oh, no. No, no. This is not good. We told you not to use magic, Ark! Fuck, I'm sorry. Please, just stay with me. Your mom is almost here. Here? Right, here, drink some of this." The man was bothered by the handprints and blood splatter on the floor, but he ultimately focused on being as gentle as could be. The man first attempted to bring the medicine to his son's lips, but he quickly noticed that the kid was on the brink of falling out due to an obvious case of severe blood loss and exhaustion. Instead of helping his son, he cut out the middleman and placed the bowl on the nightstand on top of a pile of three books and swished his finger. The liquid turned into needle-thin strands that immediately flowed into the boy's mouth. Like his son, or rather as for where Alize got his habit from, the bearded man began to speak to himself.

"I don't understand. I left for not even five minutes. What could possibly have happened to force you to use magic?"

Alize's father took a physical step away from his child to get a better view, muttering to himself all the while.

"You fell out of bed, right? I didn't hear it. I'm sorry. I'm proud of you for getting back up, but it was a stupid decision. You didn't fall asleep. Good. You would be dead if you did." The man grumbled as he examined the room with a glint of magic in his eyes. Alize, on the other hand, listened to his dad with more than a slight bit of concern.

"I see. The intensity of the magic and the vein patterning are congruent with a Mixed B type spell. Even though we told you not to use magic, I'm glad to see that you stuck to a spell within your profile. An Accord standard minor heal. Solid work. The complexity of the layering and application is similar to a standard grade cast of the [Stabilize] variant, if I'm not mistaken. It's a good choice, son. If this was a test, you would have full marks so far. It is, by far, the most efficient and effective minor heal variant spell for your condition. It requires strict control and years of practice and knowledge, which can be explained

by you sneaking in extra time in the Sim, but you forgot something."
The man's worry faded while a prideful helplessness filled his entire
being. A thick and permeating heaviness suddenly descended onto
Alize, as if he had just been thrown into an abyssal ocean with nothing
but a life raft.

*"Did Dad figure it out with just a quick glance? Hmm, wait, what
did I forget? Which lesson is he referring to? Something related to [Sta-
bilize] to be sure, but what exactly?"*

Alize still couldn't see his dad's change of facial expression or the
deadly and noble Drem warrior that floated above him in a protective
stance. He could, however, feel the weight of his dad's words and the
tempestuous but contained winds being projected by the two older
men in the room as they soundlessly exchanged meaningful glances.

"Ark, it seems that you have forgotten the issue with your profile,
and the main reason why your mother and I have forbidden you from
casting as a whole." The man frowned as he explained the situation to
his son. Alize felt his heart grip as his dad said something that he had
no reference for.

"Ha. He still doesn't get it. A dense reflection? So this is what that
bastard meant at that time, huh?"

The bearded man suddenly sneered towards the sky with a loaded
whisper of frustration and wiped the tears that silently fell.

"I cannot believe that you forgot that your spells are fueled by
Tenets, not magic. You have ruined your future, Ark. My son, you.
Hm, there's a reason...." The bearded man grabbed a chair from Alize's
desk and sat down, unable to formulate words in his absolute grief.
The kid freaked out internally, but he couldn't show it at all as he
digested a steady but small stream of medicine and news.

*"Tenets? Core Tenets! Like someone at the 7th rank and up? Are you
crazy!? None of you ever told me about that!"*

"[Sense]." A hazy halo surrounded the bearded man's crow's nest of a hairstyle. The haze generated from the neon white light and magic spread out towards the bounds of the room and then even further.

"Ha. I can only hope that I am wrong. I've been wrong about a lot of things recently...." The bearded man leaned forward and examined the patterning along his son's body with the same intensity as a starving hawk swooping toward an injured hare.

"You have already made an irrevocable mistake, so we must tread lightly and confirm my projected scans. Let us both pray that some errant god or goddess has secretly broken into our home and took a fancy to you. If not." The man stared at the fading green lights that seemed to focus around his boy's left leg.

"Well, it wouldn't matter. You already made it impossible to enter the divine rank in your future. Ha, cast again." The man's pupils dilated to the point of nearly overcoming the entirety of his irises.

"[*Stabilize*]." Alize recast the spell to show his father its effects in more detail.

"Crystallization. Huh. Just as I theorized you would have. The node points that you designated in the circuitry component of the spell is a real solid practical application, Ark. Good job. Hm, change your material coefficient by 0.03, and dial up the fifth variable in the extra modifier substructure. You should always leave a lot of room for outside interference. It's a drain on the initial cost, but it always counts when plans go awry. Potions may have a reliable consistency, but there are always exceptions, so tighten up the failsafe that you have there. Also, you are throttling the effusive intake, so raise that variable by at least double what you have placed in it. Always count on having enough magic in your environment, unless you are in a Grave or dead space like the Void. Also, remember that Accord-type profiles are entirely reliant on nature, so any spells cast with its aspects as a major component use effuse or any other external source of power before your own reserves." The bearded man completely dissected the boy's spell use with a single glance and nodded at the aftermath of his coaching. With the adjusted recast, the rejuvenating magic and the pulse at which it rocked the kid's body enlarged while the burden on his mentality lessened. The change helped him to power through a cascade of sleepiness and reignited his consciousness despite a heartbeat that slowed to frightening levels.

"Alright. Now, no matter what. Do not cast anything for the next minute. Your body is showing signs of oversaturation. For now, I want you to remember and copy this spell for when the time is up. It will help you digest the medicine that I'm feeding to you. Also, do not fall asleep. I know you cannot move right now, but do NOT, fall asleep until I tell you it's okay to do so." The bearded man kissed Alize on the forehead and prepared a spell. Once again, he skipped several steps as he explained what to do.

"In Iron Tongue, say, I give this potion the necessary wisdom for the moment so that it may breathe life into the injured, [Guidance]." In a flurry of movement, beardo cupped the back of his son's head and pressed a golden pointer finger onto his forehead. In the blink of an eye, the long, curling strand of medicine turned into needles that instantly pierced and spread throughout the kid's entire body all at once. As if a massive lightning bolt had just struck his body, Alize bounced upward as his eyes snapped open. As if pulled from the illustrations that he drew in his youth and right before his eyes, a hovering image of a veiled shade floated in the shadows of the ceiling. He briefly saw a veiled face behind a deep cowl as it faded away in absolute shock. Jarold and his father did not notice a thing, by the looks of it, but Alize just saw the face of death, and it was familiar.

"Was that? Haa, I hallucinated. Haa. Yup," the kid's shaking chest and breath quickly steadied under the hand that calmly and lovingly tapped his collarbone. His nearly stopped heartbeat churned and drummed against his ears. His blurry eyes quickly focused on his father and the golden haze that coiled in the air like some celestial spiked dragon. A second round of medicine then shot towards the parts of his internal organs that were either already ruptured or were on the brink.

"Ha. It's not that serious. I just need to calm down. I've already died more times than I can count in the training room." In seconds, Alize matched his breathing to the calming touch and pinpointed every new detail concerning the changes within his body. He quickly returned to his mind palace and got to work on translating his dad's words into the appropriate B. Type spell.

As for the older man, he frowned upon seeing his son briefly lock eyes with him before he closed them shut. Bothered but not distracted, the salt and pepper haired man removed the gem on his son's harness and recast [Stasis] using its corresponding magic type, which happened to be the Creation type that he specialized in. He froze the smallest and most easily treatable wounds in place and time, allowing the medicine and restorative energy to flood the worst of locations within his son's body. With a thought, the bearded man condensed his magic into a pure, untainted glow and refueled the Direct Type bandages. Personally, the man did not possess the profile necessary to produce the miraculous phenomena of the [First Aid] spell, but he only needed to fuel the magical item for it to automatically reactivate.

And reactivate they did. The bloodied bandages flashed with an insanely visual flare, and within the blink of an eye, the arcanum cleaned itself and everything it touched. The magical gauze adjusted, disinfected, and produced antiseptic waves of energy in a minty haze that miraculously re-stitched and decontaminated Alize's open wounds. The bandages even lashed out with fibrous threads, recovered blood that the kid lost, and transfused it back into his body. The middle-aged man grit his teeth as the wrappings inefficiently drew upon more than what he could put into it without breaking the low grade and weak thing. Thus, very slowly, and very painfully, the older man endured the suction force of the process. Of course, not everything could be saved by the low-grade wraps, so small onyx marbles the size of pearls were silently ejected and collected inside of a plastic pouch that was semi-held in place at the boy's waist.

The middle-aged man whispered something under his breath that Alize could not hear, and in less than a second, the waste material decomposed into a granular dust that then disappeared like water into sand as it was de- atomized. The boy didn't bother himself with paying attention to any of this since he knew his physical state was in safe hands. What he focused on now was accomplishing the goal his father set out for him using the restrictions indirectly imposed.

"Use a low-grade Ballast type, [Guidance], spell capable of capital-izing on all of the magic and medicine affecting your body" is what the boy actually heard in his dad's secretive undertone. As for any other issue, he would think about it or bring it up with his parents after he was sufficiently cleared of his critical condition. He flitted through his memories at quite the noteworthy pace, a process that resembled running through a rather significant library.

"One of the surgical experts over at the capital's Westempyer General, published his personal formula. What? Two hundred and two years ago? It solves the issue I have at the moment." Without a second of delay, Alize read through the information hidden within his own memory just as the golden needles began to thin out. Half a second before the final needle sank beneath his skin, his mind finished the spell he was

looking for. Thankfully, it was already translated into one of the many ancient languages taught in primary school.

"Ballenguss Piklisungen, Allg-Änderung: Ich geb-sem trask d'heiter, für den braucht, daher den verleben echeil kann: Einstrukel." Alize thought of the words, drew upon the appropriate aspects within his profile, then thought of how his body was a biological machine with certain shortcuts and awe inspiring functions. In the blink of an eye, his severed or damaged nerves vibrated, flashed, then imploded around golden needles that sunk into and drove through even his bone marrow. Glowing lines and designs similar to cell shading wrapped around his silhouette, producing a golden corona on the hard lines of his figure as his body trembled with unearthly sensations. The amber-red potion tinted his chorus of stabilization spells pink while the odd steel-blue mists produced by the harness clung to the inside area of the golden borders like frost building up on the inside of a car's glass rather than on the outside. Alize opened his eyes to something miraculous. The runic and somewhat flowering patterns of the mixed A and B type [Stabilize] spell meshed with the hard and strict lines of the B. type [Guidance], and created a swirling net just underneath the surface of his skin. It allowed any of the cast regenerative effects to move throughout his body in specific conical and self-contained bursts rather than as unidirectional pulses that tapered out and slipped through the near-vacuous amount of space between cells.

"This is great. It worked. I will at least be able to regain feeling in the areas that I focus on now. Hopefully." With a wry smile, Alize sighed under the piercing gaze of his father. Piercing in the sense that there was just an indecipherable expression on the older man's face as he scanned the Tenets that Alize just used. The crystalline casing around his boy's skin, a casing that held several layers, felt uncanny in its supernatural beauty. The charming gentleman felt something was

off about his observations, but even with his son casting right in front of him, he could see nothing but magic similar to liquid diamonds. The glimmering uniformity, mesmerizing cut, and glimmer of superior power were unmistakable. Still, something completely instinctive gnawed at the back of the man's head.

1.5 Helpful Information Semi Simplified

The bulk of the medicinal liquid ultimately landed in Alize's stomach like rocks, pushing and flooding most of the waste in his body toward the small pouch and out of his system. As a result, the kid coughed up what looked like dark red slime balls full of yellow and black stones that carried a foul smell. The plastic bag on the kid's waist also bulged as black pearls rolled out of the bandages like a broken hourglass spilling sand everywhere. Thankfully, the bearded man, his faithful father, instantly disintegrated the waste before any of it could make a mess or ruin the crappy arcane bandages. In an odd but welcome change of fate, the next thing to receive a hit from the medicine was his nervous system after its rolling hit throughout the entire process. The boy felt an oscillating burn, chill, and weightlessness that bore holes in his brain as feeling slowly returned to his mostly broken body. Similar to being struck by the gaze of a gorgon, he released a scream but found that not a single sound came out as his brain simply couldn't process the instant overload. Suffice to say, Alize didn't notice how all of his orifices and body holes ejected one nasty fluid or solid after the other due to a near instant blackout. To top the shit cake with a crap topper, the boy was, unfortunately, used to such a precarious state because of his training and instantly restarted his brain with a well timed, self-induced panic attack.

Unrelenting thoughts of the worst things that could happen to him or his family and an erratic heartbeat fought against waves of soul-deep exhaustion that slammed into mind and heart before he could even begin to catch his next breath. The pulse of any new [Stabilize] spell dulled within less than a single second, a speed that he simply could not cast at. Without even possessing the luxury of being able to think in this state, the boy grit his teeth and endured. He bided his time and allowed his exhausted magic reserves to refill one excruciating second after the next. On the other side of the debacle was the salt-and-pepper-haired and bearded man with soft eyes and curved long ears. Alize's father simply stood by his son's side with a frown and a constantly tapping foot as he watched the boy painstakingly gather his mental and magical faculties, one collapse after the other. On the bright side of all of this, the extremities of the boy's most unresponsive parts twitched and wiggled almost uncontrollably. Seconds, minutes, possibly even hours later, Alizedriel clawed his way out of the mists of his own mind and immediately got back to thinking coherently as his nerves finished reconnecting and repairing themselves.

"My insides are burning, and this aftertaste is layered in such a manner that it would be impossible not to recognize. This is something either distilled from a Parasitic Lochorn root or a Swamp Ale base or maybe it's the juice, Amberstone. Dad would most definitely not give me

the alcoholic version of the drink even if it has better medicinal effects in the short term." Alize analyzed the effects and potency of the medicine.

"Virgin Swamp ale, or amberstone juice, ground Clensis seed, powdered manglehorn from a blanchette bull, aqua-hedron sand would have to be a must even if it's not something I can taste, and, hm. It also has..." With closed eyes, the boy dived back into his imagination and completely put together the herbs and spices that his father would have needed to utilize in order to concoct this particular medicinal brew.

"Cinnamon and allspice" were the most notable of the more base ingredients.

"Rank, grade, level. The filing system for the universe. On a low estimate, what I drank would have a minimum of three stars for its rank. Since he is a perfectionist with his work, the potion would undoubtedly have a maximum grade due to its efficiency, but there has to be some margin of error so maybe this is a standard brew? I can imagine that he was in a rush, so there might have been some contamination of the ingredients. It might even straddle that margin. The problem that I have is determining the level. If it's lower than fifty, it will not be super effective on me. But if it's closer to 100, not only will it have a near-perfect effect, it will have an absolute absorption rate." In his imagination, vast rows of book-filled shelving shifted and lit up like lanterns all around him as the images or physical representations of herbs, animal parts, and the magic needed to accomplish what his dad created surrounded him.

"Medicine aside." Alize realized that he had wasted his precious time and, with a swish of his hand, the fog cleared out and parted along the path of his vision to reveal a long raised platform. In less than a second, he ran toward the edge of the circular rotunda and stood near a high-backed chair that was placed behind a semicircular bench. With

a single step, he approached the desk and twisted a checkered dial that organized itself off into four color-coded and numerated segments. Immediately, a small and almost inaudible hum in the fog turned into a mesmerizing, almost musical symphony as his mind spun with information that he could never practically use before now.

"I'm sure that I put the information I'm looking for next to the image of a Jaunting mandrake. And since I'm looking for consistency, reliability, and endurance, the information could only be in area forty-three A. Maybe 2B?"

With a thought, a massive bronze pot with a bulbous humanoid made of leaves and mushrooms rose from the mist and clicked onto the glassy round platform as if it were a puzzle piece that just slotted into its place. Three winding pathways of books and artifacts followed the plant colony out into the mist, hinting at the depth of knowledge that he possessed but could not access without purposeful recollection. A big A, B, and C stamped the sides of the three towering shelves facing Alize.

"Now, which ancient scholar altered the Guidance spell to work the way that I need it to? It should be Mardi or Tutolin. They are the most recent scholar candidates to come out of the capital's prestigious Westempyer General." All the other rising and falling shelving of the greater maze came to a haunting pause as the fog rolled back in. Effectively, this meant that all the information within the fog was not on his mind in any conscious manner whatsoever.

Only the statue of the humanoid plant remained high and solitary, towering mostly above the two shelves depicted as 43.A and 43.B while 43.C suffered a partial fog encompassing treatment. Without wasting a second, he found an author by the name of Heliocynth J. Mardi in a directory that was placed at the base of the mandrake. He carried the directory with him down the very first shelf and found himself standing by one of the very first pale blue glowing books in the section. It was a picture book for kids that focused specifically on the complexities of minor healing spells and the differences between the four magic types in terms of how they pursued healing, mending, replication, and restoration or regeneration. In the blink of an eye, Alize refreshed himself on the basics and only the basics as every related document lit up along the entire shelf like signposts.

"Accord, Ballast, Creation, and Direct type magic. Four different fuel sources that naturally grow and develop in quality and quantity in every living thing until a certain unspecified point. Each type of fuel has two controllable and observable functions. These specific uses of the fuel are separated into profile markers, Aura and Mana, which affect only ourselves and the world around us, respectively. The profiles are then further separated into Root, Aspect, and Standard Allotments. Mr. Mardi, for instance, is a Root Aura user with Mixed aspects supporting A and B type magic." He didn't open the children's book and just touched the cover as a small excerpt from his own notes that filled the sky above his head. Floating blue sparks trailed along his finger as his brain queued up the rest of the books in the aisle.

"Mr. Mardi is capable of casting less than a handful of spells and nothing else without some permanent repercussions." In the blink of an eye, Alize reabsorbed the content of some information that was assigned to him as homework.

"That is to say, Mr. Mardi developed a solid method concerning the combination of a minor restoration, Stabilize and a minor enchantment, Guidance. Exactly what I have to use now." Alize thumbed through the directory and quickly recalled some information related to someone else who pushed Mardi's work into a completely different stratosphere.

"Hehe, Rat. Dr. Rat. That's a funny name for someone who isn't related to a Dysthosian." Alize let a flood of information refresh his lacking memory.

"Rat, ahem, R. A. Tutolin, was in a similar boat as Mardi as they seemed to have shared many of the same research subjects." The only difference, as he recalled, was that Ronaldo A. Tutolin dived more into the variations of Accord spells with a fervor much like a dehydrated man gulping water. Alize rubbed his chin and returned to the central platform with an idea in mind. As if to prove himself, the fog peeled back to reveal his bench-like desk covered in scrolls, mathematics, and medical diagrams.

"These two geniuses already did the work for me. One knows how to mix A and B type magic in ways no one else thought possible, and the other somehow improved an already perfect general case spell." Not too long after, ten or so seconds, Alize frowned as he felt something blow up in his stomach and burn its way past his lungs and into his throat.

Without meaning to, his eyes shot open just in time for him to be aware of a dry heave that devolved into a coughing fit, which then turned into an exorcism of almost black blood and bile. Before the boy could even react, his father turned all the waste material into a scattering dust that Jarold immediately blew out of the room. The bearded man slowly returned his son to a resting position. Unexpectedly, Alize cracked a smile that made his father baffled. His more experienced eyes suddenly darted around the room in a brief moment of uncertainty. Delicately, like a piece of brittle glass, the old man laid Alize's head down on a fluffed pillow.

"Ark, I understand that it might be difficult, but do you know why this happened to you?"

The old man gently patted his son's head and did his best to maintain eye contact, but he could feel his own face warping with subtle guilt. Alize nodded from side to side as best he could.

"I understand. Don't try to force your memories. It will come back. Ah, your little friend. Wilfred, Wanda, Winnifell, Winniefred? That brute of a girl tried to explain the situation, but you know how that one speaks. The public education system sure is a former shell." The bearded man shared his thoughts on the matter and shook his head as well.

"Don't mistake my lack of understanding of your friend's description for a lack of information though. Before your mother left, I examined the site where you were injured. To simplify, it seems as though something tried to forcefully take your friend away while it presumably attacked you. Your mother also confirmed that there was some rather unstable magic at the site, but due to its quick decay, she could not track it down without effort and time, both of which we have all placed on you. I can safely say that, due to the time frame, we are dealing with a rather highly ranked and graded spirit since it could seamlessly blend with the area's effuse. It's the only thing that explains such a quick decay of its magic." The older man's deadpan expression made Alize gulp with an ashen and wide-eyed stare. Noticing the change, the man brushed back Alize's sweat-matted hair and kissed his forehead.

"Don't worry, my boy. I am sure you already guessed as much if you remember anything at all about the situation. If not, maybe my knowledge has jogged something loose." The man erased even more of the waste material that collected inside the bandage's pouch.

"Either way, until you are healed, or on the right track at the very least, your mother and I have decided not to pursue the matter. So for now, I want you to keep trying to stay awake until the medicine's physical effects begin to affect you. Lochorn is a bit slow acting if you remember from our lessons, but it shouldn't be more than a few more seconds now." Once again, Alize received a forehead kiss and nodded as best he could.

"Don't worry, Dad. I will definitely make it past this. After all, I secretly read through your work computer. I couldn't use any of this info before because of my Affix, but now that the cats are out of the bag, Haa. Ah, who would have thought that a duo of intern doctors managed to reverse engineer an Archon's most famous spell? A god's bread and butter. Haaha. Bayrun's Life Jacket my ass." With a painful grunt and smile, the kid closed his eyes and got back to his mage craft. The middle-aged man cleaned up the bloody floor and the sheets. After setting the room, he glared at Jarold and then sat back down. The sylph immediately slammed the crook of his arm into an outstretched palm and raised his middle finger. The bearded man's jaw dropped in astonishment as he showcased a wealth of nonverbal curse words and gestures. All of which were matched by the ancient Gaelen warrior in terms of vulgarity. As for Alize, he immersed himself in his imaginary world and scanned the symbols within the mist.

"The Indestructible Archon, Bayrun. From what I read, this recreation is called [Lesser Life Jacket] since it's not anywhere near the standard of what that seven-star god has shown. Thankfully, I did my own research, using Dad's worktable." At the center of the pedestal in his mindscape, and with the flick of his wrists, Alize conjured a piece of paper and a pen with a flustered and fearful expression. It dawned on him that, based on what his father said earlier, every instance of his sneakery appeared to be an orchestrated lesson.

Thankfully, he did not distract himself too badly as he drew on an already complicated diagram of his body courtesy of the repeated casting of [Stabilize]. Next to the diagram, a long scroll of paper materialized and unfurled as he wrote down the titles of "Mixed type: Minor Heal Stabilize" and "Lesser Life Jacket" at the top of two columns that split the scroll in half. In a single breath, he wrote down several dozen lines of mathematical and magical equations that seemingly swirled together and combined into an archaic language. Alize felt his father lightly brush his hair away from his forehead once again and kiss his brow and leave the room not too long after a gust of wind blew past his nose and a bowl clattered to the floor. He whipped out two more sheets of paper and drew two more diagrams of his body. Each one had a different color distribution and slight changes in organ placement. All in all, neither of the hand-drawn figures matched the extensive details of the magically rendered version. With a flick of his wrist, the floating pages overlapped and created a color-coded chart that showed a worst-case and best-case scenario, fixed in place by his own casting.

"First, I need to overlap and fix my diagnosis with a textbook display of Lerian biology and the findings of Mardi and Tutolin. As for the magic...." Almost immediately, the boy flipped open some books and referenced texts to different pages that held details and colorful drawings similar to the magical render. Little by little, he tweaked the hand-drawn diagrams, similar to how one used an art app on a tablet or touch screen to overlay images and trace.

"*There's also the effectiveness of dad spells, the arcanum bandages, and the medicine, but any error there is already accounted for thanks to the earlier heads up and help.*" Alize spun the pen in his hand and quickly dragged and dropped the floating lines, glowing numbers, and arcane runes of the original Stabilize spells he used from the associated scroll's column and onto the updating diagram. He traced a new image from the overlap of nearly a dozen translucent images. With a flick of his free hand, he created a rough rendering of his fall out of bed. Dragging his images over, the rough three-dimensional figurine turned into a clearly defined copy of his long-eared self.

The figurine moved just as he did, by using a single arm to pull at something and trying to stand up with the obvious result being bupkiss. Somewhere and sometime into the little holographic, green lines sprouted from the depths of its chest, stomach, and head. These lines clasped onto ripped muscles, wrapped up broken bones, and even simulated the same pulse as nerves just to keep his body from a total system shock. After a few rounds of explosive waves, the same green lines filled in the gaps between parts of his body that were completely severed. Amazingly, this temporary network completely shattered like glass the moment the imaginary figurine returned to its elevated position. In this manner of replaying the visuals, Alize purely imagined what his magic affected to gain a better understanding of the damage his body was under.

"An all-around natural compounding effect in a mystical environment and an improved conductive, reactive, and efficient transition between fuel sources. Those two additions sound easy to include, but before Mardi and Tutolin, the last improvement made to A and B type general healing spells. Hm, it was over several thousand years ago if I am remembering correctly. And I'm pretty sure that the forum on Dad's network implied that Bayrun is the one who made that improvement." Alize moved the auto-playing diagram into the column that held the word Stabilize at the top.

"Whether or not I succeed is, well, completely up to luck at this point." The kid wrote exactly what he thought at the bottom of the unfurling scroll and moved onto a different part of the spell-crafting process.

"The spoken component is the easiest to do since there is already a transitional language to reconcile and support the differences in ancient Elisha and the Iron Tongue of Resh." He collapsed the diagrams and

pulled out three different dictionaries related to languages that he knew.

"The issues that I have to deal with are purely related to the mechanisms behind the mystic rules that each magic type abides by. Following that, the final product should then be formatted and adhere as much as possible to the conventional laws of physics so it doesn't burn through my magic. The best I can do is play a matching game and cross out the variations that cost too much or run a risk of collapsing." Alize wiped the imaginary sweat off his brow and thought of something that was practically impossible but entirely plausible if he was just that unlucky. An implosion of the self, an Incast-Blip.

"Let me just try it. If anything out of the ordinary is about to happen, I'm sure my Affix will give a warning by trying to create some scenario out of the matter." In the blink of an eye, Alize condensed all the foreign words, mathematics, runic letters, and mystical symbols floating around him. With a slap of his hand, a complex and nearly indecipherable scrawling appeared on the Stabilize half of the sprawling scroll. After about a total of one minute, Alize opened his eyes to view his body with a look of determination. He could hear his father casting in the distance as he fixed the kitchen area that he had utterly destroyed a few moments before. In his mind, the kid chanted a phrase and moved the buzzing magic in his body. Unable to contain his unwavering confidence and excitement, he soundlessly recited a nameless transitory language championed by Celestials then mouthed the words "Guided Stabilize". Nothing happened except for a moment of awkward silence.

"Did I miscalculate somewhere when plugging in my numbers? Did I carry over too many extra ones? Oh, no. Do I not have the profile needed to cast this type of spell? That would be pretty bad. Dad said that I'm using Tenets instead of magic, so failing a single spell will make all of

this wasteful casting even worse." Alize spiraled for a hot second but found that his icy body began to sweat.

Without warning, [Guided Stabilize], true to its name, honed in and tightened around the damaged areas of his body with a wound-sealing gold spearhead and mint-colored trail. Unlike with the minor healing that he had been using until now, this guided variant painted his body with densely veined patterns that overlapped and improved the established amber red and pink lines all throughout his system. A semi-physical anchor, similar to a secondary circulatory system, pumped the medicine throughout and around his body with wild abandon. A flood of sweat released from his pores alongside a sickeningly sweet aroma full of honeydew and lime. Unexpectedly, the magic in the two arcanums, the harness and bandages, drained at a visible rate, blending their effects into the new [Guided Stabilize]. Alize's father entered the room a few moments later, completely taken aback by the sudden change in his son's state. This is exactly what he told his son to cast in uncertain terms, but the effect that he observed in his son was far from the norm or any expected projections. It was as though his Alize created an all-devouring ouroboros that specially searched for other spells and energy to siphon and use before its own reserves. The boy, laid there with a half smile plastered across his pale face as he jolted every other second from an autonomous recast of the snaking vines.

"Interesting. The spell overlap worked like a charm despite my errors. I did run through my calculations more than thrice, so it's no wonder it worked. But this feeling? This sharpness, and the alternating hot and cold? It's soothing but not expected. I do not like it." Alize noticed that his slowly healing body sped up only by a factor of half of its previous snail's pace. It was practically negligible, but in the grand scheme of things, it meant that he was certifiably no longer on the brink of

death. Alize's father broke out of his reverie and held his son's head up and to the side. The boy's broken body simply couldn't handle the speed at which it was healing, even if it was only a single one hundred thousandth of an increase compared to a normal recovery rate.

"What do I do here? This is too much, Ark. I told you to stay on lesser-grade healing spells. What is this? What did you do? I don't even recognize this variant." Alize's father whispered as he held the boy's tongue, afraid he would chew through it in his freakish spasms that were brought about by golden-tipped, hair's width, and green vines.

"I don't know. Is this your Affix? Is this you? Or is this something else? I just don't. Just think of your mother...." Beardo teared up and rocked back and forth as all of his wits and intelligence simply could not help him at this moment. He was afraid that his child would hurt himself by moving too much, a feat which should have been impossible because of [Stasis]. No, the older man noticed it the moment he tried to pour his magic into the harness. Whatever he put into it went directly through the bank and fueled the spell affecting his son. On top of that, he could clearly see a layer of crystalized magic completely encasing the boy in a mint green and golden shell ever so slowly, complete with a slight icy frost around his head and heart. Another layer of anguish and fear took root on the older man's face since he understood that if this gruesome sight was not related to his son's curse or his own actions, then there were only a handful of horrible choices left. All of them meant either parting as a family or killing the boy with his own hands. No, if anyone could see the older man's face, they would immediately notice that a hint of recognition flashed between his own and Jarold's despondent expressions.

"What are you gonna do about this, smartass? He can't ever leave this terrarium now. If he does, the churches and your higher-ups are going to be on us like flies on shit. Oh, and let's not forget about those bastard occultists that are still after this Apeirogon and my contractor's life." Jarold, who had been a silent onlooker up until this point, mouthed the words with a frown, narrated with his hands, and floated to the other side of Alize. Beardo read the sign language and blinked rapidly. Obviously, the man cycled through different plans and solutions but could not come to a final decision.

"I don't know. Just don't tell her about this, you old bag of farts. She'll blame herself and try to deal with the situation alone if it means making the world just a little bit safer for Ark. And before you begin to play the contrarian, know that if she attempts to take on the world, she will die, and you will be forced to make a contract with me or him by then. This is assuming that you aren't decommissioned and scraped at the treasury for Quill and Links." Alize's father replied with a soundless mouthing of the words, but it seemed as though the Fae heard him loud and clear. Jarold sneered and turned away with a reserved look of worry. The sudden gloomy atmosphere dispersed upon hearing a beautiful chime resonate throughout the air. An unconventionally tall woman with sharp features, a wide nose bridge, and glistening bronze skin over ironbound muscles, somehow, acrobatically dove through the window Jarold kept open and rolled to a complete stop beside Alize's bed.

"Mommy's back. Ark, please be okay!"

Tears streamed down her face in a never-ending flood as she knelt and raised an arm to cover her baby. Though, as if this moment were something staged in a play, she noticed the odd and tense atmosphere in the room.

Her son trembled, resembling a volcano about to blow with his violent shaking and reddening skin. A cocoon of crystalline energy and magic spun around his figure and outlined a horrifyingly fractured skeleton and torn muscle. The second thing she noticed was the sickeningly sweet and bitter metallic scent of a viscous medicine and blood that overpowered everything, even with the window curtains open and Jarold airing the area out. After more than a cursory glance and a sharp intake of breath, the third thing she examined was the somber countenance of Alize's father beneath the disguising beard and emotional facade. He was observing and secretly jotting down notes about his son's state in an almost mechanical manner despite the display and comforting words of worry. The man in question looked down and whispered, "Fuck" before he could fix his faux grief-stricken expression and hide the palm-sized notepad on his lap. Several dozen rings exploded from the abyssal depths of the woman's pupils and overlapped with a blinding vibrance.

Instantly, her jaw clenched as she closed her glimmering eyes. Her barrel chest heaved with violent shutters, almost as if she contained a painful scream and heart-tearing sorrow. Against expectations, however, the tall woman stood up with a graceful and resilient silence reminiscent of the eye of a cataclysmic storm.

"Raquelidrel Orsche Kaveri." She threw an archaic-looking leather satchel at the man.

"Yes, my love?" Orsche, Alize's father, stood up in a robotic fashion and reflexively caught the bag with his free hand. He was nearly a head and a half shorter standing at his full height.

"Save our baby." Her even tone, cold in nature, told the scruffy man all he needed to know.

"My baby..." Before Orsche could even fully depart from Alize, the woman knelt beside her son and allowed the boy to bite into her fingers as he silently screamed against mind-crippling pain. All she could do was hold her child, as Orsche did since her part was done.

1.6 Trial by Fire?

"I'm sorry. My little baby. I'm so sorry. I should have run faster. I should have waited longer and been more aware, I should have..." Alize's mom wiped her tears and caressed his ghastly visage. More than a few minutes passed by since she returned, but for Alize, it was as though he had spent hours enduring pain that would make most grown men faint in seconds. Thankfully, Orsche did not supply the harness or bandages with more magic and reminded the boy's mother also not to do such a thing. After all this time, the [Guided Stabilize] finally died down, sputtering out on the effusive fumes that naturally inundated the atmosphere. As a knockoff of a knockoff, the spell couldn't restart itself or even effectively lower its effects to prioritize longevity and stability.

"I tried to chase the bastard that did this to you, but spirits, you know? I had Jarold track it down, but there was an issue that he ran into along the way."

"I know, Mah." Alize nodded to himself and briefly remembered some encounters that his parents set for him in a Simulation that acted like a training room.

"I couldn't find a trace of it after he lost the trail, so I could not exact revenge on your behalf. I'm sorry for that, my handsome little warrior. I'm sorry." A single teardrop that the woman was not quick enough to wipe away fell onto Alize's cheek. By some miracle, the boy stared at his mom with burst blood vessels filling his sclera. He smiled oh, so slightly through the pain. She bit her lip and gently pecked her boy between the eyebrows with a soft chuckle.

"Your father blames me, you know. I can see it on his face. He's disappointed in me. I understand why. When I found you, there were only a few nasty fractures and bits poking out of your skin. You fell nicely. I'm proud of you." She hugged her son and backed off when he began wheezing.

"I'm sorry..." she squeezed his face and pouted.

"I tell you all the time, but I couldn't control myself and moved you too much. I know better. I've seen worse. I've done worse to you, but that was all in the sim and I'm so sorry! My little baby. I couldn't leave you there like that. I'm so sorry. I trained you to be like me, but I failed you. I'm a failure as your mom, and I'm sorry for that." Her tears fell once more, but she didn't try to wipe them this time; they rolled down Alize's cheeks in a stream.

"Now that I think about it, this is the first time I've ever even seen Mom cry so hard." The mental image he had of his mother: a collage of beautiful smiles, cheerful laughs, powerful but usually silly poses, and victorious sneers, usually and almost always used against his dad when he was proven wrong in an argument, suddenly gained a new folder he never expected to create. In this moment of brief reflection,

his eyes welled with tears that, under the prodding of his mother's sobs, drenched the recently fluffed pillow beneath his head.

"I will not let myself get hurt so easily anymore. This I promise you in my heart. I'm sorry for making you cry and worry so much. I love you, and I'm sorry, Mommy. And stop saying that stuff. You are strong, smart, funny, and I love you." Alize wanted to wipe his mom's tears away and give her a big hug, but he couldn't move even a single eyelid anymore. He was confident that if he so much as even breathed incorrectly at this moment, he would fall out. He wouldn't die now, of course, but it would make it much more difficult for the type of medicine in his body to work properly. Thankfully, Alize noticed some movement out of the corner of his eye before they closed.

"Verza, my love..." Orsche entered the room with a steeled heart and just in the nick of time as he placed his arm around the love of his life. He whispered at first, but with a clearing of his throat, Orsche pulled out some medicine that he had been working on for the past few minutes.

"Don't cry. Everything is going to be alright. Ark is going to pull through. This salve is for the heat that he might be experiencing. We have to be careful, so..." Orsche began to speak and was going to finish with, "So, we have to be sure that his spell is completely put out before we apply anything with magic as a component. We have to be quick and precise since we have a small window before he is no longer able to keep himself awake after the spell fades. To avoid any accidents, we will split the work and do one section at a time to not draw attention to ourselves."

Without wasting a single breath or a motion, however, Verza lunged forward at a speed reminiscent of teleportation and ripped the bandages off of her kid's body. As if she doubled, another mirage image of her stole and applied the salve to his exposed and ruptured skin like it was a common body lotion. Another phantom image then wrapped him up again like a spider would its prey. Everything finished before a single piece of ripped bandage could float a single centimeter from its initial position. Orsche stood there with a slack jaw and wide eyes, but ultimately he didn't say anything and simply sighed as he looked at their son with an ever-increasing amount of panic and wonder.

A few things stood out to both of the adults in the moments after Verza's outburst of inhuman speed and agility. The first being that there were an innumerable amount of cuts, tears, and ruptured knots of flesh and torn muscles that dotted their son's body. Insanely enough, despite the grievous appearance, not a single one bled more than a run-of-the-mill paper cut due to the tightly packed and hair-thin rose gold lines that appeared like stitches and mint colored threads that reinforced the ruptures. The second thing they noticed about their son was an unnatural lack of bruising or inflammation. An icy haze washed over these bruised sections and rippled, almost as if these locations were not only locked in a [Stasis], but they were also completely isolated away from the rest of his body. The third thing they noticed was the overall stillness after his initial frightening seizure. Alize did not move out of control in the slightest as all the trembling they both saw now only came from his naturally twitching muscles and breathing. The fourth and final thing they noticed in hindsight was that their son maintained a calm and somewhat annoyed expression throughout the entire process, even when he was gripped by a terrible quake. No, both of his parents revisited the whole thing in their minds and noticed how their son seemed to be almost pleased with how things turned out, as if everything or most things regarding his recovery were completely within a set range of expectations.

The adults exchanged a look of worry and contemplation that did not last long as Verza immediately inserted her magic into the two pieces of mystical Arcanum, the harness and bandages. The hair thin lines of Alize's spell thickened and flared in response but unlike the initial uncontrollable and painful tremors that he had to endure, the twisting canvas of tendrils spread in a manner that both of the parents simply couldn't decipher even with their knowledge and experience, respectively. Orsche, visibly confused and intrigued, began to twitch his fingers in a way that suggested he wanted to write everything down, but his brows knit as the air began to thicken with a tangible pressure. Ors raised his glittering hand toward some far-off location while Verza frowned and readied herself by standing up.

"I got it. It's just a casual glance by one of the Archon's. Just don't move like that again." Orsche quickly patted Verza's shoulder and stood by the window as he muttered something reminiscent of a madman's ravings. He swiped the air and dragged some glittering threads out of the vibrating and thick air that Jarold distanced himself from. Alize couldn't see the glorious sight, but Orsche suddenly lit up with a boreal wave of magic, like he was the sun incarnate. A tessellating but phantasmal sphere or cube, or object, with infinite faces, an apeirogon, flashed to life in his ethereal-looking hands. An indecipherable map of, presumably, the universe constructed itself inside of the infinitely sided shape that alternated between being a ring and flat two-dimensional fractals. With a tap, the illusory figure hardened into a glassy disc that popped up into a dome with another tap, then a sphere with a fourth. With a fifth, sixth and seventh taps, the sphere folded onto a single display. The entire camp and its immediate surroundings took form within the Arcane object, separated into several layers and rings of pocketed landscapes. In the direction that Ors looked at, the outermost and largest casing flattened with a red shimmer. The eighth tap boxed out the red area and separated it from the main body of the device, while a ninth tap put detail into what caused the commotion. His eyes reflected a red light in the shape of a grasping hand and arm that extended from some far-off location. Something simply incomprehensible attempted to push through and invade their little bubble.

Orsche grit his teeth and pressed his string-wrapped and glowing fingers into the jagged sphere. Without a word, the grasping hand distorted and suddenly snapped to the side, as if space itself fractured and adhered to a different set of rules. As a result, the red light rounded their camp and passed onto some location on the other side of the item's boundary. Orsche dropped the sphere to the floor, panting and sweating buckets as his waist slowly gave out. He had no strength even to sit up straight, nevermind arguing with Verza over her rash actions that ended up with him in this state. That is to say, Alize did not see or hear any of this since Jarrold prevented the sound with a vacuum and blocked the light with a wall of thickly packed dust. Instead, the kid focused on bettering himself. Specifically, he needed to ensure that every cast was made at its absolute best since Tenets were a non-renew-able, solidified expression of magic. That said, a revamped [Guided-Stabilize V.2] spell is what the parents saw writhing underneath the bandages the moment before the danger had come. Orsche, trembled as he got onto his feet like a newborn fawn and pointed at Verza.

"Alright. Now that we are still safe, huh?"

Orsche didn't dare use an invasive sensory or observational ability out of a complete sense of bafflement..

"Verza. What, um, what does Ark's magic look like to you?"

Orsche blinked and tilted his head in wonder and to get a better look at his son's Tenets. The solidified, crystalline, and divine structure that he was expecting to see seemed droopy—is the only word that described it.

"It looks like that. Huh?"

Verza blinked, with a single glowing ring surrounding her pupils. Hearing her response and seeing her body lock up, Ors immediately collected his thoughts with haste and checked his son's temperature, heart rate, blood flow, and output. In a second, the man rushed out of the room and in a moment returned with two buckets of purple-colored water that had tar-black wood shavings pooling at the bottom. All the fuss and movement made Verza somewhat jumpy.

"Ors, what is happening and what are you doing?"

Still standing and teary-eyed, she bulked up by another half a dozen centimeters as she locked onto their son. Jarrold didn't need to be ordered to maintain the vacuum where only the two of them could communicate.

"Think about what you just saw. Ah, dammit. I made another mistake or an incorrect assumption. Fucking dammit, I made a grave error. One that may have stunted our son's growth." Ors hissed through gritted teeth and left a gust of wind in his place as he once again dashed out of the room and returned with a thin blanket and the satchel that Verza brought back from wherever she was off at earlier in the day. Ors snapped his fingers to lay out the thin blanket on an empty space on the floor, but instead of dropping to the ground, the sheet floated and flattened out like it was covering a waist-high table. Without hesitation, he emptied the contents of the satchel on top of it. In a manner that did not adhere to physics, a small mountain of herbs, spices, and mushrooms piled up in different spots on the sheet as shavings, small and large parts, or pastes that were held in miniature containers.

"Explain more clearly, Orsche. I'm not following. I don't see anything wrong with him." Verza moved out of the way and crossed her arms.

"I, um, wait. 40, no 41 celsius. 28 bpm. That's, hmm, I have time. It's doable," Orsche whispered to himself, cracked his neck, then wiggled his fingers as he took his son's temperature and pulse again.

"Alright, so, I made an assumption based on the circumstances of his birth and some ancient text that I've read pertaining to similar cases." With a flick of his wrist, dozens of apparatuses used in traditional medicine and chemistry splayed out across the floating table. Miraculously, the items glowed and produced the effect of their intended uses and liquefied, distilled, sliced, peeled, and powdered the mountain of medicinal and poisonous items that were pre-portioned out.

"Ors, stop stalling and get to the point." Verza clicked her tongue in annoyance since her man was prepared to ramble and avoid the topic.

"It's necessary."

"It's not."

"You didn't listen to my explanation before we had him, did you?"

"I was listening."

"What did I say?"

"Go ahead and explain then."

"Alright, then, so due to those circumstances, there were several outcomes for our boy. The most likely, with an 86.4562% chance, is what I told you about all those years ago. That our son would be born with the Tenets of a divine being despite possessing a mortal body and profile." Orsche moved the buckets he carried in earlier and began to dump all manner of things into them.

"Orsche," Verza growled since the man purposely trailed off and turned silent.

"Forget it. To simplify, our boy doesn't have Tenets. He has a unique and delicate Ballast standard. [Shroud]." Orsche grabbed handfuls, or pinches of this and that from the floating sheet and tossed them into a humongous mortar the size of an oil drum. With another hand, he swirled the crystal clear purple water after dumping in all manner of items and watched it turn into a rancid tar black liquid. He quickly whispered [Create: Water], materializing an orb of pure and clear water above his head and motioned for some other magical plants to drop into the mortar. During this focus-intensive orchestration, Verza scratched her head in confusion and minute understanding.

"What do you mean it's unique? There is an entire branch of the Havenwood Military with casters that specializes in that aspect. There are even a few members of that branch that have a Root combo." Verza shook her head and bent over her baby boy to get a better look at her kids' Tenets. She also noticed the slightly inconsistent drooping at the corners of each crystalline fractal but only where the spell was working at its thinnest.

"My love, what I'm saying is, our son's profile mutated at some point, and I was not aware enough to catch it. Maybe my instruments were confused by your temporary state the first time I checked, or maybe the Arcanum I recovered all those years ago somehow leaked into something and messed up the testing results before we even found out that you were pregnant. I just don't know. Maybe the Tenets that I observed during his infancy somehow faded before his profiles established themselves, or maybe his Affix did something neither of us could expect. My Quill is on his curse, but it still doesn't change the fact that I missed such a vital change." Orsche conjured a small white hot flame, a kilogram of zinc, fifty-six grams of iron, three milligrams of potassium, and several other minerals. With a single hand and a few casual mental whispers, he adjusted all the formulas for his spells to match Alize's rapidly fluctuating condition. Verza, hesitantly, moved away from the flurry of concoction and shuffled to the other side of Alize's bed in order to stay out of her man's way.

"Simplify Orsche. And stop panicking. Fix the issue in front of us and we will deal with what comes next." Verza controlled her shaky breathing, but she couldn't help but silently tear up. With every extended pause, Ors bit his lip and drew blood from an already open wound.

"It was all an illusion. From the very beginning. It was fake. A passively generated ruse created by overspill. It's only showing signs of collapse now because he is burning through all the magic that he has been reserving until now. Magic, my love. Not Tenets. We ruined our son. Because of me. Do you get it?"

Orsche clenched his trembling hand and pressed on with his pharmacological process. Despite the conversation, only fifteen and a half seconds passed since he finished checking Alize's temp.

"What collapsed?"

"The passive [Shroud] that his profile can generate. Passive my love. His Aura and Mana are different from what I have been scanning. His magic is also nowhere near solidified. It was a facade," Orsche elaborated. Verza blinked a few times and gradually, her jaw dropped.

"He must have a root function in both profiles then to have a passive effect like that. Something like that needs to have been created by a rooted profile, right?"

Verza looked at Jarrold since Ors was deep in the brew. Her profile was rooted in Accord-type magic with a specific focus on an Aura-based aspect that was called [Bolster] in common parlance and a Mana aspect that was commonly called [Embody].

"Yes..." Jarold started to speak to her, but a crackling bolt of plasma whipped out from underneath the cauldron that Orsche leaned over.

"Yes. He should have a rooted profile. He should be able to use only two spells. He should, this and that, but it's obvious that he isn't barred from using anything else since he's clearly capable of using

Accord-type magic. I don't know how just yet," Orsche explained the rest of his thought process and observations without so much as a break to breathe. By the time he was done, second number 22.764 passed. In the meantime, Alize calmly and carefully took notes of his perceived internal state without a single worry or care. Then, since his parents were being respectfully quiet, he assumed that they were both engaging in their usual hushed whispers.

"What I'm doing must look pretty horrifying." Alize thought about his internal situation with the foresight of someone who lived a long and hard life and without a moment of extraneous thought, he updated [Guided Stabilize V.2]. A third and fourth variant overlapped in consecutive order to test the feeling behind two of his different thought processes.

"[Improved Guided Stabilization] won, huh? I was expecting [V.3] to come out on top." As if it were destined, the better of the two effects swallowed the other and kicked into high gear. Verza, still in possession of the magic that enhanced her eyesight, noticed that the crystalline Tenets that denoted a divine-ranked entity somehow looked even more faint and illusory now that she knew what to look for. It really was a multi-layered illusion that simply took her breath away. Like clear plastic made to look like glass that is supposed to look like an authentic gemstone, but all of that is hidden behind a transparent window. The complete uncanny break in the illusion was only for an instant, a split second, but it was more than enough for her to finally understand what Orsche meant. Beyond that, she also noticed that the rising heat of her son's body plateaued and even began to slowly drop as a chill insulated his burning temperature.

She covered her mouth and, unintentionally, backed up into the bookshelf containing all of Alize's journals and personal diaries and felt one of them fall out toward her feet. As if fate were making a mockery of the entire family, the page opened to the exact one Jarold showed Alize less than an hour ago. Verza looked away, snapped her eyes shut, and held her heart and whispered, "Why does it have to be like this?"

Jarrold, in a flurry of movement, stopped those words from reaching Orsche and floated toward his contractor. With a heartfelt grumble, the old man slammed the book back into its spot, ensuring that it was firmly secured as he tapped Verza's veiny muscles.

Orsche, with five seconds left on the clock that he gave himself, spared nothing as he snapped his fingers with grandeur. A blinding flash was instantly contained within a dark but glassy prism of magic that contained all manner of pulverized and liquefied substances. He popped the top of the glass like it was a bottle of some cheap liquor and poured the fruits of his labor onto the white blanket. A disgusting-looking spinach, broccoli, and celery smoothie poured onto the sheet and left behind pitch-black clumps of waste as the emerald liquid flowed in the air like a twirled ribbon. The medicine, after being strained through what clearly looked like a blanket, flowed straight into one of the empty buckets. The dried black clumps of what resembled coal rolled into the massive mortar along with some of the other herbs and spices that Ors prepared beforehand along with sprays of water that shot out of the floating sphere above his head. In the time it would take someone to inhale and exhale, the independently churring pestle came to a complete stop. With a frown, Orsche cast a golden light that wrapped around the paste in the mortar and turned it into bullets of emerald green and gold that pierced Alize's body.

Without looking, the man quickly took stock of the time and with a panicked breath, got back to work by retrieving a beaker filled with some strained and distilled gray liquid resembling marble. Without any hesitation, he whispered something at the speed of lightning and combined the charcoal remains of the green brew with the liquified marble and the other half of the clear pure water. With another golden flash, the twisting medicine poured into Alize's mouth. The red, almost cooked lobster-like complexion and ravenous heat that was slowly dipping, instantly froze the kid's sweat, turning him into a miniature snowman.

Alize, believing that he had made a mistake somewhere, recast his spell and got back to tweaking and improving it now that he was plunged into an icy hell. The result is he allowed the healing effects of the medicine to intermingle and amplify one another, which in turn increased his heat production, which then increased the... I don't have to explain it. Orsche, on the other hand, smiled and slowly turned around as he placed the final touches on the two vats of tar-black medicine. He saw Verza backed against a bookshelf, crying until her eyes turned puffy, Jarrold, patting her arm in an attempt to offer some form of comfort, and Alize. The damned boy's temperature nearly doubled while the icy and healing medicine did very little to remedy the situation; at best, it insulated some of his son's more vital body parts.

Orsche collapsed on the floor, panting and struggling to maintain a calm expression as the situation devolved into something he just couldn't understand.

Verza, upon seeing her man's eyes go blank, held onto her shuttering breath and dashed across the room. She lifted both of the buckets and dumped them on Alize without any knowledge of whether they were done or not. Insanely enough, centimeters before the tar could burn her child, the liquid turned into gentle snowflakes that slowly fluttered down and sprinkled onto Alize and the bed. As the snowflakes melted, they left behind miniature purple, blue, and green flickers of mist that curved toward the hottest parts of the room, which happened to be Alize's rapidly heating body.

Verza sighed upon seeing her son's burning fever quell almost subserviently to the newest addition in the slew of potions that Orsche made just for his situation. Alize, around the same time, also threw in the towel, believing that he made one mistake after the next as his temperature fluctuated chaotically. He returned to listening to the absolute silence of the controlled vacuum that Jarrold maintained around him.

"What else do you need for more medicine? I'll go get it." Verza knelt beside Orsche and steadied his heaving chest, with redness still staining the sides of her eyes.

"I. I'm sorry. Um. I don't believe we will need more of anything. His condition is...it looks fine now. No blip, no overheating, no problem. Right? Are you, uh, are you okay?"

Orsche's robotic expression softened as he grabbed his love's hand.

"I'm okay. I just saw what you meant. The passive [Shroud]. It makes no sense." Despite using a calm voice, Verza felt a sorrowful and exhausted tremor reach her from Orsche's trembling hands. Alize, from the moment he began to focus on his parents until now, could hear nothing. He couldn't even smell the medicine. At best, he tasted the most basic earthy, slightly sweet, and mildly sour notes of the liquid that entered his mouth but nothing complex enough to figure out what it was made from without his olfactory senses. Additionally, he could very faintly feel things prickling his skin but nothing intense since he was still recovering from the sensory overload of his nerves being stitched together.

"We are going to have to tell him. Jarold already showed him the page. He's smart enough to figure it out." Orsche cupped Verza's face as she spoke and brought her forehead to his. His fingers securely caressed her long and curved ears.

"My love, listen to me..." Ors whispered so softly that Verza trembled and bit her lip, eyes shaking, as if he spoke directly to her soul.

"We have to be careful with how we explain this. If he gets the wrong idea." Orsche teared up.

"I know. He will go through everything that we had to deal with." Verza wiped her man's face and held him close to her chest.

"We have a timer now, my love." Orsche immediately simplified his thoughts.

"He could have been getting practical casting experience. Not Sims. If only I had paid more attention." He couldn't handle the simple fact that he made multiple mistakes at his son's expense. Mistakes he never would have made before starting this family.

"And? We just have to prepare him for everything before the worst comes to pass." Verza pushed Orsche away and wiped her own eyes with a serious expression.

"When we started letting him go out, even in a body double, we always knew that was a timer. The only thing that has changed is we can now share that information with the most perfect baby ever." Verza held out her arm and pulled Orsche to his feet.

"Ark is not. Ha, you're right. Our baby boy is quite the little genius." Orsche couldn't even lie since he still saw a pudgy-faced and toothless bubble of mayhem every time he looked at Alize.

"I'm worried about him and what happened, though." She moved some of her son's frost-covered hair out of his face as the cold cut at her fingers.

"I know, my love. The timing we had planned was just off this time. It's not your fault. We can't protect him every time. I'm sorry about what I said before." Ors snapped his finger before responding. The massive stained blanket that hovered in the air folded into a pocket square that he snatched back and placed into one of his pockets. With a wave, all the extraneous material swished into the satchel that he quickly slung over his shoulder.

"It's fine. You made a good point. I would have said worse if you made the mistake that I did. I'm just worried about how Ark doesn't seem to remember what happened. Is it brain damage or did he just forget?" Verza trailed off and stared into the distance with a scrunched nose.

"I see where you're going with this, but it's not something that I can just check without some issues in his current state." Orsche stood next to his love and examined his son's condition with a thoughtful expression.

"And what about the spirit? It managed to get away from Jarold and avoid my detection." Verza nudged his arm.

"What about it? It is in the Apeirogon's outer shells, somewhere. We torture it for the grief given to our family and scrap its body for Ark's inheritance. End of story."

"And if it managed to escape the lockdown before you set it up?"

"Improbable."

"What if?"

"It didn't escape. It would need speed capable of drawing an Archon, and we have not been caught yet, so it wasn't fast enough."

"But if it did, it could also be something dangerous for the Tems. It was after that cute little girl, from what I could gather. It might still be after her. Are we going to let Ark's friend get hurt? What if, by not dealing with it now, we cause an issue for our baby that he has to deal with when our timer runs out?" Verza laid her head down beside Alize's chest and held her baby like he was some sort of teddy bear.

"There is a lot to unpack and resolve with that question, my love. I do not have all the answers. I do know that we should not be looking to create more events. By getting involved in her matters, we create more issues. Or did you forget the last time we tried to intervene in one of his events in such a heavy-handed manner?" Verza perked up, nearly snapping her neck with a sharp twist as she turned to the scruffy man.

"I know it's hard, but we have to plan and act around his choices now. Especially now that he'd started casting." Orsche gritted his teeth and stared off blankly.

"I promise you, my love. I will not make the same mistake twice." Ors wiped his face and controlled the bloodthirsty sneer that sprouted across his lips. Verza nodded and gave Jarrold a meaningful glance, one that informed him that it was time to take down the vacuum.

"I hope so, Ors." Verza's bulky body physically deflated like a balloon as her tension released.

1.7 Memories and Improvement

U nbeknownst to the three adults who locked in and conversed in silence, Alize went above and beyond staying awake as he dived into the depths of his mind to examine the odd coincidence Jarold pointed out not too long ago. The glassy platform and mystical library that he grew fond of faded into a dense swirl of fog behind his illusory and imagined form. Before him, his mind spread out into a massive mist room with. A blocky and semi-rendered grand staircase took up the entire visible wall to the north, leading up to a wrap-around mezzanine that bore several undetailed borders depicting uniquely marked doorways that held an illegible code on nameplates. The first three doors, set between the stairs, bore the most stability and the most barricades. Aside from the eye-catching feature of the second floor, the first floor was split into several varying portions, like pieces of a pie. Each numbered area represented an imaginary dedicated amount of his conscious thought. The fog that he had just come from was firmly placed in the portion of the room that had the number 93 on it. Now that he had left the region, the value dipped while each of the other portions grew. Sets of writing supplies and furniture filled the expanding spaces with boards and badly textured, almost unreadable, words while the several dozen doors on the top floor filled out with simple designs and plates that simply numerated titles like, "Problem #72", "Encounter # 435562", "Nightmare #365", and "Rabbit Hole #65" that repeated.

"Without a doubt, this scene is pitiful. Other casters, according to mom and dad, can just use magic to recall and work through anything in less than a second with 100 and more percent of their attention, either by magically growing additional nervous centers throughout their body or by improving the efficiency of their own minds. Even if they were forced to forget something due to an injury or any psycho-logical or magical interference, the proper spell just fixes it. Yet here I am, utilizing every trick in the book to keep my mind in order." As Alize parsed through his mental palace, he noticed a faint shadow that flickered away from one of the least loaded partitions. As he focused on the pathing, the kid noticed a stream of un-textured shadows that slipped through the mist.

Without hesitation, he chased down another flicker and thumbed along its spine with a puzzled expression. "(Minori Edition) Un-known's Grave Digger Guide to exploring Mino-Talia Vol 3: Roaming the Dead Realms of the Ual-Jisse Terrarium Substructure" was written in a small glittering text.

"This is, this is what I referenced when I thought of my current state earlier. The possibility that I may be stuck in a terrarium or a recurrent illusion." Alize let go of the massive encyclopedia and snatched an-other book out of thin air. As soon as he touched the cover, memories flashed through his mind as a nightmare and training that he once had on the matter replayed itself. In this brief flash, an older version of himself, one equipped with facial hair, stepped over a patch of blue pebbles that poked out from underneath an endless black desert. The next second, an entire lifetime condensed into a breath as he stepped into a watery sphere and drowned himself. The next second, his body stepped beyond the range of the pebbles as he fell onto the endless swath of black sand. In a panic, he scrambled to stand up and ran toward the top of a dune.

Sadly, the winds picked up and revealed a sun-bleached bone that sported gemstone veining. Completely caught off guard, the older, young adult Alize tripped over the bone and fell in slow motion. The next second, he found himself living his life as a roaming skeleton without any memory of being Alizedriel. In the blink of an eye, tens of thousands of years passed by until he finally broke his own rib bone in a major conflict that consumed the planet. Scrambling atop the pulverized and powdered remains of his allies, his skeletal figure stabbed the sharpened rib into the lady's left eye socket and bit down on her throat with fanged teeth, ripping and tearing into the surprised youth. The woman's last breath turned into Alize's ragged gasps as he woke up in a crouched position after having reappeared back atop the black rolling dune. A mere second passed before all the memories in the book imprinted themselves on the kid's short-term memory. With a frown, he let go of the book and let it flutter into the mist along with some other literature that he briefly scanned over. Very quickly, he noticed the absence of an ever-present buffering on his neck. The Affix seemed to be waiting for something.

"My thoughts seem to have set something in motion. Hm. No, looking at it like this, it's more like the Affix is holding its breath. Waiting for me to think of something that it may have already started."

Alize's frown deepened as he read the extraordinary static runes that briefly graced the hand of a mental representation of himself.

"Most likely, I need to pursue the topics that have kept me awake not too long ago." Without another second wasted, Alize examined each of the faint shadows that fluttered across his vision. The spines were each titled with something different, "Dream Journal #23", "Odd Encounters #02", "Hierophant's Depiction of Dream daddy Mourra", "A Deep Dive into the Divine Province of Nightmares and Dreams", "Terrariums and how to find your way out of them", the boy read each title, recalled most of the information, then allowed them to vanish on toward the thick mist.

"Tears, Terrariums, and Illusionary Terrors", "Hughbert's Little Pocketbook of Cultivated Existence", "Fakes, Breaks, and Stakes: A Game of Suggestive Physics and Logic", "Xeu!tye's, More of a Suggestion", Brows arched, Alize stood in the center of a small trail of text that gradually partitioned the room. After reaching fifty percent of his concentration, the small break in the fog turned into a chasm that, in the blink of an eye, swallowed his attention. The entire room spun with mist and only came to a halt after a few rotations. Behind him was a semi-rendered open door, and in front of him was a narrow but infinitely tall library that split into two halves. The see-through floor was somehow demarcated by the numbers one and two on either side of a singular line that stretched on for around five hundred steps. A double-sided arrow stopped around where the ninth step would be. The new mental construct bore a heavily inspired, almost carbon copy, resemblance to the architecture that he encountered upon briefly dying in his sleep.

"This is not great. I am immediately reminded of that peculiar masked entity who, presumably, returned my soul before I was claimed by Lady Shemishier. I am also reminded of the cartoonishly deranged hero that served as the central villain of my most recent nightmare." Alize remained still with the deepest frown that he could muster and focused all his attention on the new mental construct in front of him. The Affix on his neck was not bound by its physical location in his mind, so his interpretation of it lit up like fireworks as a little hologram at his palm. The pulsing swirl writhed and flared like a den of inflamed vipers as it expanded and laid itself across the line on the floor. The fog burned wherever the curse pulsed.

Exactly eighty-nine golden books flared up in uneven gaps ranging from the shelf near the entryway to the seemingly empty shelves five hundred steps away. Every other book filling the endless expanse was devoid of detail or vibrant color, almost as if they were merely illusions meant to fill the empty space. Similarly, the second shelf possessed golden books, but the number was pitiful in comparison, maxing out at nine, with one placed at each notch of his life in evenly spaced intervals. A tenth, pale yellow hardcover lay open on a pedestal that left a long grinding streak along the floor atop the long arrow.

A bilingual dictionary for an ancient language, something called English to Common Herzen and a newsletter by a person or group called The Crown's Eye, lay beside this tenth book but Alize did not immediately approach the obviously unfinished text and shot toward the arrow on the floor and the connection it drew between the golden texts on the left and right of the long hall.

"My awareness is changing things. Altering how I see my own life. After going over it so many times..." Alize reached out to the first dream journal he ever wrote on the left side of the hall and sat down with the first observational notebook that he would have ever written at the behest of his parents, the first book on the right side of the hall. He also grabbed a children's book called Carol's Net, and another that was a Guide to Ancient Lishen and modern Lerian Tradition. Looking at the first pages of his own texts, Alize couldn't help but sigh.

"Orange color pencil, light green crayon, baby blue highlighter, and a quick dry glitter stick glue. If I want to understand, I have to start at the beginning. Even if this leads to nothing, the Affix seems to think I'm on the right track." The pages sported sloppy and childish chicken scratch with colored paper cutouts of simple shapes that progressively grew more detailed as he flipped through. After a few moments, Alize released a breath that he unwittingly safeguarded. The mental construct of the Affix, in its holographic spiraling along the floor bound arrow, hummed a tune and waved throughout his mind as information he was always supposed to know seared into his memory as he actively pieced together the details for events that had been generated in his youth. Alize rubbed the bridge of his nose as if he had just aged decades in the blink of an eye. He silently wiped away his tears and pulled his legs closer to his chest as all eighty-nine of the dream journals were laid out in front of him, all along the line on the floor. All of their pages were ripped out, spread into nine different bands, and reorganized into a singular panoramic spread around his Observation journals. The arrow that seemingly followed his age to the very second, pointed to the very same images that Jarold had pointed out earlier in the day.

"My life is predetermined at points where there are established events. Mom and Dad definitely know about this but have not told me anything." Alize scanned the events from when he was younger and noticed that his dreams actually foretold the moment that he acquired all of his novelty items. There were even scenarios that depicted the underlying circumstances behind each time the family moved and the changes that his parents made to his training sessions. He let himself lean back against the semi-transparent shelving as he stared at the outline of his life. The guidebook that he essentially wrote for his parents to raise him in the manner that a curse wanted. The holographic infinite swirl that rebound itself to his imaginary form, as if possessed of a mind of its own, stopped hovering by his hand and streaked toward his neck in a bright flash. His head and torso snapped back through the shelving, where the fog swallowed him up and turned into a hazy but ultimately recovered recollection of the moments leading up to his prophesied injuries.

A mountain in the shape of a twisting pillar swirled out of the misty earth below him and in the blink of an eye, faced the majority of a landlocked, functionally independent and jurisdictional trading state called Jordaine. The entire country was held entirely within the bowl of a supernaturally massive caldera blooming and brimming with so much life, magical effuse, and electromagnetic radiation, that it physically manifested as an overflow of floating islands in the sky, rainbow clouds, and trees so large that their ice capped tips could not be seen as they pierced the sky above. Alize, both in the recorded nightmare held within a journal prior to his current state and in his recovered recollection, marveled at the unreal beauty before him.

"Dragonspires, Futherdere's crown, Kykeries abyss..." He whispered just loud enough for the howling wind to carry the soft words to his own ears. Three of Jordaine's more notable natural landmarks visible from his elevated position simply towered over and under everything else in terms of beauty and absolute scale. The dragonspires, a testament to the potential of the common oak. In this case, common is a relatively loose term since the tree possessed ancestral roots on another planet, one so large, it was a universe unto itself. Even while sitting within a knot on a smaller dragonspire's bark, the gargantuan roots of all the other trees lifted and curved the earth so much that the landscape was pockmarked with mountain ranges. The tops of

the spires all seemed to point toward an inspiring and fear-inducing cosmic wonder. A dark and cloudy astral body, the very same
miniature universe that the Dragonspires originated from, happened
to be slightly visible from this region of the world. Alize, even as he
recollected his memory of the visual, felt his heart wrench at the sight.
That planet, several hundred billion light years away yet still taking
up at least a fifth of the sky's background, possessed an impossibly
thin atmosphere for its size. Anyone with a decent telescope could
see that the place was a wasteland, marred and exhausted from some
ancient catastrophe that left the once habitable planet and others like
it, barren. The only thing that made the sight more horrifying was the
massive patches of ruptured bark and planet-sized smatterings of soil
that littered the entire distance between the two planets like broken
constellations.

Futherderes's crown, in comparison to the dead rock in space
and the shattered bridge between worlds, happened to be a similarly
dead-looking piece of the cosmos that happened to form a mountainous belt surrounding Jordaine. The crown prevented most of the
world's many suns from illuminating anything within a vast majority
of the region until around midday due to the mountain range's astronomical height. The third regionally visible landmark was a man-made
chasm that appeared as an ink black river stretching across the length
of the entire country from the north-west point of the crown, all the
way to the south-eastern ridges that scraped the stars. Tourists often
called the abyss "the snarling pit" in consideration of what the planetary scar looked like from an aerial view. Truly, Alize could understand
why, since even now, the entire country appeared like a pockmarked
and scarred face with a sharply crooked and somewhat sorrowful
frown. Perhaps from the northern half of the country, the abyss re-

sembled a smile, but he didn't know. As for his silent appreciation, it quickly turned into a childish and expectant joy befitting his age.

"Come on. It's safe. Trust me." He patted the ground next to him and then waved toward a friend. In both his nightmare and memories, this friend shuffled over toward him with hesitation in each of her steps. Eventually, she sat down beside him and took in the view at the edge of one of the smaller spires that towered over the landscape. To pass the time, they ate a few snacks his parents prepared and planned out some new rules for a game they invented for their friend group. The atmosphere even turned a bit dangerous for an hour or two, seeing as how the little girl wanted to show off the new spells that her parents taught her. Alize, unable to cast anything due to his promises and fear of his Affix adapting to his abilities, simply used his knowledge to very much beg her not to blow him away with what would likely be an uncontrollable demonstration. Thus, before the two kids knew it, a noticeable golden weave and velvet cape stretched across the sky as the second sun of the day set between two cleaved peaks and plunged the caldera into an earlier dusk than the rest of the continent.

A subtle mist rolled down from the top of the massive wall and dropped the country's temp by several dozen degrees in just a few moments. In the same amount of time, the forest and floating islands flickered to life akin to spotlights and cast a luminous glow onto the shaded landscape.

"Look at this view. It's beautiful..."

The two children gasped at the beauty of nature, Alize even more so since, unlike Hautzee's friend, he could see farther and with more added vibrance and clarity due to the natural disparity in their eye structures. Even without being magically fueled, his eyes were biologically geared to be better at long distances, even in dim light. The average Bluthautzee and Drem, which his friend happened to be, had eyes that were usually encased in a thick gel that allowed them to see in extremely dusty or atmospherically dense and dark environments. Comparisons aside, the blurry landscape that Alize overlooked with his friend was overtaken by broad strokes of color and sharpened detail as his reflective pupils naturally dilated to cover the entirety of his eye. With a sigh, he scanned the remaining glints of a scarlet circlet atop the mountainous peaks that confined their little Eden.

"On nights like this, Orrin's shadow glitters like the jewels of an emperor's crown. At least, that's the common descriptor used in pamphlets. It's really a shame that most people who live in the city never get to see why it's so commonly used. Look." Alize pointed to a tar-black stretch of forest and mountainside that, supposedly, never received any direct sunlight since the formation of the country and its insane geological expansiveness. As the last remaining rays of light dipped below the raised horizon, the shadow flickered and exploded with a level of illumination reminiscent of a solar flare.

"Whoa." The girl couldn't see the details like Alize, but it clearly struck a chord as a pillar of light painted the dark blot that she could vaguely see.

"My mom brought me here around two years ago. It was later in the year though, when the moons are at their brightest, so the forest did not light up like this." Alize pointed out another radiant location on the far side of the caldera with a smile. Rather than a solid pillar, this soft glow twinkled off the rolling snow that fell from the windy peaks of the Crown from the east, creating a majestic aurora of purples, greens, and blues. After a decent chunk of time passed, he stood up and approached two tents and a small fire that were erected not too far from the cliff's edge. In fact, Verza could be seen and heard leaving a third tent that was set up on the farther side of the knotted bark. Alize noted her presence but ultimately came for a small platter of snacks that she laid out near enough to the campfire. In a single breath, she leaped toward the forest below the spire, leaving a trail of faint glimmers as Jarold perfectly controlled her gliding descent. Thinking nothing of it, he returned to the cliffs' edge with a platter of snacks and prepared himself for another round of being Wynn's sightseeing eye friend but...

"I got it. Ahem. This isn't your first time! How could you cheat on me?" The girl used a low-pitched but adorable mocking voice and a pout despite not understanding what she was trying to joke about. She simply swung her feet off the edge and broke out into a giddy expression seconds later as she took in the crisp night air alongside Alize.

"What are you talking about? Wait, ha. Listen here, you brat. I told you to stop copying my comeback lines. You can get yourself in trouble if you don't understand what it means. Also, you can't spend time thinking of the best line. It has to be said right in the moment, otherwise it just doesn't work." Alize used his knuckle to bash some sense into the girl, but her half-smile, half-cry made him sigh as he sat back down next to her with a tray of pre-made smores and hot chocolate.

"I'm not a brat, you big bully. I'll have you know, I have logged more than four decades in the School's Simulators." The girl tried her best to look old and mature, but it just didn't work.

"Alright then, old lady. My bad. I can confidently say that I have only trained for a lot more than less than a quarter of that time. You're lucky that you have a whole class period every day to practice." Alize shook his head in silence since he couldn't stand the smug look that his friend put on after winning whatever game she thought they were playing. After the night fully settled into its swing, he pointed to the absolute center of the Caldera with excitement.

"Look at that. Those lights are coming from the Twin Cities. They are not as bright as what's coming from the forests, fields, or the crown, but they are some of the only spots that last all night. Well, the spires are also pretty noticeable if they have moon moss or sundrops on them but, eh." Alize chuckled as the girl's eyes widened to saucers. She was so enamored by the aurora coming from the crown-like mountain range and its ever shifting illusions that she forgot to take in the city that she lived in.

"Wow. I can see only some sparkly bits and a lot of gray. You can see both cities without magic?"

The girl covered her mouth, very obviously astonished by her friend's claim.

"Of course..." Alize smiled as he remembered explaining what he saw to his best friend. Vibrant and bustling towns peppered the landscape with wide and glowing lines drawing massive arcs through forests reminiscent of a starry night sky. Additionally, he made sure to explain that each and every city or town that peppered the overall landscape, in one way or another, led back to the two monolithic cities that stood out against the grain. Only these two locations stretched above the trees, one on this side of the grinning pit and one on the other. Even the sounds of the twin cities threatened to match the resounding pulse of life itself as the humdrum of traffic and voices carried on the wind throughout the caldera. Everything manmade revolved around these landmarks, from the clustered highways and expressways that resembled golden spiderwebs to the surreal opal and ruby tracks that lined the abyss and cut through the split peaks leading out of the country. But even then, despite the blatant industrialism of these cities, they somehow fit in with the nature around them. Alize couldn't make out anything more in depth since he wasn't allowed to use spells to heighten his sight or other senses at this point in time, but the twin cities were without question, a world wonder rivaling the natural spires, the crown, and the chasm.

"You know a lot about a whole bunch of different things, don't you, Ark. I guess you were serious about being an imperial scholar when you get older." The girl stood up and twirled with a giggle before she fell into a bed of blooming flowers that produced a faint glow reminiscent of moonlight upon being impacted. This soft radiance attracted several varieties of nighttime pollinators, which released their own vibrant bioluminescence in hopes of attracting a mate.

"Yeah..." Alize hesitantly agreed, but in that moment, he was completely aware of how little he knew. He constantly failed the tests his parents gave him, and he barely survived through all of their training despite putting in extra effort and sneaking around his father's study to learn more. He knew even less about the Affix, which made it quite the endeavor to do absolutely anything outside of a completely controlled environment. In that moment, the pain, the anger, and the dense fog of confusion that gripped his heart and thoughts came back.

"And this is where the more noticeable inconsistencies start," the nightmare came first since it was imagined and written down before the disaster that befell him. In this red-bordered recollection, he scratched the back of his head with blossoming embarrassment. In the reality that he lived through or in his memory of it, he chuckled and rubbed his nose with bitterness and a sudden spurt of anxiety. He felt his dilated pupils constrict as an overwhelming sense of déjà vu and worry flooded his senses. He even remembered that his free hand twitched at his side, ready to reach for his Glass since he felt something ominous prick the back of his neck. Sadly, he didn't catch onto the coincidental alignment of his nightmares and his reality as Jarold is the one who put him on so...

"I don't know or remember as much as you think I do. I am just using tricks to pretty much cheat my brain into working a little bit more efficiently. Trust me, it's not better or easier than having a spell. I know at least a dozen that can give someone inherently perfect memory and exaggerated thinking speeds but I can't use them like you and the rest can." Alize engaged his leg muscles almost instinctively as something inside of his gut screamed at him to run away. In hindsight, he clearly noticed that even if he moved, his instincts did not clear a path toward safety. It was like someone screaming at you to go somewhere and do something, but they were not giving directions or any instructions on what to do.

"Ark, you are like, super smart without using magic. Like, it's crazy how you think of everything even without any spells to help you out. Hehe, the group doesn't ever get into trouble anymore." The girl shook her head and laughed as some of the glowing bugs tickled her nose and face.

"I don't think you get it, Fell. Ha. Any of you could be smarter than me without even trying." Alize prattled on as he examined the surroundings based on his odd feeling. In the nightmare, he remained oblivious, but it was because he was unsettled and examining his surroundings that he noticed something dark fluttering across his vision. The moment he noticed the figure, his vision of their little camp tore vertically in an almost imperceptible manner. In less time than the blink of an eye, the ground and ceiling folded and then stretched into a panoramic and upside-down wide view. It collapsed into a space the size of a single photon. Before Alize could register the change, the twisted filter inverted the colors on everything that he was looking at. The camp's crackling flame slowed to an absolute pause as both his and Fell's bodies froze on the spot. At the moment, he did not feel, notice, or understand what he was seeing, but looking back, his mind raced with thoughts that he only now remembered.

"What is this? A spell! Something just created an instant terrarium. Right here? What just, wait, that shadow! It's...oh my goddess. Mom, where's Mom? That's bad." Alize took a single step forward as his sense of balance and vision were restored. Behind the girl, who looked at him in a panic as she tried to stand up, there was a blurry and dark figure with sickening yellow and green cesspools for eyes. It's a misshapen, blurry mass mixed in with the nearby shadows and space for just a moment as it melts into the shaded parts of the girl's features and clothes.

Whatever that thing was, Alize had barely any time to observe more as the same vision-tearing distortion singled him out. As if he were looking at the rest of the world through shattered glass, the ground underneath him snapped away from the cliff in such a clean manner it was as if the cliff side had become a mirror. In that split second before he entered a freefall alongside the dragonspire, he threw both of his hands out toward the clipped bark. Time and space and his perception snapped back to order as a sudden burst of amber liquid exploded out from a porous hole in the sheared knot. The amber liquid, the sap, coalesced into streaking threads that trailed toward the cut piece of calcified bark. After falling for a breath or two, the sap hardened into stretchy green fibers that pulled taunt. Alize, prepared for this outpour, gripped a handful of the sap as it hardened to threads capable of holding his weight and much more. With an expected deafening crash, the plant fibers pulled the cut bark back toward the spire. With a deafening boom, it created an impact hard enough to create another knot in the spire's trunk.

"Thankfully, this is still a rather young dragonspire sapling." Alize remembered that he ignored the blood that leaked from his ears and

nostrils as he remained calm and pulled on the line of sap that he caught beforehand. Nothing major was injured as he nestled himself in between a crack formed by the collision. Learning from his previous mistake, Alize immediately chose a direction and scrambled to another spot. As he expected, a perfect circle of bark just dislodged from the spire and gushed out a flood of sap. Now in a race against something he couldn't see, Alize used gravity to his benefit as he dropped from one location to the next. The nightmare he remembered didn't have his spectacular chase sequence as he just fell without a chance of saving himself during the first encounter. In his memory, he moved with a clear intention and confidence, almost as if he were doing nothing more than hopping on all fours across the ground.

Unexpectedly, he noticed that the explosions stopped just as he made it a third of the way toward the newly plastered ledge below him. In addition to the brief pause, he also noted that in the same moment, the solid stone he used as hand and footholds suddenly began to gain an odd texture and graininess. After dropping a few more times, the stone indented like wet clay and then fragmented around his fingers like sand.

Once again, his vision pulled in every direction as he slipped through the earth like a knife tearing through fabric. At first, he panicked and attempted to move his hands out of the clay and sand to grab the stone right beside him, but a lack of balance threatened to kick him away from the cliff. Thus, he doubled down and pushed his arms even deeper into the almost liquid wall despite the cuts and grinding that slowly eroded his fingertips and skin. Looking back on his panicked actions, he noticed that there were some moments where he could have pulled himself free and leaped to an accessible handhold, but that's not what piqued his attention as he ejected a ghostly figure out of his own back. His memory of the scene grinded to a snail's pace as he examined everything that he remembered with a fine-tooth comb.

"It's not a mistake that only I fell, but why? What is it after? This thing can create pocket dimension at will so it's at or above the third rank, and even if it wasn't, anything that is ranked just in general is strong enough to kill Wynnifell and I in the blink of an eye but it has not done so. Why? Also, mom? Where is she?" Alize calmly watched himself struggle to move and keep himself balanced. After a few seconds of flailing, he scoffed at his own desperate and ungraceful free climbing and returned to his body. Eventually, he landed on the knotted bark that fell in the initial attack on his person. A cloud of dust and sand swallowed him from all sides as he rolled with only enough force to twist an ankle and sprain a wrist. He kept his face down as wet clay and pebbles dislodged from the wall above him after a shadow passed through the bark. The largest and most violent disturbance in his vision and sense of balance attacked and overlapped completely with his heightened anxiety as the splotch vanished back within the spire.

In a split second and before he could recover from crashing into the ledge, the new platform that glued itself back to the tree was sheared clean off like a hot knife through butter. The only difference this time was the retention of a miniature distortion around his body and a protrusion that shot out of the spire and speared through the fallen platform. The spearhead twisted, writhed, and burrowed through the dust and bark and clawed at him as several dozen polearms.

A cudgel of wood smashed down onto his leg like an ax chopping wood. With a sickening crack, the calcified wood shattered his femur with little to no resistance. Immediately afterward, another protrusion cut toward his hip and pulverized half of his pelvic bone and coccyx. In that exact same second, some of the sand in the cloud around him coalesced into half a dozen spears and pinned his limbs to several more protrusions that resembled the ball-jointed arms of a hand-carved puppet.

"This attacker could have killed me right here. Why didn't it? Could it be distracted or unwilling? Or is it unable to do so directly?" Alize remembered the encounter with such clarity that his teary eyes narrowed to the point that a dagger's razor edge would seem dull. Thankfully, whatever attacked him retreated after a deafening crack resounded. The weird shadow, the splotch, slithered between the grooves in the bark along to the thin spearlike branch that it had created and circled the base.

"It seems to be wary of time, or its positioning. It's most likely an Aura caster connected to nature, either commanding or manipulating it through either Accords or Ballast spells. Its ability to perfectly create copies of specific weaponry like the spears and boulders is very in line with Creation as well." Alize conjured a mental image of some mysterious figure and filed away the elements of its profile since it would make any possible future encounters easier to manage.

Sadly, just as he remembered, a thick pillar shot out of the spire and crashed into the speared platform. Working in a way similar to a pinball machine, it popped the false ledge away, completely removing any further attempt for the Spire's sap to reclaim its body part. Alize's memory went dark in this moment with the last thing that he remembered being unpinned by the spears as he left the dust cloud full of wood shavings and plant material. After a second, or a minute, he woke up from the concussive ejection and coughed up blood all over the wooden arms that shackled his body to the falling ledge. He evaluated the situation and wiggled out of the crumbling protrusions and gauged the distance between himself and the spire as the piece he was strapped to spun chaotically. Below, a malformed knot surrounded by fresh bark and leaking pimples of sap popped out of the tree just enough to serve as salvation. He remembered thinking that if he jumped at the right time, it was possible to survive. The knot that he was falling onto was already too far for him to leap toward anything else but that knot. It would hurt, but he probably wouldn't die. With that in mind, and with a body fueled by shock and adrenaline, he prepared. Unfortunately, a long stretch of the massive tree's trunk sprouted rocky hands holding spears and boulders. Whatever was attacking him, the potentially crazed spirit seemed to realize the same thread of survival that Alize could grasp onto and dove down the trunk, creating more projectile-wielding hands and arms with each meter of movement. Just as he leaped from the piece of bark that was much too far away to be caught, the spirit or vile entity that lived within or around the young spire reached the knot. A forest of spikes bubbled out and toward Alize in an attempt to catch him mid-descent.

Cringing at his initial reaction and crass language, he ignored the memory of his scream that was infused with blood and watched himself swan dive straight toward the rising forest of wooden spikes. With a ferocious expression, Alize twisted his upper body in a way that only a contortionist would be capable of and rolled along the side of the closest spike before it could pierce him. He tumbled from one spike to the next, leaving a bloody trail as his skin and the mashed-up muscle on his leg and waist ruptured and oozed. With a perfectly timed push, the kid skidded across another massive spike and rolled onto his back. With another scream, he dragged himself across the broken knot that was supposed to serve as his salvation and toward the trunk of the tree. The mighty roar took his mind off of the random wooden spear that pierced and cut through the muscle on his shoulder from above.

The hands and arms that grew out of the tree released one volley of weaponry after the other, pelting the spiked forest with wooden boulders ten or more times larger than his own body. One massive boulder after another landed near him, sending thunderous rounds of vibration directly into his organs. His already bleeding ears and nostrils flaked off dark blood with each shake. Instead of enduring the dizziness and risking another stray, he rolled off the side of the knot and slipped between the bark. For a moment, he was hidden, shrouded by a cloud of dust and wood shavings.

Instead of falling into despair, Alize gathered his breath and fought off the mind-gripping pain that begged him to scream his troubles away. That is what he would have liked to have happened. Instead, he curled up into a ball as best he could and held his leg and shoulder. He cried and begged for his mom's help. He pleaded for the simulation to end and fainted several times as he forgot to breathe.

"The attacker is likely the spirit of this tree, or maybe one that roams the forest as a whole. I'm leaning more towards it being a Geist, an aberrant and volatile lifeform produced by the remains of dead or dying spirits. As for it being a proper living creature, the only ones I know that are even remotely capable of achieving some of what I've seen are in the far east. But even then, the first option is a creature that is so massive, it can shake the entire continent, while the second option is considered an endangered species due to the rarity of its appearance." Alize noted his conjecture and continued with his remembrance.

As he did so, the scenery shifted into something more action-packed as the gnarl that he hid himself within crackled and shook. Alize had no time to take in the sudden shift as the entire malformation turned into a massive plume of sand and dust. Before he could fix his mental state, he fell out of the cloud that remained in the exact same spot. The moment he exited, the wood shavings turned into a compact storm of jagged spikes that rained toward his position. The first wooden bolt lashed across his ribs while the second and third barely grazed his back and cheek. Unable to measure his movements or even see the strikes as they came at him, Alize randomly moved his body parts in a desperate attempt to be an unpredictable target. The bolts continued to cut and pierce his small frame, but none managed to deal the decisive blow before some of the taller mountain climbing canopies on the ground covered some sides of his descent. Sadly, the cover was nowhere near enough as nearly a dozen arrows made of wood shavings pierced his limbs while a massive bolt bore a hole in his stomach.

The supposed spirit dove toward the base of the spire to follow after landing a few hits, but with a sickening crack, Alize smashed into and snapped the limb of a rather tall tree that grew out of the ruptured earth. He was thrown away from the wall. To be more accurate, he crashed and fell in a manner that resembled something more like a marble rolling down an inclined but bumpy hill as he bounced off one canopy to the next. The flashing memory of losing and regaining consciousness ended with a bloody filter of him staring up at a small hole in the trees. Leaves landed all around and on top of him as he embedded into a dense bed of decaying brush and squishy moss that resembled water. Unexpectedly, the spear in his stomach bore the brunt of the fall and tugged at his body just enough to prevent an instantaneous death. His last thoughts were, "I am going to die here."

The fall replayed over and over, living through the pain as if it were just done to him that second.

"Alright. I've seen enough." Alize pulled himself out of the shelving and forcefully stopped himself from recalling the gruesome memory that he recovered.

"The culprit is definitely a malevolent spirit, a geist. It appears to have a mixed Aura root profile with aspects belonging to the accord and creation types. Hence, its necessity to pull from nature and the brief amount of time it took between each combination of attacks. It needed to pour its magic into the environment and then create molds for nature to be upended and retooled." As he pulled himself from his memory, the pages on the floor rebounded themselves to the books they came from as the shelves filtered and readjusted based on his laid out order.

"As for the specifics of the Geist's profile, I can confidently say that its Pentacode is 3:2. Movement, defense, and utility Accord aspects with additional attack and movement aspects from the creation type since it conjured its own weapons and munitions. I can't begin to know about its ranking aspects, but there should be at least one or two more. Maybe even three. Then there is...". He rubbed the bridge of his nose and found it impossible not to recall the initial shadow with heterochromatic eyes that paused time for a split second.

"I can't even begin to place the thing that hid in Wynn's shadow. It could be a spiritual lifeform or... Ha." Those alien, inhuman, and spiraling pupils practically shot a hole through his mind, forcing him not to want to decipher the origins of the entity.

"Spirits," he pivoted.

"Even if one were corrupted to the point of aberration." The actions of the creature that he labeled as a Geist, an aberrant spirit, could never be blamed for its actions.

"Ha. The nature of mystic lifeforms sucks." Spirits were the manifestation of nature itself—the good, the bad, and the ugly. Altogether, blaming his injuries on the Geist was the same as hating the air he breathed or cursing the dirt and roads he walked upon. Besides, he wasn't dead. Being emotional wasn't going to get him anywhere, so he might as well do something productive. Therefore, the gears in his head turned as he tapped his chin in thought.

"Mom was nowhere to be seen, but she was close enough to have Jarold chase that creepy thing away, considering what she said. Was it a conveniently timed return or purposeful?" The light in his eyes dimmed as an abysmal darkness encompassed his pupils. The moment the last book on the floor slotted into its place, he snapped back.

"I did say that I might need to form a contract in the future. Capturing such a useful Fae that could sneak past Mom or a Geist that could do the same and attack me without setting off alarms would make a good backup, all things considered. Even if the spirit cannot be roped into a proper contract, my parents could find a way to hire a Ballast caster to refine the spirit's magic into a Quill. I can then use that to contract a similarly graded or ranked spirit. Hmm, such a Quill would even fetch a good price in the Corridor if I ever find myself in that endless shopping mall." Alize ruffled his hair with a resonating groan. After a few moments, he rubbed his eyes and returned to the central hub of his thought processes. With a somewhat controlled imaginative flair, empty pages and books were conjured above the tables.

"According to my journals, if I survive my injuries, I will eventually get embroiled in some issues with a doctor and then the corridor in the next few events that will dictate the trajectory of my life." With a few deep and controlled breaths, he left his mind and reconnected with his body. Instantly, a potent lethargy filled him as he fought off the desperate need for sleep.

"*Was my room always so bright? Oh my, why can't I move? Right. My body is likely to be in a state of severe malnutrition after my spell. Speaking of which, I'm starving.*" Unknown to Alize, Verza rested her upper body and head on him. She woke up in his struggle to sit up against her weight.

"Ark? Are you awake? " She choked back tears and rubbed her eyes in disbelief. He looked straight at her, wanting to cry but with no energy to create any.

"Awake? Mom, I didn't fall asleep. I was focused on remembering what happened to me. Did you fall asleep? Wait, how long was I thinking? I couldn't have been gone for too long, right? Ha, should I try to speak? Hm, I don't see the harm in trying now. Let me get up first." With Verza's help, the kid managed to sit up. For a few seconds, he rolled his neck and pressured his chilly throat with his breath to warm it up.

"Mohm." His throat caught on the words and a terrible rasping cough slammed into his body like a jackhammer. Bloody bile erupted out of his mouth, followed by a weakness that made the room spin. Verza turned him onto his side.

"It's okay, baby. Mommy's here." Verza held her son tightly. A bit too tightly, maybe, seeing as how his face turned blue. Not even a moment later, Orsche barreled through the door, tears streaming down his face but not a single wrinkle in his expression. The family of three embraced for what felt like ages, but parted when Alize's blue face turned purple and his struggle began to weaken.

"Uh. Hm." Alize cleared his throat a dozen times while his parents cleaned him up and doted on his every movement. By the time the kid regained his rhythmic breathing pattern, Ors took out a small jar of magically charged medicinal water.

"Go ahead. It should help your throat and amplify the painkillers." Orsche held the cup to his son's lips and helped him drink it with a fresh cast of [Guidance]. The golden magic in it instantly brought a new wave of life to the faded [Improved Guided Stabilize] spell that continued to course on and through Alize's entire body even if the effect was recast to only appear underneath his skin. After downing the whole cup, the boy felt fortified enough to give talking another go.

"Mom. Dad. I have..." But even with the water, he paused to clear his throat nearly every single word.

"Something to tell. You guys. And it's important. Promise. Not to make a big deal. Out of it?"

"We need to discuss our future together now that I have used magic and know what you two have been hiding from me. We already decided what would happen a long time ago if circumstances such as these presented themselves, but still." Alize narrowed his eyes while waiting for his parents to communicate between themselves in silence, yet again only this time he was visually aware of the barrier that Jarold placed between the adult side of the family and himself.

"Hopefully, you three will tell me what you actually know about my Affix." To make sure that his parents didn't try anything, Alize downed his refilled cup of glowing water and popped off a few more evenly spaced rounds of yet another variant of a minor heal spell, *[V1.2 Improved Guided Stabilization]*. This new version that his parents didn't notice even after looking over him in detail worked out some of the visual kinks. A few moments later, he repeated the cycle of drinking water and lessening the visual cues, with one recast and update after the other until he heard a response. To his parents, however, he resembled a Buddha, calmly drinking tea, undisturbed by the insanity and danger that once gripped him. It was more than mildly concerning and weird for their boy not to bombard them with questions and express his own takes on matters that concerned him.

1.8 Disbelieve for Love

Verza and Orsche, through means of their own, surrounded their baby boy in a shower of hugs and kisses the moment he "woke up" despite the obvious bad state he was in. After spending a bit of time ensuring their son's safety, they found themselves in a continued heated conversation that only the two of them and Jarrold were privy to. By the end of it, they found themselves paying attention to the divine magic that their son supposedly possessed and watched in awe as the crystalline shroud that their son probably believed they didn't notice, took on less noticeable features. At best, they followed the ingrained Tenets all the way until it entrenched so deeply that the only magical presence that they felt on their son was a regular and completely normal mixed spell. The three adults could no longer keep their conversation to themselves and acted as they should in this scenario given their son's complete calm.

"Here we go. Just as we practiced," Orsche thought as he clenched his teeth so violently, he drew blood. Following the script that the family

prepared for the worst-case scenario, the bearded man whispered a spell.

"[Heavens lament]." In less than the blink of an eye, a roiling black cloud that Or's created between his fingers popped like a soap bubble before it could even generate its deafening cacophony of booms. Instead, under his masterful control, the thundercloud rolled into a web that wrapped around his hand like a glove. Lightning shot forward like an extension of his body, each bolt coalescing into something no thicker than a single needle. The insane luminance and vibration of his hand, however, made the magical darting needles appear like a spear stretching from Orsches elbow all the way to Alize's heart.

"Is this going to be something we can get through?" Verza, on the other hand, did not put as much stock into the worst outcome that their family unit prepared for since she completely believed in her baby boy. As for Alize, he finalized and thrice revised spell number [3.7] of his mixed minor spell.

"I shall call this new minor healing spell [Prevention]. It is the limit of lesser-grade spells that I have access to. As a derivative of Bayrun's Life Jacket, it holds the intention to 'prevent' destruction and death as long as there is even a drop of magic or effuse in the environment. I am satisfied with what I have created even if I may not have broached upon the likes of Mardi and Tutolin's [Lesser Jacket]." Alize took a long drawn out sip of his drink once more and found himself shifting his gaze between his parents. He was not fazed by the darting sparks that flashed and posted up all around the room. Or's face was full of intense thoughts and severe internal conflict, and Verza just stared at him with a hard face and thumbs up. That said, he also realized that neither of them wanted to start the pre-planned talk for fear of the worst-case scenario.

"Mom, Dad." Alize cleared his throat one last time.

"I know what you're both thinking, so I want to take a moment to explain what I remember and what I have managed to conclude upon some intense reflection. I would also like to discuss the underlying importance of my journals and understand why the two of you have decided not to explain the worth of my dreams..." Alize slowed to a pause as the largest dart zig-zagged to the back of his head and singed the hair on his neck.

"We promised to listen when we last prepared a similar situation for you in the Sim, so I will uphold my word. Anything untoward and I will shoot a hole through your spine just as I did then, so choose your words very carefully." Orsche looked away, unable to meet his son's eyes. The lightning darts subtly hovered away but could be activated at any time. Verza had an even more difficult time trying to respond to her son. Her mouth opened and closed, but words didn't come out. So she just nodded and gave another thumbs-up.

"Then, before I get on with my explanation, I would like to say who I am first. I think it will help..."

Alize closed his eyes, waited for a response, and drank some more water.

"Go ahead." Orsche looked up as he spoke, which only barely stopped the real tears from falling out. Alize cleared his throat one last, very serious, time.

"I AM your son Alizedriel Regencious Kaveri. I have NOT been lucky enough to experience being reincarnated by the mercy of Madam Shemishier nor have I been pulled from outside of our immortal cycle by any other divine ranked entity. I have NOT been fortunate enough to experience the process of being possessed by a Doppel of myself from a Grave or another reality outside of our cycle. Unfortunately, I am NOT someone who has been transmigrated or transfigured into Me, since I have NOT been fortunate enough to experience the reclamation process of the Gods. I am also NOT some ancient Gheist or Spirit of Possession that has taken this body, mind, or soul. Again, I am NOT a time traveler from some past or future cycle, NOR am I from some alternate universe or some such reality-bending origin. To my knowledge, I am NOT the chosen puppet or personification of a divine-ranked entity, NOR am I a Spirit of Rebirth that has taken to an empty host body after dying in my sleep. Speaking of which, I think I died in my sleep and received a really horrifying event as a result. I also know what I said not even five seconds ago, but I also met some rather odd divine entity whilst I was dead or in a state near enough to it. Also, I know that you guys have been hiding things from me about Province Mourra's involvement with my Affix. Also, also, take it as you will but as of right now, I CANNOT claim any titles or identities unrelated to being your son..." Alize brought up nearly every possible scenario that could occur or has happened to someone in the past. Most, if not all of those scenarios necessitated being reported to the regional authorities and the Immortal Empire, which would lead to either immediate execution, imprisonment, or the claim of some reputable religion with a living and respectable Divine-ranked figurehead.

"I AM your nine-year-old son, give or take. I'm not really sure how long I have spent in the Sim-Terrariums that you two have conjured." Alize didn't want his parents to worry or suffer undue stress because of what he said and finally paused to take a long breath upon seeing them both somewhat run through a gambit of emotions.

"Tell us everything that you remember about what happened to you. Start from the beginning." Verza, somewhat smiling, spoke with a whisper-like but happy quality to her sharp command. Orsche remained silent, locked in thought as his lightning bolts gave the boy some more space. They did not vanish entirely as the middle-aged man pulled out a book and used one of the glowing needles to sear his thoughts onto the page. Alize huffed, cleared his throat, and then told them everything. First, he recounted what led up to before he was injured.

To him, this played out like he was in the moment. He asked Wynnifell's parents if they could have a sleepover. After months of asking, they consistently stood by their response of no. The decision only changed after Verza followed along and gave her patented guarantee of safety. Alize even sweetened the decision by timing the sleepover around the same time that his friend's parents were planning a surprise birthday party for her tenth. For the Hautzee, birthdays were not celebrated every year and were reserved for milestones of life lived because of some ancient and most definitely traditional reason. 10, 20, 50, 100, 200, and 300 were the milestone markers between child, teen, young adult, adult, middle-aged, and old. If a Drem lived up to 300, their birthday would be celebrated every year since it would be a miracle to live every year past then. Alize explained that everything he noticed was normal up until the moment he had a strange sense of déjà vu that ate away at his nerves.

"And then it got weird." The boy straightforwardly explained that some kind of mystical being, a Fae forced a contract onto Wynn while another possibly malevolent spirit, a Geist, attacked him. Orsche put up a hand upon hearing that news and frowned. He glanced casually at Verza and initiated yet another unveiling of secrets that Alize was not privy to.

"Alright. Go ahead, you saw a wandering Fae creature and an Aberrant Spirit. For whatever reason, the Geist moved from hunting the Fae to attacking you. How did you get hurt?" Verza broke the awkward silence and addressed her son with furrowed brows.

"Well, I just didn't have the time to think more than half of the time, so I can only draw conclusions based on what I remember seeing and thinking in the moment." Alize mentioned the Geist's ability to move through the Spire and shape its bark into weaponry, and detailed its ability to create a weird spatial tearing effect that caused his vision, sense of balance, and awareness to be off-kilter. His parents and Jarold sat and floated there in stunned silence as Alize described something that most people without magic would never dream of surviving. At the end of his description, he raised a single question.

"Mom, where were you?"

Alize didn't expect a thought-out response and didn't feel anything out of place when all three adults decided to pretend that they didn't hear the question. All he could see was their lips moving and some hand gestures that said, "Let's figure out what he knows first, then share everything he needs to hear."

"Jarold, can you grab my Observation diary, the one with the number 9, and DJ, dream journal, numbers 89, 78, 67, and the rest in a similarly descending order. Turn each book to pages 9, 18, 27, etcetera, in the order that you pulled down the dream journals. Line them up like, yeah. Exactly, now use my diary as the anchor for a Derelict Jump cipher with Ancient Midwelchire Ghomeshi and modern universal Herzen as the alternating language codes for every first and ninth word." Alize commanded and watched how Jarold and his parents dropped their jaws in astonishment with his every word that he spoke. A prophetic slideshow of his life unfolded before everyone in the room. Thankfully, Jarold caught on quickly and used his winds to gather dust and hold the translated information in the air after un-jumbling and copying each page.

"This is why, even if I'm not sure about my particular situation regarding Mourra and my Affix, I know that you two have been hiding something. I'm not entirely sure, since it seems that my journals show a distinction between different types of information. Events that litter my everyday life, like say, if this goes wrong because I cannot convince you two to, I don't know, trust me enough to know what you are talking about in secret." He pointed to the moment in the slideshow where he and his parents were prophesied to sit and talk after a monumental shift in their lives.

"In addition to everyday encounters and issues, I have noticed and felt some kind of divine intervention beyond or intrinsically linked with my curse." Alize shared his most recent nightmare and the exact two moments he felt his Affix move about and attempt something out of the ordinary due to divine interference, the first being when the mysterious cocoon wrapped around his body and the second when he was caught up with the hero in the divine haze and flame. Alize sighed and finished another cup of his medicinal water.

Both Orsche and Verza looked like wide-eyed statues—no, more like robots as they mechanically turned toward each other. Verza whispered a curse and pensively stared at the cobbled floor.

"Hm. I find it hard to fathom, but..." The scruffy man's lip twitched almost uncontrollably for a few seconds, but Orsche eventually closed his eyes and nodded.

"Alright. Okay. I've read all of your journals and books, so..." The man's nodding slowed while a painful grimace bloomed like an unyielding weed.

"Am I to assume that all of your works carry the same sequence?"

Without even looking at his son, Ors nodded with implicit confirmation due to the silence and began crying without a sound. He did his best to calm his breath, but the old man couldn't help but fall apart. Logically, he knew this day would come. No, he actually ran countless simulations and found that this day and this moment were almost guaranteed to happen right now. At some point, Alize would learn the truth someday, but Ors could not bring himself to act as though this was the first time he had ever heard the conclusions that Alize came to. Verza, unlike Ors, grit her teeth and wiped away the tears that pooled at the corner of her eyes.

"You have figured it all out. I told your dad that you'll eventually get here and soon because of how much he was teaching you. Thankfully, he listened to me on a few things; otherwise, we wouldn't be having this conversation." Verza grumbled.

"Mom?" Alize tilted his head, suddenly lost.

"Listen up. You know how me and your dad have said that your Affix is called the Infinite Event Generator?" Verza tapped her arm muscles rhythmically as a sour frown darkened her face as some kind of memory seemed to leak into her thought process.

"You also know that the only limitation known to the infinite series is that it can only create things based on the owner's peak and weakest states, so no event will be so difficult that you cannot survive it in some way. Well, there's an Affix that sets the holder's life to an absolute hellish marathon, so that is not really a good limitation. There are also quite a number of Affixes that set the, eh, you get what I mean. Your Affix is part of the immortal series, so it will always balance itself out with longevity and stability in mind. That said..." Verza sat down next to Alize and held him within her arms.

"Mourra is the one who told us what your Affix is called. It was before you were born and before I met your father." Verza suddenly sneered in a way that suggested a complicated history with the Province of Nightmares and Dreams.

"The bastard also mentioned that your Affix is one of the few in the immortal series that is capable of shaping reality. It takes normal things in your life and turns them into fated encounters, desperate struggles, heartfelt and life-changing moments. We never told you about this because Mourra is a bit tricky in how it tells people things. It's why there hasn't been a major church for it in a long time." Verza released her frustration with a sigh.

"How so?"

"Well, the Province did not tell us everything. I was told some things about you, and your father was told the rest. We shared what we could when we found out you were going to be, well, that we were even going to have you, but we didn't really know what the other was missing until it was too late." Verza kissed Alize on the top of his bandaged head.

"Pie, Ark. Mourra said that the greatest desert is pie. It was so simple then, but putting that into context with what we know now. Ha. It was a sick joke, and now it's too late because your mom and I got too involved." Orsche cut in while rubbing his eyes.

"Ors! Shush. Ahem, I'm sure that you pieced it together a long time ago, that your Affix is the reason why we have been pushing you to reach the first star rank without magic." Verza combed through the small tufts of Alize's hair that could be seen through the bandages. She shot another glare at Orsche the moment he began to move his mouth.

"Pie? How does that fit into my life? Wait, it works, sort of. The number that is, not the desert. I'm guessing that my journals contain a massive life-changing event every three years, with smaller encounters sliding the specific dates elsewhere?"

"That's exactly it. The day you were born was one of the most difficult days of our lives and one of the most fortunate since we found the Apeirogon. On your third birthday, we were nearly discovered by Imperials and separated, your father and me. You were with Jarold running the Gauntlet."

"I remember." Alize frowned, not knowing whether to laugh or cry at the knowledge that his family had nearly been ripped apart approximately three years ago.

"Your father caught on to your journals by your sixth, so we left our last home and dug in here after we regrouped." Verza flexed and clenched her fists.

"Overcompensation then. My Affix had a plan when I was younger, but Mom and Dad got in the way. Then it planned even more. That explains the overlapping events that hit me and Wynn." The Affix tickled his spine as though it were nodding.

"I don't suppose Province Mourrastin offered an explanation of why I possess Tenets." Alize spoke up about something that rattled him the moment that Ors brought it up. If he knew that he possessed a nonrenewable source of energy that harmed his body with each use, he just would not have cast a spell to save himself.

"Ha. You don't have it, Ark. You never did. I made a mistake, and I don't know." Orsche collapsed and revealed something that his ego would have never wanted to admit if it didn't almost cost his son's life.

"Mourra lets people who listen to it, let US, jump to our own con-clusion based on some information it selectively chose to explain..." Verza stepped in and had Jarrold create a miniature vacuum to prevent anything Orsche said from reaching her son's ears.

"We believed that you had Tenets and if you used them all before laying the perfect foundation to reaching the divine rank, it would have allowed your Affix to create events that only divine entities would be capable of overcoming. Your dad and I made a mistake by getting involved in your last major event. We, ha, we focused on the wrong thing and made ourselves part of the problem by preventing you from utilizing your magic." Verza cleared her throat and tried to smile as she prepared to elaborate on the mistake that she and Orsche both made.

"The event that nearly killed me was generated with the intention that I would already be casting spells. Clearly, my survival without the utilization of magic has also been accounted for, but with how things turned out." Alize filled in the blanks in his head and inwardly frowned as the symbol burned his neck for a moment. Outwardly, he put both of his hands over his mother's and smiled.

"You two have done nothing but ensure that I can handle my own under circumstances that are not the best. I get it. You don't have to explain anything." Alize wiped a single tear from her face and hugged his mom. That said, his smile quickly turned into a panicked gape as he heard whispers that suddenly sounded like a cacophony in his ears.

"He is ready. More training. Sim-terr, time difference, 1 to 50, not enough, 100. No. More maybe. Weak foundation. Reach rank 1 before the year ends. Minimum, ten times the exercise..." Verza clearly didn't stay on the matter of her son being aware of new circumstances for long as she drafted up a new training regime for him in her mind. It was clear she gave absolutely no consideration to the aghast expression her precious baby boy wore. It was unknown when Jarold pulled the barrier down, but Ors sighed and released the lightning bolts with a shake of his head.

"I have no choice but to agree with your mother, Ark. We can only try to prepare you better while we have the time. Rest up for now, and we will figure out what to do with this event and your 12-year milestone at a later date."

"Wait! Wait, are you two serious right now? That's it. I just dumped all of my information, and the two of you share something that I have already guessed. That is the end of this whole talk? Oh, hell no. They are either messing with me or everything that has happened to me has been an Illusion, and it's coming apart." Alize looked at the three adults around him and, once again, checked his posters, the notches that

were hidden on his door frame, and the arrangement of the items on his shelves and frowned upon finding nothing wrong with the environment.

"Ahem. So, is there a way I can, I don't know, circumvent the events my Affix generates? I mean, I am nowhere near the divine rank, so if my Tenets are false, what does that mean for my casting going forward? And Mourra, the Province, has clearly been translating the information that my Affix is supposed to be telling me. And if that's the case, is there some wiggle room with my events, and if there is room for error, there are loopholes, right?" Alize felt that everything was going off script, especially since his parents seemed to be in another, significantly less confusing argument that ended with his dad in more tears and a tighter hug from his mom.

"You have a nine star ranked immortal Affix, Ark. It's a type of oddity that fundamentally cannot be understood even by similarly ranked individuals. So yes, there are some errors or subtle differences in your journals since you are getting a sort of prophecy from Mourra as your events are generated. That's as much as we know. I just want you to be extremely clear on the fact that Mourra did not help us out of the kindness of their heart. Your father and I were in an unusual position of power at the time, one that forced Mourra's goals to align with ours. As for helping you," Verza clarified.

"That Province is only interested in making dreams that interest it a reality. Your birth and curse are just an extension of some self-indulgent pursuit. That said, think of your journals and, Haaha. Fucking, 'the holes are in your own house', this is what it meant. May Edrial damn you, Mourra." Orsche wanted to explain even more, but his tears of sorrow and frustration over the past ruined his plans. Thankfully, Alize was smart enough to piece together and fill in the narrative.

"Holes? House? Loopholes, in the events? Mourra is or is going to use one of the loopholes of my Affix to generate events that benefit it down the road?"

"Easy, Ors. Easy." Verza glared at her man as his beard curled at its edges.

"I'm good. Ha. It's just that I spent a long time trying to figure out what Mourra meant. Burned a bridge or two that I probably shouldn't have before I met you and even more after. Ahem. Ark, let's pose a quick thought experiment." Orsche didn't feel targeted by his son's frown and silence since it was all the confirmation he needed to begin.

"In this perfectly controlled world, in this terrarium that your mother and I have kept running to hide you from prying eyes, what have you interacted with that has been capable of generating events? Hint, how is it that you have written eighty-nine journals at two hundred and fifty pages a pop that, from what I've read, are filled with a new nightmare or dream every handful of pages?"

Orsche shook his head and laughed self-deprecatingly. Alize's gaze instantly shot toward an azure-capped potpourri container sitting on a shelf in his room.

"The relics you are studying?"

Instantly, Alize noticed something off about some of his nightmares toward the latter half of the established timeline of 500 or so steps. No, in fact, he even noticed something strikingly important even in the first dozen steps of that fated timeline.

"Yes, my boy. That is exactly right. Now. Ark. Look at the damned names of the scraps and rankless arcanum that I have in my study. Look at what your life is worth to your Affix." Orsche suddenly broke into laughter as he looked up and past the ceiling. Jarold, as if scripted to act, pulled down one of the books and swept up the dirt in the room to recreate the drawings that Alize scribbled onto the pages.

"I remember this. I was just learning the art appraisal, so." Alize frowned at the images and just took in the least assuming details.

"You asked earlier why your mom was nowhere to be found when you got injured." Orsche lowered his head and spoke with a husk that Alize had never heard before.

"It's my fault. I panicked and called her over after I looked through your notes and homework..." Orsche trailed off and used his eyes to motion for Verza to say something.

"Dad, focus." Alize could see his pops thinking of a way to dance around the topic that he brought up.

"Right. I found an inconsistency with your answers and the files that I have been given by the guild. I thought you were wrong in your assessment of the scrap weight, but I double-checked because of your journal. I went into your little nook in the study and found this hidden in the pile of what you were given. It was hidden by a little and simple illusion; no magic was involved at all. Practical magic fooled some of the best scholars in history. It was right there. In the garbage, on top, placed on the inside lip of a rusted metal box. It was so close to falling off the edge." Orsche gulped air and attempted to keep speaking, but Alize cut him off.

"Dad. What is it?"

The bearded man reached into his coat and pulled something out of his vest pocket. A simple bronze key with an ivory inlay rolled out of his pocket square. With a gentle, almost reverent pinch, Orsche twisted the delicate stem of the key and showed the bright blue Roman numeral IV on one side and the silhouetted image of a padlock on the other.

"There's no way. You couldn't have. No, that was not in the pile. That's not, but is it? Something like this can be? But how did it even?

I didn't even! Proximity? No, that can't be right, right? Ye'Orajibjr's key." Alize's words barely squeaked past his lips.

Verza's entire body trembled as she shot to her feet before Alize's final three words could even be completed. Without even trying, her body sank into the ground as if its weight multiplied by thousands in an instant. A tangible level of bloodlust coated her entire body and turned a dark mystical haze into a genuine layer of demonic skin. Thankfully, despite her loss of composure, Verza rooted discipline into her body so the bloodlust didn't exude beyond the skintight and tangible coating but still. Alize looked at his mom for what felt like the first time and closed his mouth in absolute fear.

"No, Ark, you did not say that. You. Ors. Explain. That can't be right. I mean. How? How does something so important just float away from the Archons and the Gods? When would something like that have even vanished from their watchful eyes? And you, you catalog and double-check everything no less than three times, but you couldn't find something like that. Forget the Affix, you, of all people, YOU wouldn't make the mistake of misidentifying an item. Not after what happened last time." Verza dug into Or's arms with sudden panic and anger. Orsche simply stared back at her with tears and a simple but all-encompassing pout.

"First of all, I didn't make a mistake with this. I didn't even know it was something that was on my workload. I grabbed whatever I could from the guild's miscellaneous storage room to fill up my docket. We weren't exactly blessed when it was time to run away. Secondly, it's not the same key as the one in history. I'm assuming in good faith that the Demiurge of Protection enlisted another divine figure to forge copies of his key. Ark, quiz." Ors raised an eyebrow and motioned with his lips for Verza to get the details from her son.

"The original, reportedly, was stolen or lost and then recovered some centuries later with the most recent Imperial call of Buren Tenciel. I suppose, based on the numbering, that this relic is either a fourth copy of Lord Aibjrs key or it unlocks a certain level of access to something within his purview. Which I am assuming is the Jailer's Prison." Alize spoke his mind upon hearing the word quiz. Orsche's alternating smile and frown turned into an ashen schadenfreude directed at their entire family's misfortune.

"As you can see, my love, I am working on assumptions with educated guesswork and recorded precedent acting as my pillars. Not only that, we can only have faith in whatever entity, Mourra standing, that is not telling any of the other Gods or Archons about what is going on down here with Ark's Affix. It's very clear that things were set up against us and for this moment a long time ago...." Orsche twisted his wrist and made the key and his pocket square vanish.

"Ark, you got all of that?" Orsche tilted his head just a little bit.

"Yes." Alize nodded.

"What do you think of our chances? Keep in mind that this is just one of the relics that I found in the junk pile, all of which have a similar rank to this key. There are several dozen more that I am too unequipped to even look at, nevermind trying to study and appraise them." Orsche stared directly into Verza's eyes and waited.

"We don't last long." Having no choice, the boy whispered.

"Exactly. Now. Ha, my love. I am trying to keep it all together, so please. You are hurting me." Ors tilted his head back with a tear-soaked beard. He used his gentle gaze to draw attention to the bruising and blood pouring out of where Verza gripped his shoulder and wrist.

"I. I'm sorry." Verza stepped away and towards one of the corners of the room. The bloodlust that took on a tangible coating around her body slowly receded.

"You're okay. I'm okay. I understand my love. Just, you know." Orsche calmly placed a shackle of ice on his forearm and infused so much magic into a [Stasis] spell that his entire arm and rolled-up sleeve were covered in a thick casing of ice. With a crooked half-smile and wandering red eyes, Ors sat down. Alize just now realized that his father was lifted up as if he was nothing more than a rag doll.

"What are we going to do with all of this information? It's all a bit too much, don't you think? Your mom and I have tried, Ark, since you were young, but we have always been on edge because of Mourra, and you would tell us these random things at times, such inexplicably horrifying things that made us worry. I had you write everything down since that's how I grew up, and your mom and I learned how to deal with your curse legitimately when we eventually figured out the pattern. Your Affix." Orsche hunched forward.

"We did good, Ark. All things considered. I hoped that you would never start this talk, even if we prepared you for it dozens of times in different ways. Ark, we tried so hard to prepare ourselves for this. Did our best to understand the loopholes that Mourra could, would, and has used. We prevented more than half of your events from leaving this terrarium. Through trial and error, we even found an easy way to let you handle the events that we believed you could learn from. It took a few close calls. Some were even so bad when you were younger that we had to pack up and move to avoid some issues, but this..." Orsche pointed toward Alize's entire body and looked away with a knot on his face.

"Close calls. Close? Hold on. Are these trying to say that some of my Sims were real moments that I could have died?"

"My little baby. Ark, your dad wants to say that we won't be able to help forever. We have run out of ways to directly interfere." Verza stepped in and finished what her man wanted to say. Alize, with his lowered head, felt sad and lost, but at the end of the day, he guessed that his family coming to an understanding would be one of the more likely outcomes of this talk. The most likely was receiving a lightning bolt to the brain if his parents believed that he was a reincarnator, transmigrator, a ghost, or basically anything else that he said that was other than the boy that they had raised.

"I have a plan," Alize whispered with a cough.

"You have a plan? What is it? What kind?" Orsche and Verza spoke at the same time. They knew their baby boy was only nine years old, but thousands of years of magically simulated experiences and cultivated moments for growth helped him mature, reason, and conclude things much faster. Verza, feeling somewhat reinvigorated, dashed back toward her boys and sat down on the bed so they could all be close. No, well, she wanted to be close to Alize to soothe her blazing emotions, so she cuddled her son as Orsche shook his head hopelessly.

"Well, step one was limited to returning to a functional physical state and telling you two my thoughts. Preferably, I wanted to learn what the two of you have been hiding from me since I noticed something that I couldn't quite understand about my Affix's reach, my nightmares, and journals. Check on both fronts. From there, I assumed we, uh, well, would talk about it." Alize shrugged a bit as his parents' faces adopted thousand-yard stares.

"Wait though. I have a jumping-off point. Ahem. If my journals are exact or rough prophecies of my generated events and translated while I sleep. I can conclude based on your words, actions, and my training that they match up fairly well. As for the matter of my Tenets, since you said it's fake, I can only assume it has something to do with me possessing a Rooted Ballast Profile, possibly even a passive mutation because of a double root? I'm guessing, [Shroud]?"

Alize smiled like an old man who had just been caught stealing a baby's candy. Ors turned his distant stare into an intense focus. His mouth opened and closed, but he remained wordless until a laugh shook his chest.

"Without a proper scan with completely brand new tools, I can only guess that you have a synergistic mutation of your rooted profile. A rooted [Shroud] aspect profile alone is something difficult to gauge, but a mutation of it is, especially in a profile set that amplifies itself. Ha, it's something quite interesting and worthy of study." Orsche combed his fingers through his thick and tangled beard. Verza, on the other hand, frowned since her man possessed a very familiar glint in his eye.

"What you have done here. What you have cast on yourself. It doesn't fit a [Shroud] profile." Verza simplified what Orsche was preparing to explain, but Alize held up his hand.

"I know how it works, Mom." Alize matched his father's pensive gaze and felt his own eye twitch at the tiny smirk he was given.

"I also understand how my magic has been showing as Tenets." He nodded to himself.

"More than likely, my passive shroud allowed my magic to adapt and adopt the presence that Mourra's interference exuded while I was asleep. If not the province, then my Affix bled into my unused reserves. Or maybe there was a moment that one of you was about to reach the divine rank and that somehow rubbed off on me during conception or gestation." Alize nodded upon seeing his dad raise a brow and nod.

"The issue is my future application of magic. If I have a double-rooted profile, in the best case, I can only use standard spells after I stockpile long stints of magical inactivity. Such a detriment certainly changes my plans, especially if I want to." Alize stroked his chin like an old man and then suddenly paused when his parents chuckled.

"What? Don't laugh at me like that. Obviously, I made some broad-stroke plans regarding my future. Like, wait. Uh, let me start with what I was thinking about for a long time in a Sim." Alize shifted in his mom-shaped seat seeing as how she kept trying to squish his face.

"Go ahead then." Orsche pretended not to see his son's plight and nodded.

"Well, the first chance we get, you should introduce me to the guild as the apprentice of one of your friends or something. After all, you are the one who told me that it's common for an apprentice to be another scholar's illegitimate child, well. It's practically an unspoken rule to those old farts." Ultimately, Alize spoke through a squished face.

"That would be the best course of action, but not as you are. I've been putting off suggesting such a thing to you because you would barely qualify even to receive a township examinee nomination slot due to your lacking base knowledge. Now, it's even less possible if you have a rooted profile without a perfect understanding of everything in your Aspects field. You are also too injured, and your casting, despite the control I've seen, it's not exacting enough to even be considered as a spectator at such a minor testing site. That said, even if you possess vast knowledge, hold dominion over your profile, and gain the requisite skill and authority to articulate your worth, you still would not have the same practical experience as your peers. The only manner in which you would potentially surpass your cohorts is in magical capacity, and even then, a moderately talented child with thick enough human ancestry would completely overpower you in that singular field. And then there is time. Your mother and I have been trying to give you the best crash course we can, but time is not a resource that we have an abundance of, even in this Apeirogon. Now, factor in your Affix and the fixed events it has established for you, the chances of beating it to become an apprentice before a devastating event descends upon us. Well, son, they are slim to none. Now factor in your leaving this terrarium at any point between now and the next selection period for the guilds. Your Affix is certainly biding its time but once you leave and are no longer able to stay in this controlled environment, do you think it would not keep you busy all the time to make up for how long your mom and I have been cultivating you into a better us?" Ors advised.

"I understand." Alize nodded but did not continue interrupting.

"What else did you think of then? Something feasible though, and pertaining to our current circumstances." Orsche dismissively relaxed his back and leaned in the chair with an awkward sense of leisure. Alize cleared his throat and nodded thrice.

"How about you teach me what to look for to trace each event back to the roots? We have, you two have managed to intervene for me up until recently, so we can just keep living how we have except I can get ahead of things." Alize didn't really say anything too groundbreaking since nods came from both of his parents. Well, two different kinds of nods. Verza followed along with all of her heart since her smart little baby brought up a solution. Orsche, on the other hand, squeezed the bridge of his nose with a heavy sigh of disappointment.

"That's your idea? Have my lessons really taught you nothing?"

Orsche raised his other hand to put a stop to Alize's train of thought and shook his head in absolute disapproval.

"We are, regardless of whether we act upon circumventing the events in your journals hereon, beholden to Mourrastin's guidance. Thus far, the Province's translations and aid have been as accurate as they can be, but do you really think that your Affix will allow such a thing to just impede its sole function? Do you think that Mourra has not already and will not set some things into motion under the guise of intervention and assistance? Do you think it will let your mom and I keep interfering with your life? Your only line of thinking should be that as soon as you become consciously aware of such assistance, your Affix will change how it creates events. Do you understand?"

"I think I do." Alize tried to digest everything, but it was a hard pill to swallow.

"Me getting hurt despite Mom being in the area already proves that the Affix has somehow managed to overlap two or more events in a way that any external assistance I might receive is moot." Alize immediately got to the crux of the issue. Verza, finding the whole thing a bit too complicated and her son's crumpling expression concerning, placed her hand on a nerve cluster around his neck and with a simple press, the boy closed his eyes and fell asleep. The two adults froze for nearly a dozen minutes before Verza broke the silence.

"Orsche. We are not letting this boy out of our sights. No matter what. Absolutely, no matter what." Verza's loving expression melted, revealing a cold and sharp magic that oozed bloodlust. Even Jarold morphed into a tempestuous demon of storms and roiling dust clouds as the magic fueling his body's manifestation darkened.

"I know Verza, I know. But I genuinely don't know what to do. I have been repeating myself because I am stuck. What are we supposed to do now, my love? We have barely managed to power the simulator to give him just enough time to learn and grow. And we have, personally, just barely outpaced the difficulty of his Affix, but now? Ha. He has cast. It's not Tenets bad but still." Or's facade fell apart as his leg bounced without signs of slowing down.

"I'm hoping and praying that this dream shit is Mourrastin. We at least have some dealings with that tricky bastard, but I'm at a loss if it's anyone else. I don't even know who it could be that would want to use Ark's Affix for their benefit since it could quite literally be anyone, anywhere. And we can not just waltz into the churches and ask around. Once any of us step foot on consecrated ground, it's over, our cover is blown and the next thing we know, we are getting hunted by the Hounds and Ark is pulled into the Guardian program as a premium piece of clay to be molded into yet another cog in the machine. Assuming he makes it back to the capital with the resurgence of those sick monsters." Ors put a finger on his chin and frowned as he trailed off into his own thoughts.

"Raquel..." Ors snapped to attention.

"We can only roll with the punches." Verza gently moved Alize's hair and smiled.

"I know my love. I know. But I just can't. I don't want history to repeat itself more than necessary, and already our boy is in an even worse position than when either of us was cursed." Ors held Verza's hand and forced a smile.

1.9 Going Out

"**S**urely, I wasn't just knocked out by my own mother..." Alize cleared through the fog of his awakening mind and found himself thinking upon an armchair in the corner of his mental lobby. He wanted to cry but couldn't gather the emotional energy to do so.

"*No, I was very much taken out of the planning phase of my own life. Ha, I can only assume that they wanted to hit on some particularly troubling points without me reading their expressions and body language. Either way, it's also very likely that they already gleaned all the information that they needed to make a proper plan for our future. Hopefully, their thoughts align with* mine." To occupy himself, Alize completed a quick mental and mystical exercise, using magic through logic and ritualistic chanting.

"[*Prevention*]." Like the minor heal called Stabilize and its natural evolution or sequence of spells yesterday, this further improved version carried all the benefits in exchange for stricter prerequisites. This version, which retained the same name without a title update, did come with some major adjustments. A magic reduction due to the deactivation of visual effects, improvement in heat sinking, and a controlled application of the [Shroud] Aspect that he seemed to be rooted in despite the complete access to a Utilitarian standard. Confusingly, Alize wondered how he was able to cast anything outside of illusions. Understandably, one of his parents immediately pulled him out of an introspective whirlwind.

"You're up. YOU'RE UP!" Verza blinked and pounced upon Alize as if she were a starving mosquito and pecked his face with a near fanatical fervor.

"*This is the start of a day.*" Alize managed to endure a torrent of hugs, kisses, and apologies long enough to find a break long enough to speak up.

"...mom. MOM!"

The boy held his mother's cheeks in his small hands and watched her fortitude rebuild itself as she fought tooth and nail to stop herself from crying anymore that she already had.

"It's okay. I'm fine. I love you." Alize wiped his own tears away since he couldn't cry, you know.

"I know." Verza hugged her darling baby boy as if he could suddenly float away at any point in time.

"Alright mom. EPA. I have to know how long I have been asleep." Alize shook his head with a smile but forced himself to get down to the brass tax.

"Around 30-32 hours, so not a whole day. You missed the pre-light, so the sun is just coming over the crown." Verza revealed the time and kissed her little baby all over his face once again.

"*30 whole hours. Well, damn. That really crunches my timeline of things to do.*" Alize frowned as his thoughts traveled inward. For a moment, he focused on the long corridor reminiscent of that nameless Divinity's abode. The long streak of 89 golden dream journals, nine observational notebooks, and a pedestal with a tenth unfinished book, seemed to taunt him with its in-corporealness. Of course, his mind locked onto the unnatural distribution of the journals. Without wasting a breath, he recalled all the nightmare scenarios that were associated with the next round of generated events.

A fresh and sharp throbbing pain cracked like a whip throughout his mind as an entire snippet of a lifetime forcefully ingrained itself. Details that he left out of the journals surfaced as the phantom books and binders filling the shelves lit up with a cacophony of lights reminiscent of fireworks. Without realizing it, Alize's fists clenched and his breathing grew still. Thankfully, the mental imagery faded before he could start to scream.

"Mom. I really didn't want to dampen your mood but..." Alize sat himself up with a full body shiver, or tried to, considering that he flopped back down with gasping breaths.

"Careful. My goodness. Are you trying to exhaust yourself again? You don't have to rush like that." Verza helped her son sit up and passed him a drink that glittered with green light. The boy swallowed the words. "I didn't exhaust anything. You knocked me out." and swished the liquid in his mouth. For a second, his cheeks lit up as if he were swallowing a miniature sun. A moment later, that very same light burned through his esophagus and plummeted into his stomach with an underwhelming fizzle.

"Thank you. But it's easier if I tell you both at the same time to make things go faster. Red, blue, then black, right?"

Alize pointed to the assortment of medicines laid out on top of a tray placed on his bedside table.

"Yes."

"Great. We have to go as soon as possible after this, so where's Dad?"

"Your dad shouldn't be too long now. Sniff." Verza pursed her lips and grumbled.

"Sniff? You don't say it, Mom, you do it." Alize controlled an involuntary eyebrow twitch.

"He said this would happen, you know. That you would want to go. Boohoo."

"Why are you saying boohoo? If you are going to cry, do it. And what's with that look, huh? You ran out of tears, so you can only play as a crocodile. Mom, it's not going to work. You were the one who said to go all in once I decided to act." Alize released a heavy sigh without saying anything to his mom and downed his medicine like an old man with a potentially fatal heart condition. Thankfully, the thick leathery curtain that covered the hut's entrance swung open before the kid finished swallowing the last piece.

"I get why you want to head out so soon, Ark, but isn't this all a bit sudden?"

Ors burst into the room carrying two things. The first item, since it was big enough to cover the man's entire upper body and then tower over him afterward, was a metallic box somewhat meshed with camo green, blue, and various shades of brown. A massive crest of a solid humanoid fading into a dotted outline boldly flickered with a flaming light at the very center of the small obelisk.

Orsche rested the odd contraption against a shelf by the main entrance and checked Alize's temp. With a whisper, Alize's entire internal structure revealed itself because of a quick pulse of a halo over Orsche's head and the several rings that overlapped in his eyes.

"Your condition is stable enough to entertain the idea of leaving." Orsche, in the middle of verbalizing his thought, instantly froze upon slowly meeting Verza's cold gaze.

"Ahem. What I meant to say is, explain your plan or idea for wanting to leave. If the old fart, your mother, and I all agree that it requires a proper look, we will head out in the next few minutes. If not, well, you will not leave this Terrarium until you are healthy enough to beat at least one of us in a field of our choosing." Orsche quickly remedied his slip-up with a quick fix of his untamed mane.

"Are you kidding me? These old monsters are clearly using illegal spells to communicate with one another. And what kind of trap is that? If I fail to convince them right now, I am never leaving. It's possible too. Mom is a meathead, so I will have to beat her in a fight. Dad, well, I just don't have enough time to gather the same amount of information he has access to. The only outstanding variable is Jarold, but even then, the old man has lived so long as a Fae that my fake experiences in the sim are garbage by comparison. I can't beat any of these people, which leaves only, ahem." Alize cleared his throat and nodded a few times as he observed the three faces that appeared before him. Very obviously, they were conversing with one another just based on their fleeting exchanges of looks and shuffling body language.

"I am seeking to confirm the accuracy of my decoded journals. Regardless of whether this is some ploy in the long run, I, ahem, we need to find a way to decipher the Affix the moment it writes on my skin without the input of Mourrastin or some other divine entity. With that in mind, I want to directly match what is written in the journals to the runes and patterns of the Affix to learn the language it is using, and the only way that I can see that happening is by running toward the event and lining everything up. This is a learning opportunity littered with chances for me to hone my skills and wisdom, so I'm hoping that you guys don't deny me this." Alize bowed his head despite the pain and held his posture until he heard a response. He understood that there was no convincing his parents and godfather. They had to talk it out among themselves.

As if to confirm his belief, the Affix on his neck burned with a sort of sentient desire as it pushed something into motion. The boy could feel each symbol slowly etching itself, linking into some vast and unknowable tapestry. For a second, it felt as though the world bore down on him as the last symbol on his Affix struggled to complete this particular cycle of the endless loop.

"We have conditions, but let us hope that this venture is worth the trouble." Orsche gathered the dishes and waved them out of the room while Verza stood up and quickly stretched with a serious expression.

"We will put you in the Duplicator like always. If your dad or I think that the event is too much for you to handle, we will immediately terminate your connection and dispatch whoever or whatever the event is attempting to build up to. Am I understood?"

It didn't shock Alize that his mother simply looked imposing and heroic at this moment as he nodded without saying a word.

"Good." Her face softened for a split second before she left the tent to change into something more fitting for the upcoming excursion outside of their little homestead.

"You're lucky that I've made some preparations for a scenario like this." Orsche pointed to an oversized cane that he carried in a gold embroidered purple cloth. White symbols and faded patches of opalescent fabric littered the mystical wraps. Verza, on the other hand, re-entered the room in the regalia of an Amazonian queen. Her wild, curly brown hair swirled into a tight bun held together by a crown of bone and metal. A short blouse and battle shirt patched with etched bones and scales plating glitter against a skintight suit of interlocked hexagonal rings. Writhing emerald green bandages packed tightly around her calves and forearms. A long, bulky, and ornate belt hung around her hips with its excess spooled around one of her thighs, looping underneath the blooming and bladed battle skirt. Nearly half a dozen sheathed knives and pouches adorned her outfit along with spiked pads on her knees, elbows, and shin guards.

"That's a bit much, my love." Orsche paused and shook his head. In comparison, he looked underdressed in a simple button-down and soot-stained white coat that only seemed unprofessional since he rolled up the sleeves. He wasn't fat per se, but a belly protruded from the coat with a weirdly aligned monster character opening its mouth on the stomach of his undershirt.

"I know. That's why I grabbed this from your office since I don't have the Ballast Aspect that you have." Verza pulled out a mechanical disc engraved with flowering marks and placed it above her head. With a sudden flash, Verza's hair dropped along with a tasteful net of gems and metallic wire that braided her hair into a respectfully adorned bun. Her armor softened into a knee-high, bedazzled dress and bulky platform shoes that denoted some sort of muted wealth. Even the skin-tight armor turned into black pantyhose that served as a backdrop to the dress and shimmering jewelry.

"Hmm." Orsche smirked upon seeing a familiar outfit on Verza, but he didn't say anything and set up the massive box with the humanoid seal engraved upon it. As for Verza, she blushed at her man's suggestive gaze and quickly turned to something else. Her eyes flickered with the use of a spell, one that allowed her to follow the medicine inside of her son's body. Unexpectedly, the meds boiled into a mystical force that pressed against all of Alize's organs and forced him to bloat ever so slightly.

"What did you give him?" Verza asked out of reflex but crossed her arms and frowned as she noticed that Ors was just as baffled by the sight as she was. Alize's skin went from an alternating cold blue and pale to a red and warm tanned shade similar to his appearance before he became injured.

"I'm okay, Mom. The medicine is doing what it should. It's having more of a drastic effect because of the spell that I am using." Alize patted his stomach. He remained completely unperturbed by the veins that bulged all over his body and the tar-black steam that hissed out of his pores. Verza, on the other hand, examined the phenomenon with a worried frown but ultimately decided to retain the glare she cast at Ors. Exasperated, the scruffy-looking man shook his head and mouthed "What did I do?" to Jarold but he quickly rolled his eyes since the Sylph in question merely crossed his arms like Verza and rolled his eyes. Alize, completely desensitized to the family dynamic, stared at the cane that was half draped with the intensity of a newborn seeing the world for the first time.

"Do they expect to haul me around on a floating gurney at some point today? It might be a possibility with my extensive wounds, but it's not like this is a war zone. Such an item is overkill. Hm, on another note, did Dad always have one of these in the office? I must have missed it. No, that's not right. It looks..."

"Did you build that HCT-APN from the scrap pile?"

"This? Why yes! I tried my best with the tattered blueprints and wreckage, but there was very little to work with, so I had to improvise. I am, however, surprised that you know about such an ancient Arcanum since we have not gone over the Radiant Saga in detail yet. Did you find documentation referencing the Patch in your extracurricular ventures or did you stumble upon some information on the extra texts that I recommended?"

Ors raised a brow at his son's depth of knowledge.

"Fuck. He knows that I've been using his work computer. Damn it. How long has he known?"

"Of course I know of it. It's a legendary item in the medical field. I may not have read a lot on the Radiant saga but there were mentions of it in a few texts that I happened upon at some point, though at the time, the material I encountered only spoke of the devices while they were still in their infancy." Alize looked away from his dad's narrowed eyes.

"So, if I were to ask you to recite where you learned such information, would you be capable of doing so?"

Orsche leveled himself with Alize and waited for an interjection from the lovely Verza, but she seemed to be on the same page. No, the boy clearly noticed how his parents nodded to one another as if they had planned this whole encounter.

"They are using illegal spells again. Hmph, pair of vipers." In his head, the boy remembered exactly where he had seen information on such a relic. Almost instantly, the library in the fog of his mind swirled in a fervor and ejected a single book into the main lobby. In a flourish similar to Ors, the boy dramatically cracked open to the page he had in mind and cackled as he recited the words like some villain giving a monologue. Outside of his mind, the boy remained unnaturally calm and collected, almost as if he were in the middle of an exam that he studied his whole life for.

"I believe the Arcanum was briefly mentioned as one of the many contributions that the eight star rank God, Sir Tharron, made during his youth. Sir Tharron and his achievements were briefly touched upon in the forty-seventh volume of the Manuscripts of Lady Ithe, the Life Mother and patron of Bearing and Nurturing as she was titled during the Radiant Era. The Archon Tharrohn, after the natural erosion of her Tenets and in a later addition to the second newest volume of the religious text, is widely renowned as one of the cornerstones of Alchemy, biology, Accord type Utility magic and is one of the major pioneers that institutionalizing the use of Accord and Retro Ballast type Arcanum." Alize batted his eyes innocently, but within his pupils lay a challenge that only his parents implicitly understood.

"Is that so? Can I assume that you read the manuscripts to their completion? And if so, would you be willing to expound?"

"Ahem. Well, to summarize what I gleaned from my readings, Madam Tharron laid the groundwork for the current symbiotic system that the IHS, Imperial Health Services, and religious community have established. Accordingly, her work and influence have allowed a currently active Archon, Bayrun, and his more intellectually inclined contemporaries to refine the modern healthcare system as a whole over the past few millennia." Alize admired the device with a bitter smile. His gaze landed on the location where a small cube would be slotted. That empty crevice would usually be covered with a plate, but considering how the metal snapped and ripped out toward him like snaggled teeth, he could only assume that the dark stains within the socket were scorch marks. Using his quick observation as an out, the kid slowly trailed off and instantly changed the subject.

"That Quibe pack has sustained quite a bit of damage. Are you sure that it won't explode even if it gets repaired?"

"No. It shouldn't work even if I get the whole thing refurbished by a proper Ballastrate or get a Direct-type craftsman to give it a once over after it's fixed. I think so at least. The rotary circuit is already shot, and the magic scanner and register have been corrupted by some effuse that has gelled to the QC, presumably whatever spell that managed to break through the built in Gipsum. Ark..." Orsche passed his son the cane so he could get his hands on a piece of history.

"Gipsum is the name of an outdated brand of portable magic shield generators that used to have total market dominance throughout Yiruhm. They sold commercially and to the Havens military for nearly two centuries before a fatal issue caused their stocks to tank and their stalls to close on the corridor." Alize thumbed the exploded-out battery port and almost immediately became aware of what the issue was that the company faced. Ors nodded and reclaimed the small piece of history.

"The electrical adapter seems okay until you open up the casing and find that the current switching and magic regulating components have completely melted through and fused into the import and effusion reuptake pipes. It's a simple case of flawed engineering. Of course, they didn't know that at the time, and any attempts to fix the issue only made the product worse." Orsche wrapped it back up.

"That's all to say: it won't blow up if I get it professionally fixed, but it probably won't ever start. Hmm, I haven't tried it yet though, wanna see if it works?"

Ors, like a guitar soloist, flourished with eye-catching wonder as he tossed a cube in the air and spun the massive cane. In a feat of sleight of hand, he swapped the broken cane out for one without any obvious damage and slotted the cube-shaped magical battery into the slot.

"Wait! Don't turn it on!" Alize put his arm up and stopped his dad from pressing the power-on button that was on the handle.

"The adjustment might be a bit slapdash, but you can retrofit the main couplings with it. Eh, you might have to break some of the historical banks in your office. The ones that you have from the Radiant Saga in the Blessed Dump section will do the trick. Also, there's another adapter and some similar piping near the desk at, um, the fourth renaissance section? As for putting it all together, you would need a [Guidance] Spell variant to tweak the parts, erm, [Reroute] or [Tinker], I think. You could probably fit another kind of bank into a point somewhere along the circuit that is not damaged, which would completely remove the need for such a big magic battery. You would lose most of the functions due to a modified design, but it could potentially do what you repaired this one for, which is to help me walk or move around by myself, right?"

Alize advised his old man about an alternative solution.

"You used to laugh and giggle so cutely whenever I did that bit." Ors tapped his chin a couple of times in thought and put down the second cane with a pause.

"The power nodes along the original circuitry would have to be warped in quite a few vital locations, like you said. Hmm, and I'll have to re-arrange the engravings on the motherboard and the MPU, but it could work." Orsche dropped the Patch device that he had already refurbished so its tip rested on the floor and slapped it out of the Gipsum, or purple cloth that he used as a sheath. He released a massive network of golden threads that separated into dark and light variations. The dark gold lines infiltrated the cane and the sheet holding it and created an intricate and detailed wire mesh of the mechanisms, arcane stitching, and spells behind the artifacts. The cane, despite appearing small, expanded to around the length and width of a motorcycle. Pea-sized gears, pin-width metal rods, and the telltale clockwork and rigid light of Ballast-type magic condensed the massive tool into something smaller and refined.

"Nope. It wouldn't work, but I have an idea now. How about..." Orsche, excited that one of his projects received a breakthrough because of his son's out-of-the-box thinking, began to pant as he turned to leave the room. Sadly for him, an arm grabbed the collar of his white coat and lifted him off the ground.

"Alright, none of that Ors. We need to focus up if we want to get to rest before the crown's light is fully up. I also want us to get everything on the list that I've made..." Verza paused, suddenly feeling three sets of lasers aimed at her.

"What's with those looks? I like making lists. Fine, it's a mental list, but it still counts." The boys nodded along and let Verza set their family unit into motion. The first thing she did was press the fading humanoid symbol on the camo box and place Alize inside of the half that held a solid outline. Orsche, with a swish of his hand, snapped the box closed and slid the symbol to the side as he entered a code in the number pad. Like a washing machine on a full load, the device clanged and rumbled and then let out an adorable little chime. Verza pulled her son out of the right side of the opened box, the side that had an illusory outline of a humanoid.

Orsche, after a steaming Alize was pulled, twisted the symbol in a way similar to a lens shutter and turned the crest into a transparent glass pane. After confirming that his son was still inside the box with his eyes shut. Ors made his way out of the room with an enlarged mystical projection of the Patch Cane in his hands. Without paying attention, Verza received the odd purple and white cloth that Ors just used as a sash to bind it. Before she even took two steps away from Alize's tent, the experienced woman utilized the sheet as it was intended and twirled it around her son's body as if it were any other normal blanket. Carefully, both parents added their magic to the cloth and watched as it compressed atop the bandages that nearly covered Alize's entire body.

"Are you okay? Is it too tight?" Verza asked as she lowered the magic input on the threads that gave the sheet its magical properties. The wrapping loosened as a result.

"I'm okay. The pain just surprised me. Also, have I ever told you two how much I hate using the duplicator? It's slimy, and I can feel all of my organs just sloshing and pulsing. Having two connected bodies sucks." Alize felt his mother's hand tighten around his own as he mindlessly complained.

"Ah, it's okay, Mom. It's just different this time. I'm too injured, so I feel everything sting twice. It's upsetting." Alizeh smiled in his mother's arms and from inside of the box.

"Are you sure you want to do this?" Verza hesitated to move her son again.

"Yes. But, uh, don't look so glum, Mom. I can handle this much." Alize forced a smile and cast [Prevention].

Verza saw the spell's activation and closed her eyes to tighten up the wrappings. Orsche, despite being involved with the massive cane, side glanced at his family and cast two familiar spells on Alize. Similar to the day prior, an icy cloud along with a guiding golden needle storm froze Alize's injuries. Without any delay, [Prevention] deconstructed the two spells and added them to its own loop. Orsche noticed the complete envelopment of his spells and subtly nodded. As a test, he initiated a different variant of the [Guidance] spell variant called [Link] and observed how Alize would deal with the aftermath. Of course, the kid didn't even have to think as his magic consumed the spell and seamlessly blended the spell of the protective and encasement spells of blanket into his [Prevention]. That said, the purple, white, and golden blanket held a variant of [Stasis], a woven spell called [Unbound]. Unlike what its name implied, it created a space or boundary that disrupted the laws of physics in some specified way.

In this specific case of [Unbound], Alize was allowed to escape the laws of physics by being allowed to move fast without feeling the momentum. Think, creating instances of DC comics speed force. As for the [Link] spell, it allowed the gaudy arcanum to react and bleed into other things, forcing different types of magic to become compatible with spells that usually wouldn't be allowed. As a result, the white part of the fabric began to adopt a slight green tint from the

[First aid] bandages, almost as if the blanket was designed with linking, extra space, and modified functions in mind.

"Alright then. While we are searching for clues on the next event, we need to stock up on food for obvious reasons, medicinal herbs and spices for pre and after workout meals and baths, books on flavoring squire jerky and flukes, and Orsche! Are you listening?"

Verza glared at her man since he couldn't stop fiddling with the giant projection of the Patch device.

"Yes, my love. Absolutely we need to do those things that you said." Ors looked up for a second and returned to his work.

"For the love of. Ha. Fine. Since you are paying attention, we are going to have to use your connections in Rest to get Alize's name into the Empire's Social Security Registry. As much as I would like to, we can't avoid it anymore." Verza made her list known and addressed her son with a gentle squeeze of his cheeks as she carried him to the edge of their encampment.

"Hm, yes, my love. I'll see what I can do. Hmm." Orsche nodded profusely, but his focused gaze and dancing fingers made one wonder if he genuinely heard Verza.

"Ark, what did you want to tell us earlier? I remember you said that you wanted both of us to hear it." Verza rolled her eyes and squeezed her son with tender affection.

"Ahem. Well, my plans have sorta been forced to change since I woke up so late. I wanted to start off the day using some extra time before we got on our search to cross out a few of my group's hangout spots. To see if Fell is venting with the group considering what happened to us yesterday. Ah, that reminds me. One of you brought her home, right?"

"I did, on my way to the Shadow of Orrin. I left a note with her things so if anything, her parents would have forced her to stay home today even if she wanted to leave. The poor thing. I would have spent more time there to make sure that she was okay, but my mind was on you." Verza responded since Orsche was MIA.

"I also sent a voice message to her parents this morning to update them so that adorable girl wouldn't have to worry about you but they haven't responded yet." Verza sighed on the matter and motioned Jarold to begin something at the edge of the camp.

"That's fine, I guess." Alize frowned at the notion of not getting a response as soon as possible and hesitantly looked back at his tent. The image of a rectangular device made of a glassy and solidified shadow immediately came into his mind.

"*I didn't have enough time to grab my phone. Hmm, should I ask Mom to go back and grab it for me?*"

Alize thought to himself, then opened his mouth to speak, but his attention was immediately drawn to his dad's sudden laughter. Without giving anyone the time to think, Orsche left a glittering trail of smoke puffs as he teleported across the camp and entered his study. At the exact same time, Jarold waved his hand to gather everyone's attention onto the circular cloud that manifested around him. Verza stopped herself mid-step and slowly turned toward a tent on the complete other side of the long hill that they had just walked across.

"I'm going to kill your father now. I think I can handle being a single mother." Verza grumbled and was ready to give chase when Orsche popped up in front of them with a raised hand.

"My love. Wait. Look at this." Orsche dropped a pile of scrap metal, pipes, wiring, and magical batteries of all sizes and mystical colors. With a wave of his hand, all the dropped items floated up along with the giant Arcanum, reminiscent of a giant walking cane. With a simple snap of his finger, a wide array of golden light spanning the entire spectrum of shades waved around like stalks of wheat in the breeze and dismantled and reorganized the items in an instant. Verza and Alize blinked, and everything came to a conclusion.

"What kind of relic is that?"

Verza raised an eyebrow with a stony expression, clearly unimpressed.

"It's my homemade Patch.v2." Ors smiled as he secured a thick hovering chair to the floor before it could float away.

"It looks completely different. Like it won't explode if you look at it wrong now." Verza didn't even try to notice the differences since it was just too drastic. Instead of a mesh of rusted cogs, metal poles, and cracked crystals, this updated Arcanum simply looked like an upscale custom wheelchair with glassy knobs in place of where the wheels would be. The caps pulsed with a red light, but after a few seconds they turned a milk colored off white and gray. Without Orsche having to press down anymore, the chair hovered at waist height. Two yellow glowing triangles with exclamation points popped up on the armrests, but as soon as Ors touched the inlaid gems, the warnings vanished. Before the bearded man could say anything, red warning lights blared up as little projections all over the armrests. Without wasting a moment, Orsche smacked the chair several times and smiled as the warnings sputtered out. Alize shot his pops a concerned look, which was not unique to just him.

"What in the ninth is wrong with you guys? Stop giving me those looks. I promise that it's not going to explode. If you must know." Ors waved his hand and showed the previous janky and broken model with a burned-out battery slot and presented the refurbished copy that Alize assumed that he was going to have to use.

"I didn't touch these two. I still have to use my job's resources to confirm whether I did a good fix. This new one is purely of my own creation. It doesn't have nearly as many functions, but it should be fine as a low-grade mobility assistant." Orsche's smile achieved an otherworldly radiance in contrast to Verza's dark frown.

"Alright. Then, I'll allow you to get carried away right now since we are still home, but don't do this if we run into Ark's event starter today. According to the journal, the next few connected nightmares are started with a dangerous relic. In other words, it's something that we do not need you to try to study." Verza secured Alize to her body with a protective bear hug and waited for Orsche to fold up the chair that he cobbled together from more modern parts.

"What do you mean, love? I..." Orsche, as cool and calm as a cucumber, straightforwardly acted confused and innocent.

"Dad. We are serious. Please don't get carried away if the journal happens to be right about the next event then the relic that kicks off my next event is something that could date as far back as the Dark Age." Alize cut his dad off.

"Dark age, huh! Wow. That, uh, is fine. I'm a bit confused as to why that information was not on your, ahem, that was not written down, was it? My boy. What relic is it? Is it something that I know?"

Orsche rubbed his hands together as his face drained of all color at the mention of blotted-out history.

"Should be. It's on the same disastrous scale as the key, but I don't want to say what it is until we have confirmed if it's real or not, though." Alize sighed upon reviewing the events that were supposedly already in the works. With the timeline hallway, he merely had to imagine a calendar or recall the time and see how his days were booked out weeks, months, years, decades and even centuries in advance. It simply left Alize rattled as he looked at what was supposed to happen over the next few hours and months. Nevermind looking farther ahead; near every hour was packed with exclamation points and question marks. Thankfully, his lull in the conversation gave way to his mother stepping up and sitting Orsche down.

"That means do not try to study whatever it is with your hands. You have eyes. NO. AS A MATTER OF FACT, if you see something out of the ordinary, tell us and then move as far away as possible. We have tried our best to do right by Ark, but now we have to let him handle these events on his own. Am I understood?"

Verza glared at Orsche.

"Crystal, but let me make this clear, my love. You are more likely to mess with any event going forward." Orsche stepped on the glassy cloud around Jarold and very carefully ensured that Alize's entire body was firmly covered by the multicolored blanket. Verza scoffed and pulled her baby away from the man, who gazed at her with a soft but annoying smile.

"And if I do, so what? I'm only going to get involved first because you will drag it out," Verza scoffed.

"That may be the case. But who knows? All I can do at this moment is..." With a mystical glimmer, the chair frame and its cushion stretched, warped, and snapped into a normal-looking silver cane with an ivory handle. A green veining pattern cut through the marble handle with a stunning flash while Orsche wore a solemn expression.

"I promise that if I see the proposed relic that may start Alize's next event or the next cascade of overlapping issues, I will not do anything to obtain it for myself. I'm even willing to sign a pact if it makes you two..." Orsche's entire being screamed, well, nothing untoward but...

"*Why does he remind me of a snake-oil salesman?*"

Alize couldn't help but not trust his dad in that moment even if he couldn't place why he thought so. Thankfully, his mom was more experienced in the ways of Orsche and cut off his fake display of righteousness.

"Denied. I've seen you sell another man's kidney before you even had the organ on ice, just after you promised his dying mother that you'll take care of him for the rest of your life. That said, you are going to do exactly what I say, down to the letter, which means study anything out of the ordinary with your eyes only, then leave it alone to let things play out organically. Our whole goal for this trip, for sticking with Ark's timetable, is to confirm if the journals are reliable enough for him to trust in the future." Verza stepped up to Orsche and stared down at him in what appeared to be contempt to a random onlooker.

"*Huh?*"

"Did I make myself clear?" Verza paused for a breath.

"*Dad did what?*"

"Yes, my love, I will do my best." Orsche frowned and nodded to Jarold.

"Your best is all I ask for." Verza lowered her head to give the scruffy-looking gentleman a kiss on his cheek. For added measure, she also gave a peck on the forehead to the handsome little sir in her arms. Alize, around this point in time, finally processed what his parents had just said.

"What in the nine? Mom. Wait. Dad, you did what?! To whom? How long ago? Why? Wait! Are you telling the truth, Mom?"

"I am. I arrested your father the very first time we met because he was involved with an illegal organization." Verza raised a brow toward her man.

"You didn't tell him? I thought that you went over our past with him in your lessons?"

"Alleged. And not fully. I thought he would appreciate our mom and dad lore after he understood the scope of our escapades. Ahem. That is to say, Ark, your mom is sort of telling you the truth. I made a joke in poor taste about some kidnapping and trafficking issues occurring at the time, but your mother got obsessed with my good looks and followed me around like a stalker. Before I knew it, her brute squad went ahead and locked me up. Your mom had this, erm, anyway I was doing a public service and things got out of hand. At the end of the day, your mom is right." Ors maintained a calm expression, but his ears dropped down to the ground midway after seeing Verza's angry and embarrassed stare.

"Really. Am I right?"

"Of course, love."

"Then what about right after I closed up shop, when..." Verza wagged her eyebrows.

"Alright! Haa. Ha. My dear. I'm sorry. We should, uh, head out, right? It's getting late, so we will miss our transport into the city. " Ors looked at his empty wrist and tapped the cane onto the floor with his other hand. Alize smiled at his father's hurried response.

"Riiight. Let's get to it then. Jarold, send us up." Verza cracked her neck. Half a second after that, Jarold silently waved his hands in a circle and created an oblong dome around the family. A little chime broke the artificial silence once, twice, and on the third resonating bell, the family of three exploded up and forward, sucked in by a massive wind tunnel that ripped across the sky and weaved through the clouds like a snake slithering through the brush. From above, Ark noticed an intricate highway system that cut through thick forests and massive fields in the distance. A single branch of this massive network stretched and buzzed with movement and light as construction focused on expanding and connecting the villages on the outskirts of Jordaine's more modern civilization.

In the blink of an eye, Jarold lowered them through a dense sheet of clouds and into the woods near the fringes of a small nameless village that mostly consisted of around 4 to 5 thousand simple wooden and stone houses. A rather impressive aqueduct system snaked through the village, originating at a tower to the north of the village. A massive twisting sigil gathered and purified the moisture in the air and congealed everything into a massive floating hoop that mostly hovered over vast swaths of farmland.

A dozen or so of the homes nearest to this obelisk set up a small bazaar or farmers' market of sorts that stretched all the way to the village center. Even from a distance and high up, Alize and the rest of his family could see the vibrant and bustling town as everything was in the midst of a remodel. Construction workers in reflective vests and wearing all manner of custom hardhats, cast intense magic or lifted several dozen tons. They lifted cobbled streets with flicks of a finger and installed compact roads and sewers that would require no manual upkeep. The workers uprooted entire homes with families inside of them and placed everything according to a grid structure that bent and flowed with the natural terrain. Overall, these construction workers expanded and enriched the quality and scale of the village in such a way and so quickly that no one had time to process. Better yet, all of this came free of charge. As he understood it, Jordaine was one of the very few independent countries that remained an economic and political powerhouse even in the grand structure of Haven and the even vaster Immortal Empire.

That said, the quartet covered a few dozen kilometers on foot in a few minutes and ended up next to a smoothly paved road with all kinds of construction material shoved off to the side. They sat on some benches inside of a rather simple glass box and watched constructors, casually lift one or several pallets of stone, concrete, piping, or something else with either their own body, a tool, or a spell that resembled telekinesis but was nowhere as near as clean. Ors looked at his nonexistent watch and stood behind and beside the benches, watching the conveyor belt of workers look at them with odd expressions.

Honestly, Orsche couldn't deny that their little family looked pretty weird in comparison to the villagers. He was dressed to the nines. His aforementioned graphic tee was nowhere in sight, nor were his shorts since they were replaced by suit pants. Only his now snow white lab coat looked out of place over his leisurely formal clothing. His fried hair and beard were also groomed, another difference from the tangled thicket that used to hang from his face. Verza carried herself and sat down with a straightforward authority that made one believe her to be a soldier waiting to spring into action, but the pressed and beautiful ensemble and jewels made one do a double take since she resembled a humble heiress. Then there was the main attraction, Alize.

The boy looked like a weirdly bound cursed doll with a blanket over his lap, bandages covering all but his eyes, and a tuft of chestnut hair at the very top of his head. Worse still was the homemade Patch.V2. He only had to flex his fingers for the chair to move around on his intention. Thankfully, none of the construction workers could hear anything due to Jarold and the small vacuum he created.

"The bus should be here in a few moments. Until then, Ark, continue what you were saying." Orsche leaned forward just a little bit to get some better audio.

"...Okay. So after I drew in the third image for that recurring dream, I had another nightmare. I didn't write it down since it only happened once, but..." Alize pressed the forward-most gem on his armrest and circled the benches for a while

"That's incredible..." Verzas' eyes sparkled.

"It was, but I didn't think it was too important since I had another dream that repeated itself for a few weeks. I wrote that one down, the one where I ended up as merchandise in the Corridor." Alize was not prepared for the bombardment of hugs and kisses that came.

"I'm so proud of you." Verza practically jumped with joy, but her face completely dropped as her words turned to sharp and cold knives.

"Name the pigs that will hurt you, the lazy cows that stole your work, and the cretins that will abduct you if you can. I'll make sure they vanish by the end of tomorrow." Verza sneered toward some imaginary scenario and growled out her command as she prepared to go on a hunt because of a nightmare her son had once.

"I agree, Ark. Do you have any names or locations associated with these careless officials and criminals? Your journals, decoded and not, do not seem to possess such information. If you remember anything more, It would be best if you tell us so that your mother and I could discreetly remove the waste from this world." Orsche nodded with a refined air that complimented his dress but the man's rough and furious features matched his mothers wrinkle for wrinkles.

"Hey, adults whom I love and adore so much. Can the two of you calm down for more than a minute? This is why I didn't write everything down and kept the weirder and weirder things to myself." Alize sighed and gripped the bridge of his nose in the recesses of his mind.

"Mom, Dad. It's like the two of you keep selectively forgetting that we are heading to the city to confirm if we need to be more cautious of the journals that I wrote. It's enough that I remember the names of what I should probably avoid." Alize squeezed his mom's hand and scoffed at his dad for getting caught in the atmosphere several times.

"You're right, my little handsome baby boy. I love you so much, smarty pants." An onslaught of kisses bombed the poor kid's forehead and cheeks.

"I'm not telling you, Mom. You just said that I need to start handling my Affix by myself." Alize blushed and motioned toward his father.

"What? I can't give my cutest baby ever some kisses?"

Verza harrumphed and pressed her advantage with the ferocity of an ambush in the dead of night. I.e., she stood up and grabbed Alize's P.A.T.C.H. and stopped him from hovering around.

"How dare you whistle as if you can't see this. You traitor. I will remember this." Fortunately, he only had to endure for a minute or so. The thundering of drums boomed in the distance. On the singularly paved highway through the woods, a 6 meter tall eight-legged horse pounded against the smoothed-out stone highway and effortlessly dragged a similarly massive but hovering double-decker trolley behind it. A steersman pulled on the reins and brought the beast to a complete stop in front of the glass box. Interestingly enough, the coachman sat in a small cab that was fashioned to the top of a similar saddle instead of driving from the bus.

"Incredible. It still gets me every single time that such a mega fauna really exist outside of the Sim." A smile naturally bloomed on the boy's face underneath the bandages while Ors paid the toll on behalf of their little family.

Alize, not expecting it, received three apple-sized beige cubes from Verza and grinned cheek to cheek as he observed this behemoth of a horse. The gentle giant lowered its muzzle, which created a dark box around Alize as the creature's blinders hovered just millimeters off the floor. Alize raised his hand with the apple-sized sugar cubes and watched as the horse's massive tongue unwrapped into arm-width tendrils. Before he knew it, the family walked to the back door and occupied the entire back row on the first layer of the floating vehicle.

Most of the other passengers opted to take a decently sized tube up to the second layer from the look and sound of it.

A bitterness and jealousy filled his heart for the laughing kids on the second level, but instead of feeding into his disappointment, the boy turned inward.

"I should work on another spell. [Shroud] pathway spells are definitely at the top of my list now considering the possible shift in my profile. My next venture should be a memory stimulation or overall buff spell, and after that, a sensory spell. Or reverse that order. The only issue I am running into is what exactly my profile..." Alize stared out the window and tuned out any distractions. Formulas and words floated just on the window's surface as he muttered with every exhale. His working fingers constantly drew on his lap.

"Ark..." Verza turned towards her baby, waiting to hear more about the nightmares and details that were not written in his journals, but the bus lurched forward with a resounding neigh.

"He looks just like you." Verza squeezed Or's hand and moved a few strands of Alize's hair behind his long ears. They both noticed that their boy muttered nothing that even remotely sounded like words and intermittently chuckled. The thundering of hooves almost immediately turned into a thrum as the horse turned into an invisible and inaudible gale force. The only reminder that there was a lumbering beast pulling the vehicle was the saddle cab that floated just above and in front of the trolley.

"I've been thinking about that."

"About?"

"Ark. The journals. Mourra or someone who has an invested interest in ensuring that we and our son know what the curse is doing. It's weird. Odd. And a bit too coincidental." Ors frowned.

"Obviously, get to the point." Verza rolled her eyes and squeezed his hand.

"Well, we know Mourra. We know that this has its interference written all over it. I think it's a smokescreen." Ors noticed a significant lack of response from his son, paused his comments upon seeing the boy's ear twitch.

"Yeah. That's why we are going to check if things are still the same, isn't it?"

"Verza. Phew. Alright. Don't you remember those nights when he would wake up screaming, or when we had to wake him up because he was begging for help? Mourra is an asshole, but he is not a torturer." Ors reasoned.

"I get it, Raq." Verza gave Alize a big hug and despite his blank eyes and demonically whispered chant, he returned the affectionate gesture.

"Mom, I'm in the middle of. Ha, I'll just enjoy this for now." The kid let his spell crafting fall apart as he leaned into the hug.

"I can really see where I get my constant worrying and overthinking from." Alize exhaled with a musical note embedded within it.

"You heard all that?" Ors turned away with a hand on his mouth and muttered something along the lines of "He's just like his mother, acting dumb to catch a big fish", which earned him a glare and an elbow to the ribs.

"I'm not deaf, and you're both sitting right next to me, so of course I heard you two talking. I'm surprised you three didn't cut me off from listening altogether." Alize shook his head.

"So am I right to assume that your mother and I die in one of your future events?"

Orsche did not let himself get distracted and burrowed holes into his son's pupils.

"Haa, Dad, you think too much. I can not recall such a nightmare or dream, but if it happens to come up as part of a future event, I will let you know."

Alize put his hand out to shake on it, but Orsche simply snorted and looked away. The same snake-oil salesman grin bloomed across the boy's face.

1.10 An Old Haunt

Ors buried his face on the cool window opposite his son and instantly fogged up the glass with his body heat. He locked his fingers with Verza's. She and Alize then turned the conversation onto something else since Jarrolds Vacuum of Sound didn't let anything important slip out from their unit. In fact, the old Fae created an entirely different and mundane chatter using distortions and tricks to clip the family's voices. In that manner, anyone who wanted to listen in could, only to find a completely normal family.

Thus, to give Jarold the sound bites needed to craft a convincing illusion, Verza shared stories of her past with and without Orsche, while Alize shared more of the details about the dreams he wrote down in the journals. It was like he had written a game guide and was now having an interview about the highlights and difficulties behind creating it. Verza gasped and laughed with the lows and highs, as did Alize. He felt more than stunned listening to what his mother had accomplished before she met the Scholar Raquelidrel. His jaw dropped. The juxtaposition between the gruesome details behind the prim and proper reports that his dad gave him to study in his own time just couldn't be remedied in his mind.

"That's insane, Mom. I didn't know the southern-border conflict was so bad already." Alize had no choice but to cover his mouth to control an involuntary gasp. Interestingly enough, despite all the information being moved around, the Affix did not move. The Duplicator was one of the few loopholes around a curse. It was an arcane tool that, as the name implied, duplicated his consciousness, body, and soul. All the information that the duplicant was processing would then be sent through and stored in hidden relays in the event that his double perished or exited the range of the duplicator.

The loophole in Alize's case was that the doppel counted as a completely separate entity despite possessing the exact same everything as him. Of course, the Affix attempted to remedy and patch that problem several times. Alize now understood that the moments were purposeful attempts by his parents to have him deal with issues on his own.

"Yeah. Last I heard, the Crown Scale officially involved themselves in the conflict. Hmm, I saw the Isles being featured in one of your major events, so I brought up this story. You are supposed to get involved when you are older, right?"

"I believe so, I think." Alize blinked a few times and went quiet.

"Are you going to share what you left out of the books?"

"I don't remember details specifically enough to say more than what I wrote." Alize lied straight to his mom with the face of an angel. She smelled the bullshit from a mile away and appeared to be on the brink of exploding when Jarold said something that Alize was not privy to.

"Were you at least able to get into a lucid state and project yourself?"

"I was."

"Good. I remember that you wrote down being a Senior Survey officer in your dream. Do you recall that at least?"

"*Yes, actually.*"

"Then, did you happen to see the topographical data on the movements of our military or the enemy's? What about our responses? What tactics did the generals and our Queen employ? Which ones worked and didn't?" Verza leaned in.

"*Well...*" Alize readied the info but was cut off by a booming whinny and the sudden crushing clamber of hoof steps that followed.

"OLD-CHUCK SAYS IT'S TWO STOPS UNTIL GRAND HEYDEN CENTRAL. ALL PASSENGERS NOT GETTING OFF THEN, PLEASE PREPARE TO DEPART AT WEST BLUE-PIT RING STATION ON OUR NEXT STOP OR SOUTH-MINDEN IN THE FOLLOWING. IF YOU ARE GOING TO ANOTHER LOCATION, PLEASE FOLLOW THE EXIT SIGNS TO OUR TRANSFER KIOSKS LOCATED NEAR EACH TRANSIT HUB." The coachman roared above the screaming wind outside of the bus and shared the news with all the passengers. Though shared may be an overstatement, as the driver's words came out like a garbled underwater mess.

The distraction was welcome, Alize internally admitted. The lower level filled up quite a bit by now with passengers heading into the city from all kinds of villages and small towns. Most people avoided the back when they saw Alize in such a luxurious hover chair.

"If we get some maps of the southern Isles leading to the Crown State, I can draw up some formations based on what I remember seeing and experiencing." Alize whispered as a precaution, the strangers that looked in his direction made him feel awkward about speaking so publically. Her eyebrows shot up and down in thought. Orsche sighed just about as suddenly as the call broke the silence beyond Jarold's barrier.

"How does everything end down there exactly, if you don't mind my asking? Considering the next few events in that cluster of time, I assume that you dreamed of something related to the final moments of the conflict?"

Ors noticed his son's expression and Verzas' thoughtfulness and spoke out since she seemed immersed in playing some sort of chess in her mind. Alize frowned since it was like being told the ending of a movie but relented in the end since his father's side glance seemed more of a causal order rather than a question.

"We lost the war before it even began, and spectacularly at that. And before you ask for details, I only know what I experienced and reported and what I recovered from some archives in a later nightmare that I had about being a librarian." Alize put a hand up to defend himself from his mother's questioning gaze.

"What happened?" she hissed.

"Well, we found that there was an issue with our communication with the Crown Scale, so a few scholars were chosen by the Scholar's guild master and sent to reestablish and confirm the status of an alliance with the Crown state. All I know is that on our way down, the enemy simply waltzed through our borders after swiftly routing, killing, and turning all the soldiers throughout the Isles. The move was so brilliantly executed that most tacticians couldn't figure out how anyone managed to maneuver such a large scale and thorough attack until it was all over. The capital as well, everyone was either killed or turned into an undead before the day's end. My team and I were stranded in the Republic beyond the Crown State, but we quickly fell apart due to internal struggles. Wait, I'm pretty sure that I told you two about this nightmare a while ago. Mom, you had me run through nearly ten thousand simulated

scenarios where I was stranded behind enemy lines." Alize watched his mother tremble with clenched fists.

"There are almost one million troops currently stationed on the southern border across the Territories and the RIGS. When I last saw the numbers, there were at least eight thousand fleets of no less than one hundred ships headed by several dozen admirals." Veza ignored her son's displeasure and informed Orsche of what she knew.

"You did tell us, but you were too young to recognize, understand, or specify what conflict you were involved with. It's why I doubled down on you learning more about current events and stopped focusing on history before The Principal Era." Orsche tapped a finger on his armrest and rolled his forehead against the cool glass with a rigid expression plastered across his face. It was Verza's turn to clench her man's fingers as any plans in her mind suddenly went up in flames.

"Your father's right. If I had known that your event was related to the whole war and not just a battle. Are you sure that we lost?"

Verza struggled to lower her voice as she confirmed the matter a third time.

"*I only know what I experienced in the nightmares and in the Sims that Mom and you prepared,*" Alize said. A lot of the passengers, by this point, waited at the front of the bus since it would only take a minute or two in a straight shot toward the capital. Verza and Ors didn't notice since they were stuck in a stupor, but Alize did.

"ONE PICKUP AT WEST BLU-PIT. IT LOOKS LIKE WE ARE GOING TO HAVE TO STOP FOR A BIT FOLKS." The coachman did his best to roar above the wind, but all anyone got was a slightly garbled whisper.

"*Is there someone at this stop? People don't usually get on the trolley at the second or third to last stop.*" Alize raised an eyebrow at the situation. It was odd. Only one man got on the bus at the third-to-last stop. And true to the unspoken rule of the locals, the man apologized for his actions as everyone cursed and booed at him.

"Sorry, everyone. I am in a rush to pick up a time-sensitive package; otherwise, I would have just walked it." The man tipped his triangular yellow hat and flashed a genuine smile that made his silver tooth glisten in the shimmering light of the fluorescent lighting.

"*No way. This is too much of a coincidence.*" Alize stared at the man with wide eyes. Ors just happened to catch his son's momentary slip in expression despite the back and forth heated conversation he and Verza found themselves in.

"Are you okay, Ark? Is that the guy that you drew?" Ors asked in hushed tones.

Verza followed her son's gaze to the well-dressed, suede-gloved man in an ostentatious yellow and green suit. If one looked at him, they would see riches, money, power, status, and a slyness that reminded one of a fox in a henhouse, maybe because he had the head of a fox and a bushy dark red tail.

"*I'm not sure if it's him but...,*" Alize rubbed his chin and whispered back.

"No, he's not the doctor I wrote about, but I definitely remember his outfit. He was a minor character in the nightmare, but I saw him talking with the quack during my recovery period. He told you two something one of the days before we left the doctor's place. I'm not sure what it was because of all the pain medication, but you both looked upset. Well, upset in the way that you are trying to hide it, but Mom seemed more angry with you than with what he said." Alize tried to remember a few more things, but the memory was covered in too much fog.

"*Tch. I'll just have to give up. I don't remember enough about this guy to make any judgment calls. This is why magic is unfair; other people in my situation would just use a spell to instantly clear up the confusion. I need to figure something out soon."*

"How upset do you think I was, if you were to give a guess?"

Ors put a finger on his chin.

"More than when I broke your Noridian Plate but less than when I accidentally stepped on your one of a kind Ithacan howling bear tapestry," Alize said.

"Hm. He's probably associated with the... uh..." Ors looked at his love and thought of his next few words because of how she looked at him.

"Ahem. The guy must be a local fixer or an informant for the Veilseam." Orsche smiled unevenly.

"Not the Reclaimers?"

Verza narrowed her eyes.

"Not the Guild, my love." Ors wiped his sweat.

"Really?" Verza poked his thigh.

"I would..." Orsche began to speak, but Alize beat him to the punch.

"Do you think we could head over the Veilseam since you promised to get me on the imperial registry?"

Alize whispered. Verza squeezed Ors thigh with such force his face reddened.

"You want me to, Haa, what? I don't even know where something like that would be." Orsche avoided Verza's piercing gaze and sucked in a mouthful of cold air.

"Haa, payback." He cleared his throat and grabbed his mom's free hand.

"The Veilseam is not as bad as you think it is, Mom. From what I've learned, it actually funds many of the world's humanitarian efforts.

The lesser-lived species need something to protect their interests after all."

"I know." Verza smiled at her darling baby boy and let go of Or's leg. She patted it a few times with an odd glint in her eyes.

"Most countries have made that market illegal because it directly clashes with the regulations that mostly independent nations set regarding the distribution and use of magical and technological developments. Jordaine is different from other countries on Haven, so I have no issue with the Veilseam at the moment." Verza shrugged.

"Overall, I agree with you that the market is good, but that's only when powerful individuals and criminals are not the ones who have established the Veilseam." Verza's carefree smile slowly faded. She remembered a time when the vultures of Havens Capital City swooped in and locked life-saving knowledge behind the words, "danger to the common folk" and "we need to protect the interests of the heroes that seek to protect our fair citizens."

"I'm okay with you using your father's connections, but do not go into a market that has not been established by the Empire. It's very easy to get involved with the wrong kind of business with the worst kinds of people," Verza warned her son.

"*I understand, Mom.*" Alize kept his eye on the smartly dressed man and tried to pierce through the guy's presentable air of confidence.

"As for you, do you know that guy?"

"Hm?"

"Do you know him?"

"You really put me on the spot, my love." Ors scratched his head.

"No. I don't. If he were part of the Reclaimers, he would have noticed my beard right away, which led me to the conclusion that he is either a local Fixer or an informant for the market."

"You still aren't answering me."

"What do you mean? I just did."

"Don't start."

"Ha. He doesn't strike me as someone with a criminal despite the look. If anything, he could be from Drift or the Corridor since I'm sure that I would have heard about someone dressed like that in Rest." Orsche narrowed his eyes and focused on the yellow suited man as though he were a hawk glancing at a mouse in a field. The guy fidgeted and looked around to no avail.

Verza stood up, blocked his view of Orsche, and unlocked Alize's wheels. The bus slowed as the massive horse trotted toward the final stop.

"ALL DEPART. SAY HELLO TO HEYDENS REST. FOR YOU FIRST TIMERS, I SUGGEST TAKING A GRAND TOUR AND END YOUR DAY WITH A VISIT TO OUR SISTER CITY ACROSS THE WAY. EXELDRIFT MAY NOT BE AS STUNNING AS OUR REST, BUT IS HAS ITS CHARM. FOR ALL THOSE TRANSFERING ONTO THE RETURN TRIP..." The coachman gasped for so much air everyone else felt lightheaded.

"PLEASE GIVE OUR STABLE HANDS AN HOUR TO TAKE CARE OF OUR LOVELY DRIVER. PLEASE SEAT YOURSELVES AT OUR COMPLEMENTARY WAITING LOCALS DIRECTLY TO THE LEFT OF OUR DROP OFF. I SUGGEST EATING AT BENGALS PIZZERIA ACROSS THE STREET, THE ONE WITH THE RED AND GREEN STRIPES NOT ORANGE AND BLUE, THEY SELL CARDBOARD. AND GET A NICE DESSERT OVER ON 1ST AND RICHARD BOULEVARD. CARELLI'S SNACK SHOP, YOU GOTTA GO THROUGH THE SECOND ALLEY BUT I PROMISE YOU, IT'S WORTH IT. PLEASE, BE ON YOUR WAY AND HAVE A RESTFUL DAY."

The trolley pulled to a complete stop, and everyone, including the Kaverz family, departed rather quickly to avoid foot traffic and body congestion. On that note, finally being in the city reminded him of his first and oldest friend.

"I know that we really don't have the time, but can we stop by Wynn's house? She must feel terrible or responsible about what happened to me."

"We can. Once you're all better first, we don't want to make her feel responsible if she sees you like this." Verza nodded and passed Alize over to Ors, so she could head off and get the supplies that she wanted for the homestead.

"One minute. Jarold, stay with them. I don't care how you feel about it. Stay." She practically vanished from her spot, the only sign of her existence being a small trembling circle of magic on the floor that remained for a full two seconds before it fully faded.

"Alrighty then. We can follow that Vonouer guy in the yellow or we can chase a lead that I have been thinking about."

"What's your lead?"

"I was talking to the fart, Ark."

"Oh. My bad."

"No, don't worry about it. The old bag is gonna talk to himself for a while." Orsche leaned in and whispered to Alize as Jarold weighed the options seriously.

"Let's do my thing."

"Okay."

"First things first, I would bring you somewhere safe, right?"

"Details help."

"Valid. Ahem. If you hadn't chosen to save yourself by casting, the situation would be bad enough for me to act before your mother got home. Timeframe-wise?"

"Yeah, I guess?"

"Got it..." He nodded and checked his nonexistent watch.

"Then I would look around and use any means necessary to find someone to properly heal you. Not an abby and not a hospital, but something near enough." Ors exhaled deeply and put himself in the mental space needed to bring Verza to one of his few sanctuaries as a scholar.

"If your mom asks, we stumbled upon it completely by accident." An almost feral expression bloomed across his face.

"About?"

"You'll see. Gassy, let's go." Alize tried his best to follow along in the narrative, but things moved so fast that he couldn't even breathe with the rapid speed of Orsche's teleportations through the city. Seconds, maybe minutes later, and suddenly, something stood out against the backdrop of packed city streets.

"*Why is no one going into that children's bookshop?*"

"Can you see it?"

Ors rejoined the world of the mentally sane and smiled when he noticed his son could see their objective

"The building has [Shroud] pathway spells built into the very foundation. You can't see the shop unless you know the name of the establishment or the location of the building beforehand. Children sometimes break through the illusion thanks to their unestablished profiles and insane imaginations, but it doesn't exactly cater to the demographic." Ors explained with as much pomp as he could muster.

"*This is a voided market. A shop that shouldn't exist. I never would have guessed that it could look so* normal." Alize locked onto the shop's front window and scanned over a display of mostly unassuming children's books and vintage-looking stuffed animals and puppets. Nothing stood out until he went over the display a second time.

"No way. It cannot be this easy! Even the Affix would not make it this easy." He locked onto a teddy bear holding a tiny scroll. It wore a little green scarf and a little graduate cap with a tassel, but what stood out and grabbed his attention was a disproportionately large pair of glasses. Alize's memory instantly screamed and matched those glasses to the supposed relic that he left out of his dream journals since it struck him more as a fantasy than something plausible.

"We should go in and look around." Alize raised his voice very specifically but ultimately avoided staring at the initializing relic.

"Look around where?"

Verza leaned over his shoulder with a confused but ultimately supportive smile. Jarold whizzed around at her back with a huff and puff that devolved into a howl around just Orsche's ears.

"That building."

"I don't see anything there other than a garden plot." Her confusion shifted to one of muted accusations as she turned toward her man.

"Right, it says Veiled Emporium: Bookshop and Knick Knacks." The instant the title came from his mouth, Verza's brain jolted and perceived the little shop.

"Huh. I wonder what that is?"

"It's a Void Market."

"Oh, really?"

"Yeah. Apparently, Dad knew the location." Alize smirked villainously as Jarold seized up and vanished with the breeze. The old Sylph was smart enough not to get caught in the crossfire and immediately returned to placing his full focus on the barrier that he placed around Alize at all times.

"Is that so?"

"What is it? What's wrong with my dearest heart? Is it the bags? Are they too heavy? Please let me." Ors stopped covering his ears with a jaunty and worried little hop to his step as he waved the bags clear away from Verza, storing them in some magical tool that he kept on his person.

"Hmm." She didn't press the withholding of information and pushed her son across the street.

"I think the bear in the window is wearing what we are looking for." Alize informed his mother while choking back a laugh. Ors stomped about in silence behind the family unit and made a half-joking gesture that he would get back at his son.

"The bear? Really? What's so important about it?"

"I believe Ark was pointing out the material composition of its..." Ors perked up, pulled out a rubber chicken from inside of his coat and was ready to return the joke but paused in the middle of the road to getting a good look at the stuffed toy.

"Glasses." Ors flashed through his own mental library, but it was a near-instant perusal that practically blew his jaw off its hinges.

"We have to get into that shop now." Ors attempted to rush across the street, but there were far too many people blocking the magically domed walkway that flashed a gentle reminder of "No Casting while Crossing". Even more so, the roads to either side were a black blur of motion as beasts, cars, carriages, and all manner of oddly shaped and floating vehicles flew by at the speed of sound.

"What was the point of speeding ahead when you were still caught having to wait? This is why I didn't tell you what we were looking for." Alize waved to the strangers that were drawn to his father's running. The barrier that Jarold set up was briefly shattered by Orsche's attempt to depart.

"But if that's..." Orsche whispered.

"It most likely is." Alize cut his father off.

"There are only five or six others in that kind of condition in the entire universe. Most of which are in the hands of Archons or older members of the Pantheon. Oh, man. The rarity and likelihood of finding one of those, if it exists, is just like this? The chances are just," the scruffy man continued.

"*Astronomical. I know.*" Alize finished his statement since he understood his dad's level of excitement.

"What do you two think the glasses are? Also, the stranger you pointed out on the bus is about to go into the shop. Did you three follow him here?" Verza tapped her boys on their shoulders and visibly got less angry at Ors.

"Something potentially dangerous and no? Something extremely precious, and yes." Alize and Orsche said different things at the same time but very quickly, their viewpoints painted a clear picture of the event that was about to unfold.

"Ah, so is it bad that it was just pulled from the window?"

Verza smacked Orsche on the back of his head as lightly as she possibly could to express her upset in a playful manner, then pointed toward a now empty pedestal.

"*Dad. Keep an eye on him. Don't let him buy anything. And probably mom. I'm not sure. I do think this all looks a bit too suspiciously timed.*" Alize blinked and squinted his eyes to get a better look at the person who grabbed the bear, but the inside of the shop was suddenly pulled into a mystical darkness. Orsche, abandoning the law, flickered across the road and rushed into the shop. Verza cracked her neck and walked Alize across, but her eyes darted and flashed with magic as she scanned each and every face in the crowd to make sure that no one noticed the Ors-shaped hole in the barrier. A fixture that protected the pedestrians from vehicles and animals traveling at hundreds of kilometers within city limits.

"This is all very concerning. Keep holding on to your suspicions until we are back home, Ark. I do not see anyone observing us, and Jarold also cannot sense anyone hiding around in the area, but still." Verza frowned.

2.1 One Bear to Rule Them All

"Gregory. I'm here for a pickup." The well-dressed man in a yellow and green pinstripe suit waved toward an older gentleman who wore a rather elaborate monocle that possessed a length on par with a pocket telescope. This white-haired man behind the desk did not look up at all.

"Business or personal?"

The shopkeeper wiped down a small, circular, metal-rimmed piece of glass and used a tower of small, pinpoint-sized clamps and pliers to hold several of its crystalline gears and pins. Underneath this tessellating magnifying was an exposed, old, and loved watch with machinery the size of grains of sand.

"Personal. But while you're at it, I'm also looking for a gift to congratulate a coworker on being a new father. Also, I would like to place an order for two older kids if you have anything that caters to the youth of this year." The man in the yellow pinstripes smiled and perused the aisles without any particular focus. He tipped his hat toward the only other customer in the shop, which earned him a grumble and side-eye. Without looking, the shopkeeper retrieved a box from a shelf underneath the counter with a single hand and twisted some dials on the tower that he worked on. Slowly, the miniature hands moved and twisted some of the mechanisms, setting a soft and rhythmic click into motion.

"Everything should be in order. As for your second and final requests, keep doing as you are and you may find something." The shopkeeper sighed, readjusted his topping tool, and continued his delicate work. The old shopkeeper could see the story of this old mundane watch, as clearly as reading a book, and it was a tale of heartbreak and sorrow.

"All of this stuff is a bit..." The suited man pulled out a stuffed carrot and tapped its fake plastic smile with the back of his finger.

"Do you have anything cuter than this? All the stuffed animals and baby toys are a bit weird, and the older items are so old that my grandparents used to play with this stuff as children." The suited man returned the carrot and cringed away from a stuffed multicolored llama that stared at him everywhere he moved.

"Ev'thing 'ere is handcrafted. Unique in its beauty. Passed down from spit to kit. Respect their survival. To ask the shop if there is anything cute just means you can't appreciate the value of individuality." The other customer, an old balding man who reeked of alcohol, pressed the tip of his cane against the suit's arm and pushed him aside. The old man smacked his dry lips and placed a few toys and puzzles on the countertop. The llama and carrot being among the rabble.

"Pay that fool no mind. A gaudy bastard li'im don'nae possess a half wit. Hmph." The old man waited for the shopkeeper to package up his items in a small box from underneath the counter and then walked out of the store with an upturned nose.

"Haa. That old drunk must be off his medication." The yellow-suited man dusted off his arm with a hopeless smile but ultimately, he approached the shopkeeper after another quick survey around the room.

"Yeah, I can't find anything just right, Greg. Do you have any suggestions?"

The suit bent down and viewed the plethora of tiny contraptions and pieces of jewelry that were locked behind glass cases next to the shopkeeper's desk.

One tick at a time, Gregory replaced and altered rusted cogs and springs and put them back into the small pocket watch. The small disk-like coins on the table that the old man left completely eluded the shopkeeper as they rumbled and overlapped in a series of twinkling lights. A single heptacontagon ring with exactly one notch in each of its sides spun and clattered to a stop.

"I will not pick or suggest anything for a customer, especially when there is sentiment behind the supposed gift. You will either need to take your order as is, find an item, or go to another location that is better stocked with gifts for newborns, infants, and, I am assuming, children or young adults." Gregory's even voice and lack of attention on the yellow-suited man made him drop his head with a sigh.

"Come on, man. You're right, but still. What am I going to do? My friend is on his way to meet me right now. I'm already pretty much out of time since he will leave if I am not here." The suit frowned. A third, unwilling, pass around the shop proved just as ineffective as the first two. In fact, he was even less hopeful seeing as how there was an insane abundance of wood-carved dolls in ancient clothing and stuffed animals that were full of raggedy patches, teeth, and real hair or fur.

"Leave now and return as quickly as you can then. If you need a recommendation, you'll find the best toys for babies three doors down. Hmm, then again, the lines would be long considering the time of day." The shopkeeper slowly lowered the last cog. All that remained was sliding and locking the glass panel in place and tightening the shell. Thumping like a heart, the watch's droning clockwork resounded like music to one ear.

"I can't do that, Greg. It would mean more if the item I gave was one of a kind. That's why I want to get something here..." The suit tipped his hat in thought.

"Oh yeah. There was a bear in the window. The display. Is that little guy for sale?" The man clapped his gloved hands and waited for the shopkeeper to respond.

"You noticed, huh? If the bear tears or gets dirty in any way, remind your friend to bring it back so I can repair it. No charge for the service, by the way." The shopkeeper twisted the last bolt on the watch and placed it on a velvet stand that he pulled out from under the desk. With a practiced motion, Gregory took off his white gloves, placed the ring that the old man left onto a small black circle embedded in the desk, and personally grabbed the bear from its stand. After that, Gregory passed box after box behind his desk and began searching for the best package to store the teddy bear and its accessories. After he found one, another search began. This time, the box selection revolved around retrieving Dean's order.

"Thanks, Gregory. I'll make sure to let my friend know. Just a heads up though, he will probably want to stop by and thank you." The suit rubbed the back of his head as he pulled out a wallet to purchase the items he was sent for. Interestingly enough, the wallet only held three pouches. The first was an embedded silver ring with a floating mystical number on the inside of it. Another pouch was ribbed and held several dozen glowing sticks the size of sewing needles in an upright position. The third showed a metallic ID card with the words Imperial Profile on the top left and some specific details on the person known as Dean Haversham.

"How much?" The suit hovered over his wallet.

"33 thousand for your personal matter. Two hundred and 20 thousand for the watch. 22 thousand and five hundred for the bear." Gregory spoke with an even and unpressured expression, retrieving packing peanuts from underneath his countertop.

"Hold on, the bear costs that much?"

"The bear predates the appearance of all, if not most of the Archons. I have kept it from unraveling for more millennia than you could feasibly grasp, so yes. Such a vintage toy is expensive. If you cannot afford it." Gregory moved to place the toy back on the display, but Dean held up a hand.

"No. I will. Ha, I'll buy it. Hmm. That old guy who was just in here must have been a pretty important figure then, huh? To get away with buying things in here with just links, I mean." The suit flicked his wrist and with a smooth motion, he grabbed two golden toothpicks, seven silver needles, five bronze hair thin and finger length sticks that he then placed on the desk.

"Thankfully, I pooled a lot of my wrapped-up assets before coming here. Ha, but this is still quite a blow to my finances. Is there any chance you could give me a family discount or something." Dean tried to laugh but as Gregory picked up the Quill and placed them on a finger-sized black bar next to the circle without any emotions, he couldn't help but tear up. The emotional turmoil was actually so bad that he didn't notice that a long-eared man with a neatly managed beard and ruffled white coat walked in and practically breathed down his neck.

"Hello there." In a very unsettling manner, the scruffy-looking man hung his head over Dean's shoulder with a smile. Dean's tears instantly stopped in their tracks as he slowly turned his head.

"Hey." The suit returned a friendly gesture.

"Are you still buying things, or can I go ahead?"

The scruffy-looking man tilted his head in an almost possessed manner that made Dean's entire body lock up. If one could hear his thoughts, one would hear, "*I didn't hear this man come in at all. How did he walk in without the bell going off, even Gregory didn't say anything?*"

"Oh, yeah. No problem. I already got what I came for. I'm just waiting for it to be packed up." Dean stepped to the side and motioned forward with a slightly bowed head. Reflexively, he retracted his hand motion the second he noticed a subconscious tremble.

"Thank you, man." The spiffy but awkward-looking man nodded, then approached the counter.

"I'm sorry to interrupt, but I walked by here with my wife and son, and he saw something in the window that he begged for." The scruffy man maintained his smile even as the shopkeeper frowned at him.

"What was it that your son saw?"

The shopkeeper momentarily paused his work and used a pen to write something invisible on the snow-white mat situated on the middle of the countertop. The bear's glasses reflected the scruffy man's warm smile and snake-like eyes.

"I don't mean to be a bother, but it was a stuffed bear in the window. I just went over to check, but it's not there now, though. I was hoping to see if I could buy it or something similar if it's not available." Beneath the beard, pearly whites flashed.

"Talk to the customer who already bought it." Gregory used his chin, but it was adequate enough to make the guy turn toward Dean with a charismatic smile and raised eyebrow.

"You bought it already?" Orsche's voice shot up a few octaves to lighten the mood, but Dean shivered and began to sweat like a thief caught red-handed.

"I'm sorry, sir. I just bought it as a present for a friend's kid." Dean bowed his head even deeper and did everything possible to shorten himself.

"Oh, thank you for telling me. I hope your friend's kid loves it. I'll have to find something else at the store down the street." Ors walked away with a sullen expression. Gregory grumbled but returned to his work. A mysterious and thick rectangular package was placed on the table along with a black and gold velvet case for the watch. The bear was slowly lowered into its own box, scroll and glasses safely secured in packaging peanuts when...

"You know. I knew it would end up like this. I told my boy, but you know what he told me?"

Ors turned toward Dean before reaching the front door.

"What?"

"My son told me, 'Daddy. I'm scared. I don't want to see the doctor. What if I don't wake up?' Oh, when I tell you my heart broke, I couldn't stop crying." Orsche held his chest and wiped a few tears from his eyes. Dean's eyebrows came together in thought. If someone could read his thoughts, they would see:

"Who the hell is this man? Gregory doesn't frown...ever. Not only that. I didn't even notice he had come in. He walked up right next to me! That's usually a death sentence, but this man didn't even attempt to use an Analyzing or Observational spell. That said, he must know who I am now. Does he want something from me? He might be looking for

*information. It's my day off, but I can't help but notice he's emphasizing the words **son** and **doctor**. Does he need a doctor, or does he want to get his hands on a kid? I'll report to the Guardians if it's the latter. For now, let's try to get more information."* Dean fixed the brim of his hat and raised his head with determination despite the formless pressure that exuded from both ends of the shop.

"A doctor? Why is your kid scared of not waking up?"

Dean's entire demeanor shifted as he ran through names, connections, friends, and all manner of associates. He ran into situations like this all the time considering his profession. Freak meetings, chance encounters, odd gatherings—none of it was weird for him at this point; rather, it was expected. Just as it was expected of him to have answers to all sorts of questions or problems.

"Yeah. My boy was out playing with a friend and got really hurt. The wife and I have been looking for someone to take care of him, but it's been difficult to find someone who won't ask questions and will just do the work. He's such a scared and frail boy. Thankfully, my family has been hoarding arcanum for generations, so we have managed to control his physical deterioration, but if we do not find anyone today, I fear the worst." Orsche wiped his reddened eyes. He very carefully created water near his eyes.

"Why are you here then?"

Dean got straight to the point since the severity of the situation seemed pressing. Gregory's frown and ever-present grumbling turned to jaw-dropping silence as this wonderful lack of tact from both parties turned into a dramatic soap.

"Well, I told him a story about the gods. How they would sometimes act as imaginary friends to protect good little boys and girls from harm and evil..." Dean tilted his head ever so slightly, seeing as how the response didn't quite answer his question.

"I told him that story before we got to Rest. Haa. Tell me why he saw the teddy in the window and brought up the story. He told me that it was one of the gods. A lonely and scared Divine Protector who needs a friend..." Orsche's lower lip quivered.

"Can you guess what he told me after that?"

"I, uh, I don't know." Dean covered his eyes with a hat. The shopkeeper leaned over the table with an even deeper frown.

"I asked him to explain, to tell me why he was so scared and worried. My precious little boy. He said, 'Daddy, Mommy. I am scared. I know we have to see a doctor because I'm not well. I know it, but I don't want to be alone. Mr. Teddy told me I don't have to be scared of being alone because he is all by himself and it's not so bad. He said he will protect me so I can be with you two forever so even if he has to be alone, I don't have to be'. My little boy cried because the teddy in your window looked all alone. How could I, as his father, not save the teddy that told my boy not to be scared?"

Ors laid it on thick as he broke down into hiccuping sobs.

"My good sir." Dean looked up toward the sky and held the bridge of his nose.

"That is just..." Gregory exhaled with a look of absolute denial. A chime brought all three men back to reality.

"Daddy. Why did you run into the store all of a sudden? You scared me and Mommy even more." Alize wore his biggest and most innocent expression as Verza pushed him through the shop's threshold. Of course, Verza could hear what was going on inside the store. Her well-trained senses simply didn't allow her not to know what was going on in her surroundings. Dean, already on the brink of crying, stared at the boy's wheelchair, tightly bound figure, and simply couldn't handle it anymore. Like a broken dam, the water simply rushed down his face without end.

"I know a doctor. Here. Greg, I'll buy something else later. Here you go, kid..." The suit slammed his hand on the table and ripped the teddy box from the shopkeeper's hands. In a split second, the man knelt beside Alize's chair and gave him the toy and its accessories.

"I, uh, your dad here..." Dean spotted Verza's piercing gaze and felt as though a mountain had suddenly been dropped on his shoulders.

"Your dad is a friend of mine, kid. He's a very cool and nice guy. Right..." Dean stood up and wrapped his arm around Orsche's neck and held out his hand. Ors winked at Verza and then addressed Dean.

"You know my name is Zaqiel. Come on, bud, stop messing about." Ors shook his hand with a smile.

"Zaq-man. Yeah, you know I'm messing with you. Hey kid, you better take care of your buddy there. Your dad saved him just for you..." The suit patted Ors on the chest with a smile, then retrieved the watch and package from the shopkeeper.

"Wait a bit, Zaq. I'll be back with my doctor friend. We can take care of everything, alright?"

Dean tipped his hat with a grin and squeezed past Verza with a blanched expression and a shudder.

"That's too much, buddy. I'm already indebted to you for the gift," Ors said.

"Don't worry about it. And stop playing around, Zaq attack. You know my name is Dean. And the doctor is on me, no repayment needed. Just let me know if and when you need anything else, my good sir. I am quite handy at getting my hands on the things that people want or need." The suit named Dean waved from the door and vanished with a bright smile that put all of his canine teeth on display. His card somehow ended up in Ors, Verza, and Alize's hands.

2.2 The Empire's Eyes and Ears

Gregory packed up his tools and sat down with a rather unpleasant expression. It evoked a sense of...he was annoyed. Clear as day. His tone did not hide it in the slightest.

"I'd never thought you would never show your face around these parts, Raquelidrel. And though I don't particularly like your wanton attitude and way of handling matters..." Gregory held his temples to prevent a burst vein and scanned the trio.

"It is rather fortunate timing that you've turned up now." Gregory stared at Alize for a long moment and then sighed. He pressed a button underneath the counter without the family of three noticing. A flash of auroric light danced across the four corners of the shop, a magical multicolored luminance that was pure, glittering, and wavy in nature. It only flashed for a moment before the sound of traffic outside the store vanished. An empty space void of light or matter reflected just beyond the windows. Verza narrowed her eyes and twitched with an almost tangible killing intent as her muscles bulged and magic flared.

In a show of pure control, her skin tightened up and forced her body to be still. She did not move from her spot despite the agitation since neither of her boys looked particularly shaken by the shift in atmosphere. No, they both nodded instead, as if this scene were natural.

"I've had several requested pieces stolen as of late. Someone, something, or a group has begun to mess with matters of the Corridor and Vielseam."

"Bad news, huh?"

"In particular, Haven has become a nesting bed for shady dealings with the recent unexplained disappearance of..." Gregory drew out his words.

"The head of National Security." The shopkeeper scanned Verza several times to no avail.

"I understand why you would think I know where that madwoman is. Sadly, I'm just as, if not more, confused about how this works. I'm assuming this TOS update has something to do with me or her whereabouts."

"She is suspected of being involved with a string of Void Market thefts that have happened along established trade routes for the Vielseam." Gregory stared long and hard at the supposed family unit that graced his shop with their presence.

"I get it. You had hoped that there was some information I could sell or direct you to," Ors reasoned.

"Not me. My superiors hope that no member and customer will find us accountable for any losses that they may have, will, or might suffer due to this Robin Glove Hero."

"Hero is an interesting term to use for a bandit." Ors made a statement and let it hang in the air for a long while. Gregory's even tone and mechanical expression broke down slightly.

"The Veilseam and its affiliates have posted that they will generously compensate anyone with information regarding the thieves or the missing general." Gregory put a piece of paper on the table and waited for Ors to read and sign it.

"What's that?" Verza calmed her beating heart with a few kisses to Alize's forehead, but her eyes reactively darted to the pages as she examined every one of Gregory's actions. Orsche signed and passed it back rather quickly.

"A document saying I won't sue the Empire if my purchases don't come through from the date of signing. I will also be equivalently compensated for any losses I may suffer now and in perpetuity if such losses are explicitly related to the Market's extraordinary exposure." Orsche tapped the table a few times. He gave Gregory the look. You know, THE LOOK.

"What kind of purchases do you usually make here?" Verza narrowed her eyes.

"This and that you know. For herbs and stuff we need. Say, Gregory. If that's all you needed me to do, you should open the shop back up. It would make it very difficult for that Dean character to return with the doctor if we are cut off from the outside world." Orsche laughed a bit and waved his hand in a rather uncharacteristic way.

"If I may..." Gregory interrupted after breaking his calm almost all at once.

"You may." Verza passed her own glare to Gregory.

"I can only share a client's private information with beneficiaries of a private member's assets or individuals that would inherit any wealth or debts accrued by the customer. Forgive me, but I must ask you to refrain from asking for details unless you are registered with the empire or one of the two said specified relations." Gregory bowed his head with a very respectful smile, which earned him a nod from Verza.

"If that's the case, I am Verza Peachum. We are married, and he's the father of my son. Any of his assets are mine, so what purchases does he make here?" Verza smiled nonchalantly as she forced Ors to show his hand. A glowing white ring of magic and a red flower sigil bloomed on their joined ring fingers. As their hands separated, a thin red thread kept them tied together, which quickly turned invisible along with the rings. The shopkeeper completely ignored the throat-cutting motion that Ors made as he reached below the counter once more with a thoughtful expression.

"Well, he frequently trades information and arcanum of all levels, grades, and star rankings for top secret research and black site archeological services via the scholars guild Reclaimers, a known neo-veritas cult commonly referred to as The Reporters, and the market's own affiliated informant network. The trades and his requests include but are not limited to the exchange of blueprints, formulas, relics, herbs, and pills. His privately circulated file has him marked as an unsavory businessman but morally sound." Gregory closed an eye and spoke evenly.

"Ah. How many of those trades were within the last decade or so?" Verza asked the shopkeeper with an icy whisper behind her words.

"Several hundred, with the exact number being 45 trades of merit or status, 73 exchanges of physical goods, 432 funding or investment ventures, and 678 purchases and exchanges of documentation regarding forbidden or top secret information. Would you like that in percentages?" Gregory slowly turned his open eye to Ors, whose face drained of color faster than a lightning bolt striking.

"Yes."

"In total, the last decade's worth of activity accounts for 2.98%, rounded..." Gregory was ready to break down the spread of purchased but Ors jumped in the way.

"Haa. You crack me up. Those jokes, you..." Orsche laughed awkwardly but immediately stood in a corner upon seeing Verzas' smile and twitching eyebrows.

"Haa. That's very impressive. My husband managed to get quite a bit of vices satiated despite being on the straight and narrow. And here I thought he was only consumed by this little matter at home, haa. I'm just wondering, shop owner, how much quill and sway does my husband have to get what he wants so easily?" Verza asked with genuine interest, but her arched eyebrows and scrunched nose betrayed the intense amount of displeasure she tried to keep hidden.

"Madam Peachum, your husband over there has a uniquely high status within the Veilseam and a near-unlimited tab and savings account. As his wife and beneficiary you would have complete control over putting today's matters on his tab, going with the usual trade of equivalent goods and services, or using any matching denomination of the Haven Link or the Imperial Quill." Gregory aimed his only open eye on Verza with a smile.

"A tab! Interesting. Did you have a tab all those years ago too?" Verza connected some loose dots in her head.

"I have no idea what..." Ors reached out toward Gregory, motioning for him to stop talking but stopped upon seeing a devil on Verza's side profile.

"What to say." He once again moved to a corner of the shop, crouched and covered his ears.

"Madam Peachum, Sir Raquelidrel has maintained one of the highest balances in my records since joining the Scholars Guild approximately two hundred years ago. Which means that as a VIP member, he has possessed a direct line of communication with all markets established or partnered with the Veilseam subspace. According to the files I have access to..." Gregory pulled out a brand new illusory pen from under the counter and pressed the tip against the air where he wrote in a magical glowing text. Verza un-squinted her eyes upon feeling a small hand tug at her shirt.

"I'll stop messing with your father." Verza accepted the card Alize passed her and placed it on the table. Gregory's smile deepened as he wrote something else in the air.

"Is this man a fixer or a merchant? And where does he lie on the totem pole? What kind of information do I need to know if he's reliable enough to get a good doctor for my son?" Verza got straight to the point but frowned upon hearing Ors sob in the background. Alize chuckled to himself since his mother might know the rules, but obviously, she didn't understand the finer details of the game that the Market played with its customers.

"Maybe Dad should have explained that different questions are evaluated differently. Most trades of information are like giant games of chess where moving different pieces costs vast sums of capital. An expert could capture vital pieces of info (the king) using only a handful of pawns. With Mom asking questions so bluntly, oh man, it's like deliberately sacrificing every piece to capture the enemy king with your own. Though I guess as a former general, she just wants all the facts written out in front of her before making any assumptions or guesses. It probably also helps that it's not her money she's spending." Alize didn't see his beautifully dressed mother and her sparkling jewelry. Instead, he saw a woman with a tight bun of hair poking out of a metal helmet and gleaming armor layered atop cleanly pressed but Amazonian regalia covered in medals.

"Dean is the most notable fixer within the city of Exceldrift and has exceptional sway in the underground districts. Many locations in Rest are also local hotspots where you can find Dean in contact with local pill lords and arcanum runners. Since your..." Gregory motioned toward Orsche.

"Husband, and I'm truly embarrassed to ask, but is that official? I saw the spell myself, but for my records, the union must either be lawfully or religiously sealed." Gregory wrote some stuff down with his pen.

"I mean, it's not sanctified by any church, but it should be legally binding. In Haven, after some personal matters have settled down at least." Verza blushed and then quickly fumed with a stomp. Gregory's closed eye flashed a dim golden glow, which illuminated his surprised expression, but a moment later the light and his eyebrows lowered.

"I see. I wish you all the best in settling these troubling matters. Nobility can be such a burden at times, but I hope your ladyship can persevere." Gregory bowed his head and quickly wrote something else down in the air.

"Since your domestic partner has the premium deluxe VIP membership plus package, I can also tell you some currently available and complementary information regarding Mr. Haversham's competency. Dean is looking for powerful allies who are willing to secure the safety of an undetermined number of adventurers and heroes. There will be a joint venture concerning the Twin Cities, a monumental task related to the establishment of the 167th expedition to reclaim the Star-capped Fortress ruins to the southwest of Jordaine. The payment for joining as a member of the security detail under Dean's referral is a weekly stipend of 1000 Haven Links or 1 Imperial bronze Quill for the next decade or until the ruins in that segment of Futheredere's Crown have been completely mapped." Gregory shared the info as he wrote some stuff down in the air.

"I am also required by Imperial law to inform you that the Divine Faction and regional contingent of the Guardians are major sponsors of the expedition." Gregory checked over some invisible text and then nodded, seeing as there was nothing else he needed to share.

"Why would Dean need to hire people if the Divine faction is involved? Their connected holy order should be more than enough to secure the expedition's safety? If the Guardians are involved, does that mean the expedition is meant to be a state function? Ah, do you also have information on the skill of the doctor that Dean is fetching?" Verza paused for a moment and structured her questions based on what she could not guess.

"Dean's job specifically is to help facilitate a healthier and more integrated job cycle for the underprivileged and dispossessed. In other words, Dean has been tasked with spreading the word of the job opportunities available to enterprises and independent names in the Corridor as a liaison. The tasks will help expedite the process of becoming legally operating entities under the management of either a church or the state for the larger entities, while the lesser-known individuals will be given pay above the imperial minimum wage. As for specifics, the House of Representatives and the Clergy of the Jordaine's Divine Order have assessed that despite their reach and authority, Dean is the most equipped individual to assess anything that might be useful to the expedition be it relics, people, medicine, or even camping material from the Twin capitals. This is especially pertinent since the experience as a whole is meant to nurture the most exceptional youth in Jordaine." Gregory observed Alize for a long moment and frowned before he returned to writing on the air.

"I am certain that your business would thrive if you associated your brand with this venture." Gregory offered a kind of sentiment that he had extended to no one else.

"Hm. I guess it means Dean is quite handy then, huh? " Verza looked at her son with worry and then glanced at Gregory with knitted eyebrows.

"I shouldn't have to worry about the type of doctor that he is going to get for my baby boy then, right?"

"No, Mrs. Peachum. Dean is, as quoted by the Governors, 'Quite a capable force of change' and 'Integral to the honorable functionality of Jordaine's oldest criminal circles.' So, in my honest opinion, the doctor that he will retrieve for your child will likely be one of spotless reputation and exemplary skill." Gregory tapped his finger on the white square on his desk and nodded. He displayed an expanded dossier on the person known as Dean Haversham. A list of names that he associated himself with quite magically exploded forward as dozens of Doctors with no less than a century's worth of experience suddenly showed up as people under Dean's sphere of influence. Even more members of the clergy exploded out of the list as the number of healed and restored patrons were shown beside their names.

Verza read the information with an outward display of shock, wonder, and hope, but Alize watched his mother's pupils slightly constrict and buzz with movement as she committed each name to memory.

"*Ah. Well those people are in for a surprise. Hopefully, they haven't done anything unforgivably evil.*" Alize puffed out his cheeks and pursed his lips in worry. His attention quickly shifted to Gregory, which quickly turned into an awkward staring match. Instead of breaking the silence like a normal adult, the shopkeeper placed the pen on the desk and closed his eyes with rigid movements.

Verza stopped reading about Dean and pulled Alize a few steps back as Gregory's eyes began to flash in a peculiar order, as if a number were being dialed in Morse code. The keeper maintained a radiant white glow as his body slowly adopted the posture and mannerisms of a completely different person. Even Orsche, wallowing in a corner of the market, noticed the odd development and stood beside his family. Jarold, who had turned completely invisible, solidified above the family in all of his tempestuous glory.

"Someone is bypassing the Vielseam's control unit? Right now? Mom must have been recognized and pinged the Imperial archive. We must be talking to an operator in the empire's capital or someone with Imperial Access. Hm, I do think it's unlikely that the person patching in would be an operator, but the alternative is even less likely. The only people outside of the Imperial Family and Archivists with access to Vielseams like this are Archons, Cardinals of the major churches, the CEO's of the Empire's domestic brands, guild masters, and world leaders. The list of people is surprisingly large but also small. I wonder who it is?"

Alize looked up at his parents and noticed that they were once again communicating between themselves. Verza's confusion and alertness diminished in real time as Orsche, potentially, explained exactly what Alize thought.

"Virasana. A woman of your standing should not risk associating with the Veilseam or any component of the Void Market. Under no circumstances are you to come back here." Gregory, or the person behind his sudden possession, suddenly pointed his finger forward as if he were scolding a younger sibling.

"You know my identity?" Verza asked with a violent tension in her muscles. She couldn't attack, not with Alize holding her hand and Orsche pressing on her shoulder. Thus, she remained calm and collected, but if looks could kill, Gregory would have been turned to dust a long time ago.

"Of course I do. I was notified the moment your face showed up. I want you to stay wherever you are and remain hidden. It's still not safe, and the waters are only getting muddier due to some recent changes on the southern border. Raise your son and stay happy. I, I have to go now." The person behind the odd scenario smiled lovingly even if it was expressed via Gregory's somewhat stiff face. A second later, the shopkeeper's eyes dulled. He held his head and swooned the moment that the glimmer fully died down.

"My goodness, please forgive me. I did not expect that to happen so suddenly. Usually, there is a process and an agreement that has to be signed regarding matters such as this. Please excuse me, madam. I just need to sit down for a moment, and I'll be right back with you." Gregory replied, but he did not look at anyone as he blindly reached out toward a nearby seat and hunched over. The bright radiance of his eyes flowed away from him like the mists of dry ice in hot water. Any signs of life—body heat, heartbeat, or breathing almost completely disappeared or lessened to an undetectable degree. Everyone in the family could hear a slight ticking noise reverberate throughout the shop, but nothing happened after the shopkeeper sat down.

"Raquelidrel. Orsche. Kaveri. Who was that?"

Verza spoke so coldly that the room's temperature visibly dropped. Jarold, almost expectantly, smacked Ors on the back of the head and motioned that he was an idiot with sign language as he made sure to cut off their sound.

"OWW. You bastard Jarold! What did I tell you about being gentle? Damnit." Ors rubbed the bump on his head and stared at the glowing magical mists that oozed out of Gregory's mouth and closed eyes.

"I don't know, my love, but it's not someone who hates us. This is something that happens on rare occasions or with certain types of transactions. That said, the person on the other line is probably worried about you, so I can think of a name or two." Ors waved the odd situation aside as if it were normal.

"*What names, pops? Who is it?*" Alize raised a single eyebrow but didn't ask out loud since he was never told the full story of his parent's past.

"Then, does this mean that I shouldn't come back here?"

"Probably. Whoever was on the other side of that abrupt call probably paid a hefty fee to intercept your information, all things considered." Orsche touched his chin and frowned as he considered something.

"What do you mean?"

"Vielseams are neutral zones for the lawful, religious, and criminals alike since they are, for the most part, established and protected meeting or trade locations for scholars. That said, most if not all transactions are recorded by the archivists of the Empire. The person on the other side most likely doesn't want you to come back to this shop or any other Seam for two reasons," Ors explained.

"These shops share everything through the same hub, so anyone with enough influence can find anything. So if someone is after you, me, or our family, that information can be found with a simple image or name search. There is also the possibility of getting involved with an un-sanctioned or privatized Veilseam. The downsides of that aren't important right now since this is an official spot." Orsche balanced his hands and tossed one behind his back as he spoke.

"So does that mean our information is just out there now?" Verza frowned toward the unmoving Gregory and the blank space outside.

"It always is, Mom. But based on what just happened, your current location has been hidden or intercepted by whoever was on the other end of that call. Unlike Dad, I cannot guess who was on the other side since I don't know about most of the past you two have lived, but I know that person is not a joke. Anyone who can request an automatic alert has a higher status than Dad." Alize frowned as well but due to unrelated reasons.

"My Affix is something that demands being hidden because of the events it has already generated. That said, I will have to make a name for myself, one at least equivalent to whoever was on the other line of the Bypass." Alize clenched his fists as his plans for the future diversified and expanded.

"At this point. I really hope that this bear really has the relic for my event. If it does, and everything that happens in the next few hours does match my journals, my plans will have a higher likelihood of working." Alize squeezed the stuffed animal that had been placed on his lap and let go of a shuddering breath.

"Ark is right. Even though I skipped over it..." Ors spoke with a hint of nostalgia and a tinge of frustration from what Alize could hear. Obviously, they finished the real conversion privately. Most likely, they even brought up the name of the person that they both believed was the cause of the interruption. Regardless, Alize noticed how his parents both gave a cheeky smile as they side-eyed Gregory. Drawn by their suddenly shifted attention, he watched as the shopkeeper's eyelids fluttered with drowsiness.

"Then, who just talked to me? On top of that, how did they take control of Gregory? I thought mind manipulation and force spells were banned by the empire." Verza knitted her brows and scrunched her nose.

"I'm not omniscient, my love. The caller could be a family member, a coworker keeping a constant lookout for you, or a stalker obsessed with your every movement. The person could even be an investigator looking into your real identity. Actually, it's more likely to be a wealthy noble who bought your information from another attendant since your beauty piqued their interest the last time we stayed in the Corridor," Ors elaborated with a thoughtful expression.

"Forgive my abrupt shift in temperament and tone. It would seem as though a rather impatient customer was keen on contacting you as immediately as possible. Ahem. Also, I am very sorry for any inconvenience you have suffered due to my momentary inactivity. I will ensure you are compensated appropriately for your time," Gregory spoke rather unhurriedly as he returned to a standing position just behind the desk. As he spoke, the pen floated up and wrote down more than a few invisible words on the desk's white square.

"As a small token of my sincerity, all attendants of any Imperially sanctioned Veilseam are artificial constructs focused on providing an exemplary and personalized customer experience. In other words, attendants like myself are categorized as artificial Mentis." Alize watched Gregory write something down as he explained his existence and the sudden possession.

"As for repayment for my inactivity, please select one of these topics that I will be allowed to share free of charge." Gregory tapped his finger on the white square and projected a list of topics ranging from Dean's personal life to detailed reports of his connections, and greater details on all the factions and plans related to the expedition that he was tasked with ensuring does not go off the rails. There was also a small fonted topic related to Mentis and the Veilseam but, glaringly, a recommendation directly flashed, sandwiched between all the options Verza and Orsche could choose from.

This one showed, "Options regarding the medical needs of the child between Verza and Zaquel (Raquelidrel Orsche Kaveri)".

"That one. What are the options?"

Verza pointed almost the same instant she saw the line.

"Raquelidrel has ordered quite a few things from the Vielseam. Among those numerous orders, there was a rare Corridor-affiliated auction of a 7-star medicinal component. Your husband managed to procure several lesser-ranked roots. As part of your other options, I am of the opinion that you two should purchase more of this medicinal component through the same channels and allow your husband to brew recovery-related potions in consideration of his affiliation to the Cloverist Union. As an aside, the previous auction ended rather suddenly with the seller settling for much less than what was project- ed and has prevented anyone from directly contacting them due to the Imperial Privacy Act. My only suggestion for attracting the seller into cooperation is to exchange your husband's pharmaceutical and alchemical expertise." Ors immediately frowned, but Verza jumped at the opportunity.

"How do we get in contact with this person to set up an exchange?"

"At the moment, the seller does not need any related services that will allow me to broker an exchange of a good and service and as I have said before, the Privacy Act prevents me from contacting the auctioneer about business or personal requests until a specified date and time. That said, Dean is more than capable of finding a doctor or a clergyman who is able to at least restore your child to a normal, albeit not perfect state." Gregory stared at Verza almost blankly for a moment and tapped his pen on the table absentmindedly as silence permeated the room. Verza pondered and was about to answer when Ors suddenly squeezed her hand while biting his lip.

"Thank you for the recommendation. It's all a little bit too much at the moment, so I think we will let Dean's friend take a look before we regroup and come to a decision. Is that alright?"

"That is more than fine. Ahem, if it is okay with you, I can make a request to the auctioneer so that when the unspecified time and date has been reached, the seller will receive the option to decide to contact your husband." Gregory nodded to himself and picked up his pen with some sort of internal conviction.

"That's lovely. Thank you Gregory. And can you please tell whoever it was who contacted me that my family and I are going to be just fine? That person sounded sincere, so I don't want them to worry." Verza smiled so brightly that it was almost blinding. As a result, the stone-faced Gregory almost dropped his pen as he looked down and wrote something undetectable on the white square.

"*Another one bites the dust.*" Alize pursed his lips and rolled his eyes. He could somehow feel Jarold doing the same. Orsche, on the other hand, stopped acting altogether and properly observed the slight pink flush on the attendant's cheeks.

"Shut down the void seal, Terr, so we can meet Dean's friend." The temperature visibly dipped as ice crawled along the blacked out glass. Electricity crackled; no, it bent into a clean halo around Or's head.

"Please." Verza side-eyed her man, held his hand as emotion drained from his face, and smiled toward Gregory with that same soul-stealing innocence.

"Please excuse me, madam." Gregory nodded his head with a slight and mechanical smile toward Verza but instantly frowned toward Ors as he pressed a few buttons under the desk. Despite the physical theatrics, Gregory simply rotated his magic and caused the blackout window to drain like ink splats being hit by whiteout.

2.3 Somebody Called a Medic, But Not for Me...

"Veilseam. Ha. It's such a detractive translation of the original meaning. This market or location was often called a Harae'ter O'lyfai. Area of Fated Transactions. It's a shame that the original meaning was lost along with the attendants who were consumed by the very same void they serve. Gregory must have been quite the character in his life to maintain some ability to show his emotions like that." Alize quickly referenced some information that he secretly learned about Vielseams and stared out the window with another exaggerated sigh escaping his lips.

That said, a small yellow hat with a zebra print band and a squashed fox face fogged up the glass.

"Whoa! That is so creepy. How long has he been waiting outside like that?"

Alize wanted to calmly keep to his musings, but the sudden exposure to such a wide-eyed stare, almost as if a ghost were trying to rip into the physical world on a cloud, made him jump back. As if those very same clouds formed wings on the man's back, Dean suddenly flew away from the window and down the street in the opposite direction of the front door.

"What happened to him, and how long were we talking? It couldn't have been more than a few minutes, but he looked at us as if it had been years." Verza turned from the window back toward Gregory.

"Mr. Haversham, or Dean, retrieved and escorted the Doctor that he mentioned to you earlier. I just so happened to close up the shop for our VIPs' security and privacy, so the Doctor decided to part ways rather impatiently. Dean is most likely trying to invite that expert over once again," Gregory explained. Verza raised an eyebrow and was about to ask another question based on the look on her face, but it was quickly cut off with the sound of a small bell as the front door opened in what felt like slow motion.

"Doctor, please take a look at this kid. I will count that day's small matter as repaid if you can treat this child's injuries. I find his situation too pitiful, especially since the magic coming out of him is less than the flicker of a candle flame." Dean held the door and motioned for someone to come in.

"I already followed you this long. I even came back after we saw the shop was closed so I will at least take a look. As for payment, we can settle it after I decide whether to accept the patient or not," a soft, indeterminately gendered whisper came from a figure that floated across the threshold of the market. It was as though the ground itself was unwilling to dirty the saintly being's shoes. A dull reverberation of massive bodies tracked along behind this apparition of a person.

"That voice sounds familiar alright. So is the trademark sound produced by soles made of wyvern cartilage. I'll have to control my expression from this moment onward and be prepared to act based on what my parents decide to do. Personally, I'm hoping we let things play out as they are supposed to. Mom, Dad, what are you two going to decide?"

Alize closed his eyes, took a deep inhale, and clenched his fists for a moment. In a breath's worth of time, he employed a fraction of his [Shroud] presenting magic and with the most basic control, shut down the illusory effect of his [Prevention] spell. Before the floating man could completely pass over and look in his direction, Alize reversed the illusion created by his [Shroud] and manifested his wounds rather than hide them. Ors, Verza and Jarold shared a private conversation hidden by two very distinctly different brands of magic.

Ors projected his thoughts with a spell that consolidated the electrical impulses created by his thoughts into a rice grain size orb that shot out of his optic nerve and pupil, and straight to Verza, who wore a pair of earrings that received the signal.

In that same vein of spells hidden right in plain sight, a tunnel of wind silently snaked around the other side of her face and mixed with a strand of loose hair that always pointed toward Orsche. That very same tunnel hit one of his strands of hair and slithered toward his ear. Ultimately, this collection of spells allowed the two to speak to each other no matter the distance. Of course, there was a difference in transmission speed and the amount of magic either of them needed to pour into their own spells, but still, the range was virtually infinite given enough time and energy.

"White suit, silver blanket shawl, bamboo hat with a face covering, black shades, and a shaking bug-eyed creature wrapped in a blanket in his arms. The description matches what Alize told us on the bus," Verza

privately whispered her observations to Ors since she stood to the side and behind the family, closest to the window and Gregory's desk.

"Jarold said that there are four black-suited guards following behind the doctor. He counted two more that entered as soon as Dean opened the door. All of their magic is purely physical. Pop is saying that it stinks, sounds horrible, and looks splotchy? I'm assuming they are either modified humans or a type of bipedal homunculus. Can you confirm either without using magic?" Verza spoke as fast as she could think as a faint wisp just barely escaped her lips.

"I cannot. Their clothes have decent enough stitches. The workmanship appears to be of quality up to par with a Ballastrate's Silver Standard. I don't know who the crafter is since I'm not using a spell to check but it's something rather powerful, Four stars at the very least to avoid my passive detection sequence," Orsche examined, almost in slow motion, the white clothed figure with a scrutinizing eye and frowned upon seeing nothing out of the ordinary. The halo of light around his pupils vanished, as did the shimmer of glossy contacts.

"That's fine then. This just means that this event has issues that will almost certainly be bigger than what Ark wrote down or told us. What do you think?"

Verza clenched her jaw for a split second and then softened her expression into something hopeful and slightly overwhelmed.

"I think. Hmm, I think that he has been inside of our terrarium and has gone through so many of our simulations that his perspective on what can be counted as a nightmare or as danger is heavily skewed by the trauma that we have forced him to overcome. It's something that we need to address as soon as possible before it becomes an issue..." Ors spoke with a despondent coldness that cut to the meat with a razor's edge. Unlike Verza, who was physically fast and controlled enough to adjust her

entire demeanor in an instant, Ors sharpened his senses and avoided playing the fool.

"So we are going with Ark's plan?"

"Yes."

"How confident are you that this event will go smoothly?"

"Not very, but I hope things go in the same direction as what he wrote down." Verza raised an eyebrow at Ors in surprise since she was expecting him to come up with or adjust the plan.

"Really? Even after what he said on the bus?"

Ors controlled his own breathing and expression to match the rest of his family and thought about it. *"Most definitely."* Verza pinched her cheeks and blinked erratically upon hearing his stalwart response.

"As he said. It should be easier to go with the flow of this event and figure things out step-by-step with what becomes available to us." In slow motion, the Doctor's robes flutter around from behind the massive frame of a bodyguard.

"Besides, we still have to confirm if those glasses really are the whole reason why this event is so bad in the first place," Alize tugged at the hands of both his parents then nodded slightly as the Doctor's full body pushed through the door and turned toward them. The entire family of three settled into their masks. Gregory watched the scene with eyes that slowly bulged and a mouth that creaked open with each following second. Without any noticeable hints of coordination, the entire family put on the show of a lifetime.

"Brother Dean, I knew you said you would help us out with finding a doctor. But this..." Ors attempted to wipe a single barely detectable tear, but that only allowed more to flow as he choked up.

"Thank you. And thank you, Doctor, for coming all this way." Ors grabbed Dean's hand while his body trembled like a newborn fawn. Verza covered her mouth with a few delicate fingers that showed no traces of any scars or calluses, the complete opposite of the hands that Alize knew. With another hand, she gripped her son's chair so hard that her already pale knuckles turned bright red from the apparent strain, another detail that he suddenly noticed since her sun-kissed almond skin was nowhere to be found. Every so often, she moved her mouth to talk but returned to silent sobbing. A delicate maneuver that simply almost crushed Alize's image of his mother since she now looked small.

"What a horrifying performance! I didn't know Mom could act like this." He side-eyed his mother and father and simply put the final touches on his own performance. Jarold, who could and did control his contractor's volume, purposefully resonated with the surroundings and ensured that Verza's heartbreaking whispers reached everyone's ears.

"Please! Say that you can do something about this, Doctor, please. Help my baby. Please help my son. Please let this doctor be skilled enough. Please..." Verza silently bit her finger. With everyone's attention suddenly on her, she hesitated to move her pale hand to Alize's shoulder, almost as if she wanted to comfort her emotions by holding the target of her worry but remembered that the boy's current state was more delicate and fragile than fractured glass. As a result of the apparent internal conflict, Verza collapsed beside the wheelchair and held her little boy's hand with gasping sobs. The doctor tilted his head to the side, spoke words no one could hear due to some personal spell tweaking, and exclaimed with a soft hum.

"This boy. Is in quite a severe state..." The Doctor maintained an unemotional stare on Alize, having followed Verza's voluptuous figure. The completely covered man tilted his head back in a slow, deliberate fashion as he weighed a difficult matter against another. After a few tense seconds, he nodded and muttered.

"These are my qualifications..." A very specific, universally distinct, sigil sparked out from the Doctor's hand. The symbol was a staff with two snakes wrapping around it. A circle lay between the heads of the outward-facing snakes. The glowing mark flashed and produced another alteration, showing a slack rope in the left snake's mouth and a winding road in the right snake's mouth. Within the circle, spell names flashed one after the other, each one taking the shape of different bodies splayed open at various degrees or symbols related to different fields of medicine and surgery.

"As you can see, I am with DDRAD or Driad as an independently authorized physician unaffiliated with any religious order. I have dedicated my entire life's purpose and magic study toward complementing my craft, which you can see in the spells that I am capable of using within my profile. If that is not enough. You can also view my achievements for free online..." The entire sigil and viewing screen swirled into a ring that hovered near Orsche's hand.

"If that is not enough, I trust that my rank is more than high enough to assure you." An unassuming metal card with the Doctor's androgynous and non-distinct was printed in the corner of the Imperial Profile card:

Name: Leakley Nayame.

Heritage: Atalin- Terran.

Tri- Type Caster: A-C-D.

Aura Root.

Sequence: Root- 3.

The card spun around to the back, which showed a shimmering crystalline surface with 5 black stars that reflected like the most polished obsidian. Ors muttered a silent phrase and stretched his hand out. A ghostly light touched the card, releasing a flash of magic that made his eyes brighten with renewed vigor.

"I am so sorry, Doctor. I was wrong to question your skills. I can see that you have studied under the guidance of several renowned wizards residing in the Eastern Deserts and received the counsel of numerous Scales of the Southern Republic. I never expected that an expert of your height would be residing in Jordaine. I know it's a bit too much for people like us to receive your help, and even this meeting is beyond fortunate, even if it is with Dean's help..." Ors bowed profusely and hesitated for a moment before he carried on.

"And I'm truly sorry for pressing my family's luck, but we were just on our way to Dane General. I was hoping you could get us an appointment with a less busy and capable professional who will readily take cash. If there is no one you can point us toward, are there any capable physicians at Rest Clinic on Kearney and 82nd or Hope Center that would be willing to accept our family's terms? Your input would be greatly appreciated and would be more than welcome if our situation is not pressing enough to necessitate your handy work." Ors bowed once more but maintained the posture until he heard a response. Slowly and with purpose, the doctor responded.

"Dane General is a good first choice, but I would not recommend anyone in an emergency situation to go there for a while as they recently signed a renegotiated contract after months with heavy hitters from Driad's Bargaining Committee. As such, they are now the major health care provider for the Guardians and their affiliated sub-branches. Rest Clinic is more than equipped enough to handle the apparent wounds on your child, but right now, they would only make your son's situation go from dire to fatal as they are momentarily understaffed. My assessment does not account for wounds that I cannot immediately see. By process of elimination, you should go to the Hope center. The chief surgeon is well prepared and skilled, on top of being on call today. Unfortunately, there seems to be a concerning overflow from hospitals and clinics outside of the city center due to a rather severe break of Lumpet Lung in the communities in and along the Pit. Under such circumstances, I doubt the availability of the director even if I were to offer my recommendation. My professional opinion leaves me with only two options..." The doctor carefully and lovingly played with the bug-eyed creature in his arms like a parent would a precious child.

"The first is escorting you to Abbey Boulevard. I have a longstanding colleague in the temple of Om'tare Ithe, so my word will go a long way in ensuring that your son is seen. As an aside, it would be best if you donated as much material wealth as you can gather and distributed it to as many of the churches as you possibly can either during your stay or afterward. My other option is accepting your son as my patient, but I am not willing to do so in consideration of my own limitations." The doctor reached toward Orsche and assisted the tearful father back to his feet.

"Doctor, as I see it, we do not care about any limitations or price as long as you can heal our baby. We can give any amount of money that you request. If it's some material you need, we have channels and stocks of anything you can imagine, just..." Verza choked back her words as she erupted with tears and anxiety. As if to calm herself, she grabbed Alize's hand like they were the wings of a butterfly. The flush in her cheeks immediately drained as magic rose up in her body.

"Sense." Verza squeaked out the spell as she fumbled to check Alize's temperature and find his pulse. Her eyes chaotically shifted, reflecting her expressed emotional state as a single wavering ring around both of her pupils. Since the Doctor walked in, Alize toggled [Prevention] off and on in controlled spurts through the filter of [Shroud] and the blanket surrounding him. In other words, the magic in his body made him appear as though he was slowly deteriorating. Verza moved in as soon as his complexion went from pale to ghastly and drew everyone's attention to the almost imperceptible shift.

"Doctor. I know I shouldn't ask considering your status as a 5-star Physician but if you feel like it, can you at least check our son yourself? We have tried so many things, but he has not gotten better." Ors clenched his palms, drawing blood as he ripped himself away from the doctor's gentle hold. Dean's shoulders trembled as he wiped away more than a few tears.

"You said that you needed a few more things for your research the last time we spoke, didn't you? I know a guy who can get you quality material, and he owes me quite a hefty sum, so I'll foot the bill by getting what you need." Dean chimed in upon seeing the veiled man tilt his head side to side rather quickly.

"Mom. Dad. I don't feel so good anymore." Alize turned off [Prevention] altogether after preparing for his mother's signal. His entire body instantly drained of color as soon as the invisible and waveless magic retracted. The situation inside his body was similar to there being a single soldier (his natural regeneration) in the middle of a frozen (Prevention spell) enemy army (Injuries) that started to move. This singular soldier, who had been equipped with two daggers (Medicine and Arcanum) suddenly found that both of the dull blades snapped in half. A geyser of black blood erupted from Alize's mouth as his body simply couldn't handle the loss of his [Prevention]. The bear in his hand dropped to the ground along with the glasses and little plushie scroll. Instantly, the items were stained by the kid's sludge-like blood.

"Plan three. Show our sincerity, weakness, and desperation. Manipulate the situation so the quack doctor takes us to his lab that I remember from my nightmare. While I am being 'treated', Mom and Dad can evaluate the actual danger of this event. If they need more information, or if the event is bigger than what they can handle, our goal will be to ride

out the trouble and do what little we can to take control of the outcome." Alize thought about the plan and inwardly frowned as he reasoned through the thoughts and potential actions of his parents. That said, Verza played her part extraordinarily.

"My baby." She scrambled to her feet and cried two rivers in a most eye-catching and deliberate way. Jarold invisibly pushed the tears to a slow crawl so that they congealed into larger drops. Overall, she looked pitiful.

"Doctor. I, if that's not enough, I can..." Dean couldn't help pivoting his head back and forth to the heartbreaking sobs of a mother and the empathetic but ultimately evaluating gaze of someone who was deciding the worth of a life. Thankfully, the Doctor put a hand up and sighed. With a controlled whistle, four three meter tall and bulky figures who were covered in black robes and gray veils created a corridor for the doctor.

"Hopefully, Mom and Dad weren't kidding when they gave me a passing mark on my acting lessons. Ahem, let's do this." Alize thought to himself as his blanched face warped into an ugly grimace of excruciating agony. He coughed up a few mouthfuls of blood and would have doubled over in his seat, if not for the leather runes that suddenly glowed on the blanket binding his body. Dozens of straps of different widths with golden buckles wrapped around his collapsing form, locking it into a comfortable and stable upright position. The apparent pain was so bad that Alize's eyes rolled up into his head as he fainted.

"This child is certainly unfortunate." The doctor muttered something under his breath, and as a result, a massive halo expanded and surrounded his hat. Alize imagined the situation outside of his body using the magical chimes and overall atmosphere as clues.

"It would seem that my eyes are not as good as they were a few decades ago. I did not see the extent of the damage. My earlier assessment is obsolete. Hope Center's director would not know how to heal this without your son suffering some long term and possibly even permanent damage to his nervous and circulatory systems. Unfortunately, my other statement stands..." The Doctor bent over a 45-degree angle at his waist and muttered another halo into existence. This circle of light appeared near his eyes, similar to a monocle.

"Oh, my heart. I feel this guy looking into my body. It's so uncomfortable. Ew, I can feel his eyes all over me. Oh, my lady, it's actually slimy. An observational spell or tool should be quick, efficient, and undetected. Fuck, it's nasty. Hurry up, you damn quack. If my spell is off for too long, I might actually die." Concerned with the Doctor's lingering gaze and the unknowable tense expressions of his parents, Alize lost himself in hand-selecting good memories. It was a practice that helped him essentially recreate the restful state of mind associated with deep sleep.

"This type of fracturing and the extent of the muscle tearing and bruising. Your child fell from a great height, yes? He fought for his survival as well considering the spread. There are also signs of old but severe damage along the spinal column. No. The decay and effuse are centralized, which means a potion was used. A Lochorn derivative perhaps?..." Another whisper escaped the Doctor's suddenly very dry lips. He produced a smaller halo beyond the spectral glasses, which appeared as a magnifying glass that produced extensive details about whatever it was used to observe.

"Aha. Such a miraculous potion was used on this child. Yes, whoever brewed this quality of potion must be exceptional. It explains why he is not paralyzed or brain dead. Its potent effects have reversed usually irreparable damage that only..." The doctor's eyes widened and voice trembled as possibilities flashed across his mind at lightning speeds.

"It would appear that you all have already gone to the Abbey and requested divine intervention. Sometime last evening, if everything is being correctly measured. But if it also failed to stem the source of your son's agony." The doctor suddenly stood ramrod straight once more and walked back to Dean.

"We will talk later, Dean. As for all of you, follow me. Quickly. There may not be much that I do, but I will try my best." Dr. Nayame left the shop. The black-suited individuals picked up the stunned family of three and essentially carried them out of the door. Dean stood there, mouth agape for a moment before he ran behind the group with a smile and fist pump.

Gregory blinked a few times and cleared his throat, unable to truly process everything he had just seen. After a few breaths, order restored itself to his mind, and work replaced his thoughts. He almost pulled another customer's order from the shelf behind him, but something caught his eye. With a twitch of his finger, the floorboards twisted and what appeared on his desk in the blink of an eye was a teddy, a plushie scroll, and a pair of glasses that looked very similar but were not exactly the same pair as the ones that were on the bear.

"I will have to report this encounter now. The issue is deciding what to say. Should I claim that Raquelidrel hired some actors to collect a hidden relic from the Veilseam again, or are the swapped-out glasses nothing more than a red herring?"

Gregory blinked once again and interacted with a massive floating screen that connected to several dozen snippets of anecdotal evidence from other Attendants all throughout reality.

"Then there is the matter of claiming that Verza and that boy are actors. Should I ask some of my coworkers? No. If this is another elaborate weave of lies similar to the last unraveling that Raquelidrel contributed to half a century ago, then it's possible that I will expose any attendants that I interact with to unwanted trouble..." Gregory tapped the bear toy and separated the blackened blood staining it into a crystalline sphere of tenet.

"This matter also involves an individual that can bypass the Veilseam, so I can only bring this matter to her majesty directly if it is at all possible." The shopkeeper pressed his thumb on the desk's black circle and swiped the white square upward with his pen. In the blink of an eye, a snow-white sheet of paper filled with the words, "Conclusions based on inferred and collected data". Following that title, stock print text filled out Gregory's report.

"It is possible that the First-light of CAU (Cloverist All-Chemist Union) and Luscient of Havencourt were tasked with a secret joint assignment with the court's military forces. My examination has revealed that the First-Light Scholar is in deep cover with a partner who has taken up the role of his domestic companion. Further observation has led me to suspect that this partner appears similar to Guardian Pashe. V of Queen Mehraust's personal court sentinels. Relevantly packaged information hints at the 27th Queen's continued and vested interest in the progress and health of Guardian Pashe. V..." Gregory picked up the paper with narrowed eyes as the page lengthened to the point where the report nearly touched the floor. With a nod, the paper rolled up into a scroll. He squeezed gently to leave behind a crystalline band of Tenets around its center and from under the desk, he grabbed a bright magical stamp depicting a flower, and pressed it onto the band.

Six black stars pressed down into a glob of royal blue wax that enveloped the stars in colored texture. After a few seconds, Gregory placed the roll into the box on the table and closed the lid. An obsidian chain poured out of the black circle on the desk. After ensuring that not a single atom of the box was visible through the links, Gregory snapped his fingers and conjured a massive lock with the face of a bulldog but the mouth of a gluttonous demon. That deformed lock bit down on a single word, "DIVINE".

Gregory pulled another sheet out of thin air, the very top of which said,

Personal file: Orsche Kaveri. R. rank 6 Lerian- Hautzee.

- Profession: Scholar.

- Alias (s):

    ◦ Zaqiel (Peachum) Nayame- Scuttle

    ◦ Prodigy of the Whisperwood.

    ◦ First-Light Scholar, 8 Star Access.

    ◦ Luscient Scholar, 9 Star Access.

- Status: Premium Deluxe VIP Membership Plus Package

- Details: Headache. Do not accept bets. Do not engage, meaning do not let him speak or move around freely. Voided. Do not let him walk into the Veilseam. Redacted. Use a middleman. Redacted. Do not use a middleman. Voided. Try not to have any direct or indirect contact. Redacted. Triple check everyone walking into your shop. Redacted. Hope that he does not show up in your seam for any reason. Voided. If he shows up, immediately report it to the Archons and Gods and pray that he did not do something.

- Profile: Voided, Voided, 8 Star access, 9 Star access.

- Residence: Redacted Lane, Havencourt, Redacted.

- Jobs: Redacted. Fixer. Redacted. Redacted. Scholar, Voided, Redacted, Liaison for Redacted, 9 Star Access, Voided.

"Hopefully, my report gets some attention before things turn out for the worst." Gregory sighed and reluctantly pulled another scroll, one that showed Orsche's order history. Exclusively, everything was ordered online and picked up at the store in less than a minute of its delivery. The time that Orsche even spent inside of the store was recorded at less than five seconds, but this time a shudder ran down Gregory's spine as he pulled up everything on Dean and the Doctor known as Leakley Nayame. In a second's worth of time, Gregory digested thousands of years' worth of data. The frown on his face instantly turned to an ice-cold and vacant stare, almost as if all life had been drained from his body.

"It will be a miracle if Raquelidrel does not cause a cataclysmic issue in the near future. The doctor seems to be a prime target for his kind of shenanigans." With a flick of his wrist, the bear, glasses, and plushie scroll were placed in a crystal sphere rather than a box.

"There is also the boy to consider. He noticed something that I did not and, for some reason, he saw fit to ensure that this fell into my hands. Or were they trying to establish the boy's credit indirectly?" Gregory noticed a spell that was cast on the bear. It was a small, commonplace, and almost negligible utility aspect of Ballast-type magic. With his observational skill, this spell contained the most basic elements of the [Shroud] sequence, but the magic almost made his reason walk out the door when it peeled away and revealed something wrong with the bear that had been under his watch for eons.

Gregory used his thumb to press the sphere. The small bump turned into a vibration that shook the suspended teddy bear. A small slip of paper peeled away from the scroll as the simple [Shroud] spell outlined something hidden in plain sight. Gregory separated the little note into its own sphere. The message was written in a light, controlled, and impossibly elegant language that very few gods even knew. Gregory didn't know how to read the ancient text at the very least, and he was well within the rank of the Divine hierarchy as a seven-star Mentis. That said, the sigil that was on the small square of paper was so beautifully drawn and held such a mystic power that the entire store trembled. Almost instantly, the shop imploded as a sort of safety measure kicked in. The outside world, the walls, shelves, and chotchkies vanished into an inky darkness that broke the confines of imagination. Only Gregory, the plushie, and the small square of paper existed in this infinite void.

With a clawed hand, Gregory swiped at the darkness. Purple chains, as massive as entire interlinking solar systems, ripped out of the void and compressed into strings that superimposed onto the tiny page. The sigil vanished under the weight of these chaining threads. In a flash, the note resembled a miniature universe contained within a backdrop of void, with the only thing hinting at its existence being a subtle lilac outline. With another swipe, a red and silver flower bloomed from the void and withered in on itself in a never-ending cycle that made the flower grow smaller with each revolution. In a single breath, the roots tangled around the surface of the page for just a single moment before it simply blinked away. A finger-sized word, "IMMORTAL" burned into the void and would remain there for all of eternity until the person that was supposed to receive this letter, did. Gregory snapped and opened his eyes to find the shop all around him. The void was firmly outside the walls of the Veilseam as a vacant emptiness just outside the building. Pressing the pen against his temple, he pulled out another personal file.

Personal file: Ark. rank 0 Lerian.

- Alias: Ark

- Status: None

- Details: Suspected child of the Luscient Scholar and the Silver Bell Sentinel. There is no substantial evidence of the following accusation, but I suspect the child to have knowledge of her Immortal Lady or the direct Lineage of Her Lady. Conclusion, immediate VOIDING based on the terms of service agreed upon by the Upper and Lower Heavens...

The detail section remained blank beyond the word Heavens, but as Gregory thought about it, he slowly erased the information.

- Details: an interesting child. One suspected of being the disciple or child of the First-Light Scholar. As I have observed, the boy's education in religions and ancient history regarding or possibly even predating the Voided era's is on par with registered Archivists of the empire. He may be another prodigy in the making.

Gregory closed the file since no one wanted to buy such information yet and since no one wanted to purchase some obscure, mostly irrelevant, data, he didn't have an immediate obligation to submit his personal file. With a finishing blow, he slapped the page and all the other files back into his desk and frowned toward the outside of the shop.

2.4 A Convincing Setup

Alize narrowly opened his eyes as one of the doctor's black-robed guards pushed him out of Rest City's "one and only" legally operating Veilseam. Two other guards escorted his parents with the exact same rough and forward mannerisms. Passing the wall of muscle, Alize locked onto the back of Dr. Nayame. Mid-step and under the astonished gazes of pedestrians, the man simply vanished with an eye-catching sparkle emanating from his clothing.

"That's odd. Was that quack this so capable in my nightmare? There has to be someone nearby using a spell to move him elsewhere or a teleportation artifact that is tied to a set location. I refuse to believe that he could just vanish." Alize checked his memory, but this encounter never happened. He was home one instant, then trapped elsewhere as if he had skipped a cut scene or experienced time out of sync. He met the quack doctor in a sort of hyper-artistic fever dream sequence that revealed more about settings than faces and people's idiosyncrasies. That said, he simply didn't have enough time to ponder the magic the doctor used to vanish. As much as he wanted to deduce whether

the person possessed the mana required to activate such a spell, Alize had to reorganize and apply himself to control his [Prevention] and [Shroud] spells to avoid losing consciousness or getting caught.

The guards physically lifted the family of three and crouched down like springs ready to bounce. In a single heavy breath, they all touched an ornament over their chest. A hexagonally paneled shimmering barrier covered the group of guards as they rocketed forward, creating afterimages through the city as they passed a massive statue that took nearly a dozen city blocks to completely pass. To onlookers, the group resembled a long comet or thread of light that suddenly stretched and weaved through traffic, leaving small circles of magical light every 100 meters. Within a minute, the group overlooked a large crystal lake dotted with small countries and decently sized cities. Some of the islands, however, were not inhabited. The majority of the landmass on these few islands was actually pulled up from the lake floor by sprouting dragonspire saplings that resembled walls for one's entire vision if one was too close. In terms of scaling this ocean-size lake to the whole of Heyden's Rest, this Spire-island peppered body of water could only be equivalent to stopping by a pond to feed the ducks in New York City's Central Park.

After a handful of minutes, the musclemen who carried Alize and his parents ran tens of thousands of kilometers away from the city center that held a constant flow of tens of billions. Seconds later, the large lake or oceanside scenery melted into a marshland of blooming thickets full of fruit bushes that grew all over the wetlands and islands that congealed around rotting or toppled dragonspires that couldn't reach the point of exponential growth and stability. An interconnected network of vines wrapped around, connected, and dripped from calcified wood and fell into forests of twisting blueberry blossom trees. A handful of seconds later, the marshes turned into solid land dotted with broken pillars and stone monoliths that resembled a spider's nest with all the vines that weaved around and through the dry husks of older spires that simply did not have the nutrients needed to sustain their size. The azure petals of the marsh's iconic blueberry blossoms molted into a gorgeous bed of red and orange leaves that were broken up by vast swaths of emerald evergreen treetops at the base of these mostly if not fully vertical and towering menhirs.

Massive private complexes or villas of various shapes, sizes, and cultural origins very rarely broke the natural scenery that very comfortably manifested and rested beside Rest, but each spire seemed to have at most, nine different estates surrounding a different pillar. An equivalent human comparison would be Central Park South if each household or apartment was separated by hundreds of kilometers of forest and dehydrated, calcified wood. Seconds after this elongated picture of a view stretched across Alize's very blurry vision, a shadow-covered plain simply unfolded for as far as he could see. At the four corners of the massive plains, towering red tree trunks coiled upward and into a singular connected canopy. A leafy umbrella practically hovered over a seven-story mansion that resembled a small hospital without any signage.

Before the family was put down by the guards, they were separated. Alize silently and subtly shook his head as he locked eyes with his parents since he was carried off to a location where at least a dozen small and veiled figures in white waited to receive him. Ors and Verza felt the tight grips of the guards vanish only after their baby boy was pushed behind a pair of double doors. The two adults, in what felt like a silent collapse of their entire world, were then guided from the front entrance to a massive, widowed hallway. Despite the niceties of the greeters and residences of the mansion, Orsche and Verza simply kept each other in check with tight holds on one another's hand. No sound reached their ears as both of their eyes remained locked on Alize's location. That said, they both noticed that they were surrounded on either side by rows of closed doors, statues, and waiting staff dressed in black and gray, all of whom wore masks, wide-brimmed hats, or veils.

The guards who carried them over to this location followed behind them almost like circus-trained animals showing off a trick that allowed them to keep in step and stop in perfect unison with whomever they followed. Another thing that both parents noticed was the dozens of portraits and accompanying plaques that depicted the doctor's previous patients and plaques dedicated to each success story. Thousands of names and faces fluttered by. After reaching the end of this hall, two waiting staff opened double doors to a high-ceilinged study packed to the brim with medical books, scrolls, and outdated instruments or primitive arcane tech within glass or glowing barriers. A pair of veiled attendants wearing gray and white robes waited for the group almost expectantly. One of those very same attendants, a child from the person's apparent height, squealed and gently clasped her hands around one of Verzas.

"Nice to meet you, sir, madam. We love receiving patients and seeing them, oh. I'm sorry, uh. I'm sorry, ma'am, please don't cry. I'm so stupid. Everything is going to be okay, miss, so please don't cry. Dr. Nayame is the best. There hasn't been a single patient that he hasn't been able to help recover so we love seeing everyone leave our mansion happy." The attendant patted Verza's hand in an attempt to soothe her but the girl ended up bawling even harder than the woman in front of her. The attendant lost all sense of personal boundaries and hugged Verza, gasping between her own wails. At the same time, the other attendant bowed slightly and motioned towards a pair of high-backed chairs that faced a semicircular desk.

"Sir, Madam, our sincerest condolences. Please follow us to your seats." This second taller attendant stood up from his bow with the most deadpan of expressions and the darkest bags possible underneath his sleepy eyes.

"Eh, you dummy, I told you to fix your tone and lack of emotions when you talk to the relatives of the Doctors patients. You always make it sound like he can't heal such trivial injuries. I'm sorry about my brother's tone. There's something wrong with his head, but no one seems to care. Ow, damn it, did you just hit me?" The smaller attendant of the two rubbed the back of her head with a scowl but jumped out of shock upon feeling Verza lean into Orsche's arms. She rubbed her hand while crying as it turned red from pain. The little attendant looked at her own hand, then at Verza's and teared up as she instantly crouched in a corner of the room and rocked back and forth.

"I am sorry for my sister's immaturity. There's something wrong with her, but no one seems to want to say anything." The second attendant bowed once more and motioned for the two to follow him to their seats a second time. Ors and Verza exchanged a glance and nodded as they followed the boy to their seats.

"The doctor's personal assistant will be right with the two of you in a moment. Please get comfortable." The veiled boy bowed a third time and retreated back to the study entrance. After a moment, he basically hovered over to the corner like death and picked up the balled-up girl by the scruff of her clothing and placed her by the entrance.

"Please forgive us." The taller attendant bowed a fourth time and forced the girl to follow along.

"I am sorry for squeezing your hand so tightly, madam. Also, the doctor is the best. No matter how bad the injury is, you have to stay strong and be ready to see your son without crying." The girl wiped away the tears in her own eyes and bowed two times in a row.

"I am very sorry for hurting you. I hope your hand gets better soon." The girl sniffled, smiled, then ran away. The guards closed the doors behind the exiting figures and left Ors and Verza all alone. Not even half a second after the door clicked, Ors whispered a silent phrase, "Senses." A halo flashed just above his head for a moment before the pulsing ring settled on hiding in his neatly and purposefully styled hair. He suddenly let go of the tension in his shoulders.

"We're clear. For now, at least. There's a camera, but it can only pick up mana signatures below six stars so it's currently only collecting a physical video of us." Ors placed a hand on Verza's upper thigh and relaxed in his seat with a slouch and heavy sigh.

"Kids. That girl is too strong. It's a danger to her health." Verza whispered to Ors as she frowned at her hand. She wiggled her fingers and clenched them, resulting in a nasty chain of popping and squishing sounds as she reactivated the magic in her body.

"Yes. I know what you mean. Those two were at least at the fourth star rank regardless of whatever their profiles may be. They are at least stronger than the guards who brought us here. Ha, this whole quack doctor event that Ark wants us to tiptoe around is getting very troublesome." Ors squeezed Verza's leg and shuffled around in his seat to get comfortable.

"What are you counting as troublesome, the possibility that this doc might be creating new life or the relic's involvement in all of this?" Verza moved as well, trying to get the perfect image of a noble lady's posture.

"All of it. We have possibly taken the event starter off of the board by taking the Glasses from the bear, but how does this next event unfold without the spark to set it off? Will things unfold like in the journal or will there be some variation? We have already messed up by thinking the events are fixed. Ark almost died because of it. What if this event is the same? We got rid of the Relic, but there might be something that Ark

missed. No, he's not telling us. That boy chose not to tell us anything." Orsche clenched his jaw, which remained mostly hidden by the beard that "grew" out of his face.

"You are worried," Verza placed a hand over the one Ors left on her thigh.

"Yes, my love. I am losing my mind over here thinking about every-thing that could go wrong." His reddened eyes reflected the study's warm light.

"I do think that we should have discussed all of this a bit more, but you have to calm down. We are already here. Besides, Jarold is with Ark. If anything happens, we will be able to reach them before shit hits the fan." Verza exhaled deeply as she listened to Jarold's live action reports.

"No. My love. That's the thing. This event is already way beyond the scope of anything we have seen Ark's Affix generate before. I mean, you have to see what I'm seeing here. This facility is something a proper scholar should have in their home territory, but still, the research being done here is respectable despite the contents of, whew. There's so much going on underground. It's really bad. I am even getting readings on a Divine-ranked creature locked in his basement, my love. Ark's Affix. That damn thing is playing with all of our lives." Ors frowned even deeper and rubbed his eyes.

"I need you to simplify whatever you are about to say before you say it, Ors." Verza side-eyed her man as her calves, thighs, and waist tensed at the mention of an entity at or above the seventh rank.

"This doctor, who our son wrote about in his journals with the quote, 'quack hack of a physician', has a divine abomination in the basement. I'm not sure how the arcanum fits into this equation just yet, but I'm quite confident that one of us would die if we attempted to destroy this place..." Orsche condensed a whole tirade into something easily digestible.

"Then there's the matter of reporting what's going on here. Everything is on brand for a scholar of Leakly's profession and standing within the guild. In other words, under Haven's current laws, what the doctor is doing here is illegal but with the Empire's PIETy Act or Progressive Initiative Exemption for Talented "youths", the research this guy has accumulated here is definitely more than enough to pardon any unforgivable lengths that he must have gone through to make some of what I am seeing. Ninth, he might even get a medal from the Lady herself..." Orsche sighed with a sudden exhaustion filling his lungs even though he did not speak. With a sharp intake of breath, he realized that he stopped breathing altogether.

"And that's only with what I can see with my lower grade [Sense] spell. And I lost him. Is the old fart still with him?" Ors squeezed Verza's leg even harder as he suddenly lost track of Alize and his escort.

"Yes, and calm down. You look like murder is on your mind. We have to be calm. You have to be calm. It's your thing, you handsome idiot." Verza turned toward the large wooden double doors with a faux anxiety written on her face.

"How do I look? I'm going for scared but hopeful." Sneakily Verza pinched her own cheeks and wore a pitiful but expectant mask of emotion. Orsche started for a long time but before a full minute passed, he combed through the hair on his face and smiled with visible hesitation.

"Prefat ah'loys min dita lyfai." He spoke out loud, released a sigh, and turned toward the door with a fidgeting leg tick. Verza's expression did a miniature flip as a gentle and barely noticeable grin pushed against her blushing cheeks. The words roughly translated into "perfect as always, my only destiny" or "my fated love". The power of this phrase, however, lay not in the words themselves but in the personal story and emotion, love, grief, and strength behind it.

"Game face, love." Orsche, however, did not lay into the atmosphere as he wanted to and instead squeezed Verza's thigh twice. Almost instantly, she shifted in the chair. Seconds later, a person gracefully walked into the office with a glassy board that resembled a tablet in how light came off of it. A tight bun pulled this person's eyebrows into high arcs that complemented her angular, almost ethereal features. The black button-down and snow-white pencil skirt fit snugly against her body in a way that made one think of comfort and fashion before beauty, an image which was only further enhanced by the rhythmic click of black heels against the marble floor. This lady held such a presence that Orsche and Verza had to do a double take just to see two veiled figures, two butlers, pushing carts behind the tour de force that was the clipboard-holding woman. On a third glance, the two noticed that the carts were full of delicate pastries and an assortment of accessories necessary for making and serving coffee, juice, or tea.

"I am sorry for the wait. Dr. Nayame is currently performing your son's surgery. In the meantime, might you be willing to answer a few questions for our internal records?"

The woman motioned toward the butlers as she stood beside the doctor's desk. The trolleys rolled past Verza and Ors on either side and silently created an odd disharmony since the only sounds in the room came from their own breathing. In such an awkward state of silence, every other noise, like simple breathing, resounded like an orchestra of noise.

"Of course. We will answer any questions that will help." Verza sat slightly forward.

"Thank you very much. First, would you like anything?"

The lady waved to the assortment of goods as if she was the one who brought them in.

"Tea. I would like something bitter with a tang of sour, Llaro. If it's available, my husband is a fan of sweets." Like a scripted drama, Verza placed her trembling hand on Or's arm. Almost as if that small physical contact were enough to prevent the boat of her emotions from capsizing in the waves of current events.

"Right away." The lady snapped her fingers and once again let silence consume the atmosphere as the butlers blurred into motion. This time, however, an almost imperceptible clink disrupted the peace. Without saying a word, the taller of the two and the most muscular bowed and promptly walked out. The second butler did not stop his work to make the same mistake and laid out two beautiful platters of snacks and a small candle that produced a calming aroma. The butler then moved to the second trolley and soundlessly brewed and poured tea for Verza and Ors. With a bow, the guy elegantly walked out with both trolleys wheeling behind without making a sound.

Verza and Ors took in the situation and appeared thankful, albeit slightly hesitant, as they accepted the care. At that exact moment, the steam from the cup that Verza picked up, curled around her finger for less than a millisecond.

"*Don't freak out...*" Verza used the cup and her small sip to whisper directly into her man's ear.

"*Jarold is sending you information. I can see it every time a piece of him floats back. How's the situation with Ark doing?*"

Orsche grabbed a small cookie and ate the whole thing in one bite.

"This tea is phenomenal." Verza feigned surprise and mindlessly conversed with the lady about the name, history, vendor, and price of the leaves. Once that topic had run dry, Orsche picked up the with talk of the desserts. Mid-conversation, Verza raised the teacup to her face with a nervous eye twitch.

"First off, Ark Is doing fine according to Jarold. We can even reach him pretty easily. The only problem is that he is inside a chamber-pod- healing, mini-terrarium thing that is inside of another Terrarium. Jarold said we can break into the first one if there is a problem, but the second one is fixed to go through the whole building by something, so we cannot rush to take Ark away if things go bad." With proper etiquette befitting a Corridor Merchant, Verza enjoyed the tea's earthy and tart bitterness, crystal appearance, and chilling taste despite it being a hot drink. Through body language alone, she made it appear as though the tea cleared her mind and body by releasing some of the tension that she allowed to tighten her shoulders and face.

"I guess that's not as bad as what I imagined. What about the glasses?"

"Jarold moved them so it is inside of the mini-tear with Ark so..." In seconds, the Verza and Ors consolidated their information, discussed topics that would steer the ongoing conversation, and traded tips on acting in ways appropriate for the topics they chose to sprinkle in with the questions that they were answering. In other words, the "put together" looking woman was trying to get to know Verza and Ors beyond a routine background check, and they gave as little as possible while talking as much as feasible without tipping their hand.. As such, her clipboard gleamed with several instances of a familiar dog-faced sigil, but not as much as she was expecting considering her deadpan expression.

The Vielseam's mark, a monstrous bulldog, materialized above the woman's glass after quite a few minutes of talking and dropped down as a tangible object with two black stars emblazoned on a wax seal. As she conversed with the two anxious parents in front of her, the seal split apart into multiple pieces with the biggest turning into a stack of pages. Overall, she pulled their public records and placed them on her clipboard. The rest of the mark turned into a handful more unfurling scrolls. Each piece of information only possessed a single black star. Once again, the lady hand-selected the information that pertained to what Verza and Ors answered regarding their personal lives.

The first document held a synopsis of an ancient king that bed so many people that his status and influence quite literally came from the billions of children that he managed to father in merely a century and a half.

Nezaret "Noodle" Nayame. One of the most prolific kings in the history of Haven's Demo-public Meritonarchy. He single-handedly pulled the human species from the brink of extinction no less than 300 times during his 3 decade reign as the elected King of Haven. EDITED BY AN ARCHON: As the last human to gain the crown of Haven, Nezaret Nayame has left an inexorable stain on the already tarnished reputation of humanity and all related subspecies. As such, any meritorious deeds accomplished by anyone claiming the Nayame Surname will be VOIDED now and henceforth until the line has perished. The only exception is the personal accumulation of a merit total, compounded by every previously registered Nayame without said exception. Any and all known descendants, if found to possess the Noodle's profile, must be reported and escorted to Archon Irisa Ghale if not executed on sight if said report and guidance is not feasible.

The second and third documents were compiled together as a set since they pertained to the two parents sitting in the office of one of the few officially recognized descendants of said Mad King. Orscheik Peachum- Scuttle and Verza Peachum- Scuttle were the names of the two individuals sitting in front of her. Most of the information heavily focused on their youth, young adulthood, and the years Orschiek spent working for the Peachum family Brand in the Corridor. After a bit of financial trouble and after the patriarch of the Peachum family passed away, the Stall was closed, and with it, any notable mention of their family died down until decades later.

As a small-time Day Trader on the Corridor exchange, Verza gained just enough traction and influence to let her open up a new business. She even changed her name to better represent the brand, which eventually turned into a family operation after Orsche joined the venture. The well-dressed woman collected her notes and thoughts and cleared her throat to confirm a few points of information regarding their past, medical history, troubles, or concerns, their son's previous conditions or medical records or if there even were any.

On the other side of another type of grueling questioning process, Alize squinted through a pained expression as he second-guessed himself more than a dozen times after being escorted away from his parents.

"This is supposed to be a private hospital. I understand the need for a decent facade, but where are all of the messed up things that I saw in my nightmare? Did my journals get disproven so quickly already?"

Once the double doors flew open, Alize was greeted by a lavishly decorated, wide and tall hallway mostly populated by small ferns and miniature potted trees. For an instant, the hall distorted into an uncanny, gore-filled, nightmare-fueled kaleidoscope of screaming, laughing, and twitching bodies moving in ways that simply took grotesque into a new genre altogether. That is what he was expecting, so his cover almost shattered the moment that he took in the veiled figures that stood on either side of the hall. For a split second, all of their heads and faces popped and crackled with disjointed movement as their bodies bloated beyond their masks and helmets into degenerative and writhing masses of flesh and blood held together purely by magic. Genetic cohesion and stability were nowhere to be found in their form or function. Distinctly inhuman proportions boiled over into cancerous folds that ejaculated fluids both physical and mystical, and then it all just washed away from his mind like a bad dream. Just remembering the imagery made Alize shudder and mentally gag as he played the role of an injured child waking up from a sudden bout of pain. The escort of eight masked figures practically paused on the spot.

"Where are my..." Alize murmured and bobbed his head from one side to the next while batting his eyes. On his left, there was an open garden with nearly a dozen patients following a veiled man in yoga routines. To his right, the garden extended into a breathtaking enclave. A small curling tree rooted itself on a massive algae-covered rock as its sapphire petals danced along the surface of a silver pond. In the brief second that he scanned the environment, he managed to catch a glimpse of a magenta-headed fish that had a body that resembled liquid fire. In that split of a second, the miraculous fish nibbled on the azure petals and dived down into the depths of the crystal water. With a purposeful dip of his head and a second nodding pass, the boy even noticed how the petals just above the pond's surface seemed to roll with a sort of intentional waver, swirling the leaves into a language that only nature used and few understood.

"A star dancer! How does this quack have one of these treasure fish just swimming in his backyard pond? And why is Jarold following me? Does Mom want to keep tabs on my location just in case? Hmm, does that mean Dad's spells can't cover this particular area? Ah, wait, that's not right. If Mom sent Jarold, then it would mean they are still collecting information to compare the current situation to what I told them. This is good. It means they won't try to come and collect me at any second." Alize frowned inwardly. Outwardly, he seized up until the point where the escorts all around him gave him some kind of medicine. With an expertly timed [Prevention] and innate [Shroud] specifically tweaked to hide magic, hiding the fact that he was still awake was no issue at all.

The white-clothed lady pushing his chair then turned a few corners and led him to a door nestled between two peculiar and lifelike statues of half-naked people smiling and hugging themselves.

"Right. This is the door. I should have paid more attention to the nightmare, or maybe wrote it down instead of relying on my memory." The statues clawed into their own stone flesh. The unmarked door suddenly dinged. Mentally, Alize believed that he was prepared to witness what he experienced in his nightmare. This was something that he dared not to write down since putting it into words felt too raw and wholly disturbing. It was as if the attention he gave would make the worst parts of his nightmares real.

"I see. My imagination is still not as bad as what reality can achieve. Hmm, perhaps I was lucky enough to not actively remember any of this. Or maybe I was just smart enough to not write down any specific triggers," his inward grimace turned into an almost tangible disgust and anger as soon as the elevator door dinged open. The thick scent of bleach, blood, and decaying flesh wafted into his nose with the force of a flood. Through slitted eyes, he watched the well-oiled machine of progress as a single escort pushed him through a different kind of corridor. The greenery was all gone in favor of a marble and stone aesthetic that felt complete without burning runes and iron bars that sparked intermittently. Chemical press rooms passed by, spotless and resembling jail cells. The walk stretched to minutes and the minutes to days as the smell of blood and rot thickened to an almost suffocating film on the back of one's throat. Alize quickly noticed that a cool breeze slowly began to circulate in his nostrils, forcing the smell to dissipate for the most part.

The first room with iron bars to show movement after several dozen misses, held a dozen familiar black uniformed guards. All manner of headgear covered their faces, but without fail, each one pulled at chains or magical bindings. The next few cells held guards, but as the escort pushed Alize deeper down the hall, the guards grew more disproportionate, more uncanny, more inhuman in their humanity. The masks were also less common, showing disfigured people that actually all somehow resembled each other. A handsome, almost perfectly, universally attractive face came out of the pieces of disfigured features like a puzzle being put together. The next half a dozen cells were empty save for the splattering of blood and some bones piled up in a corner. The next few dozen cells were filled with figures wearing green jumpsuits. The rooms even further departed from the iron and stone aesthetic and went for a more interrogation room in a mental studies institute type of feel with one-way mirrors showing the insides of padded white cells. Rather than having cleaners in jumpsuits, the seams between the padding on the walls and floors continuously pulsed with magic and steam as the empty rooms were sterilized or purified. The rooms that were filled, however, only held single subjects rather than dozens like a can of sardines.

After a few seconds of silently observing grotesque and misshapen forms, Alize closed his eyes and counted to ten. The moment he reached one, he checked the state of the captives that he passed by only to close his squinted eyes once again. Gradually, after around 30 seconds, the imprisoned monsters settled on something more humanoid. Maids and butlers in gray and black, clothed, fed, and taught these mostly humanoid, patchworked and stitched creatures everything they needed to know. That is, until one of the malformed beasts pulled at and broke their chains with a single step toward the door. With another step, the creature charged the one-way barrier. In that very same second, a maid from an adjacent room materialized next to the behemoth and put it in a chokehold millimeters before it connected with the soundproof barrier. Like she was coddling a baby, the maid pulled the creature into her embrace and laid it down on the padded white floor. Two guards in black rushed from further up the hallway and vanished along with the body. A misshapen baby with inhuman features was then left in the maid's arms. The creature was vaguely humanoid, possessing a bird's head, scaled legs, and sparsely feathered wings where its arms should be. A pair of chubby and stubby arms curled up on its back, similar to where wings would conventionally go on a child like this.

"This quack really is using homunculi to raise chimera. I can only imagine an operation like this is self-sufficient. It would have to be. Ha, despite finding all of this abhorrent, I have this morbid curiosity." Alize scanned the other rooms as he passed by them and noticed that most of the people being taken care of were simply very deformed variations of species and groups of people that already exist or existed at some point in history. A lion-faced man with a turtle shell on his back tried to walk, but his legs and arms were swapped. A little girl with legs twisting into the bodies of snakes tried to learn how to speak, but because of her anatomy, specifically, her fish head, using verbal communication was out of the question. A small boy with the arms of a giant tried to lift them up but due to some rather horrifying mismatch of the torso, was in a constant state of collapse and pain.

The maids and butlers helped these vaguely humanoid creatures function beyond their deformities and if they could not. Alize shut his eyes to the imagery of a butler backhanding a child with three heads, six arms, the torso of a human, and the lower half of a beetle. The child's middlemost head vanished as skull fragments and brain matter splattered all over the one-way barrier.

"Is the quack recycling the homunculi corpses to create more chimera? If so, how does he get fresh bodies to create more homunculus? Is Dean somehow involved? If not, did he manage to find a method that allows

either artificial lifeform to breed? If so, does this mean the quack is a legitimate doctor? Then there is the Piety Act to think about. If I can think of these questions, any genuine scholar worth their salt can immediately tell that just this one hallway is enough to get the doctor cleared in the books of the Empire. This means that calling the authorities will only help this fake doctor bastard get imperial funding and the scholar guilds' unofficial backing. If even one one of my questions has a remotely beneficial answer to it, or if the creatures in this hallway show slightly more promise in functions more than mildly cognitive." Just as Alize thought, the following rooms were filled with maids and butlers showing the newer humanoid creatures how to behave normally in different social settings, how to dress in either the guard or servant attire, how to utilize their magic, or how to use their bodies to perform different acts or tasks that would be necessary for some other experiment or service. Eventually, the escort reached the end of the hall and entered another elevator, where she bowed to a beautiful and vaguely green-skinned lady without a veil.

This conventionally attractive and green-skinned woman carted Alize down another long corridor that suddenly opened up to a massive room with white-clothed figures all over the place. They tended to giant vats of reddish-pink liquid and tubes of suspended creatures that varied in size and form.

"Aha. This setup is incredible. This is almost exactly like what the scholars' guild would set up if this type of research were legal. Ah, wait. Oh. This is terrible. The guild might already know what this guy is doing if he has such an official setup. Also, it's very possible to churn out an entire army." Alize silently took in the environment with a very audible but dreamy whimper, almost as if the pain he was in was so great that the medication was simply not enough to keep him down and out. Hesitantly, the green-skinned woman snapped her fingers

and called several guards over. With a simple point, the guards cleared a path straight through the middle of the lab, even though there was a designated walkway that circumvented the traffic.

"Lerians and Rettons are in one corner," Alize micro shifted every so often to get a better look at the lab. To the left, he was greeted by tall figures with long ears and smooth skin. Lines and swirling engravings similar to the ridges on the bark of trees decorated every muscle or voluptuous curve. Beside these floating figures were massive vats. Suspended in pieces were giants no less than 5 meters in height if all of the parts were to be assembled in the correct orientation.

"Changlestyx, Dysthos, and Voneur are in another." To the right of Alize were spherical domes that held some sort of viscous cream. Sleeping faces and limp spectral forms of all shapes and sizes freely pressed and bobbed within the opaque liquid. At intervals of one to two minutes, an ethereal specter was pulled from the sphere through a 3 centimeters in diameter tube and ejected into a small vial the size of one's finger. Interestingly enough, once the liquid was drained from the vial, a dull shard freely clattered against the vial. One of the white-clothed and veiled individuals then pressed the vial into some arcane contraption that Alize could not recognize.

Even if he couldn't place the tool, it was obvious that it served as a sort of mystical microscope. The device projected an image of the crystal, but as it zoomed in and cycled through dozens of filters, a stunningly handsome face shone through the glimmer. Alize didn't understand the readings that popped up on another connected screen connected to the projection, but he did understand what these researchers were doing. Almost immediately, he noted a distinct difference between the three milky spheres that took up the majority of his view on the right side of the lab. The next two vats held distinctly animalistic bipedal creatures, men and women and bodies featuring both and neither traits with the heads of lions, birds, insects, or any-thing else one might imagine a humanoid creature to be. The third vat was less conspicuous than the first two as the projected readings featured scans and diagrams that were no different from any other species or human for that matter. The only difference was the veritable rainbow palette of skin, hair, and eye colors and fantastical features that departed from genetic standards or even feasibility. Quite a few of these regular-looking individuals were even indistinguishable from other species aside from hair that moved like fire, or eyes that were motes of pure light.

The underground laboratory quickly did not end there, as another section exploded out from behind the menagerie that Alize first witnessed.

"They even have Drem from all of the major clans along with Blud-hautzee." These tubes resembled the same ones used to contain the Lerian subjects. The only difference was that these were much smaller, almost child sized and smaller if one were to make a comparison. As such, Alize quickly noticed that there were people that did not develop above 1 meter and half with the absolute tallest of the floating corpses maxing out at nearly 5 feet. Most held a childlike quality, but others were clearly just adults with shortened or perfectly shrunk propor-tions. A rare few had red, blue, green, or yellow markings printed on their skin, but most did not. As for the Bludhauzche, their tubes were even less space consuming, with the containers being no taller than half a meter to at most 1.5 despite being the widest amongst the Drem. The was another two other different areas, but Alize could not turn his head more than he already was in fear of being caught, though assumedly, the final two representative species throughout all of reality were being contained in those last two spots.

"With nearly every major group of people being represented here, I can only imagine that the end goal of this lab is not just limited to developing the methodology to create homunculus and chimera. My nightmare focused on this point, but looking at all of this and getting a feel for it in person. I can't help but think there is a bigger event behind the scenes." Alize frowned inwardly as he tugged at the connection that allowed his real body to remain home. Through that connection, he could clearly feel that his Affix retained a slow and methodical buffering. Feeling the dormant state of his curse, he refocused on the scenes around his doppelgänger.

The green-skinned lady rushed him to a massive metal door guarded by two eight meter tall giants and several dozen creatures that had anything from a humanoid appearance to a multi-jointed amalgamation of limbs. The elaborately designed area behind the giant metal door separated into three different directions: a small bedroom, a small study, and a corridor that led straight to another door guarded by four guards dressed in gray and white rather than black. The long-limbed woman with green skin and sharp features squinted at Alize as she pushed him into yet another elevator. The only difference between this handoff and the next was that no one was in the elevator to receive him.

2.5 Facades All Around

"**E**mpty? Did someone not come to observe me because they found an issue in my acting? My pain is real enough without [Prevention], and so is my reaction. There shouldn't be anything wrong with my appearance. Or is there? Damnit! Calm down, I've been in worse situations. Granted, I was in the Sim, so those instances are not exactly 100% accurate, so maybe? No! I shouldn't second guess myself. If the issue is not me, then the quack must have had his people do a background check on our family. Did something not look right? Did Mom or Dad even set up a proxy identity? If so, what rank paywall is our family's information locked behind? Why didn't I ask? I just trusted they would have done the most basic of preparations when they decided to elope. Should I use magic? Surely, one of them would notice if I suddenly ejected all of my magic. They would definitely come for me. Wait, don't press the panic button. No, one of them must have prepared something since we have been able to brazenly enter Rest. Meaning, the Veilseam should also *be selling some kind of fake info before our real information. Jarold is still here; I can feel the wind on my nose, so the situation isn't too bad."* Alize pretended to briefly wake up and looked around with a strained expression that quickly turned anxious and panicked. He opened his lips to start talking, but he cut himself off and appeared as though he randomly registered a pain he simply couldn't withstand. His head thrashed about in an eye-rolling silent scream before he once again pretended to go unconscious.

"I didn't see anyone in the room, nor did I see any cameras, runes, formations or anything of the like. But considering the enemy, it's more probable that I'm too weak to even attempt to find their method of surveillance. After all, if I were in the quack's position, would I let a stranger wander freely around my highly secure facility, injured or not? No. Would I even let that person know they were being watched? No. Then, there has to be someone vastly stronger than me in this elevator if that's the case." If Alize's survival instincts and intuition were a set of twins, they would have kissed him on the cheeks at the same time and bowed three times for the pleasure of being acquainted with him. Unsurprisingly, there was a person in the elevator with him. She simply observed him in silence. Before a minute could pass, the doors opened with a small chime. A second later, someone pushed him into a brightly lit and mindlessly excessive bachelor pad.

"This is what the quack looks like without the filter of a nightmare or expensive gear. I expected something less regal." Through squinted eyes, Alize focused on the wide back of a pale-skinned man as he splashed a bit too carelessly in a pool-sized bathtub. The guy leaned against a wall and made a show of pulling some woman onto his lap with a lecherous chuckle.

"Hmm, is he putting on an act? I am probably reading into it, but his back muscles tensed for a split second. Was he not expecting me to be here? Why?"

Alize only pondered the matter for a handful of seconds longer before he returned to his academy award-winning portrayal of "the broken child suddenly waking to hellish agony". The Quack, as Alize called him, loudly complained about the noise and turned towards the screams and the direction of the elevator. His knifelike cheekbones and sharply groomed facial hair could instantly spark attraction despite his sigh and obvious frown. Dr. Quack's salt and pepper hair swooped to one side with dripping water, revealing electric green eyes that contained the youthful glow of a young man just entering his prime. No familiarity sparked as he observed the guy. Not physically, at least. The behavior reminded him of the Hero that plagued his most recent few dozen nightmares all the way until the most.

"This man is definitely trying to work some hidden angle. His facial expression shifted along with his posture as soon as he turned this way. Is he suspicious of me, a child? No, that's not it. What am I missing? And why does his face give me the creeps?"

Alize reviewed the information contained within his journals first. When nothing scratched that itch at the back of his mind, he recalled the information that he shared with his parents on the ride over to Rest. Again, nothing soothed the worry that made his heart rattle his ribcage. Even after cracking into the parts of the nightmare that he didn't want to remember, nothing settled the disgust and anxiety that dried out his mouth. He pretended to regain his consciousness for a split second and screamed before "fainting" from exhaustion. The rule of three implied that this was his last fake-out before these people began to suspect him. Dr. Quack seemed to be shaken out of his own annoyance upon hearing a child's hoarse cries. The undeniably handsome guy loosened his grip on a pair of curved horns and casually pressed his fingers into the waist of the person that he pulled onto his lap. He unhurriedly carried the stitched-up person towards a short flight of steps that led out, or into, the massive bathtub.

"How annoying. I wouldn't have gotten comfortable if I knew this would happen, ah well." The man combed through his hair with a wet hand and leaned against a step with an unsatisfied frown. An androgynous looking person with curling horns and midnight blue skin trembled as they moved off of the man's lap. The standing person bowed with a bright indigo blush across their face and retreated. The person submerged in the water alongside two other naked people, a male and a female as they stopped lathering the quack doctor's unexpectedly muscular body.

"Ah yes. Forgive the unfortunate interruption, but I will thoroughly enjoy you later, Ny-ny." The Quack narrowed his eyes at the horned woman and licked his lips with a wolfish grin despite rolling his eyes in the direction of Alize just a moment before. Right after that, his attention quickly shifted back to the rude interruption.

"The quack also noticed that his own body unintentionally tensed up and made a show of it to save his flamboyant image. Which means, like me, he is wary of someone stronger listening in or taking measure of his actions. It's possible that the elevator is a sort of shortcut. I can conclude that without the elevator and escort, this underground area is a tangle of misleading areas, a maze of some sort. That said, what I've seen is straightforward, organized, and efficient. If my journal is right and if my Affix is right, this guy is a quack who should not be capable of establishing and running this operation. Meaning, there is something or someone keeping everything this way. A micromanager, or several? Is the quack on guard against this individual? If so, did the event start because he is supposed to get rid of this person once he is supposed to get his hands

on the scrying glasses? If so, how does this change what my Affix set into motion if I have the glasses now? Does it change anything at all? I got hurt despite my parents working to circumvent the situation, so did I ensure the quack would get the glasses by taking them off of the bear? Damn it. What if..." Alize almost broke his perfect squint from how much his thoughts swirled. Jarold, as an entity that blended into the very wind, noticed the micro nose and eyebrow twitches and also began to think about what had Alize in such a state. Once he sent a breeze through the boy's clothes, his attention immediately locked onto the mini spectacles that Alize his inside of the wrappings on his wrist.

"Teeya. It's good to see you again so soon, my sweet apricot. Though despite the pleasure, I'm wondering why you brought the boy here. Shouldn't your mother be handling this matter downstairs? She should have received all the information that my hat scanned." The Quack very nonchalantly kicked his feet up, carelessly splashing water into the faces of the attendants not too far from him. One of his hands splashed water out of the tub as he pointed to an outfit that Alize had seen not too long ago. A silver shawl and bamboo hat with a sewn-in veil floated in the air right in front of a snow-white robe. Every inch of the outfit glimmered with mystical energy as a Quibe, or magic bank in the shape of a wardrobe, recharged the stitching. The kid could not turn to look at the display, so he had no thoughts on the matter, but since everyone's heads seemed to turn at the man's suggestion, Alize managed to catch something that others would not have noticed.

"There, ha. Everyone slips up when they think no one is looking. That inflection and reactionary twitch. To make it seem natural, he went with the motion, but I saw it when the Quack said, "Your mother." That mother figure must be who he expected to escort me if I was brought to this area. Is he on guard against this woman or something she is involved in? Going off of the admittedly limited information I have, the most likely

"Mother" figure is that green-skinned lady that escorted me through the laboratory. Is there some sort of internal conflict between this quack and that lady?"

"I'm sorry for the interruption, Master Nayame, but Mother shared her thoughts on the matter and estimated that the patient's restoration period has exceeded the projected range after personally scanning his condition. She forgot to tell you as she had to move up the timetable for the next project in preparation for the new Clown and Pirate material Mister Dean will provide us after this matter is over." Teeya flipped through a few pages on her clipboard and waved her finger to send a few floating papers over to Dr. Quack.

"These papers are mother's planned adjustments for the 100th experiment, findings on the ninety-ninth batch of chimera, and projections for the one hundred and first molding cycle of homunculi based on those results." Teeya did not smile or frown as the Quack rolled his eyes and swiped the pages off to the side.

"Oh. That was an admittedly slick maneuver. He just barely tilted his head off to the side as he used some type of aura to enhance his vision. It could have been a reflection of the room's light sources, but I doubt it. I'm not anywhere near the level where I could detect someone's magic as they secretly use it, but I do know that there are still telltale signs of silent casting if someone doesn't have the [Shroud] aspect of Ballast Type magic." Alize slumped in his seat as if he had suddenly entered a deep restorative sleep to match and even exceed the Quack's superb acting.

"Your mother is quite buzzing for a homunculus!" With a haughty chuckle, Dr. Quack shook his head. He sighed not too long after and walked out of the tub, which caused a blur of action so fast Alize couldn't follow. In less than a blink of an eye, the Quack's pool attendants used magic and waved their hands in unison. A silk robe snaked out of the guy's wardrobe and wrapped itself around his pool-exiting figure. A cup of some colorful liquid entered his hand while even his wet hair suddenly blew out and styled itself into a tight and refined side part that sent jolts of electricity and the smell of burning straight to Alize's body and nose. The Quack took a sip of the drink he just knew would be there and raised another hand to Teeya's face as he seemingly teleported across the room.

"Go prepare my artifact..." At the Quack's order, a fireplace suddenly roared to life as three shadows dived into the crackling flames. The pool found itself empty, full of salt water rather than chlorine or other chemicals in the meantime.

"As for you, Teeya, I only managed to dip myself in before you interrupted me. Very well done, my apricot. It seems you still haven't learned your lesson on timing." Dr. Quack placed a finger under the woman's chin with an almost hungry gulp. Teeya closed her eyes almost expectantly, but the whole sight almost made Alize want to give up pretending to be knocked out so he could barf and call the authorities.

"ILLEGAL. THAT'S DEFINITELY ILLEGAL!" Alize screamed in his mind as he watched the doctor work his magic. Even Jarold stirred as a formless pressure weighed down on Alize's shoulders to remind him to be still and retain his calm.

"That was a [Resonance] sequence] spell. That is most definitely illegal. Other than that, he is not Leakly. That man's profile is public record and something Mom, Dad, and I all looked at before we left the market. This means maybe this isn't the person from Gregory's place, or maybe he has Arcanum that replicates the real doctor's profile? Where is the real Leakley? Was he ever a person?"

Alize pondered for exactly one second before he jumped to the real issue at hand.

"It's a bit concerning though. Is the magic carrying with his voice or emanating from his body like a pheromone? Wait, is he just imagining putting this subordinate under his command or is the spell a magical distillation of the entire process of brainwashing? Ah, beyond the magic, the profile needed to accomplish what I'm seeing is insanely specific. This means that he is definitely a descendant of the Nayame family or someone who has a similar synergistic effect." Alize inwardly frowned as the Quack's lips blushed a soft shade of red. His spit, or the scent of his body, or the vibration of his words lit up with a soft haze of magic. The weird fog curled into Teeya's slightly open mouth, nose, and ears and almost instantly her exposed skin flushed. She didn't notice the spell being cast on her, nor did she notice the castoff of effuse that would usually accompany using one's mana-oriented magic.

"I will have to reward you later for being so exceptionally prudent." The Quack laughed so hard he had to take a sip of his drink to clear his throat. The magic that danced across the man's lips and swirled, dissipated the same instant he stopped casting the spell. Absolutely nothing hinted at the casting other than in that split second.

"Until then, update me on your progress finding an intact Lochorn herb and its higher-graded roots. These people are practically useless since they already used their stock on the kid." The Quack slowly seated himself on a reclining chair by a towering multicolored blaze that roared within the nearby fireplace.

"His gaze is sharper, and every movement is more deliberate. It would seem as though he only trusts this Teeya woman, but only after using his magic on her. Could it be his attendants are just here to keep an eye on him?"

Alize watched the quacks' posture change into one of focus and control rather than decadence.

"Well, sir, the information on Lochorn herbs that you have been looking for in relation to your personal issue was single star just as you guessed it would be. When I inquired privately about acquiring the herb, I was directed to the information on a private auction held at an independently operating and unsanctioned market closer to the Drip. I looked into contacting the seller but found it to be locked behind a five-star paywall, which is why you had been summoned to provide proof of sale." Teeya completely forgot about Alize and moved a strand of hair behind her ear as she followed and leaned over.

"I learned that the patient's father purchased a fair share of roots at that auction. Also, it seems that..." Teeya, who had not yet left to interview Orsche and Verza, showed Dr. Quack the files that she compiled on her clipboard.

"Ah. So, the kid and his family are distant relatives. Corridor Country elites. Haa, to think, the bush snakes of Haven missed yet another descendant of the horny dogs' bloodline. At this rate, their ranks will be overrun with lowbred mongrels. Haa." Dr. Quack smiled, but his voice carried an almost tangible malice and sarcasm.

"Go ahead. What is all of this?"

"These few pages here are a compilation of notable events in their family's history. Everything beyond this page summarizes what you need to say or know in order to act the part of their distant relative. This shows the patient's wounds, all of which are on the mend and only need a significant amount of time to fully adjust to the over-flowing magic of the Lochorn root and some other medicines. This page here is from Mother. It explains the procedures and methodology a surgeon would follow and operate with, in consideration of the patient's wounds. These documents, especially the highlighted paragraphs, show some necessary expenditures and profit margins regarding this matter." Teeya spread the pages in the air with magic and gently smiled as she separated and grouped everything in glowing brackets. Once the pages fit nicely in the air, she continued to explain the details and inform the quack of his role.

"Firstly, once the arcanum is set up, Mother deemed the patient fit enough for the medical staff to take the child's blood and other samples to distill a portion of the root's effectiveness. On top of all of that, these few pages are a plan regarding long-term profits. With a small investment of one or two homunculi, you can maintain your anonymity and potentially gain the entire Nayame family's inheritance and prestige without being targeted by other royal lineages. This is a timetable, and an accelerated projection of approximately three decades if this investment were to succeed." Teeya didn't even seem to notice that the quack's hands suddenly lashed out and wandered all over her body.

"*Wait!*" Alize raced back and forth between his memories and a massive board that suddenly manifested in the main lobby of his thoughts.

"*Holy crap. I completely glossed over what the quack just said. Horny dog. This guy looks exactly like the hero from my most recent nightmare. He's older and a bit more muscular. There's also facial hair and that overall manliness to him, but otherwise, they are the exact same person. Hmm, there's also the difference in hair color, eye shape, and then this guy is clearly mostly a Quran Retton mix and not strictly human so, yeah. My whole comparison just fell apart. But still. Mad dog is something.*" Alize pushed the thought to the back of his mind and focused on what the quack referred to.

"*Nezaret the Noodle. Unlike that king, this quack has a synergistic aspect to his profile rather than a fully rooted spell. In terms of danger, I doubt the mind control is as potent as the ancestral Nayame, but this guy's profile allows his body to naturally exude the horny dog's magic, which would get rid of the typical signs mana would leave behind. He doesn't have a [Shroud] aspect. If he did, I wouldn't have seen him casting as at all. He also doesn't have a Direct-type sensory application since he would have noticed me looking at him. This only leaves everything else, Ha..."* Alize thought about what he would do if he possessed mind control magic so potent, it could break through star rankings.

"One thing that I can be certain of is that he seems to have a Direct-type movement aspect, or maybe he has a rooted Accord, something that allows him to traverse through the air or space-time? I'm not sure. All I know is he needs to have at least one pairing Aura Aspect and a single rooted profile that complements the Mind control or a three-way synergistic pairing that supports or manifests the same effect." Alize then thought of the only reason why the horny dog failed to become a bigger name in the grand scheme of the Immortal Empire and compared it to the guy who was most definitely not Leakley Nayame.

"This guy is wary of people because he has the same issue as his ancestor, just in the opposite use case." Alize found the connection, or rather, he deduced a possible reason why the glasses he took off the teddy bear would be the spark that ignited an explosive cascade of events that revolve around this quack and the cursed estate.

"The Noodle had a potent mind control spell that, historically, seemed to even work on Archons and Gods. The only problem he ran into was not knowing who was actually under his grasp and that there was a perfect counter to his magic. Irisa Ghale, or the Cursed Pinwheel Archon, was lucky enough to automatically counter the magical effect on their first meeting and shed light on the king's profile and actions. If the noodle had the capability of seeing who his spell would work on, that never would have happened. Haven would have been fine in the end, I think, but the Empire would have gotten involved." Alize pulled up the board from the back of his mind and drew some connections.

"This guy has a different issue than what I can determine about how spell-casting physically works. His charm works regardless, just like his ancestor. It's just less effective or more subtle. Constant exposure and selective casting seem to be his modus operandi." He circled the last word that he wrote down and paid more attention to the guy's touching. It was deliberate and calculated, with flashes of magic pouring out of his fingertips and grazing Teeya's skin ever so slightly. Her breathing turned ragged and labored, but Alize only noticed the coldness that plastered itself on the quack's face as he remained fixed on the fireplace.

"The Scrying glass would fix his issue pretty much entirely. My problem is assumption. Everything hinges on there being some kind of internal division. Hmm, it's possible that he might be looking to control someone or something else? The homunculi? The chimera?"

Alize split the people he saw into two categories. Those with standard humanoid forms with only slight differences from standard people and the bodies that were composed of patchwork material that were either stitched together or blended into one whole like molded clay.

"And why do I get the same vibe from him as from the bastard hero? Is he another descendant of the horny dog that managed to be born mostly human as a genetic anomaly, or is this guy and the one I dreamed of, the same person? Is it all just a coincidence? This doctor is most definitely the precursor or possibly even the ancestor for that hero guy." Alize didn't have enough space to write everything so he pulled up another board and worked on new theories while the woman called Teeya explained some of the finer details contained within her paperwork. The first thing he did was circle and cross out the word "coincidence". "My Affix Exists" was written in the margins.

"Scrying Glasses. rank (?, probably 9). Grade (?, probably high). Level (100, most likely). With such a relic, the quack would be able to tell exactly who he could charm, who would be an asset to keep around for future use, and who would be a potential threat to his wellbeing and secrecy since it would take too long to turn them over with his casting efficiency and the implicit condition of physical touch or close proximity." Alize frowned inwardly. After some time dwelling on the matter, he rushed back and forth between his memory and the two boards that contained his multiple trains of thoughts.

"If I am to assume the real Leakley was engaged in this research under Guild oversight, I can easily conclude that this Mother figure must be his failsafe. A coworker? A scholar in her own right? Or an experiment that the real Nayame personally adjusted in a manner similar to an unchanging black box? That would make her a..." He churned through different scenarios in his mind. Trying to find something to either confirm or to disprove his conjectures.

"Alright, that's enough apricot. I get the situation. What I'm hearing is, we tie the kid up while his body is maintained in my relic so your mother can work some magic for me. Sounds pretty straightforward." The Quack laughed like a maniac and waved his wandering hand.

"Go on then, Teeya, greet the relatives then. Ah, on your way up, get mother dearest to continue preparing whatever she has in mind. I want to see what a homunculus befitting a protected lineage looks like. And tell her to make sure that the body is from the clean stock. I don't want the chimeras to leave their stink all over batch 101. Also, have some of the servants pick out the best after Dean brings us the new material. I like the plan where we secure some family ties, so I want batch 102 to include some gifts that I can give my?" The guy snapped his fingers and waved them toward Alize.

"He would be your nephew twice removed on your mother's collateral family tree."

"Great. Hm, have the neutered homunculus watch over the entire process as well. Those disgusting brats in the cellar tend to get handsy." The man sipped some more of his seemingly endless drink and suddenly frowned.

"And entertain our future in-laws until I get back into character." The quack blinked a few times and licked his lips with a satisfied grumble as three people walked out of the blazing fireplace. His posture opened as he loosened his robe with a lecherous grin plastered across his face.

"What took you three so long? I am dying over here." The quack smiled as a young man, a Voneurian-Frust with vibrant pink skin and webbed fingers, rushed over and rubbed his feet. A meter tall, cream-skinned lady, Gaelen-Drem similar to Jarold, fluttered over on a pair of butterfly wings with a panicked expression and fed him square fruit the size of grapes. The third, the chimera with curved horns and star-dotted skin, simply stood behind the Quack and rubbed his shoulders with a noticeable blush still on her face. Alize watched all of this through squinted eyes. Suddenly, the pressure on his shoulders magnified and pressed three times before it floated away.

"Jarold is leaving. Since I am still here and I don't hear any explosions, it means that he has carefully selected the information that Mom has been getting. Ah, thinking of my parents, I should probably prepare a few countermeasures for some worst-case scenarios." While Dr. Quack held Teeya's attention and put her under some sort of spell, Alize silently and very carefully shifted his head to capture Jarold's location. The latter created a faint outline in the heated air by the fireplace, a pinto second before it vanished into the rest of the warm haze.

Internally, another board slowly manifested beside Alize's current thoughts.

"Worst case, huh? What would that even be? Immediately, it would be Jarold telling Mom about the inhumane experiments and her immediate response being to destroy everything here. The result would be an investigation by not only the local Custodian force. Surveyors and possibly even an Intendant might drop by and investigate, nevermind if an issue crops up that is so large it draws the wrong attention. A proper Guardian might show up." He snapped to another thought.

'If the scholars' guild gets involved, it will be even worse. By some miracle, if we manage to run away from Jordaine's law enforcement. I'm fairly certain that the churches will send someone to poke their heads around and inevitably, even if I have a [Shroud] rooted profile, the Tenets that I am subconsciously mimicking will set off all kinds of alarms if someone is capable of scanning effuse even somewhat effectively. *For a Transgression against the Heavenly Path the Hounds will hunt.*" Alize wrote the words "PANIC: In case of the worst #1. Cry for case #2. Try to compartmentalize and disassociate for case #3" on a plaque and placed it right next to the second board in his mental lobby.

"I'll get back to this later. For now..." Leaving his mind, Alize carefully opened his eyes to find that the horned chimera with blue skin pushed his chair toward the fireplace. Intrigued, he watched in wonder as the multicolored flame parted ways to reveal a tunnel that extended out toward a mostly empty stone room. Upon being pushed into the mostly bare chamber, he noticed a porous stalactite that dripped a luminescent silver liquid into a stone basin. A custom intravenous stand, similar to a chandelier, circled the stalactite and hung low to the tub. Extension tubing snaked around the box on hooks, with each one holding empty plastic bags.

"This room. I asked Dad about Arcanum that looked like this back when I had the nightmare for the first time. This is Tharron's Corazó-Sprie. A one of a kind Arcanum that has been lost for ages." Alize's vision briefly overlapped with a blood-splattered rendition of the room. His own bloodless husk reached out from inside the basin. In a blink, the entire blue-toned room returned to normal.

"It is also called the Spring of Eternal Youth or the Heart Rejuvenating Spring. So this is the next event. My blood, fluids, and the magic that is keeping me alive are supposed to be drained and replaced by the spring's waters. It's no wonder that the next dozen or so events are all related to the quack. My recovery will be slowed by months at best, which would keep us coming back every month or sooner depending on how much of this drugged water that I am given." He scoffed and cleaned up the tangled web that he created for each thought that he possessed about his circumstances.

"I wonder how many of his patients are hooked on this genuine miracle of pharmacology." Alize frowned inwardly and waited for the horned attendant called Ny-Ny to do something related to the mess of tubing. Interestingly, they let go of his chair and turned toward the tunnel. They waited for the last spark of the flame to vanish. Once the colorful fire winked out of existence, Ny-Ny rushed to the other side of the room and punched the wall. The blush spread to the entirety of their body, almost as if an intensely compressed substance expanded within its much weaker container. They screamed and roared, beating against the stone until their hands turned to bloodied pulps. Screams thundered throughout the small room until they slumped onto the floor with heart-wrenching sobs.

"What is happening?" Alize briefly closed his narrowed eyes and did his best to remember the nightmare that related to this new event. When nothing shed light on this odd situation, he looked back on

something that his dad taught him after he wanted to learn more about how life was created and how he was born. In addition to the birds and the bees, Orsche supplemented the talk with a legitimate diagram that separated Life and its variations into three separate realms.

"Off the top of my head, it's possible that they are just venting off some excess magic as an unhealthy coping mechanism but if it's not, I can only imagine that the magic linking them together is faulty or it has been destabilized in some way. The only way to destabilize a chimera is to have an incompatible aspect essentially parasitizing the bindings and spells keeping the manufactured profile stable," Alize inwardly frowned and tried to decide if he should just observe or try to help in some way. After he confirmed the issue afflicting the chimera of course, and also after he confirmed they were alone, which goes without saying.

2.6 Artificial Life

"If I am remembering this right, it was estimated that one in every seven chimera would suddenly deteriorate after a few years regardless of how well magic is used to force life. This is due to the remnants of Aura that naturally bloom and grow within a living body. From there, only one out of every hundred thousand chimera would be able to overcome this natural destabilization after cannibalizing the Aura inside of their own bodies. The best case for these chimera is that the Aura is compatible with the spells and Mana that operates the form. Then, only one out of ten thousand of the stable chimera would be able to actually develop that initial spark beyond stability." Alize flipped a few pages in a mental book to remind himself of when he touched upon the subject of life. He skipped over the memory of mountains of homework, skimmed over weeks of Sim related lessons, and then months of lab time that his dad set up with a legitimate but very small selection of other Manaform's. One small issue though...

"Really? I can't can't find the actual topic anywhere in my mind, nevermind the details? Did I really forget? I shouldn't have, dammit.

This is why most scholars use magic to organize and improve their memory and processing speeds. I should have put a note somewhere, but where?"

He thumbed through a rather dense contents page in front of a maze of information but could not find what he was looking for. On the brink of wanting to give up, Alize spotted the name J.J. Trello.

"Classifications of life forms throughout the ages? It should definitely be here." A particular encyclopedia that he found in the shadow of a massive binder, covered some detailed information that he vaguely remembered. He checked the table of contents and instantly thumbed over to the pages on chimera.

"Maintaining a chimera's body? Developing a chimera's mental state? No, no, no. Aha. So, your chimera is starting to resemble a living being. Let's see what we have, here oh. I left myself a note? ChBi4BDls." Alize blinked a few times with a smile.

"Chimeras have 4 biologically distinct stages. I referenced them earlier, but it, 'Aurate Manifestation, metabolization, readjustment, and permanence,' are the names of the actual processes." Outwardly, Alize continued to appear knocked out, but his squinted eyes locked onto the shivering body of Ny-Ny as he looked for something.

"I can tell they are most likely somewhere near the end of metabolizing the aura that is naturally within the body parts that they are made up of but..." He did his best to hide a splitting headache that came with forcing himself to remember something he clearly didn't keep track of too well.

"It's very likely that she will turn into an aberration at this rate." Unexpectedly, a book or rather, a memory suddenly fell from the top shelf he grabbed the binder from. It was a small sticky note reminding him to look into the memory of a chimera that served as the linchpin for creating what most know when they talk about artificial life in the Manaform Realm.

"Wait!"

He parsed through the information on Manaform life and on chimeras specifically, focusing on degenerative afflictions that were the cause of death for 6 out of 7 chimeras. One of the first things that he noticed within his notes about the shelf life was that scholars used to pursue this field of study before reaching a blockade in technological advancements and spell craft. Chimera were typically or rather consistently bred or created with a minimum of one month and a max of one year to live due to issues with mutations that resulted in a mass extinction event for a whole, now nameless, country a long time ago. And two very specific naming conventions between different generations of experiments were used and adhered to almost religiously when referring to the last batch in a generation of artificial life.

"Ny-Ny. Ni- Ni. Oho. How could I have missed that? *Her name means Ninety-Nine. That would make them the product of the 99th batch of chimeras that this quack has made,"* Alize remembered that the quack and Teeya mentioned that Mother was still actively observing the 99th batch of chimeras, working on the 100th, preparing for the 101st, and was now planning for the 102nd.

"If ninety-nine here is the most recent batch of chimera, this means that the quack officially knows that this facility is able to recreate chimera capable of surviving the benchmark of 1/7. He must not know the process is on the cusp of completely metabolizing. I'm confident that the information that Teeya showed him did not possess any updates on that front; otherwise, he would most likely not let Ny-Ny out of his sight to keep track of progress firsthand." Things I should not mention to my parents." Decorated the top of a new board and, as of right now, only the cutout of the bear's scroll and an imperial sigil showed

up. A frown emerged from Alize's stony expression as a small note with the semi-translucent image of a monocle burned into its surface. Shaking his imaginary head, the image crumpled as he turned back to a picture of Ny-Ny that was sandwiched between the doctors' covered and unveiled images and the plushie bear and glasses.

"Aberrations. Magic influenced life outside of the normal or current zeitgeist." He reviewed the information he had once more and stopped looking inward since the present was rather worrying. Ny-Ny clenched their jaw and let out a sudden throat-tearing scream. They ripped at her clothing and cried about blueberries and a bird that ripped at a frog with a broken tail. After the nonsense seemed to reach their own ears, the volume of the bloody roars increased and the gibberish expanded to other languages, some of which he knew while others, Alize couldn't place heads or tails anywhere.

"Party. Beetle. Bed. You. Blueberry. Fish. Show. Hold. Boat. Hold. Help. Kill. Beetle. Save me." recurred every so often and in nearly a dozen different languages as soft, almost pale glimmers of yellow, orange, and red illuminated Ny-Ny's paper-thin eyelids.

"Forget becoming an aberration, she might become an abomination. Their mind is already a pile of mush, and its body is on the brink of fully digesting the aura spark. If I were to guess, it has another minute, maybe two before the spells holding her together unravel," A chaotic storm of magic echoed their verbal anguish. A fire whip lashed at the wall, then a gust of wind cut at the floor, a blinding light pulsed from their chest area and simply erased everything it touched, leaving a blackened line devoid of light or sound. Or it would have if they were not inside of a peculiar Arcanum that could not be destroyed. After a few rounds of discharge, all of the magically created phenomena came to an abrupt halt.

Ny-Ny collapsed onto the floor with an ashen expression. Glowing fissures of broken woven magic spread from one star on their blue skin to the next. The barbed wire unraveled. They sobbed in the corner and gasped out a few words, little phrases that cut, tugged, and resonated with Alize's withered heart. To be more accurate, they repeated nonsense that held the same kind of hurt, lost, and sad tempo of questions that he had asked himself on more than one occasion inside of the simulations that his parents curated. Even now, despite being sure that he was not in an illusion, there was always this nagging feeling that pressed the back of his eyes and mind.

"Why am I hurt? How did this happen? What's wrong with me, and why does it hurt here too? Why? Why am I like this? What am I?"

Ny-Ny clawed into their own exposed chest and banged the back of their head against the floor with tears and open wounds that drenched the maid's outfit that simply only served to cater to the doctor's vision. They pulled their mangled limbs into a fetal position, whispering in a voice just a barely loud enough voice that made it so Alize could barely make out some of the words.

"Is this hate? I hate it. I hate him. I hate this place. I hate it. I hate it. I hate it.... Why? What is hate? What is this pressure in my chest and my head? Everything hurts. You know. You see me. Why are you letting this happen?" Every so often, one of the little stars twinkling on their blue skin did its best to keep their body together by spreading some spindly threads of magic but it was similar to dragging yourself forward through broken glass only for someone to lay twice as much in your path the moment that you stopped.

"*This poor creature. Magic, spells, whatever, this is what happens when a force and energy are bound to a physical form and are forced to live.*" He watched the chimera's body split apart at the seams. Instead of blood, effuse leaked out glimmering but not bloody meat as a luminescent and dense fog that produced no light of its own.

"Based on the information I do have..." He could do nothing but observe intently as Ny-Ny's exposed muscle squirmed, deformed, and after some moments, regenerated unexpectedly as the random threads began to match one to one to each stitched together muscle fiber. Their skin, muscle, and exposed bone pulsed with life that was simply not possible for sentient magic. Sadly and almost exactly as Alize assumed, the profile that kept them alive was not programmed for living flesh that possessed magic of its own and just as Alize imagined, her body conflicted with itself as the stars turned inward and ripped into her magic infused flesh.

"The metabolization will either be a success, or the more likely option occurs and they will become an Aberrant Chimera. A non-sentient, warped, perversion of life against nature. There is also a growing possibility that the aura is snuffed out and they become an artificial monster. An abomination that takes the form of a storm of pure magic. I will most likely die if either of the two bad options happens here, so I'm really hoping for the best." Alize weighed his options and slowly turned his head to look around since he was confident that if anyone else was in the room, they would have stepped in to control the situation.

An eyeball suddenly poked out of the massive gouge in Ny-Nys chest. The wounds near the massive cavity instantly scabbed over with pustules and masses of writhing flesh. A body designed to contain but not use magic, and a spell cast to serve a specific service—a match made in the absolute pits of Hell.

"Healing magic. Some variant of Accord aura by the looks of it. Ah, that's a bad matchup if things go sour. With Creation mana and the control she displayed in not instantly killing me when it lashed out. Shh. Oh, this is very bad. Is there even a way I can escape this place?"

He gradually opened his squinted eyes, appearing as though he were just now waking from a nightmare. Exactly one second later, a sharp claw suddenly exploded out of the bubbling eye in Ny-Ny's chest and splattered Alize's face and clothes with fragments of bone and flesh that didn't bleed but was full of simple and pure water. As he examined the flesh, he almost instantly realized that the 'muscle' was made with plant fibers while the bones were made of bleached coral.

"Are their horns not bone and keratin but branches or more coral..." Alize asked himself a dozen questions but eventually decided to follow through on his decision even if someone was watching him.

"Are you okay?"

Alize croaked with a heavy rasp. His eyelids slowly fell as he bobbed his head in a struggle to stay awake. Ny-Ny jolted up with a gasp. Different from the painful spasms, but quick and horrible all the same, the horned chimera held their collapsing body and smiled.

"I am. I am okay." The magic keeping it all tucked, flashed and adjusted in the blink of an eye. Just underneath her skin, the threads, centipede-like in their crawl, reined in on their rapidly mutating body and slowed the process of regeneration.

"I am in..." Alize opened his eyes wide, completely dropped his act, and hovered himself into the farthest corner away from Ny-Ny.

"Extreme danger!"

His face paled in fright even if he couldn't stop observing Ny-Ny's rapidly deteriorating condition.

"I can die. This situation is very terrifying. But! But, If she is able to survive the war in her body and digest that aura spark as a mana-form. I would be able to observe something that is a miracle against nature." Alize thought on the subject of artificial magical constructs gaining life for a moment before a sudden flash of color and light struck the side of his face.

"Someone is coming through the fireplace. Is there surveillance in here? Dammit, I got carried away. If there is, then his person has come to deal with the both of us. But if there is no surveillance, is the quack coming here himself or did he order some servants to check up?"

Ny-Ny froze up the moment that two very voices resonated with the crackling of wood and the whoosh of the Arcanum opening. Their conversation, as far as Alize could tell, was mostly unimportant since the only thing important at this moment was that both of the strangers immediately noticed Ny-Ny's state of being. The taller, thinner figure acted first. He whipped around and then used his bare hand to smack the air and extinguish the multicolored flame. The shorter and more robust of the two rushed over to Ny-Ny and dove into a slide as she pulled the horned woman close to her flat but comforting chest. The short stranger in a maid's outfit rocked Ny-Ny back and forth even as the barbed magic lashed out against her face and arms. With a gentle hum, the girl set up a gentle and personal atmosphere as the space itself stilled under a massive inhale of breath. The hum turned into a slow and melodic tune, then a lullaby.

"Shush mi loera, quinte plus lente para' caridina. Tiena loer, tiena loer, bien rieta mi' hanyo. Beta, beta, bete mi loera. Esanda mi a'daire..." The girl's soft voice lulled to a hum that seemed to ebb and flow with Ny-Nys breathing, slowing it to a calm.

"Hush my love, quiet your, silence your heart. Take your love, take your love, and grab my hand. Breathe, breathe, breathe, my love. Beside you I am here ..." The girl held the note and rocked side to side, shifting between some ancient language Alize didn't recognize, a gentle hum, and common Herzen.

"...Sleeping babies, wave with the willow, they hush with the sheep. I will... Mom will hold you fast asleep, Dad will guard your dreams...." The little girl trailed off with a distant look but gradually hummed the rest of the lullaby. Eventually, Ny-Ny's mutating body settled down as the glowing barbed wire retreated back into the stars it came from. The magical centipedes that pulsed along their writhing flesh also fell away, but not in the normal sense, as they moved with the tempo of the song. The tall young man with deep bags underneath his eyes shook his head and calmly pointed out the obvious once Ny-Ny's chest began to rise and fall evenly.

"Ninety-nine doesn't have a mother or father. I believe that telling such lies is the sole mission of the nurses. In addition, it is a kinder mercy to put the chimera out of its misery, seeing as how its magic has begun to lash out." The tall youth frowned and untangled the tubing hanging from the chandelier.

"Idiot. They may not have parents, but we do have the Profile of someone who is connected to something in body parts in their batch. And I know that they need to be put down, but I think we can help at least one get through this final hurdle. The ninety-fives were able to survive this decomposition and metabolization." The girl lowered her head.

"Yes. Because only one of the chimeras in that mutated batch possessed an ember of aura. Ninety-five was able to accomplish what others could not by dividing its spark of aura among its accompanying batch. And look at where that evolution got them. They turned into a useless meat golem on the lowest floor. Hmph, and mother only keeps it around because it's easier to process material for our younger siblings after the mana aspects have been stripped by 95..." The young man shuddered as he trailed off, thinking about something.

"Ny-Ny, on the other hand, appears to have several slivers of aura developing in multiple parts of their body. It's impossible to help them survive this. Now kill them before it becomes an issue between mother and master. I'll take responsibility for its death." The young man narrowed his eyes and paused his actions for a moment so he could lock gazes with the short girl who looked very similar to him.

"Not yet. I am confident that I can help them. You should try too, ya moron. We have a responsibility to help this poor little baby, or are you a heartless monster?"

The girl bared her fangs at the tall young man.

"I will not stop you, since I cannot. But I am advising you that you should not take the risk considering the recent changes." The youth return to preparing the tub with an even deeper frown.

"Whatever dumbhead." The short maid rocked back and forth even harder for a good long while before something came to mind.

"Hey, do you think we have the aura profiles of one or both of their parents or siblings, or husband or wife, or grandparents, or maybe even their children if they had any?"

The girl's eyes softened as she touched Ny-Nys clawed face. The young man trembled violently as emotion beat against his still heart. The tears that wanted to fall simply did not as red dyed his sclera. His neck also bulged unnaturally for a moment, as if the beat of his still heart was too much for the rest of his body to endure. If one could read his thoughts in this moment, they would only receive screaming and crying that bordered insanity as hundreds, thousands, if not millions of voices, and physical inputs roared at him to burn the estate to the ground. Every violent impulse someone had, his mind and body were assaulted by them.

"I'm sure you are only being emotional. But to answer your question, we have the exact same origin as the donor who was fashioned into her first lumbar vertebra and some fragments of her left humerus. I believe. So yes, the molding that we have come out of is somewhat related to some parts of the Chimera. Ah, wait. Can you not tell?" The young man raised an eyebrow but didn't stop his work.

"No. I only feel a connection. Like their pain is my pain. Um, what would happen if I gave them some of my magic? Would that help her process the sparks inside of her?"

The girl wiped her tears and placed Ny-Ny's head on her lap.

"No. In fact, it would agitate the balance that their bodies are already struggling to achieve and maintain. Mother already tried that with the ninety-sixth batch of chimeras and our other siblings. Guiding and forcing the physical component of one's profile to subjugate itself to its more mystical, mana component, does not end well. In other words, her spells will stop working to keep their bodies in shape and functioning. Mother learned this even earlier with the twentieth batch." The tall but dark-eyed youth paused as he remembered something.

"A chimera or homunculus that contains or generates a spark of its diametric magic profile will experience one of three outcomes. The most likely is a slow and painful death as the magic burns itself to purify the artificial construct of all foreign bodies, even if they are not. It's how humans introduced cancer and other biologically degenerative ailments to our world.. The second outcome is a torturous and near-eternal existence of being trapped in one's own body as the foreign or developing but complete profile subjugates and absorbs the other until there is either cohesion, the Blip. Or death due to there being no more magic. The third..." the young man pressed his thumb against Alize's back and cleanly pulled the compression blanket off of his body. In a single tug and fold, the entire sheet pressed onto the hover chair's cushion. With another swift motion, Alize's clothes were stripped and folded into a neat pile above the blanket. The baggy-eyed young started toward the chill-producing harness on the kid's chest but decided against removing the Arcanum after realizing its function.

Thus, with a third and final movement, the youth raised Alize above the basin and slowly lowered him onto the rising bed of water.

"Well, we must kill it before we even get to see the beginning signs of such a devolution. And as I can tell, Ny-Ny is already on its way to becoming an aberrant chimera or maybe even an abomination against nature." The tall youth then checked the boy's pulse, temperature, and wrappings.

"That. That's insane. Why is any of that even a thing? How do you even know all of that?" The girl gasped in shock and barely squeaked out the words, but her voice carried over due to the proximity.

"Mother taught us about the caretaking duties of us highly graded and ranked homunculi. You were mostly asleep during those lessons. I can only assume you were still too underdeveloped to handle those lessons so soon after our emergence." The young man narrowed his eyes at his sister and sighed as her shock quickly morphed into annoyance.

"It's a shame, though." The young man only spoke after ensuring Alize was safe and not in danger of any complications since he had injected several needles into the boy at different spots.

"A shame? Wait, are you actually telling me what you are feeling?" The girl's voice piqued once again, but her brother doused her excitement with an unemotional and very awkward stare.

"Sorry. It's just not often that you share what you are thinking. It's all work, efficiency, pleasing the Master and mother, and blah, you know." The girl nearly woke Ny-Ny up so she continued to hum as her brother continually worked on setting up Alize's so-called "surgery".

"Hmm. Anyway, it's a shame that the master does not set aside his personal agendas to reconcile with Mother. Together, they would have managed to fix the issues with the chimera's lifespan, durability, and the abysmal success rate of getting past the first stage of development.

Batch 97 was able to metabolize a single aura aspect before breaking at the readjustment stage, and 98 was even better, capable of digesting and repurposing up to three different aura sparks and reliably taking control of a single aspect. Master and mother would have been able to go farther than this but for their squabbling. Ha, their non-stop bickering has made it so we are all without direction." The youth sighed once more and looked past the wall in front of him in contemplation.

"So you are just sad that we don't have any younger siblings and upset that the other homunculi treat us like the babies of the family?" The girl wiped away even more tears with a small laugh to lighten her own mood. The youth didn't say anything as he slowly pressed a dozen more needles into different places on Alize's body. After ensuring that the tubing ran without any kinks, the youth once again checked the sparkling bags of liquid on each limb of the chandelier. He also triple-checked the state of the empty bags all around the edge of the basin.

"Wait? Wait! Do you mean the rumors? Do you mean they are true?" The girl covered her mouth with wide eyes as the information finally registered.

"Rumors? What is a rumor?" The tall young man looked at his sister in astoundment. She opened her mouth to explain but immediately frowned upon remembering a particularly annoying memory.

"Look it up, idiot," she grumbled.

"Okay. I will when I am free. In the meantime, tell me what you mean to verify." The youth raised an eye as if his questioning was the most logical thing in the world.

"You. Muther argh. Whew. Alright. The rumor is that the master and mother used to be an item, but they broke it off because of some issue involving mind control magic and a baby trap." The girl batted her eyes, waiting for her brother to respond.

"What kind of dumb rumor is that? No, there was simply a dispute over who would raise the next iteration of homunculi after the 99th batch of chimeras were pieced together. Huh? Where did you hear that rumor?" the youth genuinely asked.

"The voices." The girl tilted her head matter-of-factly.

"I knew it. There is definitely something wrong with you. Is the problem your brain? If there is too much magic in your head, let me know." The young man stopped what he was doing and backed up as he looked at his sister.

"Hey. I'm not crazy, you idiot. You were paying attention to the lessons, so how did you forget about Batch 33? Mother discovered that I inherited a rare trait from the goop that was made from the 3w and that weird batch. My aspect allows my body to remember things that our ancestors have done with their bodies. It's an Accord-type aura root profile thingy thing, I think. Erm, it's pretty much limited to movements and memories and stuff. Well, it works differently since we are homunculi instead of real people, so, uh, I don't know." The girl stuck out her tongue and smiled. The young man sucked his teeth and looked away in disgust and annoyance at himself but forced himself to not just walk away since he was now clearly interested.

"So, these voices. What are they and what do they tell you?" The youth shuffled over with a deep frown.

"A lot of them are failed homunculi. Erm, there are a few chimera but they don't really talk much since their sparks of magic barely count as an inherited aspect. But the homunculi told me this whole story. I always thought they were trying to trick me with some rumors they heard since the homunculi that are still around from earlier generations spread some crazy stuff about Mother and the master." The girl waved her hand to dismiss her brother's attention.

"Interesting. Do you share what the voices tell you with anyone?" The youth questioned as he bent down and observed Ny-Nys complexion with quivering eyebrows.

"No. Mother told me to never tell anyone what my body can do, especially Master Nayame, since it would make everyone's lives more dangerous if he found out." The girl shrugged and leaned back against the wall as she curled Ny-Nys hair.

"It would. It's good you haven't told anyone. If you need to, and if at any point the voices get out of hand, you can come talk to me. This aspect of ours is a curse, and I am well aware of its burden." The tall youth gripped his palms out of his sister's sight and gently scooped Ny-Ny up. As for Alize, he listened in on everything as the dripping water that fell into the basin turned into a steady stream right above his half-submerged midsection.

"We should hurry out of here. The Master's relic is about to seal itself. He should have left to address the child's parents by now, so if we hurry, you could tell that woman you are sorry once again. I can feel how heartbroken you still are about harming her." The youth stepped through the flame tunnel as the girl blushed from embarrassment and sorrow.

2.7 My Eternal Spring

"Our life is strange because of my Affix. Don't you think so?"

Alize cast [Prevention] as he slowly floated toward the top of the basin. Jarold slowly materialized, but due to the moisture, he turned into a sort of misty, watery fog instead of a turbulent and aggressive dust cloud. The beard that covered most of his torso was the same, as was the billowing hair, but altogether, he was the same Gaelan Drem warrior. He sat down in the air and nodded as he stroked his beard with narrowed eyes. With a sigh, Alize observed the flow of the intravenous drips above his head and read the hand signs that Jarrold used to communicate with Orsche and Alize most of the time.

"The glasses?"

Alize moved his hands and arms to act against a rather powerful anesthetic that was flooding his system. Jarold's beard turned upward, almost as if he was trying to smile through the tangle of clouds that made up his facial hair. A tiny pair of glasses floated down from the shadows cast by the rocky ceiling.

"That's good. I thought they were still in my wraps. How did you get them out with that guy moving everything?"

"Easy, boy. **I am skilled**."

"Oh, really, old man?"

"Indeed."

"Can you do something about these IVs then?"

Jarold waved his hand and bent the tube that held the anesthetic. With another wave, the needle popped right out of Alize's arm and coiled up around one of the chandelier's limbs. The drips that held vitamins and essential nutrients were left alone, but some of the other bags were immediately ripped out in the safest way possible. All at once, the tubes with Alize's blood stopped flowing as they bunched up on either side of the basin. Visible bands of thick fog coiled around the tubes. As for the water in the basin, it began to glitter with some type of magic beyond most people's means to understand. Even Alize didn't know anything specific about the production method of Tharron's Corazó-Sprie. It was a one of a kind arcanum for a reason.

"Thank you, Gramps." Alize, despite being rather numb, put a thumbs up. Jarold nodded, gave his own thumbs up, then floated up to examine the stalactite and the water that seemed to just ooze out of the stone. As for the glasses, they floated down toward Alize's chest and remained there for a long time.

"I have pretty much two options in front of me at present." His eyes closed, and as he fell into the dark, letting the drops of the spring's silver water color his mind in ripples.

"With [Prevention] Active, I am in a bad state but I will not die as long as there is magic in the spell, in me, or in my surroundings. With the dad's medicines and the Arcanum that I still have on me, I am slowly

but surely healing." The backdrop of his imaginary descent into an ocean filled out diagram with each ripple that outlined his imaginary body. Very minutely, parts of the outline shaded themselves in patches of semi-translucent yellows and orange rings. 1% of his body was set to sickly lime green. With each drop, the yellow darkened and twisted with shadows, producing a cautionary filament that turned the mental reconstruction into a fully fleshed out three-dimensional recreation of himself. Around five percent of the body total, flashed white and slowly filled with a faded mint color that faded into the abyssal shadow between each drop.

"My first option is to follow the script and let the quack doctor take the medicinal effect of the Lochorn root out of my body and tough it out for the next few months. It might be possible to let some events pass as they should." With a splash of his hands, the imaginary picture changed. The mint green process of his regeneration turned into a drastically slower pulse that alternated between orange, red, and pitch black within his outline.

"My second option is to use this opportunity to create a bespoke spell that utilizes this Terrarium and try to maximize what I get." Alize froze for a brief second as the weird electric tether that connected his bodies frayed. His real body, the one firmly locked inside of an old military grade Duplicator, smirked. The metallic box, painted with a mesh of camo green, blue, and various shades of brown, momentarily rumbled and visibly altered the circular control panel. The solid humanoid that was on the left side of the Arcanum's sigil was a half-dotted outline, while the figure on the right bled out with an intense, almost blinding light. Every so often, the blinding dimmed, almost as if there was a connection issue and it was recalibrating something. Before Alize could even register that his connection was cut, he was slingshot back

to the smiling version of himself inside of the Eternal spring complete-ly unaware that his connection was hanging by a tenuous thread.

"If I can develop a spell specific to this scenario, I can use the spring's properties to heal myself all at once." Alize pressed a finger to the harness on his chest. The symbols that were etched into the leather dimmed and slipped through the metal clasps. Similarly, his bandages unraveled into a slack and water-soaked mess with another press of an easily accessible rune.

Almost instantly, the water that had direct access to his skin explod-ed with dense effuse and light. The initial imaginary representation of his current state shattered as it was replaced by an entirely new diagram. With the flood of blue ripples, the sickly lime green bar rose to 8% and the mint bar rose to a mind-boggling 68%. The white mist that signified the possibility of a full recovery, filled in with an icy blue, topping off at a cool 100%. The cautionary light was nowhere to be seen. Imaginary percentages aside, the most immediate effect was that Alize immediately lost the numbness that nearly paralyzed his body. He sat up without any issue whatsoever, ran fingers through his hair a few times, and waited for the fire ants to chew through the regenerating nerve endings that the potion could not affect since it focused on his brain stem. He hissed as a fiberglass scrub gripped his senses. It was only now that he looked at his hands without the filter of the bandages being in the way. All of the skin and muscle showed heavy signs of deterioration, to the point where bones were exposed and only barely hanging on now due to a golden wireframe of magic that was filled out with opaque blood-colored ice.

"This pain is good." The thin golden lines and watermelon-themed flashes of patchy skin swelled. The fibrous structure pulsed with vi-tality as the spring water, as if rolling into a chasm, pushed into the exposed wounds and gelled. Jarold materialized with a frown visible even through his beard.

"I'm okay, Gramps. I was just checking a spell that I made for myself. Look at this." Alize raised his hand to show Jarold how the blood pushed back into his exposed muscle and congealed into globs of water, but the old wind shrugged and shook his head. All Jarold could see was a mangled hand rapidly regenerating without any flair or magic.

"Oh, right. Here." Alize tweaked the [Prevention] spell so his [Shroud] would not hide his magic from other people. Almost instantly, Jarold flew closer and nodded out of pure admiration. The boy's hand seamlessly blended with the mesh wireframe that allowed his hand to function even without all of its parts and even then, the effuse that flooded the Terrarium's atmosphere and the spring water that filled in the mesh adopted a crystalline sheen that made his wounds appeared radiant rather than gruesome.

"Pretty cool, right?"

Jarold simply gave a thumbs up and returned to examining the inside of the Eternal Spring. Alize, on the other hand, squinted his eyes and leaned toward one of the two bushels of tubing that contained his blood. Bright magenta sparks of light flowed through his dark, heavily damaged blood vessels.

"What to do with these though? I cannot let the quack take the medicine out of my body but I also can't just leave here without him getting anything." After a few seconds, Alize pushed the needles into the spring and watched the glowing water essentially force his blood to come back to life with a complicated expression. "A vampire's dream, right Jarold?"

Alize looked up and smiled since the old man simply raised an eyebrow and nodded before vanishing again. It was only then that the kid looked toward the bottom of the basin. With puffed-out cheeks and a sigh, he picked up the tiny fallen glasses and clenched his fist so hard around them that his newly regenerated knuckles turned white. He submerged his head in the water and thought to himself.

"Everything is okay. Nothing went wrong. The events have all been right so far, and I have not died. Jarold is here, my parents are nearby, and I am healing. Wynn is, well, I don't know why her parents haven't responded to Mom yet, but I'm sure everything is okay. There are no insane events, and she lives in a school district. She's safe. All of my external problems are easily solved by going with the flow and relying on my family. Okay. Internal conflicts—I have a penta-coded profile, a synergy that is focused on [Shroud]. Okay, that's fine. It's not too different from the Utilitarian spread. It's just a different Ballast Aspect that I have a focus on. That's easy. Mom and Dad trained me to work with different profiles in the event that my Affix generates something. I don't personally have Tenets. That's fine. I can fake it. Let's go! I'm years behind my peers in practical casting. Bummer, but not an issue. I didn't need to practice casting in the real world, anyway. I learned enough in Sims, so that's okay. I'm okay. This is easy. The Sim scenarios are way harder than this. I can handle it. I can." Alize's face crumpled as the air in his lungs suddenly got caught in his throat. He gasped for breath while his face changed dozens of times in a handful of seconds. He avoided attracting Jarold's attention.

"This is insane. All of this is insane. I've been trying to act... I've tried to be as cautious as possible, but this..." Alize dipped himself below the basin's rim so the water splashed against his face. He cried so hard that even the imaginary version of himself slumped into a corner of his thinking space and curled up into his knees.

"I think it's finally starting to sink in..." He laughed as even more tears erupted, water splashing up into his already sopping hair.

"I am in one of three—no, four scenarios right now. One, all of this is in my head and I have already died, or I am very nearly over the precipice. I failed at killing that abomination of a hero before I perished, and all of this is some sort of elaborate illusion created by him or one of his allies to torture me. Secondly, I have somehow slipped into a smaller universe that I can perceive and live within because of an Incast-Blip. It's rare, but it's more than possible that I have simply been ejected from the Eternity. In that same vein of thought, this could also be one of Mourra's fabled Dreamcast Terrariums considering all of the Province's influence on my life, which means that I am just in a looping nightmare that I cannot leave. Then, there's the most likely situation and the most obvious." Alize thought back to what he said to his parents to calm their nerves and prevent them from jumping to conclusions about where he was drawing his calm and drive from. No reincarnation, transmigration, possession, or time travel was used in the making of his journals. That was something that he staunchly stood behind in consideration of the side effects and signs associated with each severely under-researched phenomenon in the study of mystics. All the steps had been understood as basic physics, but the magical application was not even slightly understood.

"Life is a wild series of chaotic moments, and I have been given a terrible gift capable of recognizing when it throws something my way." Alize remembered the lower half of a flat white mask eternally forged into a Cheshire grin and the forest of red hair that draped over an unfathomable entity's broad shoulders. His mind spun for a second as the impeachable magnitude of a simple throne made of writhing flesh and engraved story simply burned into the depths of his retina.

"Divinity. Hero's and monsters." Then, as a footnote to such a grand being, there was the face of the mad hero.

"Quests, visions, the future that is set in stone, and how I choose to respond to different factors." His thoughts trailed to Dr. Nayame's, the fake doctor's, appearance. The hero and the man beneath the facade overlapped in an odd and uncomfortable way. A single question, despite all the unknowns and information that he held in both fact and assumption, came to mind and filled out the top of a newly created mental board.

"Why is there no sign of any outright trouble or any of the churches getting involved with me? It's clear that at least one of the three different Divine-ranked beings has shown favorable and possibly even ongoing special treatment toward me." He breached for air and wiped his reddened eyes. Both of the kid's luminescent hands pressed into the nerve clusters and veins that attempted to burst out of his temples.

"Gramps, I'm going to work on a spell for something that will allow me to take a bit of the spring water with me, so if you can, try to find something that will keep the Terr closed for as long as possible. It should look like any other smaller stalagmite or stalactite in the corners, but there will be something off about it. It should be an internal control panel or something small enough to be a lever. I think it's more a lever or button though since this is an A-Type artifact." Alize sighed as he focused on what needed to be done now. Jarold floated down and patted Alize on the shoulder and gave him a subtle tilt of his head.

"I'm okay, old man. I just had to clear my head for a bit." Alize smiled as best he could and slumped down into the basin after Jarold nodded and tousled his hair. The kid closed his eyes, controlled his breathing and meditated. Almost instantly, he burst through the doors of his memory that led to everything magical.

"First, I need to make sure there are no issues with the spring and my [Prevention]." As soon as Alize threw open the doors, magic rings that only he could see lit up around his body and the mental image of himself. The simplified diagram of his body while in the water doubled. The first one reverted back into the heavy yellow and black rendition while the other remained mostly green and blue. The newer diagram floated over his hand and projected a pie chart into the swirling fog around his mind as if it were a projector. It contained ratios that compared the amplified regeneration to his healing factor before entering the spring, which happened to be a stream of consciousness that lit up the mist parallel. He waved his hand and traversed the long catwalk to the platform at the center of a circular maze. An authorless gold framed red book with the sigil of the Scholars guild emblem on the front and a title along its spine, "Alchemy Is Love, Potions are Life: Learn the Basics on Creating Legendary Brews", flipped over to his hand and flipped over several pages before he flicked a finger to send the whole thing to his main thought process.

"Health potions have a set limit for what they can help the body repair. Those with a Lochorn base are one of three that get infinitely close to having no limit regardless of rank or grade. The only differences are in the quantity, speed, and efficiency at which the body operates to metabolize the medication. My issue is..." Another text, one on a thin sheet of fog that resembled glass floated in front of him to show a picture of a middle-aged woman with high cheekbones, low and wide nose bridge, a rich olive complexion and dark skin.

"*Tharrohn.*" Alize paused for a moment and nodded to the air above the basin just at the mention of the ancient Archon.

"An alchemist, chemist, and physician not even seen among the gods, figured out a way to mix pharmacology with spell casting to preserve medication and allow it to persist within the body for later use. Her contribution to the medical field and the survival of every single species within eternity helped the very few resources available during the age of the Rizen Boa last long enough to stabilize the plague that many celestials wrought upon Yiruhm." History texts that went hand in hand with progress flashed within the fog. Some of which he pulled down and skimmed on his walk down memory lane, but others were left to fade.

"That said, because of Tharrohn's universally implemented changes, the spells within the medicine tap out long before reaching the state in which I am fully healed. Releasing just enough to keep me alive even without my casting to ensure that I survive." Alize motioned his hand as if he were grasping something as he took another step. The little multi-ringed wheel at his desk turned without him behind directly at the helm. The maze, by extension, twisted until a pillar with a scale rose alongside a massive collection of books and statues. Like a tectonic puzzle piece, the empty scale and the mountain of knowledge moved and clicked into place on the pedestal.

"The balanced and steady release of magic and the natural regenerative properties of the root would result in my situation, a stalemate. Injuries that are balanced between not getting worse and not getting better. One form of pseudo Immortality is within this potion as long as it stays within one's system." Several thousand books flared all around the fog the moment he thought of the matter, but instead of focusing on something that he didn't want, the boy examined the projections that were in front of him. With a wave of his imaginary hand, a pillar with two overlapping hearts and a plus symbol at the center of the Scale monument library rose from a faraway location and gradually clicked into place at the central platform as the walls, shelves, and statue gardens full of important figures parted ways.

"The spring can heal someone from near death, but only while they are in the water or while they have absorbed its effects. The water itself is also only potent because of an inconceivably massive reservoir of potions that Tharrohn supposedly brewed and concocted herself before conventional automation was introduced to A-type formulas." A huge scroll flew from the shelving and unfurled into a tattered diagram etched into the skin of some ancient creature. The hole-filled chart found itself filled in with paper scrawlings that attempted to fill out the missing components, but with each step, different phantom lights and bits of knowledge that were drilled into his mind fluttered over. These scraps filled in more missing pieces and replaced yellowed pages with glassy sheets that expanded on the artifact's makeup. A chart, a schematic, of an entire closed ecosystem filled a corner of Alize's mental view.

A multilayered spike. The head of which happened to be only slightly smaller than the tip at the bottom. Just underneath the face of the weird Terrarium, a small tree impaled a small hill and burrowed its roots deep into the conical tip of a miniature hill that poked out of the water. A pond shaped like a bowl surrounded the porous hill and acted as a sieve and filtration system that dumped the water into a reservoir beneath. In this cavernous space within the spike, the water separated into several thousand channels that flowed into separate pockets and even smaller ecosystems that served a specific and self-regulating purpose, spilling over or dripping into yet another lower layer. The channels then collected into several different reservoirs that spilled over or behaved differently based on the detailed symbols, shading, and outlining in the schematic. At the very bottom, at the tip, the waters from above collected into a final stream that dripped into a reservoir that's only job was to pour everything that it collected into a tiny rectangle at the very tip of the spike. Within the rectangle was another spike-shaped symbol, but upon closer inspection, it was just a humanoid miniature.

"That said, it's impossible for anyone below the divine threshold to genuinely absorb any of the benefits that have been packed into this liquid. Effectively, it's just an addictive painkiller, one that wreaks more havoc on anyone further away from the divine rank. Even if it's not immediately felt, the long-term effects, back before the Spring was lost, were described as more addictive than the Hero and Heroine epidemic that was brought about by the Celestials." Alize brought out his own notes on the matter and specifically remembered his dad's lessons on the difference between arcanum made for regular people and artifacts that were made by and for divine entities.

"Thus, since I am most certainly not at the divine rank and I do not actually have any Tenets, my real body will go into shock the moment that this drug enters my system..." Alize clapped his hands and sneered as the memory fog above his head parted ways. A divine statue with the image of a multi-faced woman descended from the clouds. The woman possessed six arms, a baby in two as they fed from her breasts, and a flourishing vine of square-shaped grapes sprouted from one hand while another showed the wilting of a bouquet. The last two hands covered the statue's eyes and mouth, respectively.

"I have a [Shroud] capable of mimicking Tenets. If I cast the right spell, I can steal as much of this water as my duplicant can replace and carry and burn through any of the natural divine magic in the water by using it to cast. This is quite the challenge, Affix. A challenge that I actually like since the payoff would be monumental for me down the road." Alize suddenly laughed out loud and almost lost his balance while floating.

"Cascading events. Affix, despite almost killing me yesterday. I do have to say, if this is how you balance what I'm capable of handling with what I deserve as a reward, I will gladly try my hardest to ensure that this quack loses as much as possible." Alize placed his hand on his

heart, calmed himself to float and returned to the palace within his mind. This time, instead of parsing through his memory and picking data that supported his goal, the kid stood behind the desk and looked down at everything. Habitually, he stroked his chin almost as if he was pulling at a beard.

"I'll use this relic and my duplicated body to test run a spell variant that can instantly heal my wounds or at least do as much as it can. After that, I'll share what I've deduced with my mother and father. If things lead to it, I will do my best to tiptoe around the chimera and homunculus business. Affix, I can feel that you have something planned for after this, but I will not let us draw the suspicions of any custodians or Surveyors, the Scholars' guild or any of its affiliates, and especially the churches. Hmm, actually, I should bring up the Archons to Mom and Dad. It's weird how all of my casting is focused on maximizing and expanding the foundation of only one of my Profile's aspects. Two if I count the minimization of my effusive imprint with [Shroud]." Alize tapped the pedestal and waited. A rectangular slit and circular hole opened on the floor right beside the pedestal. A book that said [Prevention] on the spine hovered up to his hand. With a tap, a familiar diagram of his body's current state popped up on one of the pages. With a smile still on his face, he added a new formula in the Book of Prevention, a formula that purposefully and specifically excluded the spring water as a usable source of magic to draw upon in the spell since he had other uses for it.

Instead, he lifted his other hand into the air and collected some of the most basic and almost universal material on healing magic that everyone in the world should have at least heard about.

The first piece of text wasn't actually a spellbook at all since it was actually an anthology of first-hand accounts. It collected the experiences of everyday people and their thoughts and feelings when they used Accord-type magic to heal others. It was a rather handy compilation of repeating pedestrian accounts and a scientific deconstruction of what was said. The summary boiled the use of Accord-type regenerative and healing spells down to a balance or sacrificial relationship based on equivalency. Things had to be balanced out in the utility that was being able to heal, regenerate, or grow something quickly.

The second text was actually a collection of mantras and verses from the Holy Book of Lady Ithe, a bible for the Goddess of Life. The Temple of Lady was THE place to go above all other religions since most if not all the officially recognized priests of The Radiant Mother held some of her Tenets.

The third item, if you can recognize the pattern, was actually a massive eight-ring binder containing the compacted distillation of the world's most efficient medical and surgical knowledge. In a sense, this was a physician's bible, one that allowed anyone willing and dedicated enough to learn everything they needed to know about diagnostic methodology, surgical techniques, and the proper application of different disciplines. Chemistry, alchemy, herbology, and the universal basics of biology were a standard given as those topics filled the first third of the tall binder.

"Imagination, faith, and the cold hard facts of reality. Magic is the manifestation of all three; thus, it should stand to reason that all three should be used to develop one's spells. I am not the only one to do this. I am not the first to have this knowledge. All official scholars have ingrained this truth into their bones. I am, however, not bound to any of the pacts or agreements that would force me to keep some information hidden and unused." Alize's smile almost split his face in two as he kicked up a storm of fluttering pages. He pulled an original song that came from a musician who used to be a cardinal at the church of Om' tare Ithe, the Goddess of Life and its sole Province. Then he grabbed an inefficient medical procedure, by modern practice and standard, that was invented after examining and recreating a forbidden healing ritual only ever referenced as "Terah's Embrace". The smile on his face slowly crumbled as an almost see-through glassy film floated out of this second book.

"I guess this is something that Dad showed me at some point?" Alize was about to move the film back into the heavy leather-bound encyclopedia, but something scratched at the back of his mind. If he was paying attention, he would have noticed that a faint infinity symbol burned into the background of the mists. If he paid attention to his real body before while his connection to his Duplicant was severed, he would have even noticed the intense burn of his Affix generating another event but next to his current task of creating an entirely brand new variant of a Utility spell, it was practically impossible that would have noticed anything.

"E of EPA." He sighed and snapped the plastic-looking and feeling piece of glass into a flat screen produced by his memory. The mist of fogginess swirled in from all corners of his vision and filled the screen at first, but very quickly, someone's pov was shown as they stood up after getting blown away from somewhere that was not caught on film.

A giant of a man covered in blood, wounds, and grime ran toward the cameraman or woman and made a show of ensuring that he showed off a broken boom mic and a side pack that was covered in all manner of fizzling crystals and a half materialized audio board.

The fallen camera person then turned to show a whole production team that had been reduced to mangled corpses, screaming assistants, or makeshift soldiers as they used the filming equipment as weapons against something that showed up as a buzzing and fragmented mass on film. The camera person immediately ran away in a wide arc, showing off insane maneuverability and speed as the giant and filmer dodged and weaved through an onslaught of attacks that could not be detected. One of these amorphous and entangled things pounced atop the Retton man, the giant, and tore into his sides and chest with the rabidity of a diseased animal. The camera person fell to the side, rolled across the floor to avoid something that could physically be seen and separated from the creature. Rushing past the chaos, the runner dove through an archway that was as tall as a seven-story building just a handful of seconds before the earth ruptured with an eight-toed and clawed footprint just in front of the entryway. The speeding perspective shot through different hallways and rounded corners with such speed and flair that it made one think that the person holding it should have been a free runner or parkour savant. In a minute, the focus zoomed in on the symbol of a circular-headed scepter with a plus symbol inside of it and two snakes separated as the door apart. Hands, soft and small, separated the massive doors, but before they could fully open, the person pushed through and stumbled into someone. The camera dropped and rolled around a bit, showing simple heeled loafers, fishnets or crisscrossing and densely patched tattoos that resembled the article of clothing, and a comfortable-looking tartan. The battery died soon after.

"Why do I have this weird feeling that the person filming didn't fall by accident?"

Alize did not rush to the next piece of oddly specific information that he wanted to use in spellcrafting. Instead, he returned the film to its spot in the book that he held and pulled out another screen that continued the only recording of the forbidden spell "Terah's Embrace". In this new screen, the cameraman refreshed the battery and focused in on a small pair of high heels that clacked against a cobblestone path. An hourglass figure that could not be hidden even with a massive white coat turned away from the camera and approached one of the massive beasts that could not be captured on film.

The person pulled two long sticks out of their tied-up hair and slammed them down in the air like a drummer testing their kit. Long auburn hair bounced and fluttered in the chaotic wind. With a whirl-wind flourish, the redhead pointed at the cameraman. In a manner similar to a puppet on strings, the camera flew so far that the woman appeared as a dot on the horizon but due to an acrobatic twist, the zoomed focus function, and an insanely steady grip, it appeared as though the camera person flew into the air by choice to get an aerial shot. Whatever conflict that struck this area received a full pan allowing anyone viewing the film to see that the unregistered creatures were just one of many that broke out of an egg-shaped and glittering dome that was above a massive field that made the entirety of Jordaine appear as a small town. Of which, the barrier began its shattering in the four cardinal directions and at the very top of its arc as a stone monolith covered in runes came crumbling down atop the shield. A colosseum the size of an entire planet in terms of total width and height surrounded this barrier, and it turned into a free for all as these creatures issued a slaughter that could not be stopped.

As for the redhead with a well-groomed beard and a shirt that showed off his hairy but muscular chest—the beautifully dressed and insanely toned man used one of the long metal drumsticks like a sword and parried a lightning fast blur without so much as a flinch. The riposte and flurry of blows that came next resembled a dance and drum solo rolled into one. The camera person zoomed out and, miraculously, spun in a dazzling display of cinematography as they caught their own dire circumstance in a full frame. The land-bound colosseum was the largest and most grandiose stage, but it was only the main part of some grander experience. The sky, all the way up to and beyond the clouds, was filled with smaller mystical domes full of stages and events and rotating grandstands. All of which were floating on shifting runic plates that were now coming down.

Creatures that were obviously different from the behemoths on the ground but just as unphotogenic swarmed all around in the chaos like fish in the ocean. The camera worker was almost caught by one of the creatures when a group of teenagers descended from the sky with a kind of slow-motion presence that screamed, Protagonists. One of the teens, a young man with hard features, blood-red eyes and short brown hair, effortlessly slaughtered the flying beast and saved the camera person after an attack separated them from their tool of trade. Another teen stabilized the closest falling stage and bleachers with an impressive and downright horrifying display of casting, a third collected hundreds of falling civilians in a lasso and stuffed them inside of a tessellating crystal that a fourth falling person bore as though it were a baby. The camerawoman's face, as it separated from her in a violent descent, immediately warped into something similar to happiness but also annoyance. Her features being an almost exact match for the guy that caught her. Alize froze. The camera spun out of control but only for a second longer since some guy caught the camera and passed it back to the girl despite the insane descent and fights taking place mid drop.

"Holy crap, I was not paying attention when Dad was teaching this stuff." Alize paused the video, rewound it, and focused on the guy's head.

Dr. Nayame, fake or not, gave himself the exact same hairstyle after he got out of his pool-sized bathtub, and the hero from his nightmare somehow maintained that same perfect swoop up until he lost his composure. The guy who caught the camera had steel gray hair, another difference, but the same stylish swoop and features as the nightmarish hero and the "good doctor". This guy, however, had a more intense innocence about him that was only heightened by his softer features and baby fat. The video played for a bit longer, but all it showed was some rather cringe and inappropriately timed hijinks.

"The kid in this found footage is either Nezaret when he was a youth or is another descendant that didn't manage to gather enough merit to break past the family curse. It's also possible that this may be a Nayame ancestor before that mad king made the name synonymous with everything wrong with humans being invited into our world by the Lord. Regardless, the guy's name isn't anywhere in the credits, so I will have to ask Dad if he knows anything about it." Alize put the video on two times speed and searched for his last reference when the scene he had in mind started to play.

The redheaded guy wearing a white coat showed up fully on camera in this much later scene. The beautiful man with a five o'clock shadow, long eyelashes, and criminally luscious locks said something to a group of familiar-looking teens who were off to one side behind a massive wall of magic. The seemingly tense atmosphere seemed completely ruined as the guy looked down at his ripped open and comfortable-looking shirt. His skin split in two, but the fishnet tats or chains reinforced his washboard abs and a bronze and somehow oily chest packed with lean muscle. Before the guy could even bleed from his open wound, the net stitched him back up and forced a slightly visible claw up and into the air. A tangled beast, one of meat and misery, tumbled back as a heavenly green radiance washed over and exposed the outline of its accursed and mangled form.

With a single reactive swing, the beautiful man made contact with the beast that recoiled away from him. In that exact same moment, with another raised beat of an air drum, the bloodied and beaten teenagers all glimmered with an alternating blue and green outline.

The creature's entire arm vanished, but before it could let out a sound or react, the beautiful man dropped to his knees and threw up a mouthful of blood. The instant the blood touched the air, the creature imploded around where the drumstick hit and vanished without a trace. The teens all rushed out and smacked the redhead on his back. The green light on their bodies diminished, but the small transfer of energy healed the guy, if only somewhat, as the full-body fishnet that covered his chest frayed and remained broken in the area that he was surprisingly struck..

With an exhausted smile, the older man began to drum against the air and dance to the kids' surprise. It was only after the camera girl turned and adjusted her focus that the older man's expression made sense. A horde of intangible things, creatures without any perceivable form yet a disastrous mass, stampeded across the landscape from practically all directions and made their presence known in the steps, claw marks, and destruction left in their wake. The kids got back to back as the older man began to tap his toe and bounce his head to a beat that only he could hear at the moment of filming.

Alize slowed the video and committed each movement, each pulse of magic, and read into each and every one of the man's micro-expressions. Flourishing his drumsticks, and striking once, the man created a circle of vibrations that tapped into the inherent flow or beat of reality. With another hit, outlines similar to his own imaginary rendition of his health tore away from the teen and vibrated on the circle that surrounded the man. An onslaught unlike any other descended on the kids, but before any of them could be hurt, the redhead struck the vibrating and multicolored outline of the teens just before they were hurt.

Since he ran through it a few times, Alize noticed that where the red- head struck, there would be a circular flash of white light and a ripple that would repel an incoming attack the instant before it connected. The instant the whole fight ended, Alize cut the memory and looped the video. Insanely enough, Alize noticed how the green outline on their bodies thickened and enlarged every time the teens landed a strike against one of the behemoths. With another watch, he remembered how the magic transferred from the teens to anyone they saved, spreading the drummer's wave of healing magic that grew larger and more potent the longer and harder that they all fought. His appreciation for the forbidden spell only grew as he noticed the insanity that seemed to be built into the foundation of its purpose. As long as the redhead played, as long as he kept the spell active, anyone affected would essentially be immortal and anyone they fought would eventually be ground to dust either by their own power and attacks being reflected back at them with the discs or due to the overwhelming numbers.

The song around the drummer turned into a blaze as the repelling and destructive force within the spell was now enough to instantly obliterate any of the behemoths as hundreds of people joined in the defense. If they were unable to, one of the first few teens that were part of the defense would enlarge a sphere that looked eerily similar to the Apierigon with the only difference being the color..

"It's very clear why this one is banned. It's basically Bayrun's Life Jacket but with much better Scaling, lifesteal, and AOE. This tethering effect is exactly what I need, though." The last thing that he grabbed—a dark YA fantasy book of all things. No magic, no gods or archons, no hundred or thousand year lifespans and plans or schemes, just a fantasy of some young lady's terrible and incurable illness (A fantasy) that was cured by the power of love, positive thinking, and probability. He returned to the main pedestal with a tower of supplementary texts that would help him with the main three in his hands.

"I have to create something specific for my profile. This shouldn't be too hard. I have already successfully altered a spell to fit my needs. I just have to use established methods to develop something similar to Terah's Embrace. It shouldn't be too hard. It's just a slightly more advanced variation of Bayrun's lifejacket, which is just a better lesser lifejacket. Ha, and the LLJ is just my [Prevention] for people with a better matching profile. I got this, I'm fairly certain I got this." Hours passed but for Alize it felt like minutes and in all that time, he only decided to try to test the spell when Jarold tapped his shoulder and woke him out of a stupor. Without even realizing it, the stalactite that had been producing a steady drop every half a minute, stopped entirely.

2.8 Benefits of Being Insured

" .. It is nice to see another member of the family trying to break the curse on our line." The quack clasped Orsche's arm.

"I am trying, but you understand how difficult it is." Orsche made sure to lean in and give a firm shake.

"I do. Trust me." The doctor nodded a handful of times then sighed so deeply that his veil parted.

"Mr. and Mrs. Peachum." The quack lowered his head.

"Doctor, please. We only use my father's last name when dealing with those who attack our business with malice rather than competitive spirit or ignorance due to old grudges." Verza's wavering voice picked the doctor's spirits up, if only momentarily.

"Exactly, my love. Doctor, we are forming more bonds and bridges today, happy ones built on mutual trust and respect even if the circumstances are disastrous." Orsche chuckled despite the tears welling on the sides of his eyes and once again clasped the good doctor's arm.

"Mr. and Mrs. Scuttle. Please excuse my slip and thank you for the trust and hope that you have placed in me." His head dropped deeper.

"I am truly sorry for not being capable enough to exceed the kindness that you have shown me." The quack's portrayed sorrow appeared to be so deep that he removed his hat out of respect and in condolence.

"I knew that your son's condition was not great. And yet I still attempted to and implied that he would make a full recovery on my watch."

"No, please, Dr. Nayame. We were already out of options, so thank you for giving our boy a chance. Yes, my husband is right. Thank you for looking after our son's health. We know it couldn't have been easy to get his conditions stable enough to have him walk out of here with us today." Orsche quickly refuted the Quacks' self-admonishment, with Verza following up almost immediately.

"You both are far too forgiving. I, like all of my staff at Umbertree, pride myself on managing to ensure that all of my patients walk out of my manor with the minimum assurance of at least a partial recovery now and a full life after the necessary amount of treatment and time. Even patients who have been cursed with Affixes in the Broken or Chronic series have left my facility better than when they entered. This is the first time an Affix or an injury has left me feeling. Ha. To offer only hope and a treatment plan, ha. It truly feels as though I have failed to meet my own standards." The quack's androgynous features and unflattering bowl cut showed a completely different man compared to the one that Alize and Jarold got a good look at. The man lowered his head in shame.

"I'm sorry. We are sorry." Verza and Orsche held each other's arms.

"If there is anything we can do to make it up to you, or anything that we can buy and donate to make up for your time. Yes, bring our son back from the bring when even the shaman that we hired off of

Abbey Road was incapable of doing so." Orsche and Verza completed each other's sentences to press the quack's sorrow into a wry smile.

"Nothing like that comes to mind aside from the selfish personal request that I asked of the two of you earlier, but the moment I think of something, I will ask." The quack tilted the bamboo hat backward and placed it back on his head. That action, however, seemed to be the straw that broke the camel's back as the parade of nurses surged forth and practically threw glass clipboards at him. Each paper-thin sheet layered on top of the other and locked into a single relic that he swiped through. The quack made quite a show of hiding his embarrassment while the nurses pulled him away.

"Forgive me. Adding your son's matter to my schedule has made things a bit..." The Quack did not finish his statement as he was lifted off the floor and dragged away.

"It's okay. Take care," Verza and Orsche spoke at the same time. At the same moment, they noticed that after the quack paid attention to the glassy tablet in his hands, his shoulders broadened and his spine straightened. With a single flick of his wrist, the quack tossed the first clipboard back to the nurse who initiated the stampede. In quick, almost blinding succession, the doctor filled out two more sheets and then stopped before he vanished behind a set of large double doors.

"I have changed my mind. If you two want to pursue some form of repayment, the only thing that I need is for you to accept my selfish personal invitation. For now, I just hope that I do not need to see any of you until your son's scheduled appointment. If either of you has forgotten anything we spoke about, my assistant Teeya will ensure that you have something to remind and inform you of some things that I may not have touched upon in my haste." The Quack's veil released from the little clasp on the bamboo hat and dropped to perfectly line up with his sculpted jawline. Without the bowl cut and a full view of the perfectly placed prosthesis that changed his nose, forehead, and eye shape, the quack's underlying looks came out. The wall of nurses piled onto the doctor like a dark swarm of locusts and pushed him through the doors, toward other "patients."

"On behalf of all the staff working here, I am sorry for not letting the doctor see you off as he normally would. I am also sorry for the spectacularly misinterpretable wording he used to say his farewells." Teeya's heels clicked against the marble flooring as she approached the two emotional parents with a controlled smile and a face full of exhaustion.

"I assure you that Dr. Nayame only meant to express his best wishes for your son's expedient and complication-less recovery over this next month." After showing a bit of sincerity, Teeya motioned towards the mansion's front door.

"Thank you, Ms. Teeya. We understand what the doctor was trying to say. I also want Ark's treatment to go smoothly. I get it. I don't want my little baby to have any of the side effects that the doctor warned us about." Orsche and Verza swapped sentences and followed after Teeya through the front doors of a waiting room just off the main foyer. She did not converse beyond the greeting and just flashed a smile and nod.

"We will have to close up shop for the month and take care of Ark, my love." Orsche whispered with a frown as he matched his steps with Verza. His words did not escape Teeya's notice. She snapped her fingers and basically summoned two black-veiled guards. The muscular beings pulled open and flanked the doorway to either side of Orsche and Verza after the small group passed the threshold.

"Regarding the details for your son's weekly treatments over the next month, you don't have to worry about remembering the instructions or getting in contact with Dr. Nayame, me, or any of our qualified and trained staff members." Teeya's customer service smile remained as she pointed to a pair of beefy guards dressed in black.

"These contain everything you will need." Teeya waved a single hand without a single pause in her even gait. The two guards at the bottom of the steps lowered to a knee and presented their held items like gifts, a silver briefcase and a thick binder full of color-coded page separators and numbered tabs. Orsche and Verza accepted with wide eyes and audible gasps.

"Wow. So organized." The two tried to contain their impressed whispers, but Teeya heard everything and exhaled with a bit of a puff to her chest. A smile slightly creased her eyes even if it was nowhere near enough to be noticed. Guiding the group, the proud assistant led the way toward another pair of guards that stood vigil at the entrance to a stunningly assembled maze garden of sculpted hedges and flower bushes.

"This next item is something that we like to give to all of our new networked members. It may be a lot, but as part of the radiant mother's teachings, any gift is never too much as long as it clearly expresses one's intentions." Teeya snapped her fingers once more. The guards standing at the garden entrance, statues amongst leafy sculptures, opened their hands and presented open ring boxes. With a little flash, Verza and Orsche found their hands significantly lighter. The briefcase and binder turned into threads of light, bound and woven into gems.

"Dr. Nayame is a big proponent of making sure things are organized and efficiently completed on time. With these gifts, he and all of us at Umbertree hope that you bring this cheque every time you come to our facility so that all of your personal documentation can always be on your person." Teeya led the way through the hedge maze without looking back.

"The briefcase contains everything that either of you will need for your son's treatment and comfort until Dr. Nayame can give him a checkup. The binder has all the information you went over with the doctor and a summary of the perks that are available to you as an insured member of our patient community." Teeya extended her hand and gracefully accepted the support of a guard that helped her remain upright as she swapped out her heels and walked barefoot atop smooth dinner plate sized stones that created a path through gravel.

"I'm sorry, Ms. Teeya, but when you said we would get a lot of benefits after changing Dr. Nayame to our family's PCP, I didn't think this was part of that package? We simply cannot accept this gift. Complementary or not. Is there a code, or lock, or something on it?"

Ors clutched the ring box in his hand with visible panic and an overwhelming sense of inferiority as his back shrunk and lips dried. To Teeya, it was obvious that the Scuttle family, despite being around money as stall owners in the Corridor, were not wealthy to the point of having interacted with this particular brand of storage device before. As Teeya understood it by looking at the Peachum-Scuttle family's reactions, Orsche knew what the ring cost at the very least, and he judged its worth as something well beyond the family's modest means. Verza, on the other hand...

"Oh, honey. Look at how beautiful this is. I don't understand why we can't accept it. Don't we have a few similar cheques back home?" Verza pretended not to know the value of the item in her hand as she innocently marveled at the intricate workmanship of the detailed golden leaves etched into its ebony and glossy surface. A miniature, almost transparent, opal folded and refracted the light around it as if it were the event horizon of a black hole instead of a gem.

"We do have cheques, my love, but nothing like this type of arcanum. We have Oncaed storage appliances at home. These rings are custom-made, so they are not something we can just get at a store, even if we have the money for them. These are, erm, custom, right?"

Ors gulped with shaking hands as he slowly returned the whole box to the guard who gave it to him. The veiled guard glanced at Teeya and, upon seeing her head shake, the silent and beefy guard shook its head and closed Orsche's fingers around the box. The very next instant, the brawny guard stepped away and fell in line with four other, now five, guards.

"They are made in-house. But you do not have to worry at all. The item, as I said before, is actually covered by your insurance since it is a gift from us to you. Think of it as our estate trying to get a tax write-off if that helps." Teeya smiled as she passed by small pockets of flower and vegetable gardens and hidden ponds with all sorts of fish or aquatic flora being cultivated. Ors trembled but eventually closed his fingers around the luxurious magical item as he trailed behind Verza. Seemingly uninterested in the worth of the item, she simply placed the ring on her left hand and fawned over how pretty it made her hand look. Teeya let the awkward atmosphere permeate for a moment and then gave her hand to the sixth guard that remained by her side. She replaced her glossy high heels and stepped onto a path made from long rectangular plates of chiseled slate. Another two black-veiled individuals bowed before Teeya and held out two finger-length silver whistles that curved into the figurehead of a four-eyed horse. The body of the whistle contained a texture that hinted at compacted muscles under a stocky and metallic silver body.

"This Arcanum is another benefit and gift of being fully insured with us." Teeya waved her hands and very slightly smiled as she continued forward. Orsche didn't appear overwhelmed anymore as confusion and helplessness overtook his demeanor. It appeared as though he had no idea what this whistle was for. Teeya, side-eyeing the Scuttles, noticed his expression and Verza's knitted eyebrows and cleared her throat.

"If you blow on these whistles and put in some of your magic while doing so, you can use the built-in spell and summon one of our many Drivers to take you anywhere within Dane proper. Now, our drivers may not be as fast as the country's public transport, but they are still remarkably quick since they are legally allowed to traverse the star road." Teeya watched Orsche break out in a cold sweat as the veiled guard practically forced the whistle back into his hand. Before he could speak or even ask about the origin or worth of the new artifact, the guard pressed on Orsche's back and forced him to follow after Teeya. These two beefy boys did not follow the Teeya train. Verza, on the other hand, accepted the whistle and skipped forward to catch up with the kind lady.

"Ms. Teeya, you said Ark's surgery and initial recovery period were over already. He's here somewhere, right?"

Verza pressed the whistle to the gem on her new ring just to see if it would work and gradually gave up on putting it away.

"Since you do not have Ballast-type magic, Mrs. Scuttle, you need to press down on the leaf closest to your palm and then push your magic into the Quill. A little screen that only you can see is going to pop up while your magic is in the arcanum's cache. You can put things wherever you want inside of its partitioned spaces. And yes, your son is waiting for the two of you just past this last corner." Teeya, almost infected by Verza's happiness, let the company smile be replaced by a gentle sincerity and continued to guide the way.

Orsche, overhearing the conversation, followed the same instructions and watched a flash of light and a web of magic consume the whistle. After showing his reluctance and overall excitement, he placed the box into his breast pocket and followed Teeya and Verza around a corner of hedges and found himself standing at the entrance to something that he simply did not expect. A smooth, uninterrupted stone path swirled around patches of mesmerizing flowers, succulent fruit trees, and juicy berry bushes. Said path snaked up a hill that was made by a tree breaking the soil and stone. One of the four trunks that served as a pillar to the massive canopy above the manor and the fields surrounding it somehow got close enough to touch. Atop the crest, Orsche completely focused on a gazebo made from stone columns and a metallic dome. Vines of ivy and colorful flowers dressed the location in what appeared to be a dress of soft greenery.

Orsche tried to find his wife as he rounded the corner, but all he spotted were the several guards that followed Teeya as she followed the path. Pretending as though he was concerned, he followed along in silence, but after a few seconds of walking on the path, he blinked a few times with a slack jaw. The full scale of one of the four load-bearing tree trunks left one feeling as though they were standing in front of a gray wall that covered everything in sight. Halfway up the hill, his dumbfounded expression changed as he heard the laughter of his wife and son. Internally, Orsche communicated with Verza.

"Everything under the canopy is part of an eccentric terrarium. Like the Apeirogon. The manor has the same setup, but it seems to be more compact with more recurrent structuring. I may have overestimated our chances or underestimated the threat that this Doctor poses. Ha. I am convinced." Orsche could clearly see that the garden that they all walked out of was not the same hedges that were placed beside the manor. From atop the hill, several dozen kilometers away, he could see the footsteps of their group imprinted on the gravel path, and they cut off as soon as they all stepped approximately five meters into the hedges. Verza's whisper carried directly over to just his ear.

"Convinced about what?"

"I am sure of my assumption," Orsche replied.

"Which one? You didn't stop talking all night, and you kept yapping while the doctor was walking. I sort of stopped paying attention." Verza chuckled and waited for a response.

"I only said one thing last night." Orsche sighed inwardly but couldn't find it in himself to call her out. Verza was rightfully exhausted after all.

"We cannot get involved with his events anymore. Well, we cannot act out on our own anymore. We have to make sure that we are all on the same page going forward." Orsche gulped and turned his head toward the gazebo with a look of wonder scribbled onto his features.

"This place is simply awe-inspiring." Orsche let himself be observed as he commented on the colorful sky that bled and then sharply cut off against a jagged knife of a mountaintop that raised the horizon to just below the clouds. He also let his vision trail along the curtain of bark that just filled everything else in his vision in a different direction.

"You can see so much of Southern Dane from here; it's remarkable." With slow steps, Orsche watched distant spires bend oh so slightly in the wind. Clouds, some filled with moisture and others formed due to the collision of calcified bark on bark, swirled through the air in a sort of dreamy fashion as multiple suspended islands began to twinkle like stars. A few moments later, Ors lowered his head out of the clouds and straightened his back with a smile.

"Ark, are you okay? Are you feeling better? Do you hurt anywhere?" Question after question rolled out of Verza's mouth as she clung to the side of her son's body and the hover chair like an oversized koala. The glowing mushroom cap on the side of the chair that Verza hung herself from very subtly lit up brighter than its counterpart and adopted a pale, almost negligible yellow tint. Orsche got closer and noticed a grand assortment of drinks and snacks arranged rather neatly on top of a stone table. At the very least, that's what the bearded man would have seen not even a few minutes ago. Alize started up at him, at the table, then backed up to him with a food-filled grin. A mountain of crumbs rolled off of the boy's clothes as he moved to stuff even more in his mouth.

"What is all of this? Is this kind of hunger a side effect of the surgery? I don't remember the doctor saying anything like this." Orsche stood on the other side of his son and blinked in utter horror. His son's face and hair were covered in an oily residue while his clothes appeared to have paint sprayed all over him. Orsche found himself ready to turn his questions to someone who was watching over his baby boy, but he froze at the horror set before him. A group of a dozen servants balanced several carts of precariously leaning towers of plates bearing the remains of spotless and cartilage-less bones, crumbs, and streaking sauces of all manner of food. Giant empty gallons of water, smoothies, and all kinds of other drinks and shakes were also ferried along a differ- ent path. Out of sight, the servants presumably exchange the physical carting of dirty dishes with easier and magical storage containers, but Orsche and any other patient of the Umbertree estate were not privy to such information.

"No, what is happening with your son is not a side effect of the surgery. As for the meals, this is simply another expression of our services and accommodations. Please eat or snack for a while. Your driver is still getting everything ready." Teeya chimed in and sat herself in a seat across from the Scuttle family.

"Uh, thank you." Orsche bowed his head a little bit and uncom- fortably accepted that the servants immediately filled the vacuum of space and assembled the equivalent of a five-course meal for nearly a dozen people.

"Thank you, Miss Teeya. This is all wonderful. The food is great." Verza spared no effort to feed herself small bites and stuffed Alize's mouth with the tender love of a parent feeding their one and only baby. Alize simply nodded his head and received the little airplanes with a smile and lively eyes. Orsche didnt touch his food and just looked at his boy with very obvious worry.

"The appetite is normal. Don't worry about bloating, overeating, or any of the normal aftereffects of a large meal. Dr. Nayame is well aware of a patient's hunger pangs and developed a medication that amplifies the body's natural ability to digest large volumes of food. In other words, your son could probably eat for the whole day and still not get hurt by eating so much." Teeya received her own meal and explained as she placed a sheet on her lap. Orsche showcased a slight inability to truly understand, but slowly, his knitted eyebrows loosened. Tears welled up, but in an attempt to appear strong and put together, he buried himself in the meal placed before him.

"I didn't notice it until now, but I was sure that Mr. Dean was following behind us while we were leaving Central Rest." He spoke up after eating his fill. Alize, his precocious baby boy, was still in the middle of a rowdy and emotion-packed meal.

"It has been a few hours. Oh dear, do you think he got lost? "

Verza wiped Alize's face, but as she seemingly thought more on the matter, something made her blush.

"I somewhat forgot that even came after us," she admitted.

"Haha, oh no, Mr. and Mrs. Scuttle. Mr. Dean is not lost..." Teeya, pulled in by the whole atmosphere, sipped her tea to stifle a genuine laugh that even she seemed to be startled by considering her wide eyes and sudden rigid posture. Laughing once more due to Alize's unfortunate yet adorable appearance, Teeya decidedly used the teacup as a mask. It did very little to hide the curve of her lips.

"He is not like Dr. Nayame or the guard that brought you here. There are traffic laws and regulations regarding the Star lanes and walks." Teeya tapped on her clipboard and nodded as though her evaluation was just confirmed by something that was sent to her device.

"He is just now leaving the Rest." She shared her information openly. Alize chewed and swallowed his food in a flurry of motion then asked, "How is that possible though? We have been here for hours."

The well-rounded assistant pursed her lips and then nodded a few times. With a small exhale that resembled a chuckle, she raised her free hand and poured magic into a bracelet that decorated her wrist. A stack of translucent papers that carried a subtle silver glow flew away from her open palm and circled over the center of the table. With a wave of a single finger, the wispy pages flattened and synced up into a wall. Under Teeya's outpouring, the Arcanum instantly warped as scrawling lines and color flooded the glass, bending and warping the light that hit them to create an image. In the blink of an eye, a grid full of names and numbers separating different streets and districts of Heydens Rest filled a handful of the glass sheets. With a flick of her finger, a dot blinked near the center of Heyden's Rest, near a massive golden blotch that said Rest Memorial Statue.

"This is the location of the Vielseam. It's also where you met with Dean and Dr. Nayame. As it was an emergency situation, the doctor decided to pay for your group's express travel through the city. Our security team, as you have all witnessed yourselves, meets the minimum requirements to travel the star roads within the city. Dean will have had to have taken local streets and highways through different districts of the city. This is simply because a two star ranked caster is neither fast nor controlled enough to use the Star Road that the doctor paid for." Teeya dragged her finger across the air. The dot split into two very minute overlapping lines that cut sharp angles through the different districts and of the city before the line overlapped onto one of the few wide paths that led out. The line mostly followed or overlapped with something called the HR-Starwalk: JD Expressway slD-15kmm 1.100.

This starwalk pathway fed into a checkerboard- like network of long gray-scale lines that only ever slightly bent in a long arc towards two places in the caldera. Similar to how a bunch of bananas might arc toward the same crown. The first cluster of roads on the starwalk intersected in a place called Kykerie's Pass while the other funneled through a place called Havengate. As for the red dot and subsequent line that represented the doctor's entourage, it cut a 90-degree angle that overlapped with a different starwalk that was colored with a yellow dotted line and a name that said Golden Rest Bridge. Though a feat of peerless engineering and fantastical magic, this bridge managed to stay aloft a massive body of water that separated the vast center of the city from an upper-scale side of Jordaine's society. In terms of scale, this dividing river made the widest parts of the Rio de la Plata look like a small trickle or a creek.

"That said, getting to and past the Golden Rest Bridge and out of the inner city is normally a multiple-hour endeavor." Teeya enlarged the map with a few more sheets of paper and extended the line all the way until it cut through the shaded patch of the map that said Rushett Dsl 15.3.

"Getting to the fields is also another journey of many hours without using the Star Road. So altogether, with the fastest commercial transports of our twin cities, Dean will reach this field in about another half a day." Teeya then extended the map even more, to the point where Orsche and Verza had to stand up and take a few steps back. Alize quietly looked at his parents for direction and smiled when Orsche pulled him back to see the map. Dots and circular rings that represented towns and smaller cities connected to and spread out from a central gray road that sliced the forest and fields in two. Different names flashed on the locations, but the point of this massive and highly detailed map was to stress the distance of their current location to the more metropolitan environs of central Rest so the names turned into a secondary blur. Teeya openly smirked while she observed the Scuttles in front of her. Orsche's gaze represented a sudden revelation as he visibly contemplated the speed and power that the guards possessed. Verza pointed some things out on the map with absolute wonder and audibly said "wow" and "look at that" more than once as she pointed out the intense level of detail and motion of the floating pages. Ark even attempted to control his seemingly endless appetite and shock as he stared at the magical sight.

"Using the fastest route. Dean will properly leave the central park area of the city in about two more days. A few hours after that, he will finally reach the border of our Dragon Marsh District. It's also called Petal borough but we like to simplify it and call this place Dragon Petal." Again, the map extended so much Orsche and Verza had to take another few steps back to take it all in.

"Our Umbrie Hill is also actually very far on the outskirts of the region, so to make it here and avoid the private property of the landowners in the area, it would take Dean an additional two or three days depending on the weather." Teeya then ended the map with a star at their current location.

"Altogether, we should not expect Dean for at least five to seven days." Teeya then suddenly put her teacup down and stood up to bow when she noticed the aghast expressions on Orsche's and Verza's faces. The duo shook as they avoided looking at any of the guards. Almost instinctively, the two also lowered their heads to take up as little space as possible.

"Mr. and Mrs. Scuttle, are either of you frightened by the rank of our facilities' private security? I know that it is typically a jarring experience when one unknowingly interacts with someone higher in rank than they are." Teeya's long ears drooped, with a few strands of her hair falling out of the tight bun above her head.

"No, Ms. Teeya, we are okay. It's just..." Verza looked toward Orsche with trembling hands.

"It's just quite a lot to take in, Ms. Teeya. We know that some transports use the roads and walks since we use one to come into the city every so often but this." Orsche clutched his wife's hand for support and stared at one of the nearby guards that remained motionless and forward facing with focused, almost blank eyes. Teeya, seeing that her explanation of Dean's travel issues led to the Scuttles going through their own minor catastrophe, used her odd Arcanum to double-check and reframe the distance for the family of three.

"If it takes five to seven days to reach a different district within Rest, I can only imagine how long it would take us to reach here on public transport from home." Verza released a tangible air of worry.

"If there is an emergency, we will be far too late to save our son." Orsche finished but practically bit his nail in frustration.

"I have seen that you filled out the address on your file, so how about I show you how long it would take someone coming from your home to here using our Drivers rather than public services?"

"That would be lovely." Verza nodded and expressed a sorrow and gratitude only available to someone at the end of their rope who received a lifeline.

"Ahem." Teeya checked her paperwork and extended a pathway from Umbrie Hill all the way south of Rest. The glassy papers lined up next to a location that was next to a new Star road that was slD-9059.

The only problem was that Teeya ran out of sheets for the GPA, Global Positioning Arcanum, to function without sliding the map.

"That is quite far." Without any hesitation, Teeya grabbed one of the less essential paper-thin glass sheets and, like a touchscreen phone with a GPS app on it, she zoomed out of her current location. The crookedly smiling country gained a long scar that trailed from the bottom of its jagged lip, all the way to the southeasternmost curve of the crown.

"But you do not have to worry. Our divers can get anyone from one quadrant of Dane to the other in less than an hour." Teeya wiped a smile from her normally unperturbed expression and walked out from underneath the gazebo. She stood right beside the cobblestone road that they all ignored until now and blew on an immaculately carved whistle. A loud whine and thunderous gallop echoed up the road. The air roiled as dust and pebbles sparked around a rectangular object that came in with the wind. A horse-shaped tornado spearheaded the object and gradually came to a halt directly in front of Teeya.

A brief second later, the turbulent wind settled to reveal a six-legged horse at the height of five or so meters and the length of around twelve. The massive creature nuzzled Teeya's extended hand and graciously accepted a small treat. An elegant black carriage with golden accents depicting trees and dragons greeted the Scuttle family. A large glowing disc, similar to an upside-down mushroom cap, flashed underneath the body of the carriage. A box on the side of the carriage similarly floated off the ground in a magical haze, splitting itself into evenly spaced steps. The carriage's lacquered doors automatically opened and revealed a splendiferous interior full of azure velvet, ivory moldings, and obsidian-paneled flooring. A screen with snacks and drinks flashed on a small display that was set between one of the two inwardly facing seats. Basically, the whole thing screamed extravagance, wealth, and go big or go home energy. As if to hammer in that particular idea or beat a dead horse, a group of guards and servants lined themselves up and legitimately rolled out an Azure carpet for the Scuttles.

"I'm guessing this is how the quack has decided to let his people kick patients out of his manor." Alize glanced toward the table that had been cleaned to the point of sparkling the instant he looked away from the center of the gazebo.

"We are already outside though, so this method of showing us our transport is more likely Ms.Teeya's doing. I'm guessing she wants to be with the quack doctor to finish their earlier foreplay." Alize broke the tense atmosphere with a giggle befitting his age.

"Thank you for the meal. It was delicious. And thank you for sparing your time to help us out so much." Alize scooted his chair forward and addressed Teeya with an innocent gleam in his eyes.

"I told you this when the doctor handed you over to me. It is my pleasure to make sure that all patients and their families eat, rest, and depart our grounds with a smile." With a gentle tone, Teeya lowered herself to Alize's height and motioned toward the horse. A servant suddenly appeared with a nutritious-looking brick of oats and vegetables that Alize gladly fed to the massive beast.

2.9 Interrogation

Orsche and Verza properly expressed their intention to wish well upon the Doctor that gave hope to their family. Orsche visibly trembled in his attempt to hold back a flood of tears while Verza openly wept as she leaned against her man for support, playing the part of trophy wife perfectly even if all she did was copy her man's behavior when he tried to act all cutesy and wanted something. The constant "thank you's" and laughter seemed to never end. Teeya, well versed in getting families to leave, settled the matter with a small exchange of pleasantries and promises. Skipping over the exact details for the sake of brevity, the Peachum-Scuttle family, after a long-winded and drawn-out goodbye, entered the carriage.

With the expected ohs and ahs of people who had never been showered in such luxury before, Zaqiel, Verza, and their baby boy Ichibaratol, settled in. The driver atop the carriage snapped his fingers and sent the horse into a full gallop in no less than a minute. As a point of reference, the carriage achieved a speed of several hundred kilometers an hour from a full stop. The most miraculous aspect about all of this was that the horse shifted into a gale force that swept the carriage up into the air and through the umbrella-like canopy of the doctor's estate. The "Scuttle" family felt absolutely none of the movement and instead, marveled like they were expected. Alize set his chair to a fixed hover in the middle of the carriage and took a moment to observe his parents as they both fidgeted with their pockets and some glittering jewelry or accessories that they managed not to draw attention to.

"They look kinda constipated?"

After a long drawn-out minute of coordinating something, his parents moved cushions, checked the smallest indents and crevices in the decorative moldings, and they even knocked against every surface that could potentially be hollowed out and used to hide something.

"I wonder what they are talking about. Probably, oh ho ho, my love, did you notice how smart and cool Ark is for acquiring the water of the eternal spring? Why, I don't believe that I have noticed that, my handsome man, but I wholeheartedly agree. I was completely overcome with pride and love seeing my baby boy act circles around the quack doctor's most trusted assistant. Well, my love, you must have at least realized that he successfully invented an entirely new spell to achieve something even I would struggle at due to my Profile? What? Ark did that? Yes, my love, it is truly something achievable only through sheer ingenuity and an impeccable mastery of many different profiles! Our baby is so cool. Or something like that," without being asked or motioned to do so, Alize unlocked his chair and moved to a spot that both of his parents and Jarold looked over already.

"Jokes aside, they are probably checking for surveillance or scrying spells and arcanum." After half a second of deliberation, Alize pressed the windowpane on one side of the carriage. The landscape was one long and torn image of trees, marshlands, azure thickets, and rolling compounds. As expected, the bottom left side of the glass held an

opaque power symbol. With a simple press and three-second hold, the window darkened. A small icon of an infinity loop with a city skyline and twisting trees burned into the center of the glass and bloomed into a UI with two squares, a little and taller humanoid. Alize pressed the child-sized icon and cycled through over a dozen different streaming and educational platforms local to Jordaine and Haven.

Rather than choose something deliberately, Alize cycled through videos until he found a popular live channel that specialized in educational shows for his age range. The current program featured a purple-haired man with sculpted features and magenta scales framing his emerald green eyes. This host and the accompanying cast of actors explored the dangers of using magic when playing games like hide and seek, tag, or some other specialized and physically active sports. Alize stared at the host for what felt like decades. The nightmarish image of a cloud-scraping bipedal dragon with deep amethyst and lavender scales overlapped with the gentle guy on the screen.

"Huh." With a speed that he didn't know that he possessed, Alize wiped a tear from eye while his parents were busy scouring the interior of the carriage. Hesitantly, he turned toward his family unit and immediately realized that only Jarold saw him. Thankfully, the sylph made it clear that he would not say anything by raising an eyebrow and tilting his head.

"I saw this episode a few days ago. Before I fell. Barnes and other hosts of the show wrap up this episode's lesson with the story of Rosencrantz and the game that led to the forging of her armor and the eventual disaster that caused it and her to shatter. Not the whole story since it's not exactly kid friendly. Haa. The song that the cast pieces together this episode, however, is practically a modern-day ode to the late Cursed Briar Archon. You know what, watch it with me, you'll see what I mean." Alize spoke up randomly and drew his parents' attention to the screen as he slowly raised the volume. Involuntarily, Verza and Orsche glanced at one another and smiled as they simultaneously gleaned their son's intention.

"Alright." Verza sat down on a chair that was closest to the window and adjacent to her baby boy.

"Does anyone want a snack? I think everything in here is complimentary." Orsche nodded along and knelt down in front of a screen that was embedded into one of the two rows of seats. The glassy box resembled the front door of a see-through mini-fridge door but without any of the protruding bulk of its many other components.

"Some cookies, please," Alize chirped.

"You had enough sweets. My love, what would you like? This arcanum can order pretty much anything by the looks of the meal options." Orsche wore an amazed expression.

"I'm okay. I am completely stuffed." Verza shook her head and returned to watching the show with her darling boy. Orsche shrugged his shoulders and ordered a churro. With a flash, the glass split open to reveal an inner compartment.

"Oh, that smells nice. Can I have one?" Alize's nose twitched.

"No. You had too many sweets." Verza pointed out a problem.

"I know, Mom, but I'm still hungry, and it smells so good," Alize pleaded and was getting ready to put on a good show of begging, but Orsche immediately caved.

"You need to be stricter." Verza pouted but couldn't help laughing upon seeing her son with a comically large bucket full of treats.

"I will be. Once his treatment is over." Orsche stretched and yawned on his way over to sit next to Verza. Outwardly, it would seem as though he leaned his head back into the cushion of his seat and wrapped one arm around Verza's shoulder so she could lean into him. Secretly, and without letting anything slip, magic burrowed into the little custard-filled gap within the center of the tubular treat. The miniature halo within his hair enlarged by a fraction of a millimeter, allowing him to gather all the information that he would need for the spell that he was preparing. Everything regarding the dimensions and orientation in space of the carriage and everything inside of it flashed within Orsche's mind. Faster than a femtosecond, he crafted an illusion that bordered on rewriting reality.

If someone used magic to sense anything inside of the carriage, they would just see an innocent and excited child in a wheelchair eating an unhealthy amount of snacks while watching TV. They would also see Verza, passed out and leaning against a pale and clearly exhausted Orsche, who was so tired that his cinnamon stick fell onto his chest and stayed there.

Beneath the illusion, Orsche held Verza by the shoulders as magic visibly glittered like an exoskeleton on his forearms. His smaller frame trembled against Verza as she attempted to walk toward the carriage door. Jarold did not stand idly by and pushed her back with everything that he had while Ors pulled. Alize was most definitely not watching a baby show at this moment as he parked himself at the door and held his hands up.

"I said let me go, Ors. Jarold, if you don't move, I will cut our contract. And you..." Verza calmly spoke to her man, telepathically warned her lifelong Fae and partner in crime, and narrowed vision onto her little boy. The sharp edges of her face softened by the smallest margin, but ultimately, she deepened her voice and restored her glare to its peak intimidation value.

"I am just going to head out on a walk." As if she were simply brushing a leaf off of her shoulder, Verza flicked her arm and shattered Orsche's magical exoskeleton.

"Don't lie, Verza." Orsche quickly stood back up and stood beside Jarold with a massive hexagonal barrier between the door and her.

"I'm not lying. I really do want to stretch my legs for a bit." Verzas' hardened expression inflamed with a magical fury as her pupils flashed like lanterns through a dense forest. Alize's innate [Shroud], no matter how complex or ingrained it was, unraveled under the maximum focus of her sensory spell. In less time that it took someone to blink, she found herself cycling through an expanded visual range of the light spectrum. As a result, Verza peered beneath Alize's skin. She did not need to be a doctor to notice that most of her son's muscles, bones, veins, and nerves liquefied and blended into a thick and viscous fluid that held or even replaced most of his vital organs. In other words, his biological interior resembled the inside of a lava lamp in constant flux.

The only two things holding his body together were a near invisible wireframe of magic that overlapped with his actual proportions and organ placement and a thick transparent gel that periodically oozed out of the surface of his, now looking at it, watery or oil slicked skin. Verza had no idea what she was looking at, especially since there was no indication of a spell even being used by her son. It was as if this was simply the natural state of his body and that left her confused and frightened since the only things that resembled this, in her mind, were a hostile and regressive subsect of creatures and a certain species of monsters that straddled the line of being biologically immortal. Despite feeling as though his soul had just been exposed, Alize matched his mother's burning gaze even if it was only for a single second. A tangible bloodlust choked the air out of his lungs and pulled the color away from his face.

"My love, you can't just 'stretch your legs' just because you don't like the way that Ark handled an already difficult task." Orsche crossed his arms and completely tanked the bloodlust that washed over him and Alize. Verza didn't move from her spot and glared.

"Then what will you have me do, huh? Sit down and listen while my baby tells me about the bloodletting that he avoided because he did something slightly smart? It's bull. I have brought down entire crime syndicates, entire countries, for less of an atrocity." Verza absolutely fumed with a reddened face.

"*Slightly smart? Mom, I am a pioneer in the practical application of spells that have been lost to the ages. People with a heavily influenced utility profile wish they could achieve what I accomplished today. Hmph.*" Alize did not speak, but the betrayal of his mother's words left him visibly agitated as his eyebrows bounced unconsciously.

"Yes, my love. That is exactly what I am saying. Listen, digest, coordinate, then act. Remember that? Ark deserves the same. Besides, we have put him through worse in the Sim. You cannot lose your cool just because we are not the ones in control of what happens to him." Orsche crossed his arms as well, but there was no sign of frustration. In fact, Alize tilted his head only slightly and noticed a slight lip and eyelid twitch that showed the depths of his father's self-restraint. No, as he thought about it...

"*Mom made a show of getting angry and tried to storm out, but Dad would not have been able to stop her if she was behaving true to her emotions. Thus, they must be putting on another act in addition to the two illusions that Dad cast to keep our conversation hidden. The question is, are they afraid that the quack has a caster following us, one capable of breaking through the illusions, or are they putting on this show just for me? If so, what exactly are they talking about that they feel the need to blatantly lie to me, their own son? Or am I reading too much into this?*"

Alize turned back to his mother and noticed that her pupils, despite being locked onto his father, seemed a little too pointed, almost as though she purposely kept him within her periphery so that he had the chance to focus on what she looked at. There was also the matter of their mirrored physical posture, the guarded, defensive nature of having one's arms crossed, and the lowered center of gravity as though one might need to react at any given second.

"I'm probably reading into it. Or I'm not. It's best to proceed with caution." Alize narrowed his gaze to concentrate on anything out of the ordinary, anything that would hint at the details of a discussion that his parents chose to have privately.

"Fine." Verza threw her hand up and paced about the massive carriage interior in a slow, almost stalking gait.

"There we go. Continue what you were saying, Ark." Orsche lowered his head as he leaned against the door frame to wait out Verza.

"Okay, but first, Mom, can you sit down?"

Alize remained in front of the door, beside his father, and waited for some type of positive response. Without saying a word, Verza sat down and tapped a finger on her thigh. She muttered something about wet work, too much prep time, enemy of my enemy, and being a little birdy for someone called the Pinwheel.

"Ah. I see. You want specific information to better plan whatever you have in mind. Ha, what should I say now? If this show isn't for me, then who are we acting for?"

Alize blinked a few times, cleared his throat and got back to telling his parents about what went down inside of the eternal spring.

"Okay. Ahem." Alize grabbed his own finger and avoided his mother's gaze.

"Skipping over the part that you do not like, Jarold noticed that the spring was getting ready to open back up. I cast a rather minor illusion under [Shroud]. Specifically, a Phys-rou pathway spell called [Felign-juris] I altered the formula a bit so I could push out a fake display of Tenets." Alize waited for his parents to finish up their communication with one another and continued only after receiving a nod from his mom.

"With the illusion, I rolled my injuries back to before the spring healed my wounds. As a result, whatever sensory spell that the Arcanum had been infused with, tripped some kind of a failsafe and locked the room before it could fully open. I used the chance to create a spell that allowed me to absorb as much of the spring's medicine as my body could possibly retain." Alize trailed off and swallowed his saliva. His mom's glare, which was often directed at his father, fell onto him.

"Now Ark, what spell did you create? I'm assuming that it has something to do with why your body looks like that?"

Verza stopped tapping for a long moment and then continued after using her ultra-focused eye movement to point down at her own hand.

"It's a derivative of two different Accord Type spells under [Embody] and the [Minor Heal] that I altered to fit my profile." Alize was preparing his next thought but noticed that his mother's tapping turned into another message, so he remained silent and nodded.

"Ahem, I'm guessing that one thing led to another, and the Doctor realized that there was something wrong with the time that you spent inside of his Arcanum." Orsche held his arm out, barring the door and practically begged Verza to remain seated with a slow gesture.

Without any obvious signs, he cast a third illusion that automatically changed everything that they talked about into something pleasing to the listener's ear.

"That's exactly it, Dad," Alize responded.

"Then, considering the circumstances, what did you say?"

"I told him that I have a Lasting Effects Suffix based on the scenarios that we went over in the Sims. After that, Ms. Teeya brought me to the garden where I met you two. I didn't really say anything important other than we used to live in the Corridor, but the business went under after Grandpa died, so we moved it to Jordaine since competition is less daunting. I also brought up the Suffix a few times in relation to other times I was hurt. I used the instances that I experienced in the sim. Was that alright?"

Alize waited for anyone to respond. Verza constantly shook her head while Orsche simply rubbed his own temples. It was only after a full minute that Orsche took a break from talking in private that they decided to speak to their son.

"What you did is good. I'm happy to hear that you remembered your training and the curse that we all agreed most represents any issues that might affect your physical state. All in all, your mother and I are proud of everything you did today. We are even amazed at what you have accomplished, but..." Orsche motioned toward Verza to take the torch of but her glare simply shifted back.

"You are not allowed to do something like this again. This whole encounter, as far as I can tell, was a trap set by your Affix to get me and or your mother to slip up and interfere with its plans for you." Orsche plugged one of his ears and threw his hands up in defeat.

"Do you understand where we are coming from?"

Orsche sat down next to his boy and waited for Verza to go "stretch her legs," as she put it. Only Alize, sitting there in his wheelchair, served as a barrier.

"I am sure that my next few lessons in the sim are going to revolve around what could have gone wrong even if I don't, so I will eventually have to experience the dangerous position that I put our family in, so yes, I understand the general danger. As for how the two of you might feel." Alize thought about for a good long minute and nodded slowly.

"He said something about my Affix setting a trap, so I'm sure Dad might feel betrayed by my lack of communication. Mom is clearly annoyed. But since they are so frustrated and Mom didn't outright leave to destroy the quacks' facility, it means that they can't do it even while working together..." Alize closed his eyes to focus on an imaginary board that represented his thought process.

"The quack's facility..." The boy started to speak, but Verza cut him off.

"You failed us, Ark." She stared at Alize as though he were the greatest disappointment in her life.

"Failed, Mama, what? Me? I failed you guys? How? And why are you looking at me like that?"

Unintentionally, Alize's face twisted since his mom's accusation didn't seem fake. From the body language and expressions that he observed on his parents, the idea that he failed his parents floated between the two of them for a while.

"We will deal with what you did to yourself in a few minutes. Right now, I am disappointed that you would keep this from me and your dad?"

"The fuck? What are you talking about? I have been nothing but open and honest. I learned how to lucid dream just so I could keep track of everything, just like the two of you asked. I wrote everything down even though it seemed stupid at the time. I even explained some parts that I didn't want to talk about because of how disgusting the nightmare felt to me, but wait, hold on. What do you think I did to myself?"

"Mom, I'm sorry, but I'm a little bit confused. What did I keep from you and Dad?"

"The doctor's identity. Leakley Nayame. Your father confirmed the man's identity the moment that he showed his Profile Sigil, but not too long ago, Jarold confirmed that guy showed some of the telltale signs of the 18th king's Profile. This tells us two things. Leakley Nayame either charmed and faked his profile before he became a scholar or someone else with the mad king's authority stole his identity." Verza revealed some of what she talked about with Orsche.

"That said, if that man decided to charm us even if only on a whim or to test the waters, we would all be in danger if not dead or captured by now. No, even if your father and I set up every countermeasure before we decided to follow your plan, we still would have been put under his thrall. You failed to inform us. No, you purposely sabotaged us and our chances of getting through this ordeal peacefully by not telling us that Leakly might be a fake identity or an imposter that replaced the original scholar." Verza laid in on thick with a derisive sneer plastered on her face.

"So. Is it? Are you claiming that I purposely left out this knowledge?" Alize squeaked out a response.

"Yes. You called him a fake doctor in your journals. Did you not?"

"I did but. I didn't mean to imply that I knew about the man's personal information or something like that." Alize almost shouted but quickly shut himself down and controlled his tone of voice.

"Then what did you mean when you expressly told us that quote, 'the man that we are going to meet because of this relic is a quack doctor that pretends to know what he is doing', end quote? You then explicitly stated that he relies on his staff, their skills, and his arcanum to do the work that genuine doctors train their entire lives to handle. Even if you didn't know, and only had a vague notion, why didn't you tell us that he was not the doctor that he claimed to be?" Verza turned her glare back to Orsche as he raised a finger to interject.

"I meant to say that the quack doctor is a liar. In all of my nightmares, he was never the one to do anything for me. It was always his minions and staff. I didn't say or imply that he was an imposter because

I have had no reason to believe that he was anyone else other than a lazy, lying scholar that got by on using the drugs of the Corazó-Sprie." Alize kept his head low and responded without a single stutter. Verza stopped tapping her finger for a moment to gauge the shaken expression Alize portrayed.

"So the validation and confirmation that you wanted to do, now that we have passed the hurdles of this encounter, have nothing to do with the doctor's possible fake identity? I am supposed to believe that you called him a fake and a quack because you think that he is full of it?"

Verza narrowed her eyes and enveloped an unending tide of blood-lust.

"I will not say that I haven't thought of the possibility..." Alize clasped his hand over his lap.

"I only assumed a false identity was secondary to knowing if the Scrying Glass artifact was about to enter that man's hands and tertiary to the location of the Corazó-Sprie. If it was truly hidden in the forsaken building. Even more so, my mind has been on formulation and sequencing spells that would have helped me overcome anything the quack might have done to me. Thankfully, the worst didn't happen." Alize completely shut his eyes and avoided looking at his mom.

"Everything that I know about the quack on a personal level, I have gathered in the small five or so minute window that I saw him without his scholar garb on." He released a long sigh and bit at his lower lip even as Verza's tangible bloodlust bore down on him like a boulder.

"I understand your worry, Mom. Trust me, I get it. My plan—no—my suggestions have not been great. At best, I have been making assumptions and creating countermeasures for scenarios and against issues that I basically had fever dreams about. I have asked the two of you to trust me and go along with my whims even if I don't know the full scale of what my Affix can generate. Based on your actions, however, I can conclude that I severely underestimated the quack doctor and what is underneath Umbrie Hill." Alize gazed upon his mother and felt her bloodlust shatter. She looked away with a squared jaw and huffed loudly and hard enough to disturb the carriage's airflow. Quickly, Alize turned his head to observe Orsche.

"I was right about the facility posing a danger. The issue is, how much did they see that I do not know about for them to act like this? It's almost like they want to go and mess with my event but they can't because it would kill them." Alize didn't know how hard he struck the nail or even if he connected with the underlying issue that his parents had and instead waited for someone to give him some information. Anything to confirm, deny, or rebut his statements.

"Ors, I'll just deal with this." Verza un-clenched her jaw, closed her quivering eyelids, and turned away from the pale remnant of her own confidence.

"Ark." Orsche sat next to Verza and rubbed her back with a small frown.

"Your mom and I have been talking, as you might have already guessed, and. We need you to be honest and straightforward." Orsche stared through his son's pupils and directly made contact with the boy's racing imagination.

"Tell me honestly. Was there anything that would have informed or helped you guess that the quack possessed the profile of Nazaret Nayame before today? Even if it was only some passing moment in your dreams or nightmares, did you notice anything?"

Orsche placed a hand over Alize's clenched fists and tried his best to offer a comforting smile, but the worry and sorrow twisted his face into a wrinkled mess.

"No. There was nothing about his profile even in the worst of what I remember. I only saw him in the background of everything. The moment Jarold and I saw him using some variant of magic, I put together why that guy might want, recognize, and need a divine-ranked scrying glass. It would be my obsession if I had magic like his." Alize looked over his memory thrice before he spoke. He didn't want to play any games of linguistics and immediately got straight to the point as he placed his hand on the tiny arcanum that was hidden within the wraps under his clothing. Verza and Orsche, under his scrutinizing eye, both released an almost unconscious physical tension in their shoulders.

"Fair assessment." Silence pervaded the interior of the vibrantly furnished carriage for a long and drawn-out minute before Orsche nodded in confirmation.

"Your mother and I have many questions regarding the things you are not telling us. We will have you answer them when we get back home and have the time to set up the sim for everything that we want to show you. Right now, we just want to know if doing this is worth the risk of losing everything our family has and if you are prepared for the consequences." Orsche used his chin as a sort of pointer to let Alize know that it was okay to speak anytime he wanted.

"The risk is worth it. Getting involved is worth it. Even if we get caught messing with the quack. The alternative is worse, I think..." Alize paused for a long moment and prevented himself from getting sucked into the nightmare of being stuck inside of Umbrie Hill.

"To cut it all down to a simpler perspective, I left out details regarding the danger posed to my own body because the two of you would have never agreed to coming to this place." Alize raised his eyebrows in wait for the argument or a disapproving sigh.

"It makes sense in my book, and yes." Orsche stroked his beard and nodded as he made one logical leap to the next, almost as if large stones were equally spaced across a river of wild conclusions.

"Really?"

Verza did not dance to the tune of guesswork and shifted her dominant leg as he snapped out of some self-imposed stupor. Orsche sighed and explained.

"Alright, my love. It's like this. Ahem, once we confirm if these plastic bifocals are indeed the artifact that Ark and I believe it is, the situation would have been like this." Orsche in a dazzling display of control, electrically charged some of the dust that Jarold was made of and created a slideshow, much to the old man's displeasure.

"Leakly or the illegal magic user who created or stole the Doctor's identity would then be able to see who he would be able to charm and how long it would take to work or wear off. As a conservative estimate, it would take one week to a year for an Arcanum of its proposed grade and rank to adjust to any language barriers and, uh, I'm droning on." Orsche slowed and nodded to himself as he brought the conversation to a private space that Alize was not privy to.

"*We have to maintain a good relationship with the quack for the main cluster of my events to play out how my Affix wants it to; otherwise, another series of events that is a trap will make things more difficult. It's even possible that my Affix will go through another unexpected overhaul and create something that might kill the two of you, Gramps, me, or all four of us. That said, everything else that we have seen here and any plans we might have for the future do not matter if these glasses are not the Arcanum that I saw the quack wearing.*" Alize clenched the little plastic bifocals that were hidden near his chest and tried to force a smile.

"Ark, your mom has the big picture now, so don't worry. We will help you the best that we can. Right now, I need to see if it's possible to remove the spring water from your duplicate without any loss." Orsche tapped his son on the shoulder.

"Of course, go ahead." Alize shook his head to clear away the absolute fear that wracked his body. Orsche nodded, then used several pieces of color-coded tape and scalpels to cut into his son's body at different spots. The odd tape disallowed any of the water to escape the balloon-like tautness of the kid's skin and created a small trickle of water that embodied a laminar flow. The pink water entered similarly color-coded vials in a seemingly unending flood.

"That was quite the risk, pops. What if my skin ruptured, and I exploded like a water balloon? My duplicant would have died, and the spring water would be lost." Alize's fake smile deteriorated into a sagging look of exhaustion.

"It wasn't a risk, Ark, and you know it. I would have never let you move onto practical casting Sims if you couldn't even develop or repurpose a stable formula for something like this. That said, what are you calling your spell?"

With a deft flick of his wrist, Orsche traded the nearly filled vials for newer containers that possessed darker caps and a mystical volume count that topped out at ten liters per vial. His mouth slowly dropped with each swap of glimmering vials.

"I was thinking of just using common to call my variant of Felign-juris, Feigned Injuries, but I was also workshopping the idea of calling it Inner Well or Reservoir as a joke. But the names Curtain, Mantle, or Overlay also feel right if I manage to expand on what I'm able to hide in my body. The only issue is that there are already other [Shroud] spells with those names." Alize lifted his chin and waited for his pops to give some input, but the man simply stared at him as though he were an anomaly.

"Come on now, pops. What's with that look?"

"Ha. Sorry, I am just a little stunned by you, Ark. You are too much. You do much. It's a great quality that you have, but it's also, ha. I love you, son." Orsche stared at a black-capped vial that topped out at 100 liters and did his best to control his sheer terror and emotion as it filled up slowly but steadily.

"That black cap, oh my goddess. There is no way that Cheque is getting filled by the water content in my body." Alize shared the same look on his father's face and instinctively raised his hands in a moment of confusion and defense.

"I didn't get everything. Couldn't get everything with the vial I have on hand. I took out enough so that your body won't explode. I don't know how much is left inside of you, but I have gotten more than enough. Have fun explaining the mystics of this to your mother." Orsche put both of his hands up and sat off to the side with just a single light yellow-capped vial. With a shake of his head, the man raised the vial to the carriage's centralized light fixture and observed the contents and his son with squinted eyes. Several rings sparked inside his pupils while his fingers danced with subtle glowing threads. The vial expanded as though it were under the world's most powerful microscope, but so did Alize's body due to the specific focus of the halo on his head.

"Explain what?"

"Nature Verz, our son went against nature in his what? Second practical application of the theory and simulated practice that we have given him." Orsche gave his boy a pitiable smile and side glance.

"Ah. That reminds me. I said that we would get into that later. Alright, Ark, tell me what you did to yourself. You might be able to hide it under normal circumstances, but if I press my sensory spell to its limit, I can see through your illusion." Verza crossed her leg a third time and leaned back in her seat.

"Mom." Alize closed his eyes and avoided meeting the glare that shut his brain in a cage of fear.

"I am..." He clenched the blanket on his body.

"I did this to myself. I must gracefully accept the consequences of my actions." Alize quickly smoothed his fists and forced a bright and enigmatic smile to his pale face. Determination and confidence hinted to his parents that everything up until now was well within his calculations.

"Sort of a genius." Orsche nearly dropped his vial while Verza's biceps and forearms twitched uncontrollably. Jarold's beard ruffled so much that he actively moved toward Orsche despite soundlessly cursing him out just moments before.

"I'm serious. I managed to do something really awesome. Dad probably wants me to explain how cool I am for doing something that may or may not be permanent. Haa, also, before I get into the meat of how amazing I am, it's a good thing that I am a duplicant right now so you should keep in mind that even if what I did to myself is permanent, my body will not be majorly impacted." Alize gathered his courage and met his mother's cold stare. Sadly, the moment he decided to put on an act, the illusory image of a bloodthirsty demon straight from the bowels of the abyss instantly burned into his retina.

"I will give you one chance, Alizedriel." Verza crossed her arms in wait.

"Alright then. Quick and simple." Alize ran around in his head to gather his thoughts and compiled everything into a digestible snippet. It took him more than a few dozen seconds to recompose himself, but the next time he opened his mouth, Verza was fully prepared to listen.

"In summary. I am." Alize, despite bolstering his resolve, squeaked out a barely audible gasp. Thankfully, Orsche cut him off with a light chuckle.

"My love, Ark is no longer Lerian. At least temporarily." Ors patted the seat next to him and touched his wrist a few times.

"I guessed as much, but what did he do exactly?" Verza shook her head in disappointment and sat down next to her man with the same hardened disdain as before. It was clear from just her expressions and body language that Alize failed almost completely under the pressure that she exuded. Orsche, unaffected by the choking bloodlust, displayed some charts.

"I don't get it. Explain." Verza, however, frowned and moved the charts out of her face.

"Ark turned himself into an Aberrant Quarian. At least less—more than a third of him is. The rest of him is more or less shifting between complete liquefaction, like an Atalin and compressed Aqua-hedrons. I find it absolutely remarkable." Ors laughed but quickly shut his mouth when Verza punched his arm.

"Remarkable? I don't see anything like that. Ors, I know that you can't see the state of his bones, his organs. It's horrible. Ark, how much pain are you in right now? Do you know what you have done?"

"Of course I do, Mom. I know that if I made a single mistake, the doppelgänger would break, and if it did, I would suffer half as much damage inside of the Arcanum. I know that I would never be able to leave using this thing again. I know that if I hadn't hidden what I wanted to do well enough or if I hadn't created the illusion of my unhealed wounds perfectly enough, I would have gotten us caught and killed. I am also aware that all the water it collected will transfer onto my own body. I even know about the trans-mutative and addictive effect once it is in my real system..." Alize collected himself after a fake breakdown and cleared his throat upon seeing the jaws of his parents drop. He hovered closer to get a good look at the graphs his father displayed.

"Yeesh. I am very happy that I cannot feel a thing. If I could feel that, it would be excruciating." Alize used Prevention as a sort of stand-in sensory spell to gauge his body's condition before casting, but the scan that his father made simply left him baffled, while whatever built in x-ray Verza possessed left him in a state of total absentmindedness. It was as though almost all the cells comprising his physical form, up and decided to break their protective casings all at once and reinforce his skin, turning him into one big, Alize-shaped amoeba. His DNA floated around in a free-form tango, a chaotic and violent dance.

"According to this chart, it's working as I intended it, nice," the kid couldn't help smiling to himself after seeing the numbers for what he managed to accomplish on embodying the spring water.

"Are you in pain?"

"No. I am not in any pain. It all passed after the first hour that I spent soaking in the Corazó-Sprie. Gramps can tell you how much it hurt." Alize sighed but quickly smiled when he felt a large pair of arms wrap around his head and a warmth that put him at ease.

"I understand. I am sorry for getting mad at you. You fully thought about the issues and chose to endure everything by yourself." Verza didn't let Alize see her cry again and held her boy as though he could float away at any point in time.

"It's okay, Mom. I'm also sorry. I know how difficult it is for you to hold back for my sake. I only saw a handful of the floors of the god-awful facility. I can only imagine what else was hidden in the halls of that nasty place." Alize hugged his mom back and quickly locked eyes with his pops.

"If you want me to show you what I scanned, it's going to be a hard no. All you need to know is that the man, whether he is really Leakley or some other illegitimate descendant of the old king, has a decent setup. One that I or you would say is standard among scholars of his particular profession. That said, he has to be unofficially backed by the local guild, has some friends in high places all over Jordaine, or he has a patron from the capital. It's possible that there is some combination of those, but anyway I say it, what he has going on in that place is punishable by death. The issue is..." Orsche sighed.

"The Piety Act right. Even if the quack has crossed the ethical and legal line of no return, if he turns over any and all of his current research and it proves useful to the Empire's grander stability, he will be free albeit under contract by her Immortal majesty." Alize shook his head.

"Exactly." Orsche nodded.

"Well then, it's a good thing that my multi-step plan involves letting people know about his profile before we make any major moves." Alize rubbed his chin as though he were an old man stroking his beard.

"Speaking of. Did you finish the list that you mentioned earlier today?" Verza leaned away from her boy and asked him face to face.

"I haven't finished it yet since it's pretty difficult to translate dreams into a solid timeline. Especially when some of the more recurring stuff had different details but I have a rough idea of what my curse wants." Alize nodded.

"Do you want to see it?"

Verza and Orsche held their breath and conversed with one another at lightning speed. Five seconds later, they both nodded.

2.10 Final thoughts

"**G**ramps, can you set up the board?"

Alize glanced toward Jarold and smiled when the old Sylph kicked up the dust in the carriage. He aggressively stole it back from Ors and turned it into a dusty blackboard. Using colored dust that Jarold pooled at the bottom of the screen, Alize began to write a bulletin.

"I am starting this from the point where my Affix has decided to try to kill me, I think, in order to soft reset the difficulty of the events that it is capable of generating. Ahem, where it forced me to start casting..." Alize put up a finger for each cataloged encounter that he wrote down.

- Wyn and my Fall (and the wild Fae that forced a contract with her).

- The Geist's aggression (attacks and the injuries that nearly left me dead).

- Profile Mixup—is it because of mortal error, divine intervention (Mourra maybe), or my Affixes manipulation?

- Dad's Relics and Job (Most of which need an Archon's attention.)

- Mom's job (We have to avoid the Guardians like the plague while exploring the validity of my journals.)

- Lochorn Root Auction (That's just plain suspicious.)

- Veilseam's Unidentified Scrying Glass (How did that go unnoticed?)

- Undetected Imperial Sigil (also how?)

"What is this about? Where did you see one of these?"

"It came with the glasses? The bear's scroll?"

Alize narrowed his eyes as though it was common sense after his dad lashed his arm out and prevented him from writing anything else.

"Dad, did you not notice it? You pointed out the glasses, so I assumed that you noticed that it was stamped?"

"What's wrong?"

Alize began to sweat seeing the anxious look his mother accidentally shot toward the dead silent Orsche.

"No, there's nothing wrong. Did you manage to read the note? If you noticed it, I am going to assume that you managed to use your [Shroud] to replicate the Tenets needed to unseal the document?"

Orsche cleared his throat and shared some choice words with Verza as he questioned their boy.

"Yeah. It was a personal letter from someone called OLM to the Paricielis. It had blueprints for the glass on it. So I guess the message was to your boss's boss, Dad." Alize shrugged and put his cotton-like pen back to the board.

"No, Ark, the letter. What did it say?"

Verza stepped in, seeing how Orsche completely shut down and covered the veins that popped on either side of his head.

"Basically, the letter said that the Imperial Scholar Assigned to run the main branch of Haven has to immediately and personally ferry the bear and all of its composite accessories toward the Imperial Iris. There wasn't anything special other than the blueprint in the note, so I closed the letter and reapplied the seal without letting my magic mess with its integrity." Alize noticed the distanced and vacant stares that both of his parents seemed to have coordinated and put some thought into it.

"Neither of them noticed my little sleight-of-hand trick. It's probably not something that either of them ever expected, even with all of my training. On another note, I am surprised that Dad missed looking into the scroll. Hmm, wait, is it possible that he genuinely couldn't see anything wrong with it?"

The tense atmosphere lasted for a long while until Orsche leaned back and combed through his hair with a light chuckle.

"Wow, I have been off my game." Orsche gave Verza a wry smile and shrugged as though he was answering some question.

"Is that all that was in the Vielseam?"

Verza shook her head and held her emotions down like a pro as she asked another question.

"No. Maybe? I'm not sure," Alize responded.

"Great, then what's left on the list for this cluster of events?" Verza dead stared into her son's eyes without releasing her deadly pressure and waited.

"Ahem, there is this." Alize finished writing out his bulleted synopsis of the future decreed by a curse and translated by a potentially friendly divine being.

- Dean's Influence in Drift (What shady business dealings necessitate him entering Rest and coordinating an expedition to the southern peaks of the crown? Will that somehow bite us in the posterior?)

- Expedition? (I don't have an event chain related to it yet, but once I am out of the Duplicator and am not piloting a doppelgänger, something will come up.)

- The man behind the identity of the Quack doctor Nayame (Who is this person and how have they managed to hide their profile and identity for so long. Or is he a scholar engaged in a long con?)

- Illegal but currently active Chimera and Homunculus experimentation (How far has that come along? And who is funding or backing such research?)

- Mother??? (Who is that and why is she at rumored odds with the "quack" doctor?)

- Tharrohn's Corazó-Sprie—how did the quack get his hands on it?

- Involvement of the Guardians?

- How does all of this tie into or shape our life together now and in the future?

"These are all the main issues that I have confirmed as current and potentially active events." Alize observed his parents and Jarold come to some sort of conclusion as they mulled over the board of dust and colorful powder.

"What do you want to do when we get back to Rest?"

Verza spoke.

"We can give you an hour or two more. Anymore than that and I cannot guarantee us safely leaving Rest without someone tailing us. The relays that I placed down would have deteriorated too much by then." Orsche checked something on his nonexistent watch as he used his finger to write something on an invisible screen.

Alize's faux smile and mercantile demeanor quickly evaporated as he stared off into the empty side of the carriage. The screen with the purple-haired man showed some end of episode musical bit where his "students" put together elements throughout the episode. They crafted a song about playing with friends in a safe designated environment, or Simulated Terrarium, along with proper supervision.

"You want to see how Wynifell is doing?"

Verza immediately butted in on her son's trailing thought upon seeing his long face.

"Yes. I know she's okay right now since there is supposedly an event where we are older and I run into her but I still can't help but feel worried." Alize tapped his finger on his lap as the worst began to churn around in his mind.

"Alright. We can head over to the Ultegra-Tem's. Her parents still haven't responded, which is very unlike Del and Fred." Verza copied her son's vacant stare.

"Like I said, we can do pretty much anything as long as it is within two hours, preferably one." Orsche nodded at something and put his wrist down.

"There we go. We will check on that nice girl and her family, but since we are still a fair bit away from Rest, what spell did you create that allowed you to retain so much of the spring water? I haven't seen your dad pull out the black cap in a long time." Verza turned to Jarold and quickly brought up a topic that never left the old man's mind.

He was with Ark every step of the way, but it still left him absolutely baffled.

"I was hoping to skip over it, but, ha, I didn't create anything even though I said that I did. There are already spell models that scholars who are light years ahead of me managed to put into any number of theories and simulations. It's just, magic costs and profile restrictions are the bane of any practical caster's existence." Alize cleared his throat, nodded in response to his father's nod and pressed on.

"To be more specific. I used a spell that was rediscovered or recreated after many expeditions into the numerous ruins of the Serelion Desert on the continent of Mino-Talia. Someone from about thirty decades ago discovered the right Profile sequences that unlocked one of the more ancient areas of Mag'aceries Domini, the kingdom of the ancient mad mage. Dad put me in a Sim that let me explore the ruins and nearby caves in the same way that the first scholars who discovered the location would have. It was difficult since I had to find my own way through a few storms of the Ual jisse..." Alize shuddered as he thought back on the horror of a legitimately infinite expanse of black sand.

"I used some of the knowledge that I learned in the sim to tie my spell together." Alize rubbed the back of his head upon seeing the blank stare of his mother and the audible silent astonishment coming from his father.

"Oh. Interesting. One of the first scholars to enter that area, huh? Your father put you in a Sim like that, huh? Interesting. Very interesting." Verza glared at Orsche and nodded a few times as she expressed a few of her choice emotions and thoughts in private.

"Alright. Ahem, so my son, you pieced together a spell that capitalized on the fortunate environment you were in, then what? What aspects are you using and in what sequence? I have seen someone retain or become water using Accord Type magic and some mix of Ballast and Creation before, but this is neither of those." Verza crossed one leg over the other and quickly brought herself back to an inquisitive frame of mind.

"Well. Hmm. How do I say this? Um, it's not really." Alize tapped his finger even faster. Verza leaned forward and stared so hard into her son's eyes that she could just barely make out the imaginary image of her baby boy pacing around in his mind.

"I mean." Alize stopped tapping his finger and sighed.

"It's like this." Alize raised a finger to his chin and explained as though he was a professor and turned to the last empty space on the board that Jarold setup for him. He drew a pentagon with a single dot in the center. He cut a line from each interior angle to the center dot and did something unconventional in terms of how one might distribute a chart of this type of information. He detailed only one of the five segments of the drawing. This single section gained five thick and curving arcs that further split into four columns with each one of those further splitting into upper and lower rows.

Despite not using them, the other sections were called Attis, Retrin, Trafo, Sensus, with the one that Alize focused on being called Injaki or General Utility.

"The way I cast makes sense for the Aspect that I have, might have." He articulated slowly as information washed through his mind.

The five aspects of magic—Attack, Defense, Movement, Observation, and Special or Utility as it was often called—built the inherent qualities of one's magical profile, just like how amino acids were the building blocks of life. That said, Alize shaded in and quickly detailed each part of the Injaki chart almost as if his explanation was something as basic as knowing the alphabet or how to count to ten. Starting from the interior angle, Alize named each of the four columns as Accord, Ballast, Creation, and Direct. Each top row, in a key on the side, represented having mana of that type, while each bottom row represented having a physical manifestation of said magic in the shape of an aura. In a quick and sure motion. Alize shaded in the bottom section for all four types of magic and added an extra fifth shaded spot to the Direct Type upper section, showing that he also possessed its associated mana.

"Upon reflection or when I looked back at how easily everything just worked..." Alize then put a brief, one-sentence breakdown of the magic types and what they represent.

Accord: Trade, deals, balance within one's body and with nature. Healing, Buffs, Debuffs, Death. MASSIVE AOE, INSANE LEVELS OF ENDURANCE. Significantly slower than other magic types, environmentally restrictive, focus intensive.

Ballast: Grounded manipulation physics and material composition. INSANE ADAPTABILITY, REMARKABLE SURVIVABILITY, restricted to the manipulation and alteration of physical matter and tool creation.

Creation: Phenomena with and without explanation. INSANE CONTROL, CASTING SPEED, AND FEWER UTILITARY USE. Less overall power and smaller AOE and is magic intensive.

Direct: Cause and Effect. THE APEX OF MAGIC. You WANT something to HAPPEN, you MAKE IT HAPPEN by simply doing it or knowing how it is done.

"The only way that I can both hide my magic and cast any spell that I want, only happens when my profile is set up as a Direct Type Utilitarian profile like this rather than a Ballast Type." Alize listed the spells he has used since he woke up and drew small little diagrams of how each spell came from his body in some way. It mirrored the quack doctor, but in a much less noticeable manner.

"Everything just works, huh? It's conjecture, but with the evidence and the manner in which you have been casting." Orsche grabbed the bridge of his nose and then slowly covered his entire face.

"This is troubling." Verza pursed her lips and stared at Jarold, who nodded in confirmation, as though he agreed with what Alize said.

"I know. Ors, if he is right, how did he get Direct-type mana? No one in our families has that on their profile. Did the Affix mess with him?"

"No, my love, there is no evidence to suggest that the Affix gave or altered his aspects. I mean, I do know that certain Prefix and Suffix variants are capable of it while there are more than a handful of Affixes in the Immortal series that are known for their Aspect alteration but this, Ha." Orsche trailed off and for what felt like hours, stared at his son absentmindedly as he tried to figure out when and where his aspects could have been changed.

"I can't say Verza. I don't know. I didn't even think of Ark having this kind of distribution. Direct type magic is already rare within the borders of Haven, so a standard spread of aspects to become Pentacoded, it's simply too unreal. The only calming element of Ark's guess is that he might only be at the first sequence all around. It supports the largest variety of spells but also the weakest and least useful without a sufficient knowledge base. In other words, I have to confirm his profile before I give him any more lessons. After all, this whole projection is only a guess based on what he has been able to accomplish so far." Orsche shook his head and completely focused on his son as he spoke directly into her mind. All the buzzing rings in his eyes and the halo hidden within his hair, spun in unison as he tried to pierce through the water containment spell and double layer of illusions that Alize cast on himself and passively possessed.

"Alright then. *We will figure it out when we get him back home. This also gives me some time to finalize his new training regime for after we get rid of any issues that we might have with our, I mean his, events.*" Verza leaned back and narrowed her eyes at Alize as well as she whispered back.

Under the immense pressure of being scrutinized by someone who wanted to dissect and study him as well as a person who wanted to turn his flesh and bone into steel, Alize crumpled. In a second, he waved the dust board away and maneuvered his chair so he could see outside of the carriage. Everything dragged into a picturesque landscape, but it didn't rip inorganically like the running guards achieved earlier in the day. The landscape simply shifted into something that he never would have guessed or even imagined. A flickering line cut across the sky. No, as the horse sped up, the line turned into a baffling crosshatched net in the sky. It was only after blinking a few times and adjusting to the nauseating feeling generated by seeing the outside world pass out of the periphery of his vision that Alize noticed where the carriage was.

"So this is the minimum speed to use the highways."

Just outside of the carriage was an almost imperceptible barrier of magic that allowed light to pass through it without so much as a misplaced photon. They were on a mystical ramp that stretched kilometers in length just to get on the legendary Starwalk, Skylane, or Highway. In less than a second, the carriage pulled onto what could only be described as an endless ocean of starlight and magic. Vehicles of all shapes and sizes, animal or mechanical, capable of running on sunlight or flight and even people moving as though they were in a speed walking competition, flashed by the carriage as it stayed on the rightmost lane of the magical highway. A dark and gleaming space that was only available to people moving at or beyond light speed.

Verza, having watched her baby boy for quite a while, frowned upon not being able to break through his Shroud and underlying filter that hid her son's profile with consistency. She motioned toward Ors with a hand and suddenly gripped a thick binder that flashed into her grasp. Upon receiving her question in a private sphere of communication, Orsche sat forward and received the binder that Teeya gave them to look over.

"Ark." Orsche thumbed through the pages in less than a minute.

"Yes," the boy turned.

"Read this." Orsche separated more than half of the pages within the binder and then passed the rest.

"Now?"

"Yes, you need to be informed just as much as we do." Verza cut in and nodded.

"Your mother is right. That is what you need to get done today. We need you to remember everything before we come back next week. You should be able to finish this by the time we get back to Rest. If not, you can finish it at home." Orsche watched his son drop the heavy collection of pages onto his own lap.

"We will give you the rest of the pages once you commit all of these to memory." Verza added.

"Question." Alize opened the half-full binder to the first page, then turned back toward the window so his parents wouldn't see his face.

"Shoot. Go ahead." Orsche and Verza tensed up for some inexplicable reason and spoke at the same time.

"Are you two worried at all?"

"About?"

Verza was the first to question her son's suddenly severe tone. Orsche's already crestfallen expression further slumped as though his skin were made of slick mud.

"Well, Mom, if the quack is backed by some third party, known or not. I have been thinking that it doesn't really matter who it is or even if we can deal with the immediate issue of the quack's illegal operation. The clues all point to some internal strife and some external pressure to produce results, as all research eventually does. I have seen it happen to scholars all the time in my studies, financial issues or intellectual differences. Those two things are always what events like this major one boil down to. That is to say, are you two not worried about getting involved with this event cluster? If the backer is the scholars, Dad, are you not afraid that you will be implicated or that some of your enemies and rivals might dig into whatever we might do in the future? It's possible that you might be terminated. Not to mention, I am not affiliated with the guild at all, yet you taught me how to create the memory palace of an Imperial scholar." Alizeh side-eyed his father.

"And mom. Any investigation, even just a cursory one, would be damning for you. Any one of the bastards in the capital would instantly jump at the opportunity to tie you up with whatever is going on in the quack's facility. I would not even be surprised if they spun a story saying that you were trying to create an army and revolt. Which brings me to my next point: is the facility a place for research, some unofficial military project, or is it something else? None of us brought it up, but how in the world has this guy, if he does have the mad king's profile, managed to remain hidden for so long? It makes no sense, especially since there is an Archon who has dedicated her life to keeping track of every single Nayame that is born. This whole operation would have been shut down a long time ago." Alize didn't turn to his parents and flipped the page. Despite speaking his mind, the boy earnestly read the documents in front of him.

"Those are." Orsche attempted to keep his talk with Verza secret, but his thoughts were a mess at the moment, so she took the lead.

"Good questions, but nothing that we should focus on. We don't have enough information, and what we do have is more along the lines of observations, assumptions, and general statements given by an Affix that we still do not know how to personally translate. We need facts and time to study the situation, and even then, we need to be careful since anything could come back to bite us in the ass. As for getting potentially caught by scholars or the law, leave that to me and your dad." Verza stood up and tousled her son's hair with a harrumph. Out of the corner of her eye, faintly, she noticed a single sparkling tear fall on a page that Alize was in the middle of flipping.

"Now, study that book well so you and your dad can come up with something to help us navigate this whole problematic series of events." Verza sat back down with a crumpled face despite her cheerful but strict tone.

"I will try, Mom." Alize kept his real thoughts to himself and wiped the tears that would have fallen if he had allowed them to.

"The quack isn't the real issue, the end of this cluster of event's is and it's not something that I want to experience," Alize retreated inwardly for a moment and stood in front of a board that took over exactly 3% of his conscious thought. A dozen or so entries from his journals were pinned up with numbers that designated their position in the timeline that his Affix created. Major bullet points that he left out of what he showed his parents pooled on this board, along with roughly drawn images and childish scribbles that hinted at his incredibly young age when these dreams and nightmares occurred.

- Dad has to give his work to the quack as payment for blackmail. I am also kept as "patient" at Umbrie Hill and am kept under "observation". I am also "treated" by the Eternal Spring's magic and medicine.

- Guardians get involved and chase Mom until she is exhausted and caught by a passing Archon sent to investigate the trouble.

- Said Archon gets involved in the quack's affairs and self-destructs, wiping Jordaine off the map.

- Scholars' guild imprisons and terminates dad.

- I am put into the guardianship program and sent to the capital of Haven where I meet Wyn under terrible circumstances, getting her and a new group of friends murdered by jackals that want to erase any trace of mom or her existence, off of the map.

Right next to this board was another section of information that only constituted 1% of his conscious thought. Most of that area was shrouded in fog, but the very first thing, almost as if it were a negative thought that constantly pressed his psyche, was a pair of mist-covered sculptures that resembled his parents. His father stood up with his back straight and a defiant expression even as the back of his skull exploded open in a spray of brain matter and magic. The same sculpture, as though it showed progression in a single slab of carved stone, showed a heavily bandaged Orsche with rotten teeth, bloodshot eyes and a hunched back that hinted at some sort of complete lobotomy of his intelligence and personality. Verza's sculpture was worse, as she stood there in chains and a full body restraint. The only difference was her head was missing, and she adopted an unbreakable sneer at her own feet. Jarold even had a sculpture, but it was more a footnote as he was there, a chaotic and formidable tornado of death and storms, and then he was a pile of interlocking rings and needle-thin sticks the next.

Alize pushed all of this into the fog and spared no effort to put his attention on a personal project that said, "Manipulating an Affix that has already decided my future problems and happiness."

Despite having different things on their minds, the family of four found a sense of unification in the silence that overtook the interior of the carriage. They settled their matters and were on their way back to Heydens Rest, preparing to confirm yet another rolling effect from an event that Alize's curse set in motion. Nearly 30 minutes after Orsche set the one to two-hour limit on Alize's doppelgänger, they arrive in a flurry of motion. They each bid farewell to their driver and coachman, the horse and the guard, and passed through the doors of the Veilseam where they were dropped off.

The silence lasted for what felt like hours as Orsche and Verza took turns pushing Alize through the densely packed streets of the commercial district in Rest. Despite the distortion of time, within minutes they stopped and entered one of the city's many public transport trolleys. One minute after the next, the single-decker bus took off and stopped at one pickup location after the next. The turnover rate for public transport was simply astonishing with seconds passing between each stop so knowing that there were only 15 stops between the Veilseam and the location that they wanted to go, the family waited for five more or fewer minutes before they departed the trolly.

"Prociente Village #37- Gate 18" flashed in bright white lettering above a colossal picket fence. Dozens of doorways of different sizes dealt with even more individuals that entered and exited the gate. Everyone, regardless of whether they walked, ran, floated by, drove, or rode, stopped to show sigils or mystical manifestations of their profiles and Imperial ID cards. These were projections similar to what the quack used in the Veilseam to prove his identity, but they were all entirely unique and personal to the person sharing the information.

Alize, Orsche, Verza, and the invisible Jarold waited across the street from this massive flow of bodies in the same silence that they cultivated for themselves through illusions, an Apeirogon, and controlled spell usage.

"I guess I should get this off my chest. Ahem. I am, most likely, going to have a very difficult time acting as though everything is normal if anything bad has happened." Alize gripped his hover chair and focused entirely on a single gate that showed signs of almost no traffic at all. Instead, a black and yellow ribbon of energy floated above this entryway and all along the road for as far as the eye could see before it turned.

After more than a cursory observation, Alize noticed a gaudily dressed and bald individual with sea foam cream colored skin that popped out of a nearby tree. His dijon yellow and perfectly trimmed facial hair danced with agitation as he swapped the ribbon with his own leafy and vine-wrapped barriers to direct traffic away from the door. Massive walls of bark filled in the empty space between the green cords of flora. Not even a few seconds later, a floating and ugly truck with sharp angles and thick plating that resembled a golf ball with incredible divots and dimples, pulled around a distant street corner with blaring sirens. Just as fast as it had shown up, the vehicle drifted through the gate and tore off down the road in the blink of an eye.

"This seems sensational. I wonder if this has anything to do with our appearance." Orsche side-eyed Alize.

"If you mean to ask if this is an event designed to pique my interest, I am going to have to say that I am successfully concerned and captivated." Alize stepped back from his initial guesses before any of his assumptions could get away from him.

"This is not in your journals, right?"

Orsche cleared his throat.

"No." Alize's jaw set as the semi-armored man showed up once more and cordoned off the gate entirely. Several vehicles showed up this time, but only their sirens wailed along as echoes of one another in a long blur of motion in and out of the Village.

"And this is not one of those details that you don't want to talk about?"

Verza's breath shuddered as her cute and illusory outfit fluttered in the wind.

"No, Mom. I don't even know what this is about." A single hand went up to where his Affix would have been. As he focused, he felt it. The small twinge, that slight burn, the minute curling of a mystical force beyond and also intrinsically woven into his existence. It was faint, but his Affix was working. It was stretching beyond his immediate surroundings back at home and spread itself into everything even tangentially related to him. It was like a fisherman who cast a net on a school of fish.

"It's a coincidence. The custodians are showing up, most likely, because of some weekend altercation," Orsche whispered but did not believe himself since he knew that fate and happenstance were the exact factors that the event generator manipulated.

"Let's get on our way." Verza pushed Alize toward one of the gates and showed a sigil that didn't look like anything too out of the ordinary. The gate guard did not speak due to the constant flow of people and simply nodded as she let them through a glowing barrier of magic.

"What if..." Alize exhaled heavily after they passed the gate and separated from a massive cluster of people that waited either to leave or to get in.

"What if nothing. Don't act based on assumptions and a minuscule amount of information. In certain settings and against specific people, doing so is tantamount to death." Ors rolled up his sleeve and revealed a tattoo on his forearm. The same arm that he constantly looked at for the time or for storing his personal items. The newfound ink resembled a massive watch face with hundreds of smaller timepieces that branched out from the central second, minute, and hour hands, almost as if they were grapes on a vine.

"Your mother and I made the mistake of assuming the worst on multiple occasions, but on this particular one, I was alone and faced off against a Spirit that could create entire parallel timelines with a single thought or gesture, not its own mind you. Every assumption that I made about its magic and spells, every breath that I took to figure it out, and every action that I made turned a simple rescue mission into millions of years of issues all in the blink of an eye because I didn't take all the limited information that I had, at face value. That said, I pushed through since the mission was built around the love of my life. And look at that..." Orsche turned the tattoo invisible once more and smiled upon seeing a wall of vines and leaves leading in the opposite direction that they were heading to.

"*Look at that.*" Alize sighed and released the tension in his body.

"That's good, right? The custodians are headed off in another direction. The school. Your friend is fine." Orsche clasped Alize on the shoulder and let a smile creep onto his face, but he did not allow the good news to cloud his judgement.

"*The cleaners have come and gone, but it still feels too coincidental, right?*"

Alize read into his father's narrowed eyes and once again felt his jaw tighten. Verza, seeing her boys jump through mental hoops, stepped forward and pushed Alize away from his father and toward their goal.

"So Ors. Even back then I was the love of your life, huh?"

"Haa, no. You made it clear that nothing would ever happen between us, so at the time, I was completely focused on my research.

Finding you and breaking that Spirit's spell just happened to overlap nicely." Orsche turned his minute smile into a playful grin.

"Now, however, I can confidently say that you are my singular passion and drive to live, at least until my job takes an interesting turn." Ors spun on his heel as if he had not just said something dangerous and bowed his head with a charming, no, a downright seductive grin. He even tilted his head innocently as he used magic to comb through his hair and instantly style it.

Verza blushed and narrowed her eyes but chose not to pursue his playful slipup as she pushed Alize forward.

"*Mydit lyfa.*" Orsche waited until Verza passed right by him to whisper the words, "My Fated One". Verzas' ears, for seemingly no reason to Alize, suddenly reddened as she pushed Orsche away from herself. Despite the blush, Vers remained focused and surefooted. Alize turned to his pops and narrowed his eyes as the guy looked like he got away with murder.

"*Dad, you are too slick,*" Alize thought for a moment before he spoke.

"I guess it's too much of me to expect a place in Dad's empty heart, huh, Mom?"

Alize wiped away a single nonexistent tear.

"Ouf. I backed myself into a corner there, didn't I? You are my boy, Ark. My one and only, of course I choose to love you every day. From now until my dying breath." Ors followed behind the rest of the family as they rounded one corner after the next under Verza's insanely quick pace.

"That's quite the response there, pops, eloquent and heartfelt." Alize shook his head.

"Yes, it is. Distracting and mind-numbing, right?"

"No. I am still thinking about Fell and why her parents haven't responded to Mom. There might be something unexpected that occurred away from her home considering the contract that I saw. Something that might have come to a head at the Schools or at her Facility." Despite finding the break somewhat lovely, Alize couldn't help sharing a major concern with his parents.

"So, do you want to find your friend at home or follow your suspicions?"

Verza stopped walking and posed a question that Orsche and Alize would have danced around as they tried to justify or denounce acting upon limited information. The conversation was already headed in that direction, and Verza wanted to avoid having them echoing each other.

"The school is where Fell would have gone if something bad happened while she was at home, but if something bad happened while she was at home, then the custodians would have been dispatched there. There is a possibility that something happened, but it was not a big enough issue to call in anyone else." Alize did loops in his mind. Rather than get fed more issues and more elaborate possibilities from his father, he kept things simple and quickly came to a conclusion.

"We should...".

3.0 An Event's Background Mystery

Alize, Orsche, Verza, and Jarrold passed by yet another familiar road packed to the brim with hundreds of the same copy pasted three story homes. The only difference between each estate was the type of fencing, garage, and gardens or lawn that accented the homes. Mixed in with simple picket fences and metal gates were dense walls of fruit-bearing trees, berry bushes, simple flowering brambles, open spaces, and entire miniature habitats or enclosures that resembled exhibits in a zoo or tanks or ponds in an aquarium. The garages were the same from one house to the next as well, but personal preference would have a slight differentiation. From one house to the next, there was a two-car building extension, a separated barn for steeds, or a simple runway, or giant pillars that allowed one to roost or glide in and away from. In addition to the insane copy-pasted homes, there were nearly empty plots of land that resembled miniature forests or isolated ecosystems, which is not to say that no one lived there. The homes were simply either on a much smaller scale or were subterranean variants of the same cookie-cutter placements. Some of the plots were even completely empty and left to grow wild or were tended to by the community by legitimate gardeners paid for by the taxes of the local homeowners.

"Machinalia, huh? A low grade or lesser spirit of Illusions, not space-time. Divine ranked but only in That's kind of interesting. Illusions that shape reality based on what other people think it is doing. What a wild time it must have been to figure that out without having the experience that a sim can provide." Alize filed away some new information about his parents and prepared his questions when he noticed that they were stopped.

"What happened?"

Almost instantly, Alize examined the floating signs that graced each street corner and noticed that they were around 50 blocks away from his friend's home. In other words, their destination was another couple of seconds of walking at his mother's slower pace. The only issue with his observation was the stone cold expressions that both of his parents adopted.

Ors waved his hands to strengthen the invisibility and silencing bubble that Jarold had created around their family as they crossed the streets. Alize did not ask any questions and simply watched his parents practically slink through foot traffic like snakes in the weeds. Ors and Verzas' faces twisted unnaturally as they closed in on their target location, like something sour suddenly landed on their tongues.

"Something happened. Something bad. Wynn is either dead or missing. I'm not too worried if she is missing since my Affix already made an event where I see her again in the future, but they don't look too enthused, so is she dead? Because of my Affix? Is it because of the Fae that forced a contract? But that was also because of my event, was it not?"

Alize felt blood rush to his head and quickly gripped his armrest to stabilize his body.

"We don't have to." Verza leaned over and held her boy's hand.

"I'm okay. Let's go."

Alize swallowed the bile that pushed toward his throat and closed his eyes. Verza exchanged a glance with Orsche and rounded the corner off of Flush Boulevard onto 45th Street. Alize counted the seconds it would take to reach Wynn's home. The first house on the right of 45th had the number 002. The first on the left had 001. He counted the even number of homes in order and finally heard the noise that his parents clocked onto from an insane distance. Voices, movement, yelling, and finally, the smell of food. Alize opened his eyes only when the noise became so loud that he could no longer choose to ignore the chatter. A parade of people choked the streets like a clogged artery. Banners full of congratulatory speeches, tied-down balloons, streamers, and unlit lanterns decorated the street from the house at 650 all the way down to where they had to go.

Massive groups of people stood around massive grilling pits, but the atmosphere was anything but in the spirit of the decorations. Ors and Verza didn't have to do anything as they flitted from one empty area in the crown to the next. After a handful of moments, they stood in front of 709, where the crowd became so thick that any movement at all meant wearing the other person's clothes. Most importantly, a silence unlike any other cut off all sound in the area to the point where one couldn't even hear their own thoughts.

"It's quiet," Orsche stated the obvious, but it meant more to Verza than it did to Alize since he did not have a great view of the entire street. Between the homes 710 and 719, there was a well-made stage full of musicians and dancers who held their instruments, steps, and lips. Between the homes 723 and 725, there was a massive array of inflatable castles and arenas that glittered with so much magic that they appeared to be made of light. Protection, reinforcement, and restoration spells up the ass were placed on nearly everything that could hurt the kids while they were playing, even each other the moment that they stepped into the play area. Dozens of screens floated in the air above these World-type arcanums and showed entire simulated spaces or Terrariums that the children of the block were allowed to play in. The moment that the children were done with their round of gameplay, their parents or parental figures standing by pulled them away and back into their own homes, all without a single sound.

Orsche and Verza once again glanced at their boy and had Jarrold clear a path with imperceptible pushes. House 732 eventually ended up on one side of the family unit while a dense and impassable crowd congealed around them. Despite being incapable of closing the final distance toward the front gate of 743, Orsche and Verza were able to focus the spells that expanded their senses and zeroed in on the cause of the stifling silence.

In front of the house that they were aiming to reach or the region that was a few meters away from it, a man in a suit held up a glowing gauntlet. Each finger pulsed with a vibration and glowing sigil that seemed to only be minutely altered from one to the next. One at a time, the man lowered his pinky, thumb, and every other finger until only his pointer finger rose to the sky. An unclear symbol briefly reflected on his suit's breast pocket as a bullhorn suddenly materialized in his ungloved hand. The man shook his head at the two other people by his side. They were dressed in similar threads with the only difference being the lack of an overcoat and the addition of multiple layers of streamlined armor that gave the two extra people a bulk that the bull-horn-holding man did not have in his dapper five-piece suit. With a tap of his toe on the floor, the slick-haired guy with the bullhorn vaulted to the top of one of five massive trucks that parked in front of house 743.

"I have read your rights as written in Jordaine's law as an independent territory within Haven. As per Imperial decree, I must ask that you all maintain this calm atmosphere and act as both witnesses and exhibits in the event that our Aides and custodians are successful in finding evidence that leads to uncovering the truth of what occurred in this home. If any of you disrupt the peace again before our investigation is over, you have, by remaining present, agreed to being detained and tried under Undine Rechen. I will now allow everyone here to speak." The suited man turned off the bullhorn and lowered his gauntlet with a breezy smile. Before he released the spell, however, he lifted the magical device once more.

"In an unofficial capacity, I would like all of you to go home and clear the streets. I know that you are all worried about Del, Fred, and the little miss Wynnifell, but I can assure you that everything is going as smoothly as possible due to the team's professionalism and experience. Officially, if any of you have any complaints or questions, you can bring them by the station after our resident cleaners have concluded their work. Give the front desk the time, date, and address after we clear out. Ask for today's public documents, you should see File 1945, Title, A09 section 3." And with that, the man wiggled his finger and allowed the crowd to speak amongst themselves as he dropped to the ground and talked to the uniformed officers about something that Alize could not hear.

"Undine Rechen and a 1945. A09 section three? This guy must not be from the local station. That or he must be straight out of the Sims. Yeesh. Undine Rechen though? It's an almost-ancient term for the Guardianship Outreach or National Adoption program. At worst, this spiffy-looking *dude is some high brow that couldn't make it in the*

Scholars' guild or was recently placed back on the force after returning from a Blip. Then there is what he said to look for. The code 1945 doesn't exist. 019400 and 0194-50 do. These are homicide codes for a murder under mystical means and one that shows Aberrant or old magic at the scene." Alize paused for a moment and fixed his vision on the man's flattering suit.

"*All said, an Intendant is on the scene huh.*" Alize stared at his parents for a hot second and just as he was about to ask them some questions, a pair of strangers stopped trying to squeeze through the crowd right outside of the barrier and illusion that

Jarold and Orsche set up.

"I told you that the Aides would show up."

"I heard you, man. You don't have to yell in my ear."

"Sorry. It's the first time that I've been in one of these lockdowns." Alize shook his head and turned back to his parents when yet another rumor broke through the churning rambles.

"I heard that some Ashen, ahem, some Hautzee girl, lost control of her magic and pulled her entire family into a Blip," a voice broke through the chatter.

"I actually heard that they managed to come back. Herod has a friend who works on the force, and she said that the little Tem girl brought something back from the blip. One thing."

"Wow. So, that means the kid earned her first star at home. Oh, my Lady above. That is horrible. No wonder the officers showed up." Someone else chimed in, but the sideshow news ended as the group retreated from the impassable wall of bodies that blocked entry to house 743.

"One decade, Yala. It has been a decade since a kid in the 37th earned a star this young. The effuse coming from that home. Ha, we lost another talented youth." Another cut through the noise and pierced Alize's ears.

"I know. Rezzora called it last year in the bones, Malcolm. In the bones. My damned old shrew broke down in the middle of bingo, Malcolm. To all rights, she went on about it. That this girl would put all of them arrogant sprouts at the school in their place, but yeesh. Ain't this a shyte show. The girl up and died." Alize noticed an older woman with long strawberry-platinum hair and crystals that decorated her rounded human ears like earrings. Other than her vibrant pink eyes and vanilla cake colored skin, and the crystals, the old lady completely resembled a human.

"My condolences, Yala. On the bingo." The old man who spoke first, most definitely stood out in the crowd as he was a two meter tall giant while sitting down on a fold-out chair. Other than his insane height, he looked completely human aside from his green hair and long mossy beard. The two old people shook their heads and packed up their different-sized coolers.

"Malcolm, she got us kicked out right as I was about to yell to her Highness and the Immortal lady. Bingo, Malcolm. On Jackpot week. My old lady lost us a free cruise of the Southern Isles with her damned harpy shrieking." The old lady knocked back her drink, crushed the can, and then disintegrated it into a slag that instantly fertilized the ground with sparkles of magic. Flowers and mushrooms instantly bloomed on the spot as the lady cracked open a cold one and left the scene in the hands of her behemoth-sized friend.

"That would explain what I saw the other day."

"What, Rezz?"

"Thalmus came into the shop with his son-in-law and grandson the other day. They bought a whole bunch of Arcanum and sunscreen that I've had on clearance due to the changing seasons." The behemoth of an old man shuffled with a hunch that drew Alize's attention but not his ear as another stranger's talk piqued his interest.

"I heard that some kids in the 37th were practicing magic not taught in the facility or the schools..." Someone threw that rumor up in the air but Alize didn't have enough time to listen in on the rest of the statement when something stood out amongst the other noise.

"I heard Fred and Del weren't on the stage to give an announcement because Wynn ran away." Someone genuinely attempted to whisper considering the tone, but Jarrold focused on digesting the severity of that statement. The entire illusory bubble shifted toward a middle-aged and buxom woman with dark green skin and curly almond hair who was addressed by a slightly younger woman with a button nose, whiskers, and dalmatian spot fur so densely packed and fine that it resembled skin.

"That's not what I heard. My man works nights at the 2nd Gate as a Guide, and he said that a silent alarm went off right as he was coming off shift. Apparently, as he was passing by the school ward and the first gate this morning, he saw them running. Look at this pic. He hasn't responded since then." The dark-skinned woman turned to the dalmatian-spotted woman with long, hanging and black-furred ears that lopped on either side of her head. With a single tap onto a golden necklace with a spiked dog collar on the end, the bracelet turned into a rectangular outline and sparked with light and fire on the interior of its borders.

"I told you that good for nothing was cheating. I know my brother, and he was a dog before he met you, lovey. I'm not even joking. When I told him about you, he loved walking around looking like some perverse werewolf, hounding every girl and the occasional guy." The Dalmatian woman scoffed and, when she saw that her friend did not react, she called out all of the flaws that her own brother possessed.

Alize, prepared to ask Jarold to stop focusing on the conversation or turn the barrier back into a cacophony of sound so he could pick and choose his rumor intake, paused the instant a text message alert chimed and reverberated throughout the bubble.

"Look at this. A group of people broke through the Barrier. He had to clock back in at the first gate and help out at the school. He's been there all night, see." Alize couldn't see whatever the buxom woman shared, but the relief and worry on her face only increased as her fingers flew into a storm of movement.

"A few of his bosses are there, so he can't really text, but... Haa. That idiot is always sending things when he's not supposed to. How much do you want to bet that he is sending a selfie?" The dark-skinned woman's breath caught for a moment after the notification chime rang out a second time. She dropped her phone and stomped on her heels. Now armed with spears for horns, the woman crackled with pure lean and violent muscle and pounced over the houses in a glittering trail.

Alize caught a minor glimpse of the image on the phone. A dog-headed man with white fur, black spots over his eyes and chest, and one green dot over his exposed chest that was obviously dyed, sat on a gurney with a dopey grin and a thumbs up. Most importantly, the image froze in his fearless pull against a group of people trying to take the phone away. He was missing an arm and both of his legs in the image, and none of the people could stop him. The Dalmatian or Dysthosian woman picked up the phone and placed a hand over her mouth as she excused herself through the crowd.

"*That's not right.*" He flipped through his memory and nearly lost it.

"*Does this have something to do with the school drama that Wynn told me about? Considering the rumors, the group must have done something dumb or hasty for it to be mentioned in the same rumor chain as what happened in her house.*" Alize ran through a list of his recent encounters and connected less than a handful of dots to the possibility of an illusory third party. Orsche and Verza, however, came up with a list that they did not share with their son.

"*Tch, fucking curse. You just had to set all of this up on her first decennary party. It's horrible what is happening to her, and it's only made worse by the fact that I don't know what's happening and only have rumors. What's the aim here? The pattern?*"

Alize closed his eyes again and imagined all of the members of Wynn's family that he had met over the two years of being her friend. In his mind, all of their bright and vibrant eyes hollowed out as he imagined their now dead and rotting faces.

"*Uncles Fred and Del were with her according to the rumors.*" Two of the bodies, in his imaginary reconstruction of events, stood up and followed after his friends leaving back.

"*By some accounts, she ranked up or got her first Star, which caused an unfortunate blip. In other words, she imploded and dragged everything with her.*" Alize drew a single root event. His mother dropped her off.

"*Franko, Jellial, Ubon, or any of her other loudmouth cousins are nowhere to be seen, which rules out a group gathering and the rivalries that I have been helping to settle. At least, at first glance—*" Almost instantly, Alize pruned any possible rumors that he may have heard that concerned Fell's friend group in the 37th ward of Prochiente Village.

"*Aunties Moua, Kefla, and Chelse would have flipped the street if they were alive and their only niece was nowhere to be seen, so I can only assume that they went down fighting or are being detained for some reason or another. That said, the significant lack of destruction in the area means that a Terrarium went up before any conflict occurred. This rules out a Blip. A magical implosion and collapse of reality would completely destroy the area even if it were contained. The officers would have also shut the entire street down."* Alize chalked up his mental board by cutting away some other rumors and snippets of information.

"Grampas Ulysses and Julio, and grandma Pinnonet haven't said anything to their friends since they were obviously part of the rumor mill. They also haven't caused a commotion yet, so it's safe to assume that they also got involved with whatever happened to Fell that made her leave. Something like that, something that would force them to create a Terrarium would have been such a threat that even those old monsters would have to be worried. Hmm, something worse than the Aberrant Spirit that attacked me. By how much, *though? The only thing that I can think of is another party completely unrelated to Wynn, the Fae, or the aberrant spirit. That then begs the* question." Alize stroked his chin.

"What else or who would cause or involve a third party to target Fell?"

A few dozen possibilities fell to the wayside as less likely than others as names, attached faces, titles, and vague descriptions filtered into his mind as he tried to find connections. His entire brain, all of his concentration, flipped into a dark, almost conspiratorial room with misty windows shuttered behind steel bars. His mind shut everything else out as he focused completely on rooting out some semblance of the truth from the snippets of info that he received. He even pulled his Affix into the mix since the root cause of Wynn's current situation, by fate and unreason, was him. Two boards mirrored each other in the small and dark room that was only lit by a floating lightbulb.

"The only thing that is different about her is the Fae that forced a contract? If that is what has caused her to get targeted, then by what means is this third party using to track her down?"

Alize stepped back and found that despite having knowledge that he should not have, he could not figure anything out at all. In fact, the nameless and rumored third party had several dozen options out of the groups of people that Orsche had either told him about or they were vague ideas of groups that he remembered from some insane dream or talk that he had with friends. Regardless, staring at the unknown and infinite possibilities left an acidic taste in his mouth as he stumbled into the darkness and away from the dimly lit thoughts that he focused on.

"Is she safe right now? Are her dads still alive? The custodians that we saw coming in through gate 18. Why were they so late to whatever happened at the school? Anything that Wynn was seemingly involved with occurred sometime between last night and early this morning, maybe even this evening, so how did all of this go unnoticed until I showed up? My Affix is involved, especially now that it can use mystical nonsense and bullshit logic, but what is it responsible for and how is it going to continue messing with us?"

After a long moment, he let go of a breath that he didn't even realize he had held and opened his eyes. Verza bit her bottom lip and held his quivering hand as she looked at her son and then back at Orsche. He shook his head to answer some questions that she whispered.

"Mom. I'm okay. I'm just worried. I know that things are fine. That Wynn should be fine. I have faith that she is. Affixes, especially the Immortal series, are consistent in their ability to guarantee anything they produce, change, or remove so the only thing I can do is hope that my Journals really are tied to it." Alize covered the top half of his face and forced a smile.

"Besides, I am sure that you and Dad have already tried to investigate or are currently scouring the scene with your spells. I won't let myself spiral." Alize briefly remembered a foray into a simulation that induced madness through controlled chaos.

"Until we get confirmation of who and how many are dead, let's take any and all of these rumors and third-hand accounts with a grain of salt. While we wait, let's state facts." Alize exhaled and spoke even as his chest burned.

"I will go first." Verza's gleaming pupils dulled to black after a moment of speaking in the magical adult manner that she, Orsche, and Jarold possessed. Her eyes and sensory spell could not break through the barriers placed by the Intendant and his Aides, so she left the scouting to the guy who had the skills necessary for this specific task.

"I dropped her off at home before I left for Orrin's Shadow last night, like I said before. I didn't want to leave that poor girl in such a state but I had no choice since you were on a timer and we hadn't gone out for groceries in a long time so." Verza immediately recounted her experience with as much detail as she could muster.

"Right, there was also something off about that little cutie." Verza paused as she seemingly confirmed something with Orsche.

"The aberrant spirit that attacked you used a lot of magic on the spire that we used as a camping base the other night. I may not have seen it, and Jarold didn't catch it, but the effuse that came off of it is not something that either of us would miss if we got near it. That said, Jarold said that the same stench of that spirit lingered on that sunspot like a dark cloud. I didn't notice that since he said it had something to do with the soul, astral stuff, and the fact that he is a Fae but before he even said anything about that girl, the whole scenario didn't sit right with me." Verza crossed her arms and pursed her lips.

"I thought it was weird that your Affix made something happen to her." Verza placed a hand on her hip, frowned, and shifted her weight as she trailed off.

"Ah, they are leaving me out again. How am I supposed to get their points of view when they shut the conversation off like this? The only thing that I can tell is that they have definitely seen, heard about, or dealt with something similar to what Wynn is going through. The issue is figuring

out what about this whole mess is the same and what is different from the Sims they set up for me. They are obviously expecting me to follow along." Alize sighed as he noticed the expressions of his parents and Jarold changing every other second.

With nothing to do, he observed the two officers beside the bespoke suited gentleman that he believed was an Intendant, a title and role that functioned as a field and combat lawyer. Both of these statue-esque soldiers, who wore eye-catching white and gold body-fitting leathers, however, were Aides or low-ranking custodians. It was difficult to tell because their left shoulders sported a striking blue-steel pauldon with the silhouette of a man holding up a tower with an umbrella-like spread of wires coiling around his person. A shield broadened the silhouette's back while a tool belt with a hammer, chisel, and other handheld tools wrapped around his waist.

Both of the well-armored Aides wore blue steel bracers with the image of an engraved dagger reflected on the wrist. The cuff that wrapped around the bracers on their right arms glittered with magic-infused embroidery that depicted a shield, sword, bow, and spear in an overlapping mosaic. A massive blue steel utility belt with half a dozen pouches and vials held a few additional loops that served as belt holsters for a few different weapons. An iridescent short sword, a dagger, a canister full of some liquid, and a pistol remained fixed to their sides as though they were both walking fortresses. One of the two Aides moved into house 743 while Alize examined the equipment through throngs of bodies looking to confirm old or create new rumors.

Moments later, 18 or so men and women in similar uniforms but without the pauldrons walked out of the household while following the Aide that recently entered the home and an angular-faced woman with sharp eyes and raven feathers for hair. The lady, under the eyes of the crowd, rolled her shoulder blades with a glare directed at the front row of wide-eyed spectators. Wings like a dragonfly but opaque with black, purple, blue, and green, fluttered out from behind her as she leaped toward the Intendant.

"Wow. That's Madam R. I didn't know that a surveyor would show up," someone's voice sounded out.

"Isn't she from the second school district? What's a bigshot like her doing all the way in the 37th?"

Alize narrowed his eyes and felt himself slipping back into a dark mindset upon hearing that a person who was essentially a local legend of a detective just dropped by his friend's house. The crowd, in any case, did not relax or relent in their rumor crafting.

"I heard that this is a cover-up," one voice reached Alize.

"I heard that those bastards from the capital are spreading out over here," another voice poked up.

"What bastards?"

"Ah, my man, have you been living under a rock?"

"Yeah, bro? Did you forget that I just woke up a few months ago after sleeping for more than a century?" An argument between friends faded into the noise.

"Another Blip case, huh? I can't believe this, can you?"

"No, actually. Fred had been near the fourth rank for a while, so I just can't believe that he dropped the ball and let anything bad happen. I mean, he is from the Ultegra household, right? Ulysses was an old friend of mine back when we were both in the army. I can tell you now that old monster would never let any child of his leave the house without knowing how to defend his own home, so this is, phew man, insane." Another rumor bled through the vibrant discourse for just a moment before something else immediately caused Alize to nearly jump out of his seat.

"I feel bad for their daughter. That little thing ran away last night because her friend died." Alize's ears buzzed as he matched a wide-eyed stare with both of his parents who heard the same thing.

"Really. Which one of those troublemakers was it?"

"Let me tell you..." The group vanished into the sea of bodies all around them.

"No. No dammit. Come on, Jarold." Alize turned his head and slightly moved his chair to try to tune back into the conversation that he was eavesdropping on.

"That's not right, bro. I heard from Chester, who heard from Ideline, who was with Anko when the news came out. I think it was at the last celebration around a week ago. They, uh, who was it?"

The speaker hummed in thought when another person took over.

"Stelle and Ichabod, the Voneur and Diran couple in 812," a deep voice chimed in.

"Yeah, them. Apparently their twins were hovering around some kid from outside the 37th on their own 1st Decennary. That boy is the one that all of those troublemakers are saying died." The people faded into the background, but a like-minded group of onlookers apparently held similar thoughts and outlooks as Alize shifted his focus.

"Those damn kids. So whatever is happening right now is because of one of their little insane games? That last time they did something like this, my house on Caldwell and Adams streets had to be completely renovated. Damn little monsters," an older voice cackled out with annoyance.

"I heard that the twins and some of the other delinquents raided the school because of Fred and Del's girl. I only heard about it because Petunia was on a call with some of her friends at the First's station," one of the parents chimed in.

"When are the faculty, staff and the custodians going to stop those little delinquents?"

"I know they have been causing trouble in the 37th for almost two years without any breaks. The Facilities either need to put them in school or the Guardians need to take them because I am getting fed up with these kids messing with people," someone grumbled.

"Calm down, Max. Does anyone actually know what's happening?"

"Well, I heard that Fred and Del left around midnight after one of those problem kids found their girl walking the halls of the secondary school's campus," someone brought up the main topic.

"Whoa. So, is the rumor true?"

Despite Alize's best attempt, he could not keep focused on just a single conversation in the veritable sea of rumors that grew rowdier and less logical with each passing second. Jarold made it as easy as possible to stay tuned in, but there was still a limit to what could be achieved with magic, especially when one wanted to remain undetected.

"I heard that the wild child who lives here killed her entire family with a forbidden spell and ran away."

"My mates are near the Secondary building in the first district right now. Apparently, some custodians were dispatched to clean up some crazy mess that is affecting the areas near the first, second, and third Gates."

"They are saying that one of the Gate Guards went berserk and slaughtered a bunch of the teachers from the schools."

"They are saying that those crazy kids from the Facilities are up to no good again."

"I heard that some kid got Blipped inside of that house and made her entire family vanish."

"I hope Fred and Del are alright. This afternoon, they ran out on the final adjustments of the planning committee, saying something about a family emergency."

"Miss Ryattidnae. It is a pleasure to see and work with you as always." The well-suited Intendant puffed his chest slightly and bowed his head as the raven-haired woman elegantly floated down in front of him.

"I don't want to hear it, Bullets. It's an absolute mess inside of there. The monsters that did that. We need to track them down quickly. I already have my team heading down some tracks left by the spirit that came in..." Ryattidnae, the feather-haired woman, didn't even meet the guy's gaze as she scanned the crowd with her head on a swivel.

"Great. You have always amazed me with your initiative, tch. These damned loudmouth fools sure are getting a show, huh?"

"It is necessary." Bullets narrowed his eyes on the woman who walked by him and squared his shoulders.

"I will never understand why you chose to become an Intendant when you can't stand listening or talking to other people." Ryattidnae side-eyed the Intendant with slicked-back hair and a smile that never reached his eyes.

"To break out of my shell and be a better person." Bullets lifted a bullhorn that manifested in his hand. A glowing dial set at the middle turned over toward the maximum setting. The mouth doubled in size and swelled with power. Like a gun, the man pulled the trigger and let loose a physically bludgeoning sound that buffeted the entire crowd.

"I will give you all a third and final warning. Please keep the overly speculative conversation to a minimum. Our officers have nearly secured the scene, so I hope that you will all be patient and wait until we can share what is going on." The Intendant lowered his bullhorn and waited for the crowd to once again get riled up, but the conversations seemingly stopped altogether as everyone waited for something to happen. A ring of magic flashed on Orsche's left eye not too long after.

"I'm in. I can see inside the building. Jarrold found a way in as well, but he can't get close. One of the Aides is a contractor like you, my love. Seems to be a blood spirit or something along the same lines considering how it is moving around through the scene. Overall, it is not pretty." Orsche tightened his jaw and cycled through different spells to see pieces of information that he wouldn't have been able to glean with simple X-ray vision, luminol solution, and dusting.

"Hurry up, Orsche. I think things are about to get..." Verza used her head to motion toward the Intendant and Surveyor that were in the middle of talking and scanning the crowd.

"Ahem. Eventful." She placed emphasis on her words simply because scanning the crowd herself revealed an irregular parting of bodies down the street.

"Ark, do you still feel the curse moving around?"

Verza grabbed Alize's chair and Orsche's sleeve as she guided them toward the edge of the street and onto a sidewalk.

"Yes. It's faint, but I can. What were you and Dad talking about? You went quiet after those randos brought up a third party of bastards from the Capital? Who did you two talk about?"

Alize followed his mom's piercing gaze toward the small parting of heads that cut the crowd in half.

"We were talking about some corrupt 'monsters' that are spending the rest of their lives in an imperial prison." Verza made air quotes around the word monsters and frowned.

"Don't worry about it. If we find anything that relates to those people, we will make a sim for you." Verza patted Alize on the shoulder and kissed the top of his head as she moved the family away from house 743. They stood in front of a walkway that cut between house 744 and

742, which was almost directly across the street from the Ultegra-Tem household.

The parted sea of bodies finally split against the glowing yellow barriers that said, "DO NOT CROSS. AIDE IS BEING ADMIN-ISTERED. DO NOT CROSS."

The first thing to cross the barrier was a rubber-tipped cane made of redwood. Pink veining along the body of the stick reflected the light and magic produced by the simple barrier and caused an almost explosive short circuiting as the yellow "tape" crackled like lightning and rolled into itself. The rods that produced the barriers sparkled and dropped to the ground from their hovering positions as the Quibe on the tip of the shafts dulled.

Sandals with socks, a wrinkled handful of liver spots, and an old man that sported a snow white tracksuit with a cherry red striped along the sides, walked out of the crowd and stood at the center of all five vehicles that the Intendant, two custodians, and the Aide officers showed up in. Despite his hunched back and chronic age, the man possessed a lusciously braided beard full of glittering beads that ended in a tight knot around a medallion that hovered exactly one millimeter off of the ground at all times. At an astonishing one meter in height, the wide-set old man slammed his cane into the floor. In the blink of an eye, the Intendant raised his gloved hand and forced a widespread silence and inability to move or think. Under Orsche's barrier, the effect did not reach Alize, and under Verza's intensely trained senses, she managed to break through whatever restriction that the Intendant placed and moved away.

"The old guy just said, 'Where is my granddaughter and the mon-sters who did that to my family, lawman?' I'm guessing that he can see inside of the house even with all of the barriers in place." Verza narrated as the old man forced his back to straighten.

"The sleazy-looking guy is going on about a main team of custodians. Blah blah, they have been working around the clock trying to clear up any confusion, okay, vandalism involving what they assume is a child-run crime syndicate." Verza let out a single chuckle as she stared at her son's baffled and upset expression.

"Is that old guy Ulysses Ultegra or Julio Tem?"

"Neither. I have not seen him before, but I've heard of his story from the kids in my club. He is Gramps. I am assuming he has that name since he is just an old Diran fella that looks out for the kids that come front the Facilities. I believe that he gave his last star some years ago and is just walking around to make things a bit neater. I haven't seen him before, but the others have. He usually shows up when Wynn starts some problem with the school kids and has to smooth things out. From what I have gathered." Alize committed the old man's appearance to memory and waited for his mom to share what she could hear.

"Oh ho. If that's the case. He is quite the observant old guy." Verza listened in and moved her family back a few more steps upon noticing that the conversation between the old man and the officers was not deescalating. The old man nodded slowly at first, but the more the Intendant spoke and requested that he return to the crowd in any number of ways, the faster his nodding became. Verza also noticed a faint disappointment that melted the corners of the older man's face. Ryattidnae, the Surveyor, and all of the officers on the scene stopped everything that they were doing and did not speak.

"This dude is an absolute idiot. He needs to stop talking before the old man blows a fuse." Verza hid her boys and waited for something insane or for the tension in the atmosphere to break. The old man in a tracksuit, standing at one and 1/3rd of a meter without his hunch, smashed and shattered his cane into the floor before Verza could share what she heard. The fine dust exploded out in a perfect circle as the spell expanded beyond the surrounding yellow barrier. In the blink of an eye, a dark pustule, bubble, or dome with a reflective and slightly red and magenta surface covered the entirety of 743 and the street in front of it. Anyone looking at the bubble would instead see past it. Anyone walking through it would instead be transported to the other side. Anyone looking to escape the interior of the dome would be incapable of doing so. That said, absolutely no one attempted to do any of those things as the crowd immediately dispersed in a panic.

"I think that old guy is the 37th's appointed sentinel. The Surveyor lady seemed to recognize him, but the Intendant did not. Either way, the terrarium is going to make looking into the house a little bit more difficult. Ors, how are you doing?"

Unlike the rest of the crowd, Verza could see into the magical barrier without much or practically any trouble and narrated the scene of the Intendant dropping to a knee and lowering his head like a knight before their king. She just couldn't hear or smell anything within anymore. As for Orsche, he shut his eyes a long time ago and clawed into his own forearm as though it were mud. The tattoo of clocks and static gears began to spin almost chaotically as tangible threads of magic from some spell began to tie his glowing eyes and hand to 743. The illusory barrier around their family also cracked and fragmented as Orsche's concentration was essentially hit with a sledgehammer.

"I'm good. Trying to keep us from getting noticed, but that new barrier is messing with my reach and vision in a way that makes maintaining invisibility pretty difficult." Orsche manually altered the gears on his wrist and muttered several things under his breath that separated the magical haze of his own magic from the environment. A corona effect surrounded the faint threads and illusion around the family and in a moment, snapped everything back into motion. Verza pulled her man and Alize further down the alley in hopes that no one saw their departure or Orsche's mystic gymnastics.

"Are you sure everything is okay?"

"I'm sure. I found out what happened inside of the house. Ark, I will have you try your hand at a similar investigation when we get the Apierigon's training room up and running for you again but right now..." Orsche spoke out loud but as if it were a natural process, he and Verza shared some even more important details through their own private channels.

"Your friend, Wynn. She is not there. It looks like she came home and packed her things. There are scuff marks and traces of her magic leading off in the direction of the secondary school, so the custodians that we saw were on their way to her like we all feared..." Ors frowned as he spoke.

"There are over 20 bodies in there. Without my tools and direct access, I couldn't tell you who each person is exactly, but there was a terrarium that went up, so it's more than likely that they are dummies from some sting. The issue with that is, there was a second terr that was used to contain the first, which is the first sign of someone trying to control the implosive range of a Blip. The effuse that I scanned also has identical traces to the scattered magic left behind by the spirit that attacked you..." Orsche turned to Alize and nodded without much of a change to his own frown. It was clear that Alize had already guessed almost everything.

"From what I know about the Guardianship Protocols and from what I could see, the Aides were not collecting evidence to find a culprit or chase down the spirit. The suspects were either captured or killed by the custodians, or the malefactors escaped through a desig- nated route so the officers could play fisherman. As for the spirit, I believe it showed up and was pushed into an artificial Blip." Orsche pursed his lips and was prepared to speak more but he also knew that Alize was well versed in Jordanian law as it was an essential course that he prepared for his son before they moved into the region.

"Dad. You don't have to spare my feelings. They were gathering Wynn's family assets and liquifying it, right? Once the last Aide leaves her home, it will immediately go up for sale. There is an Intendant on site, which already clued me in on one of the worst possibilities. He also called Section three earlier, so under Jordaine's law of Guardianship, the territory, state, or nation will serve as her legal guardian." Alize teared up but didn't allow himself to cry since he knew this was the setup for a future event. Orsche sucked his teeth and clawed into the palm of his hand while Verza chewed on the inside of her cheek. Silently, she gripped her son's chair with enough force to crack the handles.

"Okay. As long as you know what it is going to be like if you ever meet her again." Verza spoke through gritted teeth.

"Mom, I will see her. I know that she won't remember, but I do have an event. It will be a few years, but I'm pretty sure that things will be fine." Alize also clenched his fists. His vision split in half for a moment as he once again found himself in an imaginary and dark room.

"Compartmentalize, think calmly. EPA. Finding Wynn isn't impossible if I want to see her again before my Affix wants me to. The issue is that due to the rules of Guardianship, she will not remember me due to the Simulation training. And if she does, it will be as a vague whisper on the wind. How do I fix that? Do I want her to remember all of the family that she has lost if they really have died here? Did they even perish? If this is all some multilayered."

A third board filled up the dark space, but Alize only allowed the questions to build up. With a deep exhale, he left the room through a door rather than allowing himself to fade into the dark. With a creak and a massive click, he put all of his thoughts about Wynn behind him. For a moment before he let go of the doorknob, he turned back and found himself in the corner of the main lobby of his mind. Nearly a dozen other doors, unmarked, bland, and uniform, waited for him all along the upstairs section. Quite a few cracked open and leaked out an extraordinary mist.

"Ark?"

"Yeah?"

"Where did you just go?"

"Nowhere. I was just thinking about Wynn and my curse." Alize shook his head and waited for his dad to speak again.

"As I was saying, the artificial blip is still active and connected to whatever world the spirit was sent to, presumably. The officers have set up a trap for when it comes back so that is one less thing that we have to worry about coming back to bite us in the ass." Orsche nodded and was ready to list off a few other things but Alize held up a hand. Unlike his parents who were locked in two different conversations and were examining the crowd to ensure that they remained unnoticed, Alize caught a glimpse of a child that was staring at him from behind a gap in a picket fence.

"You two can figure out what you are going to tell me and what you are going to show me in the sim later. I am going to gather some information on my own if that's alright with you guys." Alize looked at his parents who regarded him with surprise.

"How?"

Verza asked first since Orsche went back to spying on the authorities.

"The friends that Wynn introduced me to. A few of the rumors have tied them to what is going on, so I am going to confirm it." Alize smiled softly and waited for his mother to let go of his chair.

"I should come with you. Where are we going?" Verza took a single step, but Alize put up a hand.

"Trust me, Mom. Please?"

After a few moments, Verza let go, maybe because she decided it was for the best or if it was because of something Orsche said to her but regardless, Alize hovered forward and locked onto the pair of eyes that darted past him on the other side of a nearby fence. A few seconds later, a small yelp and the sound of someone falling echoed out from behind the gate.

"Sorry," a whisper of a voice carried over along with the soft patter of bare feet on grass.

"Hold on, Ark, I'll get the gate," another whisper reached Alize's ear, almost as though the person's hot breath blasted right next to him. It sent a shiver all the way down his spine and turned the hairs on his neck into spikes.

3.1 In the Weeds

"*Ah. Whoever lives here really splurged on their home defense budget. A&E or Aodom & Escutcheon. The tag and symbol of the world's best and most unbreakable shield, the First Line in Home Defense.*" Unintentionally, Alize whistled to himself as a chart of brands and pricings came to mind. A&E topped the charts internationally, sitting firmly in first place for physical, tremor, blast, and trespassing protection.

"*Such an expensive and specific brand is only necessary for kids and criminals with impressive Aura-based profiles. Who do I know that fits either or both of those criteria?*"

He focused on a series of paper-thin but very distinct radiant symbols that clung to the sliding lock's crystalline engravings. The buzz of electricity inherently cycled away from the main crest and spindled out to create a thin casing around the entire densely packed picket fence. Silver fastenings tied each piece of the "wooden posts" to the next, each bearing the same magnetic field of interlocking and reinforcing defense. He examined the silver dimes that bore the A&E crest and slightly raised a brow as the enchantment and mystical magnets forced his hand away with a gentle push, glimmer, and a green warning light.

"Who do I know that lives across from Wynn and possesses an Aura that necessitates this kind of repulsive barrier from First Line Defenses? No one fits all the criteria, so why is the most antisocial member of the group here?"

Someone brought him out of such an unnecessary contemplation and said, "Don't touch the fence, Boss. Wait one moment, please."

"First decade nondescript childhood friend number twenty-three. *Carlos 'Eights' Ettoire."* A small gap between the planks revealed a small figure stumbling about in front of the side gate. A soft clinking and chatter followed a moment before an, "Aha, this should do it," carried in the wind. Exactly after a few seconds passed, the glowing A&E symbol on the sliding lock chimed and faded away in a flash. The gate opened not too long after, but Alize saw only a small gauntlet peeling the side open. A little bit of a pale or almost ghastly face poked around from behind the open gate while he hovered forward.

"Hey Eights. The club still has you acting as the lookout, huh?"

"Yes, Fell isn't here, just so you know." The boy with a voice as soft as down feathers, squeaked out a response. Alize spared a glance towards the button-nosed boy with sparkling powder blue hair and narrowed his eyes.

"I guess he was only interested in talking to her even after being invited into the group. Ha, the others need to stop letting this boy ostracize himself. He's a good kid." Alize brought his chair to a stop and turned it to Eights as he focused on the barbed wire and petal-like metallic charms that orbited the boy's Gauntlet like planets around a star.

"Hm, he has a lot more Arcanum than I remember. Those little bunch of thugs must have been busy." Alize briefly recalled that Eights only recently moved from a leather glove to a gauntlet, even though it was

now tricked out with quite a few elaborate arcane accessories. Whilst in the midst of examining each item, the blue-haired boy closed the gate and rearmed the lock.

"That's not good. He is going to trigger the 54th alarm spell if he tries to lock the door like that." The silver latch and coins flashed with a particularly violent fit of red warnings. Whips of crackling magic sparked out and began spreading throughout the entire fence like a tidal wave. Eights then used his other small hand in a panic, the very same leathery glove that Alize remembered appeared in addition to another hodgepodge of odd-looking accessories. The items almost exploded with similar, albeit less effective, spells compared to the gauntlet, but that consistent pattern of a small boost allowed Eights to generate a matching wave of magical tendrils. The twisting, almost clockwork glow of effusion coming from the boy, both matched and quelled each branching thread of red-tinted magic and the chaotic magnetic fields that were disturbed. With expert precision, the kid stemmed the leak and repulsive alarm and closed the gate before any of the dime-like fasteners could connect to one another in a meaningful manner.

"One, two, three, four, right, 16, 32, 64, oh dear lady, this kid has nearly 128 Arcanum just between his two hands. How much have these damned goblins stolen since I have been away? Tch. " Alize counted the items and forcefully held his own dropping jaw in place. In the main lobby of his imagination, a door manifested on the shrouded second floor right beside a barred entryway that held the nameplate of Wynnifell Ultegra-Tem. Alize did not allow himself to even regard the door even as he felt a dark train of thought take root inside, not yet at least.

Eights, at the moment that Alize shifted his own attention, closed the gate and secured the lock with a shaky breath. Several thousand strands of wispy magic coiled around his orbiting rings, bracelets, and charms in dozens of specific patterns that each tool was programmed or engraved to possess.

"I don't want to think about combating someone like Eights. I have not handled someone like him in the Sims yet, so I have to ask Mom and Dad to check if there is even a record of someone with a near-infinite Equip Capacity. If there is not, I can only stick to dummies that Dad can program. Hmm, if it's not possible, then there might be a theoretical package on his computer from another Scholar? For now, let me see if I can get a better read. Just in case." Alize bore holes into Eight's back before the kid turned and activated a spell that he had been silently working on. It breached all kinds of rules in casting magic specific to A, B, and C type profiles, but it adhered to the insane but balanced rules of the Direct type.

"I really hope that I guessed my profile correctly," Alize sighed internally and recited the language that worked as training wheels for casting mixed B and D type spells.

"Ballenguss, Pirly- freitzun, allgesoriyst auber funkitodenfur wiechemeine. Lo freitz allge endem mein percept bode: Zorie. Translation..." In accordance with the rules of casting a spell within the bounds of one's profile, Alize utilized the associated language, Ancient Resh, and capitalized on what his profile may be specialized in, Direct Utility.

"Mix type cast: Minor Analysis Release Location (General sensory systems within me). Target release location in every physical sense: Enhanced Senses. Hopefully, this works." Alize waited for half a second as he felt the effuse and his own magic intermingle in a manner that completely washed over his body. His illusory nerves, like a machine receiving power, clicked and synced in a manner that boasted apex efficiency, speed, and sustainability. Nothing was raised beyond their

limits, nothing was changed; rather, the manner in which his senses mingled and operated simply capped out and could remain as such until his magic turned off or until he adjusted the spell to burn his blood. A sacrifice that he willingly accepted since the spell burned through the excess spring water that he magically compacted within his body.

This one spell, in any and all variations, would usually be the limit of Pentacode casters if they chose to specialize in sensory spells. Alize, however, also chose to bank on an assumption and pushed a third spell into the overlapping effects across his body.

"Mix Type Cast: Minor Sensory Overhaul Release Location (General sensory systems excluding base senses). Target Release Location (Me): View," Alize didn't dare open his eyes or focus on any of his physical senses out of fear for what the spell might do to his ego and instead focused on creating a sensory extension of reality within his own mindscape. For a split second after the spell was cast, everything disappeared as the distinction between the world's magic and his own vanished. He could not feel the clothes on his skin or the chair under his watery butt, couldn't smell a festival's worth of food carried on the wind or taste the bitter and sweetness in regards to the fear of his curse and hope for Wynn's safety. Alize couldn't even hear any voices within the crowd or even the chime of the gate door being locked. His vision suffered the same obvious abandonment as everything darkened.

"Here we go." Alize sat himself down in the middle of his mental lobby and waited. The fog swallowed him in a split second and exploded with color after a momentary blackout. The world within three meters of his stationary imaginary body filled in his mind as though a sfumato filter had suddenly stylized and blotted everything. The constant movement and blur, wherever he focused, turned into an image so clear that it bordered on artificially sharpened. The world be-

yond this three-meter bubble of dizzying and blurred clarity featured an almost conflict-heavy sense of undetailed and blocky chromatic textures. Beyond the five-meter sweet spot, where everything was a massive adventure of abstract color and shape, the world of sfumato adopted shadows and distinction as though the artstyle of tenebrism bled into and onto everything beyond the five-meter chaos of perception. His senses fully transmitted through the moisture in the air and the water content within his own and Eights body.

"Three meters is my limit. Around five is where I can push it to if I really need to, but beyond that." Alize didn't feel phased at all by the spell and only took half a second to reorient his focus onto Eights. As if accustomed, he didn't even attempt to peer into the shadows and darkness beyond his perception since this was neither the time nor place to explore his Aberrant sensations.

"Alright then, quick time, let's see what I can see." In a moment, the filter melted away as the frozen image of Eights magnified. Each and every individual skin cell, speck of dirt, salt, grime, or microbe on, in between, or within the child's face immediately filled his perception as the kid's sweat served as a roadmap for his body. The information, however, directly entered his mind as understanding rather than interpretable information.

"Ha. This is even better than in the Sims, no wonder everyone likes playing with Direct-type spells." On a more pointed examination, Alize turned to Eight's gauntlet and gloved hands and broke through the Arcanum. He pierced straight through the covered skin. The cells did not possess a nucleus, or rather, something filled the nearly vacuous space between the cell's atomic structures and altered the way that the kid appeared under a magical magnification. Interlocking pockets of skin sported printed symbols smaller and more elusive than electrons. Under Alize's inherent curiosity, the meat and bone of Eight's

sloughed away and revealed a nebulous mesh of vibrating clusters of a near infinite number of items that were stacked into the rough shape of the blue-haired boy's body.

"That is too many items. The Arcanum ais blinding." Alize bit his tongue to stop himself from audibly gasping.

"When did Eights and the rest gather these?"

Even with a cursory glance, Alize noticed that the nebulous mass was actually micro-clustered around different regions of Eight's organs or along lengths of muscle fiber or segments of bone. There was a sort of arrangement and compartmentalization of color and dancing shape that made the entire network seem organized despite the chaos. Alize, intrigued, zoomed in on one of Eight's hands. The symbols expanded into a single bubble that held shovels, blankets, bottles, rope, and other mundane items like pencils, pens, erasers, and food. Some other items were more abstract or disconnected, like controls, buttons, levers, or some other intractable objects. In less than a pinto-second, Alize pushed his heightened senses beyond Eight's subcutaneous tissue. Most of the more separated pieces of minimized paraphernalia were now attached to larger items such as firing pistons, electrical components, tire or tread, Quibes, tanks of gas or some other chemical components, and practically any mechanical part that might act like an extension of some machine.

Within the blink of an eye, Alize pried through another layer of the kid's body and noticed gears, plates, and tubing that pumped all kinds of oils, liquids, and gases from one mystical pocket to the next. Then, he pushed his perception deeper and exposed Eight's nervous system. The silhouetted and shaded imagery consisted mostly of several dozen squares and rectangles which, upon inspection, represented motherboards, processors, entire server setups, and rows of data storage units.

"Insane. Eights is just as insane as the rest of those troublemakers." Alize sighed repeatedly as he attempted to decipher and connect the items that Eights separated into different parts of his physical inventory.

"With so many different types of Arcanum, he really could beat up everyone else in the group at the same time. Hopefully, he doesn't choose to rank up. It would be a hellish time for any world that he might end up in if he Blips." Alize gulped as he registered Eights not only as an individual but as a little monster and nightmare to behold. He wanted to search other parts of his body beyond the gauntlet and leather-gloved hands, but he could only sigh as his own sensory spell slowly fizzled out after reaching some preset limitation. In other words, the world-pausing effect of his spell faded as Eight's movements sped up.

"I can keep this spell active without using my own magic reserves and drawing out a noticeable amount of effuse for 1/100th. How unfortunate. It's good, but I shouldn't use it again until I rank myself up." Alize quickly opened his eyes with a grimace and green face before Eights fully turned toward him. If the [View] spell was still activated and he panned his vision outward to the space surrounding Eights rather than inward, he would have noticed that the boy used his own sweat as a conduit to bind all of the orbiting arcanum to specific locations along his hands and arms. Spots that happened to be the sweatiest parts of his body due to his stress and generalized anxiety.

"[View] aside, this kid has too many items in his body. From what I can see, he is running at least a few hundred at once at any given moment to power some passive effects. He must have a cheque that is just filled with banks *that he could use to power his arcanum and retain a few things that work as effuse recyclers and solar panels. The issue is where he would keep them. I would equip multiple power storage containers as*

nodes on independent circuits along my body, but did Eights? I did see movement between his inventory, but was that just maintenance or an exchange of power?" Alize wiped away the cold sweat that beaded on his own forehead and cleared his throat as Eights legitimately lowered his head and twiddled his thumbs. The kid's mouth opened and closed as he tried to come up with a topic of conversation, but ultimately, he remained quiet.

"How have you been?"

Alize rubbed his own temples and attempted a minor smile despite a headache and his reasonably growing fear of the monster in front of him. The kid bore the weight of tens of thousands of kilos yet walked around as though he were a solid 22, and he didn't show any signs of strain.

"I'm okay but..." Carlos or Eights wiped his hands and [De-equipped] his gear. Without magic to see what was going on behind the glimmer, Alize missed out on seeing each item practically implode and get sucked into the little pockets that dotted the boy's skin.

"You should know. You know. I think." Eights whispered, paused every few words, and trailed off. For a hot second, he looked straight toward Alize as though he were going to make a speech, but eventually, the kid stared at the floor and turned away.

"I am glad that Carlos has this type of shy personality. Comparatively, it is so easy to be around, talk to, and understand one another," Alize rubbed his burning eyes and frowned at the intruding headache that threatened to split his own mind.

"You are worried about Fell, right? I am sure that you are also wondering why I am in this chair?"

Alize brought himself closer and patted Eights on the head, which earned him a watery-eyed nod.

"I understand. Let's go get some answers, if possible, then." Alize hovered along a path around the side of the house that led to its backyard as he spoke.

"I don't know who lives here, but if Carlos is around without Fell, then the whole group has moved. There are only a few kids in the Facilities, or the schools that would make them move like this. Considering the barrier and the position Eights was forced to take, I can only think of one person who might have gotten everyone together," Alize rubbed his chin with his other hand and quickly shook the thought away as he addressed the kid with powder blue hair.

"Who asked you to be the group's lookout today?"

"Berry Blanc must have changed sides like I guessed so the group is sticking to tradition even if Fell isn't here to lead them," Alize waited for the short boy who dragged his feet but he did not let his thoughts end even if he placed them at the back of his mind.

"Bear." Eight whispered through gritted teeth.

"Ah. I understand." Alize nodded, but his mind pulled up the relevant info almost automatically.

"Fell was telling me about this while we were on the Spire. Ha. According to her, around half a month ago Berry the Bear and the rest of the rest of his little lackeys from the secondary school got into a shouting match with Bigs, Ranch, and Tomoe as usual. If I were to establish a timeline for the drama, that argument happened on Aōdān after a Flashball scrimmage between the school's team and one of the Facilities. A minor fight broke out the following day, Denday. Wynn supposedly showed up just in time and put an end to the shenanigans. Something happened between Eights and the Bear on the following Teresday as a result of the argument and group fight. That, what I can only assume was an after-school date, ended in a blowout that needed the attention of the Aide Officers. Fell didn't have all of the details since she was dealing with

Eden' and Shamble's situationship drama, but considering the rumors prior to what Fell told me, I can only make educated assumptions." Alize side-eyed Eights and noticed that the boy's face was stuck between anger and embarrassment.

"Hmm, then there is the following Fernday. From what I could gather from that girl's jabbering, Bear broke nearly all of the bones in the gym teacher's body and nearly killed Eights during a game of interschool disciplinary sports between the second and yet another Facility. Light seeker, if I am not mistaken." Alize raised an eyebrow and immediately drew a conclusion based on what he remembered about some rumors that floated about the group.

"I can only assume that the date went well until it didn't." Out of the corner of his eye, he noticed that Eights clenched his own small fists so hard that his bones creaked.

"As always, she left out some critical information." Alize shut it all down and focused on what he came for, Information gathering, and pushed forward. He and Eights passed another gate, one that did not possess any barrier, and entered what seemed to be a backyard forest. The path dipped down, accessible only by way of a long flight of stone stairs. Well-built but empty treetop cottages were built and strung together in the canopies with rope bridges, vaulting poles, handlebars, and pillars that served as obstacles and handholds. The man-made structures weaved almost seamlessly through the thick silver and brown branches. At the end of the treetop ninja warrior obstacle course was a well-maintained tree that supported azure leaves and amber-colored buds with yellow-green sprouts. The tree held a miniature replica of the house in front of it. The replica was set apart from the rest of the trees as a small clearing surrounded it.

"The tree and the leaves are not moving despite the rustling sounds." Alize floated down the steps and utilized the winding trail without

any apprehension. Eights walked beside and slightly behind him. Alize looked up at the empty space inside of the small treehouses and debated on whether or not to use a different variant of an observation spell but, thankfully, didn't have too after a small magical orb shot toward his forehead from one of the many treetop huts.

"Boss Ark is here, guys. Shape up." One voice was thrown down from the biggest treehouse.

Another voice rattled off, but it shot directly into Alize's head as if it was his own thought. "What happened to our big boss, boss?"

"I heard you and Fell broke up." A little kid laughed and waved down from one of the windows, but her voice was cut off by a soft thud that made the entire tree shake.

"Ow, Bear, you bastard. I'll turn you into a damn stain on the sidewalk if you hit me again. Yeah, back up, you moron. Hmph, just because you can't handle being in a relationship. Ow, you big moron, come here." The girl vanished from the window. The sound of a soft impact, like a fist hitting a pillow, resonated as a deep voice roared out in pain. The boy's voice dulled to a soft whimper after a few dozen more blows.

Several other children, like roaches being discovered in a cupboard, scattered in every direction. Some jumped out of, floated down from, or directly teleported away and out of the windows of the treetop house replica. A few others ran down a set of spiral wooden planks that grew out the side of the Azure Petal tree. A handful of the kids' firemen descended poles or carried themselves down using magical constructs of their own creation that either shot up from the ground, descended from the clouds, or simply manifested. There were also a few kids who possessed the ability to appear downstairs as though they had always been waiting in the area. All of their prepubescent voices bombarded Alize with questions that either came from their mouths, were projected in front of him as floating and glowing text, or the odd few that just directly placed their questions in his head.

"Alright, enough. You idiots are all being too loud, and back up. I need my space. Can't you see that I'm not feeling too good?"

Alize made a show of pointing out his wheelchair, then he pointed to the clearing all around him. In the blink of an eye, a group of 25 kids spaced themselves around him like he was a kindergarten teacher about to teach a class. Eights sat beside him with his back to the tree. The 26th person to enter the circle dropped from the tree with a boom that kicked up some tufts of grass and dirt. An almost 2 meter tall kid rose from the ground with messy spiky hair and a body type that was balanced somewhere between being packed with muscles and gangly. This titan of a child swayed out of the small crater with unsteady steps, each of which made Eights tense up and clench his jaw.

"Bear, do you want to sit down with the rest of us?" Alize raised his head to meet the child that stepped out of the dust. An innocent face full of tears and baby fat exited the cloud of dirt and grass. The child sat down next to Alize's chair and pulled his legs to his chest as he sobbed and held his bruised body.

"Tumble, what did I tell you about hitting kids who are younger and weaker than you?"

Alize did not spare any effort to look up toward a shadow of the 27th child at the window above him; instead, he looked toward the only empty space directly across from him with a frown. A tiny child no taller than one third of a meter, a porcelain doll with big bright eyes and dark skin that was somewhere between mauve and brick red, met his gaze with a casual pomp.

"I know what you told me, but you also said that we should defend ourselves and others, so all I did was hit him back to protect myself."

The girl crossed her arms and sat down on a lawn chair that suddenly just vanished from one side of the clearing to under her fluffy dress.

"Fair enough, I did say that." Alize nodded, rubbed his chin, and sighed out loud as he reviewed the details of his group. The names Eights, Bear, and Tumble were the first to enter his mind.

"Carlos 'Eights' Ettore. In modern terminology, one who uses simplified Aspects to describe one's profile, he is a Ballast type Root Defense and Movement Specialist. In other words, he has access to all Equip/ Rüer and Guidance/ Verälehrun Spells and the collective Aura and Mana that they represent. Like me, he can also access spells under utility. In Resh, that's either Schuvesotun or Shroudhe. And also like me, or what I am assuming my real profile is, Eights is limited to only the Aura component. That means we can both cast Phys-rou and other similar spells that manifest as illusions or facades on, over, or of physical things." Alize closed one eye and examined 27 imaginary posters that featured a portion of the friend group that was present.

"Berry "The Bear" Blanc is the group's most recent addition starting today considering the traditional rule Fell started making him the 27th thug to join Fpat, Fell's personal army of troublemakers. I know that he is an Accord Root Aura Type Pentacode, which is similar to my profile but ultimately different. He has an unstoppable regenerative speed, remarkable senses, thick skin and nearly unbreakable bones, a reaction speed that puts lightning to shame, and muscles that make steel cord resemble wet paper." Alize quickly placed the profile that he believed was his real profile next to Bears.

"He embodies the five aspects of Accord-type magic and has a perfectly rounded handle of his Rooted profile. Herecugen (Utility) - Buborce (Observational)- Denimio (Defense)- Motra-Viscote (Movement) - Kidecuéay (Attack). He does not have access to Mana, but his physical prowess. Unobtainable, better than me."

In the chart, Alize noticed the extreme skew that Bear possessed and measured his own Profile(s) against it. In one variation of his profile, he possessed a skew that gave him access to pretty much the same profile with an emphasis on Ballast's Utility. The second possible profile held the obvious skew toward Direct-type Mana and Aura. The effects of both profiles were similar, but the manner in which Alize needed to cast spells and utilize his magic couldn't be more similar to how the moon and sun cast light. The former required items and physical components; the latter required understanding and ritualistic pursuit.

"In either case. My profile remains a pentacode. My spell casting would ultimately be more difficult since it's based in Direct-type magic, but it would only mean adding a few extra steps and putting in a bit more effort to accomplish the same things as anyone else, and then some." Alize stopped stroking his chin and skipped over a few kids upon seeing Bear sniffle and wipe a few tears with a fuming red face.

"Theodora "Tumble" Umbroache. A problem child on par with Fell but more my speed since she can at least string more than one coherent thought together. Ha. She has a mixed profile, one that usually wouldn't work considering the lack of public spells and Simulated Terrariums that are built around and for people with Direct-type magic. That said, she is a true and violent genius who has managed to create her own spells for a rather uncommon Creation and Direct Type profile. She has even managed to seamlessly mix it with Accord type Aura to create an effect that practically breaches convention." He skimmed through the information on the other kids, which would have revealed to any-one else that all of the them were entirely unique but also extremely alike. For example, none of the kids possessed a matching profile, and none of them, according to Alize's knowledge, used the same spells or looked the same. Even a pair of identical twins looked different with

tiny gems sparkling above a different eyebrow. The only thing that all of the kids had in common was that they were all from Prochiente Village #37 either by moving, being brought here by their parents, or as part of Haven's Guardianship program. One other commonality was that each of the kids, bar a few, got their education in different academies. Some went to places called Facilities while a handful attended the secondary school in the 1st district, exactly three of the kids were members of the clergy and received religious tutelage, while one of the other kids aside from himself, was homeschooled out on the frontiers of Jordaine due to a cultural belief held in the northernmost continent.

Another commonality between the kids was their rank. Each one did not possess a star according to the Imperial standard of magical power. The grade of each kid aside from Bear, a comparative average set by the Empire, was set too high. An imperial standard that gauged potential rather than pure magical reserves like rank. It basically meant that each kid in this group was in the top 10% in terms of intellect, strength, and creativity throughout the entirety of reality. Bear, being the oddball and the newest addition, possessed a standard grade based on Alize's information. There was another, more in-depth imperial standard called levels that placed people on a legitimate cosmic leaderboard of sorts, but Alize was nowhere near informed enough to make an educated guess on something so specific.

Instead of guessing, he compiled all of the information that he held about the group's strengths and weaknesses. Most of the data, for better or worse, came from a simulated Terrarium that had been reformatted into an online PVP game by scholars over the past decade. In less than a second, he prepared questions, and exhausted his mind coming up with responses that might have to be used to counter what could be said. After about a minute of silently observing the group in their mad rambling, Alize leaned his head to the side and rested upon the back of his chair. The constant noise and chatter turned into a visible nervousness as the smarter members stopped talking and informed the others that he was ready. For a moment, Alize was brought back to his most recent nightmare, or rather, the inherited backstory that he just knew about his dreamscape.

He imagined himself upon a high-backed throne atop a jeweled and wood-gnarled dais overlooking a parade of genuflecting subjects. On the side nearest to his heart was the love of his life and in her arms was a little bundle of sunshine and purity that left Alize feeling all warm and fuzzy but even then, he remembered this scene only as a bit of backstory to an odd nightmare.

"Ahem." Alize blinked and found a bunch of kids around his age staring back up at him.

"First order of business, I know that there is a wandering Fae attached to Wyn right now..." Alize observed the group and noticed a sort of "So that's what it was" kind of vibe coming off of the objectively more intuitive and observant members.

"But since some of you have somehow seen or guessed what I have to bring to the table, I will bring my second order of business. *Someone in the group has either been following or scrying on Wyn before whatever happened, happened. It might even be possible that someone managed to capture something on video.*" Alize cleared his throat.

"Something that you all may not know is that an Aberrant spirit was and quite possibly still is, hunting the Fae that struck a forced Accord with her. Based on what I know, it has been apprehended by the authorities across the street." Alize closed his eyes, relaxed his tense shoulders, and waited for an eruption of confusion and questions, but all he heard were whispers and a vibe that made him more curious than at a loss for words.

"That thing did not appear to be a Spirit, but if Ark has said as much, it must be so." Someone's voice broke through the low rumblings and guided the conversation as it directly rang in the minds of all the kids present.

"That explains what you said earlier, huh, Mark?" Another child with a swirl print bowtie clapped her gloved hands and put on a loud, almost performative demeanor and was about to continue with a speech when a golden-haired girl with a tasteful bob cut held her shoulder and put an end to the play.

"I told you guys. I knew that the boss would know what was up with the captain." A smiling boy with hair the color of marigolds, long furry ears, a gem on his brow, and a tail that whipped around behind his back like a snake, pointed to the entire group in a big swinging gesture.

"Ahem." Alize cleared his throat once more, collecting himself.

"It's nice to see that you guys have been keeping each other updated on what has been happening with our leader. *It makes things easier.*" Alize prepared to move onto his third statement of business when someone interrupted his flow.

"Ark, where have you been and why didn't you shoot any of us a message? We all thought you had died or had been attacked. Wyn is, has been, it, it's bad." A girl with snow-white hair tried to unknot the worry between her eyebrows, but the attempt only made her struggle not to cry more evident.

"Well." Alize was about to use a prepared response, but someone else spoke up.

"Lady boss's situation is really bad, Mr. boss. I have nothing to add to that." A voice full of snark and laughter drew Alize's attention to a pair of glassy black eyes and a smile full of razor-sharp teeth.

"I understand. Thank you for clarifying. As for the rest of you, I've been out of it for the past few days. I died for a quick moment, for those of you who can see something wrong with me. I passed in my sleep and have been focused on recovering under the supervision of my parents and an out of network physician." Alize spoke with an air-quotes tone when he said physician. He recalled the facade displayed by Dr. Nayame.

"As for why I couldn't give you all any updates. Ha, I just forgot to grab my phone when I left home," Alize explained himself and accepted the odd looks that most of the group gave him.

"On the other hand, I somewhat understand how bad things have gotten for our leader. On that note, I am running on rumors and guesswork right now, so I would like it if all of you could let me know what happened after my mother dropped her off around two days ago." Alize waited for exactly one minute as the group whispered and shuffled around.

Eights, unexpectedly, stood up and entered the center of the circle. With a trembling hand, he retrieved an Arcanum that could display 2 dimensional footage in a 3 dimensional space.

"*[Inventory] or [Aerüntri]. I would like to craft my own version of something similar. It's very handy.*" Alize withdrew his greed as much as possible, but another door opened up on the second floor of his mind as something else took up a piece of his attention.

A 120 inches, in every direction, cube made of wire, coin-sized discs, and eight crystalline corners floated up in the middle of the clearing. The cube lit up with omnidirectional footage that started with a drone camera being pulled away from Eights. The boy was on a call with a few familiar faces in the immediate crowd with Bear being at the very top of the call order with another screen beside him depicting house 743. eights, in what appeared to be a panic, held onto a glassy remote controller and piloted the drone out the window of a self-driving vehicle. It was a two-seater car that resembled a motorcycle even as it floated off the ground via mushroom caps instead of wheels.

"*Mr. Blanc sent out a group text when Ms. Fell came back home unexpectedly, remained radio silent, and then left the morning of today. Ms. Umbroache tried to get in contact with her, but communication could not be established. Mr. Ettoire, decidedly, chose to lead an investigation on Ms. Ultegra-Tem in order to rectify the slights that have been made against our collective by interlopers,*" Alize narrowed his eyes and nodded to a girl with very disproportionate and almost synthetic features. She had no eyes or mouth, just three vertical slits of varying length where those features would have been. The only defining features that were not swallowed by leathery-looking skin were a hooked nose like that of an aristocrat and long ears that extended and wrapped into her spinal cord. Her body, altogether, was short and stubby like the majority of people that shared Drem or Hautzee ancestry, but unlike the majority of people with said heritage, she wore a bulbous suit that turned all of the surrounding grass and moisture into ice and falling snow, keeping her temperature at a breezy subzero. Her words, however, didn't reach his ears or mind. They vibrated throughout his body as a sudden and uncontrollable ebb nearly destabilized his illusion.

"*Thank you, Minute.*" Alize mouthed the words and stifled a chuckle as the girl's face, or rather, what would have been her cheeks, blushed with a mesmerizing or hypnotic lavender pulse. This girl was simply built for the cold depths of an ocean, not for land, so her inherent connection to him in this state was simply a passive effect of her own profile, something that he had never experienced as strong as this. He thought about it for a moment though, their ability to communicate and feel each other's thoughts and emotions, then remembered that he had an aberrant nature. Their intense connection was temporary, so despite taking time to reciprocate the notice she gave him with a nod, he kept one of his eyes on the screen.

The drone barrel-rolled through a group of pedestrians and took to the sky as it zigzagged through traffic, buildings, then more traffic and bystanders that used the more expensive skylanes as their main means of travel. In minutes, Eights piloted the drone near Wyns home and met up with a couple of the kids in the area that were waiting to be picked up for classes at a facility or at the premier schools of the First, Second and Third Villages.

"First problem, Wyn is up too early. She left before the buses and trolleys picked anyone up." Alize examined the footage with a scrutinizing eye as the drone shot in the direction of the secondary school after panning around Flush and 45th for a few sped-up minutes. Eights, understanding Wynn's proclivities despite her departure from the norm, floated the drone above back roads and alleyways leading toward where some kids claimed to have seen her run. By some miracle or maybe by a twist of fate, he managed to find her.

"Another problem, she is moving too fast. That level of speed is just beyond what a first rank could achieve through physical means, which means either she ranked up twice in the span of two days, she is burning herself out, or, the most obvious." Alize scanned the girl's movements in the half-second lengths of time that she was caught in frame and quickly came to a conclusion just based on the visible effuse that radiated off of her like puffs of smoke.

"Yeah. It's most likely the third option. That spell is not something from her profile, so at most, she should have only been able to cast it 5, maybe six times, in consecutive bursts of speed and rest. This, however..." The girl in the videos didn't run. She flickered without pause. After entering the shade of a house, she melted away and reappeared inside

a miniature forest. In another breath, she slinked through an alley between two five story mansions, the next moment, she rolled across the length of a one story trailer and vanished across the road as she dove through an open window and reappeared on the other side of the entire street. She traversed the residential district of Prochiente Village like a ghost or shadow. Eights lost her more than once and only managed to follow since she headed toward a predictable location in a relatively straight line.

The moment she crossed an architectural and road mapped threshold, i.e., left the residential region, the grid pattern of houses shifted into massive blocks of land that contained sprawling campuses. A mind-bogglingly long and wide educational district cut across Heydens Rest along the length of the Chasm in a parallel line to the grand world scar, and Fell ran across it as though it were merely a 500-meter dash.

Eights, from the footage, tried his best to capture her on camera, but it was just impossible as she moved across multiple campuses at just over the speed of sound, a feat seen as improbable for anyone under three stars in rank. The footage was not altogether clear, but still, it was obvious to Alize and most of the group that she was up to something, and not just her. Something in general was just off.

Almost all of the kids started whispering about the uncanny nature of their supposed leader or lady boss. For good reason, too, since pretty much everyone realized that the girl they watched was not entirely Wynnifell. The talk did confirm for Alize that this particular footage began rolling for what seemed to be the second time today considering some of the more distracting whisperers that focused on events yet to be displayed.

"I'm telling you, she hid something in the grove. Why else would she have that bag and lose it later? It's something important," someone said.

"Bro, it's a distraction. Someone is obviously following and attacking her by this point in time already. There is nothing in there, trust me. Look at her clothes though. You can tell." Another one of the kids spoke.

"Shut up. Let that smartass look at it first before you start speaking." A third kid with a buzz cut and a gem on his eyebrow snipped the conversation in the bud.

"File, I never knew that you thought that I was smart." Alize kept his eyes on the footage, but he couldn't help but make fun of his friend.

"Shut up, asshat." The boy scoffed, crossed his arms and turned away.

"Alright." Alize smirked to keep the mood lighthearted, but in his mind, chaos unfolded.

"These damned monsters 100% saw the entire video already. I can't say something that they already noticed, or whatever trust they have in me to figure this out might break apart. Might break? Break. BREAK! Break? Why am I focused on that word? Holy shit." Alize noticed that just before Wynns' "teleportations" she would look toward a location and noticeably blink one or both eyes depending on the amount of stuff around her. For example, the size and appearance or duration of the corrupted pixels varied in that it was near imperceptible upon a single eye's rapid blink then became incredibly noticeable upon a rapid double blink. The location she occupied before she moved consistently became the origin of every new videographic failure. Eights in the moment of filming, seemed to recognize the disturbance as a spotty connection and gave Fell more space to allow himself more time to adjust his piloting.

"A Ballast caster with a jammer that works on Eight's drone, An accord caster that can mess with light, shadows, tech, or something else that is unique enough to interrupt the signal, a creation caster that can just full stop bend time, or even a direct caster that knows how to code or hack." Alize hovered forward and touched the cube as he examined the forest line that was now full of splotches of dead pixels and shadow-covered landscape that couldn't really be detected unless one was as close as he was.

"The tearing is also similar to the visual or spatial warping that I endured regarding the spirit that attacked me. It could have found her within the city, having snuck past Rest's barriers undetected. Could have. Thinking about it does not help one bit. If I go off what has been said already, then whoever or whatever is following and probably attacking this mystical double of Wynn definitely has either a jammer capable of interfering with Eights or a [Shroud] spell that messes with visuals in general." Alize didn't move himself away and counted the intervals between the breaks and the locations at which the unknown third party chose to attack the possible look-alike of his best friend. The action or breaking, happened whenever Wynn tried to leave the thickets and small rivers that ran through the education strip or whenever she tried to call out or wave for help. Eight's, during the time that he controlled and focused on the drone, seemed to notice the now incredibly noticeable 1 to 5 second breaks as interference, and reacted accordingly when the first signs of a genuine danger began to appear on her clothes and body.

"The balls. To not only attack a child within a city, but in the educational district? This third party must either be insane or confident that they could get away with all of this." Alize gripped his armrests and pulled up as he pressed his body back down into the chair as the unseen attackers finally managed to wound Wynn in a meaningful manner.

Alize didn't even notice that the water tension of his flexing body parts oozed, instantly soaking through the clothes on his forearms, hands, waist, and thighs..

Tumble, having been locked onto him from the very start of this group meeting, intruded upon his personal space and sat on the empty but cushioned bar along the hovering chair's armrest. She opened her mouth to speak but noticed the watery ripple throughout his body, making her the second person to notice the unordinary, aberrant nature of his physiology. A jaw-dropping thought suddenly crossed her mind as she unabashedly crawled into Alize's lap like a cat to get a better feel for him. No one in the group seemed surprised or upset with the matter and actually sounded a bit annoyed as they commented on Tumble's actions as though she were trying to get close to Alize for a rebound. Alize tuned out the gossip and focused on one of the few ongoing narrations that constantly spewed from the girl wearing a bowtie; sadly, he only heard the closing statement of a seemingly heated argument.

"...Yeah, I agree. The person who cut her up might be at the third rank or more. My take is this though: she is moving like Ark in Battleground or Dusk when he's playing in the runner position in the Flash games that I see him in. Her profile is not even built for spells like that; that's why we all agreed to have her play the Castle position or Goalie when we are online."

"I get what you mean. I couldn't get through Fell's armor even when I altered my profile and upped my rank in the Sims. It was easy enough getting around her though."

"Exactly. I think that..." The girl kept going, stating and framing conjecture and assumption as fact as she reached the same exact conclusion that Alize found himself faced with.

"... we are seeing some doppel of Fell, like how Ark meets us in a fake body. I think that the officers across the street have something to do with all of this." The girl lowered her voice and adjusted her gloves as if what she said before was natural and this required a certain level of secrecy or delicate handling. Alize stopped listening since he knew that Bigs was about to completely jump off the rails of plausibility and fully dive into the abyss that was conspiracy. The video, thankfully, picked up in terms of speed as Eights increased the video. The drone spun around and to the outside of a forest too thick to pilot through and barely skimmed the bark of a tree as the camera pulled out of its zoom to get a better look at the general landscape. Fell, after being sliced across the face and receiving a piercing stab to the shoulder, vanished. When she appeared on the edge of the screen, Alize's eye twitched and breath caught as he noticed her bloodied abdomen and newfound limp.

Eights lowered his head as the video played, much to Alize's unexpressed confusion. The next sequence of events, however, fully explained why the shy boy cowered in front of the entire group. Seemingly unable to handle the horror of seeing a friend in such disarray, the drone crashed into a tree just as Wynnifel jumped and blinked over a river. The last thing anyone saw was that she flickered onto another patch of forest that the drone could not see. After a few seconds, the rocked arcane machine rebooted, flipped, hovered, and reoriented itself under Eight's now shaky control. The device started off toward the last position of Fell's ghostly afterimage, but the entire screen suddenly flickered and turned off.

"Is that it?" Alize hissed. His imagination burned the image of the corrupted treeline into his memory as he tried to find something out of place or anything that might hint at the figure or forms hidden within the breaking footage.

"No. I'm sorry. I forgot to connect and charge it before this." Eights jumped and fumbled around his forearms and waist.

"No problem. The TV is nonessential, so I don't expect you to always have it connected to whatever systems you have set up in your Inventory." Alize exhaled and crossed both hands over his lap, or at least he tried to. Tumble was in the way of his complete relaxation, so he decidedly leaned to the side and ignored her O-shaped mouth, shaking hands, and melting glare. As for Eights, he pulled a needle-thin quill from one of his veins, snapped a rice grain sized piece off of it at one of the notches and tapped the cube's dimmest corners. A miniature chamber split open and revealed an even smaller slot drawer containing a transparent bit similar to the soft luminance of the one Eights snapped off. He removed the dead Quill bit, Quibe, or magical battery and was about to press the new glowing grain into a now empty socket but in his haste, the kid dropped the tiny dead piece into the grass and dirt. Instead of letting it pass as a loss, Eights panicked and tapped the sides of his face to put on a pair of specialized goggles.

"While we wait, does anyone have anything to add?"

Alize shook his head, forced a smile, and found himself pleasantly surprised as a lean kid in shorts and a #56 sweatshirt spoke up.

"I saw 'er runnin boss." The kid scratched his head.

"Ah, come on, Dusk. You weren't even paying attention, so why even bring that up like it's going to help the boss figure something out?" A kid with golden hair smacked the lean kid on the back and tried to get him to sit back down.

"Sham. Let him speak. Every piece of info is good to Ark." Tumble snapped her fingers, which instantly placed the golden hair kid in another spot. Her eyes never left Alize's chest, and her other hand never stopped tugging on his shirt in an attempt to stop herself from crying about his physical state. The more observant of the group found her clinginess normal, but the crying, it sparked interest and concern. It started with one—a bald-headed young woman wearing shades and a magenta sweater. Her glowing white eyes blazed even underneath the blackout shades that protected others, but even so, pinpoint spotlights stabbed through Alize and revealed everything to the girl. For the first time that she could recall, the spotlights that revealed only truth to her at times, sputtered out as her passive effect failed to pierce through what she now understood as several dozen overlapping illusions. The most important thing was that Alize's doppelgänger now possessed magic. It was the only discovery that she cared about and one that left her darkened eyes and jaw unhinged. Several others were clued into their boss's unusual state and visibly backed away from the circle for various reasons.

"Go ahead, Dusker." Alize noticed the way that Tumble snapped as she inched closer to his body, then narrowed his eyes at the group's subtle fracturing. Unable to take everything in, he assumed that the observant members of the group were disappointed in how long it took Eights to pick up the dead quill bit with a pair of tweezers. It was very likely, to him, that those group members were capable of following the bit and knew where it was at all times.

"Aight den, I was play'n flash n dash fore I saw' er." Dusker squeezed his cheeks and pursed his lips as he actively and magically forced himself to remember something that he barely noticed.

"My team didn't scramble well laus year, so cap'n put 'em greenies on early morn' n runs. She came by in a rush along the western ridge. Round when the greenies were learnin' Spider Lunge Play." Dusker pouted and crossed his arms. A thick and heavy accent made it very difficult to understand, but most of the kids in the group were accustomed to it by now.

"If I knew what's gonna happen...." Dusk froze as almost everyone stared daggers at him.

"Oh? What happens to her, Dusk? Silence, huh? Does anyone else want to tell me what happened?"

"Ark." Tumble tried to use a soft voice, but a harsh, "Just try it" shot out of the mouth of a boy with a buzz cut, the one and only File.

"Oh? Tumble? Since when do you listen to File?"

"I don't." She glared at the distant boy, but her aggression faded away when the buzz-cut kid tilted his head and motioned to the TV.

"I want to, but I can't. We all made a pact regarding you. Please don't ask me." Tumble wiped her tears before they fell and leaned into his chest.

"Fine. How's the screen looking?"

"Sorry. I got it." Eights tapped the unfurled tips on some of the other corners and restarted the projection from where it was left off.

"I have to fast-forward a bit to the next time that I get her on screen." Eights moved to another corner and began messing with some controls. The school day, for those not given a minor vacation due to test scores, grades, and work completed, passed by in a flurry of static movement as those kids retook or made up their previous examination and placement tests. Around midday, for about two hours, the kids were given free license to take lunch, a break, and any extracurriculars that they signed up for. The only thing that felt weird about Eight's keeping a drone making laps around the school was the insane reality that it worked in finding Fell. She, now holding a duffel bag and a change of clothes, grabbed her food, ate it in a dark corner of the interior cafeteria and then left it all half eaten and in disarray atop the table.

"*Okay. She had and would never leave before eating her fill. That is definitely not Wynn. It must be a doppel piloted by an officer.*" Alize scanned the crowd within the footage and noticed that everyone's jaws dropped. Some of the more confused kids, who were on their way to pass on their extra food, formed a wall of baffled faces. He even turned an eye towards Bear, who nodded in his direction, and Eights, who tried to whisper a response then chose to raise a thumb in confirmation as he returned the speed to its normal 2x.

"Everyone thought she was possessed by whatever is helping her cast those teleportation or movement spells. There was a possibility that Big's and Ranch floated." Tumble successfully whispered to Alize after she adjusted in her seat to get a better look at where the footage was.

"Does it involve a doppelgänger and the nice officers from across the street?" Alize whispered back and side-eyed the group's resident rumor mill and smirked upon hearing an insane theory regarding the entirety of Jordaine, the result of a massive tree being uprooted. The great chasm, as a result of this rumor, was made by the impact of a cosmic shovel being driven into the earth after the work was done. Alize didn't stop the film or remain intrigued enough to tell the talking kids how on the nose they were about the creation of the country that they all called home.

It was only after this brief shift in attention that Eights zoomed in on the weird Wynn, who left school on a day when she didn't even have to go into classes. In a tracksuit similar to Dusker's, she escaped the glowing perimeter of the school by barreling through a security guard and teleporting past a dog-headed man that held a phone in the middle of a selfie. The guy, as Eight piloted his drone after Fell, sniffed the air and immediately ran towards the security guard's booth. After a flurry of movement and a remarkably fast outfit change, the dog-headed guy barreled after Wynn on all fours. The girl, after leaving the premises and leading a trail of two security guards, headed off in a straight line back home. Before Alize could get comfortable with the comedic antics and incredible acrobatic and mystical dodges that Wynn achieved on her way out of the fields surrounding the 1st district's secondary school, he felt an awkward silence and chill in the air.

"What is this atmosphere? Should I stay quiet?"

A sudden black screen filled the TV even while the corners remained lit. It was a change that caught everyone off guard the first time and sent some into a riot. Alize, however, was alone in his surprise and did everything in his power not to let his rising sense of anxiety show on his face since there was nothing for him to work with. The visuals came back not one to five seconds later. A whole minute passed as the group's attention remained locked on either the film or his every expression. Wynn reappeared in the footage, one that remained fixed in the spot since Eights seemingly learned to hover the drone on the spot. A bone-deep gash stretched across the length of her back, while black and blues covered her body through tattered clothing. The dog-headed man lay on the floor, surrounded by dead and warped pixels, while the first guard was nothing but a midsection folded around a charred tree that was peppered by sizzling spears of something that was no longer there. Wynn, faded into the background of the forest, vanished like a ghost amidst fog after dropping a black bar on the dog-headed man's chest as the numerous and encompassing visual corruption chased after her.

Just as Eights got back into the swing of preemptively moving toward Fell's intended location, the lens blacked out for half a second as something flitted across the screen. Eights miraculously managed to reboot the drone and reoriented it within milliseconds before the darkness fully grasped the device. He curled it around several trees and forced it to fall in an infinitely close to parallel curve, then with a snap twist. He shot the drone up through a canopy before several other grasping shadows closed in on it from either side. Above the treeline, he zigzagged through the clouds, following the corrupted trail of splotches that resembled a flock of birds. In a moment he caught up with Fell, making a B-line straight home.

Why she did not stay on school grounds or go to an Aide station was beyond understanding, so the Eights followed from a distance and kept the group informed of what was happening. While flying to intercept or get ahead of Wynn and the person or people following her, the drone genuinely lost connection for the very first time as a near invisible pulse wafted out from the forest. Undeterred, Eights used several Arcanums to hack into his own drone and forcefully rebooted it. The device's erratic descent turned into a controlled fall the moment all of its systems were turned on. In an uncharacteristic display, Eights stopped worrying about the camera, locked in, and masterfully piloted through brush and shrubbery in order to remain hidden now that it was clear that there were multiple pursuers who had spotted the drone from what it was.

Eight's assumption turned out to be correct as Fell stopped running. It was clear, after he got a good angle, that the decision was not by choice. There was a conjure and hooked wall that burned every single living thing and object in the region surrounding her, leaving an almost translucent box to cut her off from the environment. With a face full of defiance and an outburst of magic, Wynn's bloodied back and other wound sparkled like layers of what appeared to be scaled and chain-linked ballistic glass bubbled around her body. The girl's shadow, a barely noticeable thing in the shade of a forest, vanished between the lining and folds of her own clothes, giving her a familiar cell-shaded look. She wound up a punch, gathering force, strength, and focus as her eyes remained locked in the direction of home.

"The Fae is working with her or maybe even for her considering the ease of her movements and transitions." He observed and followed the movement of the closest broken image as Fell punched toward nothing. The dead pixels that flooded into the clearing didn't immediately swallow her in an attempt to kill or capture as they had done before. Instead, they retreated for seemingly no reason under the ebb and flow of the shadows and leaves surrounding them. Eights, in this less than one second moment in which Fell punched her cage, noticed that something was wrong and focused on ensuring that his drone was secure. Thankfully, he was aware of her spells, even if she showed something completely unknown to the group with her movement, so the device was not sucked into the devastating strike unleashed by Wynn. Her glass-covered arm smashed into the barrier and shattered it apart in a reverberating explosion that sent out exactly the same pulse that turned the drone off when it wasn't prepared. The only difference here was that all of the shadows in the forest were sucked into her closed fist as oxygen rolled back into the flash fire she created through pure friction.

The spindling darkness dragged the corruption back to the position where Fell was supposed to be. One second, ten, almost another whole minute passed by before the dead pixels managed to detangle and separate into little more than half a dozen vertical slits. Hidden and recording from a fixed location within a bramble that managed to bore and wrap itself around two boulders and a fallen tree, the drone's lens adjusted. Eights focused on getting better footage and in his pursuit, managed to get the silhouettes of the shadowy figures that simply removed themselves from his camera. As for the 7 standing figures that rose out of pockets and divots full of charcoal and glassed dirt, they waved to each other and surrounded a singular charred body that lay curled at the center of the destruction Fell unleashed. The shrouded figures stepped away from the body as a nonverbal argument unfolded. Barely discernible in the heat waves at the very edge of the perfectly circular explosion, the Shrouds distorted to reveal bits and pieces of skin-tight clothing and pieces of tactical equipment. Eights didn't stay around to get a better look at the masked and cloak-covered people and darted off toward the location that he assumed that Fell was going toward.

"These people, who in the ninth are they? What does she have that they want so desperately?"

Alize paid most of his attention to the almost instantaneous manner in which the strangers moved away from the body of their burned comrade and the heat that ruined their facades. He also noticed, even though Eights didn't seem to at the moment, that three of the barely discernible individuals with the most destabilized shrouds secured Wynn's duffel bag from under their ally's burned remains.

"And the Fae," Alize didn't mind that Eights possessed priorities and used the time to think about what he had just seen as the drone caught up. At least the boy was consistent in understanding her habits.

"The shadowy component of her spell was added by whatever Aspects it might have given to her as part of its contract. It might be able to see or allow her to see whatever is attacking, even if we can't. This is assuming that the Wynn that Eights has been following is not some Aide Officer in disguise or a doppelgänger piloted much in the same manner that I am as part of some long-con developed by the Surveyor that's on site." Alize thought of Madam R and her known exploits and really couldn't be sure about what to tell his group.

"If it is working with her to achieve something, it might know who those people are or what they want." Alize scratched at his neck and tried to imagine what kind of insane circumstance led to his best friend being wrapped up in something straight out of a spy thriller.

He unintentionally reviewed a board that he set up in his mind and quickly glanced toward pinned up images of the [Shroud] casters and their silhouettes.

"I also have to figure out how to see and handle these people. If they were sent after my best friend who is just tangentially related to my Affix and something that it set up, it is only a matter of time and misfortune before they come after my parents and Jarold, the rest of these morons, or me." Alize watched the rest of the video without blinking.

Eights could not, like all of the other times that he got lucky, find any trace of Fell and chose to pilot the drone back to her house. In a moment, house 743 on 45th, just off of Flush, came into view. In almost the same moment. The fence surrounding the plot tore upon her entry as she clawed her way out of the shade like some revenant. Fell could barely stand even as a featureless mass of her own shadow helped her hobble through a pair of open glass doors. The girl crashed into a rather open lounging space and in the blink of an eye, half a dozen some young men and women in their mid-20s to early 30s closed the doors and drew the blinds.

Eights circled the building to get a few shots of the inside of the house. Decorations, trays of food piled into mountains, and presents were all tossed to the side as Wynn's family addressed her injuries. In another circling shot, she was seen trying to sit up as older people with salt and silver hair were locked in a heated conversation. Alize, having seen it before, quickly noticed that the sentient shadow, now in a darker place and surrounded by family, solidified into a more distinct copy of Wynn and began interacting with the other members in the house as though it were an accepted member of the household.

"The Fae is out in the open, and no one looks particularly surprised by her showing up with it. Which means this is part of the gifting thing that my dad said some Drem and Hautzee still believe in. A

blessing then, huh, Affix? You orchestrated things to give her the perfect companion to slot into her Accord Aspect, and this trouble is the price? I can feel you burning up on my real body, you damned nuisance." Alize frowned inwardly and focused on the soundless interaction of the Ultegra-Tems to where he didn't even notice that Tumble was holding one of his ice-cold hands and reaching toward his cheek. Tears welled up in her reddened eyes and left trails down her cheeks as his own illusory passivity, unwittingly, fell apart as time passed.

That said, Eights pulled the camera back a few seconds later as an old woman and one of the two old men of the family left the house. They knocked on doors and pulled dozens of adults out of their homes. Decorations flew out of front doors, garages, and the trunks of parked vehicles under the direction of the old couple. In less than an hour, a silent parade exploded on the block. Fell's first Decennial festival was ready to pop off at any moment, even if everyone understood that no one would start cooking until the old couple gave the signal or until the school day was officially over. Whichever one came first was the attitude that most, if not all, of the party preppers held. Moments later, the elders of the Ultegra-Tem household were approached by one of Wynn's cousins in the middle of completing final adjustments, which prompted Eights to circle with his drone as her family went back into the home.

Around the same time, a glob of water appeared and enlarged in the backyard of house 743. The familiar glint of Blue-Steel pierced the sphere of water as a scaled man with the whiskers of a catfish gracefully touched ground in his form-fitting leathers. Immediately, he noticed the pocket of disturbed earth next to one of the fences and hardened his expression. A silken and singular mass of glossy "hair" similar to the caudal fin of a fish floated down from the remains of the thinning water globe and draped over the officer's back like a cape as he raced across the backyard. Every step rippled the ground like a stone dropped in the ocean as the earth's moisture levitated and hovered just above the grass.

A few seconds of film passed unremarkably as Eights moved from one window to the next to get better angles. The Aide first checked to make sure that Wynn's health was in order, then he proceeded to do his job and record everyone's statements. Whatever was said, according to what Alize observed, made the Aide frown in a manner that made his full and blue lips purse. Without any hesitation, the man lifted his gauntlet and pressed a metal-covered finger to the space around his fin-like ear. A bubble-like ring of water circled around his finger as he said something that the camera's built-in audio capture spell could not intercept through the home defense.

Moments later, the video began clipping, breaking. At first, no one in the family noticed, but the moment that the screen blackened, Alize felt his heart sink.

"They went into her house with an Aide on the premises! Dear goddess, who are these maniacs?" Thirty seconds later, after Eights managed to boot the drone using the same long-range hacking Arcanum after finding that his device was completely unresponsive.

The Aide was seen with a sword and shield out. Blood poured from deep wounds on his neck and waist while serrated blades that resembled spearheads somehow found themselves lodged in between needlepoint gaps in his armor. Pockets of water congealed around the wounds. They slowly pulled the weapons and colorful-looking poison out of the wounds and facilitated a quick scabbing or even full recovery. Razor-sharp waves exploded on the edge of the Officer's sword and gushed from the top of his shield to drape it in miniature whirlpools for a split second as the screen darkened for another few seconds. The next snippet of video showed a broken arcane sword and the same Aide wielding a glowing dagger as a group of cousins tried to heal the only remaining elder of the Ultegra-Tems that wasn't on the ground, face down in a pool of their own blood.

The Aide broadened his back and constantly moved his head as if he tracked multiple foes even with both of his eyes being gouged out. The air's moisture constantly licked his skin in waves and in the blink of an eye, he parried a dozen clattering needles and lodged the tip of his dagger into the neck of a tall splotch of dead pixels that was only caught on film for half a second in combat attire before the screen blackened.

In an instant, the Aide let go of his dagger and allowed the stabbed intruder to be taken away by two other shrouded apparitions. He pulled a firearm from his belt and danced in a manner that put a master of capoeira to shame as he mixed devastating jabs, whipping kicks, and gunshots together. Every movement connected with a person's body just as their illusions became warped, and each bullet resulted in a plume of either red or some other colorful blood. Some of the cousins also jumped into action as two of the near-imperceptible figures rushed past the Aide and were covered in a spray of icy mist that blew off and naturally surrounded his caudal fin throughout the entire disastrous turn of this relatively common house call. The cousins, being able to make out the vague shapes of their enemies, executed a well-timed sequence of spells that created something beyond what any of them were capable of alone. One created spiked walls of stone, another transmuted some of the stone into flint and finely ground dust, then a third moved the whole structure faster than the Aide's bullets. The projectiles and shrapnel collided and sparked an explosion that consumed two of the strange and weirdly armored intruders. The screen went black just before the explosion engulfed the entire room.

The moment that the drone came back online, the whiskered aide was seen gritting his teeth as he stared down a miniature typhoon that he and a few of the young adults created. The cousins, in unison, stood beside and slightly behind the Aide as they put up a phalanx of bedrock and jade to reinforce the man's held shield. The screen paused there.

"Yo, Eights, why did you pause the video?" File crossed his arms and barked in displeasure. More than half of the group followed along.

"I reckon the boy don't wanna revisit wutsa bouta happen." A smooth and low voice pierced through the group's noise, but no one aside from Alize paid any attention to it.

"I don't think." Eights kept his head lowered and tried to speak up, but he ended up pressing his hands together and avoiding eye contact with everyone.

"Play it, Eights." Alize placed a hand on the blue-haired boy's shoulder.

"Okay."

The screen darkened and remained for a long while before color abruptly returned. It was as if an inkwell sucked in everything that it spilled. To Alize's utter surprise and bafflement, the remainder of Wynn's cousins were pinned to walls and the ceiling in bits or with their limbs splayed and splattered, against hanging pictures and homely wallpaper. The Aide stood in front of the girl and beside the last cousin, a young woman who held her hands up in a boxing posture despite the hole in her thigh and the gouged out flesh on her cheek that slowly expanded as if a rot had taken root. The Elder, who was not a part of the dead, remained, and with a righteous anger on her face, she held onto the severed arm of a clawed hand that pierced through her own chest. A near invisible and completely transparent individual rushed from the spot as neon orange blood spilled from an exposed wound. The glowing disc of exposed muscle and blood trailed toward a blacked-out corner of the film as the only thing capable of being recorded. Seconds later, the exposed and glowing flesh vanished into a cloud of dead pixels.

The old lady, Wynn's only grandmother and matriarch of the Tem family, coughed up a mouthful of blood and pointed to the shadow with a sneer as she squeezed the near invisible clawed arm. In the blink of an eye, the entire appendage was compressed into a small marble. The old lady, with a face full of anger, tossed the marble to the Officer just as her exposed ribcage crumbled and lungs collapsed and sloughed out of the newly emptied cavity.

The Aide, a myrmidon with a cracked shield and a bent spear pointed forward, stood as sentry despite missing half of his face and possessing several fatal injuries. He said something to the last remaining cousin, and let the young lady catch the marble. Half a dozen figures dropped their illusory [Shrouds] and charged blindly to recover the evidence of their mass murder. In the chaos and without any notice, two guys suddenly appeared next to Fell and vanished with her as the Aide visually roared with magic. His throat expanded and lit up with a violent blue light that shone through his warped chest armor.

The next break showed a wild distortion as several dozen figures, all bearing the same exact silhouette, stared down at a monstrous humanoid that was a split between a dragon and a human. The cousin, who that held her hands up in a boxing posture moments before, stood backed against the wall with both of her magical gauntlets of etched stone raised. She smiled and, with one raised hand, placed the diamond full of evidence between her teeth and clamped down on the throat of an intruder with the other. She was now missing a leg, but it didn't matter since it was replaced with sleek etched quartz and tempered glass. The girl's missing facial features also received the same treatment as her face filled with gold veined marble and a lapis lazuli eye. The young woman swallowed the diamond and laughed like a maniac as she crushed yet another intruder's windpipe the moment they entered her reach. There was no skill or thought in the young woman's actions anymore as she threw up her guard and endured a magical onslaught. For what felt like hours, the young lady was thrown against one wall after the other, lifted up and thrown down onto the floorboards. She endured and traded one destroyed part of her body after the other for one of stones, gems, and another enemy's life.

Sadly, the young woman, just like the Aide that managed to pile the corpses of several masked hitmen bearing the exact same body type, could not endure everything. The screen went dark, and the next time the drone booted up, a person with a missing arm, a massive cloak, and a mask, pulled the young woman's skull and spine out of the massive golem that she had become. The moment that this person crushed the girl's skull, they dug into the golem's stomach and pulled out the blood-infused diamond. The masked person with sharp fingernails spun their only remaining hand around in the air as if to say, "Wrap it up." and had only just begun to re-enter an imperceptible state when the floorboards began to move in a manner that Alize found familiar. The drone wasn't affected, but the interior of the house began to tremble and fall apart in all kinds of directions. The diamond, in this moment of complete surprise, escaped the figure's hand before they could vanish.

That's when the footage stopped.

"NOOO." one of the kids with a reptilian exterior and solid black eyes threw her hands up in feigned sorrow while a girl who sported white gloves and a bowtie, sighed and said, "Its like watching the most perfect drama and it ends up getting canceled while on a cliffhanger".

The group was thrown into disarray as Eights put the screen back into his [Inventory].

"Sorry again, everyone. That is all I could get before the drone broke down. " Eights lowered his head and twiddled his thumbs as almost everyone consoled or apologized for the absolute rage that targeted him the first time that he shared the footage.

"No. It might not have. Do you have the drone that you used? I am assuming that you sent out another one to recover it the moment it stopped responding." Alize narrowed his eyes. Without putting up a fuss, Eights flipped his palm and pulled out a monocular dragonfly with a metallic exoskeleton. Crystalline, pyramidal protrusions poked out of the exoskeleton where the insect's wings would have been if it were a living organism. Alize twisted the long and straight abdomen of the dragonfly and twisted it into ten pieces. Each segment held an intricate internal clockwork makeup that combined electronic, mechanical, and arcane components in a perfect synergy. Each chip, cog, gear, and runic symbol was carefully and perfectly placed. The pico-scale inlay of crystal that could have only been achieved through the perfection of manufacturing, magic, and Ballast-inspired mechanics, gleamed and shimmered under the light of one of the world's many suns.

"Fashion. Fix this." Alize examined all ten segments until he tossed one toward a kid that was mostly covered in rags. A deep cowl hid their features, but for added measure, a blackened gauze had been placed over their face to cast a permanent shadow. The bundle of rags flashed forward and engulfed the 24 millimeter thick segment with the same diameter as a penny. In less than a second, the darkness within the cowl flashed with magic and in even less time, a cloth-covered hand tossed the segment. Before the piece even arced back to Alize, he twisted all of the other pieces of the dragonfly's abdomen back into place and locked it together. Under the eyes of everyone, the dragonfly's dark eye twisted as the sound of a clicking shutter reached all of their ears. Glowing crystalline wings popped out of the four pyramid tips while the Quill that was slotted into an armored casing on the underside of the Arcanum's thorax, beamed to life as though the odd drone were a bioluminescent and odd-looking but realistic insect.

"It didn't die. Nor did it break in a fall that might have occurred when you lost connection." Alize calmly revealed his thoughts.

"Mark and File, pop a terrarium around this drone." Alize moved his hand and let the dragonfly camera hover in its place.

"Aye aye, Captain." Mark hopped to his feet. His silky long hair flowed like a waterfall from a topknot and whipped around in the air like a ribbon due to his erratic movement.

"Damnit Ark. I'll do it, but use that tone again and I'll knock you upside your head. Fell ain't here to protect your weak ass, and Tumble can't do shit to stop me." An identical-looking kid, File, grumbled and stuck his tongue out at the group members that glared at him. As he slowly walked to the center of the group, he combed through his honey-colored buzz cut and rubbed the gem on his brow. He did not possess the same feline features as his twin, but he did have reflective eyes reminiscent of a sun rather than his brother's hazelnut-colored irises.

"Understood File. Now, the terrarium?" Alize didn't even register the combative expression and simply tilted his head towards Eights.

"Let me see the remote and put up the screen again." Alize received the controller and made the dragonfly do several loops and twitchy zigzags to make sure that there was no delay. After a few seconds, the Arcane drone adopted a perfectly circular pattern that required no adjustments to maintain.

"Tch. Bastard. This better pan out, Ark." File followed his brother to the center of the circle and put a hand in his pocket.

"Stop worrying, Fletcher. Ark always knows what's wrong with stuff. Just help me out." Mark hopped around and brought the dragonfly closer to his foot-dragging brother with a beaming smile. The twins, under the eyes of everyone present, high-fived each other and created a doorway with their arms. In less than a second, the tips of their extended fingers vibrated and left behind a floating crack that bent and warped any light around it. Once the writhing ring of magic was completed, the twins ducked underneath the mystical hula hoop and put themselves on the outside of the boundary. The twins each pressed one of their palms to flatten the outer curve of the coronal loop. Like a drop of dye hitting crystal clear water, the distorted ring diffused and expanded into a perfect dark sphere around the dragonfly.

"What else do ya want, Ark? Your ass never asks for just one thing." Buzz cut File pressed his back against the bubble and crossed his arms as he matched Alize's schadenfreude with righteous aggression.

"You know me so well, File. I do want something else. Cut off the inside." Alize, unperturbed, waited for his request to be handled.

"Tch. You always ask for impossible shit. We aren't even ranked, and you are asking us to control space-time like it's goddamn clay." File spit on the grass and threw his hands up.

"Fletcher, no cursing. It's nasty. Besides, we can do it." Mark poked his head around the sphere and jogged over to his slightly taller twin with pep in his step.

"Yeah, yeah." File huffed but didn't say anything rude when Mark patted him on the head.

"Alright then. Say when then, Boss." Mark nodded. Alize returned the nod and passed the controls to Eights since it was impossible to see into or past the roughly made black hole.

"Now." The sphere, under the control of the twins Mark and File, rippled from pole to pole and bubbled as though it were textured with razor blades. Half a second later, the sharp edges that poked out of the sphere collapsed into a kaleidoscopic and smooth mirror. All of the twisting images that reflected off of the surface then swirled into exactly one. All of the kids and Alize could see into and through the sphere as if it were a soap bubble. The dragonfly on the surface of the bubble continued flying in its perfect circle, but if one looked beyond the projection and into the center, the flight pattern resembled a figure eight in all directions.

"Drop the terr." Alize commanded with narrowed eyes. Mark maintained his smile, but something dangerous, almost feral, played at the corners of his eyes and lips. File, understanding the physics and magical implications behind crafting and controlling terrariums, also adopted a more aggressive posture and grimaced. Both of the twins immediately listened and removed the spheres altogether. The dragonfly, unable to ground itself in any orientation, flashed with a protective barrier, flipped in on itself along 3 main axes, spun around said dimensional marker, and cracked in the exact same way that Fell's chase footage messed up. After less than half a second of implosion, Eights, by muscle memory at this point, saved his drone from crashing into the floor by messing with the controls, forcing that thin barrier to snap the drone's body back into order.

"Again." Alize didn't have to see any footage to know what just happened. Eights returned to the circular flight path while Mark and File remade the terr. None of the kids raised their voices above a whisper even though a few questions and comments reached Alize's ears. Since none were directed at him specifically, he chose to ignore them as best he could, even if it wouldn't last.

"Ark. The fuck man?" File grit his teeth and quickly looked around as though he had just seen a ghost. No, it was more accurate to say that he was looking for a ghost that might be spying on the group.

"Oh my. Fell seems to be in quite a bit of trouble this time, huh, Boss?" Mark maintained his smile, but his big eyes sharpened to predatory slits.

The question, "What are they talking about?" floated around the circle until all eyes rested on Tumble and the rumor mill that usually rounded insane theory back into the realm of truth. The doll-like girl didn't address the group since if they didn't know, they wouldn't get it. Instead, while seated on Alize's lap, she focused on something that no one else seemed to notice about their boss. No, the kids who did possess magic, spells, or insight capable of seeing through Alize's facade, put in enough effort to remain quiet as they inched further to the fringes of the circle. The job of explaining then fell onto one of the few other kids in the group that understood the mystic and physical implications of what just happened. The rumor mill, unexpectedly and uncharacteristically, remained quiet. Interestingly enough, the silence of the crown made a certain whispered conversation seem loud. Felicity "Lily" Gionolia, preoccupied herself with explaining the situation to Eights since the boy didn't even seem to understand what he captured or the amount of danger he was in for following Fell. Other than the weird moment when the breaking images directly approached the drone, he was not aware of any moments when his drone was almost caught. Alize scanned the group with a heavy heart and did his best to ignore the tiny finger that poked his chest and the tears that rolled down a cute girl's face.

"What do I say here? Someone with Ballast and Direct-type magic was following Fell the whole day? Am I supposed to say something here? The bastards that attacked her have a similar Profile to what I should have? Is this supposed to show me how not to use my authority or what? Should I play dumb here or lie? I could say any number of things that might be possible considering every detail at my disposal, but what's closest to the truth? No, that would be lovely if what was captured on film was the truth. This is something set into motion by my Affix." Alize panned across the faces and noticed that some of the smarter kids began avoiding his gaze like he was plague. They were the few who knew the truth about his curse.

"This is really bad. Fucking Affix. You go after my parents and set up a trap to kill them if they act, and now you are trying to get rid of and set up my friends? Fuck, now Eights is probably going to get into some kind of issue if I don't handle this properly. Damnit. Most or least likely, my ass. It's possible that Wynn's entire family bore the price of a screwed-up blessing that my Affix orchestrated. That alone is guaranteed. Dammit, the officers are on site and are showing signs of protocol breaching, so it's possible that things are under control. Even if they aren't, uncles Fred and Dell got her to safety at least, right? Fuck. I got more people caught in my Affix nonsense. What should I do? If I say something that gets their minds spinning to where they act on what I say, I might get more of my friends caught in an inescapable web of nonsense." Alize wanted to rip his own hair out hearing the conversations and confusion that spread throughout the group. Thankfully, the charming sound of a skillfully played harmonica and a whistle cut through the chatter and shut everyone up.

"Boss. I am not the sharpest tool in the shed. And I am willina bet my left boot and soft chew that there're a few of us that ain't as, inner prospective az the rest of y'all that know what's goin' on So." the kid sniffed, leaned back against the tree behind him, and flicked his wide brim hat up just enough to reveal a long Quill between his teeth.

"So boss, I err on the side of caution and wonner if ya could share the fofo that seems to have the rest dem more riled than Fluke flyin' over a Squire order out on the frontier." One of the few kids who had spoken only once since the appearance of Alize, cleared his throat and carried on with a low drawl that commanded attention.

"Ha. It's always lovely to hear your voice, Cable." Alize held his blink longer than one might need to rest their eyes, exhaled, then clapped his hands.

Mark and File jumped at the sound and moved their bodies away from the terrarium at the same time. With a pop similar to the sound of a suction cup, the distortion collapsed in on itself and pulled toward one of the ten segments of the dragonfly. In an instant, the camera, Eight's Arcanum, dropped straight to the ground devoid of magic and function.

"To keep it simple. Someone with a high rank has been tailing or swapping places with Fell all day. To what ends, I have no clue. I can only assume that the officers across the street have been playing a long con on some criminal element that seems to have attached itself either to her or our group. This third party, be it a person or group, managed to create two separate terrariums every time they got close to her, one around the combat area and one around the surrounding region, cutting off or disturbing any signals. So you all understand, this person or group noticed Eight's drone from the very moment that the drone started to black out, but they chose not to break it for whatever reason. I am assuming that he, luckily, managed to keep just enough of a reactionary distance from any of those pixelated individuals." Alize leaned back during his exhale and held out a hand. Tumble waved her own and placed the dead dragonfly in his extended palm. Everyone went silent as the information sank in.

3.2 Shifting Hands and Plans

The palpitating and asynchronous breathing of more than twenty kids seated in a relatively tight circle, reaches an unsettling and drawn out pause. No one broke the unspoken vow, and no one moved a single muscle as thoughts and opinions both formed and shattered. Alize scanned the group and quickly found that only a notable few seemed to have the gears grind to a halt as a complete narrative either formed in their minds or fell apart at the seams. The rest of the circle was just about evenly split between those who had long since made up their minds to listen or wait to act on their newly formed beliefs and those that didn't understand a single thing of what they had seen even after a second watch.

"No one wants to break the tension. Ha. At times like these. Ha, Wynn is the perfect person to melt, not break, the ice." Alize scanned the crowd with a slight frown that quickly evened out upon seeing a hand slowly raise.

"Lily, thank you for being the first to bring something up. Do you have any questions, concerns, or comments about the footage, Fell, or something else that might be related to today's gathering?"

"Yes. Um. I was only guessing before you said anything, but Carlos is in danger, right?"

"I believe so, but to give my best possible conclusion, I think that it would be best to make sure that we all know who and what we are dealing with before deciding or estimating anything." Alize twisted the dragonfly open once more and tossed the same broken piece over toward Fashion. The child that resembled the Ghost of Christmas Future released a groan similar to the creaking limbs of trees in a mist-covered graveyard on the witching hour. The meaning of the kid's spoken noise resonated in the minds of all the kids.

"It's the same kind of damage. There is significantly less of it overall. The distributing cylinder is showing signs of corrosion, but it's not eaten through like before. A single AV strip is blown out instead of the whole array as well." Instantly, a wispy projection flashed in the darkness of the kid's cowl. A two-dimensional and simplified representation of five circles placed around a sixth showed up. All of the circles held a detailed function, but Fashion kept it simple by only showing power supply, memory, audio capture card, video transmitter, and onboard editing programs. Each circle was then split up into several dozen smaller circles and grids that most of the kids did not know or understand due to an incredible amount of abbreviations and personal notes.

A golden-haired boy with the nickname of Shambles, placed a hand on his hip and another on his chin as if he were about to say something profound. The kid drew a lot of attention due to his larger than average, athletic build, and striking good looks. Against expectations, the boy looked to the sky and raised both hands as he confusedly asked, "What does that mean?"

"It means Carlos was smart enough to make sure that he daisy-chained the audio and video that he captured so even if the drone's footage got corrupted, it could be streamed and stored to a different place. It's why we were able to even view the footage without the same corrosion reaching our brains or nervous center." Fashion audibly hissed, but everyone heard the meaning enter directly into their minds. Before any more questions could be asked, Alize picked up his slack and jumped ahead of the conversation.

"Thank you, Fashion. Lily, Sham, everyone else. Eights is not in any immediate danger since Ballast-type casters with his kind of profile are as rare as someone becoming an Archon. The fail-safes that he has, as Fashion put it, afford a certain measure of freedom when it comes to using his devices." Alize paused.

"That's good." Lily, hearing the news, squeezed Eight's arm and hand and smiled. Some in the group coasted on the sentiment and released a collective wave of worry.

"No. It's not." Alize maintained his deadpan expression as he could feel the tension re-engage.

"Our bosom buddy Ettiore is in possession of a rare profile. My good fellows, rare in this regard means easy to find. Those of you who have already started building tabs in the Veilseam should already know how easy it is to procure confidential information that highlights the details of a person's Profile." A girl in an odd attire fixed a pair of snow-white gloves to each of her sides and adopted a "sorry to tell you this bad news, buddy" type of demeanor. The sentiment did not get much of any traction as a girl with a toothy grin overpowered and embodied the more delinquent side of the group.

"Damn Eights. Your ass might actually end up being grass this time around. You ended up making yourself a loose thread. Haa, don't worry about it though, I will help out if anyone tries to burn you." A reptilian girl drew a line over her throat and contained an even wilder expression of misrepresented concern. Carlos, the blue-haired boy, clenched both hands to the point of cutting into his palms and bit his lip. Others in the group half-jokingly said their goodbyes or offered their support. Few, including Lily, expressed their concern in a normal enough manner.

"What are we going to do then? What can Eights do to make sure that those people cannot track him down?"

"Well, there is nothing that we can do." Alize blankly stated the only fact that he was sure about in reference to Eight's safety. He was about to elaborate, but someone unexpectedly shot a reverberating message that most heard since those with a high water content could feel their bodies tremble.

"Mr. Ettoire, might I suggest removing yourself from the problem before those people realize that they were being streamed and recorded by you specifically." Minute, still recovering from a near full-body blush, spoke.

"That's exactly what I was going to suggest. Thank you again, Minute, I appreciate it. Ahem, on that matter, Eights. You might have a network of Arcanum that separates your profile from leaking onto your remotely controlled devices. That's good, but in this instance, it creates a tangled web that those people could follow back to you if they even think that you have recorded your own drone footage and that you have built in a perception filter. To prevent those people from following any suspicions directly, if they haven't already been caught or egged into doing all of this, talk to the Surveyor outside once I leave." Alize let the group turn into a pack of howling dogs as they barked one question after the other. He instead hovered toward Eights and gripped the boy's shoulder.

"She is the Zephian woman with feathers for hair. You will most likely be put into the Guardian's witness protection for your own safety, but due to the circumstances, as long as you remain wherever they put you, you will not be put directly in the program. You will keep your memories. It will take some time, but in two years, four max, you will be able to contact everyone in the group in a legal capacity." Alize regarded the collective gasps and whispers but spoke through it with a blank expression. Unfortunately, someone's voice and movements drowned out the noise and shuffling before he could get back on track.

"Ark. I understand that our buddy Ettioire is in quite the precarious situation, but would it not simply ease his and our troubles if we set a trap and murdered the ingrates that dare harm our leader?" The resident orator, Bigs, entered the fray after a girl with a bob cut gave her the details needed to participate in the talk. The girl's perfectly coiffed hair glistened in a reflective sheen only possible with a freshly polished mirror.

"Big's. I just said that his ass is grass. It's over, girl. Ark isn't just telling him to go for no reason. Carlos is in trouble. You need to focus on common sense rather than elaborate phrasing." The reptilian girl with black pointed fingernails pulled the white-gloved girl back down onto a beanbag.

"Ranch, I simply do not—wait—that sounded nice. That last sentence." The girl with an over the top costume broke character and turned her shining head of hair toward her friend.

"Ha, you have to sprinkle one or two nice words into a talk, Bigs. Using more than necessary creates too many instances in which you might sound gauche. Erm, like you are uneducated or trying too hard." Ranch, a broad-shouldered and muscular girl for her age, shifted her neck and whispered a bit too loudly. Cartilaginous discs shifted to mostly cover empty ear holes on the sides of her scaled head. A massive mohawk unfurled behind her open leather coat and down the length of her back toward a coiled and barbed tail covered in even rougher scales than the fine and almost skin-like grains covering her hands and face.

"Oh. I see." Bigs exclaimed with a revelatory expression and pulled out a notepad and pen from the inside of her coat. Ranch's tail rose and coiled around the two of them protectively as her completely black eyes shifted toward Eights every other couple of seconds.

"I am so sorry, everyone. I could not stop the two of them from talking this time, as much as I wished to." A third girl, more petite than Ranch and Bigs but taller than Tumble, curtsied in her plaid dress to the rest of the group as though it were a commonplace occurrence. Her curly blonde hair bobbed for a little bit longer than physics would have liked. The petite girl also shared a mark of extraordinary person-ality as her still-bobbing hair settled around a featureless white mask with dark holes where the eyes would be.

"Don't worry about Bigs and Ranch Tomoe. Ahem, everyone! I am not exaggerating, like Ranch said. Eights is, after I leave here, most likely going to leave Rest and go to the capital with his state-appointed Warden after the Surveyor sees this footage." Alize waited for the talk to reach a lull and continued with his speech.

"I just want you all to be on the same page as me and the rest of us who have already drawn some conclusions. That said, let me give my final thoughts on Fell before we move onto Eights, the group, some other topic, or myself if there are still some lingering sentiments." Alize cleared his throat.

"I find that our boss, leader, and friend is most likely already in some level of witness protection under Jordaine's independence, with the second most likely outcome being that she has been put into Haven's Guardian program. The third, fourth, and fifth likely options are that she has either escaped Rest with both or one of her dads. The sixth likely option is, she is now on the run as an orphan and will meet us at the capital as per our doomsday failsafe. One of the least probable results of what we have seen is her having been chased down and murdered. If that has happened, then the Sentinels of our city might even get involved with whoever these insane individuals are." Alize sighed upon being met with silence the moment he said "murdered".

"As of right now, only Eights is in any immediate danger since the drone was under his control. If you guys don't feel safe, I suggest you talk to your parents if they are the ones taking care of you or your Warden and figure out if you want to or should stay in Rest. There is a possibility that anyone who has seen or been around her whilst she was running to school might also be in danger."

The group's silence was deafening as Alize glanced at Dusker. He fought the urge to scan the rest of the group since there was a possibility that the attack of Fell and the murder of her entire family just happened to be precursors of something else, or an event that might involve the entire group. The thought only became substantiated by a distant but piercing burn that struck his neck the moment he conceived of any unpleasant, unrecorded, and purely hypothetical events that might unfurl from this moment.

"Ahem. Right, so the group. Ahem. Effective the moment that I end up leaving this backyard, the new Captain of the group will be left up to popular vote while the new boss will be Tumble per my nomination and the results from the Proving Grounds." Alize waited for a response, a question, mindless chatter, anything that he could use to talk instead of sitting in silence with all of his friends' eyes on him.

"No one has anything to say? Really?"

"Boss, we sort of guessed that this is how it would end up and already decided who would be the next leader." Bigs didn't look up from her scribbling and pointed the tip of her pen toward Mark.

"Sorry." Mark smiled and was visibly preparing some lighthearted quip or gesture to lighten the mood for Alize but shut it all down upon seeing the boy nod his head.

"Don't worry, Mark. After Wynn, you are the most charismatic, so it makes sense." Alize waved away any misgivings and tension before something could spark.

"Now that I am not worried about you morons going too far. Ahem, now that we have things set up, do any of you have thoughts, concerns, questions, or ideas that you want to share before we move on?"

"If Fell has been attacked..." One kid in a half mask and wearing a deep cloak started speaking, but the gears spinning in his head just couldn't turn.

"Who did it? I mean. If the camera went dark every time that the assassins were on screen... No, if the screen went dark every time that they noticed the drone..."

Another kid picked up the ball but dropped it due to confusion. Worry broke out. Theories, thoughts, and questions that only led to more questions followed and filled the clearing. Alize listened as best he could and tried to piece something together without restating the obvious or outright assuming something, but a thread drew his attention more than any other.

"Why would, uh, just why and how though?"

"I mean, I'm sure Ark brought up a forced contract, but why did that lead to this?"

Another member of the group kicked the conversation across the circle with, "I don't know, but there is also the aberrant Spirit that was at the end. It hurt Ark. He said that it was chasing the wandering Fairy that attached itself to Fell. How does that factor into anything?"

"I know, right? The thing in the floorboards must've been that spirit. The issue is, how did none of the Aide stations nor the city Patrollers notice it entering Rest? It's just impossible for it to get by without being noticed by anyone."

"Maybe the person or group has an in with the city and also has a personal or inherited vendetta against Fell or the Fairy attached to her. Like maybe it broke a contract and ran away? It is even possible that her attackers might even be after the spirit that attacked Ark from the jump. It could have been associated with the Fae before, so those people made a logical leap." Someone ran with the topic and generated a flow that quickly picked up traction.

"It's possible that some illegal group made some moves, but how could they have known in the first place?"

"The only ones who knew any details about the Fae and Spirit were Fell and Ark." Someone glared at Alize. The conversation shifted toward a dangerous location, and those who understood the internal drama within the group before Fell expanded the circle of friends, frowned and glared at one of the five kids that remained quiet and more distant than the rest of the group. Her pointed statement and sputtering eyes left many in chaos.

"The Veilseam exists, moron. No one can do anything, anywhere, without their information being pulled and collected by the empire's watchdogs. A girl with an empty accord aspect suddenly gains a highly ranked Fae as her contract, one that should be on record somewhere due to its probable age. People looking would most definitely know that there is an Aberrant Spirit to be had if they make some holes in the city's security." A young man shook his head after receiving a moment to talk above the table.

"Hmph, I agreed, Noose. I'm betting everything Bigs owns that the VS has details on this shit-smelling situation." Ranch scoffed, finger gun pointed at the young man, and shut down the sentiment before it gained any traction by glaring at those that appeared to have rebuttals.

"Speaking of which, I made a run to the Drip with a few blank and lesser spirits not too long ago. Selling them fetched quite a sum at the mall down there. I can only imagine the payout if the rank is above zero and one." The kid with a half mask, shades, and a cloak crossed his arms and huffed.

"Jig, you are right. Even whilst remaining conservative..." Noose, a tall boy with pink and blue hair, fixed his glasses and projected a small graph with his magic.

"Jordaine, or at least Dane, would experience complete economic destabilization since the currently deflated Accords Repository would collapse in on itself. Conservation aside, if someone murdered Wynnifell, took the Fairy, and captured the aberrant spirit that are at least at the third rank, I estimate that it would only take a Decade or so before our country suffered so financially that it would be annexed or completely taken over by Haven. That is, if my math is correct."

Noose did not change his expression once as he said his piece and promptly inverted the holographic projection that he created with magic. Anyone who knew what they were looking at would have immediately noticed that he hopped on some kind of service that tracked the price, movement, and quality of all in-demand and rare goods going in and out of Heyden's Rest. Alize almost instantly noticed the symbol of a deformed, alien looking, bulldog as the website's logo. The Accord's repository specifically showed disastrous operation costs and a laughable profit margin. It was an Imperial-backed service that helped Accord-type casters forge and exchange contracts with other casters, natural phenomena that could be contained, divine entities, and manmade wonders.

The only contracts being made or exchanged on the market currently were imported from other countries and territories connected to Haven proper. Anything within the nation was held by independent and wealthy individuals that openly and legally, through loopholes, privately cycled the contracts through a mercantile entity called the Corridor. A free service paid for by taxpayer Quill and Links, by that measure, was turned into a private and somewhat commercialized and profitable business that made getting a good contract simply impossible for people who were not wealthy.

"Thank you for the statistics, Noose. We can be more sure that the worst hasn't happened if there aren't any waves in the Vielseam." Alize paused to clear his throat and thought to himself.

"That's right. Uncles Fredricke and Delemere got to her on time despite the intrusion, if Eight's video is to be believed. In regard to that, the person or people who were following her seemed rushed. The attacks were sloppy at best from the very start. Almost as if they were pressed for time before the Aide even showed up. No, not time. It was as if those people were under specific orders," Alize imagined the odd scene of the intruders being thrown around the inside of Fell's house. Then the reinforcements that drifted into Prochiente Village from gate 18. Those officers were headed towards the education district from the start, which begged the question, what was happening there since all the events of the day had occurred earlier in the afternoon. Jig, the boy with a half mask and a completely covered body, visibly frowned even with the completely elaborate getup that made him resemble a certain caped crusader.

"Yeah. And what about the spirit, Ark?"

"I was about to get to that, ahem." Alize cleared his throat and adjusted his seating. Tumble did not make it easy to move around as she outright pressed both of her palms against his chest and neck as though she were trying to feel for a pulse.

"I need to hurry this up. She is pressing against my [Shroud] a bit too hard." Alize ignored the sloshing of his liquified organs and prepared his piece, but someone in the crowd clicked his tongue and began to speak on his behalf.

"We all saw it on the footage, did we not? The being that disrupted the Terrarium and attacked the people that slaughtered Fell's family. It's just a matter of common addition to put things together, Jig, even you should be capable of that." Noose didn't raise his voice and simply adjusted the tie around his neck as he opened up another screen, sold some information and goods through the Vielseam, bought some others, and turned a profit in all but a few seconds.

"Excuse me. What is with that attitude, Noose? I was talking about its location now, not where it was when this shit went down. It's obvious that the Aberrant spirit tracked the Fae down and got busy messing with the dogs that attacked her." Jig raised his voice for only a moment as an even harsher voice bashed against his eardrums.

"You are squeaking, Jig." File stepped away from the discolored circle of dirt that he and his brother created and picked an empty pocket in the group circle to take over.

"Don't get into other people's conversations, man." Jig's voice, as File said, somehow transformed into that of a very young and high-octave boy as whatever illusion he was using was not good enough to fool everyone.

"I mean. I, am, I'm, ehem, I sound manly and mysterious, you brainless hothead." Jig stood up, puffed his chest, and purposely deepened his voice to regain the same stoic and manly machismo that he first spoke with.

"You still sound like a squeaker, you mouse-sounding, mummy-looking idiot. No offense to Fashion." File stepped forward once but Mark held his brother's chest and smiled the whole situation away.

"Alright fellas. A lot of mean things have been said. A lot of big-boy words have been exchanged. Tensions are high; I get it. We are all worried about Wynn. The lovely Miss Lily said it best earlier. My heart is out to you..." Mark hopped around the circle like an acrobat and maintained a genuine smile. His friendliness even overflowed as the lanky kid high-fived Bigs and Ranch, hugged Tomoe, fist-bumped Cable, and alternated handshakes and blown kisses to the rest of the group to lighten the atmosphere. Even Noose, the most mature member of the group, second only to Alize, received a single pat of acknowledgement on the back as Mark made his round. The only person he missed was Tumble, and that was because she leaned so close to Alize that they exchanged body heat. Well, her body heat sank into Alize's cool body.

"But we should all take a deep breath, step away from what we just saw, and think about it. Who has it out for Fell and would be willing to strike at any of us this hard using assassins or hitmen? Who made a similar move last year and hurt and disrespected our lovely Eden in a friendly Sim?" Mark chuckled as some members of the group started naming names with deadly expressions. A certain golden-haired boy clenched his jaw and fists so hard that he only relaxed after stepping next to the white haired girl.

"*The Drifters.*" A voice resonated in everyone's head like a gong as Fashion exhaled.

"That's right. Losers. Desperate, butthurt, sore losers that are scared of getting stomped during this year's final examinations for a third year in a row." Mark pointed to Fashion who hissed a response.

"Can anyone guess exactly who would go as far as to kill one of us outside of a Sim? Anyone? No? Well, I can't help but think that the mad lad or lady responsible for this strike has something to do with us getting the 37th into the top ten on Haven's leaderboards." Mark maintained a jovial bounce as he made another round. Those who saw it, saw it. Those who did not, did not, but Alize narrowed his vision and shook his head in a universal sign for "No, stop talking" the moment Mark locked eyes with him. Mark's smile, however, only widened.

"The way I see it, the person or people who attacked Fell didn't know about the Fae, nor did they target her because they knew about the Spirit chasing her." Mark scanned the group with the biggest smile he had ever made. His pupils, however, were completely dilated to the point where he had to narrow his eyes to barely open lines.

"Rumors Mark. We only have one piece of hard evidence in the footage that Eights acquired. Not only that, even what we saw is unreliable since Direct-type magic and pocket Terrariums were involved." Alize leaned forward and met the predatory gaze of a starved lion without so much as a shudder of breath. Tumble, who had removed herself from the group's main talks in favor of examining Alize, bit her own bottom lip to stop herself from gasping out loud. She had finally seen through Alize's [Shroud] and felt her heart skip a beat out of pure shock, fear, and sorrow.

"Rumors Ark? I can see it in your eyes, my guy. You figured out who attacked Fell and her family already, or you nearly did. How about sharing the name with the rest of us so we can take care of business?" Mark crouched as if he was a guard dog ready to pounce on whomever Alize directed him toward. Tumble, unable to ignore the underlying threat, clenched Alize's now soaked shirt and turned toward the prowling Mark.

"Go sit down before I make you, Marcelle. Ark is already doing his best to keep himself together. He doesn't have time to deal with your bullshit." Tumble gasped at her own words, turned to Alize and pressed her forehead against his chest. Mark opened his mouth to talk, but something about Tumble openly sobbing into Alize's chest tugged at his own heart. That's when he noticed it.

Alize's lips and eyelids twitched as a heavy sheen of perspiration gushed and sank back into his skin like water bubbling through sand at high tide. Mark pressed his forehead against Alize's then stepped back without saying a word as his hands balled into fists. The group fell silent at the unexpected shift in atmosphere.

"Why are you even here right now, moron? You should be in the hospital." Mark roared.

"I just came from seeing the doctor." Alize avoided Mark's pale and baffled face.

"What kind of fake-ass doctor is going to let you leave like that? Your body is fucked." Mark held his heated forehead and paced around.

"Yo, Eden. Take a look." Mark stepped back and paced next to his brother while muttering about how "insane" and "not right" Alize was.

"Anything for you, Mark. Hmph." An adorable girl with long braids of snow-white hair that reached her calves stood up with a pout and stomped away from the boy with golden hair and emerald eyes. The boy, without saying anything, scoffed, turned away from the girl, and grumbled as she cut their argument off halfway through.

"Ark." The girl skipped toward Alize and looked back toward the golden-haired boy with a smirk and a blush, but upon seeing him talking to someone else, she stomped her foot and crossed her arms.

"Idiot," the girl whispered and mindlessly cast a familiar green light tinted spell, [First Aid]. Her expression and blush, however, fell apart the moment that the spell washed over Alize.

"You even bigger idiot!"

In an instant, she placed both of her hands on his shoulders in a panic. The tips of her glowing white hair darkened to black at a visible rate. That said, Shamble rolled out of his spot in the circle and stood next to her with a sword of bone extending from his palm. The conversation he was having didn't matter compared to Eden.

"What's wrong?"

In as calm a voice as possible, Sham leaned in and pointed his blade toward everyone else in the group aside from Tumble.

"Just look. Really look." Eden moved to Alize's back and checked along his spine with an even worse blanche.

"Why did you not say anything, any of you?" Down to the very root of her hair, the mystical and almost pearlescent white dimmed to a charcoal black. Her anger directly pointed toward five members of the group, who either looked away, remained expressionless, or backed up with guilty expressions. The only one who met her gaze was a bald-headed girl with needlepoint spotlights piercing through blackout shades.

"Eden, chill. It's not even that bad. Boss just said that he came back from the doctors so..." Sham scoffed and touched Alize's shoulder after seeing quite a few members of the group get fidgety enough to stand up.

"Oh, my goddess." Sham pulled the blade back into his body and combed through his golden locks with wide eyes.

"Why do I have to touch you to see through the spell? I thought you couldn't cast spells, Ark." Shambles' words served as the straw, heavy enough to break the camel's back. Almost everyone stood up and crowded Alize to get a quick tap on their boss's shoulder or arm. Out of the 27 kids in the circle, only five who specialized in observational spells noticed that there was something wrong beyond the obvious hover chair, and only one of them managed to somewhat break through the illusions. Only now, after a few minutes had passed, did the duplicate body begin to reach its allotted operational limit.

"How are you, Aberrant, now? Is this permanent? Why haven't you said anything? What exactly is going on with you? You said that an old Spirit attacked you, so how did you end up like this yourself?" One question after the next fell onto Alize's ears and filled his mind as the kids left him no space to think with their constant chatter.

"I'll tell you about it later. Help me with everyone first, please?"

Alize placed his hand on Tumble's back and stared into her eyes with a pleading look. The tension and awkward emotions that rose between the two came to a halt as she wiped her tears away and pushed at the air. Everyone aside from Eden and Sham was impacted by an unavoidable force and practically found their bodies crashing back into the spot that they previously occupied.

"Everyone calm down." Tumble frowned and held Alize's trembling hand without saying another word.

"Ahem. I know that this is a bit of a shock to everyone, but I am now, temporarily, Aberrant. In summary, there was a relic that I wanted to steal, but since the doctor I went to was smart enough to lock it within a Terr, I was unable to take it with me. Since I didn't want to permanently lose any of my magic by casting an [Inventory] spell outside of my profile, I used my body as a container to collect one of the relic's resources. As for what that means for my Affix." Alize grit his teeth as the excited and anxious expressions of his friends slowly turned to fear and contemplation.

"I am sure that all of you can guess why Wynn has been caught up in a series of unfortunate events." Alize emphasized the word Events, which silenced the group.

"You aren't responsible for what happened to Fell and her family Ark." Tumble was the first to speak but the sentiment was not shared as File shot to his feet and rushed at Ark. Mark was the first to tackle him to the ground, Jig was the second.

"You bastard. Fell, Eights, fuck that. We are all in danger. You cursed, asshole. Why did you come here? You should have let us just believe that you died before. Before! Fuck, Marcille, get off of me, you piece of..."

Mark held File's mouth closed, but the damage had already been done as the five members who could see through Alize's spell from the beginning immediately ran away from the backyard. Mark turned toward the fleeing members of the group and put a hand out to distort space. "Wait!"

All five of those kids were pulled back to their original seated location, but that one moment of inattention was more than enough time for File to snap a finger. Jig blinked and found himself falling from the sky, and Mark found himself staring up at a Jig-shaped comet. File attempted to stand up and point a finger at Ark, but Eden just so happened to move and block Alize with her body. Tumble was not slow either as her swatting arm turned into an outstretched claw, one aimed directly at the one person who was ballsy enough to attack Alize. One universal law of being cursed or blessed by Gnoll was the sweet release of death. Any and all effects would immediately end as the curse and/or blessing locked onto its next afflicted host. If Alize died, the Affix would go with him, and the nonsense that Fell was involved with would taper out. Any events planned for the rest of the group would also never be realized or stopped in their development phase.

"Tch." File's head twitched as a distorted hand attempted to grab the crook of his neck. In a split second, the area around him warped as he appeared on the other side of Alize's chair. He closed one eye and pointed a finger gun at Alize's head; his instincts kicked in not even a half second later as both of his hands went up. Sham, eyes bloodshot, stood in front of him with a bone blade pointed at his throat. Fashion, unexpectedly, crouched beside him, decked to the nines in metallic armor similar to an exoskeleton of bones and muscles with several bandoliers as his rags and cloak fluttered open. The muzzles of two pistols were firmly lodged between File's ribs.

Some members of the group stood at attention; others sighed and remained seated. Bigs, as per normal, commentated and gave a play-by-play while Ranch kicked back in the out-of-place beanbag chair. The five members who tried to run away stopped attempting to flee due to a wispy ring of rippling space that Mark wrapped around his own forearms and around their own waists like lassos.

"I understand your anger, Fletcher. I am sorry that I did this. I am sorry. What happened to Fell is the last thing that I wanted to happen." Alize wiped his own tears before they could fall and bowed his head to everyone in the group.

"That said, I am trying to take responsibility for the event that my Affix generated before it spreads. If you have a problem with that, leave. Right now, I am the only acting leader of this club. After I leave, you are all free to continue meeting or come after me to put an end to any events that might involve or revolve around you." Alize raised his head and waited for someone to say something, but no one did. Even the five individuals who wanted to leave, hesitantly sat back down. Bear, the newest addition to the group, was the only one left confused as a weirdly thick tension filled the atmosphere.

"Excuse me. I'm a little lost." Bear didn't let his long legs move away from his chest, but he did scratch and tilt his head. His attention shot toward Mark and then the hard faces of the other members.

Mark, the smiling face of reason, noticed that no one wanted to speak, Alize included, and took up the mantle of bringing the newest member up to speed. "What are you confused about, Bear?"

"Why do you think that the attack of Fell was some personal hit and not some Accord Contract and money thing? Noose is always right when it comes to money problems, and what Affix does Ark have that all of this might all be his fault?"

File, unexpectedly, was the one to break the news as he slapped the sword at his throat and walked away from the unfired guns at his sides.

"Dumbass. Answer this first. Do you think that we have been flattening only you and your group of morons at the school in the proving grounds?"

"Yeah? No!. I mean, what?"

"Fucken idiot." File sneered, snorted, and completely separated himself from the group as he shimmered. His footsteps resounded from one of the nearby treehouses not even a full second later as he hopped onto a windowsill and calmed himself down.

"Ha, brother Bear, our club is a legitimate but unofficial representative of the best youths in all of Jordaine." Bigs switched off her commentator voice, but the amusement she gained from seeing the baffled look on the kid's face was enough to make her radio laugh come out.

"In other words, Ark is a friend whore who only wants to be involved with the smartest, strongest, and most talented people in his age group because he needs to outpace his curse and all of us to survive." Ranch chortled and was about to elaborate when a pair of hands covered her mouth. Tomoe shook her head and let go only after speaking directly to Ranch.

"Basically, Bear, Ark loves going around showing dumbasses like you and delinquents like us that he is the best. We have kept everything strictly within the Sims since before you started causing problems at the school. We have all been playing 'Proving Grounds' and made a few bets regarding, haaaa." Ranch, in a bored and slightly upset voice, crossed her arms and trailed off with a sigh.

"Bigs, I don't know how you do it. Explaining things is so blah." Ranch flipped in the beanbag and looked up at Tomoe with her forked tongue hanging out as if she had suddenly died.

"I got it." Bigs stood up, fixed her bowtie once again and opened her mouth to speak, but a pair of hands covered her mouth.

"I do not have it." She followed Ranch and lay upside down on the beanbag. With a pout, she glared at Tomoe, who pulled her slightly too long arms back into place.

"Idiots. Bear. Ark is cursed with an Affix. He can, but should not, cast spells or utilize his magic in any manner. The moment he does, problems will start affecting the people around him. In the Sims, it's fun and a bit crazy, but in reality, it's—Hmm. Noose, what was the word you used?"

Jigsaw, in his most manliest voice, spoke out before anyone else, which only served as a vocal training challenge to the group's resident newscaster and mimic. Bigs rolled out of the beanbag, brushed her suit, and struck a pose.

"He said 'untenable'. But you said it right and to the point, Jig. Berry the Bear, the newest member of our fantastical, extremely tyrannical, conclave of freaks and ghouls, I hmm. Does that work? It does? Okay, no? It doesn't? Okay." The girl paused in her speech and took in the blank stares and whispers. After a few seconds, she nodded, sat back down and wrote in a little notebook.

"I thought it was lovely. I wanted to laugh, but, eh..." Ranch patted her friend on the back and picked up the conversation.

"Bear, basically, everyone here is, meh..." Ranch trailed off again, bored with her own explanation. Thankfully, Tomoe, the most level-headed of the three, shared the final piece of information directly.

"The best students in both the schools and Academic Facilities in Dane have taken to using the Sim Proving Grounds due to our constant involvement with that game and the scenarios that Ark has provided to simulate his curse. Our private games have gained enough popularity and traction to be noticed by the Board of Ed. This year, according to talks with the whole group beyond the 37th, the Superintendents and Dane's Guardians are going to use the Proving Ground Sim as Jordaine's main ranking, grade, and level testing tool despite it initially being a Haven Sim sandbox." Tomoe's soft and regal voice resonated through the heads of everyone present.

"So..." Bear lowered his legs and adopted a more relaxed seated lotus position as his eyes practically crossed with the amount of information overload.

"Dear Goddess. Listen, Bear. The game that we have been stomping you in is a training sim Ark showed us because it simulates his curse. It is now going to decide your grade. The kids in our group, which extends beyond the 37th, have gotten to and have maintained most of the top one hundred positions in Haven." Noose shook his head and got down to business.

"So, wait. If there are more people in the group, where are they? Why are they not here?" Bear tapped his unhinged jaw and stared off in the distance, hearing that he was practically a small fish unaware of the ocean just beyond his pond.

"We, the group members of the 37th, are mostly founding members and the very best among even the rest of the group. We usually settle disputes between the others who are less invested in making sure that we all stay connected and out of serious trouble. As for why everyone else is not here, well, the larger group has been getting unruly since Ark hasn't been around for a few months. In particular, districts 1, 9, 36, and 43 have become insufferable as of late." Noose blinked and removed his spells as he reviewed some of the graphs in front of him.

"Okay, I got that..." Ranch laughed at Bear's expression and yelled out from across the circle, "You are really struggling to comprehend what it is we do and the role Ark plays, huh?"

"No, I understand." Bear lowered his legs and pouted.

"No, you don't," Ranch teased.

"Yes, I do," Bear roared so loud that the ground around him shook.

"Oh? I guess you do." Ranch touched her lip and nodded, but a crooked smile exposed her pearly white shark teeth as she thought of something to say. Thankfully, Tomoe stopped her from becoming a bully. Sadly, due to the freshness of Bear's introduction and his lack of understanding of how much trouble the group really gets up to, he asked a question that earned more laughs and derision than genuine answers.

"Then, are the kids that you guys have beef with responsible for going after Fell? The other members of the group, I mean?"

"'No shot, my man.'; 'Doubt it'; 'Those weak-ass punks?'; 'Haa. No.'; 'I don't think they have the balls.'; 'Our local adversaries and contenders are not equipped to, oh, yeah. What everyone else said.'" The tense atmosphere loosened up as everyone either laughed, rolled their eyes, or outright called Bear stupid.

"Come on. I just joined you guys today." Bear teared up again and buried his face in his knees. Almost immediately, everyone turned to

Mark, who scolded the annoyed-looking File like he was his father rather than a twin.

"I'll state it outright. The attack on our Boss Fell might have been something related to Ark's Affix." Noose set up a projection that displayed everything that he believed supported his words.

"But only marginally—" Noose paused mid-sentence and pulled his tie to the point of nearly choking himself. In a flash, he swapped his personal screen back to a display that contained a small bulldog that revealed its canines in a bloodcurdling sneer.

"Based on what I just purchased, we can look at the one bastard who has issues with all of us for kicking him out of the inner circle." Noose said nothing as he closed the screen and flicked three motes of condensed magic toward Alize, Mark, and Tumble.

"Money always gives the clearest picture about who paid who to get what done." Noose loosened his tie and shut down all of his public displays. The group that understood what information was just displayed whispered amongst themselves, but they all pretty much waited until someone among the leadership of the group broke the silence. Mark suddenly laughed. Something that was so infectious turned into a shrill banshee's call as he passed the mote of light to File.

"I was right. Haa, of course I was right." His laugh trailed off, however, and turned into a whining hum as he shifted in his position. Tumble, still tearing up, scoffed several times in a row but said nothing as she passed the mote of light onto Tomoe. File spit on the ground from up in the treehouse, grumbled, then went silent and still. Without any notice, he appeared next to his brother and hugged him without warning. After getting a read, he passed his mote of information to Jig.

"Disgusting File" Eden hopped away from the spitball that almost fell on her as was about to say something else, but she noticed that

File moved and flipped her off. She leaned close to Shambles, who had never left her side, and asked, "What's wrong with him?"

3.3 Boss Ark

"I don't know. Noose shared something and everyone kinda went quiet. Bear is, well, he just looks lost. Hmm, do what I do and snoop." Shambles scratched his head, shrugged, and leaned over to what Alize was reading. He didn't understand anything that was written in some kind of encoded script.

"Are you involved in this?"

Eden whispered in a harsh tone as she read something that held Sham's codename several times over.

"No? I don't even know what I'm looking at." The boy scoffed, but his dismissive tone only made Eden upset. An argument unfolded, one that Alize managed to push to the corner of his attention.

"*Handy Havers Comfortable constructions CO, Havam's Courtious Cleaner's, Quick-hand no ham Repairs, Come-over-to Sham's Bargain Bin, Havisham & Havarshem's LLP, Havelock's Fluke- chips and sham shack, the list goes on. Ripley, Hur'Tean, Yang, etcetera. In all of these businesses, there is a Dean. Always in some minor managerial, supervi-sory, or private contracting position.*" Alize frowned as he remembered an apparently well-connected and diverse businessman in a yellow and green suit.

"The most important business under some alias is Aave-Sham's Secure Protections Agency, ASPA." Alize quickly read up on what Noose purchased from an online information brokerage site partnered with the Empire's Veilseam.

"A dignitary from Jore's capital city recently booked the entire ASP Agency to block off and secure one of Jore's elevators and towers over and through the Drip." Alize instantly pinpointed what Noose wanted to share by following the bullet points on a graph to the same highlighted bit of information that told an entire story.

"Okay everyone. Here is what Noose found." Alize pulled snippets that told a story and revealed some semblance of the mystery beneath the insanity of a generated event.

"Some private security fellows who moonlight as hitmen in the Vielseam's Void Market recently accepted a private request. I can only assume that they believed the bounty was going to be easy since the request was only to maim, disfigure, and cripple a little girl physically and magically."

The faces of exactly ten men and women showed up at the top of the magical bulletin that Alize merely grabbed and edited via Noose's casting. Below their faces were dossiers with names, ages, family and relationship status, aliases or codenames, their job, and even their mystical profiles showing exactly what kind of magic they had access to and the spells they could cast. One of the hitmen possessed the ability to cast [Shroud] aspect spells but held an allotment of aspects that made it viable to share the illusion and directly eat away at anyone who saw it.

"Some of you may have already noticed something weird about the name of the requester." Alize pointed to a name that said, "The one above all and with no equal, Royal Arch."

"I am not saying that this person is the Prince that we all know, but I believe that there is a high likelihood considering who the leader of this team is." He pointed to a woman with short, compact braids and deep scars along the bridge of her nose and cheek. Her file sported the last name of Princeptis.

"A true assassin in that her entire profile was full of movement, and utility aspects, with a noticeable focus on aura root attack." Alize paid attention to the woman's profile. Noose, apparently, also drew a connection to someone that some members of the group knew and supplied another dossier with the picture of a haughty but adorable boy with features that Alize found unsettling due to the normal, almost non-magical appearance.

"Archibald Quimbly Rugear Le Princeptis." Alize placed the face of the young boy right under the hit woman.

"I haven't seen that nasty kid in a while, so it makes sense that he looks a bit older. Hmm, he is older, but why does he look familiar?" Alize couldn't quite place the gut-wrenching feeling that stirred his thoughts into motion.

"Hmm." Putting aside some baseless and unamiable feeling, he gripped Tumble's hand and scanned the group with more than a small amount of understanding.

"The person whom we all used to call Prince might be responsible for this attack on Fell. Despite the high likelihood, we cannot just put all of the blame on someone out of suspicion. It would get our group dismantled by the Guardians in less than a day if we crossed any legal lines." Alize firmly shut the pursuit of this information down, at least until Noose shot him with another piece of information that was just gathered in the Vielseam.

"Forget what I just said. The ASP agency has just posted a new roster of contracted employees, which seems to be missing a handful of familiar faces." Alize sighed inwardly as all of the dossiers that Noose had just collected and shared filled out all the blank spaces in the new company roster. The executor of the firing order happened to be a man in middle management who expressly handled the brokerage of externally rendered services. Basically, missions that necessitated employees of the ASPA leaving Jore.

"Dean was involved with these people in some capacity. Ha. How complicated do things need to be for my life to play out how you want it to? Damned curse." Alize touched his now burning neck.

"Ahem. According to this new information, there are now bounties on each of their heads. The poster for this new hit is the head of the Princeptis family himself, so take it all as you will and be careful if you choose to do something dangerous like seeking revenge." Alize narrowed his eyes and quickly snapped at Eights.

"That said, we should assume that they're..." Alize used air quotes for this next bit.

"...rogue agents of ASP." He then pointed to the face of Archibald De Princeptis and a new image of a pompous-looking old man that bore no resemblance to his son in any capacity.

"And these people figured out that they were caught red-handed and are currently on the hunt for whoever was using the drone to cut off loose ends." Alize's gaze did not leave Eight's once.

"Ah, my Goddess. Give me strength. Ark. No. boss, we got it. Don't worry about anything from here on out, okay?" Mark, having recovered from his downward spiral, smacked both of his own cheeks, smiled, and drew everyone's attention with a hop and a wave. Everyone in the group aside from Bear noticed Alize's pause not too long ago, a full five seconds of dead air and a vacancy within his eyes that made him resemble a dead fish. They were well aware that the Ark in front of them was nothing more than a clone, and they were all accustomed to seeing him press against the established time limits set for fully immersive clones.

"We are going to handle these people, right everyone?"

Mark's momentum from before the big reveal returned in the span of a single question as it resonated in the hearts of most members.

"Great. Almost everyone knows the deal then. Once Boss Ark leaves, split into your teams and take out the trash. Bear..." Mark's sudden shift in tone and needlepoint focus took the Bear by surprise as he buffed up with a flex.

"Since you your questions have been on the nose and considering that you have no idea what most of us have been up to or what we are talking about." Mark knelt down in front of the gargantuan boy and ruffled the kids head even if it looked like a child was consoling a grown man.

"You can come with me and the rest of the first group to head over to Jore and talk with Prince. And good job on being a productive member of the group on your first day." Mark put up a thumb and waited for a fist bump.

"Thank you." Bear wiped his watery eyes and got caught in Mark's infectious and genuine smile.

"No problem, man." Mark nodded, clasped Bear's shoulder, and walked up to Ark without a smile. Before he even said anything, Ark sighed and put up a hand.

"Before you ask me what I think you are going to, I don't know Mark. I do not know if Prince has anything to do with the mercenaries or the attack. I only ever make educated guesses and pray to her majesty that things work out or are as I envisioned. That said, the information and coincidences do lineup, so I will not say that the Prince is entirely clean of what has happened to Fell." Alize rubbed his temples and made a proclamation.

"If you want to, however, wait until I leave and start looking into what happened yourself. Or work with everyone else to get a better picture. I am done with you all either way." Alize ignored the talk and questions as he maintained eye contact with Mark.

"I am leaving today. This group, Rest, probably even Jordaine in its entirety in the next few months if this chain of events doesn't pan out how I want it to." The reference to an event, especially in the context of Alize, perked up the group's collective ears and shut the extraneous noise off.

"You and Tumble will be the next leader and boss respectively, so I hope that you two will have good enough foresight to think about what it means to have everyone look into the information that has been gathered and shared here today." Alize, older than his years, pressed forward on his chair and clasped Mark's shoulder with one hand as he squeezed Tumble's waist with the other. Tumble bit her lip once more and leaned even closer into Alize's chest in a similar grip that a baby might hold on to their favorite stuffed animal. Mark simply nodded and forced a smile.

"Right then. I'm going to head out now, then, everyone. You all can see through my [Shroud] which means that I only have around 30 minutes left to get back home." Alize chuckled as the group's palpable silence resonated with a magically transmitted conversation that he was not privy to. Whatever they were deciding on was too difficult to parse and infer from their faces and body language, so Alize continued on since time was now of the essence.

"Eights, walk and talk with me." Without looking back, he hovered out of the encirclement of kids. Before he could exit the clearing with Eights hot on his heels and the doll-sized Tumble who crawled onto his chest and into the crook of his neck, a boy with a wide hat and quill between his teeth blocked the path. A single tear rolled down his eye as he placed both hands on the holsters on either side of his waist.

"Cable, is there something that you want, either to say or do before I leave?" Alize paused his forward hover as he stroked Tumble's hair. Her shoulders constantly moved as the sound of muffled hiccups only reached his own ears.

"Boss! I, " the dull hum of magic and the movement of lips that indicated the group's silent debates, came to an abrupt end as Cable took off his hat.

"Ark." One word was enough. Nearly everyone in the group shed some varying levels of tears. Alize shuddered, but his eyes remained locked onto the stone staircase that led out of the backyard

"Y'ain't lookin' back, and no one can stop ya. I know it. They know it. As a partin' gift, let me share somethin' 'bout Fell's strike." Cable didn't look to the side and remained faced toward the group. He controlled the tremors and the tears that fell from his eyes.

. "I dunno if what I heard is accr'ate but I ain't one fer readin' into what folks say." Cable cleared his throat several times to get rid of the sudden cold afflicting his body.

"Shoot, Cabe." Alize didn't point out the emotion and leaned forward with intense focus to ensure that the boy's shuddering was fully out of his periphery..

"Well, it goes like this. A while back, my old man rode in from Kykerie's Eastern Gate City to look fer a pesky brood' o monsters settlin' in the mountains. While he was wranglin' the ma critter in, the lawmen told him to sniff out any clues 'bout a lost soul from a nearby town. My pa, as good as he is at trackin', didn't find a lick of a trail. I didn't think much of it, but a few days back, he looked all bothered 'bout bein' asked to hunt down a missing shipment. I pried a bit, but all he muttered was that what went missing only had two kinds of folks lookin' for it." Cable cleared his throat one last time, placed his hat back on his head.

"Now, I ain't learn much from what my pa said, but I sure did get a name. Now that I heard it enough times, I now know that the ASPA was in charge of wranglin' the shipment from Kykeries west gate and haul'n it to the east where my pa was. Somewhere along the way, it vanished." Cable waited for Alize's response or input.

"Cable. You may not know this, but that was the last thing that I needed to hear to confirm the depth of this event." Alize snapped all of the puzzle pieces together and got a picture that rapidly began to resemble a nightmare he once had.

"Bodies. Dead or not, Dean or the companies under him are gathering, selling, and moving bodies for the quack doctor. The severity of the issue changes based on the status of those bodies. Corpses would be fine without a permit as long as they are not sourced through means of murder or kidnapping, living people are also fine if there are volunteer release papers submitted to the proper Commerce, Workers, and Scholar guild or unions that handle research permits. The issue is Cable just said that someone went missing. My best guess is that the 'person' is actually a group of people and rather important ones at that since a cowboy like Cable's dad was asked to look into it. Not only that, Aides are not seen as lawmen in Cable's eyes, so he must've been directly talking about someone with the military rank of a Sentinel or maybe even a proper Guardian."

Without verbalizing his personal thoughts or addressing the massive upheaval that occurred in his understanding of the issues that his curse presented, Alize opened his eyes and said, "Thank you, Cable. It may not seem like much, but what you just told me has made a few personal issues clearer. I will be heading out now. Please take care of yourself and everyone else as best you can."

Alize tipped an invisible hat and received the same respectful gesture in kind, even if he didn't see the boy return it. Just as he and Eights passed by the first obstacle, two of the five kids that noticed his Aberrant state from the very start of the grouping barred the path.

"Boss." One of the kids bowed deeply while the other held up a hand that printed, "I'm sorry, Boss" in neon colored magic.

"It's not a problem, you idiots. If I were in your shoes, I would not have left anything to chance and secretly called an Aide out of consideration for the worst. Thank you, though, for not saying anything. I appreciate and understand the amount of trust that all of you placed in me." Alize squeezed the two of the kids on their shoulders and smiled as he passed by. Yet another blockage stopped him from traversing the path that led to the stairs out of the backyard.

"Ark. All things considered, the moment that you leave this group, I will be hunting you down with the aim of putting an end to your Affix." File was allowed to stand in Alize's way even if it wasn't close enough to close the distance or clear enough to get a shot with all of the people surrounding him.

"File, honestly, only Wynn is for sure tied up with my curse. You and the rest are bystanders for now with the only exceptions being Eights, Noose, and maybe the Prince if he is behind the whole attack." Alize combed through his hair and nodded.

"But if you want to come after me and serve the function of an antagonist, then go ahead. If the roles were reversed, I would plot, scheme, and exhaust every option necessary to remove or even murder any negatively or even ambiguously Affixed individual that could influence my existence by mere proximity and familiarity." Alize waved to the rest of the group.

"That said, I will be leaving Jordaine in a few months if not a year or two due to some personal matters regardless of how all of you handle yourselves so If I find a way to perfectly telegraph my events and generate stuff that is purely beneficial, I will let as many of you as I can, know." Alize briefly broached the topic with his parents the moment that he figured out that his dreams and underlying thoughts were tied to the Affix's bag of tricks. Without meaning to, he sank a good portion of his mental processes toward examining his own life and all of the uncontrollable factors that culminated in odd, dangerous, or outright unfortunate encounters.

As he looked back on his own past and the actions of his parents, he immediately noticed that almost everything they owned outside of what Orsche and Verza planned to run away with, was granted or taken away by his Affix in some manner or another. The divine ranked terrarium that the Kaveri family and Jarold lived in, the duplicator that allowed Alize to leave the pocket sized world for a brief period of time, even some of the relics and artifacts that Orsche possessed within his study were impeccable and completely random finds. Alize even remembered all of the times that his family entered an antique shop and found a piece of junk that ended up being something important or just useful enough that Orsche thought it was best to purchase. The parts for the hover chair that he was currently using happened to be the product of said junk collection. Gnoll's Urn, the hand-size pot with the royal blue seal and golden runes, happened to be a purchase of the Affix's influence category since Alize didn't know the inherent reason why he felt the urge to collect it.

As for the punishments, Alize clearly remembered the multiple times that his family was forced to pack up and leave an entire country due to the appearance of Surveyors that asked a few too many pointed questions or Intendants that just happened to be in an area while off duty. Alize didn't understand or recognize any of the threats back then, nor did he know what his parents were running from until they arrived in Jordaine. Putting the way in which his Affix balanced being a curse and a blessing aside, Alize noticed that no one else blocked his path.

He floated up the stairs and put Tumble down after she begrudgingly let go. Lifting her as if she weighed nothing. Alize pressed his forehead to hers and whispered, "Thank you."

"*T. I would not have survived coming into the city and meeting everyone in a duplicant if it weren't for the attention and care that you have given me. Thank you.*" Alize forced an even expression even as his eyes reddened.

"*Outside of the Sims, I really have nothing other than my thoughts to offer, so thank you for always thinking of me.*"

"*Why does it sound like you won't ever see us again? You just said that you will reach out when you get a handle on your Affix. You have to.*" Tumble tried to contain her tears, but the dam had burst long before Alize decided to set off.

"*That was for everyone else. Theo, I am, most likely never going to see any of you ever again. It won't be because of anything bad, mind you. Well, eh, I am just preparing myself and all of you since I might never leave the hell awaiting me once I leave Rest.*" Alize imagined what his parents might be conversing about in their free time. Surely, it revolved around his new training regime, altered daily schedule, and the new level of simulated cruelty that would await him inside of the homestead's training room.

"*Your magic—you have to get real-world practice now, don't you?*"

"I do. If I don't contact anyone in the next couple of months, assume that I have either died or been locked up by my parents. I will work like there is no tomorrow to regain my visitation privileges, *but with my magic now being in the mix, I am unsure of where the bar is."* Alize squeezed Tumble's hand and faked a smile.

"I am sorry," he said, but the remainder of his speech was cut off by a pair of small lips landing on his cheek..

"You are a horrible person, Ark. A bad guy." Theodora pulled away, wiped her mouth and the tears streaming down her face, and hardened her expression.

"You never showed up to any of our stuff unless you needed something, you never spoke to any of us outside of group meetings and games, you never took the time to reach out to anyone other than Fell and you let me." Tumble clutched the hem of her dress.

"You always knew that we would never be together in the way that I would want. In any way that any of us wanted. I hate that you always lie to all of us. I hate that you think that you will never see us again. You didn't say it, but I get it." Tumble huffed and collected her emotions as she stared hard and long.

"Ha, this girl just stole my first kiss." Alize could think of nothing else as he touched his blushing cheek.

"I hate it." Tumble hopped onto Alize's chair and looked down on him as she lifted his chin.

"I don't know what your parents are gonna have you do, but I'm pretty sure that the Sims that you have shared with us were part of their training. So here is what you are going to do. Beat everything that they make or find for you and come see us after you can solo everyone in the group IRL. If I am not with someone then, I might give you a chance to be my boyfriend. How does that sound?"

Alize, despite being stunned, registered the tail end of Tumble's speech and smiled for a hot second before he banged his forehead against hers in a playful manner.

"The first thing that I will say when I see you is..." Alize picked Tumble up and placed her on a rock beside his chair. Without looking back, he pushed forward. Eights, jaw dropped, shifted his gaze between the blushing Tumble and the smiley Alize and quickly followed.

"Say something, you idiot! Don't just go around headbutting people and blowing air into their ears, you freak." Tumble spoke in Alize's mind as steam flushed around her head.

"I am a freak, so be on the lookout for me after a few months to a year. If I can complete whatever hellish torment, my parents are concocting, I will be asking you to be my girlfriend the moment I see you." Alize waved and waited for Eights to open the first, non-alarmed gate. The entire group faded out of sight. The moment they "lost" eye contact with their boss, the real conversation started. At least, that's what they wanted him to think. Noose shot out motes of light to everyone besides Alize and Eights and held a private mental conversation on top of their arguments about nonsense plans that may or may not be legal. Without looking back or using a spell to confirm, Alize could feel the eyes of all of his friends shift onto his back even as the sound of their talks returned to the distant backyard clearing. Eights, in silence, pushed him toward the second gate.

Just as he crouched in front of the silver lock, Eights gave voice to the turmoil in his heart.

"Do I actually leave Rest with my Warden and go to the capital? Should I?"

Alize considered the meaning of the question for a moment and sighed.

"That is up to you and what you do with the footage. The way I see it, you have three options, and only one allows you to leave the group along with all danger and any possibility of my Affix affecting your life." Alize understood that he was not just talking to Eights. He could feel everyone standing behind him in complete silence even as their voices came from the backyard.

"Go into witness protection. It will take time, but the Aide officers and custodians will do their jobs and clean up the problem. The whole system works to make sure that kids in our positions can always return to a mostly normal life. The other two options are joining the program of your own will and hoping that you get sent to the same place as Wynn. That comes with a few caveats of course, one being that she is in the program and not witness protection. Then there is just the simple probability that you are even blessed enough to remember her or anyone else in the group after you go through the process. That option results in the same outcome as the next since you could get roped into her event due to your greater familiarity instead of a whole new event generated because of your connection to me." Alize paused to make sure that Eights was following along.

"The last option, as I stated previously, is dealing with the people who are most likely hunting you. You could share the footage with the Intendant and Surveyor outside, but you also could just handle everything with the group and then use that as a field report since all of us are part of the Board of Ed's fast track."

Alize was confident that Eights and everyone else in the group would be capable of outsmarting and murdering the assassins if they worked together. The Sims that he had access to due to his parents were the very same Sims that he customized for his group as their Boss. His training, and by proxy, theirs, were not the the run-of-the-mill school or facility standard. They were personally tailored Sims designed and used by scholars and soldiers at the caliber of his parents who were, in their own right, nearly Divine ranked. He shared this training material with his friends and threw in his own twists in the hope that they would eventually become good enough to help him overcome issues that he was not competent or confident in being able to handle down the road. It was a failsafe, one that became supremely important now due to the change in his cure's modus operandi.

"Ha. Eights, just like anyone else in the group, has committed several atrocities inside of the tailored Sims designed to bring the worst out of someone's character. They are all capable of murder and treachery, the only issue is, are any of them capable or willing to take someone's life outside of a realistic game." Sims, especially the top most ranked ones like the Proving or Battlegrounds, were virtually indistinguishable from the reality. That said, even with an infinitesimally small difference, there was still a missing component that a Sim, even at the pinnacle of the divine rank, would never be able to replicate. That train of thought led him to the image of the kid called Prince.

'That nasty ass kid. Thankfully, I cut him off from using my Sims the moment Wynn told me what he was up to on the server." Alize frowned as he examined Eight's growing agitation.

"The prince, out of a lack of wanting to understand him, took the roleplaying aspect of the Sims to a very dark place that reminds me of the hero and the man masquerading as Dr. Nayame." Alize shook his head as he realized why his old friend seemed uncannily familiar despite not seeing him in years.

"I guess being a sleaze is just in some people's nature." Alize hovered out of the way of the gate to make room for Eights.

"What were we talking about? I seem to have lost my train of thought." Alize eased the tension as he heard the sound of several hands smacking their own foreheads.

"My options? You were explaining the last one." Eights got to work on the gate's defenses.

"Right. Your third option is to deal with the assassins, be it through murder, an anonymous tip to the officers across the street, or turning yourself in to be protected." Alize picked at his fingernails and held a deep breath.

"Personally, I would go through the Veilseam and collect their new bounties if I had the power to do so. The next thing that I would have done is figure out if the Prince really is the person behind the hit on Wynn or if this was some kind of higher order chess move from a third party that knew about our group's internal conflicts and has beef with us and him. He is most definitely capable of organizing and funding this kind of thing, don't get me wrong, but most of us have played Sims with him when he was still, well, less of a degenerate. That said, I find it odd that his name would be attached to any of this considering how much he desires to be me. I'm thinking that if you pursue this path, look into the Drip and the Aides in the area. Someone who maybe knows Jig and what you all are usually up to." Alize could practically hear Bigs scribbling things in her notepad as Eights slowed the unlocking process.

"Specifically, as Noose said, follow the money. The corridor is at the bottom of the Drip and since we are a major trading city, everything in Rest is run by the elite down there so Wynn might have actually been attacked by someone who needs a good Accord and is wealthy enough to block out any info of her Fae and the Spirit. That said, such a play would have to be handled through corrupt but legal channels, so that's something. It's also just possible that a whole bunch of random events just coincided. That is more my Affix's speed, I'm finding." Alize raised two fingers and then lifted a third.

"You guys, ahem, you, Eights. Ahem, I would also check the fields between the schoolyard and Dusker's facility. Her duffel bag, despite being of a similar make, was swapped out somewhere along the way before it got taken by those people. I'm sure you didn't notice, but the gash along the base of the duffel had a different stitching style." Alize smiled as the gate chimed open.

"Oh right, my personal and genuine opinion of the question that you posed is a conditional yes. Do whatever you can to go to the capital. I can tell you without a shadow of a doubt that Wynn will be there in around five years attending the Imperial Academy." He said nothing else and left Bear's family home through the same alleyway gate that he had entered from.

3.4 Return to the Trusty Market

"I'm ready to go now." Alize hovered himself toward his parents and mostly ignored how they silently motioned toward one another as if they were in the midst of an insanely physical arm-waving competition.

"It would be nice if we could drop by the Veilseam before we go back home. Ahem, if there is time," he whispered.

"Ha, they must be putting the final details on whatever hellish existence that I am about to enter." Jarold, who had appeared behind him as per normal when he was sent away from his mother, engulfed and included him into an invisible vacuum that prevented their words from being listened in on.

"Scan first, then train him until he gives up wanting to leave, my love. And before training, we need to create a replication of today's encounters before even teaching him anything new. You should already know by now that Ark wouldn't be able to focus if he doesn't personally see and feel what happened to his little friend, Fizzle, Freckle?"

"Wynnifell or Fell. It's not that hard. And no, Ark needs to train first before we put him in any Sims. He will learn what happened after he can clear the danger himself." Verza stamped her foot down as a final warning.

"Mom and Dad, I already saw what happened." Alize hovered over and grabbed both of his parents' hands as he led them through the rest of the alleyway and away from 45th Street.

"One of my friends recorded the whole thing, well, as much as he could have given the spells and unnatural phenomena at play." He ignored the blank stares and instead used his eyebrows to motion for Jarold to explain and share everything since it was now obvious to him that his ghostly grandfather figure never left his side. After a few seconds, Verza, having received a full play-by-play, shared the info with Ors.

"Yeesh, that info complicates things. Our Affix is getting pretty nasty," Orsche and Verza exclaimed simultaneously, then promptly cut Alize out of a more in-depth dive into the legality and feasibility of handling things for their son.

"Once again, I am left out of the loop. Ha." Instead of feeling upset, Alize revisited the information that all of his friends put on the table and evaluated the chances that his Affix might generate something.

"Fell is embroiled in an event already. My Affix, despite not being directly attached to my duplicate, has moved and sent out cosmic feelers to weave a net around my parents and Eights. There was also another instance of something happening while I was at the Quack's place, but that might have just been progress in the main event or minor additions that were added due to how I and my parents handled the encounter. Those are all given examples of how my Affix evolved to affect things be-

yond my immediate physical sphere of influence." Alize turned inward as his parents led the way back to either the Veilseam or home. Several dozen boards full of pictures, information, and tasks warped around him.

- Fell and my Fall is now Fell, My Fall, Friends, and Foes.

  ○ She is most likely alive.

  ○ The Fae's identity is still unknown but is an ally (?)

  ○ The group as a whole is now easy pickings for my Affix, at worst. At best, their lives will only intersect with mine at certain points that don't cause too many problems.

  ○ Carlos (Eights) is being tracked or hunted (?)

  ○ Noose purchased some rather specific info. It might bite him in the future.

  ○ Cable is, well, hopefully his father stays safe but, if he gets involved in the monster hunt or looks into the missing "persons" request, things might get bad.

  ○ The Group might take matters into their own hands, which leads to an obvious cascade of chained events that will ultimately lead them all back to me for better or worse and by some intolerably connected sequence of chance.

  ○ The Prince has a connection to Wynn's would-be assassins, and Dean's network may or may not be responsible for the massacre of her family.

- Dean's Influence in Excel Drift (What shady business dealings necessitate him entering Rest and coordinating an expedition? Will that somehow bite us in the posterior?)

  - He is connected to ASPA, a security agency that recently fired and blacklisted the assassins that went after Wynn.

  - What is Dean doing with his shipment to the quack doctor? Is it bodies, medical supplies, both, or neither? Is the missing "Persons" request that Cable brought up tied to the protection agency or some other shady business that he "works" at?

  - What if Dean is the one who is funding the quack's research? He is, after all, a well-connected and apparently thriving merchant. Having a scholar who can re-purpose corpses and grow sentient and physical spells is impossibly lucrative. If the science behind the Homunculi and Chimera is perfected and reintroduced to the world through the Corridor, it would upend everything. The empire would have to send someone to manage the situation directly. Is that the goal?

  - Then there is what Mom said about the cold state of war that we have had along the southern border for the past two decades. My Affix already made plans for me down there but if Dean is the one behind the quack in more than a supporting role then he would be almost directly responsible for disrupting and possibly even toppling the monopoly of contracts that the Scales have on the Accords Repository. The cold war shifts and the war would begin anew. The Southern Isles will once again become an undying and self-perpetuating engine of war against the Empire and all of its vassalage.

"Oh, that's not good. Verza, we should move a little bit faster." Orsche did his best to whisper, but it was difficult as he smacked his lips out of pure shock.

Alize, about to update a third and fourth lingering threads of thought, opened his eyes upon hearing the muttering and immediately guessed that his dad had done something that got them caught. There was the possibility that someone in the crowd saw through a two-layered illusion and informed the authorities, but that was less likely than Orsche overstepping his own skill. Despite the worry, Alize didn't panic. Verza pushed his chair and left the pedestrians far down the road from where Bear and Wynns Homes were. The more he paid attention, the noticed the sounds of erratic movements and panting breaths between distant screams.

"Ah. I was only joking, but it would seem something went terribly wrong." Alize scrunched his face in concern as he focused on the people closest to him. He first noticed that a very weird tentacle-looking tunnel retracted back into the apeirogon in Orsche's hand. It briefly sported the compacted dimensions of a cube before it folded onto the man's middle finger. Orsche's consistent illusion spell was heavily reliant on the divine rated artifact that could effortlessly create and sustain terrariums; the observation spell that he used to infiltrate Fell's home also relied on the space-time defining arcanum and right now, it showed signs of destabilization in the form of cracks and warping.

"What happened?"

The boy knew he wouldn't get a straight answer but still asked with a slightly raised eyebrow. Before either of his parents could respond, a pitch-black dome expanded and washed over several dozen homes that they left behind them. It visibly shimmered until it resembled a gargantuan soap bubble. In less than the blink of an eye, the homes vanished as an explosive eruption of magic clouded the interior of the instantly popped terrarium. After a full second, the translucent bubble shimmered once more and returned all of the houses to their normal state, allowing the fleeing pedestrians to continue on in their panicked fleeing.

"I was retracting my last sensory spell as slowly and carefully as I could and..." Orsche trailed off upon feeling an annoyed glare stabbing into the top of his lowered head.

"Your dear dad here thought it would be a good idea to try to crack into the suitcase carrying all of the Officer's evidence." Verza explained calmly at first, but her feet started to leave imprints on the sidewalk as she stomped off with Alize in front of her. Ors scratched the back of his head and picked up speed with a guilty smile as he pulled something out of the Apeirogon.

"I took this after I noticed that one of the officers was lingering. Based on what you and Jarold saw, and what your mother shared with me. Haa, my boy, I took it before it was stolen." Orsche pulled out a crystal-clear gemstone with glowing orange blood congealed at its center.

"I purposefully set off an alarm." Orsche chuckled and pointed to the bubble that flickered between a mostly opaque black and translucent with two differing environments being displayed.

"I'm fairly certain that the officer that I spotted was not actually part of the Guardians, soo..." Orsche shrugged and tossed the gem to his son. The instant Alize caught the evidence, the sound of glass shattering resonated twice over. A small bubble, one that was only big enough to cover a single house, popped open in a violent twist and revealed a home in rubble and a monster of a kid duking it out with a 10 meter tall giant. The second bubble, a few meters in size, popped at the apex of the dome. Alize immediately looked toward the smaller and less eye-catching explosion but felt his eyes water over and brain numb.

"It's okay. That is all being controlled. I saw your friends talking with the officers before that all happened." Verza, without the same delay as her son, digested the information, picked her boy out of his chair and ran off as she mouthed, "Thank the goddess." Orsche, without needing to communicate, folded the Arcanum and teleported behind his Verza as she dashed through a developing crowd without letting herself be seen.

"Seconds then. We avoided getting caught up in that mess by no more than a few dozen seconds." Alize looked back toward the mess that he created by proxy and pushed a sigh through his pursed lips after hearing what his mother said and noticing the relieved expressions on his father's and Jarrold's faces. Within a breath's time, a baker's dozen of uniformed Aide officers led by a slightly better armored Custodian whisked past the hidden family like revenants on the hunt for the warmth of life. On their way, they dispersed the crowd and ensured that everyone had the space to run or drive. Most importantly to Alize, the lead custodian was a familiar figure with Dijon yellow hair and the ability to bend and create plantlife. It seems, them going in the direction of the school was a ruse that was built up for this moment.

"My problem with this whole event isn't that the assassins are confident enough to retrieve the evidence from under the officer's noses. My gripe stems from the insanity that is making itself known to the public. This is all way too flashy, so there must be a play here, a ploy, or diversion." Alize thought back to the shadow of a muscular boy against a ten meter tall young man.

"You always do this. No matter where we go, you always make a mess."

Verza stopped moving for a brief moment and held out a single arm. Almost as if they had been practicing this move for their entire lives, Orsche teleported and wrapped his arms and legs around Verza's arm. She pulled him close to her chest and bulked up a few inches due to her own casting.

He smiled at Alize as they faced each other and mouthed, "Your mom is faster than me."

"I know, pops. *I'm just worried about my friends. If these assassins were ready to attack in the open like this, that just means that their confidence is or was high considering the number of Guardians that have been lying in wait to capture these people red-handed. Confidence, for people like this, should mean certainty in whatever job that they have taken. This—*" Alize watched yet another person-sized terrarium pop a hole in the massive dome.

"*This is not controlled on the third party's part. Not smooth. They have most likely already been apprehended, and this is a Terrarium to show the people what would happen if they weren't caught. Most likely, the assassins are operating out of anger, resentment, and possible desperation, not knowing or just now realizing that they might have already been caught. That means, the group probably took my recommendation to make this a career test,*" Alize felt his heart skip a beat as he reviewed the profiles of each of his friends and the monsters that were most likely responsible for the potential massacre of Fell's family.

"*But say. If the officers have not orchestrated this terrarium and Madam R's reputation is just that, over-hyped talk, these assassins would be out for blood. They were outrun by a girl with no rank. They were stopped from completing their mission in a smooth manner by a hard to kill family. Then they were outright slaughtered or held in the house by an Aberrant spirit that no one aside from Wynn and I would have known about if they were not part of whatever secret plot to let it pass into Rest,"* Alize bit his thumb and crunched his thoughts as Verza carried him further down the road.

"Eights and Noose are in an incredible amount of danger. Not only that, if those assassins were watching us the whole time or if the Prince really is involved, then it's more than likely that my identity has also been brought up at some point. Depending on who looks into everything that is happening or what has already happened to Fell and the rest of those misfits, my parents might also get discovered. Then there is the risk, no, the guarantee that Gregory, as an extension of the Vielseam, either hinted at or directly implied my relation to dad already which means that anyone worth their salt would be able to buy enough information to read between the lines and find my pops, which, would most likely lead back to my mom. And if that happens, any change of info involving me might also be tied to the layered alias and identities that we have given the quack. Which will then lead to fuck. Calm down. Fuck this Affix. Ark, calm down. I need to calm down. There is too much. Slow down and observe. Slow. Down." Alize squared his jaw and tried to rein in the thoughts that spiraled out of control. All of the threads that he began connecting between the board that he mentally placed around himself, weaved together to create an inescapable net that slowly enveloped and choked out everyone that he knew and loved. Some indeterminable figure made of mist smiled down on him as a luminous infinity symbol swirled and burned into the floor beneath him.

"Right now. What is happening right now?"

He blinked and focused all of his attention on the kid inside the dust. The destroyed street periodically flickered into a clear and un-damaged road full of pedestrians and previously curious and gossiping festival go-ers on the move. Everyone within the radius didn't seem rushed to escape the larger terrariums radius, but it didn't change the fact that the stream of movement did not stop whatsoever as the officers motioned for where people should leave. Reorienting onto the dusty and demolished landscape, he noticed nearly two dozen members of the group combining spells and movement to pressure and even push back several figures in large coats that darkened their features and warped the light around them. Out of absolutely nowhere and in small groups of three to four kids, the several assassins that found themselves on the back foot vanished into different elliptical discs.

Tumble, Eights, Mark and File, and Noose all stood in a unit as Tumble pushed the dust away to reveal five different glassy reflections of the same street in varying states of disarray. Without wasting any extra movement, she swiped at the air and pulled Bear from a spine-crushing backstab. A giant dagger the size of a great sword tore up the earth where Bear stood not even a second ago. Eights, unexpectedly, did absolutely nothing and stood as close as possible to Tumble as if he were a shadow. As if they were summoners, Mark and File cracked the reflections that they supported and called other members of the group at different intervals in their own fights to access spells that neither of the boys would have been able to cast without permanently losing some magic. Noose, in the middle of the constant rotation of friends, shot orbs of information like a Gatling gun while he projected several dozen screens and graphs full of almost indecipherable material.

"Something is wrong here. The group is defending itself way too easily." Despite being pulled away by his mother, Alize couldn't help but notice something.

"They are all fighting one person." Alize immediately remembered the profile of one of the assassins. Accord and Creation with an em-

phasis on cloning spells that separated, replicated, and consolidated the body into magical constructs. It was a spell that predated the study of artificial and completely autonomous life and something that one of the assassins possessed.

"I am sure that they have a plan." Hopelessly, Alize watched as all of his friends held their battles without much, if any, trouble.

"They just have to be on the lookout for..." Tongue bitten, Alize's widened and moist eyes turned bloodshot as he recalled the video that Eights shared with the group. Black nails, blue-tinted fingertips, and pale skin covered in tattoos, pierced straight through Eight's heart.

"Seakier Princeptis," Alize followed the bloody arm to the person who wielded it as a spear. His pupils uncontrollably constricted the moment he reached the woman's biceps. His vision stopped at her shoulder, liquid streamed from ruptured blood vessels in his eyes. The pinkish, almost clear water of the eternal spring oozed out, repaired the damage, and seeped back into his skin as it trailed down past his squared jaw and grinding teeth. Forcing himself to power through some Direct spell that prevented him from looking directly at her, Alize pushed his waning sight until it passed over the woman's shoulder. In that recursive torment, he just barely made out another figure standing next to the now ex-member of ASPA. This assassin with the thickest shroud covering themselves held the very same briefcase that the Aide officers placed all of their collected evidence into.

Since the lackey didn't have any defining physical characteristics and a muted silhouette, Alize couldn't place a dossier next to the person but he did notice that the assassin presented the case then used some military grade arcanum that he couldn't see to scan Eight's body. Despite not seeing the make, model, or brand of the Arcanum, he did manage to glimpse a screen that held a nebulous icon for a familiar-looking Monocular Dragonfly and a familiar cube. Seakier pulled her arm out of Eight's chest without any rush whatsoever and stored the case inside of some unseen but flashing Cheque as the lackey pulled the two devices out of Eight's rapidly withering body. She then motioned to the rest of Alize's friends and murmured something that Jarold was not at liberty to overhear in consideration of the old Sylph's orders to keep the family hidden and moving.

"This is a simulation. This has to be. I was brought home and put in a higher-ranked Sim after getting back. Ha, but on the off chance that this is all actually happening," Alize, in bullet time and shaking from the amount of adrenaline in his body, glanced over each blade of grass, building, and person in his field of view. Every splatter of blood became highlighted with the intensity of precision focus, as did every strand of hair or article of clothing. Despite looking for the telltale sign of an illusion, not a single thing stood out as artificial or out of place, only reflective or shadowed in the way that physically rendered Terrariums bent space—time, light, and reality. Seeing that the possibly rendered space around him was in order, Alize scanned his own memories.

"That's right, they're missing." The singular assassin that split itself into several dozen figures to attack the group, duplicated itself into hundreds of more versions upon receiving an order.

"Mark and File are out in the open along with Bear so they must have all made the same decision." Alize noticed how the large kid, despite being in possession of stellar footing and a remarkable physique, constantly lost ground in order to move and avoid blows that he could easily match. The number of clones meant absolutely nothing to Bear since the kid, before the extra bodies showed up, completely overwhelmed the giant clone before the sudden backstab. Mark and File being out in the open also clued Alize in on a well-rehearsed tactic

that the group was planning to use during the upcoming exams and Proving Ground tournament.

"If they are trying to pull off the DCR Fade, then Bear will have to lose his footing right about." Alize imagined the chaotic battle that his friends were in and visualized all of the moves and feigned deaths that were about to occur and by complete chance, he and Noose locked eyes. The kid tapped the middle of his forehead in an attempt to send out another message, then suddenly coughed up a mouthful of blood the instant Alize subconsciously mouthed "Now". Dozens of bloody cavities expanded throughout the silhouette of Noose as a radiant explosion cast by several hooded clones blasted him to death with all kinds of spells.

"Now." Even though Alize didn't give any order, it was almost as if Bear could hear the command. The rhythm that the muscular kid held in his constant back pedaling, stalled as he slammed a foot down to forcefully stop and close the distance between him and the long-range clones of the assassin. With unstable footing, Bear was blown to the side and had no choice but to once again engage with the giant clone. Locked in a grapple with near to no time to reorient himself, the bone in his forearms snapped and speared through either lung and through his heart as the giant crumpled his body in a single clasp of his hands.

Tumble, in the middle of staving off more than a dozen enemy attacks with forceful pushing and cavalier teleportation, somehow missed a single clone in the chaos. This small-scale but perfectly proportionate clone to all of the other silhouettes snaked out from behind a wall of bodies and twisted a serrated dagger deep inside of her tiny ribcage. Mark and File were no different in that they suddenly fell to a clone even in the midst of controlling the battlefield in its entirety. The terrarium was their domain, but the constant subdivision and transportation of friends just before a fatal blow left their concentration strained, at least, that seemed to be the case from an outsider's perspective.

Due to what any normal observer would call inattention or the fraying of nerves, the twins could not handle their own onslaught and the continuous pressure of supporting their allies and plainly received a bullet to the head and spear through the heart, respectively. The small terrariums they sustained and the pockets therein collapsed. Blood-curdling screams rang out first before the sound was abruptly replaced with squelching and piles of ground meat that just fell out of the air. Alize's friends were squeezed through rips in the fabric of space-time along with the clones that they fought.

"It's slow. They all died at the same time, but Mark and File were too slow. If the Prince was smart enough to share the details of our tactics, I don't doubt that these assassins will see through the trick. Please don't see through it. Don't see through it. Just believe that they all died. Please." Alize furrowed his brow and glanced toward the shadow cast by Bear's family home. All he saw was a long shadow, darkened and unnaturally elongated by the collapse of a terrarium and twisting with magic and unstable radiation.

In another small pocket, hidden and folded within the house, Tomoe and Fashion crouched at the front of the alley of Bear's family home. They both resembled unearthly apparitions or alien creatures that evolved or were designed to ignite one's flight response. Tomoe's ivory mask peeled back into a jagged and warped mockery of a face while her golden locks elongated into a writhing tent of snakes around her ivory and spindly figure. With a pulse, Mark squeezed out of a cocoon made of her hair and immediately rolled to his feet. Without any communication whatsoever, he clapped his hands and pulled File out of a rift in space. Together, they created a gate and pulled their friends out of a near certain death. Fashion, in a similar manner to

Tomoe, stood vigil in a bestial quadrupedal form. With a flex of his armored body and in the blink of an eye, he reappeared with Bear's body slung across his back. The kid immediately sat up and waited with a look of confusion and excitement as the group seemed to pull off something that he never expected to be a part of. Both of his now missing and not crushed forearms and hands grew back over the course of a few passing seconds.

Tumble crossed her arms with an annoyed pout as Fashion lowered her to the floor with his long, lupine maw. The tear along the center of her dress visibly knit itself back even as she glared toward "her own" skewered body. Noose fixed his glasses and loosened his tie as Dusker placed him down from a princess carry. Ranch, leaning against the dim A&E brand fence, grinned from cheek to cheek as her spiked tail impaled the back of Big's neck, pulsing with magic that poured into the loudmouth's body. The girl lay on the floor, panting and sweating a storm. Several misshapen outlines of bodies and blobs with rough and mostly distinct features, almost as if they were bad clay molds, piled around her. The alleyway was full of massive divots, as if someone gouged out the earth and turned them into action figures. Eden, now with short black hair, wiped the sweat off her brow as she stood next to a jumpy and worried Shambles that held the same amount of small dolls. Each one held the features and clothing of group members and a belt of brightly colored gray hair. Eights was the only member of the group that was nowhere to be seen, but none of them looked particularly concerned or sad.

Unable to see that his friends were okay but trusting that they were safe despite their obvious-looking deaths, Alize examined the changes beyond the scope of Mark and File's last surprise. The twisting and re-flective shockwave of their collapsed terrarium tore through the larger illusory pocket of space-time and revealed a temporary battlefield that spanned the entirety of three streets and several dozen homes. The juxtaposition between the idyllic suburb and the blood and ash filled sky sent shivers down Alize's spine as he briefly compared the current conflict to the remnant turmoil within his most recent nightmare.

"A reminder. I don't need one Affix." He watched the shrouded silhouettes of ex-ASPA members, who were most likely behind Wynn's attack. The butchered remains of several officers were strewn across a glassed and pockmarked landscape. A handful of custodians in much more elaborate gear barely stood on their own weight as they used cracked and warped weaponry to stand. The greasy Intendant Bilvey Bullets was nowhere to be seen, nor was the odd old man who set up the very first terrarium that prevented the public from viewing the final moments of the investigation. Only two roughly humanoid silhouettes remained where they once stood, and even then, the bodies slowly chipped away and diffused into the environment as flashes of obstructive magic and effusion.

Madam Why, the surveyor, stood at the front of Rest's finest with a mace and dented shield as she spread her broken wings. A disgusted and angry snarl spread across her once emotionless face as she examined the perpetrators of a heinous crime. From the looks of it, she was locked in a serious conversation with the assassins and found out some pretty valuable information based on how the custodians glanced at their officers and back at the criminals that were ballsy enough to roll in on an active crime scene and impede an investigation.

Everything occurred too fast for Alize to think. In the next moment, the largest translucent dome turned an opaque black. The new space inside of the terrarium turned from a cataclysmic environment back into one full of life and buildings. Any pedestrian who was trapped with the beautifully timed Officers used this chance to quickly escape the effective radius of the spell that warped what onlookers were seeing. Many continued to run. Others, once they left, waited for the environment to shift once again so they could see the conflict that wrapped them up inside of an inherently protective spell. Alize did not have the chance to wait for the next shift as Verza bounded through the streets and around frantic busybodies like a panther through the jungle. Her explosive calves and thighs nearly burst out of the illusory dress, forcing her more barbarous attire to clip through the pristine facade she and Orsche held.

Without any warning whatsoever, Alize blinked and found himself floating over the 18th Gate into Prochiente Village #37, through a different barrier that covered the entire residential district. From this heightened position, Alize kept his eyes on the cracked dome surrounding 743 with an unhinged jaw.

"What's so funny?"

Verza, despite breaking through a Terrarium with pure physical force and presence, took the time to pat her baby boy on the back and take an interest in his contained chuckling.

"Nothing. I just thought that Fell is smart but not in the way that would help her plan several steps ahead." Alize outwardly laughed again, but in his head, he readjusted his plans and thoughts.

"Is that all?"

Verza, seeing her son drift off, pinched his side and let herself be carried by Jarold as he carted them through a cloud and back to the ground using the shadows of the surrounding skyscrapers.

"No. I was thinking about." Alize dumped his thoughts and process onto his parents as they decided on whether or not to let his timer run out at the Veilseam or bring him home as soon as possible.

"So yeah, that's why I think that everyone in the group made the same choice to follow in Fell's footsteps. I don't know if they already came to that decision before I came along or I influenced them but I will definitely be able to see them again if my Affix doesn't outright try to kill them before my next big event." Alize verbalized his final thoughts as he scanned a familiar-lookin. shop window.

"I am worried for them and for you, but I cannot find any errors in that logic. I just hope that things play out like that. The guardianship program isn't infallible. Things go wrong all the time. Child placement, Warden vetting, resource allocation, criminal activity. " Orsche nodded along and caught Verza staring at him toward the end of his speech.

"Anyway, I'm just trying to say that we have only confirmed a few events related to the Quack doctor and can only assume the worst with a few of the Arcanum and chachkies in your room but as an extreme, we can say that those are also going to be problematic if left unchecked or verified. Then there is what you said about feeling your Affix. We have to make sure that your duplicate isn't generating events from afar for obvious reasons. Then we have to look into the events that will probably be generated from everything that you have learned today, and those will not be so clearly defined considering that you will probably not be getting any more hints in your sleep. So, something like meeting your friend in the capital nearly half a decade from now is." Orsche rambled on and tried to keep a smiling expression, but he just couldn't as he ran the scenarios and probabilities in his head.

"Don't be too hopeful, okay, baby. Life is already full of too many uncertainties. You can not bank on anything happening the way that you want it to or think that it will. Umm, what I mean to say is, me and your dad need you to understand and always keep in mind that whatever your Affix promises or plans, might not always be exactly what you have written down even if it looks to be that way right now. The quack doctor is a good example of that." Verza used her eyebrows to pass on the conversation.

"Yeah. Your mother is right. He is, or rather, the operation that he controls is a problem and raises some serious questions and concerns. We all believed that he would act a certain way due to the events planned, but by grabbing the glasses preemptively, you were not locked into him behaving a certain way or doing anything that you didn't want to. The quack was not guaranteed to get the Arcanum even if he still could with enough fortune." Orsche was ready to dive deep into the matter, but Verza cut him off since they stopped in front of the door to the Vielseam.

"Basically, Ark. Things happen. Your Affix exaggerates and links those things together so they are unavoidable, but overall, be wary of relying on the information you get from the curse or, you know, whoever else is translating for you." Verza pointed up, down, and then towards Alize's own heart. She kissed him on the forehead and whispered, "Be careful. I don't have my own personal account in the Veilseam, but I have heard enough. Don't say anything for free, don't move unnecessarily, and don't ask for anything outrageous. Your father is quite rich there, so we can afford to put everything on his tab, but..." Once again, Verza kissed Alize, but this time her lips landed on both of his ruddy cheeks.

"7:3 in your favor, Ark. Choose your words carefully and spend your information deliberately. You have 10 minutes at most before your duplicate shuts down and forces you to sleep." Orsche, having been cut off moments earlier, stroked his beard and nodded as he pushed the Vielseam's door wide open.

*Ding.*Ring.*Ding.

The door's little bell chimed several times as a single hand pushed against the handle. Gregory narrowed his vision to the cuticles of said hand and immediately scoffed upon seeing familiar wrinkles on the knuckles.

"Raquelidrel, I regret to ask why you have returned once more. I am still trying to recover the losses I made during your last visit." Gregory placed his invisible writing implements away with a flick of his hand and glared at the pointy-eared man that poked his head through the doorway. Orsche, being quite the knowledgeable scholar, scoffed at the passive accusation and opened his maw to form a rebuttal, but...

"Nuh-uh, none of that. We are here for our baby, not for you. So keep it to yourself." Verza held Orsche's jaw closed for a brief moment as she pushed Alize toward the counter.

"I'm sorry for any of the trouble that my husband may have caused for you." Verza respectfully bowed her head a little bit and flashed her flawless smile toward the blushing shopkeeper.

"It's no problem, Ma'am. Your husband has historically caused quite a bit of trouble with all of our establishment's staff, so we have protocols and regulations in place just for individuals such as him. But if you need any help, I can gladly place any and all of your matters on your husband's tab." Gregory leaned forward almost expectantly as a smile brightened up his ghastly expression.

"Thank you for the offer, but I am afraid that my husband and I have made the decision to let our son handle this personal matter of his. He was very keen on talking with you alone so he could work on his own balance sheet." Verza gripped the handles of Alize's chair and forced herself to smile and let go.

"If you can, please take care of him." She let go of the handles and took a few steps back. Gregory, an entity that represented the building itself, blanched upon feeling the impact of Verza's movement across the floorboard. If buildings could feel pain, he would have been crying from the weight behind those footfalls. Instead, the floor creaked and groaned like any other old building.

"Of course, madam. You have nothing really to be worried about. Your son, just by merely existing, has actually accrued quite the eye-catching sum of purchasing power in relation to its fledgling establishment. In addition to that, he has been given a sizable income based on your husband's beneficiary package. As for any possible detriments to the development of your son's account." Gregory grabbed a stack of papers out of his desk and placed them right on the edge of the desk, the side closest to the customer.

"Any and all overdrafts made by an underage account holder will be transferred onto the legal guardian or warden registered on the child's account." Gregory spoke louder and faster all the way until his very last sentence. He drew out every single word and stared directly into Orsche's eyes. In a flurry of motion and mind-boggling speed, Orsche read through all of the documents on the desk and collected his dropped jaw.

"Oh, my gods. No! Gregory, please ..." Orsche didn't get to finish his statement as a sudden explosion of magic forced him outside the shop. Verza and Alize could see the man banging on the window with tears in his eyes as he begged Gregory for something. They could even see him stomp around in circles as he produced dozens of needle-thin bolts of lightning. In the span of exactly seven drawn-out seconds, they all watched Orsche go through all the painstaking stages of grief.

Verza raised an eyebrow and aimed to pick up the documents that fluttered into a single pile after they scattered around, but Alize turned around and held his mom's hand.

"Mom, don't worry. I will only be a few minutes. Five at most." Alize met his mother's narrowed eyes and nodded as she steeled her resolve.

"Don't do anything your father would do. I'll see you in a few minutes then?"

She kissed Alize on the forehead and walked out the front door. Orsche briefly poked his head in, but Verza pulled him away just as he motioned and mouthed, "I'm watching you" to Gregory.

3.5 Activate the Scrying Glass?

G regory treated the boy in front of him like one might a languid dragon basking in the sun, with respect, fear, and general caution. Without setting off any alarms, as in, without making an obvious gesture to a document, he pulled up the information that he had prepared but hadn't put into the greater Veilseam and imperial hive mind.

"I guessed that bastard would make another appearance considering his track record, but this is quite the change of pace. Haa, I might even get some information on that troublemaker if I play my cards right." The building trembled once as a second and third file showed up next to Alize's. At the moment he flexed a single finger outside of Alize's view, an inaudible rumble ricocheted around and through the boy, giving Gregory a near-perfect scan of the kid's physical state.

- Personal file: A.R. Kaveri. 0 star (Aberrant) Lerian.

  ◦ Alias:

- Ark

- Ichibaratol Scuttle: Carrier of the Consequence Series: Lasting Effects Suffix

○ Status: None

○ Details: An interesting child. Confirmed to be the illegitimate child, through the birth of the First-Light
  Scholar and the Hyperfold Blood Fairy. As is observed,
  the boy's education in religions and ancient history
  predating the Voided era's is on par with registered
  Archivists of the empire. He may be another prodigy in
  the making and a threat to Eternity if left unchecked.

*"What kind of fortitude does this child have to endure an aberrant
state of being without fully devolving? It's remarkable. If his state is
temporary, reversible, or even an illusion, it would spark so many questions and interesting ethical debates."* Gregory possessed half a mind
to applaud the child in front of him, but he chose against it as a
number increased next to the boy's name by a fixed amount. It was
something that only keepers of the void could see, but it didn't stop his
credit from skyrocketing. The moment it passed an internally tracked
threshold, Alize gained a status: Pre-Approved.

"You should be done scanning me." Alize, having counted ten seconds, hovered forward as if he were taking a single step. Gregory,
stunned by the words spoken to him, controlled an instinctual flinch
and instantly used a spell to freeze his expression.

"Calm down. I'm not going to bite you for casting a sensory spell
on me without consent. And I am not going to take advantage of your
slight breach of Veilseam protocol as payback. I'm not my mom and

I'm not my father." Alize hovered forward once more and skimmed over the documents that were placed on the desk.

"I have five minutes, so I want to make this as quick as possible. I am assuming that these documents are related to my cut of the inheritance that my pops has paid. Since he is a notable scholar, the guild should have matched whatever he put in. Oh. My. Ahem, so this is how much my old man invested in my future. That's enough, Quill, to live comfortably in the Corridor for at least half a decade." Alize side-eyed the shopkeeper as he flipped through and nodded.

"*This child is so similar that it's uncanny.*" Gregory tapped his finger a few times on the desk and projected a poster full of rules and minor regulations.

"Since you have been Pre approved, and your legal guardians have consented to allowing you to build your own credit. Ahem, this is a free warning to all new patrons of the market. Do not say or do any-thing you cannot afford. The moment you ask me a question or make a gesture alluding to anything recorded within the Vielseam's preset sign language in any establishment, or make a request, you will have to pay the corresponding price. If you somehow offer or ask for something that has never been recorded in the Vielseam, you will be waived of any outstanding or related fees. If you accrue a debt surpassing the worth of your life's evaluated potential, status, or provided material offerings, wealth or Quill, all members of this network will be issued an order to capture or kill you depending on the severity of the order. If you are unsure about the rules and regulations, I suggest returning home with this document. It contains all of the Vielseam's TOS and TAC. If you intend to back out, do so now or state that you are putting any and all of today's outstanding transactions on the balance of your Legacy account. Since you are still a minor under Imperial law, the Legacy account establishes your guardians as the cosigners for anything you do, but in this case, since your mother is not an official member of the Vielseam, all consequence is held by your father." Gregory wrote something down on an invisible sheet and used his other hand to gently tap the table. A scroll with a weird dog-headed seal unfurled and revealed several long documents full of rules and regulations. Alize, unexpectedly, did not stop to read any of the half dozen scrolls before he signed them all.

"I understand the rules of the Guardianship and the process of becoming legally autonomous in the eyes of the Empire. I am cognizant of the Corridor's free market and rights of trade under the supervision of the IAIC. Additionally, I am aware of my complete independence and liability in all Veilseam proceedings henceforth." Alize didn't have any time to waste and immediately separated the documents into what Gregory needed to file away first.

"Oh. I can see that you already know what these documents are." Gregory, with a raised eyebrow, removed the fear and caution that he held in regard to Alize's potential and fully focused. As he understood it, the boy in front of him was not a miniature Raquelidrel. He was an entirely unknown kind of beast that was, apparently, prepped for the Veilseam and all of its intricacies.

"I do, and I would like to spend at least a minute to get things done quickly and in a timely manner." Alize motioned for something to write with and on.

"I would like to liquify the assets of my Guardian's legacy account and access any trusts that either of my parents may have placed under my name or as a private legacy account. I would like to invest my Quill separately from anything that they might have placed my future into. I do understand that 38% of my life's current estimated value will not be liquidated due to the inherent PHIC of the funds under the IGM. With the reserved funds, however, I would like to establish my own legacy account and trust for any and all of my future wards if I am ever fortunate enough." Alize pointed to several documents with his dad's signatures already on them. Several dozen other signatures with the Kaverz name dotted the long scroll, and even more names with several different surnames dated even further up the scroll.

"I will, after all of my liquid funds have been gathered, allow for 18.6 percent of my remaining total to be used for the governmental investments rather than taxes. Specifically, I want all of that money to be put directly into Jordaine's Guardianship and Haven Exchange programs." Alize smiled as he readily accepted a piece of paper and pen from Gregory. He wrote down several companies and percentages without looking up from his fully locked stare. Gregory found himself being pulled into a different kind of tempo from anything he had ever felt as the child's expression softened from a shark-toothed grin.

"I would like the remaining 43.4% of my assets to be invested evenly and annually spread in increments of .0001% over the next 200 years or until the funds run dry. The brands with bullet points are to have their R&D departments expanded exponentially, while the filled squares prior to their notation are for field supply and personnel acquisition related to heritage preservation nonprofits only." Alize slipped the paper and steeled his expression to make his intent and instructions as clear as possible. Gregory, without saying anything, compiled several copies of the note with several formal documents that Alize signed.

"In addition, I would like to formally transfer any and all forms of ownership of these investments over to the Imperial guardianship program's EAD." Alize clenched his fist and pinched his own leg after nodding off for a split second. He waited several seconds to be asked questions that he really did not want to answer.

"This child is farsighted and generous. Thankfully, it would seem that the worst parts of what other attendants told me to worry about

with Raquelidrel aren't present in his son." Gregory presented multiple stacks of paper. One minute. Alize finalized everything after one minute, for a total of 1 minute 78 seconds or 178 seconds of universal time. At 1 minute and 90 seconds, Alize turned the awkward silence into something Gregory found was more Raquelidrel's speed.

"Now that I am officially a patron of the Vielseam. Ahem. I will get down to the real business that I wanted to discuss with you." Alize crossed his fingers on top of his lap and imagined himself upon a throne, overlooking throngs of semi-worshipping retainers and servants.

"You have made a mistake, Gregory. One that could cost you your position as an attendant to the Void."

"This boy. I get one read on him, then his entire demeanor shifts." Almost immediately, a hint of anxiety somewhat poked at the back of Gregory's nape, but it quickly washed away. After a short moment of silence, no more than half a dozen seconds.

"Whatever do you mean?"

"Well," Alize scratched his cheek.

"All of his courage is gone. What a cute kid! Reminds me of my son. That rowdy shed must be a full-grown garage by now, maybe even a one-story with a family of its own to look over or a shop of its own to run. Go ahead." Gregory wrote something down, but his eyes stayed locked on Alize's half-confident and pleading expression.

"Well, my dad made sure that when or if I ever encountered the Veilseam or the Void market on my own, that I understood several things very clearly. I have learned the basic procedure for creating a separate account. I also know that every shopkeeper or attendant to the void has the bare minimum requirement of a seventh star divine being and should be treated with the appropriate respect, so." Alize immediately bowed his head after saying as much.

"Thank you for being as nice as you have been to my father, mother, and I. The second thing after the basics that I have been taught is that, as the keeper of a major market, beings in your position have to go the extra distance and acquire a certain base level of omniscience and a supporting variety of knowledge so you can properly evaluate the people, information, and goods that are moved through or because of the Vielseam." Alize held his head high and spoke with the cadence of an exceptional student repeating their professor's words, even and uninterrupted by doubt. Almost word for word, the small synopsis that he spouted was a textbook summary of what has been established and reiterated by the Scholars Guild in an official capacity.

"It is no issue simply to be kind. I am more interested in your education. Ha, you certainly seem to have been taught well. Ha. Ha. A right little scholar." Gregory's bottom lip quivered almost imperceptibly as he suddenly realized how much Alize was giving him. He was both happy that someone, even if they were a child, had given him such valuable information about their personal capability. Of course, due to his parentage, Gregory held some reservations about the boy's endgame.

"Ah. Yes. I have not formally taken any tests or exams, but I have passed many Sims with flying colors." Alize cleared his throat upon hearing an old nickname that his parents used to use for him until he started to fail almost exclusively in his more complex studies.

"That's not to say that I am anywhere near the intellectual benchmark that my father is at. I am just specialized in a few topics related to my Ballast pentacoded and rooted profile and a few supplemental areas. Ahem. It's the reason why I decided to help you out despite my parents advising against it." Alize, noticing that Gregory guarded himself out of nowhere, sighed and slowly lifted his hands to the top of the desk. Small glasses rolled onto the table.

"Oh. Here, this is yours by right." Gregory, feeling foolish for at-tributing Raquelidrel's reputation and history to his son, tapped his desk and pulled a scholarly-looking bear out from underneath it.

"I would certainly get in trouble for not ensuring that this gift entered the appropriate hands, so thank you for bringing it up. Now that you are here, it is only right that I return what is yours. I am sure that you'll notice my choice to redress the stuffed animal with new and matching attire. I hope that you are okay with my vision." Gregory wrapped the bear and its new accessories and placed them in a nice bag in front of Alize, but he simply pushed them over to the side.

"Thank you, but I'm not here for the bear itself. Other than getting myself established, I am here to discuss the future and how this meet-ing could change both of our lives." Alize did not spare a side glance toward his gift as he hopped it across the handle of his chair. Gregory narrowed his sight on the act and realized that the boy in front of him kept one hand on the desk and clenched it.

"What does this child know?"

Gregory's mind shot back to the note that held a weirdly distorted version of an Imperial stamp. His attention then lay on Orsche's fran-tic pacing just outside of the window. He seemed to have received a confirmation message regarding his guardianship status and all of the other documents that Alize requested and signed.

"Go ahead then." The shopkeeper returned his attention to the customer in front of him.

"First, you should look at these glasses really carefully. I think that there is something that you might notice about them. Second, whoev-er brought the bear in, with its original accessories, is also an individual that you should keep your eye on if they happen to show up at any point in the future."

Gregory spared a quick glance at the plastic glasses, then raised his head about to speak, but the kids' focus made him think twice about writing off the suggestion. Alize shifted uncomfortably and coughed to clear his throat.

"Before you proceed, I must stress the importance of you scanning this item as hard as you possibly can. It is extremely important to your safety, position, and this conversation going forward."

"I will look into it to the fullest extent to ease your mind and mine." Gregory made a show of looking at the glasses. The shopkeeper's pupils and irises vanished underneath a divine aura that couldn't be contained in his body. In fact, the entire shop trembled with a vast and unknowable aura as the gaps in the floorboards lit up with Tenets. Then, a ring of light reminiscent of a massive wheel or halo exploded behind the shopkeeper's body as several dozen more sparked into existence and collapsed in on the glasses. The high ceilings that faded into endless shadow, burst with spells and swirls of magic reminiscent of Vincent Van Gaugh's starry night. In less than a breath. Several hundred twinkling eyes beamed iridescent energy into the spiraling hoops that flared out into even more rings.Gregory also produced a barrier around Alize so the boy could see everything without being crushed under the sheer pressure of the dense magical atmosphere.

"Your stuffed bear's glasses are made of a blend of materials consisting of polyethylene and a common auric-dicarbonate derived from the discarded shells of the northern Blue Sea Crab-ling and storm reef sand. *Created from a now-extinct species, huh? It's weird to see anything made from their shells since they are notoriously difficult to melt and mold, even if it is worked.* The item was produced in a single small batch of 30,000 with a serial number of 1474291198374 in official imperial reports. Ah, it says here that the manufacturer went bankrupt several dozen centuries ago, but the related licenses and production rights of this bear and a few of their other products were purchased by Oncead Logistics. *Weird. Why does a Ballast Electronic brand have rights to a stuffed animal and its accessories? And why are there no exact dates of bankruptcy and dissolution or a name for the previous copy, production, and distribution right holders?* Oh, it happened during the fifty-third imperial restructuring of the corridor under the Brand's 145th CEO just before the company joined the economic and industrial pipeline of Jordaine. *Huh, that's an odd bit of information. I was under the impression that Oncead's official establishment occurred much earlier than their 145th CEO. I should look into it a bit more. There might be something of note. Even if there is not, just the hint that something is wrong with a Corridor brand will net me a nice boost of reputation amongst my peers,"* Gregory trailed off in his own thoughts then smacked his own forehead as he laughed.

"You are just like your father. He did teach you well. Ha. I was fully snagged on the lure that you presented. Haa, I'll take a loss of Tenets just this one time since you are still a kid." Gregory wrote something down on a little notepad that rested on the desk, but Alize genuinely couldn't help crying since Gregory did two things wrong. As an attendant of the Vielseam, either of those mistakes would result in an instant demotion or getting his memories "corrected" by the empire's Archivists. First, he wasted Tenets rather than magic to create a sight that would mesmerize and impress any other kid, possibly due to some personal feelings. Second, he shared his findings free of charge, even if some information was left out.

"This guy. This has to be a joke. Things are going too easily. Affix, are you up to something right now?" Alize wiped the two tears that rolled down his cheeks, habitually touched his neck, then picked up the glasses.

"Sir. Mr. Greg. No. Gregory. I need you to understand something." Alize shook his head and raised the glass.

"This is a nine-star artifact. If you didn't get that information right as you scanned it, then I can only assume that you have zero suspicion and ability to crack through the items built in Shroud," he revealed the truth.

"Really?"

"Yes. To be more specific, this type of tool became known to people outside of Rendira during the closing millennia of the Second Age of Greetings, the Aeon of Bounde, after it had already become a legendary artifact. In the original iron tongue of the people at the time, this relic would be called the Alli Initui." Alize used just his right hand to model the tiny pair of glasses. Gregory's face warped uncontrollably, as though he was forced to drink a gallon of lemon juice.

"As translated by the Fredionian's of Rendira during the Third Era of Pillars or the Aeon of Younite, artifacts of its like were called the Gla d'oer unisi." Alize restated the relic's history with a new pose, but Gregory shook his head with a pale face and glassy eyes.

"Ha. *Alright, it looks like no one other than Dad's team actually looked into history that far.* You should at least know about the massive conflict surrounding the Age of the Fallen, right? It should be the period of time just before the Veilseam was established." Alize raised an eyebrow while Gregory completely shut down. Even the building's tremors stopped.

"Oh man, okay. So basically, this is a scrying glass. Or the relic that the Arcanum is inspired by, you should know that name at least." Alize lowered the plastic glasses with a begging look.

"I do..." Gregory's mind connected the dots, and the picture left him very much in disbelief.

"That's good. Then, you should know that after a few ranks, Scrying Glasses are capable of breaking the limit on what its user can and cannot see due to the limitations of biology, DNA, magic, etcetera." Alize raised a finger and waited for a nod before he continued.

"Well, before the Veilseam was fully established under the empire, the Alli Initui was said to be the end all be all for artifacts that enhanced sight and overall perception. Keep in mind, this would have only been during and through the First Age of Greetings. A relatively under-researched period of Yiruhm's history. Yes, Gregory?"

"I am sorry. I am unfamiliar with the time period and the artifact, but there is something here." Gregory, in a stupor, used his personal account to purchase the right to look into yet another subject that Alize brought up.

"The Alli Initui is a peak rank and graded divine tool. Theorized to be a set of at least 2 dozen pairs in varying states of disrepair. Believed to have been developed at the height of Rendira's power by several unnamed Ballast Engineers and Ballastrates [VOIDED LIST]. There are no known means of production, restoration, or replication. There are 5 known carriers of working, unfragmented copies of the lost original work. There are 3 destroyed sets in Havens Vault, 4 destroyed fragments and two working fragments are in the hands of the Scales, 3 destroyed pairs are known to be with Wizards of the Western Coast, 2 destroyed sets are in the hands of registered Hunters with one working fragment in rotation amongst the local chiefs, one fragment is in hands of an unknown party and one semifunctional copy is unverified. All five copies of the functioning Alli Initui are in the hands of the Grand scholars of each nation and the emissary Iris." Utterly baffled, Gregory attempted to digest the information that pierced his wooden brain. Unintentionally, he let go of the pen in his hand and allowed its built-in Ballast

and Accord-type enchantments to write everything down that he was supposed to.

"That is a professional. Even while bewildered, he is verifying my info. Everything I said is common knowledge to scholars at and above the six stars in dad's field, but the fact that I am starless and not registered with the guild yet holds the same information, is a huge security risk. Not only that, merely mentioning the name of Erased History is an imperial taboo." Alize clasped his fingers together.

"Things that the Empire doesn't want normal people to know, I have learned. Anyone else, including my father, would be unable to share what I have told you today. Not only that, you have been saved by me. The second that these glasses enter my dad's hands, without them possessing a legal owner, he would have been oath and contract bound to report the discovery, which would in turn, bring up your failure to identify and secure the artifact yourself, to light." Alize watched the puppet of the Veilseam building twitch uncontrollably and finally, hover backward to address the floorboards themselves.

"Gregory. You will find it near impossible to verify most of what I said, especially regarding the eras before the Vielseam. The past, sadly, is a casualty faced under the erasure that the gods employ. It will be impossible for you to get anything through firsthand accounts and channels if you do not have a deeply personal connection to the scholars directly responsible for this research." Alize stopped talking and waited as Gregory barely managed to wrestle control of his faculties.

"Haaha. You are a funny kid. Haa. Good fishing tactic, but other customers have done it so much that there is a guidebook amongst us shopkeepers. Ahaaha. Those are just plastic glasses, kid. Meant for a stuffed bear, see." Gregory flipped his palm and displayed everything that he scanned. He was so amused and in denial that he wasted even more Tenets to prove a point as he unwrapped the gift Alize was supposed to have received.

"Those glasses that you have are no different from these replacements that I prepared. The model number is ultimately different, but the materials and manufacturer are exactly the same according to my documents." Gregory smiled as he waved to the extravagant wrapping, boxes and bags that he played out along with its contents. He stole the bag that Alize had placed on his chair's handle to prove a point, another mistake that made Alize sigh.

"Ah. Ha. Alright. Let me see if my [Shroud] can do anything to help stress the importance of what I am giving him here." Alize dropped his pretenses and suddenly stared at Gregory as if he was less than insignificant. In a second, he imagined himself back in his most recent nightmare and the curse induced dream state where he fully embodied the steadfast, controlled, and death defying nature of an old and magic-less Imperial Consort.. The sudden shift nearly sent Gregory into a tizzy but before he could raise any protest or questions, Alize opened his left palm. Similar to the quack doctor's display, he produced a sigil with a dropdown cylindrical wheel to show the magic types he possessed, the spells that he knew and had access to, and his overall profile.

"You couldn't find anything confirming what I said, could you? Let me tell you something about my life. I have been, since birth, engrossed in Sims dedicated to fixing, applying, and repurposing different ancient tools and artifacts with a focus on Arcanum that can be used with my profile. I have had a streamlined and dedicated experience cultivated by one of this era's greatest minds, so I am, without having been tested by the guild in an official capacity, on par with other specialized experts in a purely simulated environment." The sigil shifted to the utility aspect of all four magic types for added flare.

"In addition to my simulated experience, I also have hands-on experience with relics and enchantments that are so old that they cannot even be dated within the span of our Universal time code." The sigil shifted through hundreds, thousands, tens of thousands of spells that most people would have never even heard of. Alize locked eyes with Gregory and flashed a proud smile as he waved the glasses around one last time. At 3 minutes and 42 seconds in, Alize went silent and waited as he leaned back.

"Ha. I have limited omniscience and about as much knowledge as a shopkeeper of my rank, grade, and level should have to support my sight. Just as you have said. My aura is beyond that of a normal attendant, having reached the point of omnipotence within the set boundary of my foundation and frame. I am not a ninth star, so I cannot speak with absolute certainty as her highness does, nor am I an eighth star, so I cannot simply force my way to the truth due to similar powers and their interference. I can, however, defer to someone who is an undisputed professional." Gregory frowned a little bit, but his strangely bloodless face and bulging eyes only made his lightheartedness come off as chaotic. Alize only imagined that Gregory thought of Orsche when he said undisputed professional since the guy nearly spat the words out to the side. Unexpectedly, Gregory sat down and lowered his head to the desk as if he was out of energy.

"Young Scholar. How are you going to prove to me that this little trinket of yours is a Ninth Star relic? With that man's personality, if he noticed such an item before you, my shop would already be in shambles, so I can only assume that he is operating on trust in you and instincts that have always gotten the better of even my superiors." Gregory raised an eyebrow and put the tip of his pen back to the invisible page as he addressed Alize.

"I am going to make this relic mine by attuning to it," Alize revealed. With [Shroud], he showed off the profile that both of his parents raised him to know how to use. A Utility Aspect Root with a focus on Aura and Ballast Type Mana, making him a Pentarooted caster.

"And if it does not work?" Gregory raised an eyebrow.

"Then you can subtract all of my accidental purchases from my dad. I may have a separate account, but my credit can only go down to zero due to my age. Also, I think the both of us made too many mistakes today, so I cannot afford it if I am wrong." Alize waved his hand, but the expectation on his face made the shopkeeper hope that the kid was correct. Even if he was wrong, the only person who would hurt in this entire scenario was Orsche, since an expenditure of Tenets meant nothing to a building that would continue behaving as a shop regardless of whether it was divine or not.

"Ah. Before I start, do you mind setting up as many defenses as you can? I don't want the activation sequence to cause you any damage if there is something like an effuse buildup function that is on this relic. Also, it would be best if you placed us in the void. Since it's a Ninth Star, its activation will ring throughout reality, and I don't think either of us wants that kind of attention."

Gregory nodded and shot to his feet.

"I'll humor you, kid. If you are right, then you are. If you are wrong, your old man will foot the bill just as you said." Gregory felt himself returning to his rowdy youth, when he was just a young plank of wood not yet out of its initial sanding. Obviously, he wrote down everything he needed to even despite the fear, curiosity, and excitement that seeped into his foundation. He placed a few defensive spells on himself, the desk, and the invisible walls that Alize couldn't see.

"If I do this right, you need to be prepared, Gregory. None of the magic from this relic can seep into the void or the world; otherwise, we might start a whole new war." Alize reminded Gregory with a serious expression, but it only came off as a kid trying to look like an adult. Upon seeing the boy's determined gaze, the shopkeeper decided to double the defenses with personal effects. Even Gregory didn't know why he was persuaded as he prepared everything that he possibly could. Perhaps it was Alize's faux confidence that reminded him of his own child, maybe it was the promise of Raquelidrel's infamy that made him wonder if he was the target of one of that man's many schemes, or it might even be shock and intrigue that made him regard Alize's words and requests. He didn't know. He didn't want to examine it. Instead, he dived headfirst into something that would either backfire spectacularly, pay off, or not harm him in the slightest while besmirching the Vielseam's worst customer.

"I'm ready." Gregory nodded as the entire shop faded into an inky nothingness, a place where its existence was only denoted by the shop's overall boundaries.

Alize, fully mentally prepared, used the only tried-and-true method anyone could use to activate a magic item. His magic stirred and pooled within his palms. Ballast magic worked through physical states and perceivable and scientific mediums, so Alize immediately imagined that his magic was inherently tied to his body and mind as electrical discharges and magnetic pulses. With a Shroud stating that his magic was purely of a Ballast typing, he moved into action. His blood, or the waters of the eternal spring that was tinged pink from his blood, poured out of a sudden split in his palm and physically shifted into a radiant but rigid magical sphere around the glasses. In less than a second, he cast [View] and controlled the pinpoint spurts of blood. The divine Tenets of his facade stabbed into the nose bridge of the tiny glasses as his glowing blood congealed and hid what he was actually doing from Gregory.

A vast magical storm enveloped Alize's senses as he focused on the object.

"Just effuse." The chaos of dense magic nearly ruined his comprehension. The general Tenets that he encased his perception in did their job and almost instantly swelled as his spell sucked in the magical radiation that inundated the plastic. Instead of being pushed aside by the chaotic tide, the strand twisted the effuse into a drill that bore straight toward a hidden chrysalis deep within the bridge of the frames. In less than a millisecond, Alize observed and copied the color and shape of the Tenets that slumbered within the frames and released his control over the whirlpool that he made. Instead of breaking into the protective and mostly hidden shell and replacing the pieces with his own magic and Tenet like he should have under normal circumstances, Alize allowed the effusive whirlpool to suck in the waters of the Eternal spring that was mixed in with his blood. The divine ranked waters flooded into the whirlpool of magic as if the glasses were a drain and...nothing. His sensory spell shut down less than a millisecond after he used it, and several precious seconds later, nothing occurred other than him getting a nosebleed and losing focus.

"Ah, how disappointing. I am not as smart as I thought. I am sorry." Alize bowed his head.

"Is it not the Alli Initui?"

"No, it is. My magic just isn't enough to do anything to its barriers. It was like trying to fill an ocean with a single pocket of sand. It was completely useless." Alize recalled the chrysalis that attracted and was illuminated by his fake Tenet. Even now it devoured his 'blood' non-stop to no avail.

"I see. Since this did not work, I will cancel my defenses and—." Gregory's face blanched as glimmering eyes all focused on the glowing pink sphere in Alize's hands.

"Focus, child, it's activating." Gregory, with a flourish, spent everything in his personal account as a shopkeeper to purchase Arcanum capable of withstanding the compression of a black hole. In an instant, he swiped at Alize to move him away. An item that looked like an iron casket slammed shut around the Nine star Artifact along with several boxes that snapped, clamped, and folded in on themselves. Gregory then held the resulting black box with sweat flooding down his face as if he was standing in a running shower.

"That will not hold. Also, sorry for this." Alize, despite all of those barriers, felt a tug against the skin of his palms as a hair-thin thread of his blood remained connected to the glasses. With a gentle smile, he pushed his magic to present in its most basic aspect and directly pushed the package of his magic along the line, much to Gregory's absolute shock. Before he could deal with Alize's trick, the box in his hands imploded into a single glittering chrysalis.

The lights and shadows within the awakening Arcanum, interchangeably folded into a physical shape. The brilliant item first adopted a familiar form as the frames of the toy glasses. Alize instinctively reached out, and before Gregory could react, the glasses morphed into an ornate monocle with a long chain that widened into a long and ornate ear cuff. With a tug on the string connecting the two, the relic morphed into a thick and very wide pair of goggles. A third harmless pulse once again altered the relic, making it resemble a single glass pane helmet that covered every facial orifice. The scrying eye pulsed one last time as it settled on an elegant pair of rounded but face-forming silver frames with black accents. An absolutely underwhelming stillness settled as Alize and Gregory looked at each other.

"Is that it?"

"I don't know. I've never activated a relic at the divine rank before. Never even seen someone do it firsthand."

"Gregory. What do you mean?"

"Well..." Before the shopkeeper could say anything whatsoever, a boreal array of magic and vibrant light wafted off of the relic and Alize, almost as if the boy were at the epicenter of a mystical tornado. A blink of an eye later, the countertop simply evaporated along with Gregory's entire body. Wave after wave of energy crashed into the invisible boundary that separated the space of the market from the void beyond it. In fact, silver and red cracks cascaded across the walls and threatened to burst like a broken dam.

3.6 Void Master Status

"AHHHHHHH." The disembodied voice of Gregory came from all sides as a completely unharmed and unbothered Alize stood on top of a crystal clear and splintering floorboard.

"Oh. This is pretty bad." Alize rather blankly, examined the rate at which Gregory broke apart and legitimately had nothing else to say. If Gregory died here.

"At best, I would be trapped inside of the carcass of a sentient building that would bob across the Void for who knows how long or if I will ever be found. The void itself is a concept that exists as an, and I quote Dad thinking this, a forbidden love child between death and the abyss, adopted and raised by the Nine Hells and loved by her immortal majesty, end quote." Alize slid his foot slightly over toward the center of the broken boards. Wood chips fell away from its edges and filled in the cracks all throughout the illusory box that Gregory projected.

"In other words, the amount of fucked that I would be if the good Ole shopkeeper can't handle this is beyond my worrying. Ha. I may have miscalculated the explosive friction between the relic's natural Tenets and the environment's effuse. Please endure." Alize separated the temples of his new glasses and dissected Gregory's roar in response.

"AABAa. Ooouuu. Aaaaaahhhh."

"No, don't say that. You absolutely can do this. Just keep fighting. You can do it." As serious as he could muster himself to feel anything other than scared into calmness, Alize raised a fist and crouched down.

"OUUUUUAAAAAAED."

"Come on now, Gregory, name-calling, and toward a child no less? There is no need for language like that. Besides, it's not even that bad." Alize patted the mottling plank underneath him and tried to smile even while more than half of it appeared to have been fed to a wood chipper.

"AAAHAAaaaaaa."

"Ah no. It already accepted me as its owner, so I am fine. You don't have to worry about protecting me, so just make sure that everything is contained as best you can."

Alize thought back to his dreams and nightmares as an older gentleman in the court of the Empire. At one point, he was awarded a fragmented version of the relic he now possessed. In that pseudo-nightmare that he kept to himself, he made the erroneous mistake of activating the artifact. Thankfully, the Empress herself managed to circumvent the danger and...

"Ahem. Now that I have the time, how would the quack have managed to turn this thing on if he got his grubby mitts on it? I thought of this before, but unless one is in the void and has a meat, huh, I guess just a shield that is as strong as Gregory, activating or attuning such an artifact would draw too much attention. Attention that he couldn't. Ah.

Afford. His only option would be to sacrifice the Eternal Spring and the creature that's in the basement of that awful manor." Alize knelt on one knee as Gregory deteriorated to the point of becoming unstable. Half of his body hung off the side.

"The issue is time or the placement of events as planned or designed by my Affix. Everything..." Alize slowly lowered himself onto the broken bar of splintered wood and left himself freehand as he thought about how things would have proceeded if he hadn't caught himself falling out of bed or decided to cast.

"...that has happened so far would be different and more than likely, worse for my family and friends."

Alize reviewed the information he pinned up in his head and found that if he showed up at the quack's manor anytime before or after meeting the fixer Dean, then the butterfly effect would have done its magic under the heavy-handed edits of his Affix. Alize remembered the instance where his father used the Apeirogonal terrarium Arcanum to redirect the gaze of a higher ranked being then briefly replayed the later audio of his parents talking about how they would have dealt with the quack if things broke out in a manner similar to what Alize subconsciously translated into his dream journals. In the worst scenario, he tried not to remember it, but his memory flipped to an alternate nightmare where his parents tried to retrieve him from the underground lab where he was being contained and "healed". Dean's personal referral, apparently, went a longer way than he imagined. In this nightmare, different from the "observational stay" that effectively blackmailed his parents, he "died" before any treatment could be given to him, and his parents were sent on their way. He could even see death itself or some related chthonic entity reaching for his soul in a bid to disperse his consciousness, but the pink goop that he was suspended in kept his entire being in a stasis. He was at this moment reminded of the Homunculi siblings that had come into the Eternal Spring before his "treatment".

"Things could be much worse." In this pink-filtered nightmare, he could only watch as his parents eventually figured out that he was forced to keep living and came to collect. They were apprehended and killed right in front of him in such an easy manner. Sadly, that is not where the nightmare ended, even if the imagery faded away from his primary stream of memory.

"Ah. Now that I think about it. The nightmares have been used to inform me of the many potential routes that my Affix planned for. That is a scenario where I would be turned into a Homunculus, a Chimera, or something else. The curse must have calculated or known about these glasses somehow and prepared this better alternative." Alize thumbed along the bridge and nose pads of his glasses with his free hand.

"It wants me to have this Arcanum more than any other possible route that it could come up with. Ha, just how far ahead are you planning?"

Without realizing it, Alize touched his neck and breathed to the tune of his own heart.

"SOOUUUUAAAAAAHaAHA." Gregory's guttural roar turned into a defiant laugh as the invisible box full of cracks that shaved the boundaries into a skin thin Veil, began to fill out with the dotted out-line of planks of wood. An army of floor tiles gleamed as they formed a bulwark underneath Alize's feet. The fingers' worth of wood that he held onto, sprouted a single leaf and hair-thin roots that connected to each phantasmal piece of architecture.

"Congratulations." Alize didn't even look up as he caught a glint of light reflecting off the lens. Gregory, the building, not the puppet that he used to accommodate humanoids, trembled in excitement as the dotted planks filled out and turned into a simple cube with four solid walls, a floor, and a ceiling. All of which was illuminated and given color by the activating Ninth Star Relic. This was a universe-generating, big bang, kind of explosion. A violent and continuous burst of energy and radiation that would have sent waves to anyone with half a brain — but here it was, contained within the dimensions of a 14x16 box. And here Alize was, completely unharmed and visibly unmoved by the danger.

"Just a few more seconds. You can do it." With a small raise of his fist, Alize cheered Gregory on as he slowly leveled the glasses to his own face now that he was no longer in danger of falling into an endless void. He lied through his teeth and didn't know how long it would take for everything to settle. It was just a hope. As he stared through the glass, he paused and allowed his thoughts to linger.

"Relics capable of starting and ending wars. A mysterious and unknown Fae, in addition to an aberrant spirit capable of getting in and out of a major city undetected, assisted or not. A quack doctor with personal issues, a possible artificial army, and the resources needed to possibly recreate a genuine human. A people's man that maybe has a finger in too many pies. Assassinations, a missing person or persons case that is being kept under wraps. And a whole bunch of mysteries and rumors that only make things more complicated and interconnected." Alize checked himself, or his mental and emotional state. In a moment of clarity and dissociation, he recognized how fragile and close to rupture all of him was.

"WUAHAAAHII." Unintentionally, Alize shuddered as the floor beneath him parted. Feeling his heart leap out of his chest, he could only scream with Gregory's echoing battle cry. Laughably, the moment his eye closed, his body shook as the hover chair that lost its function and fell away, floated up through the void and caught him as it hovered over a newly crafted plank. Releasing a shuddering breath, Alize opened his eyes to see new blaring feedback. The glass flashed and warped with icons, text, and magic as it cycled through scribbles, block letters, hieroglyphics, binary, and all manner of text and pictures.

"It's okay. Breath. It's just a few more seconds. BREATH." The falling parts of Gregory swam around in the void, swirling back to the expanding piece of wood that now bore a total of three leaves and larger roots.

"[Shroud]." With a quick and purposeful recast of an aspect that seemed built into his body, Alize immunized himself against the effusive tide that rolled back in with Gregory's movement and allowed the relic to flood him with its own built-in Tenets.

"Oh. So the icons are not because of an identity error." Using context clues, Alize noticed that only yellow and black letters and shapes vanished from the projections that were produced by the lenses.

"The rest of this must be operational or boot-up details of some sort. Or maybe it's trying to communicate with me as the person attuned to it. Sadly, I do not recognize any of these languages. They are getting more familiar but not, oh. Interesting." Alize placed a finger on a hinge and hummed.

"This Arcanum might be even better than I or Dad believed it was." Alize referenced his father's work with the estimated time periods that he gave to Gregory and marveled at the relic's ability to alter itself. He recognized the very odd final word in the twisting display.

"Initi'latinit. *It's initializing. My best guess is that the Arcanum is going to go into an immediate power-saving or rest mode to update its language and setting operations."* Alize glanced down at the new wooden plank that was the epicenter of the solidifying room. It held a calf-sized sapling bearing exactly eight leaves.

"Did you contain it well? There were no leaks, right?"

"YOU, kid." Gregory, the humanoid representation of the building, rose out of the wooden sea of planks that reconstituted the building with an exhausted pant. He rolled onto his side and threw up in a violent fit of exhaustion.

"Congratulations once again." Alize, beyond his years at this moment, bent as much as his chair allowed, rubbed circles into Gregory's back, and lifted his head. He handled the ancient shopkeeper as one might nurse a drunk friend.

"I did. I did it. You were right, and I... It was kinda underwhelming if I am being totally honest." The old shopkeeper, half within the floor and half materialized as a man, cried in a pool of sap, sweat, and bile.

"You did it. Good job. I mostly guessed and had faith, and yeah. The Arcanum might be at its ninth star, but ultimately it is only a pair of glasses. You are amazing. A really solid building." Alize mindlessly praised as he focused entirely on his new Arcanum. A long white and gray bar slowly filled in as icons and filters flashed across the lower edge of the frames.

"I am, aren't I? I went all in from the start. I, you. Thank you. I am not sure that I would have been able to contain the relic's activation unscathed if I hadn't put everything in from the start..." Gregory fully waded out of the relatively bare flooring and collected himself. Remembering his position as an attendant to the Vielseam, the old building stomped his foot, wiped his shoulders, and restored the interior of the room to the finely manicured experience that was entering a Veilseam locale. In the blink of an eye, his entire tempo epitomized a calm and collected professionalism. If Alize wanted to, however, it would have been easy to call out how Gregory's eyebrows quivered or how his pupils constantly contracted and dilated with a moisture sheen. Life. The man was a puppet of the Vielseam, a building made from fabricated parts but now. His jaw dropped slightly as he stared at Alize.

"You knew that this would all happen, how? Are you..." Gregory's eyes knotted in confusion. The very same thought process that the entire Kaveri family went through regarding Alize's uncanny guesswork and demeanor.

"Absolutely Not! No time or rebirth shenanigans. I made a series of educated guesses based on what my pops told me about the minimum level, grade, and rank of someone in your position. I expressly stated that I am familiar with the rules. That doubles when I have encountered enough Veilseam attendants within Sims that have been rotating within the scholars guild. EPA you know." Alize leaned back in his chair and couldn't stop himself from telling the truth. The alternative, letting Gregory travel to the land of assumptions, was just about the same as a death sentence.

"Whew, boy am I glad this paid off though, Greg. This particular outcome had a 2 in 73 chance, so big ups, huh? We just pulled off a miracle. That's not so bad, my divine friend. Not bad at all." Alize couldn't keep still as he came off his adrenaline high and collapsed into his chair.

"2 in, no. You are. Oh, my goddess. Are you serious?"

Gregory examined his own body in a panic and realized that the kid, even if he wasn't being 100% truthful, was not too far off from how miraculous activating the artifact was. Then there was the matter of the boy attuning to it in seconds. The Tenets stored within the device were not corrupted or unstable despite the duration of time that it had been unassociated with anyone. It activated without a hiccup, then there was his own body. Not only did Gregory withstand the initial tide of effusion being pushed out of and away from a source of infinite power, it all just so happened to be just enough to crack his foundation and inundate it to the point where adaptation or collapse were his only two options. Then, to top it all off, he managed to contain everything without a single leak.

"A child assisted me with a grade improvement and allowed me to come back to life. A child, based on a guess, gambled his own and my sentience on a reality-altering hunch. This child, rankless, attuned a Nine Star artifact without so much as seconds worth of passing time and calmly cheered me on through a struggle that I believed would be my end." Gregory, using sleight of hand so fast that Alize didn't even form an instinct to observe it, wrote a note, stamped his personal sigil onto the page, and sent it off through the void with a bulldog-esque seal on it.

"Ahem. Please forgive my previously uncouth appearance, sir."

"Sir? Hold on. You don't have to start doing that now."

"Do you know about how the Veilseam handles the status of its patrons?"

"I do." Alize nodded as he sat up straight to combat a feeling of unease.

"Then you should also know that the moment in which you successfully gained ownership of the Arcanum, your status in the Veilseam changed."

"I do, but you didn't. Ah, you already sent an update to the Empire."

"I did. My referral has just arrived at the Veil's Imperial reception, so your new status should be official in just a few more moments."

"Ha. Great. Just remember what I said about you getting fired because of this." Alize bowed his head even deeper than Gregory.

"I accept your apology and offer my own thanks in kind, Sir. Thank you for choosing me to be a part of such a monumental event, even if it was only sparked by my inept appraisal abilities."

Gregory gripped his own trembling hands and released a sigh through a slight smile. It was around now that he realized the shaking did not come from his body. It was the entire shop that rumbled. Alize wanted to shut down any kind of kindled emotion or respect that Gregory might develop based on this encounter, but something shot across the void in a blinding arc of something that Alize had never seen before. He couldn't even describe the resulting aftermath of some blindingly bright light tearing through layers of the void akin to a relativistic jet with the pinpoint accuracy of a needle. A letter pierced through the boundaries that Gregory placed and stopped just within Alize's reach in a startling crunch of crystalline magic.

"Approved Referral. Patron status expedited. Finalization pending final review." Burned into the space just at the top of Alize's vision, a confetti gun's worth of stamps, sigils, and signatures rained down. The related paperwork, according to the regularity of a repeating signature, seemed to have been completed in quite a rush.

"Is it always this quick?"

"No."

"Well, then." Alize retained his outward calm, but the chaotic storm within his mind had him scrambling to figure out what to do with his newfound authority.

"*From a pre-approved patron of the Veilseam straight to an approved and referred member who is waiting to gain the highest level of status. Ha, 20 seconds should be enough time.* Ahem, I have a few seconds, so the first thing I need before I go is for you to show me the recommendation letter that you sent and the official report that you are going to send to your bosses after I leave."

"Of course Sir, this is a copy of my evaluation regarding today's transactions but if something is not to your liking, please feel free to adjust any of the information and I will send a letter expressing my errors and haste whilst in an elevated emotional state." Gregory, a professional in the art of servitude and catering, shifted into high gear and unveiled a copy of his faster than light speed letter. He also shared several invisible pages with the boy, who he was confident would become his new direct boss after his referral got approved.

"Also, I couldn't help but notice that you are pressed for time. As my preferred patron, I am at liberty to use my power and knowledge to help you as long as I do not break any of my oaths in my role as a shopkeeper and attendant. If you need more time here to finish your tasks, I can grant it." Gregory snapped his fingers. The result was an inversion of color and a reversal of space, as if Alize were suddenly placed in the universe of a funhouse mirror that flipped an image rather than mirrored it.

"Thank you." Alize didn't pump the brakes on his focus and simply nodded as he let Gregory's casual disregard for the laws of physics wash over him.

"Right now, I have gained the status of a preferred member due to Gregory's referral. The issue is this next step." Alize examined the burning and rebirth of his void file along with the update that Gregory's letter initiated. Under his personal details, the details showed that he was the sole owner of a previously unregistered and ownerless divine ranked artifact. There were no further changes or details that gave away specifics other than the emboldened words that dictated his rank and profile.

"A rather eye-catching *disparity."* The next thing that he spotted was a footnote that showed him exactly what was waiting for a final review. Gregory's update within the update. It gave exact details in word-for-word transcriptions and adequate descriptions of his observations. Nine stars burned in this footnote.

"Well written." Alize praised almost absentmindedly as he realized that Gregory also lived or worked based on the scholars' mantra of EPA. Going down the immediate list of thoughts that the old shopkeeper fluffed to appear official, Gregory's detailed account, unlike Alize's mental account, contained so many variables and pieces of information that the kid couldn't even wrap his head around the first page's 0.0001 sized font.

"At least, the conclusion of the report is easy enough to understand." Alize read the words, "As such, I defer the assignment of status to our Immortal Lady of the Void". Alize sighed and edited his own information with a fine-tooth comb.

"This time-stopping thing, what is the time differential?" Alize didn't look up as he used the official Veilseam pen that Gregory loaned him.

"No time will have passed for you physically or on the world outside starting from the moment that I stopped the flow inside of here."

"Huh. *How horrible. I have to roll back the clock and endure my duplicate's deterioration."* Habitually, yet another door appeared on the second floor of Alize's mental palace.

"How would I circumvent, deal with, and/ or endure an effect like this if the caster is someone looking to do harm to me or someone I know and love? There is not much, but there are options." He did not allow the door to close, unlike the thoughts surrounding his own friend group and family.

"Thank you once again. I am sorry to ask, but since you have given me the time, and the Veilseam has approved my authority, I would also like to look at all of my paperwork again."

3.7 Home

"Are you sure this is what you want to be sold if someone looks into your information? And these individuals, are you sure you want to create tailored accounts?"

Gregory sifted through seven different mounds of documents, lifted a handful of papers to his face, then combed through his disheveled hair with an ink-stained hand.

"Yes, on both counts." Alize lifted a thumb from the front door and waited for Gregory to release the magic that stopped time and displaced the shop.

"And all of these, ahem. Events. Are these truly going to happen due to your Affix?"

Gregory looked up at the cursed boy—no, his cursed, ahem, his regular boss— with bulging eyes, trembling hands, and a newfound understanding of existence.

"Probably. In some manner. Maybe. Might not. Hope not for some. *Of course, fate is an unstoppable wrecking ball rolling down a hill, and we are all obstacles in its way. The only bright side is that I can, due to my Affix's gentle and sometimes insane nudging, get a glimpse of the rolling ball's* direction, *but...* Ha, just make sure to release all of that information on the dates that I specified and, oh, before I forget. The note that you picked up from the Bear's scroll. Ensure that it ends up only in the hands of her Immortal Grace. No one else is allowed to see it." Alize adjusted the glasses on his face and blinked a few times to follow the boot up sequence that the relic prompted.

"Yes, sir." Gregory nodded his head almost profusely as he returned the shop to its original place. Alize could now see beyond the void that shrouded the windows and the glass portions of the front door. Everything was still frozen, inverted in color, and flipped along the X-axis of his vision.

"What were those two doing? Have they been screaming at each other?"

Alize's face somewhat pinched upon seeing his parents through the glass. Verza seemed to be stuck in explaining something, but Orsche adamantly stood by whatever belief he held, based entirely on an evaluation of their postures and the movements of their lips.

"Ha. Hopefully, it's an argument that won't cause our family some troubles." Alize turned the doorknob and looked back at Gregory.

"Before I go, I'm sure I don't have to remind you, but I will state this one last time for my own peace of mind. Officially, my Arcanum is going to appear as a refurbished seven-star Scrying glass, the Cracked Eye of the Lucent Hierophant. Any and all mention of it will be transferred through the Scholars Guild and led back to my father's research." Alize's stern expression reminded Gregory of his own son's serious expression when the kid moved out on his own.

"Yes Sir. I will ensure that our dealings today are handled with the utmost care and regulation." Gregory nodded.

"Good. I'll be on my way now, please take care of yourself and try to get your hands on the Sims that I wrote down for you. The scholars have been keeping stuff like that locked up, but I'm sure that you can find an illegal copy somewhere if you look hard enough. I can almost guarantee that after you use them for a while, you will fully gain enough experience talking and haggling to outmatch your run-of-the-mill scholar. And I'm confident that you will be transferred to a field position after this, so if you are not assigned to me, please keep as much of what I have given you today secret."

"I will." Gregory nodded from his half-submerged position within the pile of data that Alize provided. With a snap, the building shivered as if with indigestion and popped the temporal alteration like a sheet of brittle glass being struck with a hammer. Alize's mental clock, with five seconds on the dot remaining, pushed the door open.

"That was a headache to get through. Ha, it somewhat reminded me of all the paperwork I had to get through as a deputy Survey Officer in the sim dad made. Ha, it must have been weird now that I think about it. He compiled his own experiences and memories as a Scholar's apprentice and let me figure it out. I wonder what he cut out of the sim, out of his life. The same can be said for mah." Alize hovered towards his parents after what felt like months of back-and-forth conversation and writing and found that his parents did not have the most welcoming of faces even as they turned to validate that they saw him. Verza and Orsche were both as red as tomatoes despite their natural bronze and pale skin tones and complexions.

"Five minutes on the dot outside of the Vielseam. What happened in five minutes?" Alize glanced toward Jarold for some kind of sign, but the old bag merely used his wind and hands to sign, "I was not paying attention, kid."

"Oh. I get it now." Ors pounded a fist into his hand as if a lightbulb suddenly switched on.

"You did not run away in jealousy. You were suddenly caught off guard on your way back from the bathroom and had to deal with some enemies." Orsche nodded.

"Exactly, I've been trying to tell you all these years, but we have always gotten interrupted when that day has been brought up." Verza's attitude dropped since Orsche suddenly accepted whatever it was she told him. She moved a hand to soothe her wildly beating heart.

"Haa. My love, you really are quite capable. After all these years, I have always thought you left me to deal with that whole cult situation while you took a crap." Orsche scratched his nose with a hearty laugh. Verza left an afterimage in her previous location and smacked him on the back of the head.

"A crap? What kind of refined lady craps for three hours? I had to cuff the people who ambushed me, and then I had to track down their leader after that. Hmph, I even found a way to destroy their anti-magic scrubby vacuum thing before they could blow up you and your girlfriend. And even then, I only took that long and blacked out afterward because of the curse you handed off to me to play around." Verza blushed, but the anger and annoyance on her face hid the muted splash of color almost perfectly.

"MY GIRLFRIEND, HA. I have never dated that octopus even once in my life, not even in a sim, my love. You always bring that up, but she has just been overprotective of me since we grew up together. I am sorry, though, for believing you to be jealous of that annoyingly clingy woman. I love and have always ever loved you." Orsch sincerely bowed with an apologetic tone, but because of the angle, Alize spotted his father's cheeky smile.

"Hey son. We are just getting each other's perspectives on some adventures we had back in our youth. I'm sure your mother will want to bring it up at some point since it involves our entire family. Ah, about that. Have we ever told you about the epic journey that your mom and I went on just to conceive you?"

Orsche directly dropped a loaded bullet into the chamber of Alize's mind. Instead of trying to scour his memory for a mention or a crumb of parent lore, he decided to respond honestly.

"No, I could never get the full story. I only know the little bit that you two told and showed me in Sims, and the origin story and myth of my name."

"Okay. I mean, it's to be expected. I'll try to get your mom and the old fart to help me tell you the story. It might not happen until you are older because she is a bit, well, you know. But, If we ever get around to it, I want you to keep it in the back of your mind that I always helped your mom out because I thought she was a cute airheaded klutz." Ors scratched his nose as he mostly ignored the verbal berating that Alize also tuned out.

"I am sorry, love." The moment Verza scoffed in annoyance, he stood up on the tips of his toes and kissed her on the cheek. Alize smiled maliciously, seeing how things were just going to be blown over as usual, which earned him a deadpan look from his dad.

"Love at first sight, right, Dad?"

"You little shit. Haah. Watch how I make your Sims unbearable." Orsche looked shocked and innocent.

"Bring it, old man." Alize smiled sweetly, which only enhanced his charming and adorable features that were still full of baby fat. Verza, having been around Orsche long enough to know his tricks and ticks, instantly realized what was happening.

"Hey, sneaky bastard. Were you telling my baby something stupid just to make yourself look cooler than you actually are?"

Verza narrowed her eyes and squeezed Orsche's cheeks with a frown.

"Absolutely not, my love. I was trying to explain to our baby boy that, ow, if we ever get around to telling him about our youthful adventures that he needs to keep in mind, that hurts, that you were a steadfast beacon of strength, beauty, and poise whenever things got a bit dicey." Orsche rose to his full height, which was still shorter than Verza, and grinned as his hands played around her waist and trailed along her arms. Completely caught in a romantic trap, Verza pushed Orsche away, covered her blood-red cheeks, and muttered something about not liking being tickled in public. Orsche, having extricated himself from the doghouse with flattery, a handsome smile, and expertly positioned tickles and skin grazing, turned to Alize with a thumbs up.

"*My boy, that is how you make the love of your life melt into the palm of your hands. Just be an adorable idiot, and you are golden.*" Orsche spoke directly into his son's head, but at the same time as this message, Verza whispered.

"*Your dad is such an idiot that he's cute. Make sure that you find someone who you love even when you are mad at them.*"

"Okay dad. Mom." Alize shook his head in disapproval, but he couldn't hide the smile that was simply etched onto his face.

"Oh, by the way, those are nice glasses. Nice. Glasses. Glasses. Glass. You Activated. Glass. Scrying eyes. You." Orsche was the first to change the subject as he flashed a beaming smile in response to the cheek pinching Verza gave him. His body, however, locked up the moment that his brain began to process what it meant for his son to possess an active divine-ranked artifact.

"Oh, how handsome you are! The glasses look nice on you. Is it the relic that you spotted earlier today?" Verza squished her son's face and then kissed his cheeks and forehead with a radiant smile.

"You look very cute." She then pushed Alize's chair toward Orsche so they could be on their way back home.

"Thank you, Mom, but I'll move myself until I can't anymore. You have to pick Dad up. I think he is in shock." Alize carefully evaluated his father's noticeable vacant expression.

"Really. I thought he was playing dumb again. Ah. You might be right, baby. I haven't seen your dad like this in a while." Verza raised an eyebrow toward her husband, looked at the glasses, then suddenly giggled.

"*The fuck was that, Mom? Since when do you, nope. No, not asking myself that. When was the last time Dad was this shocked?* Ahem." Alize cleared his throat and shut the door on yet another stream of thought.

"I guess you managed to activate the artifact in the market? I knew it was possible since your father did something like that before, but you said that this relic was an Eye of Argus back on our ride over. Your dad was explaining how rare and how powerful this relic was and still is, and it made me worried. Are we safe?"

Verza effortlessly slung Orsche over her shoulder like he was a sack of feathers and followed behind her son as she expanded the conditions of her question, "What I mean is, who is that Munch person that left the Arcanum here and why was it supposed to end up with the Quack doctor like your journals hinted at? This kind of relic, even if it was 'coincidentally left', would not just be inside of a Veilseam without being noticed for a long time." Verza stopped there, walked beside her son, and watched his pensive expression of pride and slight concern etched across her still-red face. Alize looked around and noticed that his father's illusion barrier was still active, so he spoke un-worriedly as he led them back to the trolley depot. It was clear to him that his dad shut down his own motor control for a certain amount of time to prevent his greedy fingers from lashing out at his son's new equipment.

"I don't know, Mom. I know what you are trying to get at, but I don't know. I found out that you and Dad have been treating my dream journals as a guide to avoid danger today. I used my magic for the first time today. I have interacted with more people outside of a sim today than I ever have in the total amount of time that I have been using this duplicant body. I don't know who brought these glasses to the Vielseam. I don't know which god or entity is pulling the strings behind my curse or if there is even more than one." Alize, as calmly and evenly as he could, hit cords within Verza's heart.

"I don't know, and that's okay. I do know what my Affix can do. I know what it wants to do, and I have already put a few plans into motion while I was in the market." Alize overlapped his hands on his lap and gazed in the direction that he knew the Dragon Marsh District was in.

"Therefore, until we sever our ties with the quack doctor in a month, we are safe to live our lives in line with the fake identities that we are using." Alize corrected his posture with a relaxed sigh, but he suddenly froze up after seeing a new prompt on his glasses.

"Okay then. Live as normally as possible and let the Affix run its course. I get it, but pfth, haa, and what are you doing? " Verza narrowed her eyes and stifled a laugh, finding it slightly weird and funny that her son had suddenly started to spin his chair in circles as he rolled his head in circles.

"I am trying to see if this works. The language that the Initui, Argus, is using is an old and regionally phonetic language that was pretty unpopular way back in history. I am trying to follow its prompts but..." Alize began throwing his head from side to side.

"I don't think it's working. I think that I have to recalibrate my vision and equilibrium. It just needs a baseline, but I'm fairly limited while sitting down, so I'm trying to give it as much information as I can so it can better adjust to my preferences later. I think. I would have asked Dad, but..." Alize held his head with a hand and clenched his jaw to avoid spewing it all over the floor.

"Okay. Uh, you said that you made plans at the market. How and what plan?"

Verza found her head spinning to keep up with Alize's sudden doughnuts. He said everything that he did for the most part within the Veilseam and made sure to stress the importance of his new status and how it was completely tied to the relic.

"...So. Hold on, mah. I'm sorry." Alize stopped moving, took his glasses off, and used his wrist to flick them about in all kinds of directions. In less than ten seconds, Alize finished narrating his preparatory work when he suddenly heard a voice reverberate through his mind.

"***Nah, du' cont. Biwea uv acclime pas'tivit, attune du'cont.***" In the blink of an eye, Alize put them back on and spotted the prompt.

"Ha, such a pain. *I guess I will have to let it passively acclimatize. I can't complain though, can I Argus? You seem to also be aware of the language barrier between the two of us.* Conwe'av d'acclime pas'tivit." Alize looked up and found his mother staring with wide eyes as he casually spoke another language that she had never heard of.

"Are you okay, Mom?"

"I am okay. I am just thinking about what you said. You are a preferred patron, but you are at the top of the waiting list to become a Void Master." Verza adjusted her grip on Orsche.

"Yeah. Apparently, the status only needs a referral from an attendant or some other divine-ranked being, and it can just be bestowed onto anyone after her Highness gives the okay." Alize shrugged his shoulders as if it wasn't a big deal, but Verza shook her head and pinched the side of her own waist.

"It's that easy. Wow. Hmm. How does that work? With everything else, I mean." Verza asked with overflowing pride, but her tone and cadence slowed to a low, almost sad, timbre.

"Mom, anyone with a divine rank or a similarly rated artifact qualifies after a referral. It doesn't mean that everyone gets it. I am too weak, I don't have a credit history, and with how I filled out my paperwork, the Arcanum that I put in leads back to dad's Legacy. As the relic of a Veilseam inheritance, I doubt that I will officially receive the status." Alize faked a smile and pushed down the anxiety that rushed through his mind.

"It's possible, no, more than likely that someone will have their interests piqued by Gregory's referral. I took a gamble. A potentially horrible gamble. Anyone, literally anyone, with even a slightly higher status than him will be able to look into and see that I made edits as his preferred Patron. The circumstances behind my insane boost in status will then lead to someone or many someones figuring out that I have an Alli Initui, or Eye of Argus scrying glass. The blowout could break out in any direction, and my Affix would have a field day making the lives of everyone I know and love a minefield. The problem is, if I didn't get ahead of it and proactively set up informational dugouts, I would be at the mercy of whatever it cooks up. I can't allow that. Can I? Has the Affix hurt anyone that I care about other than myself?"

Alize bit the inside of his cheeks and exhaled.

"I was hurt, but I gained more than I am hurting. Wynn is alive, and so are her parents. Eights is most likely okay along with everyone else.

The quack didn't do anything outright sinister or bad to my parents or me, and I mean, that whole manor and the lab is morally corrupt. But is it? All of my information that I have about what exactly is going on in there is based on a skewed understanding of my Affix, theory, and scattered observations. What is happening down there is horrifying, but under the PIETY Act, it is scientifically and mystically just to push the boundaries of understanding." Alize rambled on at near light speed as he laughed to his mom about how things will eventually turn out completely fine. He was only snapped out of his dual chatter when a small chime sounded in the back of his mind. An unobtrusive red dot suddenly filled a gray circle at the corner of his vision.

"The Initui is starting a passive scan now." He folded the glasses over the collar of his shirt as the lenses blacked out, similar to transitions.

"What was I saying, Mom?"

Verza placed a hand on his shoulder and stopped him from moving forward.

"I have been through this with your father already, baby. He is too smart for his own good and gets caught up in plans and backups and this and that, and ha, I've dealt with his secrets and hiccups longer than most people with our heritage even stay together." Verza placed Orsche on the floor like he was a wet towel and knelt down in front of Alize. She locked eyes with her son. Neither of them noticed that even as Orsche's body remained rigid, his eyes narrowed on his wife and child.

"What I'm trying to say is, you are too much like me and your dad. Ah, don't speak because I know you, Ark. I know you. That smile, the way you speak and how you choose your words. What makes you happy, sad, angry, your fears, *you*. Ark, you are my baby, and I know how me and your father raised you to think and act." Verza held Alize's face the moment he tried to look away.

"I know that you are trying to tell us as much as you can. I know that you have kept the worst parts of your nightmares to yourself. I know the horror that an Affix can plan and put someone through. I know that whatever it decides and whatever happens, regardless of how strong I may be or how smart your dad is." Verza teared up but didn't let them fall as she did her best to mirror her son.

"I. We know and understand how bad the worst scenarios can get, so I am not asking you to reveal your plans or your worries. I know that you have been skipping over the specifics for a reason, and I'm not going to ask you to share your thoughts if you don't want to. I just don't want you doing that—not to me, not to your father, not to us. If you want to vent, go ahead. If you need to cry, do it. Don't force yourself to be strong. To be okay and not worry." Verza caressed Alize's cheek and didn't wipe the tears that rolled down his shocked face.

"When you feel that you are ready, please tell us what you planned for in the Veilseam in more detail. I don't like when serious issues are glossed over since it makes me feel like I am not strong enough to deal with the problems. Do you understand? I'm not very good at speeches and stuff unless it's in fighting. I usually leave it up to your grandpa or dad for situations where I have to get a point across." Verza tried to hide her embarrassment by admitting something that she never expected to give voice to. That truthfulness, however, seemed to be the straw that broke the camel's back. Alize reached out, bawling to high heaven as he gasped for breath. In his mind, the doors on the second floor of his mind, half hidden in the fog, all swung open and released a tidal wave of negative thoughts that came crashing down.

"Breath baby. Breath." Verza rubbed Alize's back and didn't seem surprised when Orsche wrapped his arms around the two of them.

"First. My first. And. And, Wynn. And Carlos, and you two. And. My, me. Affix. Ahhhh." Alize leaned back and between sobs tried to say exactly what bothered him throughout the day. He had acted his heart out, putting on an Oscar-worthy performance. He had done his best, but now, as they waited in a dark corner of the trolley depot in Grand Rest Central.

"It's. It's been so hard. I tried. I tried so hard. All the way. All the way until now, and it hurts. I tried not to let it show, but it hurts so much. It sucks so much. The water. The pressure. It's been hurting me so much." Alize just couldn't keep it going as he clutched his liquified body after pushing his parents and Jarold away. Every other second he was reminded that his [Prevention] spell retained the shape of his body and even then, he was reminded of how close he was to breaking the surface tension of his own skin with how much his effuse and spring water that the Felign-juris spell burned through to keep his passive Shroud, active and on throughout his body.

"I had my first kiss. Wynn's family was executed right in front of her, and all of my friends are in danger. All because of my Affix. How is that fair? How is any of that fair? I nearly got the three of you killed, and that's just the beginning of what it has planned. How can I outpace something that even gods don't want? How am I supposed to keep you guys, my friends, and the world safe if I have to end up in this much pain just to avoid being killed by a random Geist?"

Alize shivered and bawled unendingly. This time he accepted his parents' suffocating hugs and fell asleep in their warm embrace. Verza and Orsche let go of Alize only after the shadow of night threw its cloak over the amethyst sky. In other words, they stood in the middle of a street for a few minutes, allowing one of the world's many suns to fall as their son was forcefully disconnected from his duplicant. The bright lights of Heyden's Rest and the constant stream of pedestrians that avoided their family unit did not suggest that night fell at all, since it only meant a new skybox to the natives of such an active and brightly illuminated city.

Verza and Orsche stared into each other's tearful eyes. The pain, grief, and unexpected understanding that flashed between them hinted at some underlying history.

"Looks like I was right again, Verza. I told you my plan would bite us in the ass..." Orsche wiped his tears and clenched his palms so tight that he drew blood.

"His first kiss? With who? I thought he was dating that adorable girl, Wynnifell." Verza's face hardened into something only a demon would make as she picked her baby like he was a glass flower. The thought, "*Is my son an unfaithful playboy?*" flashed through her mind for a hot second as she looked at Orsche, who folded the chair into a cane.

"What? What did I do?"

"There is no handling it later, my love. This is our later." Verza motioned toward Jarrold to set up a path straight toward the edge of Rest. Alize didn't know it, but she and Orsche had already decided to get home as quickly as possible the moment he left the Veilseam. That meant they allowed his lead the way only until he fell asleep.

"What are you talking about?"

Orsche, a bit confused, followed Verza in a series of consecutive teleportations as she ran through the streets unimpeded.

"Sims. The simulated terrariums that we have been getting and creating for Ark. We need to raise their rank." Orsche nearly buckled under the weight of a task he had long since believed Verza would not let him pursue.

"Are you sure?"

"I am. We also need to check his profile again, so do what you have to. I will prepare an even better training regime."

"Hmm, how long do I have to scan and create Sims?"

"One month. After we return to that accursed manor and make sure that things are not going to end up with us being indebted to that monster, we will have him dive into sim's until he breaks out or breaks down." Verza squared her jaw and avoided looking at her delicate baby.

"You know, I love you, Verza." Orsche gently elbowed his lover's arm as he weirdly alternated the grip he used on the Patch hovercane.

"I know. And I hold a great amount of affection for you as well." Verza's expression somewhat softened.

"Oh, look at who is picking at old problems now." Orsche lightheartedly chuckled, but his mind couldn't help turning back to the old adventures he and Verza used to have. What scenarios has he left out that their son could learn from? What stories has he heard or even lived through in a sim created by another scholar? What lessons and skills did Alize need to learn to be a better caster, a smarter scholar, a stronger soldier, a better person? What would forge and temper the boy's attitude and resolve, and how far could he, as a father, teacher, and scholar extraordinaire, push the envelope before he broke down?

Personally, the mental exercise was just as much of a torture as it would be for Alize to live through considering that Orsche did not want to see his son give up and falter. Not again. Orsche gripped the handle of the hover cane and shuddered out a sigh as he repeated, *"Never again"* in his own mind.

3.8 Remote Access

"Four. Ninety. One hundred and eighty seconds... Three hundred." Alize counted in the darkness that he awoke too and settled in mind.

"Three hundred. And. One? Three hundred and two, Three. Four. *Fuck*. Mom! Dad? Haa, did either of you put me inside of the training room? Did the Duplicant get returned to the machine properly? There might be an issue with the disconnecting procedure if you can hear me. I know that you two wouldn't forget what I told you, but I remember that I lost connection when I was at the quack doctor's spring." Alize waited around 3 minutes again and turned to the fog of his mind the moment he reached 301 seconds. Whispers floated out from the back of his mind and drew his attention toward the ever-expanding second floor.

"Okay? Okay! Something obviously went wrong. EPA. What are the possibilities? First, there is the more probable chance that I never left home in the first place." He briefly imagined his father's divine Apeirogon, a terrarium-generating artifact that doubled as an illusory domain and the only key to the Kaverz family homestead. In scenario number one, he was back at home, sitting in his hover chair in the middle of a completely white padded room with a blank expression. Drool spilled out of both sides of his mouth as his parents were off in some corner deciding what to do next as he created a whole outing into town in his own head. To summarize, he never left with his parents to find the divine Scrying Glass or the quack doctor, and they simply constructed an illusion based on his journals and allowed his brain to fill in the rest.

"That doesn't seem to be the case though since I haven't noticed any sensory inconsistencies or breakages in my perception of time aside from Gregory's influence. It's also impossible to replicate or forge any Imperial sigil with Terr tech and spells. Additionally, there haven't been any pauses, magical influxes, or spontaneous effusive spouts pushing my senses or memory around. Which makes my second point moot." In the latter scenario, he constructed a silhouetted object floating in a vat of pink goop using anatomical information of a Lerian's brain and the layout of the Quack's underground lab. In this possible "he never left" idea, he was little more than a preserved corpse or a suspended brain cut out of his physical shell, hopeless and at the whims of a person called Mother and a Quack doctor that found him and his parents a little too suspicious to just allow safe passage in and out of his Manor.

"There is also the chance that I did not wake up after closing my eyes to either dilute my pain or to focus up at any particular point." The points at which he could have died were numerous. He fell out of a tree that touched the clouds, fell out of bed while severely injured, and spoke to his parents after freely using magic that resembled divine Tenets. Then there could be a change at any point during that time and entering Rest, where his parents could have believed that he was being suspiciously similar to a reincarnator, time traveler, or incarnation of a divine being. And all of this was assuming that the reality he experienced so far was not some elaborate setup, trap, spell, or volatile ecosystem like the Ual- Jisse on a far-off continent.

His errant imagination twisted his thoughts and the fog. A writhing shadow kicked up the clouds and enveloped him almost entirely as the ghostly rendering of a bloodbath coalesced. A rampaging "hero", a pretender and sheepskin-wearing wolf, tore through the snapshots of fog and decapitated and trampled over two people that he was supposed to love in the future. The anguish, the defiance, the sorrow, and the power behind those faces pulled at Alize's heart in a way that made him want to scream out. With a swipe of his hand, his imagination backed down and pushed out of the lobby, receding and encroaching onto the main area of his mind in a similar fashion to when there is a neap tide.

"If my future is set, to an extent, by my Affix, then will this or something like it, happen?"

Alize held his mouth shut and symbolically placed an arm over his gut. A migraine of untold proportions was coming on, and he wanted nothing to do with it. Closing his mind, he reached out to any part of his body if it was at all possible in the darkness around him. Not expecting a change in the dead synapses of his body, he examined the dark and sighed. It reminded him of the weird noise beyond the visual limit of his [View] spell.

"Huh." It was extremely similar. Alize raised his hands to his face and shook his head slowly as he became less clearly defined and more artistic. The moment the darkness began mingling with his skin, he realized he was within the abyss beyond his own perception. Wherever he was, was not safe. Whatever he was in, it lived and breathed chaos. The Affix didn't burn. It did not writhe or twist or mingle with his senses. It wasn't playful or even almost childish in its warnings. It directly pulled at his musculature and smashed into his vertebrae, moving his eyes away from a serpentine eye that broke out of the abyss. A hand ripped out of the textured ink and fully grasped his head and flailing body before the Affix's heavy-handed interference could snap his neck.

"Fuck!"

Something he simply did not understand gripped his temples and pushed him back while another entity, vast and horrible, thrashed within the abyss and sent a shockwave throughout. Bioluminescent and almost runic eyes, eldritch in nature, spiraled out of control for as far as he could see. Half covered by a dark hand that was covered in a lace glove, the small portion of the sentient abyss embodied change and growth as the more he viewed the spirals, the more they fanned out and looped into one another. The grand display reminded him of his Affix. The instant he drew a connection, the body of whoever was holding him became more visible. An embroidered black corset was the only thing that he actually noticed between the fingers that covered the upper half of his face.

"Who are you?"

His question landed on deaf ears as the figure slammed what he assumed was his body through the abyss and scattered his mind. Unintentionally, the dispersal forced him to blink, with the next moment being him falling away from a hand that ripped open the fog of his imagination with a swish. His mental lobby shook and cracked away as a deep Tartaran plague swirled in behind the wraith that stood between him and a creature full of deep purple and scarlet but deeply chthonic scales. That beast pressed and crashed against his internal perception like a tower of drums crashing into a wall of cymbals, dispersing the fog to reveal an archaic stone ruin atop a vast landscape of fading and ashen imagery.

Alize crashed and skidded across the floor of his mental lobby and curled up as the remains of some forbidden pit sloughed off of him and into the floor. Migraine was an understatement. It felt as though someone had gouged his eyes out, burst his eardrums, flayed his skin, ripped out his tongue in small incremental portions, and de-brained him through the nostrils all while keeping him alive. Hyperventilating and internally screaming to collect himself, Alize looked up toward the wraith that blended into the abyss surrounding it. Screams, cries, and cacophonous laughter wafted in from the breach within his mind as each phantom particle from that abyss coalesced, shifted, and ground against the dense mass of ash that had been taken in with him. The fog closed not too long after, taking with it the haunting image of a divine being that left Alize focused on nothing but his curse. The chaotic breeze that remained, despite not clinging to him in a physical sense, spread itself in every direction except for the grounded Alize that was beside a crack in the floor that spewed out gray mist in an attempt to restore the tile.

Unable to break through the densely packed fog, the chaotic apparition shot toward the second floor and spread itself into every single negative thought that the kid ever had after being unable to permanently or even noticeably destabilize the already chaotic tangle of information that bound and loosely connected the several boards all across the ground floor.

"Stop." Alize tried to get to his feet, but the ash clawed at his ankles and brought a mess of dust with it. The wind, or a more violent cousin of it, rattled the chains that barred entry to the contents behind the first three doors and specifically bore down onto the numerous chains and locks with the least protection.

"I don't know what's happening. I don't know what you are, but please." The pain of having his deepest secrets forcefully ripped into was something he had never before experienced, but this weird and somewhat sentient shade made the whole messy business somewhat better. The thing, to Alize, resembled a child throwing a tantrum after being placed in an unfamiliar environment.

"Try to understand me. You are going through my memories, and I cannot stop you. I just don't want you to have what's in those rooms." Alize pleaded and threw up to the side. All he received in kind was a banshee's call as the thing took on a humanoid shape. Its head and upper body dispersed around the locks. In less than a second, some of the chains holding one of the doors closed snapped and revealed a doorknob.

"Do you think this is enough?"

Verza's leveled and loving voice came out of the cracked open door first, trailed by a pulse that completely overhauled the aesthetics of the lobby. Gym equipment, yoga mats, and machines that were reminiscent of ancient, medieval torture devices shattered the tile all over the lobby. His imagination turned those broken pieces into pockmarked turf, free weights, and water bottles filled with all kinds of medicines and supplements. The shade noticed the alteration and scattered itself to play with everything all at once. In less than half a second, the creature adopted a form almost perfectly matching Alize, albeit vastly more muscular and masculine. It returned to the door and punched the locks. Another chain snapped. When the room didn't change, it burst another then another until the iron and steel barred door was revealed and broken down. It shamelessly barreled through the door and beyond the threshold. Silence.

"I told you not to go in there for a reason." Alize cried and forced himself to lay straight as a cacophonous laugh turned into a terrible shrieking. The darkness beyond the door frame swirled around an amorphous shade that was full of holes and was bent out of shape irregularly even for a chaotic being with no set form. Just as a tendril of abyssal smoke exited the room, a violent swirl of iridescent fog burst out in the shape of Verza and Jarold. The demonic force of nature that the two of them became was unstoppable as they grappled the retreating grainy ash, cut off what they grasped from the main apparition, then slammed the door. The chaotic spirit recoiled and splattered across the entire hall, opening and slamming doors to no avail as the main tangle of ash that was connected to Alize swirled around his body and attempted to almost, complain?

"What is this stuff?"

The ash that was once on his body, coiled around his finger and hand, then around his arm and neck for a hot second before it reconvened with the rest of the turbulent magic that attempted to ruin his mind or at the very least destabilize it.

"I told you not to go in there. Don't try it with the other two either. It's only going to hurt you. Just wait here with me. Eventually, whoever it was that left you in here will take you out. *Hopefully.*" Alize raised an eyebrow as the shade skipped past the second door in his mind and banged on or barged into everything and everywhere else. It was bent and warped beyond belief now. Blood, flesh, and weird fluids bubbled and oozed from the now broken hinges and frame, glueing the space closed. Spears and jagged splinters of bone and soft pink of exposed marrow erupted from the fleshy crags like geysers and created a new, weird barrier that kept Alize's fears locked in a prison of his own creation. The ash, seemingly unshaken and undisturbed, recalled the parts of itself that invaded other parts of the kid's mind, and tried barging into the last two doors that it was unable to crack. The arcane locks and runic symbols keeping the first door shut dimmed and shattered one after the other due to the simple proximity, but now that its focus shifted, the glimmering barrier shattered like glass. The main hall returned to its semi neat chaotic spread with the only difference being that everything was made or sustained by some elaborate, fancy, or crystalline arcane tool or spell rather than simple wooden furniture, bound hardcovers, parchment, and boards of cork, porcelain, and dry erase.

Orsche spoke only after the shade set a single one of its feet in the doorway and hesitatingly moved forward. A wall of fog suddenly pulled the shade in. After several screams in low tones, the wall went down. The chaotic entity attempted to rush out, but the instant that it reached the doorway, the fog went back and prevented its escape.

"So what have you learned this time?"

The poor thing roared in defiance but whimpered toward the end violent series of explosions. The wall went down, and the shade limped out of the room with needlepoint holes all over its body, each one crackled with electricity that formed a net around each limb, slowly cutting into the inky storm surrounding it.

"What have you learned this time?"

The wall went back up as the creature cried out as the net pulled taunt and reeled it back in. Alize curled up and covered his ears. He was not ready to deal with whatever he left behind those doors, but since this creature happened to volunteer as tribute, he might as well get some rest.

The door opened again some moments later. The shade, in a knee-high and skeletal frame, calmly walked out of the door one step at a time. Fog smaller than threads of silk, whipped out of frame and completely encased the residue of the winds in a cocoon, leaving behind only a solid humanoid shape similar to Alize only in that it possessed his rough features. The door frame writhed and twisted for a long moment as the textured chaos attempted to break out of the arcane wrapping to no avail. Alize noticed the weird silence, uncovered his ears, and examined the small copy of himself that shivered uncontrollably at the top of the second floor of his own mind.

"I told you. I do not fear not knowing what you are. I am only afraid of what I am familiar with." Alize stood up and held his breath, seeing that his mental library had been cannibalized.

"Ha. If you don't kill or hurt me more than you already have, you are more than welcome to a hug." Alize tilted his head and opened his arms to the chaotic little thing that stole his appearance. He could see the small amount of liquid ash curl along the creature's inky splotch of a body and rest within its glassy eyes and in the middle of its forehead.

He blinked exactly once after staring at the ashen pupils of the creature and found himself falling. Now surrounded by explosions and by a ghoulish heat and sickly flame, he subconsciously cast spells that he had the most experience in, [Prevention] and [View]. In a weird artistic rendering of time, he noticed that he was once again an old man covered head to toe in remarkable equipment. He was missing the accessories on one side of his body as in the original nightmare, but now, he was able to examine the Hero's raucous behavior as his spell simply had no limitation, spreading across the entire continent in a single breath.

"The Hero's ash! This is not a chaotic spirit! This is. What? What is this thing?!"

The moment that Alize thought of the origin of what was assaulting him—glowing steam, fog, mist, exploded from his lower body and brought clarity to the abyssal waves that attempted to break him mentally. His body jolted as the smell of burning hair and oak wood filled his nostrils. The tiny, chaotic thing wrapped its arms around his calf and trembled. A slight tinge of color peaked through the crown of its head.

"Hey, are you? I mean. Do you have a name?"

The second that the question came out, his hands shook, eyes spasmed, and body locked up. If he was attached to his regular body in whatever state that he was currently in, he would have noticed that his blood ran cold, and his heart stopped beating momentarily. His Affix moved a single time then immediately turned into a knife of pure frigid cold that straightened his back and lifted his head away from the tiny thing at his side. Hands, ranging from snow white to as dark as the abyss that the entity came from, wrapped around his body and squeezed.

The tiny creature released a cry that was immediately stifled but one of the hands lashing out to silence it. Alize, looking straight up in the midst of losing his vision, noticed a single arm as dark as the night itself piercing through the fog. It was frozen in its place, along with the divine entity attached to it, half submerged. A pair of fangs, like swords of judgement, hung on either side of the apparition. This image burned into his memory as a pair of tiny hands closed his eyes.

"HAAAA." Alize gasped for breath and fell backward as he started toward the empty fog-covered ceiling. His Affix, having been frozen for a long time, splintered across his back in a way that made it feel as though his brain released a flood of dopamine. His lobby returned to its normal serenity. The only difference being the grainy napalm that filled in the cracks on the floor. Even the first three doors returned to being shut behind layers of maximum security. Inherently, however, Alize knew that two of those were changed by something that burned a mark into his mind. The problem he faced now was that whatever surrounded his physical body right now, or surrounded whatever his consciousness was currently connected to, was dangerous.

He sat there staring and going through his memory for a long time to make sure that there wasn't any permanent damage and sighed. With nothing left to do, he curled into a ball and replayed the events several times over, trying to understand or narrate what happened in a way that made sense. He could feel his Affix bleeding. His body felt it. The dense coil and wheel of fate was just unraveled. The proverbial boulder had been shattered. Whatever it was that his curse really wanted by loading events into his life like a bullet into a chamber, whatever it was aiming at. He could feel it. The infinity loop on one side of his neck unfurled and lassoed around the base of his skull and fixed itself to the base of his spine.

"I am *not Dead. Not* in *an* illusion *or a terrarium. Something* is wrong. *Not seeing. Not sensing. Can't comprehend?* Simulation? *Incomplete information.* I can only work on my *best assumption."* Alize gasped for air as the metaphorical bullet that wrecked a path straight through the back of his head, passed through and out of his forehead. Books of memory rained down on him, opening to pages with highlighted words that exploded into walls of text right in front of him.

"I get it. There is only one reason for something like this." Alize instantly tried his best to imagine the golden-eyed and mask-wearing Divinity that supposedly guided, put up with, and believed in the Hero.

"Something unexpected just happened, and I was privy to it because of Gnoll's influence. Affix, are you there? Am I right? Did you do something? You saw an opportunity to create an event for me and took it, right? I can't feel you behind this curse but this has to be your doing." Alize touched his neck and waited but rather than a chaotic warmth or a playful pause, there was a coldness and emptiness as any heat from the curse washed down his spine and out of his tailbone. By habit, he checked his hand only to see that the dual loop of infinity hadn't transferred.

"Something bad is happening; something really bad," he concluded. The negative thoughts that he kept locked behind the doors on the second floor turned into oblong and treacherous beasts. Out of absolute necessity, he went upstairs and firmly secured each and every door.

A shiver ran down his spine again and remained there as he suddenly remembered the shadow that twisted within the fog just before his imagination brought up the ash and the Hero. Whatever it really was, whatever the unknown goal or aim was or whoever it was that resided within his mind, it bore the semblance of an Ourabouroureal snake. If only for a moment, the shadow of the writhing beast encircled the entire lobby, fading in and out of mist like a thread amongst needlework. It was only now that he could feel it—a creature of fate, a beast of burden, a protector and fear-inducing nightmare. He was not divine. But his Tenets, even if only passively and subconsciously sustained, came from somewhere, and he knew that this immortal creature was tied to his curse. Standing up at the very center of the lobby, he shifted his stance so one foot remained on the solid floor and the other stood atop multicolored black sand. Without skipping a beat, he crossed his legs over one another and meditated.

"I'm still alive. Meaning, nothing untoward has been found within my mind or soul. It's obvious from that encounter that there was a conflict between Yiruhm's oldest beast of burden, Gnoll, and..." With a blanched face, he straightened up his back and examined the lobby.

"Lady Shemishier." Other than the fallen books that floated back to their spots, the corrosion and breakage on some of the doors, and the constant reminder of his parents, the lobby remained completely the same. Minus the floor that is. In an almost robotic fashion, he turned to the right of the lobby and noticed that the fog had already cut the outline of a doorway and corridor straight to the magically oriented center of his mind. Without showing any haste, he reappeared in the mental space that he dedicated solely to the use of magic that he was taught about and learned to use in Simulations. The central platform was just as he left it, a mess with a glassy book set upon the pedestal that was set atop a rotating dais. The word "View" was carved into the crystal book's spine. The only difference was the addition of his [Prevention] book and a statue that contained the iconography of what one would assume to be a demon at first glance.

It was a tall, feminine figure with a long cowl drawn over an un-carved face and a dress that one would typically wear to a funer-al. This statue did not possess any of the conventional trapping or regalia of a romanticized divine being and instead carried two rings on a small necklace in one hand and clutched at the Dual Loop of Immortality that was carved into a pendant on their own chest. The only other piece of remarkable sculpting was a corset that bore all of the known names, symbols, and rules for every Prefix, Affix, and Suffix in existence. These words were on such a minuscule level and woven so intrinsically into the sculpture that many scholars were still discovering new patterns that revealed new curses and blessings that could be or already were bestowed upon someone.

"Gnoll." Now swaying side to side unsteadily, Alize returned to the lobby, half expecting to come back to find his thoughts ransacked. Unexpectedly, almost nothing changed.

"It's gone. Did you take my curse away?"

The timeline generated by his Affix was missing, even if his ability to recall the past was not hindered in the slightest. In fact, when he did so, the lobby's mist parted and revealed vast bookcases containing his memory, but to see any of the golden books or an arrow tracker on the floor, even in his memory, was impossible.

"This isn't like the times when it's been waiting or stalking my environment for a chance to do something. This feels like a full retreat. Or maybe an entrenching? Affix, or rather, Gnoll. Are you trying to hide something? It doesn't appear to be from me, so who or what are you trying to avoid getting caught doing?"

Alize sat down in his mind, stretched his neck, and stroked his chin. For half a second, he reminded himself of the chthonic entity that mistakenly came to claim his soul and recognized that there was a distinct lack of said being right now.

"Shemishier? Lady Death. Was I supposed to enter your embrace and my Affix, ahem, Gnoll, got in the way of that?"

Alize wasn't expecting a response, nor did receive one as his mind slowly returned to normal. The only piece of the puzzle that did not fit was the odd little chaotic creature. He could not understand its behavior or why it reminded him of the hero, so instead of attributing more attention than it was worth. The encounter was placed behind a locked door on the second floor.

"Hm. Anyway that I slice this problem, I come to the conclusion that I am not dead yet. Which is saying something." Alize stepped out of his mind once again and took in all of the sensory stimulation as if he was simply being tasered. This grain film and napalm burn was not the effect of the Void. That was an emptiness and desolation beyond the reductive descriptors that language could provide; it was nothing, and anything below the divine rank would become that. At best, it was a still canvas that Alize only comprehended as an "unknown" or an "other" because Gregory did his job almost perfectly. Then there was dead space. A lightless expanse that stretched so far that it was impossible to reach an end or see another light even if one traveled forever. The word space implied that it could be filled, even if it would be impossible to sense anything within it. This ashy, almost spectral grain was not that either since there were sounds and smells, and feelings that accompanied the burning, shock, and pressure. As far as Alize could tell, this was the opposite of space, of expansion. He was physically observing or perceiving a state of harmless compression beyond physics. "Abyssal" and "Primordial soup" came to his mind as he started to imagine and dissect the possibility. Everything, all at once, pressed and moving, and communicating, and conscious, and molding, splitting, spinning, birthing, decaying, recombining, and life and death, and matter and matter, everything beyond and in between. The impossibility of being able to perceive this was just, it was all too vast, so he fell back into his mental lobby as even the fog in his imagination thinned out, trying to force his brain to rationalize and understand.

"Am I so exhausted that even my Gnoll decided to back off and let me rest? Pfth, absolutely not. Based on what I have already been through, this is the calm before the storm. The primer. The Affix is finally digesting magic." Alize allowed his subconscious thoughts to bubble up and habitually covered his neck. After steadying himself, he returned his senses to the umbral expanse before him. This was not the dark of night, or an excessively vast shadow, nor was it an inescapable canvas of space devoid of light and feature. Above all of that, this was not the Void, a fate far worse than nothing and death and dark.

"It feels like I should see something but can't. In a weird way, this all reminds me of the Apeirogon..." Alize scanned what he believed was a horizon.

"And my [View] spell's outer boundary." At this moment, he was reminded of a saying that perfectly represented why he didn't want to push the spell beyond its limits. "If you stare into the abyss, the abyss stares back at you." View, his spell, worked on that concept and pushed the boundaries of his senses in a way that only Direct type spells could, but scientifically, he used magic to artificially increase the spin and charge of the physical forces that constituted his body. In other words, wherever he was, it was too fast and foreign. A physical body, as he had become aware, was too slow to exist wherever he was, and the mind was only capable of grasping at the foundational reality behind the veil. The abyssal and inky, almost textured chaos.

"My consciousness, my soul, has escaped my body yet again, but considering the conflict that just happened, it seems that I have just been pushed too far away from my own body." Alize immediately figured out that he was like a fisherman thrown overboard at sea and at night. He could either take on water and sink in the vast darkness around him, or float and roll with the waves and hope for survival. Thus, instead of drowning in despair, he moved all of his willpower toward observation. If he died peering into the unknown, then that was the reality of his situation. Thankfully, all that focus did was point him in the direction of a pinpoint splotch of color that folded into the unfathomable waves of grain at the corner of his vision.

"Holy crap." He examined the dot for a long time and felt his jaw drop.

"Have I been looking into wherever this is, through the Alli Initui?"

He didn't have the churning or the Affix to inform him of any correct guesswork, but the dot happened to be a life raft in this situation.

"Argus, Frogret." The tiny red dot within a grayed-out border enlarged and then showed **2.4562%** at the center of it.

"Is that enough for you to understand me? Can you help me?"

A soft whistling rang out in Alize's mind like a ringtone for a few seconds. A rustling sound, one that sounded eerily close to an object being lifted from one's chest, resounded at the end of the fifth tone.

"Hello? Argus?"

"Hello?"

"Argus?"

"Argus?"

"Alli Initui, I mean?"

"No. I am not Alli but ha, wow. That name brings me back."

"I am sorry. I was just trying to communicate with my artifact, and now I am not sure what's happening." Alize reached out with nothing but naïve sincerity.

"Haa, crazy. Not you shrimp. Look at this. That light means that someone found another copy fragment. Haa, I got it. Next time, if we are home, **okay. Mhwa, I love** you, **monkey. Ahem. Hey, mortal, good luck and good job getting your hands on one of these fragments."**

"Thank you?"

"You're welcome. Now, **take care of yourself and those around you. Hold love in your heart at all times and never show mercy to those** who **don't care about life. Goodbye."**

Before Alize could find the right moment to cut in, the red dot flashed orange in a specific sequence then minimized back into the corner of his vision.

"Argus. Frogret. Progress. Fuck. M'onen- durustra innokan. Can you understand me?"

Once again the dot enlarged, showing no progress beyond the 2.4 5%, flashed orange then chimed with the very same familiar whistling.

"Hello?"

"Hello?"

"Is this the Gla d'oer unisi?"

"**Haa, hoho. How dare you call my precious Alli one of those knockoff glass eyes. Presumptuous mortal, I don't know how long it's been for** you, **but such disrespect is unforgivable.**"

"Knockoff? Really? Uh, wait, please! I am sorry, sir or madam. I was just trying to confirm if my Scrying Glass could understand me. I'm in a really weird situation, and I'm trying to figure it out and..." Alize noticed something about the abyssal ash and the distribution of what he could only assume were swarms of magical gnats in the penumbra. The horizon turned into mounds and molehills, indistinct towers and riverlets, and swirls of constant motion indescribable, beyond dark, fantastical, and mesmerizing.

"**Oh. Is that so,**" the person on the other side of the call cut in.

"Yes, and—" Alize was about to speak when the call was abruptly dropped. The red dot flashed yellow, then orange, and finally minimized as a red dot. Without even having to be prompted, the Alli Initui or Argus initiated yet another call and held the tone for more than a minute until the call was picked up.

"**The time differential must be up because of this event. No, it's just another person who stumbled upon a fragment. Ha ha,** hello there, **mortal. Who are you?**"

"Hello, it's me again and...."

"**Itsumi Ayganan. Weird** name, **but I am not one to judge. Where did you get your** relic, **and what time period are you in?**"

"No, it is I again. I just called you two times before. I am the person who has the Alli Initui. I called it a Gla d'oer unisi, and you laughed at me. It couldn't have been more than a handful of seconds ago." Alize shot his shot and waited for a response. An uncomfortable amount of time passed by before he heard a response.

"Yeah. That's what I said, Ititsumi Agan. And of course you have a fragment of the Alli Initui, so you **have contacted me. Dumb** mortals, **am I right? Haa, exactly."**

"I am the same caller as the previous two times. I have a fully functioning Argus. I am trying to communicate with my relic but it is connecting me to whoever you are." Alize observed the shade and noticed how the constant buzzing and mixing slowed, no, rather it stilled as if someone stopped moving and he was attached to their position. It was not all too dissimilar from a lucid dream except he could not separate himself from the forced perspective.

"You are the same caller?"

"Yes."

"The fragment did not stop working or explode either of those two previous times?"

"I'm not using a fragment? But if I was, should it have become inactive or taken my life?"

The sounds that came through the call were enough to paint a vivid image of what was happening.

"Hold on, guys. **Save me a** seat. **I have to use the bathroom. Excuse me. Pardon. Let me** just **squeeze through** there **and thank you. Thank you. Hey** man, **how are you aHaaha, yeah. The kids? Oh, they are** troublemakers, **just like their mother used to be. Haa, what about you and yours? Nice, me? No, I'm going to the restroom."** That went on for a while as the person connected to Alize's Alli Initui rushed somewhere. The buzzing background chatter that Alize slowly parsed through and recognized as distinct sounds and voices, dimmed to a reverberating thud that felt like pressure buildup in the head.

"*Footsteps, maybe.*" Alize heard the other person running through what sounded like an empty, wide, and long hallway after the pressure of noise faded to the background. A bass boomed and a creaky door was thrown open, and just as he managed to comprehend the distinct footfalls of the person on the other side of the line, the sounds stopped.

"You have called me through three different fragments, **right? They are so** rare, **and here you are, wasting them."**

"No. I am using the same arcanum."

"Impossible. There is only one completely functioning Alli Initui and I have it. What you have is some fraudulent copy or some knockoff Universal Glass Eye. It's not Auntie's Alli' Intuition. Check your facts, **mortal."**

"I wouldn't even know where to begin. I was cursed either by misfortune or by Gnoll and ended up with this divine ranked Arcanum and now I am talking to you." Alize made sure that the being he spoke to understood his predicament.

"Well, **that really** sucks, **huh?"**

"Yes. It does. I am supposed to be home right now, waiting for...."

"Wow. It was a rhetorical question. Keep up, **mortal, damn. This stupid** cheque. **It never gives me what I want."** Alize heard the same ruffling and covered his ears to reduce a piercing clanging sound.

"Are you okay?"

"I'm doing fine, **you dumb mortal. I'm just trying to. No, I don't have to explain myself to** you." The movement continued for a while until the red dot at the corner of Alize's vision expanded unprompted.

"Hmph. This should do the trick. It was nice talking to you, **mortal,** but **it's time to say goodbye to you and your knockoff scrying glass."** The dot flashed through several dozen colors that Alize didn't even know existed and then blacked out, leaving an empty gray and white sphere floating in the corner of his vision.

"What did you do to Argus?"

Alize didn't feel or see anything wrong at first, but that didn't stop what was going to happen.

"Motherfuco, kay. Maybe this then. Figure it out mortal, C'est le but de la vie, " Before Alize could even parse through his memory for an even remotely similar language to what the entity on the other side of Argus's line said, a milk white whirlpool swept up his perception.

"I should have expected this. Curse, divine artifact, magic, change. Ha, of course the person on the other side of this call would be some careless god or playful demonic entity. I am going to die here. An errant consciousness, whisked away in a chaotic storm of something that I cannot perceive or fully understand. Thank you, Argus. You killed me faster than my Affix ever could. At least this is painless." Alize allowed his mind to fall inward, into his lobby of thoughts as he was swallowed by something remarkably unfamiliar.

"Alright. Wow. It didn't blow up again. Haa. Wow, you mortals really are drama queens, huh?"

"Huh?"

"Huh! Sorry. That was mean. Open your mind, **kid. You should be able to see me in three, two."**

Out of nowhere, Alize dove through the floor of his mental lobby and, similar to when he lucid dreamed, felt his body turn ethereal. Impossibly bright light, esoteric shapes, and vibrant colors that didn't have names burned into his, not retina, but his mind and soul. This ethereal dream state heightened and directly highlighted how impossibly slow light was at getting visual cues across and how rugged physical matter was at translating tactile senses.

"Look at that, I was wrong. There are two, a set. Haa. When did you mortals manage to develop a fully functioning Alli

Initui? Something must have been erased by her, something that she doesn't want anyone to know. Haa. Incredible." Alize couldn't register it at first, the abstract nature of everything that came out of the grainy abyss, out of the umbra and penumbra but the brain is an evolutionary miracle capable of working wonders all by its lonesome, nevermind magic so whatever the Divine messenger did completely updated his senses. That ghastly whirlpool that Alize fell through, pressed the boundary of his consciousness and translated the abstract colors and shapes, and penumbra into a familiar sfumato filter. His other senses came in a flood as the smell of freshly spritzed lemongrass and lavender assaulted his sense of smell. The soft cosmic hiss of a supergiant star or the rattle of an old and vibrating incandescent light bulb beat against his ears in whatever ethereal state he was now in. He couldn't feel anything, but for whatever reason, a salty, earthy, almost meaty, and somewhat soapy medley touched exactly four points on his tongue. As if he were licking someone's skin. A watery and fibrous and almost celery-like taste coated the rest of whatever sensory organ replaced his tongue. The only sense that felt muted and practically gone was his spatial awareness. He was no longer constrained by the memory of his physical body.

"Mortal. My bad. I really thought that." The person in front of Alize, someone who was slowly becoming more solid, stopped whispering the moment a nine-bell chime resounded.

"TESTING, TESTING. Ahem. Everyone, please report to the amphitheater. Mom. Ahem, Our Immortal and Eternally Beautiful, Graceful, and Benevolent Empress, is coming back from standard. A Yiruhm. She has an important announcement to make. That is all." The voice cracked through Alize's ability to comprehend speech, and forced him to simultaneously hear and understand every dialect, language, and body motion that was associated with the meaning of the words spoken over a PA system. The result was a fracture across Alize's lobby as thousands of books shot all over the place in an explosion.

"Sorry mortal. Let me uh. Here **we. Go. Is that better?"**

Like a camera coming into focus, Alize's perception equalized before the new environment. He wanted to clutch his non-existent beating heart, or graze the back of his neck, or complete some other habitual and calming act, but he quickly realized that he was stuck looking in the direction of the person that Argus connected him to.

"YOU!"

"Calm down. It's not like I planned for the feedback to crash into you like that."

"No. It's you. You are that guy. You are that teenager?"

"Mortal, I am 'That' guy, but I have not been a teenager for far longer than your cycle in Eternity has been in rotation."

"Oh my. No, you are the one who caught the camerawoman. THE Camerawoman. The one who caught the only known recording of Terah's Embrace on film." Alize recognized the guy even with his beard and more respectable haircut. His face, without the hair, would have been a slightly more muscular copy of the camera woman that briefly lost her tool of trade.

"Ohh. I haven't heard about that in a long time. Haa. It's nice to see that someone still knows about my sister." The man scratched his cheek and lifted Alize to his eye level.

"I am Red Leica. You can call me Red or Leica, or whatever you want."

"Hello Leica. I am Ark. It's nice to meet you. I would hold my hand out, but..." Alize trailed off as the world became less broken apart and more solid.

"Is he in a bathroom stall?"

"**I get it. Also, I can hear your thoughts and subconscious. Yes, I am in the bathroom. I was not joking when I told my family that I had to go.**" Red, as if Alize were an object, moved the kid's vision away from himself and used the bidet and toilet wipes to finish his business. Every stall, urinal, or waste disposal box was empty, aside from the one Red was now leaving. Observations would have ended there, but Alize couldn't help but gasp at the overly extravagant display of wealth and architectural design. Cloud veined marble, gleaming frescos made from precious metals and gemstones. Even the presence of fully autonomous constructs with porcelain skin, holding warm towel trays, mints, and utensils necessary for grooming one's person or clothing, all hit him like a truck.

"Are you in the Corridor?"

"Yes, **and No. I am inside the Corridor's Omnidome. The one over in Iris, in Yiruhm Proper.**" Red spoke, but his lips didn't move whatsoever.

"So you are on the Divine Continent. Ha, are you speaking to me directly?"

"**There are a lot of people here who would love nothing more than to overhear someone talking with a mortal outside of** Iris, **so no. I am talking directly to Argus just as you are. We can see each other's** conversations, I think. **I am not sure how this works quite yet. Seems to be a new** feature." Red lifted Alize once more and retrieved a cloth from his coat.

"Am I stuck looking through your lenses?"

"**I am assuming** so." Red cleaned up his glasses and wore them like any other person would.

"How long am I going to be stuck following you?"

"**How should I know? I thought you were some pushy Ballast Caster that hacked me using one of those knock off universal**

eyes or one of those idiots that keep asking me questions about the fragments and where to find more." Red graciously accepted the primping of the standby servants as they restyled his hair, combed and clipped his beard, and freshened up his clothes with different spells and sprays.

"Leica?"

"Yes?"

"Am I dead? Or in a sim?"

"No? That's a weird thing to ask, **though."**

"I know." Alize, to preserve his own sanity, paced around in his mental lobby and kept a singularly focused eye on the screen that appeared in the middle of the room. Everything that Leica looked at, his mind picked up, and not just visual cues.

"This is a remarkable setup, kid. Ark, I mean." Red Leica's voice appeared directly behind Alize without any warning.

"Thank you!? I was wondering how long my natural defenses would hold up against an eighth rank?"

"Haa. If only. I don't have the discipline or the death wish to push myself that far. I am a seven-star." Leica appeared on the second floor of Alize's mind and peered into one door after the next. He even slipped the chains and peeked through the keyholes of the first three doors and cringed. Beads of sweat rolled down his face the moment he turned away.

"You have quite a lot going on in your life, huh, kid?"

"I told you that I was cursed. It happens to be a very dangerous one, and my parents haven't taken to just letting me get killed." Alize didn't feel as though any of this was out of the ordinary, nor did he make a fuss as Leica perused his thoughts like an open book. This was bound to happen, in some way, by force or not, the moment that someone or something pulled his consciousness out of or away from the Duplicator. The only thing that Alize knew to do in this situation was follow the devil she knew instead of trusting the one she didn't. And in this case, that familiarity was the connection that his relic initiated with this strange guy called Leica. Alize paused as the guy spun one board after the other, reading everything about Alize's life in the few steps that it took him to walk from one desk to the next.

"I can see that. Hm, strange. You had a whole bunch of memories in this direction, right? Stuff related specifically to your curse?"

"Yes. My Affix shut down the whole region. I'm not sure how or why, but what can I do other than accept it?"

"Yup, I know how that is. One of my kids was born with a Prefix." Red tapped out of Alize's mind and memory. Without having paid attention, the only two people to ever wield in the manner that connected them like this, entered a crowd and fell in line with the rest of the even stranger bodies and forms that were trying to get somewhere.

"What's the series and name if you don't mind me asking?"

"**Broken.**" Red paused for a long time before he said anything. Alize, even if he wasn't connected to his body and was nothing more than a mass of thoughts and ego floating inside of someone else's glasses, felt his heart drop into his stomach.

"**The name is Sightless Life.**" Red stifled a self-deprecating laugh.

"**I saw it coming, you know. Before I inherited her Initui. I saw the Prefix hitting my kid. I tried to avoid having kids but, ha, Prefixes. They are more like getting a promissory note from fate and being kneecapped by reality until the thing that is supposed to happen, happens,**" Red excused himself as he moved through a network of halls and up dozens of flights of steps.

"**Happy accidents, one after the other. Kid, Ark. My bad.**" The divine guy sighed and shook his head slightly.

"I know you are trying to be respectful by not asking, **but Phase is her name. My youngest."** Leica straightened his back as the crowd turned a corner and up a ramp that led to a blindingly white exit.

"That is a beautiful name, especially despite the Broken series." Alize imagined how Leica hoped that the Prefix would end up taking after his daughter's name, and end up being a broken or cursed phase in her life.

"It is. I know what a Prefix can do to a person, to a family, and tried to pick a name that would always be a reminder to be hopeful. To be happy. To push through anything that might come her way to make life difficult or scary. Even without a magical curse, life **can shut down a bright kid's entire** future." Red covered his eyes to adjust to the glare of a passing entity that embodied and set the limit for Light.

"I can only imagine what that Affix of yours will end up doing. I can tell that it's an immortal series just by looking at the gaps in your memory. It's woven into you more than anything I have ever seen on my own daughter. I couldn't see the name or any reference to it, **so I'm assuming Gnoll personally ripped out any mention of** herself, **but just looking at the problems on your mind. Shit, the Eternal realm is about to get into it again. Ha. And here I thought Mourra finally put an end to the nonsense with his intervention."** Red passed through the threshold of the radiant doorway with a confident step.

3.9 Tired, Tested, Tried

Alize, somehow within the Alli Initui, faced a mind-altering, perspective-rewriting, enlightening, divine revelation the moment that the flash of the doorway faded. Unfathomable entities of all flavors, makes, beliefs, and concepts gathered in an amphitheater befitting the infinite scope of reality, a reality beyond what Alize understood or could imagine. Thus, he focused on what was familiar. High-backed walls, columns, and free-floating overhangs of a uniform but densely decorated and chiseled stone sported drapes depicting pantheons, legends, heroes, hellish incarnates, demons, gods, and all manner of impossible idols and figures.

Cascading velvet carpets rolled up and down every step in a varied enough color patterning and stylization that there seemed to be some semblance of order in all the chaos, even if Alize only grazed the surface of the intricate arrangements. The next thing that he noticed through the port that was Argus is that every spot was filled. Notably, giants stood out. They were so large that only the bottom ridges of their shoes or toes could be seen, colored in the same barely off gray scale or slate as Jordaine's unscalable mountains. The only difference was that even as he shifted his gaze, the giants appeared farther and larger with every single blink of an eye. The next interesting stimulus was a seat that replicated the same amphitheater on an impossibly minuscule scale. The only difference in the occupants was a simplicity of form and detail that went so deep Alize found himself gasping and grappling with the impossibility of complex sentience on such a scale.

On that same miniature, the same amphitheater mini was equipped with an even smaller nano replication that went even further down. Almost inherently, instinctively, Alize realized that whoever or whatever occupied the seat in the theater embodied the very nature of minimization. Leica, almost as if he could foresee Alize's revelation, turned back to the largest of the giants that the kid first noticed. The entire theater now seemed to be completely overshadowed and surrounded by a single crag in one of the giant's skin cells. Unable to wrap his mind around the still-expanding titan, Alize moved his attention. Hawkers who wanted to make a quick Quill found ways to peddle their wares up and down the stairs as if this gathering was a common fair.

"There are. Too many. It's almost as if..."

"There are more divine beings gathered here than in history?"
"Yes!"

"There are. At least, more than in recorded history. This is the Corridor's Omnidome. Specifically, we have all been gathered in or on Iris, the absolute center of everything from across time, space, reality, existence. However, or whatever is easiest to rationalize."

"The Omnidome? Center? Hm, what about..."

"**The vast majority of these people aren't in Yiruhm, in Eternity. Freely that is. I'm sure the orator will get to it. Haa, but in case it doesn't come up.**" To explain it better, Leica projected the thought of himself inside of Alize's mental lobby and hijacked a blackboard. With a casual spin of his wrist, he drew up the amphitheater's seating arrangements.

"**The seating follows any** run-of-the-mill **theater's format. The only difference here is** in the **specific conditions regarding attendance. For example, the VIP and reserved seats...**" Red filled out the central most cluster of seats and its surrounding.

"**Are for the current pantheon of Gods, spirits, Fae and everyone else that** has **reached the** divine-ranked **benchmark and** has **fallen in line with our Immortal Lady. In other words, they are the shield looking out for the mortal like you and the sword that is pretty much forcing everyone else in this gathering to protect their own little slices of existence and time.**" Red didn't outright point toward the section and only offered a little bit more than a passing glance. Alize committed the faces that he saw to memory and connected each one to a name that Leica wrote onto the blackboard.

"**The sections around the VIP seats are for other** modern-day **bigshots but those who didn't make it into the inner circle or left it for personal reasons. You can see some lesser-known Archons, some lords and ladies of the balancing Scales, the Magi of the inverted desert and Wizards of the far shore, and even a few Apex hunters and Legends that are scattered about. All of them, and you, are from the modern age of Yiruhm. The group on the fringe, aren't registered with any of Yiruhm's leadership and have never made their identities known so I can't tell you who they are, however, they still support and remain with Our Lady despite being mostly antagonistic and downright evil at times.**

My best guess is that they survived some experience that showed them the alternative of Eternity and represent the Abyss." Red trailed off as he briefly trailed off toward another group of people tucked away in a back corner of the amphitheater. No one looked, interacted, or even noticed this relatively small group. No one except for Leica, that is.

"Speculation is all I have, and observation. Sadly, I didn't inherit my sister's relic until recently, **so I missed my window to see the truth."** Red guffawed upon seeing the incredulity written across Alize's face.

"The group on the other side of the theater, functionally, is **a neutral party in the grand scheme of creation. We all like to call them retirees. People who have done their part in ensuring mortal life, so they just want to enjoy after all of the hassle of establishing this balance."** Red stopped looking around and allowed a small unit of ghastly, skeletal gibbons to pass by him. They wore feathers for crowns and luxurious painted bones and hides for clothes, and communicated with nearly inaudible intonations of their massive leathery throats and diaphragms. They all tried to convince, beg, or even bribe a golden-armored guy that resembled a monkey with the proportions of a human. Seemingly upset, he transformed into a gnat and flew toward one of the few regions of the amphitheater that was themed and controlled by a single banner and one of the largest groups.

"If you look over there." Red drew colorful lines all over the blackboard and tied them to his shifting gaze as he explained one group after the other. One contained animals in primeval, almost exaggeratedly savage appearances. Another had heroes and villains in loud costumes ranging from spandex to robes. While most held some religious or symbolic reference that Alize placed them as dating back to the Celestials and the needlessly long Void Era. A period of time dominated by humanity and its insane ingenuity, short lifespans, and conflicts. He put a star on the notes that he committed to memory and copied the information Leica shared with him into long-term memory, almost entirely because the topic of humans had been broached.

"In that section in the back, it's **the largest and is one that is full of the most outsiders."** Leica didn't have to say anything for Alize to understand what he meant.

"Those are the Divinites? And the creepy things around them? Are they?"

"Creepy is right; **uncanny is the word that I would use. The Outer Gods, the first children of our lady, I understand that there wasn't a lot at the start of Eternity to work with to create or birth them. That's understandable. But those** humans. **Yeesh. Even the ones that have fallen in with our Lady's camp are a bit mental."** Red scanned the crowd at large, zooming in on groups of humans that were more akin to legitimate shapeshifters as they wore an assortment of clothes, faces, and bodies that truly spread across a spectrum so varied, it hurt the mind to comprehend. The gnat-shaped monkey man reappeared in the back of the human section, separating himself but still overlooking the crowd with several other figures that split the single-bannered area into different internal camps.

Alize followed Leica's panning gaze and took in the insanity that was before him. These people were so varied that they could have integrated into practically every group and served in roles or in positions so varied that it was impossible to say anything specific about what unified humanity, other than being weird and chaotic. The eldritch and varied appearances of the first divinities and their similarities to the youngest sentient life to join eternity did not lessen as Red parsed through the crowd and recognized a notable bunch. They sat by and propped up a banner that was just a blue and green flag that bore seven interlocked silver rings.

"They are neither here nor there, fading in and out of this world at the flip of a thought. Mourra loves them, even after. Well, you already know what has come out of the Voided era." Red frowned as he once again noted the mysterious and unnamed group all the way at the back corner of the Yiruhm support camp.

"The almost total collapse of our history?"

"An unfortunate loss. Thankfully, our lady had the foresight to preserve some of what happened with the Vielseam. Ha, you have questions. Speak your mind."

"Thank you. I just have two, three things that I want to ask. First, why haven't you filled out the section that we are heading toward on the blackboard? You explained every other group here. Second, you didn't say who those seats at the center of the VIP section are for. I have never seen the pit of a theater elevated like that. Thirdly, I am just plain confused by what the orator said during the PA announcement that I heard. I've been trying to read into it, but I can't figure it out. I know that there is chronomancy, dimension hopping, plane shifting, and Incast Blip stuff that regular people could do if given the resources or strength of will to sacrifice their magic or contents but is there a distinction between using A and THE as descriptors for the mortal realm that I am not understanding? Or can she travel freely outside and back into Eternity, examining multiple parallel scenarios?"

Alize didn't waste any time and stood right beside Leica as the older gentleman stopped drawing on the map.

"The answer to your first question is, this region is full of dead people."

"Thats..."

"Not impossible. Death is the finish line for all life aside from Our Lady's. Anyone else at the divine rank is just good at moving horizontally to avoid the outcome. That's just reality. A lot of people in this section just haven't done everything in their power to prolong or escape the inevitable. That or they are actively courting our Lady's shadow for some weird fantasy or power play."

"Does that mean..."

"Am I dead? No. The box seats that you and I can see around this region are for special cases. Typically, we are treated as fate makers, seers, truth sayers, oracles, or advisors of a pantheon if we are part of one. You can see small motifs on the box seats if the Seer is willing to advertise their connection. The latter are 'free agents', as our Lady likes to say. Free to rebel, fight, and change the world and her designs if they so choose. It's an endeavor that usually comes at the expense of their own life or the death of an era." Leica smiled as Alize slowly turned toward him with a blanched expression. He tried to conceptualize what a divine-ranked, self-acclaimed seer and truth-sayer had just told him.

"Wait! You just said..."

"One moment." Red slowly lost his smile as he examined the amphitheater in ways Alize simply didn't understand. Based purely on the expressions, body language, idle conversation, or lack thereof, the divine guy was able to see a conflict brewing on a scale that left him breathless. His pupils constantly twisted and splattered like an inkblot as the future unraveled in a way that made him uncertain of Yiruhm's future. He locked eyes with an individual that sat within a massive tent, who began brewing tea for themselves.

"Sorry. I saw something that gums up some of the plans that I had made for my kids. What were you talking about?"

"You knew that I would contact you today, right now? If you knew, why did you pretend not to know it was me?"

"Oh?"

"The Initui. There is not a pair, or a mortal-made copy capable of connecting to this relic. Everything that I am seeing is a recorded message, isn't it?"

"I am sorry for doing this again." Leica vanished from Alize's mind, from the space that Argus allowed him to occupy.

"Did I guess wrong? Could it be that..."

"Congratulations." Leica reappeared in a flash of crystalline magic and new clothing that bore a weird resemblance to the armor of Jordaine's Haven officers. The only difference was the unique placement of weaponry, extra armor pieces, a color palette change, and a distinct lack of symbols that tied him to Haven, Jordaine, or any other authoritative power. The Red Leica that Alize had been 'talking' to thus far, calmly walked through the amphitheater using a silken cloth to wipe his lenses during this change.

"I have to focus on sending a message to anyone noticing and recorded this bit a few centuries before getting in contact with you." Within Alize's mind, Leica bowed. The position was slightly off, as if he was not looking at Alize.

"I know things are a bit confusing, but once you are with the relic for a bit, you will see how things aren't necessarily in a linear order. That said, my future friend and I are going to set everything up for you, so just know that as my successor, you may have to step it up. I just have one thing to remind you of. No matter what, do not let our Lady's shadow get in the way. Intentionally or not, try not to die or let yourself get close. Make sure to remain steady, focused, and open-minded." Leica laughed even harder and then suddenly looked over to his side.

"**I gotta go. My future friend is a bit hangry, so I gotta deal with that.**" Leica of the far past left Alize's mind. The flash, however, turned into a trail of sparkles that encircled a dot in the corner of his vision. It now showed 35.245% complete toward something. Red of the present, or a more recent past, once again sported his bifocals and drew Alize's attention to his sly wrist flick. The cloth that he used twisted into a thread smaller than the entire diameter of a single electron and snaked along the floor toward the person who brewed tea in a canopied box seat. In the millisecond-long duration of the distraction, Leica reappeared beside the blackboard that contained a detailed breakdown of seating arrangements.

"**Sorry about that.**"

"No problem. My parents had me learn how to get my bearings in non-Euclidean space so I understand, somewhat. It was in a simulation, so it wasn't exactly the same as all of this."

"**I saw that when I looked. The next time that you find yourself in a looping jumble. Stand still and fill out as much space as you can around you. Preferably, don't use magic. It agitates space-time, helping you anchor yourself.**"

"Thank you."

"**Of course. As for your next question. Those raised seats are for Our Lady, our lord or ladyship consort, and the main pillars of Yiruhm's managerial pantheon. They are, in most cases, the kindest and the most hardworking of all of us so-called immortals. As for your third question, it will have to wait a minute or two. Things have been unraveling and becoming less clear.**" Red wanted to answer Alize's third question but paused given the circumstances of his situation. His eyes bore an ink splotch that resembled the loop of infinity. If Alize could see them, he would have noticed that the loop began bleeding in the exact same manner that his own Affix broke apart and leaked across his spine.

"Hey kids. I'm back, thanks for getting them to their seats." Despite walking as slowly as he possibly could to extend the duration of his talk with Alize, Red Leica could not stop himself from reuniting with the group that he parted from.

"Red, you have to train your children better. They are incorrigible." A woman with an extra eye on her forehead waved Leica aside and frowned.

"Honey! It wasn't even a thing, Red. We got you, man. Just take it easy next time. You have to accept that your stomach just isn't what it used to be." A ruggedly handsome but pot-bellied man standing at a full 30 cm nodded as he floated onto the woman's shoulder and kissed her cheek.

"Got it, thank you two again anyway. And you, my little shrimp, what are you laughing about?"

Leica approached the back of his family's specially arranged box and stared suspiciously at a roster of five kids that mostly bore a striking resemblance to him.

"Daddy, Oly and Lumix got me a bomb stick and a rainbow swirly. Do you want some?"

A mischievously chuckling little girl, no more than 4 or 5, stood up on her seat and attempted to show off a massive shish kabob full of different hard candies and pastries and a cup that was around the same size as her. How she managed to hide it, no one would ever know. That's a lie, Red immediately tied the deception to a pale, almost bloodless girl with long hair and a far-off gaze that put too much emphasis on how little she was interested in the little girl's antics.

"Oh? So you weren't hungry at the buffet but now you are?"

"Yes, do you want some?"

The little girl definitely attempted to show off her strength and balance by standing on her chair, and in absolutely no time at all, she tripped on the armrest and dropped everything. Leica's priority was his daughter, so faster than Alize could process, the little girl was already in her father's arms. The spear of sweets and the tankard of fruit-flavored ice, however, did not drop forward onto the hand-sized man and the woman with a third eye. Instead, the treats ended up near the mouths of two miniature giants.

"Boys, don't give your sister things that she can't balance with." Red sighed and stared up at his sons. Each one sat down with frames triple the size of their father but with features that undoubtedly proved their ancestry. The only difference between the two boys was the shorter height and baby fat on one and the peach fuzz and bit of musculature on the older of the two. Each one held one of the almost-fallen snacks and munched or sipped while looking shocked at having been blamed or pretending not to listen.

"I tried to get them to stop."

"Liar. Dad, Canon is lying. She is the mastermind."

"Nice job, little bro. Lying to dad. Haa."

"Shut up, Oly. Dad! Canon told Niko to pay for it. Look at her wallet."

"Linux. Lying really doesn't look good on you. I'm not even mad that you would blame me. I'm just worried about how you forget that you paid?"

"Niko, don't even. I didn't pay."

"Check your wallet then? I'll even do mine right after that." While Leica's children fought, he took in the sight with a smile and sat down next to a young woman who resembled him the least, even if she was the only one who bore the same colored ink splotted pupils as him.

"I paid for it, Dad. I didn't expect them to start fighting over the snacks. I am sorry." The oldest laughed at the antics of her siblings.

"NO! I bought the snacks. I got hungry."

"You nasty little gremlins. Ha, shrimp don't fall for any of their nonsense. Don't you start lying to me too." Leica ignored the tug of war behind him and tickled his youngest, Phase.

Alize observed this heartfelt interaction twice over. The first time, he noticed that Leica's oldest was anywhere in her late 30s to mid-20s. The others were anywhere between their late teens, based on their outward appearances. Leica, however, only saw all of them as little ragamuffins no bigger than his youngest. Put on the sidelines of his current patron's attention, Alize moved around the mental space that Argus reflected and focused on the peripheral vision that was recorded.

"Where is Gnoll on this distribution of multiversal placement? That cursed spirit is not only responsible for my Affix. It rearranged my memory before the Initui connected me to Leica. There has to be a reason. The most likely one is that Gnoll does not want to be tethered to me right now, but why? Would it be possible for. Dumb question, obviously, some of the divine beings in this crowd could undoubtedly notice that I have the residue of the spirit's Tenets. The only thing probably hiding the effuse of Gnoll is little miss Phase." For a split second, Alize looked at Leica's youngest and noticed that her pupils had essentially been ripped out of her eyes. Covering her irises was a massive X-shaped reflective sigil that resembled barbed wire as it spread, constricted her blood vessels, and possibly even trailed along the optic nerve and onto the occipital lobe of her brain.

"It must have been horrible for Mr. Leica's entire family. To know what would happen and just accept this outcome." Alize held his stomach as a deathly pallor spread across his face.

"Thank you for not taking out any of your anger on me." He respectfully bowed toward the screen and continued to examine what the older user of the Initui recorded for him. His attention shot to the stage. There wasn't anyone on it, not yet at least, but there was a setup. A long bench with a seat faced the audience, dressed by a table set on either side. His thoughts raced as he tried to guess what kind of meeting of the Divine that this gathering would turn out to be. Never did he expect, even in a least likely scenario, that some of his burning questions would be answered in such an extravagantly straightforward way.

"It's about to start, Ark. I forgot to say this when I was voicing over the footage the first time, but there is a distinction between 'The' mortal realm or Yiruhm and 'A' Yiruhm. The former refers to Eternity, or the mortal realm, since it is always the first life-bearing solar system in the universe and the last to be destroyed when a gathering like today happens. You can refer to the Age of Burden for what it looks like when Yiruhm is close to being renewed. It was the last time that one of these meetings had been called." Leica didn't appear, and instead, a floating red piece of chalk wrote everything down on the blackboard.

"A mortal realm is everything else not created or molded directly by Our Lady's hand. They are old realities, parallel manifestations of the world created by some bored divine entity, or a different time code and cycle that people from Yiruhm can fall into if there is an Incast Blip. A mortal realm also refers to a self-sufficient terrarium that is on a scale that is similar to or is a replica of Yiruhm as a whole." Red stopped writing and allowed Alize to restructure his own understanding of history as he saw fit. For the kid's sake, he also kept his eye on the pit platform with 14 seats and continued to swivel in his seat to pan across the crowd.

Keepers of the Void, people in uniforms similar to what Gregory wore but more primped, proper, and uniquely designed, adjusted seating, laid mats on the long risen platform, placed cushions on seats, and draped blankets over the high back rests on all 14 seats. Each blanket, aside from the two seats at each end, was embroidered with an overall design or patterning that echoed throughout the amphitheater. The resonating tapestries overwrote the background of banners and sigils of pantheons and groups and split the entire endless structure into roughly 13 sections if one included the "Dead" or "Free" gods. Once those attendants were done, they prepared the stage. A microphone was placed on the podium, and a banner was rolled down its slate-gray face.

A black banner, as deep and soul-crushing as the void itself, dripped from a silver cord and bloomed into a tangle of yellow and green stems that unfurled with wide, almost splashing leaves. Blue, purple, white, pink, and red flower buds seemingly popped out of the banner as silver and orange trichomes dribbled out of and down the leafy greens and yellows, into silken and free-floating strands. As the banner rolled out, an iridescent array of flowers similar to the Queen of the Night bloomed in a never-ending cascade that completely pushed the encroaching void out. A sea of green, pink, red, yellow, blue, white, and silver spanned half of the tall podium. The moment it hit halfway, an uncountable number of similar banners right beside each pantheon or independent 'Free agent' miraculously appeared and unfurled. The silver and orange threads that dripped throughout the first tapestry, wove and weaved through the beautiful chaos of life and connected each banner, knitting into a tangle right above the floating platform that was above where the pit should have been. Magic, similar to pollen, rained down on the crowd, sprouting crystalline flowers across nearly every empty surface.

"It feels alive." Alize gasped as the spindling silver and orange threads pushed upward and above the amphitheater and filled the Omnidome with a heavenly fragrance and body-numbing ease. For a moment, Alize was reminded of a spider lily, but only for a moment as a single orange bud rose from the silver sprout and bloomed into a flower that defied physics as it completely detached from the tangle and rose above it. Like a sun, the luminescent and gargantuan petals overshadowed everything but only for a single moment. Almost as if its own size and power were toxic, a single petal collapsed inward and boiled with energy. The single point of contact liquefied, putrefied, over the course of the banner's unraveling and imploded. Twisting and snapping, and squealing as if the flower were a body that was pushed through a meat grinder.

Tar, void black, and rotten in stench, oozed out of the luminous stamens and burned the silver tangle in less than a few seconds of blooming, almost as if the flower was trying to singe the rot and protect itself. The immolation did not discriminate and ate away at everything. Beauty and horror in a petrifying union were displayed as a grainy, textured, abyssal ash, like a slurry of dried blood that hydrated using venom instead of water. The sludge rained down and coalesced around the once stunning tangle of floating roots. The void banners swallowed their sprouts and cut each other off, destroying any chance of ever reuniting. In seconds, all that remained was a disgusting and writhing mass that somewhat resembled a seed or a sphere, floating right above the 14 raised seats. Alone, it pulsed and splattered onto the void that now composed each of the independent banners. A single silver tear was pressed out of the tangle and splattered onto the very first tapestry to be rolled out over the stage. It rolled along the inky tarp in such a manner that everyone could see, hear, and feel the ripple that it caused as the blooming life that followed after this drop repeated itself several times over. Each time, it was more beautiful that the last and infinitely more horrifying when it all collapsed back.

"It's not alive. It's a reminder of how we all die. How we all leave our Lady alone to deal with the aftermath of our infighting and the troubles that we all leave behind." Red interjected only after the attendants began to retreat.

"It reminds everyone here of what Our Lady loves and what she hates. For whatever reason, I couldn't tell you what the banner actually means. There is a rumor that the Divinities know, but there hasn't been a single one of them that has decided to break their silence. Some humans too, but they make every attempt to understand more complicated."

Almost instantly, Alize recalled the hero's patron. An ancient divine being that had and held no modern references despite being entirely aware of everything going on in his own and the Hero's life. The idea that it was an ancient divinity sent a chill down his spine.

"I'm not sure about who that is. There has never been a divinity **here that matches the appearance of the entity that I am seeing in your mind. I can only assume that the person you met is one of Our Lady's children. And one that isn't particularly involved in whatever is going on with us mortals and immortals."**

"Something is wrong about what you just said."

"I agree. But..."

"BUT?"

"But I do not know what else to tell you. I only see facts, **and my sister's intuition only sees truth. Right now, the facts that you have are not enough for the relic to help me give you answers."** Red shrugged his shoulders, seemingly out of nowhere to the rest of his family and friends, and turned his gaze over toward a familiar sight. Dense fabric covered the sides of a simple squared tent, but now, two extra people wearing matching clothes pulled back a curtain that hid someone that Alize only saw once before. This person in robes sat down in a lotus position and sipped tea as they played a simple game Alize recognized as Tact. As far as Alize understood, it was a board game with 120 pieces spread across 3 different boards along 3 separate axes, all of which was duplicated nine times over and overlapped across differently colored squares. On the other side of the amphitheater, 3240 people all had a single game in front of them, one resembling chess but detailed and colored similar to a city or landscape blueprint. Each one ripped out their own hair or banged their heads while despondently crying as their board fragmented and overlapped on the boards of their still playing allies like a tower.

"I have a friend who I can ask about your circumstances, **but I am not sure if I will have an answer before my recording runs out. I am still unsure on how Argus has managed to connect us."**

"Is there going to be an issue if you look into that Divinity and Hero for me?"

"Hopefully not. I do know that if there is a roadblock, **I can always ask Gnoll. That one seems to be responsible for your meeting with that entity and with me. For now, keep an eye on the stage."**

"Thank you."

"Mhm, don't worry **about it. Helping you just gives me anoth-er excuse to confront that cursed woman."**

As Leica said, the stage lit up with movements unlike anything Alize had ever seen before. Dancers, acrobats, and pyrotechnic displays raced across the stage and up the steps of the amphitheater. The lone podium that held the very first void banner expanded and rose up into the sky, putting all of the focus on a handsomely dressed man that reminded Alize of Bigs. He had tall hair, blinding teeth, a loud outfit, and a personality that filled and overpowered the entire space. Which is a remarkable feat considering the several dancing phoenixes, raging dragons, flashing Nephele, twisting Rocs, and prancing unicorns that synchronized an eye-catching recital.

"Stars! Large and small, burning with life, magic, and humility. Stars! Loving, burning, hating, feeling, and yearning to be better by providing more not only for yourself, but for others. My fellow stars! We are gathered here today for a special occasion. For a once in an eternity announcement. Light bringers, life bearers, and children of the one and only Immortal, bring your hands together for mom- OUR LADY!"

Silence. Muted. Blank. Hyper focused silence. Alize didn't hear anything that the man said as his gaze fully locked onto the raised platform with 14 seats. He snapped through his entire life and found that all nine years of life that he has been granted, the decades that he spent inside of Sims curated by his parents, and every nightmare that stretched on anywhere between days to millennia due to a curse, all of that time was nowhere near enough to prepare him for what he beheld. Raucous, almost ravenous cheers, crying, and emotional outpouring was met with gaudy flare as everything turned white, then black, then mesmerisingly colorful. Up on the raised platform that should have been a pit, where simple and high-backed armchairs were made unique and comfortable, people and odd objects materialized. As far as Alize understood it, other than the Divinites, these were the only ninth ranked, divine beings in all of creation.

"Poayact, Shemishier, Noune, Ye'or Aibjrs, Canaemort, Om' tare Ithe, Belladore and Belldore, Tolltalitus, Innasearte, and..." Alize gulped as he noticed that three of 14 seats did not have a primping attendant or an incomprehensible entity occupying it. Putting aside whatever that vacancy meant, Alize felt his attention draw to the 13th occupied seat.

"Gnoll!"

A divine [Shroud] enveloped a spherical region just above the table and unfurled into the wings of a butterfly to either side of the ragged sphere. In the blink of an eye, night, constellations, and life manifest, gently lowered onto a cushion. A distinctly feminine form crossed one leg over the other as a hand plunged into a cowl so deep that the spirit's face was nothing but a tangle of shadows. A necklace, now worn, bore two rings, and an outfit so intricately detailed and scribed that all curses and blessings could be seen writhing along its surface. This was the creator and mother of all Prefixes, Affixes, and Suffixes and the target of Alize's anger, sorrow, and capitulation.

"It seems that Our Lady. Ahem, that we have all come a bit earlier than the designated time, so while we wait for Our Lady to show up, how about we get this show on the road." The Orator at the podium stared at and seemed to communicate with the 11 beings up on the raised platform and began hyping up the crowd with mindless drivel that painted the picture of, propaganda. It was propaganda. All in all, Alize did not hear anything worth paying attention to as he completely locked onto Gnoll. He counted the frequency, duration, and depth of each of the spirit's breaths, committed the names and movement of each curse and blessing that danced along the spirits outfit, to memory. He even counted the number of times that the spirit moved and when its gaze shifted even minutely. Nothing else entered or filtered through his mind as he focused entirely on the divine being that had hooked itself into his life. That is, until Leica purposefully looked at his close friends and forced Alize to hear his conversation.

"The rumors are true then?"

Alize tuned in only after the older gentleman tapped his imaginary shoulder and motioned him to follow along.

"What?"

"Red." The 30cm man, who twinkled with a blazing white flame, sprung from his seat and closed the distance between himself and Leica. The spirit raised a fist and was about to strike, but Leica gave him a pair of puppy-dog eyes.

"Fuck you, man." The flaming spirit sighed and consciously steered his fist off course.

"Ohhhhh. Tio Ure said a nasty word." A cascade of parroting and childish voices beat the spirit called Ace into submission.

"Hand it over" was the next phrase to be said five times over.

"Damn extortionists." As if it were a common occurrence, Ace took out a handful of Quill that varied in color and in the number of notches along their surface. The lady with the third eye massaged her own temples as the kids once again chirped for their swear jar money.

"Boncheit kin, you lot are leeches. How could you raise your kids like this, Red?"

"Easy. Give them a good home, food, love, and a little bit of an education and bam—next thing you know, they start conspiring to fleece you. You specifically. By the way, kids, the word he used means." Leica said something to his kids that Alize couldn't hear. Thankfully, it didn't matter in this case since he knew the language that the wily spirit used.

"Little bastards." Alize tried not to be rude by eavesdropping on the conversation, but he couldn't help it. It was funny seeing all of Leica's kids gasp after Phase came to the slow realization that it was a bad word. They all followed her lead, chanting, "Bad word, pay up."

"Is this what you wanted me to see?"

"No. But don't you think they look cute?"

The scene played out for a while as the fiery shorty continued cursing at the absurdity of losing money to a bunch of kids that all glued the words "Swear Jar" across the front of their cartoon animal themed wallets.

"I've been robbed, hon!"

All of Leica's kids laughed as they waved down some hawkers.

"Well. Think about being helpful before you get violent next time." Red stifled a laugh as Phase puffed out her chest and asked her aunt and uncle that if they wanted something to eat, that she would loan the money. Obviously, considering the state of Ace's empty wallet, they accepted and shook hands on the matter. After the girl paid, she offered Ure a napkin that had scribbles written in crayon. Without any warning, the flaming spirit puffed out a mouthful of smoke as his flaming hair snuffed out. He was hit with an IOU, complete with a tidy compounding interest rate of 27% per minute that Phase's food loan remained unpaid. It went without saying that Phase held onto the original and only gave her uncle a copy.

"Red?"

"I got you. Come here, shrimp. I'll make sure that you little gluttons are fed, so let your uncle off the hook just this once." Red waved down the same hawker and paid for a small mountain of food before any of the kids could use their newly acquired funds. Having successfully called off his own kids, he passed the original contract napkin to his best friend and brother by choice and watched the man eat and burn it up with a ghastly shudder.

"Thank you, Red. I wouldn't have been able to. You know." Ure spoke through bouts of spitting ash, and he motioned toward his wife.

"No problem. Shrimp. Don't use your contract with your family, please."

"Okay. Sorry, Tio Ure."

"Don't worry, little Phase. Please don't cry. It's okay. I'm alright." The Spitfire, suddenly overwhelmed, tried putting on a funny face but only made it worse and got stuck in a cycle of trying to make it better. The woman with the third eye quickly found herself annoyed and pushed the hovering firefly off to the side.

"To answer your question. Yes. The rumors are true, or the one that this loudmouth just said is true. Mourra apparently overstepped his given authority in a mortal realm that Our Lady was personally visiting for ideas, and it somehow affected Yiruhm proper negatively."

"Gossett, that can't possibly be true."

"It's true."

"Which parts then?"

"All of what I said is true, ass-ho-ciate. Associate friend." Ure cut in after he finished assuaging the little devil with a blank check. He dove into the cleavage window that Gossett possessed in order to recover his emotional energy. The maneuver also served as a protective measure to avoid the demonic gazes and twisting smiles of Red's spawn. Whatever they were telling Phase to write on her blank check was surely going to come back and bite him in the ass at some point.

"Azure is telling as much of the truth as he can. His memory isn't doing its best right now." Gossett did her best to whisper, but even as she did so, there was a distinct lack of noise around the Leica family box.

"My memory is fine, woman! I have the mind of a pyre." Azure waved his fist and glared upward but found that his fire turned from snow white to a flickering blue.

"Oh, then what happened when you were hanging in Mourra's dream cast?"

Leica raised an eyebrow, tilted his head, and waited for a response.

"Hmph, someone or something erased, moved, changed, or placed something inside of Eternity. Obviously."

"Obviously?"

"Yes!"

"Then what happened exactly? Give details."

"Mourra did something, and something happened. You know what, shut up. Use your dam-ang, dang glasses to see what happened."

"Gossett?"

"I don't know. Whatever occurred in that mortal realm was so disastrous that he was forced to sign a pact with the Lady upon being released from questioning."

"So what type of future was it that Mourra projected?"

"Depending on the person that you ask, it was either an outsider's miniature of Yiruhm, or one of Our Lady's personal projects. I couldn't find anyone who knew exactly." Gossett crossed her arms and popped her husband out of her breasts with a frown. Anyone who was looking would immediately notice that he was not actually resting on her in a physical sense. He was ejected from a small green and white tattoo that started on the top half of her sternum and fanned out across her entire body, remaining mostly hidden by clothing.

"Azure also didn't leave a trail for me to follow like usual, so I can only assume that he had been pulled into whatever was going on either by force or secretly. All that I know for sure is that Lady Shemishier dropped him off with me after going missing for around thirty millennia. He was drunk as a skunk, stinking of human and ash." Gossett glared toward the floating platform of 14 seats and nearly crushed her man. She focused on an amorphous shadow that roughly assumed a bipedal form and remained standing despite the high-backed chair behind it. A massive cloud made of pitch-black fabric, similar to a shawl a bride or grieving widow might wear, concealed the Lady of Death's features and form completely.

"That sounds like Az might have." Red swallowed a mouthful of saliva.

"This little spark knows better than to cheat on me. Aren't I right, honey?"

"Absolutely not, you crazy, face-changing, Bwitch. I am a beacon of integrity and passion. To even suggest that Red. Hmph, I'll get you after your brats are somewhere else." Ure's emerald eyes blazed as his iridescent pupils fragmented and spilled out into his irises like stoked embers. Gossett blushed as a fleck of sea-green flame danced across the surface of her third eye.

"You'll 'get me'? Sure. If we are ever in the same time period, I will let you 'get' me a meal that is. It sounds nice. Kids, if we ever see your uncle outside of the Omnidome, he is going to 'get' us a meal."

Like vermin, three of his kids scurried around squeaking about food despite the mountains of trash and empty containers that filled every empty seat in the Leica family box. Azure, stunned and frightened, escaped back into the safety of the tattoo that sat on Gosset's chest.

"So the Mourra stuff. How is the Province of Dreams in trouble this time?"

"Like I said. I couldn't find out much, but from what I could gather, Mourra messed with or cast a spell during the creation of the Void Seal. Or rather, it has been or will be called the Veilseam by the present-day Pantheon." Gossett made sure that all of the eavesdroppers knew that she was talking to them by looking around her immediate area very slowly.

"The spell is simple, really. I noticed it the moment that I heard the rumor, but only after I became aware of Mourra's involvement."

"Gossett, how simple would the spell be if Our Lady called this meeting because of it?"

"Hmm, not very. It was simple to me. Is that better?"

"Yes."

"Alright, then. By looking into it myself, I learned that Mourra really did cast a spell on the Vielseam. One that will spread or already has sent a message into the minds of everyone in Eternity at a specific date." Gossett was about to get to the meat of her conversation when the orator announced something that most people expected but didn't really understand given the scale of this gathering.

"It seems that Our Lady just received a personal message and is not going to join us at this time." The orator read a note and wiped sweat from his brow at an inhuman speed as boos and slurs rained down on him.

"Wait!"

Another piece of paper carried by the wind entered the orator's hand and forced the crowd to bring it down a notch or two.

"Okay. We have been given permission to proceed. Ahem. So, as I was saying before. Sleep. A natural, almost necessary process undertaken by most, if not all creatures, conventional and not. It is, when done right and safe, a rejuvenating, calming, and ultimately enlightening experience. It allows a dreamer to parse through difficult subjects, confront and possibly remedy fears via nightmares, and even allows oneself to provide guidance through usually abstract imagery or straightforward lucidity." The orator hopped off the raised podium. In the blink of an eye, the speaker resized himself to match the scale of the mind-bogglingly large stage and placed his microphone on the podium that he was just standing on.

"We have here the embodiment of a conversation between the mind and soul, and the ultimate goalkeeper of every sleeper, dreamer, and thinker, the Province of Dreams, Nightmares, and the Intangibility itself, Mourra." Like a host of some daytime television show, the orator waved his gargantuan hand toward the bench and snapped his fingers so spotlights would reveal the object placed atop it.

The amphitheater erupted into camps at the exact moment that a black pearl appeared and began to bloom akin to a water lily. Almost unanimously, the amorphous creatures littering the back of the theater roared and chanted in some indecipherable language that felt, intended, and encompassed everything. Many of the Divinites that no longer associated themselves with Eternity, with Yiruhm, gasped and attempted to hide the fear and worry that brewed behind their eyes and shifting forms.

The humans throughout the theater had undergone the largest transformations, whether they were beside, behind, apart from the Divinities that behaved as their stewards, or were elsewhere in the rows of seats. The constant shifting and fading was a thing of the past as almost all of them one of three stances in this moment, worry and concern, anger and vitriolic hatred, or absolute neutrality due to either confusion or a level of understanding or grasping of a greater picture that Alize didn't or couldn't fathom. As for the rest of the Divine-ranked beings in the audience, the camps pretty much followed the same trend as the humans, simply less controlled and infinitely more confused.

"We are all here for one reason and one reason only." The orator spread his arms wide and projected millions of scenes and points of view that simply spread into an omniscient and present-day layout of Yiruhm, the heart of Eternity and the home of the Immortal Lady. Mourra, an amorphous tangle of speech and abstract imagery, remained caged within the translucent barrier that retained the shape of a pearl despite its being cracked open.

"To serve as a jury of peers in the case of Mourra V. Yiruhm." There were gasps, laughter, then slow, daunting, almost deafening silence. It did not last long as many rushed out of the amphitheater screaming bloody murder. Others directly lost their composure, few simply vanished from their seats and from the minds of their cohorts, never to have existed at all as banners and pantheons burned to ruin.

"I haven't seen this level of bloodlust since Our Lady Invoked Buren Tenciel at the last summit." Red sat down inside of Alize's mind, inside of the Initui, and released a full-body shiver as the real him continued to examine the crowd. The VIPs and those surrounding them were silent from the very beginning of their appearance. Some of them, under the piercing gaze of Argus, even appeared bored, as if they had known this information for quite some time. Red turned over toward the back of the section that he sat in and was going to show something rather remarkable about the dome and its ability to work omnipresently and concurrently throughout time, but Alize already took off in his own thoughts.

"HOLY CRAP. MOURRA IS ON TRIAL!? WAIT. Wait! Wait? When was this? Is this? Leica, when is this happening?"

Alize threw a handful of boards on the floor and cleared just as many desks as he restructured his understanding of the communication between his Affix's fated events and his dream journals.

"Divine intervention. From two gods, two. At once. Wait three? Four? Does Argus count too? If so, that's five. Leica, do you and the Initui count as two separate divine beings, or should I just put one? And Gnoll, why is that cursed spirit at the main table? Why am I just now realizing that?"

"Ha. Kid. Ha, Ark. You're missing some pretty cool exposition here. You can think about it all after you are out of magic."

"Alright. Wait, what do you mean?"

"Shush. Pay attention. This is a truth that no one will ever tell or show you until you make it to the Omnidome. Specifically, the one at Iris."

4.0 One Eternity under Our Lady

As of this moment, Divine entities, unfathomable and sometimes eldritch in both appearance and behavior, gathered alongside similarly matching beings of immeasurable wisdom, intellect, power, and presence. All of them felt their collective breaths catch on the words spoken by the orator.

"Presiding over this case are the Honorable Divinities, Judges and Arbitrators of the Divine, and the Gods and Goddesses of Yiruhm proper." The orator snapped his finger and put up a small screen of a much smaller hearing with only the managerial staff that sat upon their opulent thrones serving as the adjudicators of Mourra's fate.

"Mourra, proven guilty of charges of consanguineous treason, is here to plead his case to the Aleph Council as an ordained right and act of piety towards our fair and just mo, ahem, Lady Immortal." The orator didn't explain the contents of the video and stopped talking to let it play. A small internal meeting, consisting of 11 members of a 13-seat managerial staff, including Mourra, voted to punish the dreamy Province or let PIETY stand. Without Mourra receiving a vote, it ended in a split vote of 5 and 5. Leica, upon seeing that Alize was completely lost, filled in the gap in his understanding of the Yiruhm's Aleph Council.

"Our Immortal Lady is currently without a spouse and is generally unconcerned with giving a vote on matters that she has deemed as having an easy solution. The problem is, Our Lady has quite a skewed outlook on **life."**

"So, breaches of conduct and treason are beneath her?"

Leica didn't have to say anything as the video explained it all. From the very first and unadorned seat on the platform, a small black dot expanded into a human-shaped outline. The Immortal Lady's seat almost immediately produced Gnoll as a tiebreaker the moment that tie occurred.

"Yes, **and no. Thankfully. Our Lady always has better things to do and delegates."**

The new vote, once Gnoll was brought up to speed, broke in favor of Mourra's PIETY but only by one, which was far from the unanimous decision needed to swing an action. The video showed an immediate expansion of voters with the inclusion of the VIP section and the summoning of surrounding supporters, retirees, and antagonists that lived in and around Yiruhm proper. Their collective vote functioned as a singular entity on the council, a temporary 15th seat, but instead of swinging the vote toward a 7:5 break, the room voted against Mourra. Splitting the chamber once more. The third step in the process was a larger meeting spread across all of creation and time. Which brought Red and Alize to the next statement of the orator.

"Mourra also stands accused of Orchestration in the First Degree with a potential of 77 googol counts of genocide."

A list of names, locations, and estimated tallies filled the entire airspace behind the bench where Mourra was placed. Everything was written in the language of the Gods and practically flew over Alize's head, so he could only focus on what was said and what Leica examined.

"Orchestration?"

"It also means Divine intervention."

"Oh? Interesting. Does that mean you can get in trouble for Orchestration since you are talking to me?"

"I am recording a mental note on my personal relic. Why would I get in trouble for thinking to myself? Also, what Mourra is being accused of is completely different from whatever the council could pin on me. At best, I'll get a slap on the wrist and a fine for recording without a permit."

Red didn't comment on the matter any further as visions of the future danced within his pupils. Without missing a beat, the Orator grabbed everyone's attention the second that the massive wall of information stopped updating.

"As a unified jury, we must rule as a majority for whether or not Mourra reaches the benchmark for PIETY."

The orator pushed through the noise and raised his hand toward the two tables on either side of the bench. Two counters showed up, a deep emerald green and an apple red, both of which started at zero percent.

"We will gauge the Province's karmic imprint on Yiruhm and evaluate the events that have been, are, and will be guaranteed to occur as a result of his impudent decisions." The orator, despite trying to remain unbiased, clearly couldn't keep his work and personal gripes separate and closed the video with a snappy side-eye thrown at Mourra. No one said a thing. The only person who wanted to voice their concern simply couldn't due to an obsidian-esque cage surrounding them. Mourra constantly twisted in a fog of letters, numbers, basic shapes, and chains of esoteric objects but gave up after seeing the tallies of lives lost that everyone else seemingly lost their minds over. To Mourra, this loss was better than the complete destruction of Yiruhm. Under the collective gaze of the amphitheater's gathered crowds, Mourra adopted a humanoid shape. For the first time, even after being put on this stage several times before for similar crimes, the youthful kid, dark-skinned and golden-eyed, leaned back against the bars that contained it and crossed its arms. Long braids draped over the kid's shoulders in a manner that fully displayed the artistic vision the Province held. Its most favorite passages, songs, and images were woven into each lock of hair.

"Is Morra hated by everyone here? This feels personal for some reason."

"Not really, no. Provinces, by their very nature, are well liked, respected, and oftentimes, loved. Mourra is most definitely at the top of the list of the provinces **that are most loved. What you are sensing in the crowd is a hatred for anyone and anything that intends to harm Our Lady."**

"Is it that bad?"

"Eternity nearly crumbled the last time someone hurt her, **so messing with the future is worse than making a temporary mess of things in whatever** era **they happen to live in."**

"Oh, how old are you, Leica? I mean, hm, I have a feeling that you are talking about the Void Era, but that was so long ago that the best information about what happened is directly tied to some Celestial recordings likening it to something called the Dark Ages."

"I am from Luidelri- Eonavavil in my native tongue. I believe that an approximate translation is The Eon of Divine Retribu-

tion. We don't use years to tell the passage of time and instead use the creation or discovery of new civilizations, lifestyle-altering technologies and spells as milestones to tell Yiruhm's age. But if I were to place it on a timescale using the metrics you know, I would have to say that I am joining this meeting with my family somewhere between 900 billion and 50 billion years before your time?"

"Are you still alive?"

"Haa. My death and the outcome of my children's fates are two of the only things that elude my vision. The third would be you, beyond knowing that I would meet you and have this conversation. So, probably not. If I was, you would not have my sister's inheritance. That same stands for if any of my children or any of my descendants were alive during your time. I'm not even sure that my body would hold up until then."

Red didn't hide his annoyance as he directly looked at Gnoll and scanned over the five other managers of Yiruhm that voted in favor of expanding the decision-making process. His gaze idly shifted toward a nonchalant Mourra not too long after.

"That makes sense."

"Doesn't it just?"

Red adjusted his glasses and wiped them with a cloth.

"Go ahead."

"What?"

"Speak your mind?"

"Who?"

"Ha. Ask your questions, kid! It's okay to feel lost. You haven't been introduced to the Dome or the Council in the usual way, so it's normal to be confused, so ask away."

"The orator is having his people do something to the amphitheater. If I see this new footage without being at the divine rank, will I be okay?"

"Hmm, I'm actually not sure. There has never been a rankless person inside of Iris's branch of the Dome."

"Should I look then or not? I can see something starting. Should I just turn away from Argus's screen?"

"No? I'm sure that it is a sufficient enough buffer to protect you if anything weird happens."

Alize and Leica went back and forth for a while as the orator and the Dome tech hashed out some details regarding the case of Mourra V. Yiruhm. The flashy guy prattled on about how Mourra saw fit to instigate an upheaval in one of their Lady's personal projects, confirming some of the floating rumors that Gossett got her hands on. He didn't commit much of the propaganda to memory since Leica, Gossett, and Azure were closer to the pulse of information, even more so than the Orator due to the rumor mill courtesy of Leica's inherent predictive and passive foresight and the Alli Initui. Moments later, an egg with several discs of light and magic materialized above the stage but around half a meter above the mic that the orator used as both a walking stick and pointer. Faster than the Alize could blink, a seemingly spherical explosion spread to the infinitudes across the theater.

"Whoa."

"Calm down. The spell eases the senses for what comes next. Not everyone is built for omniscience. Hmm, then again, you are seeing this through a recording via Argus, so I don't actually know if the spell is affecting you."

The egg, after ejecting whatever it contained, floated toward the Orator and sank into the screen that he created. In less than a second, the flat, movie theater screen gained several dimensions and enveloped every jury member.

"It's about to start. Be careful from here on out. If you feel dizzy or tired, turn away from the Argus and Hey? Are you good? I can't hear your thoughts anymore, **kid."** Red closed one eye and used the back of his eyelid to focus on the lobby that was constructed within Argus. His set jaw loosened all at once. Instead of a pretty smart and incomprehensibly lucky kid running around desks doing his best to memorize the crowd in an incomprehensible scratch, there was an inescapable abyss deeper and more archaic than depictions of deep space and the all-consuming Void.

"Alizedriel? Damnit." Red was about to ask Argus to run a diagnostic, but something stopped him dead in his tracks. The scene out in the Omnidome, it exactly matched what was going on in Alize's mind, for a moment at least. Leica was privy to a firsthand account of a single point in existence. A teardrop fell toward the Abyss that was Alize. In the omnidome, a black, dark red, almost ichorous and vicious blood boiling out of a singular point in the footage was going to be used to either convict or free Mourra.

"What is this?"

The grainy darkness within the Initui, looping and exhaustive in its shifting, morphed into a face that left Red shaking in his seat due to the familiarity with the immortal lady. The footage, however, from that expanding spot, began to play every single moment that Mourra lived. Each of those moments was inhabited by the entire crowd, and in less time than half a second, the votes were all in. Mourra's PIETY, as decreed by Yiruhm's Staff and members, the Divinity's Presiding, and the Aleph Council at large, was...

Just around the same time as Alize's sudden breakdown, The family trio, Jarrold the old silent Fae, Verza, and Orsche, stepped out of a wind tunnel and found themselves standing at the center of a 3x3 meter clearing between henge stones and trees that had their limbs woven together into a ring.

"My love. This one is for sure the place. The Apeirogon is pointing here." Orsche scratched his chin and began kicking at the scattered rocks, rotted bark, and grassy patches that poked through swaths of moss.

"Two times, Ors." Verza pursed her lips and adjusted Alize's replicated body with a frown.. Any features that the kid might have had were completely gone. Replaced by a flat and slightly pink and transparent shell of what resembled a wax balloon filled with water. The clothes on his body were half submerged, while his exposed skin was covered in rivulets.

"Figure it out soon before his duplicant explodes." Verza tried to be firm, but worry bled through her facade as she examined her son's clone and the glasses that had reached 98.526% of something.

"I will. It's just hard to remember where I left the relays. It has been a while since I placed everything." Orsche sped up his prodding of the environment and used the PATCH in its hovercane form to try to hit the floor. Jarrold, annoyed with the unpleasantness of Orsche, puffed his chest and blew out the surroundings.

"Impatient geezer. I was trying not to leave a mark or use magic. Now the Guardians can track your Effuse." Orsche wiped away some dirt and sidestepped an extraordinary number of stones and branches that were more than likely deliberately tossed toward his face.

"Who is going to be in this exact spot ever?"

Jarrold signed with an expression that was no more grim than his usual stone focus. The old wind floated over the clearing after throwing his question out and examined the area.

"Maybe an Archon if they have been deliberately sent after us. The Hounds might also figure something out, as unlikely as that is."

"I told him to hurry it up, Ors. I don't know what's going to happen when Ark's glasses reach 100% but I want to be inside of the Apeirogon when it happens."

"I understand my love, but again. I have been Arcanum and only spells that I am allowed to use in civilian life to retain my secrecy, and you are being hunted. I understand the rush, but we cannot afford to make any mistakes at all." Orsche sighed and moved one step toward Verza to give her a hug or kiss and accidentally tapped the cane on something that was now slightly exposed. A small camo printed and palm sized disc with the symbol of two humanoid bodies fading into one was revealed in the shadow of one of the many monolithic stone henges. With a light press of a button between the two heads, Orsche pulled the popped out handle and revealed an additional spiked component that was planted into the dirt. With a bit more button pressing and dial turning, the femur length cone collapsed into a relatively thin cylinder that lit up on the button with a pyramidal Quill.

"That is the last of the Duplicator's relays. I'll open up the Apeirogon after we get away from..."

Without any warning, prompting, and beyond any calculation or guesswork, Alize's replicated body liquified and congealed around the glasses that had sunk into the center of his goopy head. Before Verza could even blink, the floating sphere of pink liquid turned black and imploded.

"RAQ!"

Faster than any of them had ever moved, Verza, Orsche, and Jarold rushed at the youngest in their familial tribe. One of Verza's hands snatched the imploding dot in an attempt to impede whatever was going on, Orsche tossed the Apeirogon up and at an angle. Jarrold, using the principles of a Brachistochrone curve and the barrel of a sniper rifle, compressed air to the point of collapse and shot the divine-ranked Arcanum with absolutely no hesitation. Light, in this moment, froze and parted in liquid-esque fractals as the Apeirogon ripped through space-time and collided with Verza's outstretched palm. In an instant, the terrarium-creating device exploded open and swallowed everything within a 100 kilometers. In this fraction of a second, Verza screamed as her clenching fist was too slow to prevent her son from being ripped away from right between her fingertips. The last thing that reflected in her eyes was the Alli Initui and the small loading bar that faded away on its lenses. It jumped from 98.6 to 100% faster than she could even process as the Apeirogon's infinite reflections caught the divine shades and smashed them into a mirror that bore a snapshot of Alize's room.

About the Author

Jimmy Joshua Paulino was born in the Bronx and moved to Pennsylvania at fourteen, where he has lived and grown ever since. Though he hopes to relocate in the future, he's content where life has placed him for now. A lifelong lover of storytelling, Jimmy draws much of his inspiration from games. He aims to bring the same sense of immersion into his own writing.

Jimmy originally pursued a computer science degree in college, a path he admits he struggled through and ultimately hasn't applied in his career. He missed his chance to switch to literature. While he humbly claims not to possess all the skill or determination he wishes he had, his passion remains unwavering.

Today, Jimmy is simply doing what he loves: writing stories and sharing them with you, the reader.